A BOOK.

That's what starts it all,

the bloodshed & the violence, the romance & the sex.

a goddamn book.

LIMITED EDITION

2024

Dearest Reader,

You might be wondering what this special edition is all about. Allow me to explain, my darlings.

In your hands, you hold a book filled with magic, sex, and violence. Not necessarily in that order. In fact, if you are expecting order in this book, you'll find none of it. This is an *Alice's Adventures in Wonderland* retelling, and it's curious and curiouser at best.

"What if I don't like Alice in Wonderland?" you might ask.

Well.

Hold my tea.

I think you'll like *this* version.

This hardcover contains the complete *Harem of Hearts* trilogy, a story about a woman sent to another world who then discovers love … nine times over. Yes. Nine. She has nine fucking husbands and well, there is more to the plot, but that's the important bit right there.

It remains unchanged from the original version (but for a few typos and fixes here and there).

This edition is/was (depending on when you're reading this) only available for a short period of time in 2024.

It's also a version that I will *only* sign in person. When I sign it, I'll emboss it, too. How does that sound?

If you're new to this tale, I hope you enjoy the ride.

If you're old to this tale, stay weird, you strange motherfucker.

Much love (and also books, tea, cats, and crumpets):

C.M. Stunich

C.M. Stunich

BOOKS BY
C.M. STUNICH

ROMANCE NOVELS

HARD ROCK ROOTS SERIES*
Real Ugly
Get Bent
Tough Luck
Bad Day
Born Wrong
Hard Rock Roots Box Set (1-5)
Dead Serious
Doll Face
Heart Broke
Get Hitched

TASTING NEVER SERIES
Tasting Never
Finding Never
Keeping Never
Tasting, Finding, Keeping
Never Can Tell
Never Let Go
Never Did Say
Never Could Stop

ROCK-HARD BEAUTIFUL*
Groupie
Roadie
Moxie

TRIPLE M SERIES*
Losing Me, Finding You
Loving Me, Trusting You
Needing Me, Wanting You
Craving Me, Desiring You

DEATH BY DAYBREAK MC*
I Was Born Ruined
I Am Dressed in Sin
I Will Revel in Glory

THE HAVOC BOYS*
Havoc at Prescott High
Chaos at Prescott High
Mayhem at Prescott High
Anarchy at Prescott High
Victory at Prescott High

STAND-ALONES & BOX SETS
If You Don't Love Me We Both Die
Devils' Day Party
Baby Girl
All for 1
Blizzards and Bastards
Fuck Valentine's Day
Broken Pasts
Crushing Summer
Becoming Us Again
Taboo Unchained
Taming Her Boss
Kicked
Football Dick
Stepbrother Inked
Alpha Wolves Motorcycle Club
Glacier

HERS TO KEEP TRILOGY
Biker Rockstar Billionaire CEO Alpha

RICH BOYS OF BURBERRY PREP*
Filthy Rich Boys
Bad, Bad BlueBloods
The Envy of Idols
In the Arms of the Elite

LOST DAUGHTER OF A SERIAL KILLER*
Stolen Crush
Payback Princess
Endgame Romance
Game Over Boys

SCARLET FORCE
Fuckboy Psychos
Unholy Terrors
Vile Bastards
Stalking Nightmares

ADAMSON ALL-BOYS ACADEMY*
The Secret Girl
The Ruthless Boys
The Forever Crew

FIVE FORGOTTEN SOULS
Beautiful Survivors

BOOKS BY

C.M. STUNICH

A DUET
Paint Me Beautiful
Color Me Pretty

THE BAD NANNY TRILOGY
Bad Nanny
Good Boyfriend

SCI-FI/FANTASY

FOR THE LOVE OF ALIENS*
Pheromone
Seminal
Venery

***THE SEVEN MATES OF ZARA* WOLF**
Pack Ebon Red
Pack Violet Shadow
Pack Obsidian Gold

HAREM OF HEARTS*
Allison's Adventures in Underland
Allison and the Torrid Tea Party
Allison Shatters the Looking Glass

KINGS OF UNDERLAND
a Bride for Beasts
a Marriage of Monsters

ACADEMY OF SPIRITS AND SHADOWS
Spirited
Haunted
Shadowed

THE FAMILY SPELLS
The Family Spells
What The Hex?
The Heart Cantrip
Witch Mates are Fated?

TEN CATS PARANORMAL SOCIETY
Possessed

THE WICKED WIZARDS OF OZ
Very Bad Wizards

OTHER FANTASY NOVELS
Werewolf Kisses
Gray and Graves
Indigo & Iris
Stiltz
She Lies Twisted
See No Devils
Hell Inc.
DeadBorn
Chryer's Crest
Under the Wild Waves
Seven Wicked Creature

CO-WRITTEN

HIJINKS HAREM*
Elements of Mischief
Elements of Ruin
Elements of Desire

THE WILD HUNT MOTORCYCLE CLUB
Dark Glitter
Cruel Glamour

FOXFIRE BURNING
The Nine
Tail Game

OTHER
And Today I Die

UNDERCOVER SINNERS
Altered By Fire
Altered By Lead
Altered by Pain

*Complete Series
Out of Print

HAREM OF

HEARTS
the complete trilogy

Harem of Hearts

the complete trilogy

c.m. stunich

USA TODAY BESTSELLING AUTHOR

Harem of Hearts (Limited Edition)
Allison's Adventures in Underland © C.M. Stunich 2017
Allison and the Torrid Tea Party © C.M. Stunich 2018
Allison Shatters the Looking Glass © C.M. Stunich 2018

For information address Sarian Royal, 1863 Pioneer Pkwy. E Ste. 203, Springfield, OR 97477-3907.
www.cmstunich.com

ISBN-13: 979-8-3303-8660-4(2024 Limited)

This special edition is dedicated to the fandom, and to anyone who has ever wanted to take well-loved classic literature and turn it into a bloody smut-fest.

Peace and love to all my fellow weirdos.

I heart the fuck out of you guys.

XII
XI
X
IX
VIII
VII
VI

1
ALLISON'S
adventures in
UNDERLAND

All In The Wicked Darkest Eve

All in the wicked darkest eve
In blood and shadows alike;
We strive to live through mighty pain,
By mighty arms unite,
Oft mighty hands make plain romance,
A traveling heart's plight.

Ah, cruel Nine! In such an hour,
Beneath such dreadful weather,
To beg a tale of life so bleak
To stir bound wings of feathers!
Yet what can one lone voice avail
Against ten tongues together?

Imperious Alice tumbles forth
Her edict "we will end it"—
In wistful tones her people hope
"There will be justice in it"—
While her men carry on the tale
And also help begin it.

Shit, this sudden war's begun,
In ire giving chase
The young woman moving through a land
Of wonders dark and base,
In friendly tryst with man and beast—
The darkness she would face.

And ever, as the story changed
The wells of knowledge lie,
And hearty strove that weary one
To put her subjects by,
"I am not brave—" "True fear is fine!"
The frightened voices cry.

Thus grew the tale of Underland:
Thus slowly, one by one,
Its queer events are fucking wrote—
The tale is far from done,
And home is where, the girl may ask,
As she debates to run.

Alice! A terrifying story,
And with a skeleton hand
Lay it where graveyard's nightmares bury
The rebels no longer stand,
Like magic's withered throne of corpses
Plucked from a far-off land.

CHAPTER ONE

Down the Fucking Rabbit-Hole

A book.

That's what starts it all, the bloodshed and the violence, the romance and the sex.

A goddamn *book.*

"Are you seriously reading right now?" my younger sister, Edith, asks as she stands next to me in a silver dress covered in sequins. Her hair is twisted into a bun and secured to the side of her head with about a hundred bobby pins. The design looks like a snail shell to me, but I decide not to say anything.

I close the book in my hands—some whimsical fantasy of a life I'll never lead—and watch her eyes latch onto the cover.

"You're reading for *fun*?" she asks, bending down and snatching the book from my hands before I get a chance to grab it back. *I knew I should've brought my Kindle outside instead.* At least then she wouldn't have seen the werewolves on the front cover. "This *whole* thing?"

"Sorry it doesn't have any pictures in it," I joke as I rise to my feet and give her a smirking grin in response. "I know that's the only type of book you *can* read."

Edith rolls her eyes and swipes at her forehead with the back of her hand.

"Whatever, it's hot as hell out here and we have a party to get to. Come on."

I roll my eyes right back as soon as she turns around, and take the daisy chain out of my own hair, tossing it onto Edith's perfectly coiffed head without her noticing.

"This is a big deal tonight, so try not to screw it up for me," she says as I cross my arms over my chest and follow her from the backyard, past the pond and my father's prized koi fish, and into the house.

"How could I possibly ruin a high school party? Isn't the whole point *to* screw up?"

"Seriously, Allison?" she says, yanking the sliding glass door open and stepping inside. She kicks her flats off near the door and heads for the stairs, probably to put on a pair of heels that would most certainly break *my* neck if I put them on. "And no tennis shoes!" she shouts down, just before slamming her bedroom door and making the whole house shake.

"Shit." I run my fingers through the ratted, tangled strands of my hair, all mussed up from lying in the grass and reading all afternoon. "And you think *this* is gonna impress Brandon?" I whisper under my breath.

Grudgingly, I pound up the stairs and kick open the door to my room, digging around in the clean clothes pile on the floor (I'm not big on folding stuff and putting it away) until I find a fresh pair of jeans and a plain white tank.

"Is that what you plan on wearing?" Edith asks, leaning against the edge of the doorframe and looking down at me from under a pair of false eyelashes. "Jeans and a t-shirt?"

"It's a tank top, Edy," I say as I stand up and tear my grass stained tee over my head, trading it out for the new one. "It looks good on me," I blurt, defending myself before she can say anything mean. With Edith, it's always best to stay on the offensive.

"You're into Brandon, right?" she says coyly. I cross my arms over my chest and stare her down. The bitch sneaks into my room and reads my journal; I have no secrets. I don't even bother trying to hide them anymore. "That chess geek or whatever?"

"Fuck you," I tell her, pushing past to get to the bathroom before she does.

Edith chases after me and shoves her way in anyway.

"I've got a dress for you," she tells me, sucking her lower lip under her teeth and smearing lipstick everywhere.

"I don't fit into your dresses, Edy," I chastise, pulling out a box of tampons and waving them at her. "Can I please get some peace to put one of these in?" I'm not *actually* on my period, but you know, privacy comes with a hefty price when you've got a sister.

"Not until you agree to try it on," she says, heeling the bathroom door shut behind her.

As soon as she does, I see it hanging there on the back of the door.

Shit.

"What is that effing monstrosity?" I ask, pointing at the blue and white *thing* dangling from the hook. "I'm not wearing that."

"Oh my *God,* Allison, give me a break. When's the last time you wore a dress?"

"Three years ago when Aunt Margaret passed away; Mom made me."

"You're *eighteen* years old for crap's sake. Just try it on. If you hate it, I won't make you wear it."

"I hate it now. How will putting it on change that?"

Edith stares me down and then glances over at the mirror, adjusting the daisy chain so that it sits even prettier atop her perfect white-blonde hair. I have the same hair, but I always put a few colored streaks on the side. Today, I've got a miniature rainbow woven in.

"I bought this with my own, hard-earned money and …"

"Fine."

I reach over and snatch the dress from the hook, giving it another once-over. To say it's not my style would be an understatement. The skirt is too short and the color …

"I hate blue," I groan as I take my top off and drop the dress over my head. It slides into place like it was made for me. *Crap.*

"Turn around," Edith tells me, making me spin so she can zip it up and tie the white bow in the back. As soon as she knots it, I get this awful feeling in the pit of my stomach.

"I'm wearing this, aren't I?" I ask miserably, staring at the brightly colored fish on the shower curtain. I can *feel* my sister grinning maniacally behind me though.

"Oh, yes," she tells me, purring in my ear as I swat her away, "yes, you are. Don't you want to get laid sometime, Sonny?" I wrinkle my nose because I *hate* the nickname Sonny, but Edith knows it and if I reveal my cards … it'll only make her say it more.

"I have been laid—several times actually," I tell her as I turn around and try not to sigh.

The dress, it actually looks great on me.

By the end of the night, I'll get to see how good it looks covered in blood.

To be fair, it looks pretty good like that, too.

The party is this overblown nightmare affair at the house of a student I don't even know.

"This is so fucking great," Edith gushes excitedly, yanking me out of the car and slapping my hands away from the dress. I keep trying to smooth the skirt down, but it flounces right back up. I paired it with a red waist cincher, black and white harlequin patterned tights, and some buckled boots, but still … it's ridiculously uncomfortable.

"Please don't get puking drunk," I warn as she bounces into the kitchen and immediately starts filling a plastic cup with vodka. "If you do, I'm not covering for you this time."

I watch my sixteen year old sister splash pink lemonade into her drink and then chug it.

"Whatever," I mutter, shaking my head and adjusting the big black headband pinned to my hair. It has a small top hat lilting to the side, red silk roses clustered around the base. I can't decide if I look … *okay* … or ridiculous.

Weaving through the crowd, I keep an eye out for Brandon, a fellow senior in my class and the only guy at my school who's not a fucking asshole. I'm tired of dating immature, spoiled little boys. I can't *wait* to graduate and head off to college. But at the same time, there's no *way* I'm spending my senior year alone.

Once I find the backyard—this hormonal mess of groping teens and flickering torches to keep the mosquitos away—I spot Brandon. He's sitting on the edge of the pool with his jeans pushed up and his feet dangling over the edge.

If I'd known then that I'd later see him with a bullet in his head, I'd have run away screaming.

"Hey," I say softly, sitting down next to him and crossing my legs. I shove the skirt down between my thighs and it fluffs right back up. *I hate you, Edith,* I think as I watch Brandon swirling his feet in the heated waters of the pool.

"Hey," he replies, just as softly, pushing his glasses up his nose and smiling over at me. "I don't usually see you at these things."

I shrug my shoulders loosely and pick at the edges of the blue and white dress.

"I don't usually come," I tell him with a smile that says *he* is the reason I'm here. Either it doesn't come across or else Brandon's too naive to notice that I'm flirting with him. "So … what are you doing here? This doesn't really seem like your scene either."

Brandon sits up and tosses a shy smile my way.

"My brother dragged me here."

I grin at him.

"Sister," I say, pointing at myself and we both chuckle. *I've got him,* I think as I scoot a little closer and keep smiling.

The pool is lit up with small round lights in the bottom and sides, turning the water a brilliant turquoise that casts strange shadows on Brandon's face. He stares into it like there's something there that he wants—and that he wants a *hell* of a lot more than me.

I guess even chess geeks can be assholes.

"Do you like to read?" I ask him, lifting up the book clutched at my side and trying to pass it over. Brandon glances casually my way, fixes his glasses yet again, and smiles.

"I don't have a lot of time to read," he tells me, and although that's a common enough thing to say, there's an edge to it. His hand tightens around his knee, knuckles going white as he squeezes it. *Fuck, what the hell is this guy's problem?*

Now I'm already trying to figure out how to get away from Brandon, so I can read. Why are guys in books so much less dickish than ones in real life? Cuter, too. Oh, and they never have pimples. Brandon has one on his chin which is fucking fine, or would be if he wasn't being an apathetic dick.

"Okay," I whisper under my breath, noticing that his eyes have glazed over and he *really* isn't paying attention to me anymore.

I stand up, feeling flustered, and start off toward the trees near the back of the property. Whoever's house this is, their parents are *loaded* and there are all these beautiful white lights strung up across the yard. I make a beeline toward a bench beneath the voluminous folds of an oak and take a seat, lying on my back and wishing I hadn't let Edith put any makeup on my face.

"What a waste," I murmur as I crack the book and try to find my place.

"I love you, baby," he says, cupping the back of my neck and pulling me close. Our foreheads touch and my breath falls out in a rush. His fingertips burn; his mouth is hot. I've never wanted anything as much as I want him.

"Lucky bitch," I mutter as I flip to the next page.

I'm so into my book that I don't notice Brandon making his way across the sweeping lawns toward me, his dark hair shimmering under the strands of Edison bulbs strung from the trees. The only reason I look up at all is because I hear the distinctive clicking sound of a hammer being pulled back.

"Oh, for Christ's sake, I'm *late*," a voice snaps, and my head whips up, goose bumps taking over my arms, crawling down my back.

The book falls to my chest as I struggle to sit up, gaping at the man standing not six inches from the end of the bench.

His hair is jet-black, his eyes red as blood. And on his head, a pair of white rabbit ears sits, one perked and standing upright, the other flopped in half. He stares at Brandon for a moment and then with a gloved hand, reaches into the pocket on his red vest. Pulling out a watch, he checks the time with an agitated sigh.

"Fuck," he says again, and then he lifts up a gun with his opposite hand and points the barrel in Brandon's direction.

"No, wait!" Brandon calls out, falling to his knees and putting his hands together in a prayer position. "I just need more time for—"

The red-eyed boy's floppy left ear perks up at the same time he raises an eyebrow.

"King's orders," is all he says, and then he's pulling the trigger and putting a bullet through Brandon Carmichael's forehead. Blood spatters the lenses of his glasses before he slumps to the side into the grass.

"Brandon!" I scream, scrambling off the bench and stumbling over to him. I sink to my knees in the mud and feel the side of his neck for a pulse. In my heart of hearts, I know that he's dead, but I have to check. I just have to. "What did you do?!" I shout, but Brandon's murderer just stares at me blandly and checks his pocket watch again.

"Hearts, I really *am* late," he scowls, tucking the watch back in his vest and tossing the gun to the ground at his feet. With one last glance at me, he turns away. The rabbit ears on the top of his head twitch (something I should've wondered about, but at the time seemed the *least* weird of all the shit happening around me) before he takes off across the yard at a jog.

I might be a bit of a loner, more likely to sit and read on a Saturday night than go out with friends, but there is no fucking way I'm letting a murderer run free.

Yanking the cell from my pocket, I dial 911 at the same time I stand up.

"I've just witnessed a shooting," I gasp, adrenaline surging through my limbs. Before I can second-guess myself, I start to run, picking up the gun as I go.

I blurt the address out to the operator and then shove my phone back in the dress, leaving the connection open so if anything happens to me, the police might still be able to find my body …

Thinking about it later, I'd realize that I wasn't just a stupid teenager making an even stupider decision, I was *compelled* to follow the White Rabbit.

"Hey!" I shout, stumbling after the psycho, the murder weapon clutched in my sweaty hands. "Stop, asshole!"

My breath screams in my lungs as I struggle to keep up, heart pounding, brain scrambling to remember how exactly I'm supposed to hold this revolver in case I need to take a shot. Isn't there a spot that'll blow your finger off if you touch it there while firing? Or was that an internet rumor? I can't remember!

The rabbit-eared nutcase dives into the bushes with me following after him, my dress catching on branches as I follow the rustling, quivering motions of the foliage.

They lead me right to him.

Or more specifically, to the edge of a very large, very suspicious looking hole.

There's no time to think, to wonder, to question.

One minute, my feet are safely on the ground. The next, I'm tumbling into blackness.

♦ ♠ ♣ ♠ ♣ ♠ ♦

My scream is fear made sound, tearing from my throat unbidden as I plummet down through the darkness. At first, that's all I feel: sheer panic. But then … I just keep falling. And falling. And falling.

There is way too much fucking time to think.

If I'm falling long enough to have thoughts, this is going to HURT.

My heart whimpers one last staccato cry before I manage to pull myself together, blinking into the darkness until I start to notice curious things … *really* fucking curious things.

The walls around me are made of packed dirt and lined with shelves and cabinets, maps and photos, jars of … God only knows what. Small animals float curled in formaldehyde, their grimy glass coffins stacked next to taxidermic dogs and birds frozen in flight, racks of antlers and decapitated lions' heads, mouths forever molded into silent roars of rage.

It's only then that I notice the gun still stuck in my hand.

As soon as I do, my mind floods with that image of Brandon's glasses, spattered and stained with blood. I toss the revolver onto a passing cabinet and shiver, wiping my hands on the front of my dress. As soon as I do, I realize they're covered in blood, too.

Turning my palms over, I stare at the violent red stain, carving little valleys in my skin. The stink of copper overwhelms me, mixing with the pungent musky odor of damp earth and rot. My stomach roils and a lightning bolt of fear strikes me hard.

I'm falling down a fucking hole.

Chasing after a murderer.

And I just chucked my gun.

Fortunately—hah, *fortunately* is such a subjective word—the cabinets and shelves in this place are chock-full of weapons. I've seen knives, whips, rifles, even a guillotine. As I continue to plummet downward, I take a chance and snatch another handgun off one of the shelves.

In the process, I knock one of the creepy jars off and hear it crash to the floor far below me.

Fuck.

A scream tears from my throat, but it's short-lived.

The long stretch of dark, damp well comes to an abrupt end and I land with a loud *oof* right in the arms of the bunny-eared murderer.

"Oh, my ears and whiskers," he breathes, his voice like bones and ice. It's a little weird, I'll admit, hearing such a sinful voice slip from the lips of a boy wearing bunny ears. "How late you've made me."

I'm so shocked by the sudden change of scenery that it takes me a moment to react. Instead, I just sit there and stare into his eyes, the color eerily similar to the stain on my hands. His heart beats rapidly against mine, echoing the adrenaline fueled thumping that's ringing in my ears.

His arms are too strong, too sure, and he's holding me up like I weigh nothing. Plus, his body is ridiculously warm, and he smells like earth and growing things.

If he hadn't just killed my classmate, I might've considered asking him out.

"You … fucking shot Brandon," I say, and the boy abruptly drops me in a pile of bones and dead things, their flesh stripped away, leaving nothing but fear and ivory. "What … the … where …"

I can't even make myself finish the question; I'm too horrified by the pile of corpses underneath me.

"I'm gonna puke," I groan, standing up and stumbling back until I hit the hard-packed dirt wall of the cavern. My hand clamps over my mouth as I glance up at the boy, his red eyes focused wholly on me, his ears twitching like they're *alive.*

He's wearing a red vest over a short-sleeved black button up with a pair of well-pressed slacks and slick black Oxfords with red hearts on the toes. As I stand there, he adjusts the cuffs on his shirt and gestures at the gun with his chin.

"Nice choice. Good grip, not much recoil. You could take down a jabberwock with that thing."

The boy's full mouth twists into a sinuous sort of smile, not at all like something you'd expect to see on the face of a teenage kid wearing rabbit ears and a waistcoat.

"Well, I'd best be going," he says with a small salute of his gloved hand. The motion causes the muscles in his bare arms to bunch, highlighting the fact that he's literally covered in ink, brilliant swarms of tattoos that I can't quite make out in the shadows. "Fare-fucking-well, Miss Alice." He pauses before turning away, shiny shoes scuffing against the filthy stone floor beneath our feet. "Try not to die before we meet again?"

He takes off around the corner as I stand there gaping at the long, dark length of the corridor, the borrowed gun clutched in my shaking hand. Lifting it up, I realize that this … this is no modern gun. There's a *fuse* on it that I don't have a damn clue what to do with.

"Wait!" I shout as I drop the gun, and even though I know I'm chasing after a murderer, I also want to get the hell out of this place, wherever it is.

Underground in a swanky suburban neighborhood, apparently. I always knew those people with their HOA fees and white picket fences were hiding *something …*

Taking off around the corner, I stumble into a long hallway with a harlequin patterned floor, much the same as my tights. Up and down both sides are doors with big, gold locks. And hanging from the ceiling above my head, skulls with flickering candles inside their mouths.

"What fresh hell is this?" I whisper as I slow down and start carefully across the floor, my boots scraping loudly against the tile. "Rabbit Dude?" I call, biting my lower lip and trying to avoid the eerie sense of déjà vu washing over me.

It's not like I haven't read Lewis Carroll's *Alice's Adventures in Wonderland.* It's not like the similarities have escaped me. Narrowing my brow, I try to remember what happens next—and how Alice got herself out of that nightmare in the end.

Or if she ever did.

"Shit, I read too many books," I curse, digging around in my pockets for my cell. For the life of me, I can't remember what happens in the *real* Alice's adventures. I've read so many adaptations, played so many games, seen so many movies and TV shows.

But then I stumble upon a glass table, cracked in pieces and strewn across the floor.

Okay, now I remember, I think as I stare down at a tiny broken bottle with the words *FUCKING DRINK ME* scrawled across the tag.

Bending down, I tuck my blue and white skirt under my thighs and dig through the glass shards, looking for a small golden key.

"Although it's just as likely to be a *skeleton* key in this nightmare," I grumble, my heart in my throat, sweat sliding down my spine like tiny spiders. I know how fucked this whole situation is. And I'm more than aware that Edith probably just slipped me some LSD before we left the house. "I've never prayed so hard for hallucinations in my whole life."

Slicing my finger on a piece of glass, I curse and lift it up to my lips, getting ready to suck on it.

But I stop when I remember that it's not all *my* blood.

"Damn it, Brandon," I curse as I stand up and kick the useless shards away with my foot.

There's no key here.

And I know for a *fact* that there was one in the original book.

"This confirms it," I say with a hysterical laugh. "I am out of my goddamn mind. It was Edith. It had to be. It just had to."

I start off down the hall and pause in front of a long, black curtain, hanging in tattered shreds from the wall. Behind this, there should be a tiny door, right? One that I can barely fit my head into?

Instead, when I pull it back, there's a man sitting on a red chaise lounge, leaning back and smiling wickedly at me.

Around his neck, there's a tag that says *DRINK ME.*

"Oh, *heeeell* no," I say, backing up suddenly, until my feet crunch over the shards of broken glass. Thank *God* I decided to wear combat boots instead of the awful heels my sister'd picked out for me.

"What's the matter?" the boy asks, tilting his head to the side and letting the corner of his lip twist up in a smirk. "You're not thirsty?"

"This isn't happening," I tell myself as he stands up and makes his way past the curtain and into the main part of the hallway. "Clearly, I've taken some serious drugs and wound up with my unconscious mind all wrapped up in boys who *obviously* do not exist."

"If you think we're made of wax," a voice says from behind me, "you ought to pay, you know? What do you think this is? An exhibit? A show?"

Hot fingertips trail along the back of my neck, and I jump, whirling around to find an identical looking boy with an *EAT ME* sign around his neck.

He has blue-streaked black hair rather than violet like the first one, hanging over his forehead and covering one brilliant sapphire eye, giving him this cheeky look that matches his twin perfectly. Because there's no doubt in my mind that these boys are, in fact, twins. Except for hair and eye color, they match each other perfectly, right down to the half-erect curves of their cocks.

"Contrariwise," Mr. Drink Me says, "if you think we're alive, you ought to fucking *speak.*"

He walks slowly—*languorously*—toward me, until I've got one naked boy in front and one behind. They're both sculpted gods, Adonis in the flesh. Made of wax he said? I honestly wouldn't be surprised. They both look too perfect to be real.

"I just want to go home," I say and the boys exchange a look over my shoulder.

"You'll want to go to the garden then," Drink Me says, and a warm shiver slides over my shoulder as Eat Me steps up close from behind, his breath feathering against my neck.

"Yes, the garden."

"Although that won't get you home."

"Stop speaking in riddles," I say with gritted teeth, because even if these guys are, like, seriously next level hot, I'm not about to stand here and play games. "Then what *will* get me home?"

"How should we know?" Drink Me says with a dramatic roll of his amethyst colored eyes. "We hardly know where you live."

"And even if we did," Eat Me continues, trailing his fingertips down the backs of my arms and making me shiver, "what makes you think we'd tell you, Alice."

"Alli*son,*" I say, stepping out from between the two of them, my boots loud against the harlequin patterned floor. I take another careful step backward, putting some distance between myself and the creepy twins.

I open my mouth to keep talking and then snap it shut. I just corrected them about my name … but how the hell did they know it in the first place?!

"She's going to panic and run like a rabbit," says Drink Me, like he's bored out of his skull. He looks me up and down with a sigh. "For an Alice, you're awfully jumpy. What's your fucking problem?"

"*My* problem?" I ask with a snort, pointing a single finger at myself. "I just saw some dude with rabbit ears *murder* my crush. He shot and killed him."

"How hard were you crushing?" Eat Me responds, crossing his arms over his chest and looking down at the broken glass on the floor like he's thinking way too fucking hard about this. "Enough to make diamonds?"

"Did you not hear what I said, you fucking psycho?!" I ask, taking a few more steps back. "I said a guy with *bunny* ears *murdered* a kid from my school!"

"You didn't say *bunny,*" Eat Me corrects, offering up a shit-eating grin, like this is all some sort of game, like he's not standing there naked and chiseled with blue-black hair dripping across his forehead and a sign that says fucking *EAT ME* hanging from his neck. The little blue ribbon slides across his muscles as he moves closer to me, and I see that his back is covered in tattoos. "You said *rabbit.*"

I turn and run then, like any sensible person would do, back down the corridor and toward the pile of bones and ivory littering the floor. It's a dead-end down here, a wall of rough stone that leads to nowhere. And when I look up? The hole I fell down is a good ten feet above me. Even if I *could* reach it, what am I going to do? Go all spread-eagled and crab walk my way to the top?

Sorry, but I got a C in gym last quarter specifically because I *refused* to even try to climb that damn rope. I have a thing about heights.

"Oh? Is that where you came from?" Drink Me says, making me jump as I drop my gaze and scoot away from him, keeping both twins in my sight as I bend down and pick up the gun I dropped, the one with the fuse. I might not have anything to *light* it, but they don't know that. With my other hand, I pull out my cell and find that I have zero service.

Of *course* I have zero service because what heroine in any story ever *does*?

I turn on my phone's flashlight app and spin it to face the twins—and honestly, I'm not stupid, I figure these have *got* to be Tweedledee and Tweedledum although they're not really supposed to show up until book two, *Through the Looking-Glass, and What Alice Found There.* Hey, if there's one thing I *do* know, it's books.

"Stay back, this thing is powerful enough to burn the flesh off your bones." I figure if I'm *not* actually on the grass at the party, frothing at the mouth and having a seriously bad reaction to some drug Edith slipped me, then I'm rolling with this whole magical world thing. And my bet—these assholes have never seen a cell phone before.

"Your phone has the power to burn flesh?" Eat Me asks, looking like he's trying his hardest to hold back a laugh. "Well, now, who's being the ridiculous one here?" He ruffles up his blue and black hair with his fingers and tilts his head at me. "If you need to make a call, *my* phone is back in my pants pocket."

I drop my hand back to my side and just stare at the two naked men, doing my best to keep my eyes *above* their waistlines. It's hard to miss the fact that they're both fully erect though. Like, why the fuck are they sitting in this weird hallway naked anyway?

Screw it—I'm going to ask.

"Why are you both naked?"

The twins turn their gazes to one another, clearly bemused at the state of my confusion.

When they look back to me, Eat Me has a smirking smile stretching across his full mouth, his tongue sliding across his lower lip and making it shiny and pink. I can't seem to look away.

"We're gifts for the Alice," he says, as Drink Me smiles at me, a tad caustically. "Gifts for you. The King sent us."

"The King?" I ask, but I can already see where this is going. I'm a smart girl. I can make leaps of logic. "The King … of Hearts?"

Drink Me's smile—or wait, is he Tweedledee or Tweedledum?—gets a bit more real.

"Yes, the King of Hearts is waiting for you."

I tuck my phone back into the pocket of Edith's awful dress and cross my arms over my chest, still holding onto the strange gun. I might not be able to *shoot* somebody with it, but I could bash these guys over the head if I had to.

"I'm sorry, but I think you've got me confused with somebody else. Look, I was at a party; I was running; I fell." I glance down and notice the blood smeared across the front of my dress, bile rising in my throat as I relive Brandon's death all over again. *That rabbit-eared son of a bitch …* "I don't need any gifts, don't need to see any king. All *I* need is to get back up there."

I point at the hole with a single finger and Drink Me sighs, like I'm the dumbest person he's ever met in his entire life. *This* from a guy who's standing there naked with a *DRINK ME* sign hanging around his damn neck. Like, really? Talk about throwing stones in glass houses.

"The Rabbit-Hole only goes one way, Alice."

"Alli*son*," I repeat and Drink Me sighs, putting both hands on his face and dragging them down.

"I know your *name* is Alli*son*, but you are *the* Alice. The one and only." He scoffs and turns away, shaking his head, his purple and black streaked hair falling across his forehead. "I can't believe we belong to you now. How ridiculous."

"I'm sorry, what?" I ask as Eat Me takes a few steps forward and offers me his hand. "You *belong* to me? People can't belong to people."

"We're gifts from the King," Eat Me repeats, like that's just a fact of life; the mellifluous quality of his voice never changes. "We're yours now. If you don't want to see him, that's your choice. All we can do is what you ask. But Tee is right—the Rabbit-Hole only leads *into* Underland, not out of it. If you want to leave, you have to start in the garden."

"Tee?" I ask, raising my brows. I'm not taking the naked weirdo's hand, not even if he's every woman's wet dream with his sapphire eyes, artfully disheveled hair, and that careful slash of a smirk across his face.

"That's Tee," Eat Me continues, gesturing in his brother's direction with his chin. When he drops his hand to his side, he doesn't look disappointed. No, he looks fucking *intrigued*, like I'm some sort of challenge. *That motherfucker …* "And I'm Dee."

"It's an easy one to remember," Drink Me continues, giving his brother a look and reaching up to untie the purple ribbon at his throat, letting the little tag at his neck drift to the ground near the pile of bones. Now that I'm standing here looking at them, it all makes sense. I bet those are the bodies of animals that wandered into the brush, tumbled down the hole like I did … but had no bunny-eared murderer to catch them when they fell. "Easy because Dee is a d-bag."

Tee crosses his arms over his chest and looks at me in defiance.

"Aren't you Tweedledee and Tweedledum?" I ask, because I'm still on the fence about the whole LSD trip/this is actually happening sort of thing. And if it *is* happening, then … I'm probably in shock because I don't feel anything. Not all that surprising considering it's been a hell of a long time since I felt anything at all. Not since my mother was convicted of murder last year. No, since then I haven't *felt* much. Why should I? All it does is *hurt.* When you let the world in, it cuts you and makes you bleed.

I rub sweaty palms on the red waist cincher, trying to get off the last red-brown streaks of Brandon's blood.

"Only if that's what you want to call us," Dee aka Eat Me says as he tugs on a strand of his blue-black hair. He's smirking at me again, like we're not all standing around in a dead-end tunnel next to a pile of bones and ivory.

"And isn't this … Wonderland?" I hazard, but I should've known better.

The murderer with the gun? The mound of corpses? The chandelier with the skulls?

I've read/watched/played enough fucked-up Alice interpretations to have figured it out.

There's always trouble in paradise.

Otherwise, I wouldn't be here, right?

"Wonderland …" Tee says after a moment, surprising me by speaking up. He turns away and I see that his entire back, from his neck down to his ankles is covered in tattoos … *and* scars. Two big aubergine angel wings wrapped in chains take up every inch of available space, even covering the backs of his arms. "Hmm," he scoffs on the end of a sigh, glancing over his shoulder at me. His smile, when he gives it, is nothing short of *devastating,* both beautiful and melancholic all wrapped into one. "Not anymore."

Chapter Two

The Pool of Drugs and Tears

The chaise lounge I found Drink Me … sorry, *Tee* lying on when I pulled back the tattered black curtain has a small door next to it, about the perfect size for a baseball to fit through. In the original Alice books, she drinks the uh, *DRINK ME* bottle and shrinks to the perfect size.

It only goes to show how sick in the head I am that I'm expecting the same thing to happen here.

"So," I say, standing up and keeping my gaze focused on the burgundy striped wall in front of me. It has vertical stripes in alternating columns of shiny and matte paint. To me, it just looks like blood. *Blood on the backside of a boy's glasses, blood all over my dress …* I hazard a look over my shoulder and find that both twins have *finally* wiggled into their pants, their beautiful cocks hidden from sight and never to be seen by me again.

Because, like, I have no interest in ever seeing them again.

"So what?" Tee asks, digging into his pocket and producing a phone.

Holy shit.

The twins were telling the truth—they *do* have a phone. And it looks … a bit like mine, too. Tee taps a button on the side and the screen lights up.

"Didn't you want to make a phone call?" he asks as I stumble over and snatch it from his outstretched hand. As I do, the rough whorls of my fingertips slide across his palm and his amethyst eyes snap up to mine, heat curling down my arm and coiling inside my chest. I jerk my arm back and pretend like it was nothing.

Because it *was* nothing.

Nothing at all.

Looking down, I find three simple apps on a plain black background—one to make calls, one to send texts … and something with the symbol of a *bomb* for its icon. I'm not even going to fucking ask about that one. When I turn the phone over to inspect it, I see that it's sitting inside a glass case with gold and copper gears and cogs, spinning and ticking away beneath the surface.

Huh.

I flip it back over and start to dial Edith's number.

"If you're trying to call outside Underland though," Tee continues as Dee looks at his brother in annoyance, "then you'll be sorely disappointed. There *is* no service outside of Underland."

I feel the edge of my mouth twitching in annoyance as I start to hand the phone back to him and notice the corner of *his* lips tilting up in a small, self-satisfied little smile. What a freaking asshole, man. He holds his palm out for the phone, but I just chuck it his way and watch as he struggles to keep it from hitting the floor.

"This is the door we're going through?" I ask as Tee glares at me and Dee grins like a gothic anime *GQ* model on crack.

"It is," he says as I kneel down and, like the original Alice in the books, peer through the lock and into the garden. "King's personal gardens," Dee continues as I blink and try to make sense of what I'm seeing. A white and red castle *towers* over an intricately planned and meticulously maintained series of hedges, flower gardens, and … giant fucking mushrooms. They're the size of *trees.*

I blink stupidly and lean in closer, barely listening to Dee as he talks.

"There's only one way out of Underland and that's through the Looking-Glass, but you need permission from the King to use it. And this door here, it's the only direct portal into the garden—or anywhere *near* the castle grounds really."

As I watch, a man—*another* ridiculously handsome specimen of masculinity—marches down the white gravel path like he's on a mission, pausing at the rustling of a nearby bush and stopping at a crossroads, next to a white bench covered in red hearts.

Based on the crown he's wearing, the cruel set to his jaw, and the hard glint in his eyes … it doesn't take a genius to make the connection—the King of Hearts then?

"I can see the king," I blurt and hear Tee grumbling from behind me.

"I can see your panties," he adds, and I clench my teeth, reaching back to tug my skirt over my ass. Doesn't help much, but I can't seem to pull myself away from what I'm seeing. From the rustling bushes … steps the rabbit-eared murderer.

I can't quite make out what he's saying, but I stare in fascination as he kneels before the king, a pair of white kid gloves in one hand, and a knife in the other. He offers the blade on his outstretched palm, his chin dipped in deference. The cruel king reaches out and tousles the raven-dark hair of the rabbit-eared boy, almost mockingly.

'King's orders.'

That's what he said just before shooting Brandon. So somehow, my classmate, chess geek and senior year crush, Brandon Carmichael was mixed up in all this Underland stuff?! I don't see how, but then, I also didn't figure on him getting shot in the face at a high school party. Things aren't always what they seem, right?

But shit if I can look away from the king's face. I don't think I've ever *seen* a man quite as beautiful as that, both infallible and yet … also flawed. It's a strange conundrum—his perfect hair, red as blood, his perfect clothes … and that ragged scar that traces from his lower lip and down his chin, across his neck. It's as if his throat was slit at some point, like someone tried to take off his head.

"Oh! The Duke, the Duke! Oh! *Won't* he be savage if we've kept him waiting?" a voice says, much more clearly than the murmuring voice of the king and his rabbit. A foot steps in front of the door, effectively blocking my view of the two ethereally beautiful men. Whoever it is continues forward and I notice that he has rabbit ears—just like Brandon's murderer—*and* a puffy white little tail.

What the fuck?!

I pull myself away from the keyhole and stand up, brushing my hands down the knees of my harlequin patterned tights. There are tiny red spatters of blood on the white, but I ignore it for the moment. Brandon's killer is on the other side of this door; I'll be coming face-to-face with him again soon enough. But frankly, I'll march right past him if it means getting out of here.

"So, where are the other FUCKING DRINK ME bottles?" I ask, crossing my arms over my chest as Dee moves closer—now dressed in a black and white striped button up … with all the buttons undone, as well as combat boots with buckles. Like the rabbit-eared murderer, these too have hearts on the toes. He kneels down and picks up a *tiny* key that I overlooked before, so small he has to wet his fingertip with his tongue and touch it to the shimmer of metal to make it stick. He rises to his feet and then slips it into the pocket of his black denim jeans. They're so tight, they look fucking painted. "Let's shrink to size and get this over with."

Dee and Tee share a look which scares the shit out of me, this perfect pair of dream boyfriends in front of a tattered black curtain and walls the color of blood. I know most of my classmates would flip their shit to be stuck in a room with these men and all I can do is wonder how the hell I'm going to get out of here.

"Rab took one and smashed the rest," Dee says with a slight shrug of his shoulders, and then his smile … it takes on a torrid twist that makes my throat tight, pebbles my skin with goose flesh. Oh dear. That look … I can't tell if it promises either pain or pleasure. "But that's okay—you have us."

"Rab?" I ask, reaching up to rub at my temples.

"Rab," Tee breathes, like he's trying his very hardest not to scream at me. He moves over to the chaise, getting awfully close. As he passes by, I get a whiff of what smells like cool mountain air, crisp and fresh, like a virgin layer of snow's just fallen. I pretend that scent does nothing for me and turn to watch him as he picks up a pair of leather belts with pouches, holsters, and sheaths attached to them, and hands one to his brother. "The king's favorite lackey, the White Rabbit."

Tee turns to look at me, his violet eyes flashing with irritation, like he's trying ridiculously hard not to stab me with the giant fucking *knife* that's hanging from the belt in his hands.

"The White Rabbit," I breathe because, you know, *of course.* In the original book, Alice's adventure starts when she meets the White Rabbit, just before she falls down the fucking rabbit-hole …

"Rab, yeah, the guy who shot your assassin," Tee grinds out, clearly frustrated with me already. It's been what, fifteen minutes since we met? That doesn't bode well.

"My … my what?!" I don't generally like repeating myself, nor am I a fan of asking too many questions. But come on—when a supernaturally sexy stranger tells you that your high school crush, the nerdy one with the thick glasses and a pimple, is an assassin, you question that shit.

"Your assassin," Dee says, coming over to stand in front of me. Now that he's not nude, I'm starting to notice other things about him, like how damn tall he is. He reaches past me to the chaise and snatches up a hat, tucking it on his head. It's a black wool and leather motorcycle peaked cap with a red heart on the very top. My heart skips a little when he leans in close to me, his sapphire eyes ringed in black liner. "What was his name, Tee?"

"Brandon Carmichael," Tee says, pulling out a silver pocket watch similar to the one the White Rabbit—*Rab*—was using before. Talk about a cliché—these people have *all* the Alice ones down pat.

"Right," Dee says, grinning impishly at me. "*Brandon Carmichael,* the private assassin for the King of Clubs." He whips a long blue trench coat off the back of the chaise and shrugs into it, the silver heart buttons on the front catching the flickering candlelight from the wall sconces.

I cross my arms over my chest and cock a brow.

"Brandon Carmichael, the geeky king of nerds, the kid I've known since preschool whose hair I used to pull, captain of the chess team … Sorry, but I've seen him fill his time with after-school cram classes and SAT prep courses. When the hell would he have time to learn to kill people?"

Dee grabs a second hat off the chaise lounge and moves over to his brother, settling it onto his head and carefully arranging the loose tufts of hair that are sticking out over his forehead. He steps back, puts his hands on his hips and nods like that's that.

Neither twin bothers to acknowledge my question.

"Hello?" I say, waving a hand in their direction. "How the *hell* would Brandon Carmichael have gotten involved in … whatever the fuck all of this is anyway?"

Tee gives me a look that speaks volumes as to how he feels about me—he thinks I'm an idiot. Well, I'm also a *reader* and I've seen every trope in the book. *Please. Treating the human newcomer to the supernatural world like she's stupid for not automatically knowing all their strange customs? Not cool, bro.*

"Brandon Carmichael is a Rabbit. He was sent Topside with the sole purpose of keeping an eye on the Alice," Dee says, his smile ratcheting up a notch as he affects a sharp bow and then straightens up with his smile-turned-rictus-grin. "Now, Tee, you know what you have to do …"

Tee's jaw tightens and he glances away sharply, raising his palms to rub at his face. When he does, the sleeves of his black and white striped button up slide down his wrist a bit, revealing flashes of the tattoos on the backs of his arms, the edges of those purple and black wings.

"Wait," I say, holding up a hand. I don't mean to stand here and force these guys to info dump but … Brandon's a *Rabbit?* And what is all this Alice business? But then … I'm about to go home anyway, right? Does it *really* matter? Either none of this really happened and I'm still tripping hard on one of Edith's fancy party drugs or else, I'm about to jump ship and never come back, so who gives a shit? "Never mind."

I put my hands on my hips and nod at the guys.

"You ready?" Dee asks, and the look on his face is … envious? Of what, of *whom*, I'm not sure. Definitely not the girl with the dress covered in blood, right? "Alright,

Tee, unbutton those pants."

Tee reaches down to the button on his black jeans and pops it open before I can even think to protest. He's got the zipper down before I can remember how to make words.

"What the fuck are you doing?!" I snap, moving over and snatching him by the wrists. My fingers feel like they're burning in all the places we touch and my breath catches, heart thundering as my throat gets tight and I struggle to swallow. "You just put pants on, so why the hell would you take them off again? I already told you—I'm not interested in gifts from the king and I'm *really* not interested in human slavery, alright? This is the twenty-first century; that shit is barbaric."

Dee laughs, like this is all just a silly misunderstanding.

"We need to shrink, Alice," he says, pointing down at the little door. "And Rab drank the last potion and broke the rest, remember?"

'But that's okay—you have us.'

Oh.

Dee had said that, hadn't he?

Then again, what the fuck does that have to do with Tee taking off his pants?

As if he can read my mind, Dee points at himself first.

"Eat Me," he says and then swings his finger over to his brother. "*Drink* Me."

I just stand there for a moment and stare, gaping in shock. As soon as the implications of those phrases hit me, my hands on Tee's wrist feel … almost lascivious. Jerking backward, I step away from the twins and bump into the chaise lounge, nearly falling on my ass. I manage to keep my feet and find myself in some sort of weird crouching position, like I'm preparing for a fight. One hand rests over the large dress pocket that holds the gun.

"You're not implying what I think you're implying … are you?" I ask, my voice husky and quiet and dangerous. I might be a little nerdy, a little more into books than people … but I still know how to kick some ass when needed. "Are you asking me to suck him *off*?"

"The previous King of Hearts slaughtered our people," Tee snaps, and … are his cheeks turning slightly pink?! "Why do you think we're the only ones left?"

"Clue—it's not just these handsome faces," Dee says, grinning maniacally and then he coughs, snapping his booted feet together and clasping his hands together behind his back. "*Tweedledum and Tweedledee agreed to have a fight,*" he sings and his brother groans, releasing his hold on his pants but not bothering to button or zip them up. "*For Tweedledum said Tweedledee had fucked up his Saturday night. Just then flew down a monstrous witch, who'd witnessed their full quarrel. A rather powerful but judgmental bitch, she cursed them both immoral.*"

"What … what the fuck does that mean?!" I ask, and I realize I've probably asked this question about a hundred times in the last ten minutes but … come the hell on!

"We were cursed with … well, the same magic the king's bakers put into his tinctures and cakes. Tee here can make you as small as a mouse." Dee gestures at the door and then points at his bare chest, his muscles visible between the lines of his slightly rumpled dress shirt. "And I can make you as big as a house."

"A house and a mouse," Tee repeats, taking back up the creepy twin mantle. "Right now you need to be a mouse so …"

"Drink Me is *literal?!*" I snap because, like, that's fucking gross. "Whoa, buddy, you've got another thing coming if you think this is happening right now. I'm not giving some guy a blow job just so I can go through a goddamn door. Are you stupid?"

Tee's face crinkles in anger and Dee sighs.

"Well, you don't have to give him head *per se*," Dee begins, but I can already see where this is going. Drink Me, huh? Well, I'm not drinking *anything* related to these twins, their dicks, or anything else for that matter.

"No."

Just one word, simple and succinct. Nostrils flaring, I stand up straight from my battle crouch and glare daggers at the boys.

"If we don't go through to the gardens, we'll have to go the long way around …" Dee muses as Tee angrily buttons and zips his black denim pants.

"I know what you're thinking about, but it isn't so, no-fucking-how," Tee growls, marching over to the chaise and grabbing a purple trench coat that matches his brother's. He shoves his arms into the sleeves like he's picking a fight.

"Contrariwise," Dee continues, eyes sparkling mischievously as he studies me. I might find him cute if he hadn't just asked me to suck his brother's dick and swallow. Gross. "If it was so, it might be; and if it were so, it would be; but as it isn't, it ain't. That's logic."

Ignoring their nonsensical banter, I decide to add my own two cents.

"Can't we just stick our arm through that little door and wave around until someone notices us? They can pop a few potions through from the other side and voilà, problem solved."

Tee snorts at me and I snap a glare over to him.

"That's not how the portals work," Dee says, giving his brother a look. Sapphire eyes meet violet ones and I just *know* they're having some sort of private twin conversation. "You really don't want to know what'll happen if you simply stick your arm through without the rest of you following after. We'll have to go the long way."

"The king won't be pleased," Tee whispers, but I cross my arms over my chest and hold his gaze.

"You said you belong to *me* and that it was *my* choice what we do. I'm not sucking Tee off, so we're going the long way."

"You heard it from the Alice herself," Dee says, sounding a little … too excited at the prospect of the 'long way', whatever that means. "What choice do we have but to comply? And truly, isn't this all Rab's fault to begin with? If he hadn't been such a brute and broken the other DRINK MEs then everything would be just fine, wouldn't it? Or, perhaps, you just weren't charming enough."

"The long way will take days," Tee adds, glancing over at me. The weird part is, he seems almost *relieved.* Maybe he didn't want me to suck him off either? "A week or maybe two depending."

"A week or two?!" I ask, pointing down at the little door. "But the garden is *right* there."

"No," Tee snaps, swiping his palms down the front of his shirt and then beginning to slowly button it up. His brother doesn't seem inclined to copy him in that respect. "The gardens are hundreds of miles away, and the going's rough; Underland is not a kind or forgiving place."

As if my world is, I think angrily, keeping Tee's stare and holding it until Dee steps between us. I feel like that's what Tee's insinuating, that I must've had it easy. As if. My mother's in prison for *life* and my father's disconnected and checked out. He spends more time with the koi fish in his pond than he does with his daughters.

"However it is," I say, gritting my teeth, "I can handle it."

"Come now, let's take the door to The Pool and rent a boat, shall we?" Dee asks, turning and leading the way back through the tattered curtain and over to another one of the doors that lines the hall. He pulls a ring of gold keys off his belt and unlocks it, the scent of brine and mold drifting into the strange hallway.

Sucking in a deep breath, I follow after Dee and into Underland.

Secretly, somewhere deep down inside my chest, I'm actually … relieved that I don't have to go back.

Secretly, some part of me wonders if I'd be disappointed if I never did.

The Pool is a disheveled old building, made of rotting wood and sitting precariously on the edge of a large river. The waters are deep blue and volatile, frothing as they crash into rocks and part around the stilts of the old dock. Boats bob and bounce, barely secured in place with thick rope and heavy knots.

The whole place stinks of salt and mildew, like the very wood boards I'm standing on are liable to fall apart and crumble into the water at any moment. It's dark out which is a small relief—this place is strange enough without worrying about time warps or whatever the fuck. I just tell myself it's the same time here as it is back home and try not to think too hard on the subject.

Across the river, I can see a thick stand of woods, with trees as tall as the redwoods back home, their trunks as wide in circumference as my father's SUV. No, wider. Big enough to drive through if there were a tunnel there. I can see more of those giant mushrooms, too, like the ones in the king's garden, breaking up the blackness of the trees with white and red and purple, their gills glowing with a faint luminescence.

Glancing over my shoulder, past Tee's frowning face, I see more of the same. Trees and mushrooms and nothing else.

"Let's go," Tee says, unwilling to follow his brother across the narrow dock until I do. When I refocus my attention on him, he looks nervous as hell, one hand resting on his knife, his eyes narrowed with careful focus.

"Why?" I ask caustically, flipping some of my long blonde hair over one shoulder. "Is the jabberwock going to get us?" It's supposed to be a joke—because the White

Rabbit *had* said the gun I'd chosen could take one down—but when Tee looks at me, he doesn't seem to find it particularly funny.

"Do you have matches to light the Queenmaker?" he asks me, and I have no clue what he's talking about. Tee steps in close, so close that I can feel his warm breath on my lips when I tilt my head back to look up at him. I'm tall—five foot ten, actually—but Tee still towers over me. I figure he must be at least six foot two. At *least.*

His hand reaches down and grabs mine, placing it over the pocket on my white and blue dress.

"The gun," he whispers, "because if a jabberwock *does* come, you're going to be the only one that can stop it." I suck in a small breath, and that cool mountain air scent fills my lungs, cutting off the almost rancid stink of raw fish and salt. A saltwater river? I'm not sure such a thing *exists* back home. "Let's go before we get our throats slit."

He takes my hand in his, but I jerk it right back, marching ahead of him and starting across the slippery surface of the dock. There are no handrails on either side leading out to the deck of The Pool and the building itself. One wrong move and I'll go plunging into the navy blue depths.

I don't think too hard about it, trusting in the thick soles of my combat boots, and reach the other side without incident. As I get closer to the building, I can hear the ruckus inside, even with the roar of the raging river all around me.

I pause just long enough that Tee moves around me and pushes the door in, holding it open with his back and waiting for me to go inside.

The smells of booze and smoke and sex waft out—honestly, it doesn't smell *that* different from one of Edith's high school parties. Crude laughter mixes with the clinking of glasses as I step inside and find Dee already at the counter, leaning his elbows against the polished wood surface and making eyes at the pretty young bartender.

As I come up behind him, I catch a snippet of their conversation.

"Ain't nobody rentin' out boats at this time o' the night. Not for the king, not for anyone. Besides, Dee, you're not in Heart territory right now and you know it. I can get you a room for the night, but not a ride. Not until morning."

The bartender glances up past Dee, pauses on Tee and then … focuses on me and stays there, like she's seen a ghost. I swear, I can see her skin pebbling with goose bumps. She looks like a pirate in her black tricorne hat, a white pleasant blouse partially unbuttoned and showing generous swaths of ebony cleavage. Her hair is long, much longer than mine, and hangs nearly to her ass, a warm caramel brown color that matches her eyes.

"Who's the girl?" she asks, but there's a tenseness in her shoulders that wasn't there a moment ago. I feel like she somehow *knows* who I am. Hell, maybe she's more aware of who I am than … well, than *I* am.

The Alice.

What the hell is an Alice anyway?

"This," Dee says, standing up straight and tossing a sapphire glance in my direction, "this is our new mistress."

I sigh, but I don't bother to correct him. What's the point? I have no idea what the rules are here. For all I know, denying that fact could get me killed. As Tee stated, Underland doesn't much seem like the original Wonderland from Lewis Carroll's books. Whereas Alice's world was a dream … mine could easily be a nightmare. It *smells* awful enough to be one anyway.

"Mistress, huh?" the bartender says and then she nods her chin at me. "What do you want to drink, Mistress?"

"Oh, uh …" I start, but I don't have any money here. I mean, unless they take US dollars which is probably a serious fucking no. Then again, the twins *do* have cell phones … that can't call out of Underland. Ugh.

"A cup of Earl Grey ought to do the trick," Dee says and Tee makes a noise under his breath.

"No tea tonight," he tells his brother, but Dee just grins and raises his dark brows, tufts of black and blue hair sticking out from beneath his hat. "Dee …" Tee growls in warning, but his brother's already ignoring him, turning back to the bartender.

"Give us a pot of Earl Grey and we'll share," he says, slapping his palm on the counter and then reaching down to pop a silver heart-shaped button on a leather pouch attached to his belt. He digs a few coins out from inside and sets them on the counter.

I can't imagine why Tee gives two fucks if his brother orders a pot of tea, but his fists are clenched at his sides and he looks furious.

"Comin' right up," the bartender—or should I say *barkeep*—drawls, her eyes following me as I turn in a slow circle and take in the crowd.

Men and women dressed in fantastical costumes, like the twins with their striped shirts and peaked caps, decorate the tables, sipping from chipped white teacups and laughing raucously. The background music is slow and sensual and vaguely reminds me of Marilyn Manson. I try to figure out where it's coming from and find my gaze drawn to a stage in the far corner, a man clutching an old-fashioned microphone, voice crooning into the speakers. He has a full band with him—drums, a bass, even an electric guitar. Well, at least it *sounds* like an electric guitar. On closer inspection, it has the same glass covering as Tee's phone, the same cogs and wheels inside, ticking away as the musician strums her fingers over the strings.

In front of the stage, couples and groups dance in slow, swaying motions. I've been to enough parties—not a lot, but enough—to know that they're either drunk or high or both. Some of them look like they're about to strip down and have an orgy right there in the middle of the dance floor.

"Thank you, Lory," Dee says, taking the pot of tea and a stack of cups on a silver tray. He holds it up above his head with a single hand and winks at his twin, moving over to an empty table against the wall, just below an open window.

I can both hear and smell the river from here, but even that salty reek is better than the scent of unwashed bodies and sex that fills this place.

"Is this a bar … or a brothel?" I ask as I look around and see a disproportionate number of men to women. In fact, the longer I look, the more I notice a pattern: one woman with multiple men. Several of the groups both sitting and dancing follow that pattern and I cock an eyebrow.

"A brothel?" Dee asks, frowning as he pours three steaming cups of tea and passes them out to his brother and me. "What would you need a brothel for? You've already expressed your vehement disinterest in both me and my brother. Even if this *were* a working-house, you'd be hard-pressed to find a man as beautiful as either of us."

"I meant …" I start, but Dee seems fairly serious and his brother is staring into the cup in front of him like it holds all the answers. I can see something shining in his eyes as he bites his lower lip and looks away, reaching out to push back the teacup.

Dee rolls his eyes but doesn't comment on the move.

"So this isn't a whorehouse with … women?" I ask, looking back at the mix in the bar. Or wait, is this a bar? It smells like alcohol, but on closer inspection, I notice that everyone's drinking tea, just like us. So it's a teahouse then?

"There are no whorehouses with women in them," Tee says quietly, looking up from the smooth surface of the table, polished by dozens of elbows and hands wearing away at the wood rather than because anyone had sanded or slapped a coat of poly on recently.

"Why not?" I ask, but like, I'm literally thrilled to hear that. Skeptical, to be certain, but thrilled. Coming from a world of sex trafficking and forced prostitution, sitting here in this weird one with salt rivers and a smelly teahouse doesn't seem quite so bad, now does it? *Even if the twins did try to get me to suck them off …*

"Because of the Riving," Tee whispers, looking up and blinking his long-lashed eyes at me. With the easy sweep of dark liner around them, his eyes seem even brighter, like two amethysts wedged into a superbly handsome face.

"*Ry-ving,*" I say slowly, digging through my mental dictionary. I read a lot, so the word seems familiar. Doesn't that mean to tear or rend? To split open? The *Riving*? Ugh. That can't be anything good, can it?

Dee scoots my cup of tea closer and then lifts his with a grin.

"Drink up," he says, pausing to take off his cap and setting it aside on the end of the table.

"Magic surged through Wonderland, killed half of all the women and turned half of the ones that were left into men," Tee says, as if this is something that happened a long time ago, just simple fact. He doesn't even seem all that bothered by it.

Magic.

Wonderland.

"Going off of *your* calendar," Dee continues, sipping his tea and shivering with pleasure. I pick up my own cup and do the same, feeling this warm surge in my belly that surprises me. The tea is good and musky, the hint of bergamot oil sitting on the back of my tongue lending for a pleasant sort of aftertaste. But … my throat gets tight and as soon as I swallow, my mouth feels dry, like I've just eaten a *really* good pot brownie with my friends and the THC is starting to kick in. "The Riving happened in … 1865. Isn't that right, Tee?"

Deciding for the moment that I'll just roll with it—because how can I question *magic* after I just fell down a hole into a pile of old bones and met a boy with rabbit ears?—I ask, "Why would the women turn into men?"

"Women have a much higher affinity for magic than men, so when the Riving happened, their bodies absorbed most of it," Tee continues, and for the first time since I've met him, he actually looks pleased, like reciting historical lessons is definitely his fucking thing. "Many of the ones that were strong enough to survive had their magic essentially burned away, leaving a weaker shell of their former selves. Thus, they became men."

I blink a few times and then sip my tea because I don't quite know what to say to that. In a strange sort of way, it actually makes *some* sense. I mean women *are* equipped to give birth to babies; men can barely stand to have a single eyebrow hair plucked without screeching in pain.

After a few more sips, I'm starting to feel … tingly all over, that needlelike feeling in my arms and legs, like my limbs are asleep but absurdly more pleasant. I find myself swaying with the music as Dee hails Lory and she brings a plate of cakes over to the table. They're frosted with bright colors, dotted with little black currants that spell out *EAT ME.*

As soon as I read that, I snatch it up and start to giggle.

"If I eat this, will I get as big as a fucking house?" I ask, swaying side to side in my seat and trying to blink through the colored haze that's just slid over my vision. "The same as if I gave you a blow job and swallowed, huh?"

I take a bite and find that it tastes like pineapple and custard, nice and bright and fresh.

"This," Dee whispers back, leaning in close to me, his breath smelling like cherry tarts. He wraps his hands around one of mine as I lift the small cake to my lips again, pausing me mid-motion. "Is a different sort of cake." His face is just as dreamy and far away as my own as he leans forward and flicks his tongue against the corner of my mouth, licking off a bit of yellow frosting. "Dance with me?"

"Oh, for fuck's sake …" Tee growls from across the table, still sitting stiff as a board, arms crossed over his white and black striped shirt, his tea and the plate of cakes completely untouched.

"It's been ages since I've danced," Dee slurs, taking the cake from my fingers and slowly, sensually sucking fingertip by fingertip into his hot, wet mouth, cleaning off all the frosting. I can't even move, frozen there but blinking furiously, my heart thundering in my chest. I can feel my nipples pebbling beneath my dress, my thighs clenching together as a warming sensation surges through my core. "Ages and ages."

Dee pulls me up from my seat and drags me to the dance floor, both of us stumbling and giggling as we go. When we get close to the stage, he pulls me into his arms and hugs me close, like we're not complete and total strangers, but friends … *lovers.*

I want to fuck him so bad right now, I think as I close my eyes and lean my head on his shoulder, breathing in that sharp, fresh scent of his, like snow and ice on a sunny winter day, a snowboard beneath my feet and goggles on my face. He smells like … family vacations when my brother was still alive, like happiness, like winter. *Mmm.*

The world around me spins and tilts, but when I start to lose my balance, Dee is there to catch me and hold me up.

"Alice," he whispers, his mouth against my ear, his breath warm, "you're going to change the whole world, aren't you?" Dee drops a kiss to my neck and I sigh, my knees giving out, my body slumping to the floor.

And then I pass out.

Chapter Three

A Cock-Race and The Long Tale

A loud knock at the door wakes me from the best sleep I've had in *years*, the type of sleep I had when Fred was still alive, when mom wasn't in jail, when the worst part of my day was having to deal with Edith's bullshit.

"Leave me alone, Edy," I growl as I drag a musty smelling pillow over the back of my head and clamp down hard on both sides, trying to block out the noise. The knocking only seems to get louder.

"Open the fuck up, you idiots! Ship leaves in ten and Dodo wants full payment *now.*"

I blink my way through a foggy haze and into the darkness beneath my pillow, sitting up with a sharp gasp in my crumpled blue and white dress and tights. Dee is lying passed out next to me, his blue and black hair rumpled and tangled, his shirt missing.

As I stare down at him, I hear a door open behind me and glance back to find Tee in a towel, cursing under his breath as he moves over to another door, dripping water across the floor, steam rising from his pale skin like mist. He unlocks a good half-dozen bolts and chains and then tears the door open to reveal Lory, in her tricorne hat, skintight brown pants, and boots.

"The Long Tale leaves in eight minutes, and I need your fare *now.*" Lory holds out her hand, gold bangles dancing across her chocolate skin.

"You said ten," Tee growls, turning and noticing for the first time that I'm awake. His eyes meet mine for a moment, but I have trouble holding them because … wow. His body is glorious, all wet and speckled with beads of moisture like that. *I sure would like to lick …* Whoa. What the fuck is wrong with me?! As I turn around and lean back into the pillows, I can feel my head swimming and I groan.

Was I … drugged last night?!

I look down at Dee and then snap my attention back to his brother, watching as he digs through the leather pouch on his belt and produces a handful of coins. He passes them over to Lory and she nods sharply.

"You said ten," he repeats and Lory just grins, her white teeth bright in the shadowy room.

"It *was* ten, but you took too long answering the door. Now it's six. Hurry up."

She glances over at me, lying on the double bed next to Dee, and winks. "See ya onboard in five."

Lory turns on her heel and leaves the room as I struggle to collect my thoughts.

"What the *fuck* happened last night?" I ask Tee as he heads toward the bathroom and pauses, the tattoos on his back making my breath catch. The feathers look so real, like I could reach out and touch them, feel the soft down against my fingertips … And those chains? I have to blink a few times to convince my tired eyes they're not shining in the weak morning light from outside. It streams in the dirty windows and highlights dust motes, floating in the air like faeries.

"You had a tea party," he says with a roll of his eyes, stepping into the bathroom and slamming the door closed. I grit my teeth because, like, rude much? Throwing my feet over the edge of the bed, I see that somebody removed my boots last night.

Lucky them that they didn't remove anything *else.*

I pad over to the heavy wood of the bathroom door, trying not to take *too* close of a look at the decrepit room. I slam my fist a few times on the door and then cross my arms over my chest, running my tongue over my dry lower lip. My mouth feels chapped, and my head is swimming like I drank a dozen tequila shots in a row and passed out. And don't even get me started on how I feel about sleeping in bloody clothes.

'A week or maybe two depending.'

If I have to be in Underland for that long, then I'm in serious need of fresh clothes. *One* night soaked in Brandon's blood was more than enough.

"I don't know what a fucking tea party is—" I start to scream and then Tee's ripping the door open just as the knot on his towel comes undone and the black fabric falls to the floor at his feet. He's rock-hard and quivering—both him *and* his dick.

"You don't have tea Topside?" he asks me, and I wonder for a second why they call it Topside. But then, *Under*land … and I did fall down a hole to get here … I shake my head to clear it and take a deep breath, trying to stay calm and *not* look at Whichever-Tweedle's cock is currently pointing at my face.

"Not tea that makes me …" I pause as snippets of last night flicker to mind, of Dee sucking on my fingers, of slow dancing, of … well, I don't really remember anything after that, actually. "Tea is just, like, boiled plant water back home—sometimes with cream and sugar."

I exhale roughly as Tee sighs and bends down to gather his towel, covering up his bits before he rises to his feet. I notice he's lined the floor with more towels, like he's afraid of touching too many things in the grubby bathroom.

Don't blame him.

Not one hundred percent sure I'd have showered in there at all.

"You don't boost your tea," he says slowly, like it's just dawned on him. He swears under his breath and then flicks a raging glare toward his brother as a groan sounds from behind me. "If I'd known that, I never would've … well, shit, I would've warned you."

"Boost our tea?" I raise both blonde brows. "It was drugged."

Tee sighs, his purple-streaked black hair stuck up all over the place, wet and spiky and kind of … like, adorable. If he were a boy back at school, I'd have hit on him for *sure*—even with that personality of his. Hell, who am I kidding? It probably would've *drawn* me to him.

I have a problem getting attracted to assholes …

My last boyfriend …

No. Nope. Not going there, not today.

"Tea *is* a drug here," the purple-haired twin explains, looking down at me with a *slightly* less bitchy than usual expression. Tee reaches out and tucks some strands of rainbow-colored hair behind my ear on impulse. I think the move surprises him as much as it does me and we just stand there staring at each other for a moment before he blinks and shakes his head slightly. "It's blended from the get-go to have certain properties. I can't remember the last time I drank normal tea." He pauses and looks right at me, his eyes the color of violets, this beautiful purple that shimmers beneath long, dark lashes. "Maybe never. People stopped drinking plain tea after the Riving."

I rub a hand against my forehead and glance over my shoulder as Dee throws his feet out of bed and groans, the blue and black wings on his back catching the light. I wonder what the symbolism is there? I mean beyond the obvious *you are slaves, you will no longer fly free* vibe that I'm getting. But why angel wings and chains specifically?

Doubt I'll ever feel comfortable enough with this pair of weirdos to ask.

"I'll remember that," I say as I take a step back, suddenly aware of how hot the air between us has gotten, and how much like soap Tee smells. It's intoxicating, that warm, wet muscular god smelling like shampoo and soap … *Fuck.* I turn around and glare at Dee as he leans over and puts his head between his knees. If I hadn't seen the look of genuine concern on Tee's face, I might've thought they did it to me on purpose, drugged me up like that. Lucky them I don't think that anymore or balls. would. *roll.* And by balls, I don't mean sports equipment. "Is there somewhere I could grab new clothes?" I ask and Dee's face whips up, pale but with a sinful little slash of lips.

"We could always ask Lory to borrow some?" he says, standing up and groaning, like the effort's just too much to bear. I wonder if he finished off Tee's cup last night? The last thing *I* remember is collapsing on the dance floor. "But otherwise, no. We're in the middle of nowhere which is to say, we're as far from everywhere as we can get."

I roll my eyes because I'm not in the mood for riddles and games, and head straight for the door.

If Dee thinks I'm too scared to ask the cranky pirate lady for a change of clothes, then *he* has never slept in a dress soaked with his crush's blood.

The boat we're sailing the river on is called The Long Tale and the crew is a motley assortment of weirdos that make the *twins* seem normal. Lory seems to be the least crazy of them all and she *did* lend me a pair of black breeches, a pale blue peasant blouse, a black and gold jacket, and some clean undergarments. Took me about fifteen minutes to try to figure out how to slip into said undergarments before Lory burst in the bathroom door, ignored my screams of protest, and laced me up in a white corset with hidden pockets for knives.

Hell, she even *supplied* the knives for me.

I keep my headband with the top hat, the red waist cincher, and my own boots, but at least I'm not wearing Brandon Carmichael on my dress anymore.

"Are you bloody stupid?" the captain—a *huge* hulking beast of a man named Dodo—shouts as he stands on the dock and watches several men carry large crates onto The Long Tale. "Do I have to do fuckin' everything around here?" he growls as I stand on the stern … er bow … uh, whatever the front part of a ship is called.

And when I say *ship,* I mean *floating hunk of rotted wood covered in barnacles that smells like rotted fish and looks like it has an equal chance of sinking as it does floating.*

"Are we sure this fucking thing is sturdy enough to get us upriver?" I ask as Dee unlocks our rented cabin and opens the door. The smell that emanates from inside there is almost *worse* than the one out here. Wrinkling my nose, I step up close to the blue-haired twin and act like I don't notice the spark of heat that jumps between us when our shoulders brush together. "What the hell is this?" I ask as I examine the room—if it can even be *called* a room.

There's a ten by ten square—a *wet* ten by ten square, mind you—that's taken up by an odd square bed covered in what looks like burlap sacks. No pillows, no blankets, nothing else in there except for a small, dirty round window and a trunk that, when I step into the room and open it, is also partially filled with water.

I purse my lips.

"Bet you wish you'd sucked my brother off now, huh?" Dee chortles, and I swear to God, I almost punch him right in the nuts. "A mouthful of cum or this room for two nights—which sounds worse?"

"*Two* nights?" I ask, and I try really hard not to shriek.

"Dee, knock it off," Tee snarls, and it sounds like *he* is now trying really hard not to punch his twin in the family jewels. I glare at the two brothers as they engage in a stand-off, and I see Dee's hands clench into fists at his sides. That strange poem that Dee recited for me yesterday comes to mind, and I wonder what the brothers were like before they were enslaved by the King of Hearts. Were they princes or paupers? Based on that poem, it doesn't much seem like they got along any better then than they do now.

Sibling rivalry, I can definitely understand though. Edith and I have *never* had a peaceful relationship, and my older brother Frederick and I were sworn enemies. Until he was murdered, anyway. I close my eyes against a rush of emotion and slam the lid closed on the old trunk, standing up straight, and keeping the satchel slung over my shoulder—another gift from Lory. It's an old, wrinkled, cracked leather bag that smells like salt, but it works for keeping Edith's dress safe. I know I *should* probably just throw the hideous thing away, but … I already lost one sibling. I won't throw away a dress—no matter how grotesque or bloody it is—that my sister bought with her own money.

After a moment, the twins break their relentless stare, stepping away from one another in near unison and clearing the doorway for me to slip out of the cabin. I pause on the deck of the boat and cringe when Dodo starts shouting again.

"Oh for fuck's sake!" the captain snarls and I glance over to find Lory smoking a cigarette on the dock, watching as her fellow mates get their asses handed to them. Dodo's red beard and disheveled appearance make him look like a fucking Viking, but he's handsome in his own way. I'm not into guys the size of tree trunks with hairy arms and permanent scowls, but I bet my mother would find him cute. If we saw this Dodo guy on a movie or something, I know she'd sigh and tap me on the knee a few times, maybe toss a piece of popcorn my way. *'He's a bit attractive, don't you think? But just a bit.'*

I sigh.

I'll never watch movies with Mom again, so what's the point?

"Why do they all have animal names?" I ask, referring to the crew: Duck, Mouse, Dodo, Eaglet (a baby eagle), and Lory—a nickname for lorikeets that I only know because I read the original *Alice's Adventures in Wonderland* and had to look it up, thank you very much.

"Why shouldn't they all have animal names?" Dee asks, jumping back into the whole riddle game again. "Don't animals often have people names? It only seems fair to make it an even trade." One day I've known these guys and I can already tell that when they start to get a bit singsong-y like that, I'm in for some of that awful lyrical nonsense that made me love the original book so much in the first place. But like, in real life? Not a huge fan.

I decide to ignore Dee and make my way over to the edge of the boat, on the side opposite The Pool, glancing down into the salty waters and wondering how a geographical anomaly like this came to be in the first place. Lifting my gaze, I see the forest and the giant mushrooms again, their caps as big as the roof on my parents' house. Some are spotted, some striped, but they all seem to have white stems and gills.

As I gaze out at the weird as fuck forest and wonder *why* I'm not freaking out about any of this, I hear the sharp slap of rope against wood and glance over my shoulder to see Lory untying big, fat knots from the railing of the dock.

We're getting ready to leave—*finally.*

I wonder why she was in such a hurry to get *us* down here this morning?

Tee and Dee stay ridiculously close to me like guards. I watch them surreptitiously and try to decide if it feels like they're guarding *me* from the outside world … or if they're escorting me like a prisoner. But after a few moments of watching them—Tee, especially—I can see that they're constantly scanning the environment, looking out at the woods, down at the water, and even up at the sky.

Shit.

I do *not* want to know what comes down from the fucking sky.

"Why are you so concerned with what happens to me?" I ask as Dodo shouts orders to his crew and I feel the boat start to move. My stomach lurches and I clamp my hand down around the railing to try to gain some stability, heart racing in my chest as we drift away from the dock … and then start to fly down the river at a speed that whips my blonde hair back from my face.

"Because," Tee says, and even though his voice is fairly low, he's not hard to hear over the wind and rapids. "You're the Alice."

"What's …" I swallow hard and lock my knees as the boat jostles and bounces on the water, swerving this way and that to avoid the hulking shadows of stones. We're moving so goddamn fast, I have literally zero idea how the small crew is keeping up. "What the fuck does that mean?"

"The Alice," Dee begins, and when I glance over at him, he actually looks a tad serious, "is the only one that can save Underland."

♦ ♣ ♣ ♦

Besides the small, shitty cabin we rented for the trip, The Long Tale also sports a dining hall and kitchenette, a storage area, bunks for the crew, and the captain's quarters. Not a one of them is much nicer than the original cabin I saw. And everything is wet, every damn inch of that fucking boat.

Thank *God* for my combat boots—they keep most of the saltwater at bay. Well, you know except for the fact that after eating breakfast in the 'mess hall' my butt's soaked. Nobody else seems to be bothered by it, so I do my best not to complain.

Although, you know, I *am* eighteen and liable to go there on occasion.

"How long did you say this, uh, portion of the trip's going to take?" I ask Dee as I sit smashed between him and his brother on a narrow bench in the dining area, staring down at a plate of dried crackers smeared with some sort of salty-meaty paste—i.e. my lunch. My nose wrinkles and I try to pretend like having two big, warm, male bodies on either side of me doesn't matter at all.

But holy crap.

Holy. Crap.

When the twins move, I can feel the muscles in their bodies sliding beneath the skin, these powerful pistons stretching and contracting, and I have a seriously hard time keeping my mind out of the gutter.

Being a hormonal teenager blows.

"Two days," Dee answers as he picks up one of the crackers and takes a bite. Somehow, he even manages to make eating our weird lunch sexy.

"Or two nights, depending on who you ask," Tee adds automatically, staring at his plate in a similar way to how I'm staring at mine.

"Two nights and two days, really," Dee continues, "because you can't have another day without having a night, now can you?" I sigh and, giving into my rumbling tummy, reach down and grab a cracker, closing my eyes as I take a bite. If I have to sit here and listen to nonsense, I may as well do it with a full belly. Surprisingly, the giant cracker is flavorful, herby, and the paste on top turns out to be something like pâté. "Say, you like poetry, Alice?"

"Alli*son.* Hell, you can even call me *Son*ny, like my sister does if you want. But not Alice. Whoever this mythical Alice is, she's not me."

"Mm, what an interesting segue into a non-sequitur, wouldn't you say, Tee? This Alice is good at roundabouts. You'll make a fabulous mythical Alice, Alice. Now." He finishes his cracker, slaps the crumbs from his palms, and then swings a leg over the bench so that he's straddling the wood.

He scoots closer to me, so close that our faces are only inches apart.

"Do you like poetry, Allison-who-isn't-Alice?" Dee asks again and I sigh.

"Depends on the poem," I hedge, taking another bite of my cracker and trying not to like the way Dee's lids drop, heavy and sexy. Bedroom eyes, that's what he's got. Fucking bedroom eyes.

"Can I tell you one then?" he continues, and I hear Tee sigh from behind me. "It's a long one, though."

"I have nowhere else to be," I say, and I realize with a start that I don't even really care. I *should* be at school right now, sitting in my statistics class and staring out the window, wondering if my dad's going to get a Christmas tree this year, or if it'll be like last year when he made us go and sit in the cold, sterile visiting room at the prison with Mom. "Go on," I continue as Dee's face splits into a grin and he slides back and off the bench, standing up straight and tapping his boots together. He clasps his hands behind his back and clears his throat.

"*The world was wrecked and withering,*
wrecked and full of fright:
The Alice did her best to take ...
In the horrid sights—
But this was hard, because it was
The corruption of her life.

The moon was bathed in blood and hate,
It blotted out the sun
The kings had got no business there
Because their time was done—
'It's very rude of them,' she said,
'Slaughtering everyone!'

The blood was red as red could be,
The bones were dry as dry.
You could not see a star because
Gray clouds were in the sky:
No angels flying overhead—
There were none left to fly."

"Tee?" he asks, but his brother just glances up from his plate and narrows his eyes. "Would you like to finish the rest of the poem?"

"Not particularly, *Dee*," Tee says, taking a deep breath before pushing up the sleeves of his purple military coat and grabbing the cracker. In three quick bites, he eats it, stands up, and wipes his hands on the napkin he had tucked in his lap. "Allison doesn't want to hear an epic-length poem about a prophecy she doesn't believe in."

He turns his gaze to me and pauses just long enough to make me uncomfortable before he flicks his eyes back over to his brother.

"You'll stay with her for a while? There's hardly enough room on that bed for the three of us. I'll sleep the first shift." Tee adjusts his peaked cap, nods briefly at me, and then turns on his heel and leaves the room.

Well, shit, now I'm intrigued to hear the rest of the poem.

A prophecy she doesn't believe in, huh?

"What's his problem?" I ask as Dee sighs and takes his cap off, twisting it around in his hands. His blue-streaked black hair is sticking up all over the place and his sapphire eyes seem to flash with something before he looks up at me.

"He hates this world and everything in it," Dee says, moving over to one of the round port windows and opening it, letting in the pungent reek of salt. He turns and leans his back against the wall, watching me carefully. "There's not a person we know or love that's still alive." He pauses for a moment and I see yet another flicker of seriousness on his face. "Well, except for each other. Tee doesn't want to see Underland restored. He *likes* seeing it fall apart; he *wants* it to crumble away into nothing, and I can't blame him."

"You don't feel the same way?" I ask as Dee stands up straight and spins his hat around on a single finger, throwing a grin my way that makes my heart stumble and fall, scraping its damn knees as I try to pick myself up off the proverbial pavement.

"Me? Do you mean does Dee feel the same as Tee?" He winks at me and moves over to the bench, putting his boot on the end of it, leaning down close again. "No. Because, like I told you last night Allison-who-isn't-Alice, you're not going to *save* this world." Dee's grin ratchets up a notch and he reaches out to play with a strand of my rainbow hair. "You're going to *change* it."

He straightens up, my heart still racing, and holds out his hand.

"Come, come, it won't do for the Alice to be running around with the Queenmaker when she's as likely to blow off her own head with it as she is a bandersnatch's."

♦ ♠ ♣ ♠ ♣ ♠ ♦

"These might be the only things on this ship that aren't *wet*," Dee says, looking at me with such an innocent expression that even though I'm pretty sure he said *wet* with a lusty bite to this tongue, I let it go.

He pulls out a box of matches from inside one of the stiff leather pouches attached to his belt and passes them over to me.

The current has slowed some since we left The Pool, so the wind isn't quite as fierce and the rapids not quite as loud. I can, however, still hear Dodo screaming orders at his crew, and when I glance back, Lory gives me a small wave from the crow's nest, a cigarette clutched in her opposite hand.

"So this thing's called the Queenmaker?" I ask as I look back at Dee and heft the gun out of the leather satchel that still holds my sister's dress.

Dee watches me with his sapphire eyes, his voluminous blue coat billowing in the breeze. His smirk is crooked and way too endearing for his own good. Or mine. Definitely not good for mine.

"Here," he says, reaching out and taking my hand, using his fingers on mine to turn the gun over so I can see the crown stamped onto the bottom of the grip. The wood grain has this striped look to it, like the antique guns my grandfather used to collect; I'm pretty sure the ones that looked like this were made of maple. "The Queenmaker, a weapon designed by the former Queen of Hearts. It had the sole and very specific purpose of being used in a Royal Hunt."

"For a jabberwock," I say, because my mind just can't seem to get over the fact that something like that might actually be real. John Tenniel, the original illustrator of Lewis Carroll's Alice books, certainly painted a nasty picture of a jabberwock. And the idea that something like that actually exists? Must still be in shock.

Because … standing here on the deck of this boat with the cold air stinging my face, my lips dry from the constant splashes of saltwater, and my wet—from the *river* water, not arousal—panties stuck up my butt crack, I'm pretty damn sure I'm not in an LSD induced trip anymore.

Standing here next to Dee, his warm hands on mine, his sapphire eyes bright and curious, I'm positive I'm not imagining this.

"The same queen that slaughtered your people?" I ask, and I wonder if I've said too much, if he might shut down and shut me out. But no, Dee just shakes his head and releases me, stepping back and whipping out an arm to point at the river, his blue coat flapping in the wind.

"Aim this way," he says as I turn and point the gun out at the water and the strange, creeping woods on either side of it, "and I'll tell you a little story."

"Another poem?" I ask as I wonder how to light a match *and* hold the gun at the same time. Certainly not very gracefully is the answer to that question. As I bite my lip and push the box of matches against my hip to open them, Dee reaches over, plucks one out and tucks it behind my ear.

"The Queen always kept a match or two here and there—in her hair, behind her ear, in her *brassiere.*" Okay, I do *not* miss the way he emphasizes that one, leaning too close to me and letting his breath tickle my cheek. "And no, not another poem although I can recite exactly two hundred and thirty-six different ones from memory, if you wish."

Dee crinkles up his face in an even bigger grin. I can't decide if he really is just this happy-go-lucky or if he's hiding from that same darkness that seems to take over his brother's face.

"What's the story then?" I ask as Dee moves behind me and puts his lips next to my ear.

"Permission to touch the Alice requested," he whispers and my skin feels suddenly tight and achy as I nod and Dee steps in close, sliding his fingertips down my arms, tantalizing me even through the fabric of my borrowed jacket. When he gets to the gun, he curls his fingers through my own, repositioning them until my grip on the weapon feels natural and easy. "The key is maintaining a certain level of confidence when using a weapon like this," Dee continues, putting a booted foot between my legs and kicking them apart. The suggestive nature of that movement doesn't escape me. "Feet apart. Don't forget to brace yourself, Allison-who-isn't-Alice."

Dee steps back suddenly and the icy chill of the air and water surrounds me again, trying its best to douse that wild heat his nearness summoned up in me. Doesn't work. Ugh. Insta-lust drives me totally crazy insane. Like, I'm no good at resisting impulses. It's one of the reasons I prefer to stay home and read—it's a lot harder to get into trouble with your nose buried in a book.

Nah, I'd much rather watch hapless literary heroines bury themselves in shit … *liiiiike* giving into absurdly attractive men like Tweedle-fucking-dee.

"Strike the match on the gun," Dee says, and I notice a charcoal gray strip on the side of the grip, just like the ones you see on any matchbook. I hold the Queenmaker in a slightly unsteady left hand and use my right to pull the match from my ear, light it, and then transfer the flame to the fuse, flicking the used match over the railing and into the river. "And don't worry *too* much about aiming—the Queenmaker is more like … a directional sort of weapon."

"Huh?" I ask as I watch the tiny orange flame chase down the fuse.

"Now, where was I?" Dee snaps his fingers and nods, reaching up to adjust his peaked cap. "Yes, yes, of course, a *story.* Now, how could I forget?"

"What do you mean by *directional* sort of weapon?" I ask, but it's too late because the fuse is just about burned all the way out and Dee is leaning casually against the railing, not at all concerned about what's about to happen.

"What kind of story would it be if it didn't start off with *once upon a time*?" Dee asks, and I can't tell if it's a rhetorical question or not as the fuse disappears and … a violent fucking shiver echoes out from the gun and into my arms, up my neck, into my teeth. I'm clenching my jaw so hard, I'm afraid I'm about to bite off my tongue. "Once upon a time …" Dee starts as the gun goes off with this sonic fucking *boom*, like a goddamn cannon, rocking me on my feet and lobbing what looks like a metal baseball out of the barrel and into the water.

It hits a rock on the way down and … Jesus fucking Christ.

"Once upon a time there was a fair and just Queen of Hearts," Dee continues as an explosion rocks the ship, sending us bouncing on violent waves, the river pulsing and thrumming as a red and orange ball of *flame* shoots straight up into the sky, alighting the grass on either bank … and basically dragging my jaw to the wet surface of the deck in shock. "She ruled with compassion and grace and—"

"Seriously massive fucking firearms," I add, staring at the weapon in my trembling hands with my very first dose of—and here it is folks—*shock.* I am shocked shitless. I just shot what's basically a goddamn missile out of an ancient looking flintlock pistol. Color me impressed.

"—seriously massive fucking firearms," Dee adds without skipping a beat, humming slightly under his breath and lifting his hands up, fingers splayed, and spreading his arms wide as he continues with his story. "Never had the land known such peace, such prosperity, but …" He pauses and rises to his feet, coming over to me and taking the gun. With a single flick of his arm, he opens the chamber and looks inside. "We'll grab some ammo and fuses when we get to where we're going."

"And where's that?" I ask as Dee makes that same arm motion and the gun clicks shut. He hands it over to me and I tuck it back in my satchel with a certain level of respect. Now that I know what it can do? I'm treating this thing with kid gloves.

"Why, exactly where we need to be, silly." He stands up and gestures with his chin for me to follow along. "Now do you want to hear the rest of the story or not?"

"Continue," I say with a small sigh, walking alongside him and passing by the rest of the crew. I notice as I walk that they watch me with a certain level of curiosity that makes Dee narrow his eyes and curl the corner of his lip.

"But the queen's reign of peace wasn't to last long. The Riving hit and tore her to pieces—literal *pieces* that had to be scraped off the walls and floor. After that, her daughter, the crown princess, yet another powerful sorceress, found herself in the magic-less body of a broken man. Princess became prince became tyrant king."

"And that's the current King of Underland?" I ask, trying to jump ahead in the story. Dee pauses at the front of the boat and looks out over the railing, his blue and black hair whipping back against his face.

"There's no King of Underland, per se. There are four completely separate kingdoms with their own ruling families," Dee explains, holding up a fist. I figure he's about to tick off the kingdom names, so I beat him to it.

"Hearts, Spades, Clubs, and Diamonds?" I ask and he pops up a finger with each, adding onto the end with another big grin. The dark woods flash by behind his head, growing more ominous as the day's shadows start to fade into night. Just like back home, it must be winter here because I feel like the daylight didn't last long. Already, some of the giant mushrooms are starting to glow—an eerie blue here, a sickly green there, a vibrant pink on that one.

"See, you know more than you think you do, Alice."

I sigh, but I don't correct my name this time. Why bother? Dee seems like he's going to do what Dee wants to do, the rest of the world be damned.

"So the King of Hearts is the tyrant then? Or the King of Clubs?" I was told the former slaughtered Dee and Tee's people while the latter sent an assassin after me soooo … they're both villains?

"The current King of Hearts is a great-many-times-over-grandson to the queen in our story and her son, the princess-turned-prince-turned-tyrant. He's a massive improvement over his father except …" Dee pauses and unconsciously reaches up a hand to touch his shoulder. For just a split second, his eyes are melancholic and far away, filled with a longing so deep it would take two seas just to fill it. "Except he's not perfect either."

"Because he gives naked boys away as presents?" I ask, folding my arms over my chest and noticing that the smile on Dee's handsome face is tinged with bitterness. He copies my pose and leans back, meeting my gaze dead-on.

"Boys? Didn't you see what we had to offer? We're certainly men, don't you think?"

"How old are you?" I hazard and his grin reminds me of the Cheshire Cat … Speaking of, am I going to run into him, too? Fuck, I need to ask someone about those damn books and see what they say. I don't believe in coincidences. Well, I don't believe in fate either. So … maybe I just don't believe in anything anymore except pure chance?

"Nineteen," he says as he salutes me and I roll my eyes.

"Boy," I say and Dee shakes his head.

"There are many ways for a boy to become a man, but being bathed in blood? That puts us above all else. If anything, we're men amongst men, the manliest really." Dee glances past me to the woods and we both pause as this *awful* screeching sound echoes across the water, the shock of it hitting my eardrums literally driving me to my *knees.*

My hands clamp over my ears and I feel a hot wetness against my palms as the screaming, wailing roar cuts through the landscape. Dee kneels down beside me, seemingly unaffected by the god-awful noise. But when I look up, I see that his ears are literally bleeding, red rivulets running down the sides of his face.

"It's the jabberwock," he tells me as I pull my hands away from my ears and stare down at palms that are just as red as they were yesterday—*yesterday*—because it's only been twenty-four fucking hours since I saw Brandon Carmichael shot in the face. Then again, if the White Rabbit works for the king, and the twins hate the king, then really we're on the same side, aren't we?

"*That* is a jabberwock?" I ask, and I feel this cold shiver pass over my skin, something more than just the sting of saltwater and the brutal arms of the wind. My voice sounds fuzzy and distant, even to my own ears, and my head is ringing like I just spent all night at some shitty underground punk concert, standing next to the speakers in front and not caring that I can feel the bass inside my brain.

"The Tulgey Wood is full of them," Dee explains, looking into my eyes and reaching out for my hands. For some reason, I let him take them and watch in fascination as he pulls a black handkerchief from his pocket and starts to clean them off. "You don't have jabberwocky where you come from?"

"Not exactly," I say and then pause at the sound of scuffing boots on the wood behind me, glancing back to find Tee, his face stoic, the corners of his mouth pulled down in a slight frown. His ears are bleeding, too, but as I watch, he uses an identical handkerchief and scrubs the sides of his face clean.

"If you're tired Allison, you could sleep. Or else I'll send Dee to bed."

"Or two in bed is more than just twice as fun," Dee says, leaning in close enough to kiss. I notice he doesn't try though which is nice—he might be crazy but at least he's not a totally sexist prick like some of the guys at my school.

"I'm not sleeping with you," I tell him and he shrugs loosely, dropping my hands and reaching out to mop up the blood on my face instead.

"Suit yourself, but the offer is open. We belong to you, after all, Allison-who-isn't-Alice." Dee rises to his feet and pulls me up along with him. Tee watches us both with a tenseness in his shoulders and hands that I don't quite understand.

"I could sleep," I say and Tee nods briskly, handing over the key to the cabin. As I start off toward it, he calls out to me. "Wait, Allison."

I turn back as Tee shrugs out of his purple jacket and hands it over to me.

"It's awfully cold in there," he tells me with a sharp nod. "And wet. Sleep on top of this; it'll keep you dry."

"It's awfully cold out *here*," I start, but Tee is dropping the long trench over my shoulders and moving away before I can protest. Dee gives me a look and a wink as his brother saunters off and I reach up to tug the jacket closed across my chest. It smells good, too, like fresh leather and soap and clean air. I bury my nose in it for a moment, but just to get away from the reek of fish and the stink of salt.

"Don't bother arguing with him—he's one of those pesky, chivalrous types."

"And you?" I ask as I head to the cabin and unlock it.

"Me?" Dee asks as I open the door and glance back at him. He has bedroom eyes again, heavy and half-lidded. "I'm the cheeky asshole. If you want someone to fuck while you're here, I make an awfully nice bedroom buddy."

I raise both brows.

Scratch what I said—he's just as much of a dick as the guys back home.

"Yeah, thanks, I'll remember that," I say caustically, stepping inside and closing the door behind me.

♦ ♠ ♣ ♥ ♣ ♠ ♦

I don't expect to fall asleep right away—not in the cramped, smelly room with its uncomfortable bed and musty stench. But I guess literally stumbling into a brand-new world that I never knew existed, one that matches up with one of my favorite childhood reads, has really taken its toll on me.

One minute I'm curling up on top of Tee's trench and wondering how the hell I'm ever going to sleep again, after hearing the roar of that goddamn jabberwock, and the next …

Sunlight is streaming across my face and … Dee is snoring beside me.

I roll in his direction and narrow my eyes. *This motherfucker ... when did I ever say he could share a bed with me?!* But then I realize that it was getting dark when I went to sleep and now it's bright as hell outside. There's literally nowhere else on this ship he *could* have slept.

With a sigh, I sit up and scoot off the end of the bed, heading outside to find Tee at the edge of the railing, watching the shore.

"More trees?" I ask as I come up behind him and offer up the coat. Whatever it's made out of—some leather or suede or something like that—water beads off the exterior, and I was careful to keep the interior facing toward me. It should still be dry enough for him to wear, even if that burlap sack covered lump they call a bed is like a damn sponge. "How vast is this Tulgey Wood place?"

"It seems to go on forever sometimes," Tee says as he shrugs into his jacket and casts an annoyed *look* in the direction of one of the crew members. This one is young and blonde and honestly, he's pretty goddamn handsome, too. Like, every fucking man in this world is beautiful. That's what makes it feel the most like a fairytale, I have to say. Where are all the ugly blokes, huh?

"You guys do know that back in my world, there's a book called *Alice's Adventures in Wonderland,* right? And all of this …" I pause and sigh. "Including *you* are in it."

"You've read it then?" Tee asks, turning his severe face to look at mine. I can see with my own eyes that he has the same full lips as his brother, the same long, curved lashes, the same smooth jawline and head of mussy hair. But the way he carries himself, his expressions, even the cadence of his voice when he's *not* chortling singsong nonsense is so goddamn different. If I hadn't seen them standing right next to each other, I might not've believed they were *brothers* let alone twins.

"Of course I've read it. Basically everyone back home has. There are *hundreds* of *Alice's Adventures in Wonderland* adaptations. Now, tell me, why the *fuck* there's a book back home that … somehow echoes everything that's happening here."

Tee stares at me for a long moment and sighs.

"The prophecy—the one you don't believe in."

"You're telling me Charles Dodgson aka Lewis Carroll was a prophet for Underland?"

"Well, it wasn't called Underland back then, now was it?" Tee whispers, casting another mean look over my shoulder. I turn and it's a different crew member this time, a brunette. I think the blonde's name is Duck and this one … is Mouse? Shit if I can remember. "Did we sell tickets?" he asks, his voice as sharp as the blade on his hip. "Because as far as I can recall, we did *not.* If you want to see a show, visit a box office."

The crew member scurries away with a roll of his eyes before Tee looks back at me, the amethyst color of his irises striated with a range of other shades, the darkest aubergine shadows and the brightness of lavender. I have to blink myself awake before I get caught in them.

"Lewis Carroll fled Wonderland after the Riving. Whatever you think you know about him, it's a lie. He was a coward and a prude and possibly even worse things. Mad as a hatter with all his visions." Tee's coat whips around him in the wind as The Long Tale takes on a particularly sharp turn and he gestures toward the mess hall with a hand. "There's breakfast waiting, if you're hungry."

My stomach is rumbling like fucking crazy and honestly, I don't care if it's dry crackers and meat paste again—I'll eat six.

"So Lewis Carroll wrote the book as a prophecy for … me?"

"For the Alice," Tee says, sounding exasperated and annoyed with me as he opens the door to the mess hall and gestures me inside. I'm surprised to find the captain, Lory, and … another brunette, one with darker hair this time who I think is Eaglet? But fuck if I know. "It didn't matter which one, so long as *an* Alice showed up here. But the book is jumbled and broken, and whatever survived of Carroll's mind after he became a man was fractured at best. He was writing the prophecy from memory only because after the Riving, he didn't have a lick of magic left."

"This old story?" Lory says with a sigh, flicking braids over her shoulder as I take a seat at the table and Tee moves over to the kitchenette to fix us plates. I'd do it myself, but I have no idea what the rules of propriety are here, what I'm supposed to eat, how I'm even supposed to fix up the meals we're being served. Lunch yesterday might've been crackers, but breakfast was slices of fruit smooshed together with a cream cheese filling dotted with nuts and currants. Not even sure if there's a name for that back home. "You tryin' to bore your mistress to death?"

Tee just sighs, but I can see that his back muscles are stiff and tense. The twins don't seem at all interested in sharing with anyone else that they think I'm this Alice character. They haven't said as much to me, but I'm smart enough to pick up on social cues. If Edith were in my place, she'd be dead already. Well, either that or she'd have fucked one or both of the twins. Shit, maybe she'd even be home? Because I'm not a hundred percent sure that she wouldn't have sucked Tee off and swallowed, just for fun if not to get into that minuscule little door.

Now *that* part certainly wasn't in the original book, now was it?

"Here," Tee says, putting down what looks like some sort of breakfast scramble in front of me. It actually smells *good* and I vaguely recognize the yellow fluff and bits of meat. The only question now is—what *kind* of eggs and what *sort* of meat is on my plate? I don't think I'd have much problem eating any species of egg but the meat … could be an issue. "Bacon and eggs," he explains, like he's reading my mind … or maybe just the expression on my face.

"Bacon from pigs?" I ask, but the look Tee gives me is another of those *are you stupid* ones that makes me sigh. He sets a glass of water in front of me and when I reach out and bring it to my nose for a sniff, Lory laughs.

"We might be pirates and thieves and all-around assholes, but we're not stupid enough to drink salt water, missy." She laughs, this husky, throaty sound that makes my skin pebble with goose bumps. The captain—Dodo—stares at me blankly, but the other guy? He's for sure checking me out.

"We're on the Long Stretch," a voice says from behind me, and I glance back to see the last two crew members stepping into the mess hall, their hair twisted and teased into peaks from the saltwater. But if they're in here … then who the fuck is manning the ship?!

"The Long Stretch is a segment of river that's straight as an arrow and free of rocks, as slow-moving as the Tulgey Wood River ever gets," Lory explains at what's probably a look of sheer fucking terror on my face. "We've sailed it a million times—try not to piss yourself, missy."

The other men gather plates as Tee sits down beside me and I swear, I hear him growl when the blonde—Duck—sits down on my other side.

"So, what's your name, miss?" he asks, looking at me with eyes so pale they're like chips of ice. He's handsome, but definitely not my type. The way he's smiling at me though, I figure I'm probably his. Fuck, if he's like most of the men I know, *women* are their type period. As long as she's biologically female in that she has tits and a pussy, they're into her.

"Sonny," I say when Tee's hand comes down on my knee and squeezes tight. I've never been so happy for that stupid nickname as I am in that moment. Tee's hand relaxes and he takes it away. It's weird, but I almost *liked* the warmth of his palm on my leg. *God, I need to get laid.* That was sort of the point with me getting all close and cuddly with Brandon Carmichael and look how *that* turned out. Add in the mess with my last boyfriend and we're really getting somewhere fast.

"Sonny, huh? I like that name," Duck says, digging into his eggs and bacon with a voracity that makes me raise my eyebrows. I poke at my food for a moment and then finally hazard a bite. Well, hurray for small miracles—it tastes like scrambled eggs with bits of crispy bacon in it. "So, Sonny, how on earth did you manage to get the last two angels in existence out of the king's grubby grasp?"

I choke on my food and feel tears prick my eyes as I try to swallow the eggs down my throat instead of inhaling more into my lungs.

Angels.

Did he just say fucking angels?!

"That's none of your damn business, Duck," Tee says, taking small, dainty bites of his food. The way he eats reflects his personality, that meticulousness that demarcates him from his twin. I'm still sitting there gaping and trying to make sense of what the hell is going on, but the conversation moves on without me anyway.

"I thought Sonny here was the mistress?" Mouse asks from the other side of the table, seated next to Lory and the still silent Dodo. Eaglet's crowded in on his other side, watching me with curious hazel-gold eyes. In fact, all *three* men are staring right at me like maybe they think I'm some kind of prophetic Mary Sue, too. Meanwhile, my mind is stuck on angel wing tattoos and curiouser and curiouser things. "Let her do the talkin', why don't ya?"

"Eat a dick," Tee snaps and I raise my eyebrows. Whoa. Underland might be creepy and weird as fuck, but I guess they're up-to-date on modern slang? His purple eyes drift around the circle of men—and Lory—sitting at the table with us. "Sonny isn't interested in fucking any of you."

"Or maybe you're just jealous and you wish it wasn't so?" Eaglet says, and he's got some of that same rhyming quality to his voice that Tee and Dee get when they're about to start spouting nonsense.

"I know it isn't so," Tee says and I slam my palms on the table before this gets out of control.

"I think I can speak for myself," I say as I glance over at Tee and he purses his lips. They look extra full, all pinched together like that. I try not to notice, but then … that would be a lie. He really is handsome, this Tweedledum dude. Glad he's not just called *Dum*, too, because there's nothing sexy about that at all. I much prefer the name Tee.

"Underland has so few women that sometimes men act irrationally," Tee growls out, giving the crew members another round of glares. "They hit on anything female and they forget their damn manners."

"Not all of us grew up with silver spoons in our mouths, *your majesty*," Duck says and *weeellll*, there's another one. Angels. Your majesty. Ugh. I hate being out of the loop. Makes me feel liable to hang my damn self in it.

"That silver spoon was shoved up my ass by the king and you know it. Feel lucky you grew up poor and too worthless to pay attention to."

My eyebrows shoot up as Tee tosses his fork onto his plate and it clinks against the chipped porcelain. Duck, Mouse, and Eaglet all stand up from their seats like they're about ready to gang up on Tee and beat him senseless.

Tee stands up from the bench, coat flying out behind him, and grabs his knife from his belt, spinning it around in his fingers as he narrows his eyes on the three men and takes a fighting stance.

"Let's have a cock-race then," Mouse suggests, tousling his pale brown hair. "And see how you fair in a *real* fight, your highness."

"A cock-race?" I ask, just as the door swings open and Dee appears, his jovial face dropping into a deep, almost exaggerated frown when he sees his brother facing off against the three pirates. Yanking the knife from his belt, he narrows his eyes a bit. Or maybe they're just droopy and half-lidded as usual? Hard to say.

"A cock-race," Dee says, spinning his knife much the same as Tee did and moving over to stand next to me and his brother. "Is when two or more men fight it out for the same woman. Well, if she's not inclined to have them both or all. Usually it's all, but I think some women just enjoy a good fight, too? Do you enjoy a good fight, Al—"

"*Sonny* never said she was interested in having a cock-race," Tee snaps, cutting his brother off. All the eyes in the room go to me. Frankly, I'm more interested in hearing about *angels*, about *royalty*, about these fucking weird as shit twins I seem to be stuck with for the next week or two.

"I'm not looking for lovers," I say, staring at each of the three sailors in turn and then glancing toward Dodo and Lory. They're both finally smiling at me. "And I don't need to see a cock-race. Like, the words alone are giving me some pretty awful imagery."

"You're certain?" Mouse asks, biting his chapped lower lip and sitting back down at the table. "Because, for you, miss, I'd take part in a hundred cock-races."

"Uh, that's … nice of you, but thanks, no thanks. I'm on a mission here and I'm not looking for sex of any kind. If you have a cock-race it'll specifically be for your own enjoyment." I take another bite of my food, refusing to let something as normal as bacon and eggs slip past me. Never know when fruit with cream cheese or crackers with meat paste are going to be on the menu again. "Now, sit down, tuck your junk back into your pants, and let's move on."

I've dealt with enough asshole teenage boys to know how to handle myself.

Fortunately, after a few seconds of tense silence, the other two crew members take their seats and the twins sheathe their knives.

"You're a tough broad, like Lory, ain't ya?" Eaglet asks and I see the pirate woman give him a look that shuts him up quick. "Nothin' wrong with that, just a compliment."

I expect more fussing out of the men, but it's like, as soon as I tell them no, they go back to their food and stop staring at me like I'm the second coming of Jesus. It's kind of … nice, actually.

"Why is it you always find women *not* sleeping with you the ultimate compliment?" Lory glances over at me with honey-brown eyes and lifts a dark brow.

"He gets attached too easily, Eaglet does—to women he *doesn't* sleep with. And those he does, he always finds something wrong with."

"It's never the women," the man hedges, reaching up and adjusting the white bandana over his dark brown hair. It's decorated with black diamonds—something that I imagine isn't a coincidence in a world where the four kingdoms are named after suits of cards. Or is it the other way around maybe? "It's their other lovers I can't stand."

I finish my breakfast while the crew gossips and Dee *squeezes* his fat ass—okay, his gloriously sculpted ass—in between me and Duck, chowing down on a plate of food piled twice as high as his brother's.

Once again, I find myself with one twin pressed against either side of me and once again, I find that I kind of like it, too.

"After this, get outside," Lory says, standing up and flashing a white-toothed smile at me. "And I'll teach you somethin' useful to take with ya."

Four hours of learning to tie ropes with the crew of The Long Tale leaves me with blistered hands and a seriously sore back from hunching as I try to concentrate. I've always been a bit of a homebody, a reader, the kid who gets good grades whose worst sins are smoking pot on the weekend and having safe, consensual sex.

I've never really been a person who works with their hands.

It's not exactly my thing, but I have a good time with the crew—especially since the men stop staring at me and hitting on me. That's nice. After breakfast, they're about as polite as Lory, which is to say, not very fucking polite at all. But while their talk and mannerisms are crude, they aren't lascivious or pervy or anything of the sort.

No, the only person left on The Long Tale that's like that is Dee.

"One more night in this shitty shit ship," he says, and I don't know if he thinks he's clever or if he's just that easily entertained because he chuckles, lying on his back next to me. Tee is on my other side in a similar position.

He was right about the three of us not fitting on this bed—as it is, we're smashed even tighter between the two walls than we were on the bench at breakfast this morning. But it's pouring ass rain outside now and there's another jabberwock screeching in the distance. I'm not exactly sure how I feel about either twin, but I'm not so heartless that I'd make them sit outside in the rain.

"What's next?" I ask, because although it's wet and smelly and the food is weird as fuck, The Long Tale isn't the worst place I've ever been. No, I can think of four places right off the bat that beat this out a million to one in the *shitty shit* department.

Number four—the cold, sterile visiting room at the Humboldt County Women's Correctional Facility.

Number three—the courtroom where my brother's murderer was found innocent.

Number two—the blood splattered alley where I found Fred's body.

Number one—and does it make me heartless that this is number one instead of the alley?—the floor in front of Liam Carpenter's couch where he and his friends tried to gang rape me.

So, smelly, wet, rotten boat with a bunch of crude pirates and two weird twins who recite poems and speak in riddles?

Not really that bad, after all.

"Well, first we'll stop at Rab's place and see if we can't get a royal escort back to the palace. Otherwise, we'll have to stop by the Duke's …"

Tee makes a sound under his breath, and I vaguely recall that other man with the rabbit ears muttering something about a *savage* duke. Interesting.

"The Duke's and then … the Hatter's."

"The Mad Hatter's?" I ask, because I can already picture that chapter in the original book. I don't remember anything about a ship and a bunch of pirates and mushrooms the size of houses though, so I suppose it's not exactly *on-canon*, now is it? Who knows what I should expect from the rest of this stupid trip?

"Oh, we're all mad here," Dee says predictably, and I narrow my eyes, turning my face to the side to look at him.

"Is this where I'm supposed to say *but I don't want to go among mad people*?" I ask and Dee laughs, closing his eyes as a fat drip of saltwater from the roof splats right in the middle of his face.

"You've mixed up the order some, but I'll forgive you," Dee says, smiling but keeping his eyes shut tight. After a moment, I can see that his breathing is slowing, his chest rising and falling at an even, steady pace.

"Here," Tee says after a moment, and I'm pretty sure he was waiting for his brother to pass out. I turn back to him and find a small, leather bound book in his hand. Where it came from, I have no idea. Maybe from one of those mysterious belt pouches of his? Or from inside a giant pocket on his magnificent purple coat.

I take it from his hands and find that it's an omnibus copy of both Alice books, the same text, the same illustrations that I remember from back home.

"Keep it," he tells me, and then he's turning away to face the wall and I'm left staring at his back, at the part where his black and white striped shirt's come loose from his pants, revealing a tantalizingly small square of tattooed skin.

"Thanks," I say, holding the book against my chest and wetting my lips. I want to ask about the angel thing, and all of that *your majesty* and *your highness* and *silver spoon* crap, but it's too closed-in inside the cabin, too claustrophobic.

Later.

Yes, I'll just ask the mysterious twins if they're angel princes from a dead and slaughtered race.

I can't wait to hear the answer to *that* one.

Chapter Four

The Rabbit Gives Alice a Little Thrill

Watching The Long Tale take off down the river leaves a sinking feeling in my gut. I actually sort of *like* the weird, gruff crew, the bitchy pirate, and the silent captain. I don't imagine I'll see a single fucking one of them ever again.

But also …

"I assumed they'd be leaving us at a town of some sort?" I ask as I stand on the tiny dock and look around at … the woods. We're standing at the edge of the river with trees and mushrooms towering over us from both sides, a small dirt path, and a five by three rectangle of old dock. That's it. Just us, the trees, and the fucking fungi.

As I take in the forest and all its mysteries, something white flashes in the corner of my eye, like a smile without a face. But as soon as I turn to look at it, it's gone and I'm left blinking and wondering if I even saw it at all.

"That's the problem with assumptions," Dee says, whistling as he starts off down the path. "They make an *ass* out of you and shins—two of which we all have." He pauses for a second before turning around to look at me. "Unless of course you're an amputee which then you could have one shin or none shin and then the only person that's an ass is you."

I just stare at him because, like, what the fuck is he saying?

"There are jabberwocky in these woods, right? And we don't have ammo or fuses for the Queenmaker, so what happens if we run into one? You guys'll fight it off with your knives?" I mean to sound sarcastic, but honestly, once we start walking and I'm engulfed in the shadows of trees, I feel a chill pass over me that has nothing to do with the weather.

"Something like that," Tee says and his brother makes an amused sound in his throat, turning forward again and picking up the pace. I walk between him and Tee, letting them do their guard thing because, like, I hardly know what the food in this world is called let alone what threats to look out for. I'm independent and fierce, but I'm not stupid. To actually *be* a strong character, you have to have more than snark and stubbornness—you have to have brains. And I am *beyond* determined to be better than half the girls I read about.

"If the White Rabbit works for the king, then why does he live all the way out here?" I continue, somewhat relieved to hear birds chattering and animals rustling in the underbrush. There's nothing more frightening than dead silence; I can't stand it. When it's quiet, that's when the bad memories and the awful thoughts ring loudest. I'd rather not hear their sinful soliloquies just now, thank you.

"Because he likes it out here, because it gets him away from the palace," Tee says, and he sounds gruff—which seems to be normal for him—but there's an edge to his voice and I can't decide if he despises this Rab guy … or if he feels sorry for him.

"You said Brandon Carmichael was a Rabbit," I continue, noticing the hundreds of little mushrooms dotting the forest floor, clustered at the bases of trees, hidden beneath the glossy green fronds of the jurassic looking ferns. Some are as tall as I am. "But I didn't see any ears on the guy and I've known him since he considered crayons covered in paste a delicacy."

"A Rabbit is the official term for a ruler's righthand women and men," Tee explains, and at least he sounds *slightly* less exasperated with me this time. Heck, maybe he's starting to like me? I slow down a bit, so I can walk side by side with him, the fabric of our jackets brushing at the arms. His shirt is buttoned up and tucked in today while Dee's is rumpled and half-tucked, completely and totally unbuttoned and flashing smooth swaths of muscles when he turns back around to look at us.

He puts a finger up on either side of his head, mimicking the look of rabbit ears.

"They make them shift the ears, so their positions are easily identifiable. Well, except for Brandon obviously because he was working as an assassin, and they didn't want to tip you off." Right. As if seeing a boy with rabbit ears in the human world would automatically make me think I was being targeted by a ruler from another world. Tee and Dee are clearly clueless as to how things work back home. Case in point: a *tea party* is a fuck of a lot duller there than it is here. Much less hallucinogenic.

"Shift?" I ask, my satchel swinging as we walk, the book, the gun, and the dress tucked safely away inside of it. I thought Lory might ask for the clothes back when we disembarked—or at the very least the beautiful jacket—but she didn't.

"All Rabbits are shifters," Tee explains which doesn't much help me because I didn't know *shifters* were a thing to begin with.

"Like werewolves?" I ask because, you know, I read a lot of books. Fuck, I read about wolf shifters, bear shifters, dragon shifters … But I have a feeling that this is nothing like that. Underland is … strange, to say the least.

"Shifters …" Tee begins, and something passes across his face that makes my stomach flip. He looks like a man who's seen horrid things, awful things, things that haunt his waking hours *and* his sleeping ones. I recognize that look. My nostrils flare, but I ignore the emotions welling up inside of me. I wouldn't be here today if I acknowledged them every goddamn time they asked. "Some could be wolves, maybe. Don't you have shifters where you come from?"

"Not really, no," I say, but before I can think to ask anymore questions, I see a house through the trees, smoke curling from a stone chimney. It's picturesque as fuck

—at first glance anyway—but also … kind of creepy. The house doesn't seem to quite sit right, almost like it's leaning to one side. And the purple and black paint seems to make it sink into the shadows of the forest. There's a single dead tree in the yard with something … some*one* hanging from it. "What the hell?" I whisper as Tee puts a hand in the center of my back and encourages me forward.

The rope creaks ominously as we approach and I find my eyes glued to the corpse, rotted and bloated and just swinging there like rotten fruit. Bile rises in my throat and I look away, focusing on the dilapidated white picket fence and the crooked gate.

"Why is there a body in this man's front yard?" I ask as Dee leads the way to the front door and lifts a fist to knock, hitting a rusted metal plate with the words *W. RABBIT* on it. When I glance up at Tee, I can see that his violet eyes are dark and his mouth is twisted in a slight frown.

"Because he does whatever the king asks him to without question," is the only response I get.

"Goddamn it, Mary Ann! I thought I told you to get lost? You want a fuck buddy then—" The door swings open and there he is, the rabbit-eared murderer with the bloodred eyes, blinking stupidly back at us. He looks at Dee first, then Tee … drags his eyes over to me and pales considerably. His skin's white enough as it is that when he blanches, he looks like a goddamn vampire. "Why is the Alice here and not at the palace with the fucking king?"

"Because you smashed the DRINK MEs and we couldn't get through the door," Dee says, shoving the shirtless man out of his way and stalking into the house. Tee puts pressure on my lower back and I follow after, although I'm not sure how I feel about being in the house of a man who keeps dead people swinging in his front yard like macabre wind chimes.

"You didn't need those," Rab says as I pause in his foyer and meet those chilly eyes dead-on, "you have Tee."

"You just thought you'd smash up all the bottles and I'd suck some dick to get where I needed to go?" I snap, and I can already feel my hands curling into fists, my jaw clenching, memories of Brandon slumping forward into the grass replaying in my mind over and over again. Sure, the twins say he was an assassin, but … I just don't fucking know anymore.

"Actually, yes," Rab says, his voice as cold as it was two days ago when he shot my classmate in cold-blood. "That's exactly what I thought. What the hell are you doing all the way out here?"

"We're taking the long way," Dee says as he wanders out of the foyer with its purple and black striped walls and into a living room decorated with the same hint of gothic whimsy. Rab looks at me for a long moment, shirtless and wearing only a pair of rumpled slacks, unbuttoned *and* unzipped. They're sagging fairly low on his hips too, showing off all sorts of beautiful muscles that I don't need to see. "We thought you might want to give us a royal escort?"

"There aren't any escorts set to come out this way for *weeks*," Rab says with an exasperated sigh, putting his fingertips up to his temples. That glossy black hair of his is mussed up, the white rabbit ears twitching on the top of his head. He narrows his red eyes at me. "Fuck, the king is going to be pissed." He pauses and reaches into a pocket, pulling out a pocket watch and checking the time before slowly looking up at me. "Although I can't say I'm disappointed to see you again, Miss Alice."

"It's Allison or Sonny, but it definitely isn't Alice. I'm not cool with being the chosen one. Too much responsibility, not enough reward."

"Wow, caustic and jaded, aren't we?" Rab says, and I know within seconds of meeting him … that he's a psychopath. I know, I know, not a *huge* leap to make considering I saw him gun down an unarmed teenager. But still. "It's not like you have a choice on whether or not you're the Alice. That's like a lizard saying it no longer wishes to be a lizard. Too bad though, right? It can shed its tail, but it will always be a lizard."

"I don't believe in fate or destiny or any of that crap. I make my own choices, thanks," I snap, feeling Tee bristling at my back, but ignoring him. I don't know what's got his panties in a bunch, but I know damn well how to expertly untangle a pair of lacy bits. Rab holds my stare and lets his mouth twist into an awful smirk, one that's as cold and cruel as his corpse decoration dangling in the wind.

"Then make the *right* choice and come with *me* to see the king."

"I thought you said there weren't any escorts out this way?" Tee breathes from behind me, and I can hear hatred thick and heavy in his voice. Again, I can't decide if that's *for* Rab or for the king, maybe?

"There aren't," Rab says as a kettle whistles on the woodstove and he moves over to it, snatching up a knitted black and white striped mitt and pulling it off the heat. "I just think it'd be best if I were to accompany you the rest of the way." As Tee and I step into the living room, Rab sets the kettle on a ceramic tile embedded into a small wood table and lays out four teacups. "The Tulgey Wood is … well, it's *fucked* and you both know it. You stand a much better chance with me. Tea?" He gestures at the steaming kettle with an inked hand.

"No tea for me, thanks," I say, because I can already see where this is going. I'm tripping hard enough on Underland's overall weirdness without adding 'boosted' oolong to my list of problems.

"None for me either," Tee adds and Dee groans from his position on Rab's purple sofa.

"Come come now, we've had several days of hard travel and it's time to unwind, is it not?"

"Contrariwise," Tee says, his expression stern and his frown carved into his face like he was born wearing it, "if there are no royal escorts, Rab can at least feed us and we'll be on our way."

"Contrari-contrariwise," Dee snaps back, taking off his peaked cap and tousling his hair with his fingers. "We've been crammed on a smelly, salty boat for days. I want some tea, a snack, a shower, and a nap—and in *that* order."

"For a slave you're awfully demanding," Rab says as he takes two tea bags from a tin and drops them into two of the cups. "Must be that princely blood that runs through your veins. What say you, Miss Alice?"

"Please don't fucking call me Alice," I breathe with a small sigh, taking in the mounted animal heads on one wall with a wary eye. I recognize the face of a pig, a crocodile, but the rest … I have to blink several times to make sense of them all. One of them looks suspiciously like … a *dragon.* There's a bird with its massive beak open wide, pointed teeth glistening in the light from the roaring fire. It's almost cozy in here … almost. But then, like with the outside of the house, there's just something off, something not quite right.

"There's the stink of blood on you," Rab says, slouching against the wall, his rumpled slacks sliding so low on his hips that I can see a dusting of dark hair leading down to his cock. *Jesus Christ.* He twitches one of his white ears at me and blinks bloodred eyes.

"Really?!" I ask, storming into the room and across the plush white rug on the floor. I don't look too closely at it because I'm fairly certain it's the skin of … something. It's huge, like it came off a damn polar bear. You know, except for the *purple spots.*

I stop in front of Rab and try not to notice how good he smells, like spruce and damp earth. Maybe he smells that way because he has to dig a lot of graves? He certainly seems good at killing people.

"I smell like blood?" I ask, trying not to fly off the handle. But I've always been just a *tad* confrontational so … I rip the dress from the leather satchel and shove it against Rab's deliciously muscular chest, shivering as my knuckles brush against the warmth of his skin, all those tattoos he'd so tantalizingly flashed between his gloves and shirtsleeves revealed in their full brilliance. "*This* is why—you killed my friend."

"Your friend?" Rab asks, tilting his head to one side, his eyes wide and unblinking as he stares at me. "I saved your life—I killed your assassin. As it were, he was probably on his way to rape and kill you that very night."

"I …" I shove the dress back in the bag, a blue and white bit of fabric stained with red hanging out the top. It's one thing to be *told* that Brandon Carmichael was someone awful, but I don't know these men from Adam. All I know is that I saw this rabbit-eared piece of shit shoot an unarmed teenage kid in the head. They can *say* all they want about Brandon, but I knew the guy for like fourteen years and he was never anything but nice to me. "I was going to ask him to prom."

"A rapist and a murderer? My, my, you certainly have low standards, don't you? What, then, exactly, was the problem with wrapping those pretty lips around Tweedledum's magnificent cock? If you had, you'd be at the palace by now. As things stand … Hearts and Clubs, you're *late*."

"You shot him in the *face*," I growl and Rab cocks a dark brow.

"You'd prefer I shot him elsewhere? In the intestines so he could suffer and die a slow, agonizing death from infection? In the spleen? The kidneys? The head seemed most efficient to me and quite frankly, it was more than the little worm deserved anyhow."

I just stand there gaping and wanting to punch the White Rabbit in his smug, handsome face.

I settle for growling under my breath and turning back to face Tee and Dee.

"Let's get food from this motherfucker and go. I want to go home."

"Home?" Rab asks from behind me, and I see Tee flick an amethyst gaze in his direction. "Oh dear, you haven't told her, have you?"

Closing my eyes against Dee's expression of alarm, I take a deep breath and turn back to face Rab.

"Told me *what*?" I snap, blinking and shaking my head to clear it. *Could've sworn I just saw one of his tattoos move ...* But then I open my eyes and refocus and Rab's tattoos really *are* moving. He has several pocket watches and clocks etched into his skin, several of which have second hands that are ticking away the sands of time. "What the … fuck?" I ask, forgetting for a second what I was so angry about in the first place. My feet move back in the rabbit's direction without bothering to consult my brain.

"Oh, you like?" he purrs, his voice like bones and ice. There's something sinful but intriguing about it. I get close, too close really for propriety's fucking sake, but Rab doesn't seem to mind. His smile cuts across his handsome face like a scar. "This one," he continues without waiting for me to reply, lifting up an inked finger and pointing at a black and gray pocket watch on the bulging curve of his right bicep, "tells me how long until I'm due back at the palace." He slides his finger up his shoulder and onto his chest, to the face of a magnificent grandfather clock buried in the rest of his brilliant ink. "This one tells me how long until I'm executed." And he says that without a hint of irony or a drop of fear, but like it's simple fact that he'll have his head lopped off one day. Or, at least I'm assuming that's how they execute people around here. *Off with their heads*, right? "And this one …" He slides his palm down the smooth expanse of his chest and belly and lets it rest over his hip. "This one tells me how long until teatime."

As I stare at it, the second hand hits twelve and the minute ticks over, lining up with a single red heart on the face of the clock. After a moment, the heart fades away and pops up at a different time, almost twelve full hours later.

The hell ...

Nice as his ink is though, his words beg another question, one that I can't let myself forget in the majesty of this place. It's fucking cool that this guy has tattoos that move … fuck, tattoos that predict events in time, but that doesn't change the fact that I'm not from here and I don't belong here, and the last thing I want to be is somebody's savior.

How can I save anybody when inside, I'm being drowned by my own demons?

Swept away by my own sins.

Haunted by ghosts and mistakes and what-ifs.

"Told me what?" I whisper, stepping away from Rab as he smiles lasciviously and goes about preparing his and Dee's tea, dropping a lump of sugar in each, adding a splash of cream.

"We were given to Allison as gifts and so we can only do as she asks. She wants to pass through the Looking-Glass, and we'll do whatever it takes to get her there," Tee says, standing stiffly in the doorway, one hand hovering near his knife, the other clenched into a fist by his side. His purple eyes are dark with shadows, and the muscles in his shoulders are tense as fuck.

"Allison, huh?" Rab says with a laugh, picking up a saucer and moving over to

Dee. He offers up the steaming teacup and then settles into a leather wingback chair in front of the window. "Well, you gave me choices and if you refuse to let me call you Miss Alice … I far prefer Sonny." He winks at me as he lifts his teacup to his lips and takes a sip. Dee's already halfway through his. "*Sonny*, you do know the king is never going to let you use the Looking-Glass? Or were you planning on sneaking her through, Tee? Yes, that seems like something you might do, sneak the Alice through and then run away with her."

"Why wouldn't the king let me use the Looking-Glass?" I ask and Rab laughs as Tee growls, low and menacingly behind me.

"Because," Rab says, looking at me over the rim of his cup and grinning, "he wants you to be his *bride*."

♦ ♥ ♣ ♠ ♣ ♥ ♦

Brushing my hand across the surface of the mirror, I clear the steam away and lean in close, staring at my reflection's blue eyes, her wet blonde hair, the rainbow streaks woven into the right side. I'd expected the salt water to mess with the dye, but it's holding strong, the colors just as vibrant as they were last week when I put them in.

"His bride," I scoff and roll my eyes. "Puh-lease. The King of Hearts can kiss my ass."

Although, you know … he was *ridiculously handsome with that bright red hair and those scars …* I don't want to admit it, but I'm intrigued.

Curling my fingers around the edge of the countertop, I sigh and drop my head, closing my eyes for a moment and letting the steamy, candlelit bathroom soothe away some of the stress I'm unwittingly carrying around with me.

Knowing Edith, she's probably freaking all the way out about my being gone … and Dad? Fuck, Dad's probably losing his damn mind. I bet he's already talked to Mom and told her and now she's stuck in a cell wondering if one of her two remaining kids is lying sliced up and dead in an alley, too.

Lifting my head back up, I take another look at myself in the mirror, at the robin's egg blue of my eyes, my pale blonde lashes, my long hair. It's about halfway down my back now, but it used to be longer, like I would sit on it a lot at school. But then Fred died and … I cut off about a foot of it and put it in his coffin with him. Everyone—including my parents—thought that was weird as fuck, but I didn't care. I did it anyway, damn them all to hell.

Is it so wrong to want to give a little piece of yourself to the dead?

Fred's hands looked so cold clasped together in that casket, and maybe … as they rotted away underground, my hair would keep his bones warm.

"His bride," I repeat again, stepping away from the porcelain sink and taking a look around the bathroom. I can't quite figure out where this world is on the industrial revolution scale. Like, Tee and Dee have cell phones and I swear that first night at The Pool, that woman was playing an electric guitar. But we traveled on a ship with oil lamps, like medieval sailors, and I haven't seen a car or electric lights, haven't seen a plane fly overhead, haven't heard the roar of an engine.

But then … the indoor plumbing? It's fucking fabulous. I think I just took a two hour long shower without ever running out of hot water. I glance at the toilet and then reach out and flush it. It works like any normal toilet back home, and it's a fuck of a lot better than that chamber pot I had to use on The Long Tale.

I throw on the red dress that Rab provided and purse my lips tight at the lacy panties and bra that he included with it. He told me it all belongs to this Mary Ann chick—whoever she is—but he also promised to have both my blue and white dress *and* the outfit Lory gave me washed and ready to go for when we leave in the morning. No clue who's *actually* going to do the washing considering both Dee and Rab are completely out of their minds on English breakfast tea, laughing and playing one *looooong*, slow game of chess, but whatever.

The red dress is tight, clinging to my curves and falling to mid-thigh, a heart cutout over the cleavage that shows off the whiteness of my breasts. It's sleeveless with a plunging V in the back that goes nearly to my ass crack. Honestly, it looks like something meant for a night of clubbing, not for hanging out at some weirdo's house with a corpse dangling in the front yard. I feel like the body out there should disturb me more than it does, but frankly, as long as I'm sleeping in a room with a window that *doesn't* face the swaying lump of bloated flesh, I'll be fine.

When I open the bathroom door, Tee's waiting for me.

For a split second, I see his eyes widen and flick over the length of my body, taking in the tight, clingy fabric of the red dress with a shimmer that he quickly hides by glancing away and scowling.

"I just wanted to let you know that Rab's house servants—Pat and Bill—are here. One of them is in the kitchen preparing dinner and the other's washing your things. I just didn't want you to run into them and be alarmed."

"Thanks," I say, watching as Tee reaches up, like he's about to adjust the bill of his cap. Only, he's not wearing it right now, just a pair of black linen pants and a … ribbed purple tank? They have fucking tanks here in Underland? Well, shit. That's … very modern of them. And holy damn does Tee look hot in his.

His nipples are hard and pebbled beneath the fabric, and I can't help wondering what it would feel like to run my hands up the smoothness of his belly and feel the stiff peaks beneath my palms.

"You're welcome," Tee says, hesitating for a moment like there's something he wants to say. Instead, he turns away and heads back toward the guest room the three of us are supposed to share.

"How come I got a snazzy red party dress to wear and you got pj's? I don't believe in gender divisive clothing so … could I like snag a pair of Rab's pants and a tank, too?"

Tee pauses with one hand on the doorframe and then nods his head.

"Follow me," he says, moving into the guest room. There are two beds in here, both of them twins—hah, good pun—but I figure Dee'll end up stuck downstairs in a drug induced haze the rest of the night anyway. "We keep clothes here for when we're on long trips. Rab hates it, but King's orders so he can't complain." He pauses and rummages around in the top drawer of the dresser. "You can have some of mine."

He hands over a white ribbed tank with red hearts all over it and another pair of black linen pants with a drawstring, just like the ones he's wearing. Our fingers brush when I reach out for them and I feel my throat get tight. My body responds with a wave of unwanted lust, washing over me and making *my* nipples pebble. The change is immediately obvious in the red dress, but I don't bother trying to hide it. What's the point? I've been around plenty of slut-shamers and pearl-clutchers in my life and they're some of the most miserable human beings I've ever had the displeasure of coming across. Who cares if my nipples are hard? It's a natural biological function and I can't help it.

"There's a small library downstairs, if you need a place to read," Tee tells me, sucking in a long breath and taking a seemingly purposeful step away from me. "You can go into the yard if you want as well, but don't step outside the fence, not one foot."

"After hearing the jabberwocky screeching in the woods? No thank you. Besides, sitting outside in the dark and cold with a book and a corpse? Not my idea of good reading time." Tee smiles slightly, nods and then climbs into one of the beds, curling up on his side in the flickering candlelight. There are a lot of candles in here, too, dozens and dozens.

I take a few moments to blow some of them out, my stomach grumbling and protesting at the lack of food, and then drop the pajamas Tee gave me on the foot of the other bed.

I think I'll eat first and change later.

Besides, I might not want to admit it, but there's something about the racy little dress that I like.

But just a little.

Heading downstairs, I peek into the kitchen and find a man humming as he stirs a large pot of soup, the smell of fresh herbs and chicken broth making my stomach clench painfully. As I watch, he removes a tray of rolls from the oven and sets about buttering them, his thick hands cloaked in white gloves, his round body dressed in a meticulous apron and black slacks. This blonde guy—Pat or Bill, whichever he is—might be a slight bit overweight, but he's got a handsome face and a headful of glossy hair like everyone else.

Maybe it's like natural selection or something? Not enough women to go around, so the guys have to be like extra hot?

Backing away from the kitchen, I decide to leave the man in peace for a few while he finishes up, ignoring the lazy, languorous laughter from the living room. I spend a few minutes exploring the downstairs and then pause in the dining room, the table already set for four. I guess Pat and Bill won't be joining us then? Makes me more than just a little uncomfortable, the idea of servants and … naked guys as gifts.

I pause at the dining room window and stare out into the darkness of the woods, the sun quickly retreating into the distant sky and leaving the landscape with a dusty, hazy sort of look, the shadows it casts almost worse than the total darkness that's on the way. As I'm studying the trees and the brightly colored mushrooms that make up the forest floor, I see it again, a flash of white in the darkness, a toothy smile without an owner.

Fuck, I knew it! I wasn't imagining that shit before, when we were disembarking. There's definitely something there. But once again, I blink and whatever it is … is gone.

Well, that's not creepy *at all*.

I roll my eyes, but what am I supposed to do about it?

As long as it can't get in here, I'll be okay. Tee seems to think I'm safe enough that he can go to sleep while Dee's out of his mind on drugs, so I decide not to worry about it. Besides, I still have those knives Lory gave me to slip into the hidden pockets of the corset. They're in my satchel upstairs, but maybe I should carry one around—just in case.

There seem to be two entrances to the dining room and as I stand there, studying the forest and hoping to get another glimpse of whatever was out there, the swinging doors to the kitchen open and the man in the white apron walks in. When he sees me waiting there, he grins.

"In the mood for some pumpkin soup with a little jubjub bird?" he asks and I feel the corner of my mouth twitch.

Jubjub bird. Right.

So it wasn't chicken, after all, was it?

♦ ♠ ♣ ♥ ♣ ♠ ♦

Some nightmares are so persistent as to become an unreal reality. They're so frequent and so jarring that even though the dreamer *knows* she dreams, she can't seem to wake herself up. And when those dreams are based in the awful friction of reality to begin with? Well, that just makes things that much worse because waking up … you know there's no reprieve from the boogey man that hides beneath your bed.

The monsters are real, and they've gotten inside your head.

After a few hours of restless sleep, dreaming the same dream about Fred over and over again, the one that *actually* happened, I give up and climb out of bed, glancing down at Tee before moving into the darkness of Rab's house. Pat and Bill left after dinner, but not before letting me know that my clothes had been hung up to dry in the shed out back. Oh, and did I mention that this Bill guy … had a fucking lizard tail?

Yeah, like, long, green and scaled.

No joke.

I didn't even question it. That's the state of my existence right now. I ate soup with bird meat that I couldn't name and I *liked* it. And I didn't even care that I was the only one at dinner. Nothing different about that. I've been eating alone in my room for the better part of two years. The last time we had family dinner was the night my parents and Fred got in a fight, he stalked off, and then I found him dead in an alleyway.

I pad down to the kitchen and find the leftover rolls wrapped in black and purple striped cloth on the wood topped island. I snatch a few out and head back to the dining room window again, looking for that flash of white teeth in the darkness as I eat.

Instead, I spot a blue glow from the top of a nearby mushroom—one of those towering, house-sized ones—and hear the shuffle of feet on the wood floor behind me. When I glance back, I find Rab, his eyes bloodshot and his dark hair a tousled nest on the top of his head. But holy damn, if his pants aren't hanging low and showing off … well, *everything.* Glancing down, I can see the base of his cock, half-hard and tenting his slacks.

"Caterpillar," he says, his voice hoarse and his tone laced with irritation. Rab looks down at his low-slung pants and just when I think he's about to yank them back up, he does the opposite, pushing the slacks over his hip and flashing me a whole lot more of his erect dick than I really need to see. But then I see the clock tattooed over his hip bone, the second hand ticking down, the red heart just fifteen minutes away. "Damn it," he grumbles, lifting his eyes up to mine and narrowing them slightly. After a moment, he smiles, and the expression is wicked as hell. One of Rab's ears twitches slightly and flops in half.

The urge to reach out and rub it between my fingers is almost overwhelming … I wonder, does he have a little cotton puff of a tail hidden in those slacks of his somewhere? If so, I'd like to pinch it.

"I don't suppose you want to meet Lar, do you?" Rab asks, yawning and scratching at the flat, muscular expanse of his lower belly.

I swallow hard.

"Who's Lar?" I ask and he shrugs, turning away and heading toward the front door. I follow along behind him and watch as he slips into a pair of black slippers. My combat boots are already sitting there, so I decide what the hell, and put them on, too. Stealing Tee's coat from a hook, I try not to look too closely as Rab finally reaches down to fix his pants. Not sure if I'm excited about that or disappointed.

"Come with me and you'll find out," he says as I shrug into the purple coat and follow him into the frigid early morning air. The corpse is still hanging from the tree, but at least the wind's not blowing, so for right now, the body is still, its clothes in tatters, its face swollen and purple in death.

I look away and stare at Rab's muscular back as he opens the gate and steps aside, waiting for me to follow him out. Tee *did* say not to leave the yard, but I figure Rab works for the king, too, and even if his motivations are all screwed up, it seems highly doubtful that he wants me dead.

"You didn't like the red dress I gave you, Sonny? For shame, for shame. I'm sure you'd look brilliant in it."

"Actually, I *did* like the red dress, and after all the shit you put me through, I have to say that I stuffed it in my satchel and I'm taking it with me when I leave. You can just tell Mary Ann too goddamn bad—her boyfriend killed my crush and is a serious asshole and she owes it to me."

"Mary Ann is *not* my girlfriend," Rab says with a husky laugh, his flopped ear standing at attention and swiveling around to face a rustling in the bushes. The humor in his face dies away as quick as it came and he holds out a hand, splaying his palm wide against my belly. The warmth of his fingers teases that little bit of skin between my pants and the bottom of my tank and makes me shiver. "Shh," he whispers and in the distance, I hear the faintest scream of a jabberwock, not enough to make my ears bleed this time but enough to make the fillings in my teeth hurt. "Mm." Rab reaches into the back of his pants and pulls out a gun I hadn't noticed he was carrying. It vaguely reminds me of the Queenmaker, with a fuse on the back, but it's much bigger and solid black with gold accents.

"It didn't sound all that close, did it?" I ask as I cross my arms over my chest and follow Rab down one of the three roads that lead away from his house. The one straight ahead obviously goes to the river, but we've turned right and are heading toward the mushroom with the bright blue glow on top of it. Its gills glow, too, but the light coming from above is distinct and concentrated, this Caterpillar guy I guess.

"Maybe not, but jabberwocky move fast," Rab says, tucking the gun under one arm and digging a cigarette out of his slacks pocket with his free hand. He takes a match out from behind his ear, reminding me of my lesson with Dee, and lights it up. "Better prepared than eaten alive, I always say." We walk for a little while before I start to notice bats hanging upside down from nearby trees, watching us with wide eyes that glitter in the glow from the giant mushrooms. "But you can keep the dress. Mary Ann never wore it anyway, and I have a feeling she won't be back for a while no way, no how. She just married her ninth husband, so she'll be busy for a spell."

"Her ninth?!" I ask as I rub a hand over my face and find myself under the umbrella of the massive mushroom's blue and white cap. "Jesus Christ, how does she keep up?"

"Here," Rab says, ignoring my question and gesturing toward something I can't quite see around the curve of the mushroom's stem. I walk a little closer and find a ladder waiting, nailed into the spongy flesh of the giant fungi. "You go first and I'll pretend I'm not checking out your ass from behind."

"Wow, you're a real piece of work, aren't you? You think you're clever, coming up with a bunch of lines that make you feel like a real man when all you really are is a shred of patriarchal bullshit?"

Rab's brows go up and he laughs, his right ear flopping over and partially obscuring his forehead. He tilts his head to look at me with bloodred eyes, smoking his cigarette and letting that evil little smile of his take over his full mouth.

"Why did you break all those FUCKING DRINK ME bottles anyway?" I ask and he shrugs.

"Because I could?" Rab says, and I feel my hands clench into fists at my sides. Turning around, I grab hold of the slick, cold surface of the metal and start to climb. At first, it doesn't seem like such a big deal, but when I get about halfway up, I look down and realize why I hate heights so goddamn much.

The ground is … well, it's fucking far away and it looks hard as shit. If I were to slip and fall from the damp ladder right now, there'd be no one there to catch me. My body would crack against the earth and I'd bleed out from the inside, twitching and writhing in agony from my many broken bones.

My attention snaps forward and I force myself to keep climbing.

There's no point in having a freak-out now, halfway up the side of a mushroom the size of a damn skyscraper.

I make myself climb the rest of the way, crawling through a hole carved into the mushroom's cap and collapsing onto my back on its spongy surface. Staring up at the canopy of trees and the stars beyond, I try to catch my breath as I wait for Rab. My heart's beating crazy fast, and I'm already freaking out about having to climb down again, so I don't even notice the man sitting less than six feet away from my face until a puff of sweet tobacco scent rolls over me.

Sitting up suddenly, I turn my head and my eyes immediately meet the large, blue ones of a man, quietly smoking a hookah … and taking a *very* keen interest in *me* and nothing else.

CHAPTER FIVE

Advice from a Caterpillar

The Caterpillar and I look at each other for some time in silence. At last, he takes the hookah out of his mouth and addresses me in a languid, sleepy voice.

"Who are *you*?" he asks, raising one skeptical brow.

I just stare at him a minute, taking in the pale sky blue color of his hair, his lazy slouch, the slow moving smile on his pink lips as he takes a drag on the hookah, exhaling colored smoke and making the air smell like fresh blueberries.

"I could ask you the same question," I reply as I rest an elbow on my knee and wait for Rab to pull himself through the hole and onto the top of the mushroom. I don't really look out at the horizon, or the sloped edge of the mushroom's cap. Fuck, I'm not even going to *stand* while I'm up here because knowing my luck, I'd probably trip on one of the big white spots and go tumbling over the edge to my death.

"You can call her Sonny," Rab says, the gun tucked back into his pants as he grabs a seat next to the Caterpillar—Lar, I guess is this one's name—and borrows the hookah for a moment, taking a deep drag. I wonder if it's just flavored tobacco that they're smoking or something a little more … interesting? I hope not, sitting up here a good sixty feet off the ground.

"Sonny?" Lar says, watching me with those wide blue eyes of his, his blue-blonde hair feathering across his forehead and teasing his neck and shoulders with a textured, razored sort of look. At first, I thought he had a blanket wrapped around him, but as I watch, he unfurls a pair of massive butterfly wings and my breath catches in my throat.

For several seconds there, I forget to breathe completely.

Lar's wings are sprawling mosaics of color, like two stained glass windows attached to his back, the tips curling softly in gentle spirals. Based on their size, it feels like they should look awkward or out of place, but they don't. They move in these slow, easy sweeping motions, like the man himself.

My sister's always been obsessed with butterflies—mostly because she finds them cute—but since she's not really much for studying, she also thinks it makes her sound smart to rattle off random facts and Latin names for the winged insects. That's why, looking at Lar's wings, I make the connection between the *papilio ulysses* or the Ulysses butterfly and his coloring.

The only difference between his wings and that of the Australian butterfly is that instead of the simple two-toned blue with black edges, Lar's wings are tinged with a dusting of gold.

"Sonny because the Alice doesn't like being called Alice," Rab replies and I grit my teeth. Tee and Dee still haven't said anything outright, but it was pretty clear they weren't comfortable letting anyone else know about this Alice thing. "Relax, Sonny," Rab says, sucking on the end of the hookah and giving me this stupidly wicked little smirk. "The Caterpillar's the one and only soothsayer for the King of Hearts—he knew I'd find the Club Assassin at that party … and he predicted you'd follow me back to Underland after I killed him."

"Predicted?" I ask as Lar's mouth lengthens into an almost disturbingly self-satisfied smile.

"Here," he says, taking the hose of the hookah from Rab and handing it out to me. He fluffs his wings a bit, sending a light breeze in my direction. "Have a drag and we'll see what Underland's wild magic has to say about you."

"I'm not interested in taking drugs sixty feet up in the air, so … thanks but no thanks." I flash a winning smile and glance around at the canopy. There are birds up here, a lot of them, in brilliant colors that are easy to distinguish from the shadows. Not only is there the mushroom's glow to illuminate them, but the Caterpillar has a lit lantern with blue glass, the flicker of color I saw from Rab's dining room window.

"No drugs, just a special herbal blend that'll allow you to see beyond the humdrum of reality. Isn't that right, Rab?"

"That's right," the White Rabbit says, watching me carefully, that wicked smile still resting on his face. The way he's lounging, with one knee propped up, elbow resting against it, his chiseled body covered in tattoos. It's almost too much. I look back at Lar instead, but he's not much better. He's wearing a white coat with gold filigree and epaulettes over his shoulders, no shirt underneath. His *nipples* are pierced with gold keys and he watches me with this easy, laid-back sort of look, like he's got all the time in the world. "It's not a hallucinogen, Sonny, just a little tobacco. The worst it'll do is make you feel lightheaded for a few minutes."

"Beyond the humdrum of reality?" I ask, because that's just the sort of nonsense bullshit these people have been spouting since I got here. "I don't understand."

"Just take a single drag and you'll see," the Caterpillar says, his wings ruffling softly in the night breeze. He's quite pretty, with his shoulder-length hair and his lackadaisical smile, just like all the other assholes in Underland apparently. "And if you're worried about falling, don't be. I'll catch you, little Sunshine."

"Sonny," I say with a weary sigh, but really, I'm getting tired of repeating myself. Hell, if these guys want to start calling me Mabel or Ada or George Washington, I'm sort of done with the protesting. If there's one thing I hate, it's repeating myself like a goddamn broken record. "I'm not really into peer pressure, you know?"

There's a sound, like boots on metal, and we all pause.

After a moment, Dee's head pokes through the hole in the mushroom and he drags himself up and onto his back, panting almost as hard as I was. Not ten seconds later, there's Tee with a violent scowl etched into his face.

"I thought I told you not to leave the yard," is the first thing that pops out of his mouth as he climbs through and stands up, seemingly unaffected by the soaring height of the giant mushroom. His amethyst eyes stare accusingly down at me, and it's interesting to see that *he* isn't winded in the least.

"And I thought *I* was the mistress here and could make my own decisions," I say and Tee looks away sharply, redirecting his anger toward Rab and Lar. He looks cold without a coat on, dressed in black linen pants and a tank and boots. I feel a little guilty for taking his, but when I move to shrug it off my shoulders, he looks back at me and holds out a palm.

"Don't. Keep it," he says as Dee groans and rolls onto his belly, crossing his arms under his chin and looking at me with a small smile.

"Have you seen one of Caterpillar's prophecies yet?" he asks, sounding groggy and hungover but also in a good mood, as usual. "They're a real trip."

"Something dragged the corpse out of the tree," Tee says and this is enough to actually grab Rab's attention. He turns his bloodred eyes up to Tee and blinks a few times in surprise, tapping his fingers against his knee. "There's no sign of the body anywhere."

"That's not good," Rab says, musing for a moment as Lar takes another drag on the hookah. "The house and yard are spelled—nothing should be able to get past the fence without taking a huge hit from the wards."

"And yet something did," Tee says, putting his hands on his hips.

"Something did," Dee repeats as he pushes up to his knees and prods one of the large white spots, digging his fingers into the mushroom's soft flesh.

"Dee, Hearts above, do you want to get your head lopped off?" Tee snarls but his brother ignores him and yanks a piece of spongy meat out, handing it over to me.

"The King would want his Alice delivered to him at all costs," Dee says as I stare at the hunk of white flesh and wonder what the fuck it is he wants me to do with it. "If we'd had a little bit of this to begin with, we wouldn't be sitting up here wondering what slithered over Rab's wards and ate the POW in his yard."

"Prisoner of war?" I ask, but then there are probably a million other questions worth asking right now. "You think something … ate that corpse? Like a jabberwock?"

"A jabberwock, a bandersnatch, a jubjub bird … it's hard to say," Dee continues, gesturing with the mushroom meat in my direction. "Take this Allison-who-isn't-Alice."

I reach out a palm and let him drop the spongy flesh in my hand, wrinkling my nose as I bring it close to my face for a sniff. It smells like almonds and blueberries, making me wonder what's in that hookah. Seems a bit coincidental that the smoke and the mushroom meat would have the same smell.

Dee scrambles to his feet and walks across the slick, blue surface of the cap like it's nothing, like he's done this a million times before. As far as I know, he probably has. He stoops low on the opposite side and digs up yet another handful of flesh, bringing it back and offering that to me, too.

"Just remember," the Caterpillar says, giving me his lazy smile, "one side will make you grow taller, and the other side will make you grow shorter."

I take the second hunk of mushroom flesh and tuck each one into a pocket on either side of Tee's jacket for the time being.

"You're telling me this mushroom has the same properties as the FUCKING DRINK MEs and the EAT MEs?" I ask, although the only *EAT ME* item I've seen thus far is Dee himself.

"Rather the drinks and the cakes have the same properties as the *mushroom*. The king has his men harvest the flesh and use it to make the cakes and tinctures—when they can't get a real curseworker in the kitchen, that is." Dee grins at me like that explains everything and takes a seat so close to me that his arm brushes against mine and his body heat seeps into my skin.

My head is spinning with spells and wards and curseworkers and magic mushrooms … but I just blink and refocus on Rab and Tee, both of whom still look worried over the whole missing corpse situation.

"Normally, the king has anyone who takes a bit of mushroom flesh executed but, well, I figure he'd make an exception for you," Dee adds, not at all worried by the prospect of decapitation. "You never know when we might find ourselves in a bit of a tizzy again, right? The next time we run into a little door, you won't even have to *consider* sucking that asshole over there off."

"Shush, Dee," Tee growls and then squats down next to Rab. "Do you have *any* idea what might've taken the body from the yard? Or how?"

"Not a clue," Rab says as Lar hands over the hookah hose and Tee, surprisingly enough, puts it to his lips and inhales. He passes it to Dee next, and his brother takes it, doing the same. With a long sigh, I follow suit and hope like hell I'm not going to regret this later. "I just suppose we'll go back, collect our things, and head out? If the yard's been breached, it's just a matter of time until the house is as well." He sighs and glances in Lar's direction. "Let's get this over with, shall we? The Alice is late enough as it is."

"All in good time, my friend," Lar whispers, his voice low and even as he flicks his blue eyes to mine and smiles like the cat that's got the cream. "You can't rush these sorts of things, you know."

He spreads his wings wide, extending them to their full width. I blink several times in awe as the blue in the center begins to ripple and change, the colors morphing and twisting until there are moving images trapped in the black and gold edged frame of Lar's wings. It's like watching a TV screen but … fuck, no, it's like looking through a window. There's not a goddamn screen in the world that can blow hot rancid breath in your face, echo a sound like shattering glass that makes your ears bleed, and show you a vision that's so detailed you can make out each individual feather …

"The fuck …" I breathe and my heart starts to thunder in my chest as the image zooms out, away from the snapping beak of a bird with teeth like a shark and eyes like an insect, fractured prisms of green and gold that reflect the blue glow of the giant mushroom. Because, whatever this prophecy is about, it's taking place *right here.* For a moment, I have to look away to catch my breath, take in the gently swaying tree limbs and the distant chatter of night birds. It's quiet and peaceful here, but in the vision or prophecy or whatever the hell it is that's going on in Lar's wings, it's violent and messy and bloody.

The bird lashes out at the cluster of people—i.e. *us*—sitting on top of the mushroom, claws raking through our bodies and spilling bright spatters of red. Its massive wings—as wide as Rab's house is long—are splayed out, flapping and thrashing the limbs of the trees with violent gusts of wind, its feathers glossy black but with a green undertone that blends it into the surrounding landscape with flawless ease.

It's why we didn't see it coming until it was too late.

The vision sharpens and I find myself staring in abject horror as the monstrous bird tears Dee's stomach open with shiny black talons, spilling his entrails across the blue and white surface of the mushroom, his mouth open in a silent scream that he never gets to finish.

"Oh, well, *that's* not very pleasant, now is it?" he breathes, curling his hand around mine as the nightmare continues to play out in brilliant color and detail. It seems so real, so goddamn real … But the feel of Dee's hand against mine makes it a little bit better, his warmth seeping into my skin, taking away some of the chill. I thread my fingers through his as my prophecy-self runs for the ladder and gets snatched up by the *head*.

It's about the moment I get fucking decapitated and then *eaten* that I look away.

With a gasp, Lar curls his wings in, tucking them close to his body at the same time he rises to his feet. Rab and the twins follow and somebody's foot hits the hookah, sending it rolling down the curved surface of the mushroom and off the edge. I have to wait several seconds before I hear it hit the ground and shatter.

"A jubjub bird," Dee explains as he reaches out his hand for mine again and yanks me to my feet. "Lar, take Allison-who-isn't-Alice down to the house and wait for us. Rab, how much time do we have?"

"Two minutes," Rab says, checking one of his tattoos, his skin even paler than usual. He nods with his chin in the direction of the ladder. "Start climbing, boys."

"May I, Sunshine?" Lar asks, but he doesn't wait for me to respond. Shit, I don't blame him. What did Rab just say? Two minutes? Two minutes until the prophecy we just saw comes true? Two minutes until a bird the size of a fucking house swarms down and starts eating people?!

Lar picks me up and tosses me over his shoulder—a move that doesn't really float my boat but, when faced with a goddamn man-eating monster, I will choose this any day. He smells like blueberries and tobacco, my face pressed into the back of his jacket, my stomach lurching as his wings spread wide behind us and … we drop off the edge of the mushroom.

My eyes squeeze shut, but there's only a split second sensation of falling and then, it's like we're being kissed by the wind, lifted up and buoyed by clouds. When I crack my lids, I can see Lar's massive wings beating gently, these smooth, slow strokes that end with us settling easily onto the dirt path in front of the house. He sets me down on my feet inside the confines of the gate and turns to glance over his shoulder, a tightness in his jaw that seems at complete odds with his usual personality.

"I ate a jubjub bird for dinner," I say, blinking and shaking my head, teasing strands of rainbow and blonde hair around a finger. "I *ate* one of those."

"Yes, well, better to *eat* than be eaten, I always say," Lar says with a loose shrug of his shoulders, blue eyes focused on the distant glow of his forgotten lantern. The ladder's on the opposite side of the mushroom, so it's hard to say how much progress the other three men have made, but I can feel my heart in my throat, sweat beading on my palms.

"Do we just stand here and wait?" I ask as Lar casts an amused glance in my direction.

"What other action do you suggest we take?" he says, just before a wild screech tears through the woods, sending the glittery-eyed bats and the colorful night birds into the sky in droves. They scatter across the round, white surface of the moon like broken glass. But that sound? Holy shit, that fucking sound. It's as violent and painful to listen to as the jabberwocky's, but worse in a way, too. It feels sharper and less sentient, the scream of a beast.

It explodes from the trees on the side of the road nearest us, heading straight for the mushroom with another one of those raucous screeches. I can feel hot liquid on the sides of my face—why is everything in Underland so goddamn loud?!—and watch in horror as the creature's claws rake across the surface we were just sitting on.

The blue lantern goes rolling off the edge of the cap and plummets to the ground, shattering to pieces in a rush of orange and yellow flame. As soon as the blue glass breaks and the color changes, the bird goes completely insane, hopping down from the top of the mushroom with another violent scream, attacking the burning undergrowth with a sharp black beak and pointed teeth.

"Is that what the blue glass is for?" I ask, glancing at Lar, his white jacket slung over his shoulders. It's cut short in the back, sitting above his wings, and hangs in two long tails on either side of him. The bird's powerful flaps are so intense, they create a breeze that reaches all the way over here, stirring the fabric against Lar's legs. "Because it seems to have a thing for fire."

"The jubjub bird's attracted to flame, but it can't see the color blue," he says, frowning and shaking his head. "It doesn't make any sense for it to have attacked us up there—on the cap of a blue and white. Not once has that ever happened to me, and I've been signaling Rab from that same spot for years."

He takes a few steps back and sinks into a lazy crouch next to me, his wings opening and closing like a butterfly at rest on a flower, those blue eyes focused on the bird as it shreds the flaming fronds until there's nothing left but ash and upturned earth. It pauses then and lifts its head, cocking it from side to side like my brother's parakeet. She died soon after Fred did, and I always thought it was from a broken heart. I know I felt like I might from mine.

The jubjub turns and looks in the direction opposite us, and I see a small spark of orange flame in the darkness of the trees. Rab steps out, looking shirtless and deadly in his tattoos and don't-give-a-fuck smirk, moving forward with his gun outstretched, the fuse burning steadily down to nothing. He even holds it one-handed, like a boss.

The gun goes off at the same moment the bird screeches, lobbing a metal ball about the same size as the one the Queenmaker fired off the edge of the boat. It hits the jubjub in its full, red breast, the mark there disturbingly similar to that of a black widow spider. Flames rush up on impact, rocking the forest with a wave of heat and a tremor.

I expect that to be enough to kill the bird.

Fuck am I dead wrong.

Batting its massive wings, the bird rises up several feet off the ground, twists its head in a circle like an owl except … you know, it *keeps* going. All the way. Three hundred and sixty degrees. As soon as its head comes full circle, it rears back and hocks a ball of red phlegm in Rab's direction. He barely manages to dodge out of the way, the red liquid spattering the ground and trees like blood … blood that sizzles and burns and leaves holes in the bark.

Jesus fucking Christ!

I take a few unconscious steps back and watch with wide eyes as Rab scrambles to his feet and faces the bird, flames still dancing on its chest that it barely seems to notice. It drops its head low in a hiss, a long tongue uncurling from its mouth before it shoots a stream of white at Rab, tangling him up in what seriously looks like a dude's cum.

"Spider silk," Lar says, standing up, his shoulder-length hair blowing in a breeze that doesn't quite seem to touch me. His wings glow and I watch as his pale blue eyes light up, the sapphire earrings dangling from his lobes dancing in the same wind. "Fuck, Rab, what on earth are you doing?"

Rab thrashes around in the silk as the jubjub bird makes a pleased trilling sound and tucks its wings close, hopping toward the man as I stare in openmouthed shock. I mean, he *did* shoot my classmate, but I don't really want to see the guy eaten by a giant fucking spider-bird with shark teeth, do I?

The twins come around from behind a tree, using the jubjub's moment of distraction to make their way over to us, hopping the fence and landing on the path beside me.

"Mistress," Dee breathes, panting and looking at me with wide, sapphire eyes. "We need your permission to—" He cuts off, his head whipping around at the sound of a *different* roar, one that doesn't quite make my ears bleed but rattles the windows in Rab's house. Looking back toward the lump of silk, I find a … another fucking unidentifiable *thing* tearing its way out of the silk.

With another snarl, the creature bursts out of the webbing and takes off, tackling the much larger jubjub bird and knocking it onto its back with a screech. The second beast, whatever the fuck it is, has a thick, white fur coat with black spots … much like the rug on Rab's living room floor. It has a long muzzle, thick paws, and a fluffed tail, like a dog or a wolf, with long rabbit-like ears and bloodred eyes.

Rab is nowhere to be seen … but the wolf-rabbit-cat monster looks an awful lot like him.

Shifter.

The word rings in my head as my mouth drops open and I watch the two creatures duking it out.

"Go Rab!" Dee says with a whistle, like he's mighty impressed. "He's kicking ass. Won't last forever though. Bandersnatch are *not* a match for jubjubs, no way, no how." Dee turns back to me, but I'm so focused on Rab and what he's become that I can barely hear what he's saying. "Hey, Allison-who-isn't-Alice," he croons, swiping a hand in front of my face. "Tee and I need your permission to—"

Once again, Dee's words are cut short.

But this time?

It's not the jubjub or the … the *bandersnatch* … it's a fucking jabberwock.

The now familiar screech makes my poor ears ring as blood drips down my face and onto the shoulders of Tee's jacket. The ground beneath our feet begins to shake and I can hear both twins cursing under their breath. Without waiting to see the jabberwock in person, I turn and head into the house, flinging the front door open and flying up the stairs to the guest room. The Queenmaker is just where I left it, tucked away in the leather satchel, and the twins are right behind me.

"Don't be scared, Allison," Tee breathes, sliding into the room, panting with adrenaline. He blinks in surprise as I turn around, hefting the gun in my hands.

"Rab must have more fuses and ammo around here, right?"

Dee snaps his fingers and turns to his brother.

"She's right—the Kingmaker uses the same fuses and the same musket balls. Do you have the key to the weapons' room?"

"No," Tee says, short and sharp, but then he's turning away and flying down the steps, calling for us to follow after him. Dee and I scramble to keep up and come around the corner at the bottom of the stairs just in time to see Tee lift up his boot and kick the goddamn door in. The wood of the door stays intact, but the hinges rip from the doorframe and the whole thing just lists to one side. I follow him in there and find … a fucking army's worth of weapons. There are guns of every shape and size, swords, axes, knives, even obscure things like nunchucks and garrotes.

For a moment, I just stand there gaping.

But then the sound of the jabberwock's scream echoes outside the house and I cringe.

"Can't we just grab a different gun?" I ask as Tee starts yanking drawers out and digging frantically through them. "There seem to be a lot of, uh, choices in here."

"Not like the Queenmaker," Dee says as he joins in the search, scattering items across the floor and not giving two shits about the mess he's making. "You saw what the Kingmaker did to the jubjub—fucking *nothing.* And with a jabberwock involved? We need to shoot that motherfucker and *run.*"

"Here," Tee says after a moment, turning and taking the Queenmaker from my hands. With that same smooth motion in his arm that Dee used on The Long Tale, Tee opens the gun and inserts a big, metal ball and a fuse. Closing it up, he passes it to me and then hands over a matchbook from inside the drawer. "Don't bother aiming for its face—just shoot at the bulkiest part of its body."

"Me?" I ask as Tee wraps his hands around mine and sends a shiver of warmth through me. His amethyst eyes lock on my face.

"This gun is designed to work with the user's natural store of magic. And it's called a *Queen*maker for a reason—it's not for the clumsy hands of men. Now *go.*" Tee turns me around by grabbing my upper arms and spinning me toward the door and Dee reaches out for my hand, curling his fingers around my wrist.

The twins drag me back outside where Lar is looking up … up … *up* at a fucking …

"It's a goddamn dragon!" I scream, my hands trembling as I look up and find a dragon with scales as black as night but burnished with gold when it moves, the wicked muscular length of its tail swishing across the ground and crushing mushrooms and ferns in its wake. It stalks toward the jubjub bird like a cat on padded paws, curling its lips back from its white-white teeth.

"It's a jabberwock," Dee corrects from beside me. But the creature I'm looking at doesn't much look like the drawing in *Alice's Adventures in Wonderland.* I mean, it has massive webbed wings, feet with claws, and a large scaled body, but that's where the resemblance ends. It, too, has that feral, wild look of a cat or dog or some strange combination of the two. Opening its jaws wide, it lets out a scream that drives me and the three men around me to our knees. Gold eyes flashing, it takes off across the clearing and heads straight for the jubjub bird and the bandersnatch … who I guess is fucking Rab?!

Without thinking too hard about it, I yank the match from behind my ear and strike it against the Queenmaker, lighting the fuse and gritting my teeth against the explosion that I know is coming. *Shit, I hope I don't kill Rab in the process*, I think as my pulse races and my heart thunders so loud that I can hear it echoing around my skull.

The jabberwock snatches the jubjub bird by the head as its screeching reaches a wild crescendo and I wonder if I'm ever going to be able to hear a goddamn thing after this. Before the fuse has even hit the bottom, the dragon—because, dude, it *looks* like a frigging dragon—snaps the bird's neck by shaking it with a horrific amount of violence and strength.

"Oh my god, it's the fucking duke!" Dee screams. "Alice, don't shoot him!"

At the last second, I lift the muzzle of the gun up and the metal ball explodes from the end, flying in an arc and landing on the other side of the jabberwock. It's like a bomb's just gone off, flame rising into the sky as a rush of heat and light washes over us and sends both the jabberwock and the bandersnatch rolling across the forest floor.

Rab's big furry body crashes through the fence and nearly kills us all, skidding to a stop just inches from where I'm kneeling. The dragon—the duke?—collapses where he stands with an earsplitting groan.

"Oh shit, oh shit, oh shit," Dee says as both he and his brother take off toward the downed monster.

"What … what the fuck is going on?!" I scream as I rise to my feet and look over at Lar as he slowly climbs to his own. He just smiles, the expression slow and bemused.

"You almost killed the duke," he says with an easy laugh.

"Who the hell is this duke anyway?" I ask, panting as I come around to the front of Rab's comatose body and watch as he shifts back into his human form—if you can even call it that. This guy is anything *but* human.

"Who the hell is anyone, really?" Lar asks, leaning down and picking Rab up from the grass. He tosses him over his shoulder the same way he did me, moving into the house without bothering to answer my question. I just stare after him and then turn, just in time to see the massive dragon … sorry, *jabberwock* melt down into the body of a naked man.

Opening the gate, I take off down the road in a jog, past the dead body of the jubjub bird, and pause next to the twins. The forest beyond is on fire, but I don't see what the hell I'm supposed to do about it. How was I supposed to know the fucking screeching monster with the gold eyes was another shifter?! Not exactly like we have a lot of those back in my world. Not exactly my first thought when a monster comes raging at me, that he's a goddamn duke.

"What do you suppose he's doing all the way out here?" Dee's asking as I stand next to the twins and try not to gape at the handsome man lying on the ground in front of me. Holy fucking shit. Are there no ugly or even average looking people in Underland?! The man in front of me is *stunning* with tousled golden hair, and a body without an ounce of fat. He's just as muscular and pretty to look at as the rest of them … except, you know, he's got a long black tail and *horns.*

"Who is this guy?" I ask as Tee checks his pulse and sighs in relief.

"The Duke of Northumbria," he says, nodding at his brother. "Help me lift him and we'll get him inside." Tee grabs the comatose man by the arms while Dee grabs his feet and they start to carry him back toward the house, ignoring the rancid stink of burnt mushrooms and the choking thickness of the smoke.

As if summoned by magic, on our way back to the house … the sky splits open and rain starts to pour over the woods. I jog back and wait at the fence for the twins, opening and then closing the gate, locking it, and then doing the same with the front door.

The jubjub may have been able to steal the corpse from the yard, but I'm from a world without magic, and I feel safest in a house with a closed door and a goddamn lock.

"Shit, what the hell happened out there?" I hear Rab cursing as I come around the corner and find him sitting up on the couch. Where the duke is naked, Rab's at least still wearing his pants and boots. Not sure how that works with the dynamics of shifting, but there it is. "The Kingmaker should be able to take down a jubjub. It hardly even *looked* at the flames once it saw me. And can somebody tell me how it stole the corpse from the yard in the first place?"

"You're assuming the jubjub was the one who stole the body," Dee says as they lay the duke down on the wingback chair Rab was using yesterday. "Assumptions make an *ass* out of you and shins—"

"Dude." I cut Dee off with a wave of my hand, tossing the Queenmaker onto a sofa table and moving into the living room to sit on the edge of the fireplace surround so I can stare at the five men in the room—even if one of them is still passed out. "What the *fuck* just happened out there?"

"What do you think just happened out there?" Lar asks as I narrow my eyes and he lets out a low, self-satisfied chuckle, perching on the edge of the couch with his arms crossed over his chest and an easy smile on his face.

"Do you answer every question—every *valid* question, I might say—with another question? Because if so, you and I are *not* going to get along particularly well," I growl with narrowed eyes, looking at the sexy bastard and hating that he knows how damn hot he is, too. Like why can't pretty people complain and moan and gripe about their appearance with the rest of us? Such a turn-off when they know they're hot … such a turn-on, too. God, I'm just a fun little bundle of contradictions, aren't I?

Lar just smiles at me, his eyes droopy in a lazy, cat-got-the-canary sort of way.

"Must be compensating for a seriously small dick," I mumble. Not the most creative insult in the book, but eh. After giant spider-birds, shapeshifting dog-cat monsters, and fucking *dragons*, I'm about at the end of my rope today. And the sun hasn't even come up yet. What a way to start the day, huh?

"Is that what you think?" Lar asks, flicking some hair back from his face, his earrings swinging as he gives me this easy, languid grin. "What size *do* you prefer, Sunshine?"

"I'm not particular as to size," I say, giving him a smirking, sarcastic smile of my own in return. "But three inches is such a *wretched* cock length, don't you think?"

"Oh, so you're admitting to having seen my cock then?" Lar asks, tilting his head to one side, his hair swinging prettily against his shoulder.

"Are you admitting to having three inches below the belt?" I ask with a little sneer and I'm not at all surprised when he reaches down to unbutton his pants.

"Would you like to see how very wrong you are?" Lar says, in an apathetic, lilting sort of voice.

But our banter is interrupted by a spectacular amount of cursing from the wingback chair.

"What in the bloody hell am I doing here?" the golden-haired man asks as he sits up and rubs at his forehead with the heel of his hand. I can't stop staring at him. His hair is just a little *too* gold and those fucking horns … They're black as shadows, curving wickedly over the top of his skull while his tail swishes in irritation. Looking at the wall of mounted heads now, I can see that the thing I thought was a dragon before is in no way large enough, more like a giant lizard. Shit, maybe it's Bill's cousin or something?

"Your grace," Tee says carefully, standing stiffly on the opposite side of the coffee table. "How are you feeling?"

"Like I've been fucked in the skull by a—" The Duke cuts off abruptly, noticing me for the first time, and then rises to his feet. "You're the bloody Alice," he says as I stand, too, and try not to look at his cock. There's been a whole lot of that since I arrived here, a lot of staring at the ceiling or the walls or a man's hardened nipples instead of his junk. "What the hell is she doing all the way out here?"

"We had to take the long way, sir," Dee says, and although he uses the word *sir*, his humility definitely leaves something to be desired. He doesn't much sound like he respects authority at all. The twins exchange glances with each other as 'the Duke' and I have a stare down.

"Alice," he breathes, the hint of an English accent in his words. Shit. I'm a serious sucker for a good British accent. Although, if he's from Underland, he can't very well be British, now can he? I have no idea where these people get their accents from or how the hell they speak the same version of English as I do, but whatever. I'm just glad there isn't a language barrier cherry on top of this shit sundae. "The king must be *furious* to find you missing." He flicks a glance of his gold eyes in the direction of the twins and Rab, but I can see from his facial expression that the idea of the king being angry is amusing to him. Great. Another psycho. "Have you called him yet?"

"The network is compromised again," Tee says, the edge of his mouth twitching slightly. "We're not to discuss our whereabouts or anything to do with the Alice over the phone in case the Clubs are listening."

"Right, right," the Duke says, snapping his fingers in a way that makes me grit my teeth. Here's a man used to privilege, used to people doing what he says. I can already tell by the way he stands, chin up, shoulders back, his mouth curving into a sure smile. "So, you're making your way toward the palace, are you?"

"We were just getting ready to leave," Tee says, exchanging yet another look with his brother. "We'd planned on asking for refuge at your estate tonight. I must admit, we didn't expect to see you so far south …"

"I've clearly shifted in my sleep again," the Duke says with a long sigh, his tail sweeping across the floor like an angry cat's. He never takes his eyes off me, though. No, apparently I'm worthy of his *full* attention—even his dick is pointing in my direction. "You seemed to be struggling quite mightily with the jubjub. Have you lost your skills, Rab?"

"That was no regular jubjub," Rab says, his voice cool and deadly as he sits with his elbows on his knees and stares straight ahead at me. I meet his bloodred eyes for a moment and then look back at the Duke. "It certainly didn't behave as such. Besides, someone or something crossed my wards and stole a prisoner of war from the fruit tree. Not that I miss having a bloated corpse hanging outside, but it shouldn't be possible or even plausible for a jubjub to do something like that."

"Mm," the Duke muses, glancing over at the Caterpillar. "And you're here, too, are you?"

"Am I? Or perhaps I was here first and it's you who is *too* in this equation." The Duke narrows his eyes at Lar's nonsense as Tee quietly bows out of the room.

"Any interesting orders from the king?" the Duke continues, crossing his arms over his chest. The movement does nothing to hide his junk from view, but oh well. At least I can see that *he* has more than three inches for sure.

"I was planning on heading back to the palace as soon as I delivered my vision to Rab, but I can see now that I might do with some company," Lar muses as Tee moves back into the living room and offers up a pair of pants to the Duke.

"Do you happen to have a name?" I ask because, come on, *the Duke* is just a title, and I kind of have a problem with authority. He finishes putting the sweats on, letting them hang as criminally low on his hips as Rab's slacks. I can see though, that there's not exactly room for his tail, so he doesn't have much choice.

"You can call me North," the Duke says, his smile an arrogant twist of privileged lips. I can tell we're not going to get along very well, me and him. "It's a *pleasure* to meet you, Allison Liddell."

Chapter Six

Big and Better

"I've never walked so far in my fucking life," I say as I struggle to crest the next hill, sweat sticking the pale blue peasant blouse to my skin, my heart pounding inside my chest. I'm past the point of simple complaining—like, I am *not* built for this shit.

"Really?" Dee asks, grinning brightly at me. "They don't have legs where you come from?"

"We have cars," I gasp as I slump against a tree and reach into the leather satchel for the gold flask Tee gave me before we left. It was filled to the brim with water, but I can feel from the heft of it in my hand that it's running dangerously low. "And bikes. And trains. Shit, we have *horses*. Don't you people have horses?"

"Here," Tee says, handing over his own flask. "You can have some of mine." Whereas my legs are shaking and I have to blink past thick gobs of sweat to look at him, he seems perfectly fine, not at all taxed by the miles and miles we must've walked. I'm not kidding when I say I've *never* walked this far in my life.

After throwing on our clothes and eating a quick breakfast, we left in the pouring rain, walked through sunrise, and now … the sun is *setting*. Like I said, pretty sure it's winter here, too, so the days aren't overly long, but my guess is that we've been hiking through this damn forest for close to eight hours now.

Eight hours.

When's the last time *you* walked for eight hours straight?

I'd so much rather be at home reading a book.

"We have horses," Rab says, taking advantage of the break to get out a cigarette and light it. Lar bums one off of him, his wings opening and closing in this mesmerizingly slow pattern that makes me want to stare. When he sees me looking, one corner of his mouth curves up in a smile and I plant a purposeful scowl on my lips. "But there are things in this forest that like horses even more than we do—jubjub birds, for example."

"Considering we have both a jabberwock *and* a frumious bandersnatch," I start and hear Rab chuckling, this low, deep sound that scrambles my insides like the eggs we had this morning—the jubjub eggs. They were red as blood and I had to close my eyes just to eat them. Granted, they *tasted* just fine, but I couldn't get the image of that *thing* spouting web and poison and shrieking like a damn banshee. "Don't you think we could handle ourselves just fine?"

"You saw how I was faring against the jubjub," Rab says with a smirk that makes me want to slap the arrogant right off his face, "it was a close fight. I don't know about you, but I only enjoy gambling when the odds are stacked significantly in my favor."

"What about you?" I ask as I notice North watching me with his arms crossed over his chest, tail twitching. He's dressed in a pair of black breeches, brown boots, and white button up that's only half-buttoned. The sleeves are pushed up, his tan skin striking against the stark white of the shirt. He looks every part a duke … you know, except for the horns and tail. But really, those are sort of the best parts. I find myself having trouble looking away.

"What about me?" he purrs in that accent of his, tilting his head to one side and watching my throat as I drink.

"Can't you, like, shift and fly us back to your place or whatever?" I ask, knowing I sound like a whiny bitch but seriously tired of holding in questions I've been wondering about all damn day. Holy crap though, it was worth it to stay quiet and listen to these men talk.

Underland is *beyond* fucking weird, and listening to their casual conversations gave me some serious insight. Apparently the ratio of men to women here is like, ten to one. No wonder this place is such a fucking nightmare.

"There are several female jabberwocky in this area looking for a mate," North says, smiling at me in a pleasant sort of way. It's a smile that says, *hey, want to fuck*? And the answer to that question is a resounding *yes*. Yes, I'm attracted to him. To the twins. Even to Rab and Lar. Hell, maybe I should move here and start my own harem? "I got lucky this morning that they didn't sniff me out. But I won't risk that again." He runs his tongue over his lower lip and glances away for a moment before flicking his gold eyes back to mine.

"Already have a mate?" I ask and sure, it *sounds* like fishing but … Okay, so I'm fishing for information, big deal. Also, I'm ridiculously curious to find out if the Duke, like, mates with other dragons … er, jabberwocky. I think *jabberwock* is singular and jabberwocky is plural? But hell if I know for sure.

"I was cursed with this affliction," North says, narrowing his gold eyes slightly. "I wasn't born like this. I'm no more a jabberwock in my blood than Rab is a bandersnatch." He gives me a crooked sideways smile and looks up into the darkening canopy above our heads. All around us, little mushrooms start to glow like their bigger counterparts and night birds start to chirp again, a replay of last night.

I shiver and finish off my flask, waving Tee's away for now. Hopefully we're getting close to the estate? If not, I'll probably end up gobbling his down, too. I'm not trying to complain so much, but I'm literally just not in shape for this kind of a hike. The last time I went hiking was for an end of the year field trip in eighth grade and even then, it was only a three mile walk along relatively flat terrain.

This is like that … except on crack.

"How much farther?" I ask as I push off the tree and we keep walking, Lar and Rab leisurely smoking their cigarettes as Dee threads his hands together behind his head and looks up at the moon. It's round and white and if it's any different than the moon back home, I can't tell. The only difference here is that there's, like, two of them?

"About four miles," Tee says and I try not to groan. Some random fact in my head tells me the average person walks at a speed of about three miles per hour. Great. Just over an hour to go, right? I try to be optimistic, but that's not really my thing. And besides, the people from Underland don't seem to be all that overly optimistic themselves.

"Shall I recite a poem or story to keep you entertained, mistress?" Dee asks, adjusting his peaked cap, his coat billowing out behind him as he walks. I've given Tee's purple coat back and have taken to stuffing as much of Lory's pirate jacket in my bag as I can, the sleeves dangling as I walk. I'm too overheated to wear it anyway.

"Please don't," I say, and Dee tosses me a little grin.

"Are you *sure* you don't want to hear the rest of the prophecy now? It's a lovely story, the way Tee tells it." I glance over at Dee's purple-eyed clone, but he's frowning and looking at me like he doesn't know quite what to make of me. I wonder if what Rab said was true, if he really did … does? … plan on fleeing through the Looking-Glass with me. I guess I wouldn't blame him if he did, considering what happened to his people …

'Must be that princely blood that runs through your veins.'

Rab's words echo inside my head. Paired with the conversation I heard on The Long Tale, I get the feeling that it's more than just an empty adjective.

"Maybe later," I say, because the more time I spend here … the curiouser and curiouser I get.

This prophecy though, I have a hard time believing it's about me. Well, okay, as Tee said quite clearly—about *the* Alice. But how do they know I'm her? And why should I be? What is an Alice anyway?

"You ask a lot of questions of yourself," Lar says, flicking his cigarette onto the path and stepping on it with the brown boots he borrowed from Rab. He looks a bit like a prince, too, with that white jacket slung over his shoulders, his blue-blonde hair fanning across his forehead as he turns to look at me. "I can see them running through your head, flitting behind your eyes."

"So your prophecies extend to more than just … HD video on your wings, huh?" The joke falls flat and it's pretty clear none of the men have a damn clue what I'm talking about. I just sigh and keep walking, the smells of the forest familiar and foreign all at once. I recognize the rich scent of wet earth, the gentle pungency of rotting foliage, the muskiness of the mushrooms. But there are strange scents, too, ones that seem so out of place—the bright kiss of a rose, the copper stink of blood, the whisper of overripe fruit.

"I can read palms, tea leaves … entrails." Lar flexes his wings as he speaks and I notice both Tee and Dee watching him with a certain amount of envy. Dee does that thing where he reaches his fingers up to his own shoulder, touching it softly and then drawing his hand away abruptly when he realizes he's doing it. "Whatever you like, little Sunshine."

"How do you all know I'm *the* Alice?" I ask, my eyes flitting from Lar's blue and black wings to North's thrashing tail to Rab's bloodred stare and twitching ears.

Compared to the other three men, the twins look almost *normal* in their long military coats, striped shirts, and jewel-toned eyes. "I mean, how do you know I'm not some random girl that found herself in the wrong place at the wrong time? I literally *fell* down that hole into Underland. It could've happened to anyone."

"It could've happened to anyone," Lar repeats, his voice as smooth as silk. He doesn't hurry with his words, instead letting them fall from his lips like each syllable means something important. He has a deep, husky sort of voice, and I can only imagine what that'd be like in the bedroom, slow sweet things murmured into the shell of my ear as … as I drag my mind out of the gutter because there are *far* more important things to worry about than getting laid. "But it didn't, did it? It happened to *you*."

"And you saw that in a prophecy?" I ask as we pass over a large stream, booted foot loud against the curved wood of the bridge. As we cross, the wind hits the water, chilling and pressing against my heated skin like a caress, giving me a brief reprieve from my overheated body.

"We all did," North adds, his voice a growl that matches well with his horns and tail. "All the king's horses and all the king's men." He flashes a grin over his shoulder at me, and if his teeth are a little sharper than they should be, who would notice with a face that handsome? "Clear as day, *you* are the Alice, Miss Liddell."

"Is that how you knew my full name?" I ask as we step off the bridge and onto a dirt road that looks much the same as the one we've been traveling all day. "Because of the prophecy? Because I haven't told anyone here my last name and it's been bugging me for hours."

"Lar's prophecies are just snippets in time," Dee explains for me as Rab pushes one of his sleeves up to stare at a clock tattoo on his left bicep. "Like what you saw with the jubjub bird. We knew your first name from what little we saw, but your last? It was just a matter of fact that you'd have the Liddell blood—that's what makes you an Alice."

I blink a few times and then scrunch up my brow, the satchel swinging at my side. As promised, the dress Edy bought for me is completely free of blood. Even the harlequin patterned tights are clean. This Bill guy might be a lizard, but he's also one hell of a housekeeper.

"My mother's family has always insisted the women keep their last name and pass it along to their daughters," I say, and look up just in time to see Dee and North looking at me like they're not quite following. "Back in my world, women usually take the last names of their lover."

"Which one?" Rab asks, smoking another cigarette. I'm over here panting and he's puffing away like he's on an afternoon stroll instead of a grueling daylong walk.

"Back in my world," I repeat with a sigh, "most people only have one lover."

I can feel all five men turning their eyes in my direction, their curiosity as piqued by the idea of monogamy as mine was when they started discussing the tapped mobile network and how useless their phones were without a reliable safeguard against spies. Considering we're walking on foot through medieval looking woods, that was certainly interesting.

"One lover," Dee muses and then shakes his head like he's having trouble imagining the idea. "Why?"

"Because in most parts of the world, there are equal numbers of men and women …" I hedge, adjusting the strap of my satchel. It's almost pitch-black now, the only light coming from the stars, the moons, and the mushrooms. It's barely enough to see by, so I stick close to Tee's left side and hope he knows where he's going.

"And that means what, exactly?" Lar asks, his wings glowing faintly in the shadows.

"Just … that … I don't know. Fuck, I'm so brainwashed by the patriarchy and society's heteronormative expectations that I don't even know how to answer your question. It's just the way things are in most places—one man and one woman. It's stupid, I know, and I'm not saying there aren't any gay people, just … even they usually go the monogamous route."

"Sounds dreadful," Rab says, his cold voice sending chills down my spine—good ones, too. That's how nutty this world is making me. I'm even attracted to the guy who turns into a giant wolf with rabbit ears. "Boring, too. How can *one* person fulfill the needs of another? Doesn't that get tiresome after a while?"

"I …" I start, but I don't really know what to say to that. I think of my parents, of dad sitting alone in the living room with his head in his hands, missing his wife and his son and hating the whole world. "The only boyfriend I ever had was a total prick, so … I guess I'm not qualified to answer your question. He could've been one of a dozen boyfriends and he still would've been a total piece of shit." I shrug my shoulders like it doesn't matter, like I didn't try to break up with Liam, didn't find myself drugged and lying on the floor helpless while he and his friends removed my clothes …

If it hadn't been for Frederick, they'd have gang-raped me and then what? The look on Liam's face as I lay there that night, the violent scowl as he tore his hard cock from his pants and put it near my mouth … I don't doubt there was a chance he might've killed me. But then Fred came in swinging that baseball bat and there was just suddenly blood everywhere …

I squeeze my eyes shut to block it all out and nearly end up face-first in the dirt. The only thing that keeps me upright is Tee's hand on my elbow, his fingers warm even through the fabric of the shirt. When I open my eyes, I can see him staring at me with a curious expression on his face. *Wonder if they'd still think I was the Alice if they knew how messed up inside I am?*

Or that my brother is dead because of me.

That my mother is in prison.

That my dad's forgotten how to do anything except breathe, eat, and work until he can barely stand up straight, his shoulders drooped from exhaustion.

"So you're telling me it's my bloodline that makes me an Alice?" I ask, and if that's the case then I feel a slight sense of reprieve. I'm not the only living Liddell woman. Besides my mom and sister, I have three aunts and six cousins. Any one of them could've fallen down the Rabbit-Hole … Any one of them and yet … it wasn't them, it was me.

Lar is probably right.

"It's in the blood," Lar confirms, his wings curled slightly at the edges. I wonder if he's like, considered fae or something. Or if they even have faeries here in Underland. I guess if they do, they'd probably call them something outrageous—like a *mome rath* or a *borogove*. "When your ancestor fled the Looking-Glass after the Riving, she left with all of her magic *intact*. And she left knowing that her or someone in her line would be needed to set things right again."

"So what, exactly, is it that you're expecting me to do here? Hate to tell you, dude, but I don't have magic and I don't have powers and even if I *did*, I wouldn't know how to use them." As we walk, Tee reaches into his pockets and then pauses, extracting the white mushroom meat first from one pocket and then the other before handing both pieces over to me.

I take them, liking the way my fingertips feel against his warm palms, and then tuck them into my satchel. I wonder what it would feel like to shrink … or grow to the size of a house? Maybe before I leave this place, I should sneak a bite just to see. After all, when the hell else am I ever going to get a chance to try something so fantastical. No, as soon as I get back home, that gray fog that's been sitting over my life for years will get just a little bit thicker, a little bit harder to see through.

"But you *do* have magic and you *do* have powers or else wielding the Queenmaker would've been impossible," Rab says, his left ear swiveling in my direction. "Nobody expected you to drop in fully trained and ready to fight a war. The king is well aware of the limitations of his new bride."

"I'm not anybody's bride until *I* say yes," I snap and feel both Dee and Tee tense up.

"Normally, that would be quite the obvious statement," Rab continues, seemingly unbothered by the fact that some guy's declared himself my betrothed without my even having *met* him. "But not when it comes to the King of Hearts. Nobody says no to the king."

"Yeah, well, he hasn't met *me* yet, now has he?" I ask, noticing a rainbow twist of mushrooms in the brush. They curve between the trunks of towering trees like a colorful little river, mimicking the streaks in my hair. As I'm admiring their vibrant colors and faint glow, a *green* fucking pig trots out and starts rooting around with its snout. I cock a brow, but really, a pig's a pig—even if its skin is the same color as the grass on either side of the pathway.

"Oh, I can't bloody *wait* to see his reaction to *you*," the Duke purrs, his tail flicking in amusement. "He isn't used to being challenged by anyone but *me*." The look he casts over his shoulder is wicked, and I remember once again that other Rabbit, the one I saw through the keyhole of the little door, calling him savage. He looks savage right now, his teeth white in his tanned skin, the moonlight causing his horns to reflect strange shadows across his face.

"Just to be clear—my sister could've easily slipped into the bushes and fell and then *she* would be the Alice, *she* would be the king's betrothed. Am I right?" I ask, just trying to gather some clarification. Maybe it should bother me that I'm not *the* one and only chosen one. But it doesn't. If anything, I feel relieved. I don't want to be this world's savior. How can I save a world I didn't even know existed until a few days ago if I don't even have the strength to save myself?

"There was a ten percent chance your sister would come instead of you," Lar admits, looking back at me, his earrings and hair swaying with the movement. His smile leaves his entire face an enigma, making him impossible to read. I imagine he's one of those people that are fucking *insufferable* to be around on a regular basis—like Edith. Fuck, these guys would've been better off if she'd fallen through instead of me. Of course, Edy would've had a conniption at all the weird shit, but she also would've swooned at these guys' feet, too. From what little I could see of the king, he was hot as hell. She'd have happily married him—especially if it meant being a *queen*. "If she had though, there was also only a ten percent chance she could save Underland—as opposed to your thirty-five percent."

"Thirty-five percent?" I ask, raising both brows. "Those aren't great odds."

"They were the highest possible odds out of all the living Alices," Lar says, slowing down to walk in line with me and the twins. "The king had me check every possible divination source and the results were clear. Well, as clear as a fogged window ever really is. You can make out shapes and color, but you never really know *who* is looking in at you until it's too late."

We stare at each other for a long moment, and I realize that his eyes are the same color as mine—a gentle robin's egg blue.

"What are you anyway?" I ask and he cocks a pale brow at me. I keep trying to think of an adjective to describe his unique blue-blonde hair color but it's as elusive as the man himself. "A faerie?"

"What are you?" he replies, that same sardonic smile plastered across his face. "An Alice?"

I roll my eyes and keep walking, focusing on putting one foot in front of the other. In the distance, something screams, a bloodcurdling nightmare of a screech, like death and dismemberment made sound. Something out there is dying a painful, painful death.

"Maybe we should walk a bit faster, Rab?" Dee suggests and the rabbit-eared man sighs, dressed in a black waistcoat and purple button up with the sleeves rolled to his elbows, pinstripe slacks and loafers with hearts on the toes. He flicks his newest cigarette out of the way, shakes allover like a dog, and then starts to melt. His hands drop to the ground and his back arches, thick strands of white fur bursting through his clothing as his mouth elongates, filling with razored teeth.

I always thought seeing or hell, *being* a shapeshifter in real life would be fucking awesome.

Watching the hideous malformation of Rab's body, I'm not so sure. My nose wrinkles and I take a small step back as he rises to his feet and shakes out his black spotted coat. At the shoulder, he's easily as tall as I am—maybe taller.

"Would you like a leg up, Allison-who-isn't-Alice?" Dee asks as I raise both brows.

"This was an option before?" I ask, trying not to feel so goddamn relieved at the prospect of riding on a beast's back—riding *Rab*.

"Not much of an option," he growls, turning to look at me with a ferine smile, his lips pulling back from his teeth. His bloodred eyes look into mine as his warm breath feathers over me. "Considering the cost to my dignity?"

"He'll draw other bandersnatch our way," Dee explains as I grab two fistfuls of fur and feel the twin wrap his hands around my hips. His fingers dig into my bones in the most pleasant way, a reminder of how good it feels to be held like this during sex. Swallowing hard, I let him boost me up onto Rab's back, feeling the thick, warm muscles of the beast between my thighs.

"Female bandersnatch?" I ask and Rab growls in what I assume is an affirmative. "Are all the female creatures in Underland starved for sex or something? I thought there were plenty of males to go around … although it probably sucks to be a lesbian here, huh? Not a lot of choices."

"Females in Underland are sexually aggressive, a counterpoint to the harshness of the males where you come from," Tee explains, and I can tell by the way he relaxes his shoulders that he finds comfort in reciting simple facts. "You'll see a lot of that here—the opposite of something you might be used to. Underland and Topside are in direct opposition to one another. When the balance is off …" He pauses just long enough that Dee decides to fill in.

"It causes catastrophic events like the Riving. It's why we lost most of our women—because of the way they're treated in yours." Dee shrugs his shoulders, but he doesn't know the half of it. I have a feeling everything these guys think they know about my world is hearsay and speculation. "If we don't get Underland sorted, your people are next—and it'll be *much* worse than the Riving. You won't just see your women turned to men—you might not *see* anything at all."

"You're telling me that if I don't stay here and rescue Underland from … whatever the fuck I'm supposed to rescue it from, *my* world suffers, too?"

Tee purses his lips and Dee chuckles.

"If you believe in the prophecy, then yes."

Fuck.

I sigh because I know I'm going to have to listen to that stupid poem now. I think about asking Dee to recite it as we walk, but now that my slow ass is perched on Rab's back, he starts to run and the other men follow suit. Not a one of them has much trouble keeping up.

God.

If I were staying here—and I say *if* because I'm definitely *not*—I'd need to workout more. Reading is nice, but it definitely doesn't tone the calves or build up cardiovascular endurance, does it?

I lean forward and curl my hands around Rab's long rabbit-like ears to keep my balance and hide my already chapped lips from the rush of cool air. He shudders a little underneath me, but doesn't protest and before I even realize it, I've fallen asleep.

♦ ♠ ♣ ♥ ♣ ♠ ♦

Cold, wet droplets against my cheeks wake me from an easy sleep, one that—thanks to the day of hard exercise—is dreamless and peaceful, even on the back of a sprinting dog … cat … whatever the fuck it is. A *bandersnatch.*

The rain that dogged us at the beginning of the day's walk starts to come down in thick sheets, and I dig around frantically in my satchel for the black and white striped umbrella Rab lent me this morning. I pop it open and hold it above my head as Rab's sprint slows into a careful jog and we come around a bend in the road, pausing before a soaring white and red manor, lit by lightning against the darkness of the trees. Thunder cracks in the distance and I feel my throat tighten as something *else* screams in the woods, something predatory that *isn't* a jabberwock, jubjub bird, or bandersnatch. What the hell else is out in this goddamn forest?!

The house itself is beautiful, with red-roofed towers and disturbingly detailed carvings of women and men in mourning, tears streaming down their faces. They shimmer with the rush of rain against the white stone and make me shiver, like their crying is all too real.

Rab comes to a stop on the white stones of the circular courtyard and kneels down, waiting for me to slide off. This time, North is there to help, taking my hips and pulling me down the side of the beast, his body crushing me into Rab's warm haunches.

"Welcome to my home, Miss Liddell," he growls, stepping back into the rain and letting it plaster his blonde hair to his head, droplets sliding down the slick blackness of his horns. With the umbrella for protection, I ignore the incoming thunder and lightning for a moment to gape at the manor. Most of the windows are stained glass, decorated with red heart motifs that are as pretty as they are redundant. Looking around at the heart-shaped hedges, the heart-shaped stone statues, the decorative heart shapes built into the stone mosaic under my feet … it's not all that difficult to remember what kingdom we're in. It feels like I'm being hit over the head with the message.

As I take it all in, Rab shifts and then reaches down for my hand, curving cool fingers around my wrist. His pale face is almost eerie when another lightning bolt crashes into a nearby tree and lights up his expression.

"This is no ordinary storm, Sonny," he says in that cruel, cold voice of his. "Best come inside before you end up cursed."

"Cursed?" I ask, but I let Rab drag me toward the front door. As my boots splash through puddles, I notice another flicker of white in the shadows of the trees, high up this time, perching on a branch like a bird. Again, it's just a smile, no face. But I'm a smart girl—I know how to figure things out.

That has to be the cat, the damn Cheshire Cat.

I flip him off just before Rab drags me through the doorway.

We must've just used a servant's entrance or something because as soon as I step inside, I find myself in a kitchen with a roaring fire and a massive cauldron. A woman stands next to it, stirring carefully, and glances away sharply when I meet her eyes. Behind me, a footman in red, white, and black livery—full-on powdered wig and all—moves to shut the door, pausing at the last moment as another man in a similar outfit approaches and bows low.

He hands over a letter, his eyes flicking up briefly to find the duke staring at him with interest. I can see the letter carrier's throat constrict as he tries to swallow.

"An invitation from the king to play croquet," he says, his wig soaked with water and dripping down the sides of his face. God, I hope they're going to let him in for the night at least?

"Come come," North says, snatching the letter from between the two servants and gesturing for the rest of us to follow him out of the admittedly cozy little kitchen. It has stone floors, a fireplace as tall as I am, and smells like fresh dough and salty butter. *God, I'm starving again,* I think as I pause at the entrance to the dining room and look back.

Now that the duke's gone, the cook rushes over to help the dripping messenger in and I blink in fascination as she kisses one man on the lips and then the other, holding one hand against either of their cheeks. Interesting.

I turn back around and find Tee waiting for me, dripping wet, his purple and black streaked hair stuck to his forehead. When I catch up, he starts walking and leads me down a series of halls with black and white checkerboard floors to a hunting lodge.

As soon as I step inside, I'm surrounded by dick.

Every man *except* Tee is kicking off his boots, tearing off his shirt, and shoving his sopping wet pants to the floor. *Oooookay,* so Lar wasn't lying about having more than three inches inside his breeches either.

"Allison?" Tee asks as I stand there, trying to blink through my shock. It's not a *bad* sight per se, all these attractive men stripped down to nothing, their bodies lit by the dancing orange flames of the fire. This room has mounted animal heads on the wall, too, just like Rab's living room. Except this collection is much larger, much more impressive. Now that I know what a jabberwock looks like, I spot one on North's wall right away, the decapitated head posed in a silent scream. "You need to strip out of your clothes. That's a wild magic storm out there."

"Huh?" I ask, turning back to look at him and seeing that he's already got his jacket off and his shirt undone. "Wild magic?"

"The same stuff that caused the Riving," Dee says from behind me. I keep my attention on his brother, on the slow, careful way he peels the wet fabric of his shirt away from his skin, turning to lay it over the back of a red leather chaise and flashing those magnificent tattoos of his. Before I can stop myself, I reach out my hand and brush my fingers down the wet muscles in his back, watching as he shivers and hunches over, curling his hands around the chaise and holding on tight. "Oh," Dee whispers, his voice curious but husky.

I feel like I've made some sort of social faux pas, something beyond just, you know, feeling up some random dude's back.

"Sorry," I start as Tee glances back at me, his face tight, but his eyes so much softer than they should be. It's the first time I've seen that expression on him, and I can't for the life of me figure out what it means.

"Don't be sorry," he says, and his voice is even huskier and thicker than his brother's, like he's having trouble catching his breath. "Dee and I belong to you—you can do whatever you want to us."

"Although Rab doesn't belong to her and she seemed to have no trouble feeling up his ears. Would you like to touch my tail next?" North asks, moving over to a liquor cabinet on the far wall and not giving two shits that his firm ass is right fucking there in my goddamn view. He fishes a key out of a small wooden box and unlocks the cabinet, stepping back and gesturing for Dee to take his place.

I turn back to Tee as he sits down and starts to pull off his boots.

"You should really take your clothes off before you get cursed," he repeats and I sigh, setting my satchel aside and shrugging out of my jacket. Before I can even think to ask about replacement clothes, there's a knock at the door and at a word from North, several servants enter and start passing out clothing.

I'm given what I guess is a nightgown, made of silk and trimmed with red lace. It's a lot fancier—and a lot racier—than anything I'd wear back home, but the fabric is smooth as butter against my fingertips and as soon as the woman puts it in my hands, I don't much feel like giving it back. Lifting the gown to my cheek, I resist the urge to rub it against my skin.

Behind the lounge where Tee is sitting, there's a decorative screen that I slip behind before I strip off the rest of my clothes. I can't decide if I'm doing it so that the boys can't see me … or so that I don't have to see them.

"I'm guessing Rab's ears … North's tail … Tee's back … those parts have a more sexual affiliation here than they do back home?"

There's a chorus of male chuckling from the other side of the screen, but I can't decide who exactly it is or if I even care. That answers that question. And then, of course, I feel guilty because Tee feels like he doesn't have a choice. And I know what that's like, to have someone try to take choice away from you. It isn't a pleasant feeling. Fuck, it's one of the worst.

I dry myself off as best I can with the towel the servant gave me and drape it over the top of the screen, slipping into the cool silk of the dressing gown and shivering as it caresses my body. It hangs nearly to the floor, but has a slit that goes all the way up to my hip, flashing a whole hell of a lot of white thigh when I move. If I were a different person, I might care, but I'm not a prude and I step out from behind the screen with confidence.

Thankfully, the guys are all wearing at least *some* clothing, although Rab seems more than content to lounge around without a shirt on.

"Oh, look," he says as I pop into view and his red eyes shimmer in appreciation. Rab slides his palm down his chest and taps his fingers against the tattoo on his hip. "It's almost teatime."

"Tell me more about this wild magic shit," I start as I scoop up my clothes and trade them out for the Queenmaker and the book, handing the satchel over to one of the waiting servants. Before I let go of the strap, I glance over at Tee, wearing a loose black top and pants. "I will get this back, right?" I ask and he nods.

"They'll hang everything to dry. Once it does, it's safe to wear again," he tells me as I flip through Alice's pages and find only a few water spots here and there. Glad I wrapped it up in Edy's dress. "A few drops are okay, but you don't want to wear clothes soaked in wild magic. A storm like this, as charged as it is, could be as bad as the Riving—especially for someone like you."

"Someone like me?" I ask and Tee smiles slightly to soften the words.

"Someone seeped in magic of their own," he says as North flashes me a savage grin.

"Don't want to turn into a man, do you?" North asks, sliding onto the couch next to Lar, taking care to stay away from his wings. I raise my eyebrows.

"You're telling me that rain," I start, pointing a finger up at the vaulted ceiling above our heads, "is capable of turning me into a dude—like dick, balls, the whole works."

"Spend enough time out in it and yeah, it's a possibility," Dee says as he folds his hands together behind his head, standing next to the fire and warming himself by the roar of the flames. I give a little shiver as I sit on the edge of the chaise with Tee and hold the book and gun in my lap.

"Sorry, but that sounds like a nightmare in the making." I pause as something occurs to me, watching as Dee pulls a kettle off the fire and pours hot water into a blue and white porcelain teapot from inside the liquor cabinet. Even here, in the duke's house, I get the sense that he's worse than a servant, a slave maybe. That, or maybe he's just an addict and wants tea badly enough to make it? "How is that even possible?"

"The magic that was stripped from all the women in the Riving …" Tee starts with a small sigh, his elbows on his knees, hands folded together. "It's just … in the air now."

"Like acid rain or toxic waste or some shit?" I ask, but everyone looks at me like I'm speaking a foreign language and I sigh. "Never mind. So, what's the plan then? We stay the night here, leave in the morning again?"

"That's the thing about plans," Lar says, flipping open a silver box on the table next to him and extracting a cigar with careful fingers. "They're like doors—they swing on hinges."

"Meaning what?" I ask as he smiles back at me, pushing damp hair away from his forehead. "We're stuck here until the storm passes?"

"It's not so bad here," North says, gesturing in Lar's direction and waiting as he passes over another cigar. "There are worse places to find yourself trapped."

His gold eyes bore into mine and I hold his stare. He might be royalty here, but I'm from another world. His title doesn't mean a damn thing to me.

"How long could it last?" I ask as Tee rises to his feet.

"Hours, days, weeks," North replies with a loose shrug. "Can't predict the weather, so why try?"

"Don't you have carriages or something we could use?" I ask, but my protests sound weak, even to my own ears. I don't sound like someone that gives a whole lot of shits about how long it takes to get to the palace, the Looking-Glass … my *life*.

"We have carriages, but what or whom is going to pull them is the question?" North asks, tail swishing slightly. "In a wild magic storm, a horse is as likely to be a pumpkin as it is an equine. In an emergency, we could make the trip, but why rush it? It's safer and easier to ride it out."

"Okay," I say with a small sigh, glancing over at Tee. There's something comforting about the amethyst color of his eyes. "Okay. We'll wait the storm out."

In the back of my mind, I know that Edith's probably spending most of her time in the bathroom, puking and crying and begging for me to come home. Because that's what she did when Fred died. Of course, Fred was buried six feet under; he was never coming home. But I can. I can go home … I'm just not sure if I want to.

In the morning, I wake to find my clothes dry and hanging in the misshapen wardrobe in the corner. It looks like somebody took a match to it and let it melt, one side flopping lazily toward the floor. It almost looks like I could mold it with my hands, like clay. Pressing a hand to the side though, I can tell it's perfectly solid, just wonky—like everything else in this world. Off. Strange. I equate it to the Leaning Tower of Pisa, that nagging sense of something not quite right.

Moving over to the window, I can see that the rain hasn't let up even a little. In fact, the black grandfather clock in the corner of the room says it's past noon and yet, I can't see a damn thing beyond the sheet of water cascading over the glass panes.

Swiping my fingers across the foggy surface, I turn and survey the room with its two king beds, both of them covered with luxurious canopies, falls of black and red velvet cascading from the ceiling to the floor. The curtains even have those old-fashioned rope pulls to make them easier to open and close.

Dee's still asleep in one of them, snoring, one arm tossed up over his face. His brother's missing, but as soon as I move away from the window, I can hear the shower going in the attached bathroom. I was too tired after dinner last night to protest being stuck in the same room as the twins. Honestly, I don't even mind. It's just … the idea that it's assumed they have to stay with me, like they're dogs on a leash or something, is annoying. If I were them, I know I'd fucking hate it with a passion.

Taking advantage of Dee's snoring and Tee's showering, I turn toward the window and slip the silk dressing gown over my shoulders, letting it pool on the floor at my feet. As I'm bending over and sliding the panties over my foot, I hear the bathroom door open.

Jesus Christ.

There's a long pause there as I stumble and turn, grabbing up the pile of clothes from the chair and holding various folded pieces over my bits. Tee, though, gentleman that he is, looks away sharply and exhales, stepping back into the bathroom and closing the door quickly. I dress myself as fast as I can, back in Lory's pirate gear, and then head over to knock.

Tee opens the door, fully dressed in his usual clothes and frowning severely.

"My apologies, Allison," he says, glancing away from me and toward the window. "I didn't realize you were up."

"Yeah, well," I say with a small laugh, ruffling up my blonde hair with my fingers.

"I got to see yours, so it's only fair, right?" When I turn back to Tee, he's not smiling. I think it takes a lot to get him there.

A long moment of silence follows, and I realize I'm blocking the doorway. Moving to the side, I watch Tee slip into the room and grab his boots, perching on the edge of a high-backed red chair to put them on.

"Was that … I mean, *is* it really your plan to come with me through the Looking-Glass? I could help you get set up in my world if you wanted." Tee pauses, his purple-black hair wet and tousled. I have the strongest urge to run my fingers through it. "I can only imagine what it's like for you here. I … lost my brother two years ago and then my mother a year later." I chew on my lip. I could clarify that she's just in prison, not dead, but why even go there? Why start a story I have no intention of finishing? "The pain is enough that the longer I stay here … the more I wonder what it'd be like if it were permanent. What if I never went back? What if I never thought of all that bullshit ever again?"

"You can't run from pain," Tee says suddenly, fixing the laces on his right boot and standing up, that fresh, clean smell of his wafting around me and making me feel dizzy. "When you do, it chases after you."

"So you weren't planning on skipping town?" I ask with a raised brow and Tee sighs, his purple eyes looking down into mine, his hands curling into fists at his sides.

"I don't have any pain anymore, just numbness. There's nothing left in Underland for us and there never will be. Let the four kingdoms tear each other apart, murder the whole world. I don't care. They deserve whatever they have coming to them."

He moves around me and heads for the door, but I'm not done, following after him and into the hallway.

"What are your wing tattoos about?" I call out as he storms down the checkerboard hallway with long, confident strides, purple coat billowing out behind him. Tee doesn't bother to look back at me, but before I can start running after him, I hear Dee's sleepy voice from behind me.

"It's a curse," he says as I glance back and find him sagging against the doorframe, eyes half-lidded, his voice thick with sleep, "from the previous king of hearts. Like a bird with clipped wings, he said." I turn around and Dee steps back, letting me into the room with him, looking down at me with an expression of such deep melancholy, I can hear it ringing inside my chest like a chorus of bells.

"You're … angels?" I ask, because that's what Duck said—*the last two angels in existence*.

Dee just smiles in a way that tells me the answer is *yes.*

"And princes?" Another smile as he reaches out and trails his fingers over the back of my hand, giving me chills.

"Not anymore. Now we're just … yours."

"Well, I set you free then," I say as he sighs and takes a step back, turning away from me to pad towards the bed again in bare feet. Dee isn't wearing a shirt, so I get a nice, clear unobstructed view of his wings, the blue-black feathers disappearing beneath the waistband of his pants, bleeding onto the backs of his arms.

"That's not how it works," he tells me as he climbs under the covers and leans back against the headboard, looking between the curtains toward the closed window and the pouring rain outside. "If you don't want us, the king will just take us back and use us … for whatever." He turns his head to look at me and flashes a grin that I don't buy for shit, not after seeing the expression of sadness on his face. "Should I tell you a story? Recite a poem? We'll be here all day and despite what the duke says, his house is dreadfully boring."

"So if I go back through the Looking-Glass, you two are … what, gifted to somebody else?"

"The king's been toying with the idea of making us high-class whores for the nobility," Dee says, closing his eyes and sighing. "I imagine it'll be something like that."

"You're kidding me," I whisper, sitting next to him on the edge of the mattress.

"I wish I were," he says, cracking one lid and smiling at me. "But it wouldn't be a particularly humorous joke, now would it? If you're looking for a laugh, I have much better quips up my sleeves."

Our gazes lock, and I can see as many emotions running through his eyes as I have colors woven in my hair. He's acting like he doesn't care, but he does. And he's looking at *me* like I can help.

The scary part of it all is … I can, right?

The king gave the twins to me—their fate is in my hands now. Staring at Dee, the idea's a lot more substantial than the thought of being some mystical chosen one. I don't have to hear a prophecy or unlock some secret powers that I'm not even really sure I have. All I need to do is look into the dark blue of his eyes and see shadows dancing there, shadows of grief and loss and pain that mirror my own.

My hands curl into fists in the blankets for a moment as I take a deep breath.

"What were you asking my permission for?" I ask him, scooting a little closer. "During the fight with the jubjub bird. Twice, you asked me for it. To do what?" The expression on Dee's face brightens up a bit as he looks at me, his eyes searching mine for a long, quiet moment.

"What would you think if I asked you to kiss me?" he whispers, and almost as soon as he's finished talking, I hear my heart thundering inside my chest. My pulse races so fast, I feel almost dizzy when Dee leans toward me, feathering his breath against my lips. "Have you ever heard one of those fairytales where a prince kisses a princess and wakes her from a long and troubled sleep?"

"Of course," I reply, and Dee is so close now that when I talk, I feel our mouths brushing together.

"This is like that … only better. So, if you're curious … kiss me and put your fingers on my back."

Taking another deep breath, I reach out and put a hand on either of Dee's shoulders. The position is awkward from where I'm sitting, so I turn and crawl up onto the bed, straddling him through the thick blankets. I try not to think too much about the hardness of his cock underneath all this fabric. Instead, I close my eyes and lean in close, slanting my lips to his.

Dee groans violently and puts his big hands on my waist, parting my mouth with his tongue and teasing me with long, careful flicks. I lean into him, my breasts pressing against his bare chest, my fingers gliding down his arms and … across the gentle softness of down feathers on his back. My fingertips bump against the warm metal of chains and I gasp as I hear them clinking against one another.

"Don't stop," Dee groans as my heart stutters, stops, starts up again, and I feel my body respond to the heat and husky need in his voice. I part my lips and let him kiss me deeper, harder, tasting the sweetness of his mouth, a fresh crispness that matches that wild airy scent of his. "Now, take the chains off …" he whispers and I start to push the metal links down his wings, feeling sharp surges of satisfaction as they slide over the feathers and land in silver pools on the pillows behind him.

Pulling back, I watch in openmouthed awe as Dee spreads his wings out, these two glorious expanses of black and blue feathers that shimmer in the weak candlelight from the single taper flickering on the wall.

"Holy shit," I whisper, sitting up on my knees and reaching out with my right hand. I stroke my knuckles down the length of one glorious wing and Dee groans like I've just licked his cock. When his eyes flick up to mine, they're heavy and half-lidded with lust. "Does that feel good?" I ask, my body pulsing and throbbing in all the right places. My nipples are pebbled, hard and desperate beneath my blouse, and my thighs are clenched tight against a surge of heat between my legs.

"It feels incredible," Dee groans as I do it again, stroking and petting his wings. His head falls back and he moans with reckless abandon, his hips rising unconsciously beneath me. Leaning forward, I press my lips to the side of his throat, kissing and licking his suddenly sweaty skin. His hands tighten on my waist as he continues to thrust beneath me, these slow, undulating motions that make me question whether or not I have any self-control at all.

Grabbing two handfuls of feathers on either one of Dee's wings, I yank hard and he grunts in a mix of pain and pleasure, following me forward and pushing me onto my back. He covers my mouth with his at the same time he covers my body with his own. Our tongues swirl together as he curls his wings forward and slips them underneath me, creating this cocoon of feathers that has me writhing and thrashing with need.

Dee wraps his fingers in my hair and pulls my head back, taking his own turn to kiss and nip at my throat as I struggle to kick my boots off and reach for the button on my pants. He doesn't stop me as I undo the breeches and push them down as far as I can.

"Allison-who-isn't-Alice," he whispers as he licks the curve of my ear and slips his left hand into my pants to cup my ass. "Did you want me to fuck you?"

He asks that question just before pulling away and sliding off the end of the bed. Dee's expression is wicked as he curls his fingers under the waistband of my pants, taking my panties with him as he yanks and pulls them down my legs and over my feet, tossing them aside.

Dee drops his own pants, revealing the hardened length of his cock just before he climbs back on top of me and starts kissing my neck again.

"Alice," he whispers, teasing me with gentle thrusts of his hips, slipping his shaft between my folds and teasing my clit. "You have to tell me *yes* or I can't do it. I have to hear the word *yes* from you, mistress."

"Do you have protection?" I ask as Dee pulls back a fraction and tilts his head at me.

"I'm all the protection you need when I'm in this form," he tells me with panting breaths, his sapphire eyes dark with lust, so dark it's hard to make out where the blue color ends and his pupils begin. "This is what I was asking for, during the fight. Unleash me and my brother like this and we can fight for you, Alice. That's why the king sent us—he knows we're the best."

He smiles at me and leans down to kiss my mouth again.

I let him, twirling my tongue around his for several seconds as his hands explore inside the peasant blouse and free my breasts from the confines of the corset, lifting them up and over the top so he can palm them, cup them in warm hands and flick his thumb across the swollen peaks of my nipples.

He misunderstood the protection question … Shit.

"Do you have condoms here?" I ask after another moment and Dee pauses.

"Condoms?" he asks, blinking down at me. "Uh …"

"Like, to protect against diseases? Pregnancy?"

"Oh," Dee says, his expression falling. I reach up and put a palm on either of his cheeks so that he'll look me straight in the face. "The king had us stripped of our fertility—another angel will never be born in Underland."

I lick my lips, my throat tightening at the sound of despair in his voice.

"As for diseases …" he starts and shakes his head. "I don't have any. You can use your magic to check if you want, I don't mind." He reaches down and takes my palm, putting it in the center of his chest, like I have any idea what to do with that. "Just close your eyes, Alice. Tee and I belong to you now. As soon as you crossed the barrier into Underland, the gifting was complete. The king arranged the whole thing—there's nothing about me you can't know if you want to."

The moment is so surreal that I actually find myself surrendering to it, the way I would a dream. My eyes close and I suck in a sharp breath, feeling this … *something* between me and Dee, like a tether binding his heart to mine. It feels uneven, this connection, like holding the leash for a dog. But there's nothing I can do about it, so I relax into it, follow it to its source … and feel myself being swallowed by blackness.

♦ ♠ ♣ ♥ ♣ ♠ ♦

It's night out when they come, the blackest black, an evening of ink and stars. They surge up the side of the mountain like shadows. They shouldn't be able to get up here, not without the power of flight. But they come anyway, hordes and hordes of soldiers in red metal, climbing the sheer rock face as easily as if it were a staircase.

Magic.

Someone gifted ... someone powerful *has given them the ability to break down the last barrier that stands between us, taken away our last hope, our only sanctuary.*

I fly out of bed to wake my brother, but he's already up. We exchange a look in the dark that speaks volumes. Slipping into clothes and strapping on what weapons we have, we move down the stairs, our wings dragging against the stone floor behind us.

I can already hear the screams, already smell the blood.

The things that rush in the door at us ... they aren't even people. I don't recognize the flat faces and the silent screams of rage frozen on their faces. They're soulless, empty, with as much heart as a deck of cards.

"Get to Mom's room!" Tee screams as he heads in the direction of the nursery. I'm torn between wanting to follow him, and wanting to check on my parents. If we're going to run again, we need the queen and her kings with us, just like last time. Last time, we escaped together and started again. They found us, all the way up here, buried in the clouds, but we can try again. If we're still alive, there's always the hope of starting over.

I burst into my parents' bedroom just in time to see a spear slide through my mother's stomach, blood spattering the stone wall behind her. She spreads her wings wide one last time and collapses to the floor at the feet of the King of Hearts.

When he turns to look at me, I feel my blood turn to ice.

"Just in time to see the show," he says, stepping back and waving a single arm in my mother's direction. "Off with her head."

Before I can get a single step into the room, the king's guard swings a massive claymore in her direction ... severing her head from her neck, painting the white roses on her nightstand red with blood.

With a gasp, I come to, Dee still resting on top of me, his sapphire eyes looking into mine. I can feel my body trembling and shaking beneath him as he leans down and kisses first one eyelid and then the other. I think he mistakes the quivering for lust or want—there's no way I can tell him what I just saw. That is, if I even had a damn clue what it is I just saw.

Was that a memory? A prophecy? It was *me* in that vision and yet … it wasn't. No, I'm pretty sure I was watching the world through Dee's eyes.

"Did you see?" he asks, pinning my arms gently above my head, pressing my skin against the silken cocoon of his feathers. His smile is devastatingly sweet, turning my heart to mush, making my throat tight. "I'm clean and ready for you, Allison-who-isn't-Alice."

"I saw," I whisper, wrapping my legs around him as he releases my wrists and reaches between us, finding my opening and pressing the head of his cock against me.

"Yes?" he asks again as I fight my way out of the vision. I don't want to see Dee's most painful moments, not when I have plenty of my own. Why would the magic … or whatever it is, show me *that*? That's about the last thing I'd ever want to see.

"Yes," I breathe, our eyes locking, my heart stuttering.

The grin I get in response is wicked and sharp, but soft enough at the edges to make me swoon. I can feel him pressing against me, encouraging my body to open for him. And when I do, he thrusts his hips forward in a smooth easy motion, making me gasp as he fills me up, stretching me in the most pleasant sort of way. I've only ever done it with condoms before so I'm surprised at how warm he feels, the scalding length of his cock teasing the ridges of my pussy with easy strokes. I squeeze Dee tight with my thighs, sliding my fingers over his shoulders and playing with the skin and feathers where his back and wings meet.

Dee's mouth crashes into mine in a rush of heat, pleasure teasing me in almost equal measures from all the places he's touching—my breasts, my mouth, the silken softness under my back where his wings hold me in what feels like a giant hug. He moves inside of me nice and slow, taking his time, making me groan with each forward thrust and gasp each time he pulls away.

The sounds he makes are half-relief and half-pleasure, the muscles in his wings trembling beneath my fingers, making me wonder how long it's been since he last felt them spread wide and glorious behind him. Weeks? Months? Years?

"Thank you," Dee whispers against my ear, and I know he's not talking about the sex … although he seems pretty thrilled with that, too. I smile against his mouth as our kisses grow deeper, hotter, more desperate.

When I feel his body tensing up, sweat pouring down his sides, I convince him to roll us over by putting a single palm to his chest.

Once I'm situated on top of Dee, his shaft buried all the way inside of me, I start to move my hips, looking down at him with his blue-black wings spread across the bed, his hands on my hips, our gazes locked. I work him until I feel his muscles getting tight again, leaning down so I can kiss his mouth and work my clit at the same time. His orgasm hits first, but I don't stop moving, refusing to let him rest until I'm done, too. Fortunately, it only takes me a moment, and I find myself collapsing on top of him with a long, embarrassing groan.

As soon as I do, I feel Dee's arms go around my waist.

"Hello hello," he says, lifting his neck up to look in the direction of the door. I get the feeling he's most definitely *not* talking to me. Sitting up and jerking my head around, I meet Tee's violet stare and feel my cheeks flush with heat. "Something we can help you with?"

"No," Tee says, but his eyes flash with envy before he turns away. I can't decide if that envy's over me … or the wings. Oh, who I am kidding? It's probably the wings. "Allison, the Duke would like to see you downstairs when you get the chance."

Before I can respond, he's stepping back and closing the door while I curse and clumsily extract myself from Dee's body.

"Would you like some help in the shower?" he asks, sitting up with that lazy, heavy-lidded bedroom look of his, wings splayed open and resting against the mattress. "Because that's what I'm here for, Allison-who-isn't-Alice, to *serve*."

"Right," I say, my emotions twisting into a strange bundle inside my belly. "But I think I can manage this part on my own."

Dee raises a dark brow at me as I scramble inside the bathroom and slam the door, turning around and leaning my back against it as I take a deep breath and close my eyes for a moment. *What did I just do?!* I just fucked a guy from another world, a world that … shouldn't even exist. Christ almighty, I screwed Tweedle-goddamn-dee.

Who's a prince.

And an *angel*.

And then his brother walked in on us?!

And I thought Underland couldn't get any weirder …

Oh how wrong I was.

♦ ♣ ♣ ♦

After a quick shower, I get dressed again and step into the room to find both Tee *and* Dee missing.

Huh.

My body is sweetly sore, and my heart is pounding like a teenage kid with a crush.

Oh … wait. I *am* a teenage kid with a crush.

Groaning, I lean my back against the wall and put the heel of my hand to my forehead. Brandon died, what, four days ago? And I've already replaced him with some weirdo from another world. I need to seriously check myself.

I just let some dude I don't even know come inside of me. Because I *believed* him when he told me to use magic to check for diseases?! Then again, I have to give myself a little credit because the man was sporting a wingspan that was easily thirty feet from one wingtip to the other. And only after a magic kiss released the glorious appendages from the tattoo on his back in the first place.

Still, Mrs. Davenport, my sex ed teacher, would fucking kill me for being so stupid.

With a sigh, I stand up straight, smooth my palms down the front of my shirt and resolve to *not* act like a weirdo when I find Dee and look into his blue eyes and remember him *fucking* me just before his brother walked in.

Yeah.

Like that's happening.

I'll probably stumble into him, gaze up with glimmering doe eyes, and forget my own name.

That's what got me into trouble with Liam two years ago—all that misplaced passion. He took advantage of it, took advantage of me, and then he killed my brother.

Exhaling sharply, I let myself out into the empty hallway and start walking in the direction I last saw Tee go, and down a set of curved stairs. The house is grand and whimsical, with soaring ceilings, delicate black glass chandeliers and walls as red as blood. As pretty as it all is though, after a few floors and a few hallways, it starts looking like I'm going in circles.

At one point, I pause and backtrack, pushing open a set of glass doors into a solarium where I know for sure I've never been. The trees, flowers, and—you guessed it—mushrooms kept in here are like nothing I've ever seen before. As I pause to rub at a plant with fuzzy orange leaves, I notice it again, that white-white smile in the shadows.

When I blink and take a few steps closer, I can see that it's a house cat, sitting in the bough of a tree. The cat only grins wider when it sees me. Knowing how the story goes, I'm *fairly* certain it's not going to hurt me, but still … it has *very* long claws and a great many teeth. Besides, it looks like a cat now, but who knows what—or whom—it might shift into. I decide to start off with a respectful greeting although it *is* tempting to call it out on being a creeper. Shit, it's been following me since we disembarked from The Long Tale. *Weirdo.*

"Cheshire Puss," I quote, referencing the original book as I cross my arms over my chest and study the black and white striped cat. It blinks big, gray eyes at me and stands up, arching its back in a languid, sleepy sort of way, grinning a little wider. "Would you tell me, please, which way I ought to fucking go from here?"

"That depends a good deal on where you want to get to," he purrs in a rich, deep baritone, sitting down on the tree limb and swishing his fluffy black and white tail at me. As I watch, parts of him fade in and out—his tail, his paws, his ears, his head. The only thing that seems to stay consistent is his grin.

"I don't much care where—" I start as he crouches down to look more closely at me.

"Then it doesn't matter which way you go," he replies as I roll my eyes.

"—so long as I find the Duke. Do you know where he is? And don't think I haven't noticed you following me the last few days."

"Oh, you're sure to find him," the cat continues, ignoring the latter part of my statement, "if you only walk long enough."

With a yawn and another stretch, he hops down off the tree, shifting as he goes so that when he lands, I'm looking at a man instead of a cat.

The Cheshire Cat rises to his feet, towering over me and flashing that same maniacal grin, his two front teeth pointed slightly, like a vampire's. His eyes are the same steely gray, a mimicry of the storm outside, the ears sticking up from his black hair striped and pierced through with several silver rings. In fact, with him leaning over me like that, I can see that he has a ring on either side of his lip, too. And one in his eyebrow.

"In *that* direction," he says, sweeping a hand out the way I came, "you'll find the Caterpillar and the White Rabbit." His grin turns into a wickedly curved little smile as he leans in closer and I take a small step away from him, my back pressing against one of the glass walls of the solarium. "And in *that* direction," he points the opposite way, toward a path in the bright foliage, "you'll find the Duke and the twins. Visit whomever you like: both sets are mad."

I lick my lower lip and the cat watches the movement. He smells like woodsmoke and flowers, an interesting mixture to be sure. But it's almost intoxicating. I blame Dee for waking up my hungry sex drive. It's been a while since I got any, so to speak, especially in a situation that felt as safe and normal and easy as it was with Dee. Even without whetting my voracious appetite, I was checking out every goddamn guy in Underland anyway. Guess I can't really blame this on the angel prince, huh?

I know what I'm about to do, follow the script from the original book … but I can't help myself. It's like the words are slipping from my mouth before I can stop them. *Magic.* It feels like fucking magic, the same way I felt compelled to follow the White Rabbit in the first place.

"But I don't want to go among mad people," I whisper as the Cheshire Cat puts a palm on either side of my head and leans in even closer.

"Oh, you can't help that. We're all mad for *you* here." I blink a few times as I try to process what he just said. Pretty sure *that* wasn't in the original book. "I'm mad. They're mad." He tilts his head in the direction of the foliage, just as the twins step out from behind some thick fronds. Dee's wings are still out, spreading wide as soon as he's free of the trees. When I see him, my heart skips a beat and I feel a rush of heat inside my belly that has nothing to do with the gorgeous man penning me in against the glass.

"How do you know they're mad?" I ask as the cat grins at me again and takes a step back, casting a haughty look in the twins' direction.

"They must be or they wouldn't have come here," he says, looking particularly gorgeous in a pair of leather pants and a black and white striped tank. Another very modern looking outfit. But after witnessing the three-way fight between the giant spider-bird, the dragon, and the werewolf with rabbit ears … I've forgotten how to be surprised.

"And why is that?" Tee asks the cat, flicking his eyes to me and away again. But he can't hide it. Even that split second look was long enough for me to see the longing and desperation in his gaze. He wants his wings, and I can't blame him. I wonder if what I did to Dee is permanent or something that has to, like be renewed on a regular basis?

The cat just smiles mysteriously and takes a few more steps back, perching his—admittedly gorgeous—ass on the railing that lines a small bridge. Underneath it, there's a small creek filled with koi that makes me think of my dad. My heart constricts painfully and I glance away, noticing as I do that the cat's eyes are following the movements of the fish with more than just simple curiosity. He looks like he's hunting, and when he flicks his gaze back to mine … he still does.

I shiver and swallow hard, curling my hands into fists.

Dee moves up to stand beside me, his arm brushing against mine and making my breath catch in my throat. I glance his way and watch as he flashes a grin of his own in my direction. It's flirty and full of promise, and I have a *really* good feeling that promise is for more sex before I leave Underland. Just looking at him makes me start to sweat. I want to, like, hold his hand or something but I've got too much pride to reach over and try.

"If you get tired of playing with boys, Alice," the cat purrs as he turns his gray eyes in Dee's direction and I roll my own at the name Alice. Even the damn cat knows who I am. "And decide you'd prefer to play with men instead, just let me know."

"Hmm," I say as Tee bristles and grits his teeth, the muscle in his jaw ticking with anger, "Dee is bigger and better than you'd ever be, I'm sure. I'm just fine with these *boys.*" The cat laughs, stretching his arms lazily above his head and giving me a piercing sort of look.

"Well then," he purrs as he fades almost instantly from view, "message received. I'll just be on my way then."

I search for his grin in the trees, but don't see anything. Of course, I have no doubt that he's still around here somewhere.

"Can I ask you something?" I start, turning to Dee and trying to forget that just twenty or so minutes ago he was buried inside of me. It's hard to forget that though, considering how much clean up I had to do in the shower. There's no denying what happened between us.

"Can you? Or should you?" he asks, getting that playful nonsensical edge to his voice. "Or could you? Would you?"

"How long does this last?" I continue, ignoring him and gesturing in the direction of his wings. He pauses and glances back with a small sigh, curling them around his body like a shield, so the only part of him I can see is his face.

"Only until midnight. Like all fairytales, it has to end sometime."

"Oh," the cat's deep voice coos from up in the branches of a nearby tree. "It just occurred to me—did you say he was *figger* or bigger. Because, you know, *figger* is not a word. A fig is a fruit and not an adjective. Unless you meant to say *figure* in which case, either your or my spelling is wrong. And to be quite frank, Alice, I don't think there's anything wrong with *my* spelling."

"I said *bigger* and you know it, now fuck off," I growl as the cat grins again and starts to fade from view, starting with the tip of the fluffy tail sticking out the back of his leather pants, then his legs, his muscular torso, his head, and ending with his grin.

"The duke wants to give you the Vorpal Blade," Tee says, as I turn to look at him, standing farther away than seems reasonable for a normal conversation. Sucking in a deep breath, I move over to stand in front of him, put my hands on his shoulders, and lean up on my tiptoes to kiss his mouth.

I don't quite expect the explosion of passion that erupts between us.

And the groan that escapes his lips? It's nothing short of a growl.

The fabric of Tee's jacket stretches and bulges beneath my fingers, his wings rising from the tattoo like a submarine from the navy waters of the sea. I try to break our kiss, but his strong arms wrap around me, holding me tight. When I lift my suddenly droopy lids, I can see him looking back at me, his purple eyes as dark as a night sky, full of constellations and drenched in mystery.

I did not think I'd be getting a kiss like *this* from the brother that hates me.

Tee kisses me with this fury, this possessiveness that makes me wonder what the hell else is hiding under his constantly bored and pissed off facial expressions. Fuck, now I'm the one that's intrigued. I lean into him, putting my palms on his chest, drinking in the beautiful fresh scent of soap and snow as he caresses my tongue with his own and I help him shrug out of his jacket.

Our kiss is a violent frenzy of lips and teeth and tongue, a twisting avenue of desire that I want to explore further, shine light into every shadow and see what secrets it might hold. I fantasize about what it might be like to fuck him as my fingers tease each button of his black and white striped shirt apart, exposing his perfect abs and chest, my fingertips exploring each crevice. I don't hold back when I get to the hardened points of his nipples either, rubbing my thumbs over the peaked points before the shirt comes down his muscular shoulders and drops to the floor.

"Free me," he growls out, like a chained animal. "*Please*, mistress."

The only sound that seems capable of coming out of *my* mouth is a groan as I dig my fingers into his purple and black feathers, the heaviness of the chains weighing my hands down as I explore Tee's wings. The sound of those metal links hitting the floor in a heavy clatter is so satisfying that for a moment, I forget where I am and what I'm doing. It doesn't help that Tee's cock is hard, straining against his black jeans for release.

My right hand slides over the bulge and he bites my lip with a little snarl, encouraging me with his tongue to undo his button, pull down his zipper …

"Well, now, look at this," North's voice growls from behind Tee as he appears out of the foliage with his tail swishing, his golden eyes narrowed, and a cruel smirk etched into his lips. "The king will certainly be pleased to know Miss Liddell is enjoying her new toys." He's smacking a large knife against one hand and grinning at me. Right away, I recognize that knife as the one Rab was holding on his palm, outstretched as an offering to the King of Hearts. "If you have a moment, though, I'd like to share a few tricks with you—you're going to need them if you want to survive one of the Hatter's famous parties."

CHAPTER SEVEN
A Mad Tea Party

The Duke of Northumbria and I seem to have varying opinions on what *a few tricks* entails. I assumed he was going to give me a few pointers on etiquette, or a quick lesson with the Vorpal Blade like Dee gave me with the Queenmaker.

But no.

I find myself standing in the middle of a room with polished wood floors and white painted lines. There are leather punching bags in one corner, and mats filled with down feathers—the feathers of *angels* I'm told. My stomach churns at that, thinking of that memory or flashback or whatever you want to call it that I got from Dee. If the duke had said it with pride, I'd have probably punched him in the nuts. As it were, he sounded matter-of-fact about it and not much else.

Staring at him with that awful grin though, I start to get nervous.

"I'm not really the fighting type," I tell him which isn't *necessarily* true. If I have to kick ass, I can. I can scrap with the best of them, but I don't have any formal training. That, and I'm ridiculously out of shape. Like I said, I'm a reader, not an athlete. "Can you just give me a few pointers on how to use the knife and we can move on?" I don't bother telling him I won't be in Underland long enough for it to matter—the duke seems convinced that I'll be marrying that tyrannical nightmare of a king.

"The Vorpal Blade isn't a *knife* anymore than Excalibur is a *sword*," North says and I raise my eyebrows.

"But Excalibur *is* a sword …" I start when North moves around behind me and takes my hands in his, mimicking that moment on the boat when Dee fixed my grip on the Queenmaker. North does the same with the Vorpal Blade, curving my fingers around the black hilt. It's smooth and polished to a shine, its surface as reflective as a mirror.

"The Vorpal Blade's hilt is carved from the horns of a jabberwock," North explains, ignoring my protest, his body warm and solid behind mine. I can't help but flick my eyes in the twins' direction as he gets a little closer than necessary, sliding his fingertips over my own. They don't *look* jealous, but who knows? I can feel the muscular length of his tail curling around my ankle and giving it a bit of a squeeze. Not sure if that's intended as a come-on or not. It's hard to say when I've never met a man with a tail before. "And the blade is made from a fractured piece of the previous Looking-Glass. There were only three shards recovered after the Riving, and this is one of them."

"Why do you have it?" I ask, because if this blade is as special as North is making it out to be, wouldn't the king have it in his possession?

"Because it was *owed* to me," he growls, and the hair on the back of my neck stands up straight. His accent is pretty, cultured, melodic … but the way the duke talks? Like he's on the verge of letting loose in a violent roar? I can see why they call him *savage.* He's got this feral, primal quality that both frightens the fuck out of me … and interests me. Can't explain it. It's just … there, this pulsing bestial quality in my chest that makes me want to growl right back. "And now I'm giving it to *you*, Miss Liddell because it *is* mine to give."

He steps away from me, black tail thrashing as he pads across the room and spins back to face me, the flickering torches on the walls making the curved, deadly shapes of his horns look like they're glowing. They also serve to highlight the big, white grin in the corner of the room. So much for leaving me be. The damn cat's back.

"Now, Miss Liddell, come at me with the blade."

"You want me to … try to stab you?" I ask and North gives me this utterly irritating self-assured little smile that really seals the deal. Fine. Crazy son of a bitch. He wants me to chase him with a giant, magic knife? If he's going to have *that* sort of attitude, then he doesn't even really need to ask. I'll fuck him up with the Vorpal Blade for *fun*. "Suit yourself, *Duke*."

I look down at the blade, grasped clumsily in my hand and think about the twins, spinning their knives around their fingers on The Long Tale. They made it look so damn easy. Holding it in my fist now? There's nothing easy about this. Just the weight of the blade feels unfamiliar. The only time I ever hold a knife this sharp is if I'm about to cut into a piece of steak.

I have no goddamn idea what I'm doing here.

"Well?" North asks, crossing his arms over his chest. "I haven't got all bloody day." He pauses, flicking his gold eyes up to the glass ceiling above our heads, the rain still coming down in violent sheets. "Wait a moment, please. That might not be an accurate statement. Rab?" I glance over as the door to the training room … gym … whatever the fuck it's called, opens and in walk Lar and Rab. Lar immediately takes a seat on the floor, sitting cross-legged and smiling at me with this *I know you're about to get your ass kicked* facial expression.

I glare at him and refocus my attention on the White Rabbit, watching as he unbuttons his waistcoat and shirt, shrugging out of them to reveal his tattooed arms, chest, and belly. With a single fingertip, he traces his way up his abs and over his shoulder, locking his bloodred eyes with mine as he goes about it. *Fucking tease,* I think as he pauses on his bicep and taps at the clock there.

"We're due back at the palace *now* so suffice it to say, you do *not* have all day. In fact, we're late."

"And if you had to give me a timeframe to go by?" North asks in his crisp English accent.

"I'd say you actually *owed* the king a half or maybe even a full day," Rab adds and North nods like that makes any sense at all.

"So you see, Miss Liddell, we don't have a day. We don't even have a *second.* We're in the red now. If you please." I roll my eyes at the nonsense and take a deep breath, holding the knife out to the side as I run forward, straight toward North and his beautiful bronze skin, blonde hair, and gold eyes. He looks wicked terrifying with that savage smile, the black horns, that whip of a tail, but I keep going, swinging the Vorpal Blade at him with every ounce of strength I have.

As if he's picking fucking tulips on an afternoon stroll, North reaches out and snatches my wrist, twisting it just enough that I cry out in pain and drop the knife. Before I can even register what's happening, he's used my arm to flip me over and onto my back, my body crashing into one of the feather mats that line the training room floor.

"That was dreadful, Miss Liddell," he says, looking down at me, his gold eyes sparkling with amusement. "It won't do for the Alice to be so … soft. You're liable to get yourself killed *far* before you even make a difference in this world. Stand up." North steps back and holds out his tail for me to grab. I'm not quite sure *what* the etiquette is with extra body parts and all that, but he *is* offering.

I curl my fingers around the muscular end of his tail, the black scales smooth and silken beneath my palm, and North yanks me to my feet like I weigh nothing at all.

"North, you're quite the little pervert, aren't you?" I hear Lar whisper as I glance back and find him with his butterfly wings spread wide. "If you're grabbing his tail, you may as well be grabbing his dick." He brushes razored pieces of blue-blonde hair from his forehead and gives me a bemused smile.

Wrinkling my nose, I ignore North's raucous laughter and swipe my palm against my shirt.

"Again," he says as I sigh and pick up the Vorpal Blade from the floor. Under different circumstances, I might've *liked* this, learning to use an actual weapon for self-defense … or in this case maybe, offense? But knowing my ultimate goal—to go home and get back to my life, it just doesn't seem like a practical use of time.

Still, when North directs me to start again, I do.

I try a different method, throwing my body at him and keeping the knife close. I figure he can't grab my arm if he can't reach it, right? Instead, he steps nimbly out of the way and I end up sprawling across the ground, rolling over at the last possible second and lifting up the knife in self-defense as North brings down a wooden practice blade that I hadn't seen him grab. I manage to just *barely* block the blow with the Vorpal Blade, but that's enough.

Magic surges through me like electricity, and I realize then that the violent tremors I felt when using the Queenmaker *weren't* from the gun itself. No, they were from *me.* Those same tremors travel through me and into the blade, sending North *flying* across the room.

He hits the wood floor with a grunt and rolls, coming up to his feet with his brows raised in surprise. But he doesn't stop. He comes at me again, so quick I can barely think of what move I *want* to make, let alone act on it. At the last second, I get a booted foot up and into his stomach, but he's anticipated the move, curling his fingers around my leg and yanking me hard enough that I slide across the floor and underneath him.

North straddles me, grabbing my wrists in his hands and pinning them to the floor above my head, a mockery of the gentle way Dee held me only an hour or so ago. The thing is, it's not entirely unpleasant to have North above me like that.

Sometimes, I wonder though, what it might've been like if Fred hadn't burst in that door and saved me. Would I still feel the same way about moments like this? Or would they be tainted? *Are* they tainted already? If Liam and his filthy friends had … Sometimes I have nightmares about it, about what *could* have happened. Sometimes I wonder if something worse did.

Liam and his friends killed my brother.

Claimed it was self-defense.

Got away with it.

And my mother killed *them*.

"Are you crying, Miss Liddell?" North asks, pausing our sparring session as I tear my hands out from underneath his wrists. He stands up off of me and I raise a hand to my face. I'm not crying, not yet. But he must see something in my eyes that makes him think I might.

"I'm fine," I growl out, pushing to my feet without his help, the Vorpal Blade still held tight in my hand. "Let's go again."

North raises his eyebrows, but he doesn't question me when I set up for the exercise again.

And again.

And again.

By the time I'm done for the night, my body is soaked in sweat and the twins' wings are … gone.

The clock's struck midnight and the fairytale is over.

Dinner is served in the formal dining room, a black glass chandelier dripping low over the table's black lacquer surface, place settings and silver trays already laid out and waiting. My stomach growls in protest as I sit my freshly showered ass down in one of the tall chairs with the heart-shaped backs and try to figure out where to start first.

Working out all day and not eating? Not my idea of a good fucking time. I'm *starving.*

I'm also wearing the skintight red dress Rab gave me, and it doesn't take an especially observant person to see that all the men in the room are appreciative of the outfit. I could probably tell them off like I did the sailors on The Long Tale, but … as long as they're polite, they can *look.* After all, I've spent all day ogling the way North's muscles dance beneath his skin. About halfway through our training session, he took off his shirt and I couldn't help but look, really.

And having all that sweaty, muscular flesh pressed against mine?

It was just a tad tortuous, I have to say.

"Do you want your wings back?" I ask, finding myself at the head of the table with the duke and the twins on one side; Lar, Rab, and the cat sitting on the other.

"It's not our decision to make," Tee says carefully and North laughs, lifting up the top on a silver tray and revealing a whole roasted miniature pig. The scent of pepper teases my nostrils and I sneeze, rubbing at my nose as North snaps his fingers and a servant appears to carve the meat.

"Don't be shy on my account," he says, flicking his golden eyes over to me. "The king doesn't like the twins to use their wings unless it's an emergency, a life or death situation so to speak. If you were to, say, unlock their curse every night just *after* the stroke of midnight. Well, I can't say that he'd be pleased."

I narrow my eyes as another servant steps up on my right side and starts lifting the tops off trays, filling my plate with a variety of things that at least *smell* good—even if I don't quite recognize everything being dished up. Once the other servant is finished carving, North lifts up a slab of juicy pork with a pair of tongs and lays it on my plate without asking.

My eyes narrow even more.

"Don't the twins belong to me now?" I snap, hating that I'm saying it even as I do. After all, if what Dee says is true—that the king wants to turn him and Tee into high-priced whores—I have to step up and take responsibility, don't I? Besides … and I won't tell anyone this, so if you spill my secret, I *will* lie … I like knowing they're mine.

I'm attracted to them both, and I genuinely like their personalities—even if they're a little weird. I'd proudly keep them … if I were staying. And by keep them, I mean, like, let them live their own lives while under the guise of my control of course. Even if we did have to meet up every night at the stroke of midnight to break the spell again …

"I should be able to do whatever I want with them," I say as Dee grins and piles his plate with a sweet smelling tower of what looks like orange mashed potatoes. Taking a careful bite of the matching pile on my own plate, I find myself with a mouthful of buttered yams with brown sugar. Mmm. "If I want them to have their wings out, it's my prerogative."

"Well, I suppose the king might make an exception for his future bride," North adds and I have to resist the urge to roll my eyes. Why sit here and announce that I have *zero* intention of marrying the piece of shit, some jerk that thinks it's okay to gift me two naked men and then demand I be his bride. Not happening. But I'd rather keep my cards close to my chest so to speak. If I need to sneak into this Looking-Glass —or make a run for it—it's always better to have the element of surprise.

"What's your name anyway?" I ask as I glance over at the cat, sitting with one elbow on the table, lazily sipping milk from a wineglass. Please. What a cliché.

"Isn't it Cheshire Puss?" he asks, letting the last word roll off his tongue in a purr. "It's what you called me earlier, and I quite like *pussy.* Cats, that is."

"How vulgar," I say, engaging his stormy stare and refusing to look away first. "But if you want me to call you *Puss* while we sit at dinner together, I will."

"His name is Chesh," Tee adds helpfully, drawing my attention over to him and his violet eyes.

"Chesh?" I ask with a small sigh. "That's almost as creative as *North* or *Lar*."

"Almost as creative as the name *Allison* is for the Alice," the cat says, his striped ears swiveling around on top of his head. He folds one back in irritation, and I hate that his voice is a Lucullan feast for the ears, far too rich and sumptuous for his own good. I can already see that he's an arrogant prick like all the rest of them.

"It's not like my parents knew I was some magical Mary Sue, now did they?"

"I'd hardly call you a Mary Sue," Rab adds, drawing my attention over to him. One of his long white ears flops in half as he picks up a small teapot and pours himself a generous cup. Great. Here we go again. I push my teacup and saucer away, picking up a clear pitcher of what I assume is water. "To be a Mary Sue, everyone has to like you. I'm not sure that everyone at this table does."

I glare at Rab as I give the pitcher a quick sniff; I can tell it's anything *but* water.

No, it's vodka.

"Isn't there anything to drink around here that won't give me a hangover?" I ask as Lar gives me another one of his sardonic little smiles.

"Why does it matter if you have a hangover?" he asks, his wings curling gently at the edges. I wonder what they feel like, if they're soft to the touch? If I *were* to touch them, would I get powder on my fingers the way you do with real butterflies? "Even if the rain *did* let up, we wouldn't leave until morning. And when we did, we just might take a carriage. So a hangover would hardly preclude you from participating in any of your previous plans."

"If you think you're being clever," I start, searching through the various other pitchers until I find one with something that looks, smells and … with a lick from the swipe of a single finger, *tastes* like iced tea, I pour myself a generous glass. "You're really just annoying."

"Am I?" Lar asks as I glance his way and try not to compare him to Howl from the movie *Howl's Moving Castle.* But like, that's sort of what he looks like. And although I'm not normally one to have a 2-D crush on a Japanese anime character, Howl is fucking *hot.* And so is Lar. Plus, he's like, basically a faerie. That's one of my absolute favorite sub-genres to read, too. Ugh. "Are you sure about that?"

"Am I sure that I find you annoying? Yes, absolutely."

"That's your problem then," Lar says as he accepts the teapot from Rab and pours himself a generous cup. "*Nothing* in this world or any other is absolute."

I roll my eyes and glance over at the twins. After spending even a small amount of time with these other assholes, they're starting to feel almost *normal.* I notice that Dee passes on the tea tonight and I smile.

I'd rather not have him high when he could … you know, be doing other things.

Things that involve me … and naked bodies … and beds.

After I'm finished eating, I head upstairs to change into my silk dressing gown, intending to stir up some drama with Dee … or Tee … or like both?

But as soon as my head hits the pillow, I'm out.

"The Walrus and the Carpenter
Were stalking close at hand:
They grinned maniacally to see
The forming of her band:
'If this were only cleared away,'
They said, 'it would be grand!'

'If nine big men with nine big cocks
Presumed to hold her near,
Do you suppose,' the Walrus said,
'That we could get her clear?'
'I know it' said the Carpenter,
And gave an awful leer.

'O Alice, come and walk with us!'
The Walrus did beseech
'A pleasant walk, a pleasant talk,
And mend this bloody breach:
We can still slaughter nine or more,
So say goodbye to each.'"

I blink, coming to slowly, the lilting sound of a semi-familiar voice drawing me up from the sheets and into a sitting position. Sweeping a hand through the tangled blonde strands of my hair, I see Tee sitting at a desk in the corner, singing to himself.

"Is that the rest of the prophecy?" I ask and he startles, glancing sharply over his shoulder at me, the color draining from his face as he licks his lower lip and I'm reminded of that violent kiss in the solarium. *God, whoever would've pegged you to be an alpha male?* I wonder as his purple eyes meet my blue ones and we get caught staring at each other.

"Part of it. There are twelve more stanzas," he hedges, and I notice that Dee is lying on the same bed as me. I vaguely remember him whispering in my ear as I drifted off, and since I *was* planning on trying to get into his pants again, I probably mumbled yes to whatever he was asking. I stare at him, sleeping on his side, his tattooed back catching the light of the candles, and I have to fight the urge to lean down and kiss him.

I will …. just not yet.

"The Walrus and the Carpenter, huh?" I ask and Tee sighs, closing a small leather journal, locking it with a golden key and slipping the key into his pocket. He moves over to sit on the edge of the mattress. "Sounds a lot like the poem I read in the original Alice book."

"The Walrus and the Carpenter …" Tee starts and I can see his brow crinkling up as he shakes his head, lifting a severe stare in my direction. "They're nothing like the characters in that book—they're much worse."

"Worse than men who prey on naive children and then eat them?" I ask, cocking a brow. Dee stirs in his sleep, wiggling closer to me, and I suck in a sharp breath as he throws an arm over my stomach and nuzzles in close to my side, his breath warm through the silk fabric of the dressing gown. I don't know him for shit, but I feel this … *urge* to protect and care for him. Rubbing a hand down my face, I drop it in my lap and glance back at Tee.

"When that's a euphemism for the things they really do, then yes. Worse. The *worst*, actually."

A shiver crawls down my spine, and I can only imagine what exactly he's implying. No, I can't go there right now. If I let myself drift down that dark stream, I might drown in it.

"Nine big men with nine big cocks?" I ask next, trying to lighten the mood. But it's dark in here, lit by a single flickering taper on the desk where Tee was sitting. Outside the duke's manor, the wind howls and rain pelts the windows, tree branches scratching against the thin panes like claws. "That seems oddly specific."

"It's a prophecy," Tee says with a sigh, looking down and into his lap. His expression is far away and conflicted; I don't understand it. Then again, like I said, I don't know him at all. Maybe if I did, I could figure out what he's thinking. "An old one. And it has to be, if we have any chance of …"

"We?" I ask, carefully removing Dee's arm and crawling out of the blankets. I stand up and then turn to face Tee, putting my hands on his shoulders and drawing his gaze to my face. "What do you mean *we*? I thought you were leaving this place."

"I never said …" Tee starts, but then stops when he realizes he's not fooling anyone. "I'm reconsidering."

"Because of me?" I ask, but he says nothing, his body going stiff as I straddle his lap, putting a knee on either side of him and settling over the heated warmth of his crotch. "You think I can be this savior?" I grin, because I'm in a damn good mood. The best mood I've been in … since Fred. Since Mom. And in this clusterfuck of a world? It must be the sex, all those feel-good hormones flooding my brain. "Hate to break it to you, but I can't be anyone's savior—although nine big cocks sounds like a fun prophecy to fulfill."

"You *are* the Alice, whether you like it or not," Tee starts, swallowing hard as I lean in close. He knows I'm going to kiss him again, free his wings from their awful prison. He won't stop me now. "But if you don't want to try, I don't blame you. Maybe there is nothing left in this world worth saving?"

"Something changed your mind though. I mean, enough to even consider staying, right? What was it?" Tee refuses to look at me, staring out at the storm until a gust of wind whistles under our bedroom door and blows out the candle, plunging the room into blackness.

"My brother thinks you can change the world. I saw it in his eyes today. It was more than just words this time; he believes it with his whole heart."

"That was just the sex talking," I whisper, and when the word *sex* flits across my lips, I feel Tee stiffen up beneath me—in more ways than one. His entire body goes taut, and his cock thickens inside his jeans. "He was riding the afterglow high, that's all."

"Allison," Tee says slowly, and I realize he's the only weirdo here that calls me by my proper first name. "It's more than that—I know Dee."

"And I don't. And *he* doesn't know *me* from Eve, so if he thinks I can—" I start, but Tee's cupping the back of my head in one of his big hands and crushing his mouth to mine, stealing the words from my lips. I forget whatever rant I was about to go off on and relax into him, pushing my breasts against his chest as we struggle to tear Tee's shirt off before his wings rip it to shreds.

The chains sloughing off hit the floor and wake Dee with a start.

Based on the scraping sound from the side table, I think he even grabs his *knife* before he relaxes enough to realize what's going on.

"Shit, you scared me," he whispers, and I can hear him panting in the darkness. Tee and I aren't kissing anymore but our faces are pressed close together and I can feel his breath against my lips. Tears sting my eyes, but I have no clue *why* because nothing's happening. Well, nothing except for the fact that I'm straddling a stranger's lap. In a world I didn't know existed. With my fingers tangled in his *feathers*.

Angel prince.

God.

No, even worse—*twin* angel princes. It's like the most clichéd cliché ever written, but … like, if I were reading it, I would totally be envious of the main character.

The bed creaks as Dee crawls closer to the two of us, putting his mouth near mine. When I turn my head, he leans in and kisses me hard and fast on the lips, groaning with pleasure as his wings unfold from his back in two glorious swaths of darkness. A flicker of lightning from outside illuminates them, stretched out to their full width and casting terrifying shadows on the wall behind him.

"I could get used to that," Dee says, and his mouth is close enough to mine that I can feel him grinning. "I could get used to fucking you, too, Allison-who-isn't-Alice, if you were into it."

"Does it at all bother you that I'm sitting on your brother's lap?" I manage to choke out, feeling Tee erect and wanting between my thighs.

"No," Dee says, sitting back on his heels, another quick flash of lightning revealing his sapphire gaze and that face, so easy on the eyes. I could look at that man all day and not get tired of seeing that perfect curve of lips, his straight nose, or those sculpted cheekbones. Looking at him now, he really does look like a prince. "Should it? *Nine big men with nine big cocks*," he repeats in that singsong voice of his. "It's in the prophecy that the Alice should have nine husbands. Which, of course, is actually one less than the national average here in the Kingdom of Hearts."

"So you don't care if I check Rab's naked torso out or get off on the feel of North's sweaty body pressing against mine while we spar?" I mean to sound snarky as fuck, but actually I come across a little breathy and weird, like I'm wistfully dreaming of the two men I just named. Which, maybe I am … just a little. What can I say? I've been thrust from a nightmare at home into a … well, another nightmare with giant man-eating birds, but at least this nightmare has men who all ring an eleven or higher on my scale of one to ten.

"*Nine big men with—*" Dee starts and Tee cuts him off by making a low, growling sound in his throat. "No, it doesn't bother me. We have different rules here in Underland than you do back home."

"What are your rules then?" I ask, not because I actually care though. Because I … well, okay, fuck I *am* curious to find out how this whole dating multiple guys thing works.

"*Weellll*," Dee starts, and I can tell he's feeling playful by the sound of his voice, even if the rapid flickers of white-hot lightning in the pitch-dark are killing my night vision and making him hard to see. "You fucked me first, so maybe I'm the primary?"

"You're a slave, Dee," Tee corrects, his voice low and thick with agony … the agony of being chained, trapped. It makes me sick to my stomach, and in the darkness of the room, I throw my arms around his neck and … hug him?! Surprisingly, he lifts his arms and hugs me right back. "We don't get to make choices—we belong to the Alice."

"Keep going, Dee," I say, ignoring Tee's words and nuzzling my face into the side of his neck instead. I might not know him, but sometimes I suppose, it just feels good to be touched? "Then what?"

"Then you would tell me who else you were interested in, and I would either approve or disapprove of them. With each guy I approved—like say, Tee here—we would add him to our discussion. And then he would also have to approve or disapprove of the next man you were interested in."

"This is common practice?" I ask, leaning back and looking into Tee's face. It's so dark I can barely see his eyes, but I can *feel* his fucking gaze all over me. That, and the hardness between my thighs.

"It is here," Dee says, and I can hear the blankets rustling as he crawls back into them. "I can already tell who you're into, and I suppose I don't much mind any of them—"

"Any of who?" I ask with an indignant snort.

"Rab, Lar, North, Chesh," Dee says, and I can hear him chuckling stupidly. "It's pretty obvious."

"It is not," I say, but maybe it is. Just a little. "Doesn't matter anyway because as soon as we get to the Looking-Glass, I'm going home.

"Sure you are," Dee says with a sleepy smirk. I can see it reflected in the next flash of lightning. "Goodnight, Allison-who-isn't-Alice. Keep dreaming."

"You're a real piece of work, you know that?" I snap, feeling my skin heat as I get flustered. "I can't even *believe* that I slept with you." But as soon as I finish talking, I can already hear him snoring.

"He learned to fall asleep quick, in any available moment or … else he might not ever get to sleep." Tee exhales sharply as I turn my attention back to him, wishing the candle hadn't gone out so I could see his face. I want to ask about that vision, that awful fucking vision that I *know* was just a quick flicker of the pain Dee must've suffered. As I faded out of it, I could feel his heart shattering to pieces.

Seeing your mother murdered in front of you?

It's not something anyone ever gets over. And besides, if the boys are nineteen … and they didn't look much younger in the vision, then what happened to them can't have happened all that long ago. Their wounds might not be scars yet—they might still be festering, bleeding sores. I know mine are. People act like time heals all wounds, but all it really does is make the torn flesh rough and hard with glossy pink scar tissue. That's the best-case scenario, and I don't think any of us are even there yet.

"Do you want to have sex?" I ask him, stroking my fingers through Tee's feathers.

"Do you?" he asks and I swallow hard.

"Yes. As long as you don't mind that Dee and I—"

"I don't mind," Tee growls, reaching his hands down between us and freeing the erect length of his cock from his pants. He grabs my hips with a level of possessiveness that I didn't expect and yanks me forward, shoving my silk dressing gown up my thighs, and guiding the slick head of his shaft to my opening. He's clearly aroused, his penis already glossy at the tip with pre-cum. That's the view I get in the next flicker of lightning, the thick hardness of him that's about to go inside of me.

Without another word passing between us, Tee puts pressure on my hips, sinking his shaft slowly into me and then wrapping his arms around me once we're fully joined together. I lean my forehead against his and exhale. I can't help but feeling … like a queen who's found a knight.

It doesn't make much sense, but there it is.

Slowly, I rock my hips against Tee and hear him groan low in his throat. It's the sound of a man who's finally coming unhinged—in a good way.

"How long has it been?" I whisper, and I can't decide if I'm asking about the last time he had sex … or the last time he spread his wings.

"Two years," he gasps out and either way, I feel bad for him.

My arms rest on Tee's shoulders and my fingers play with his feathers, digging in between them to brush at the bare skin underneath.

His mouth tastes like violent want, and his hands clench tight with raw *need.*

It feels gluttonous almost, to have both twins on the same day. But they offered and I was more than happy to accept. Why shouldn't I take something for myself? Especially when these two guys are willing to give it?

Tee's hands slide my nightgown up and over my head, breaking our kiss for a moment to toss it aside, so he can palm the heavy weight of my breasts, knead the white flesh between his fingers. More lightning flickers outside; the rain comes down even harder. It's nothing compared to the storm our mouths make when they clash together again, greedy and grasping, and I realize I'm not the only one here who's drinking this all in, absorbing every ounce of pleasure from the situation. It feels like Tee's been suffering for a long goddamn time. If in this single second, we can pretend to be friends or lovers or whatever, maybe it'll calm some of that inner turmoil inside both of us.

"Allison," Tee breathes as he slides his palms down my naked body and cups my ass.

He curls his wings around us both, shielding us from the lightning and the storm outside, making me feel protected. Hell, I felt like that from the very beginning, when Tee stood outside The Pool in the darkness, watching the shadows with wary eyes.

It feels good to be protected—even if I know how to take care of myself.

Throwing my head back, I can feel strands of blonde hair tickling my skin, my tits pressing against Tee's chest as we grind our pelvises together in a sweaty, slick slide of bodies. My orgasm is a much slower, much more languorous build this time, starting in my lower back and working its way into my limbs, making my fingers and toes tingle. My body tightens naturally around Tee's as I drag my fingers through the sweat on his chest and he wraps his wings even closer around us.

He comes inside of me with a ragged sounding growl as I slow and then stop the movement of my hips, panting heavily and then yelping stupidly when he suddenly flips me over.

"Tee," I start, but he's already pushing my knees apart and sliding his fingers up my inner thighs. He doesn't hesitate to put his hot mouth over my cunt, tasting me with a flick of his tongue and making my back arch up off the bed. My fingers curl into the blankets as he cups my butt cheeks in either hand and buries his face in my heat. "Holy … fuck …" I murmur, my eyes watering and my throat getting tight as Tee slides the tips of his wings up my naked flesh and over my breasts, licking and teasing the wetness of my folds at the same time he tantalizes my skin with his feathers.

Two hooked fingers slide into my core, rubbing my G-spot as Tee circles his tongue around my clit and drives me into a violent, messy orgasm. He doesn't stop working his fingers or his mouth until I'm practically sobbing with pleasure from the release, moving up to lie beside me and kicking his boots and pants off and onto the floor.

"What just happened?" I whisper to him as he curls up beside me in the dark, wraps an arm over my belly and pulls me close. My skin prickles with energy and I bite my lower lip, heart thundering as my pussy throbs and my nipples harden again. Sex I can do, that I can handle. I'm not sure about the cuddling.

But Tee pulls me against him with a firm arm, that same alpha male edge to his actions that I felt in the solarium. I want to protest, but my eyes are heavy and I feel sleepy from food and sex. Besides, if Tee is going all alpha male on me … then for a moment there, I'm not in charge. I don't have to pay the bills because dad's too tired and sad to remember. I don't have to set alarms to check on Edith all night to make sure she doesn't drown in her own puke. I don't have to rush to answer the phone when we get a call from the prison, so I can hear mom's voice for a precious few minutes.

No, if Tee wants to give me the illusion of safety and freedom from my responsibilities, for tonight … I guess I'll take it.

"*Nine big men*," Tee whispers in my ear and I laugh, a smile stretching across my face. It almost hurts, how strange that smile feels. "I think I'm number two."

I fall asleep wrapped in his arms … but the smile stays.

♦ ♠ ♣ ♠ ♣ ♠ ♦

"Busy, busy, busy last night, were we?" the cat asks when I step out of the bedroom the next morning and find him crouching on the railing, his black and white striped tail twitching with amusement. He's a big cat for sure, but nothing out of the ordinary—not when it comes to size anyway. But his coloring is certainly … unique. He looks like a goddamn zebra.

"Gross. Were you fucking spying on us?" I ask, crossing my arms over the peasant blouse and the red waist cincher. I have to admit, when I woke up this morning and found myself naked, curled in Tee's arms, and in desperate need of a shower … I was a little nervous. It felt like more than just a one-night stand, what happened between us last night. And I *really* don't need to be forming emotional attachments to men from another world.

Now I'm going to get my ass kicked by Mrs. Davenport, the sex ed teacher, *and* Ms. Reed, the school shrink. *Sorry for acting like a weirdo, but I just traveled to another world and started falling for some winged princes who also happen to be the last two survivors of a brutal genocide; I may need to be medicated.*

"Spying?" Chesh asks, his body melting in this agonizingly slow stretch of limbs until he's sitting there in leather pants and a red tank with a rose and a gun on the front of it. "Why the fuck would I bother with that? I had more important things to do last night. Didn't you see—I left you a *gift*. Well, several of them in fact."

I follow the cat's stormy gray eyes and look over my shoulder … to find a sea of dead rodents in front of my bedroom door. I was so busy trying *not* to look at the twins as they got dressed that I didn't notice the corpses when I first stepped out. Now, I'm gawping. No shame there.

"Well, look at that," Dee says as the door opens behind me and I feel my heart start to pound. I turn back to the cat as the twins step up on either side of me, taking their places as proper guards. "Somebody has a crush—hard enough to make diamonds."

"What does that even *mean*?" I whisper, because I'm having a hard time not staring at the pile of mutilated rat and mice bodies on the floor. There are like, *entrails* hanging out.

"Diamonds … marriage," Dee says, like I'm the silly, stupid one. Uh-huh. Okay, fine. *One* of his random ramblings actually makes sense. I'll give him that. I flick my eyes his way and he smiles at me, folding his wings together against his back. "Pressure makes diamonds. So if one is crushing hard … then diamonds are made. Ring, marriage. It makes perfect sense, don't you think?"

"I *am* crushing that hard. Can't you tell from my offering?" Chesh asks, tucking his feet up on the railing, his hands between them, fingers curled around the banister as he flicks his tail and folds one ear back. His gray eyes stay locked on me as I head toward the main staircase and, hopefully, breakfast.

"Why were you following me through the woods?" I ask as I pass by, figuring he owes me an explanation.

"Was I?" he asks, cocking his head to the side. I don't know why his voice has to be so low and booming, this deep baritone that reverberates inside my chest. It'd be a lot easier to hate him if every word he said wasn't dripping sex and dark innuendo.

"You were," I state as I glance briefly at Tee and he catches my gaze, licking his lower lip.

"I were what?" Chesh asks and I throw up my hands with a sigh.

"Never mind," I say, moving past him and trying not to be impressed when he stands up and easily walks along the railing *down* the stairs with me without falling. Before I hit the bottom step, he leaps off and cuts me off, putting an arm on the banister and leaning close to block my path.

"I wasn't following *you*," he purrs—*literally* purrs—blinking big, round eyes at me, the piercing in his lips, ears, and brow winking in the early morning light. "I was following the duke. Sometimes, when he sleeps, he shifts. And when he shifts, he wanders. I simply tracked him through Tulgey Wood is all and *you* happened to be there."

"Right." I push Chesh's arm out of my way and ignore the fact that he has black and gray tattoos that I somehow missed before. Must've been too preoccupied with the ears and tail to bother noticing the ink. *But holy shit he has nice arms.* "Now move. I'm starving."

I head past him, the twins following along beside me, to find Lar, North, and Rab already waiting at the table.

"You're awfully late," Rab says, his voice this cool blast of ice against my skin. His left ear swivels to face me, but he doesn't bother to look in my direction, already settled in with a plate of cakes and a cup of tea.

"Isn't it a little early to start getting high?" I ask as I check a few of the silver trays and find jubjub eggs—can't mistake that red fluff for anything else, right?—slabs of meat that I think are the fried slices from last night's pork, and sliced bread with butter. It's an interesting spread, but I'm pleased to see that it's all edible.

Good.

Because if we're not leaving today—and based on the weather outside, I take it we're not—then I'd like to try practicing with the Vorpal Blade some more. I mean, why not take it with me when I go home? I've already found myself in more than one situation where a big ass knife might come in handy. And if I actually know how to use it? Even better.

"It's never too early when you're already late," Rab replies, smirking at me as I take my seat at the head of the table again. This time, the twins sit directly on my right with Chesh next to them, the other three men seated across the table.

"We have nowhere to be today," North says, sipping a cup of what I think is actually … coffee? Is that coffee?! "The weather simply isn't favorable enough yet."

"Don't you have a date to play croquet with the king?" I ask as I search through the silver teapots on the table until I find one with the distinctly bitter aroma of a good French Roast. *Thank fucking God.* I pour myself a heaping cup and dash in a load of cream and sugar.

"Next week," the duke says, and his voice sounds tight. When I glance up at him though, all I see is a careful smile on his lips. "If it comes down to it, I *will* shift and fly to the castle—it'll be worth the risk. But let's just hope the magic rolls on by before then and leaves us with some sunshine, shall we?"

"Can't Lar just predict the weather in some tea leaves or something?" I ask as I take a sip of my coffee and try not to groan in pleasure. Tee and Dee both keep casting glances either at me or at each other, and I have a feeling if I let out an orgasmic whimper of ecstasy over this caffeine, that it might just get them—and me—all riled up.

"I don't get to choose my visions, just like you don't get to choose whether or not you're the Alice, Sunshine," Lar says, flipping through an old book with long, careful fingers. He flicks his pale blue gaze to mine and smiles sardonically.

"I beg to differ—I think everyone has the freedom of choice. Or they should anyway."

"I didn't say you couldn't *choose* not to act as the Alice, but the simple fact is: you *are* her. You can leave Underland and forget all about us, plunge both your world and ours into darkness, but just as the sun will rise tomorrow, so too are you the only Alice we'll ever have."

"What if I dropped my cousin down the Rabbit-Hole?" I joke as I set my coffee aside and steal the tray of scrambled jubjub eggs from Dee's hand, spooning a mountain onto my plate. I want to eat well and train hard today. Walking through the forest made me realize how out of shape I am. It'd be nice to tone up a bit. "She's got the Liddell blood, too."

"There were many choices for the Alice, but you've already claimed the title; it's too late now." Lar closes the book he was reading and stands up, his hair and earrings rustling gently in a non-existent breeze. This is the second time I feel like I've seen that, his clothing swishing when everything else is still. It's strange enough that I don't even get distracted by the gold keys pierced through his nipples. "I'll be in the library if you need me."

"There's a library here?" I ask as Lar takes one last sip from his teacup, blue and black wings spreading wide before he disappears out the way we came in.

"Of course," North says, leaning back in his chair and looking over at me with gold eyes, his sinuous black tail twisting around my ankle. Lar equated North's tail to his dick so … I kick it with my other foot and he jerks back, eyes going wide in surprise. "You're quite the brazen one, aren't you, Miss Liddell?"

"Don't wrap your sexual appendages around me without my permission and I won't have to be," I say as North narrows his eyes and lets out a low growl. I have a feeling he isn't used to being told no. Good. That's a lesson a person is never too old to learn properly. "Now, can you tell me why you thought it necessary to give me the Vorpal Blade just so I can attend the Hatter's stupid tea party? What's so frightening about that? I feel like I've already been witness to quite a few since I've been here."

I stare at Rab across the table, both loving and hating the way his lips carve a sinful slash across his handsome face as he sips slowly from his tea. Those bloodred eyes of his are locked on mine, the tattoos in his arm muscles bulging and flexing with the movement of bringing his cup to his lips.

"The Mad Hatter is a mercenary; he doesn't care for crown and kingdom. But he also can't be ignored. You'll have to stop in and pay him a visit, at the very least. The king would've taken you himself, if you'd gone straight to the palace first. As thing stands, we'll have to go ourselves. Otherwise we're highly likely to get … *lost* on the way to the palace."

"You're worried this guy might try to kill me?" I ask, as Tee makes a frustrated sound on my right. When I look at him, he's clenching his fork in a tight fist.

"He might," he admits as I catch Dee's worried glance. "You never know with him and that's the problem—he's impossible to predict."

"So this guy's basically a king in his own right?" I ask. "*Another* tyrant king?"

"Basically, yes," Tee answers as North shakes his head and slicks a hand up the side of one of his horns. He acts like he's just fixing his hair, but there's something vaguely sexual about the movement and I can't seem to look away.

"Another tyrant king … I assume you mean the King of Clubs is a tyrant? Because nobody in their right mind would discuss the King of Hearts in such a manner." North drags his finger across his throat and shakes his head with a caustic laugh. His words come across less like a threat … and more as a warning.

"Do you think we could keep training today?" I ask, ignoring his previous statement and focusing instead on what's to come. So. No matter what I decide to do, I have to get past this Mad Hatter guy first, right? And to do that, both Tee and North seem to think some skills with the Vorpal Blade could come in handy.

Great.

I don't admit to myself that I'm more than just a little excited for this—and for all the wrong reasons, too. *Fuck, I think I almost … like it here.*

"I don't see why not," North begins as I shove the last bite of egg into my mouth and rise to my feet, brushing my palms off on a red cloth napkin and tossing it over my plate.

"I'm ready when you are," I say and North's grin is almost as bad as the damn cat's.

I'm going to get my ass kicked today, aren't I?

"Have fun," Chesh purrs as both Tee and Dee finish what's left of their food and stand up to join me. The sexual tension between the three of us is palpable, but I do my best to ignore it—for now.

Later … is a whole different story.

♦ ♠ ♣ ♥ ♣ ♠ ♦

I do not expect to get my ass kicked by every man in the goddamn house.

Tee flips me onto my back, his knee at my throat. No pressure, just enough to let me know that he *could* kill me if he wanted to. Our eyes meet and he gives me this secret, private little smile. I would find it cute if he hadn't just pinned me to a mat.

"Hearts above, *again*," North says, lazily waving his hand above my face. Tee pulls away and the duke hands me the Vorpal Blade—Tee sent it flying across the room with a single swipe of his own knife. "What happens if that crazy bastard, March, tosses a blade in your direction during teatime? Will you catch it? Or will it embed itself in your pretty face?"

"Wait. March … the March Hare? He would throw a knife at me?!" I ask as I groan and, despite my better judgement, clasp Tee's hand so he can pull me to my feet. My body hurts *all-fucking-over*, muscles I didn't even know I had screaming in protest. Add to that the delicious soreness between my thighs and … I could really use a hot bath. "During a tea party?"

"Or worse," Tee says as I try not to notice how warm his hand is wrapped around my own. "Dee."

"You guys aren't seriously going to double-team me, are you?" I ask, but as soon as I say it, heat flushes across my skin and all I can fucking think about is them double-teaming me. One twin on either side, their hands skimming across my flesh, feathery wings entwined above us … Oh God. "I can barely handle one attacker, let alone two."

"The March Hare and the Mad Hatter never work alone," Tee explains, looking hot as hell with his purple-streaked black hair falling over his forehead, his amethyst eyes set in steely determination. He gives me one more intimate little smile and … then runs at me.

Dee comes from the other side, his face in a brilliant grin as usual, as I try to figure out where to go and what to do. These boys seem determined to make me learn the hard way, withholding crucial information until I fail at the exercise a good dozen times or more. And *then*, maybe I'll get a tidbit.

On a positive note, I *do* get some Underland gossip while I spar.

"The March Hare was a Rabbit for the previous Queen of Spades, but he defected and joined Hatter some ten odd years ago, was it?" Rab drawls, one of the only men not participating in the sparring. Instead, he seems content to lounge without a shirt on, his tattooed muscular body on display and providing quite the ample distraction.

Dickhead.

"Right after his Inaugural Feast, I believe," Lar says, his pale blue eyes focused on me as I dive to the floor between the twins and roll onto my back, kicking out with both feet and managing to clip Dee in the arm and Tee in the hand.

It doesn't slow them much though and within a few seconds, we're right back where we started except that *Dee* has a knee to my neck while Tee knocks the Vorpal Blade from my fingers with an easy flick of his own knife. When I *do* get the chance to hit them with the weapon, they go flying. The magic in the blade … er, I guess in me? … is powerful enough that I don't even have to be good, just adequate.

"Don't get frustrated," Dee whispers, pulling his leg back and helping me to my feet again. He presses a quick kiss to my cheek and I get all flustered, my skin heating to the point where it feels hot and achy. Damn it. Damn it, damn it, damn it. I don't want to get so excited about a stupid kiss to the cheek. How long have I known this guy? Five days? For fuck's sake … "You're smart, Allison-who-isn't-Alice. You'll figure it out."

"What's an Inaugural Feast?" I ask as I stand there panting, surprised to find Chesh waiting with a glass of cool water. He passes it over to me, his inked fingers sliding across my knuckles and making me shiver. I hide the reaction by tipping the drink to my lips and finishing it in three long gulps.

"An Inaugural Feast is when a Rabbit is presented with his or her three meats," Rab continues, sitting up suddenly and pushing his pants down to check one of his clocks. His long, white ears twitch and he lets go of his waistband with a yawn.

"Three meats?" I ask, even though I'm not sure I want to know. I swipe the sleeve of my blouse across my forehead to collect some of the sweat.

"A shifter can't shift until they've consumed the flesh of three different animals—those are the forms they take on," Lar says, rising to his feet and stretching his beautiful blue, black, and gold wings behind him. They really do look like stained glass, delicate and ethereal. "At the Inaugural Feast, the king or queen presents their Rabbits with the flesh of a bandersnatch as well as two other creatures—or *people*—of their choosing."

"You have three forms?" I ask Rab, but he just smirks at me and winks one red eye. "What are they?"

North claps his hands, interrupting me. Not that I think the White Rabbit has any interest in answering. No, I'm sure he'll save his other two forms for the most inopportune moment, just to give me a little shock and remind me how goddamn weird this place really is.

"Start again, Miss Liddell, if you would. Perhaps we should switch tactics. Caterpillar?"

"You think little Sunshine can handle it?" he asks, shrugging his coat off his shoulders—he never does seem to put his hands through the sleeves—and coming over to stand in the center of the rectangular training area.

I grit my teeth as Tee hands me back the Vorpal Blade and steps aside.

"Show me what you've got," I growl, a pretty ballsy move for someone who's been kicked, punched, and tackled a good three dozen times already. Lar smiles lazily at me, stretching his arms above his head as I study the gold keys pierced through his nipples. I doubt they're purely for decoration.

"Good. I won't hold back then, Sunshine."

Lar's hair and earrings start to move in that same supernatural breeze I noticed before, one that doesn't touch a damn other thing in the room except for him. As I stare, he starts to glow faintly and then … picks up a good dozen practice knives from the table behind him *without* even touching them.

My mouth drops open as the wooden blades arrange themselves in a semi-circle above his head … and then come flying at me. I react on pure instinct, swinging the Vorpal Blade in a wide arc and catching the whole lot of wooden weapons with that same trembling force I felt in the Queenmaker. Lar's weapons go flying in random directions across the room, clattering to the floor in a raucous that sounds like rain.

But Lar is nowhere near done.

He holds his arms out straight in front of himself and claps his hands together.

A wash of cool wind hits me like a hurricane, making my eyes sting, my hair whipping against my face. It's all I can do to stay standing upright, let alone realize that he's coming at me, grabbing the wrist with the knife and turning it at a sharp enough angle that I have no choice but to go with it, falling to the side and hitting the floor with my shoulder.

Once again, I'm on my back but this time, I grit my teeth and swing the Vorpal Blade at Lar, knowing it won't actually hit him, but trying to throw some of that power I felt inside of me at him like an invisible weapon. Lar moves two fingers across his body, like he's warding off evil and I see this ripple effect in the air as my … fuck, I guess I have to call it magic, don't I? … hits his with violent force.

"Enough!" North shouts, pounding over to stand above me in his black boots. He waits for me to sit up and grins, his teeth white in his tanned face. "*That* was brilliant, if a little dangerous. If you'd done that to anyone else, you might've killed them."

"What did I just do?" I ask as I shake my head and climb to my feet without any help this time. "I'm not a huge fan of the possibility that I might kill someone without even knowing what the hell is happening."

"You're using your powers, Miss Liddell," North says as the Cheshire Cat reclines on one of the training mats and plays with a stray feather, batting it back and forth with his hands as if he's still in cat form. "The magic in your *blood*."

Exhaling slowly, I slip the Vorpal Blade into a belted leather sheath North gave me this morning. Without waiting for further explanation, I head over to Rab and plop down on the cushion next to him, so close that one of his inked muscular arms brushes against mine as I grab one of the tiny orange mushrooms from the plate.

"These aren't hallucinogenic?" I ask and he gives me this infuriatingly sexy smile.

"Not the orange ones," he tells me as I pop one into my mouth and chew it. The texture's a bit weird, kind of spongy, but it tastes like peaches and cream. And holy hell, it tastes good after all that exercise.

The other men gather around us, taking seats on the scattered cushions and browsing the variety of silver trays North's staff brought in for lunch. I notice they all sit closer to me than would generally be polite in new company.

Well, except for the twins. The twins can sit as close to me as they want while I'm here.

"The magic in my blood …" I whisper, grabbing another tiny mushroom in my fingers and staring at its little white spots and delicate stem. It reminds me of the mushroom flesh in Lory's pirate jacket. Small as a mouse … tall as a house. Maybe I'll take some of *that* with me to the Mad Hatter's? He couldn't very well throw a fucking knife in my face if I crushed his ass to death, now could he? "Why is the Mad Hatter well, *mad* first off, and second, who is he to have so much power?" It's not a very subtle change of subject, but if I'm going to keep functioning here without slipping into shock, I'm going to try to take the magic thing in bit by bit. Ease myself into it.

"The Mad Hatter is an enigma," Chesh purrs, swishing his tail and looking at me with half-closed eyes. "Nobody knows whose side he's really on or what he truly wants. His loyalties are predictably unpredictable." He blinks a few times and twitches his black and white striped ears before licking the back of one inked hand and sliding it over his hair to wash himself. In a strange way, he reminds me of my cat, Dinah. Fuck, I hope Edith or Dad remembers to feed her while I'm gone … "One minute he's friend and the next, foe."

"And his name?" I ask, not expecting anything spectacularly creative. How about *Mad*? That would fit the pattern here.

"Raiden Walker," Tee supplies and a small chuckle escapes my throat.

"Right because the Cheshire Cat is Chesh and the Duke of Northumbria is North … and the Mad Hatter is Raiden fucking Walker. Makes sense."

"He's not from our world," North explains with a lazy, expectant wave of his hand. "He's from *yours.*"

Hmm.

Well, shit, now I'm interested in meeting this guy.

"As for why he's mad," Rab continues, gesturing with a thumb in Chesh's direction. "Weren't you listening to the cat? We're *all* mad for you here—even the Hatter."

"*Nine big men with nine big cocks*," Dee sings and little chills chase across my skin.

Nine … and there are six people sitting around me who fit that description.

Coincidence … or … no.

I don't believe in fate.

No matter how compelling the evidence seems.

Because if I do, then I have to believe that Fred was fated to die, and I won't accept that.

"Let's go again," I say, rising to my feet and knowing that I'm going to regret this come morning. "Show me how to kick Raiden Walker's ass."

By the time I'm done sparring that night, I'm not sure that I know how to kick ass …

But I sure as fuck get mine handed to me.

Shower, food, sex.

In that order.

Or at least that's my intention when I finish eating and excuse myself to follow the twins back to the room, but at the last second, I change course and veer off, finding myself standing back in the training room.

"If you push too hard, you'll hurt yourself," Tee whispers softly from behind me.

North is there—I'd wondered where he'd gone to after leaving dinner early. He's shirtless and beautiful, sweat soaking down his back as his black-scaled tail thrashes in agitation. It might look like a dragon's tail, but it moves like a cat's.

"I'll be okay," I tell Tee, glad I slipped into the borrowed white and red heart tank and black linen pants he gave me at Rab's house instead of my nightgown. "I just … want to blow off some more steam."

"Let us know if the sex is good," Dee says, grinning sharply when I glance back at him with narrowed eyes. He brushes blue and black hair from his forehead and raises his brows at me. "What? You like North, don't you?"

"I'm not having sex with him," I say with an exasperated sigh. "I just want to work on a few more things before bed." Or maybe I'm just scared of going to sleep? Five nights I've been here and only one of them was plagued with nightmares. The rest were peaceful. I doubt I'll get lucky again tonight. "If you're still up when I get back …"

"Dee won't be, but I might," Tee says, his voice low and husky, his eyes meeting mine and making my heart pound.

"And if you both are?" I ask, wondering if I'm pushing my luck.

"We'll see," Tee tells me, turning and gesturing for Dee to follow along with him.

The heavy doors to the training room close and I'm left alone with a sweaty, angry dragon, his gold eyes staring at me from across the length of the gym.

"Haven't had quite enough yet?" he asks, his accent crisp but his lips curled back from his slightly pointed teeth. "I admire that quality in an Alice."

"Have there been many other Alices?" I ask and he just closes his lips and keeps smirking at me.

"What did you want to learn?" he asks, tilting his horned head to one side as I pad into the room and pause on the mat in the very center, underneath a circular stained glass window that makes up part of the roof. It has heart motifs in it, just like everything else, but it also has diamonds, spades, and clubs. Interesting.

"I want to know how to protect myself in close combat, like if a man were to grab me …" I almost can't finish the sentence. I can't stop thinking about that night when Liam drugged me, how woozy and disoriented I felt. He came at me from behind and grabbed my wrists, pushing them against my lower back and slamming me into the wall as he rubbed his hard-on against my ass.

It was awful.

Fucking awful.

And I couldn't do a damn thing about it.

"Close combat," North says, shirtless and beautiful, his gold hair and gold eyes making my heart flutter in my chest as he walks over to me, sweat sliding down his muscles and drawing my eye to the waistband of his pants. "That I can do."

"If you were to come at me from behind," I start boldly, lifting my chin. Maybe if I face the nightmare while I'm still awake, I'll be able to fuck the twins and then fall asleep and wake up in the morning without a single dream tearing at the inside of my skull. "How would I defend myself?"

North steps in close and takes me by the hips, turning me away from him so that he's standing at my back. I can smell him, this musky sweet mix of fresh scent and *male*. It's hard to describe exactly what he smells like, only that it's primal and bestial and it turns up the flame of heat in my belly to a roaring fire.

"Usually if someone comes at you from the back," North starts, his voice a low growl of testosterone and wild energy. When I close my eyes, I can picture him in his dragon … sorry, *jabberwock* form, crashing through the forest and snapping the jubjub bird's neck like it was *nothing*. Must be nice, to be that powerful. How refreshing to know you could take care of yourself in almost any given situation. I *want* that. I crave it. "They're trying to surprise you. The key," he continues, his breath stirring my hair as I struggle between two emotions—want and … *fear*. Gross. No, I'm not like that. I'm not fucking afraid of anything.

Except the loss of control.

"He grabbed my wrists and threw me into a wall," I say without meaning to, and I feel North's fingers tighten on my hips. "I was drugged, so it wasn't exactly a fair fight, but maybe if I knew what to do …"

"I can help with that," North says, moving his hands from my hips to my wrists. When he pulls them behind me and presses them to my lower back, memories of that night flicker in my head and I feel sick. My brother saved me from being raped; Liam and his asshole friends never forgot that. They followed Fred into an alley and they killed him. "Are you ready?"

"Ready," I whisper back, my eyes focused on the floor in front of me.

"Don't bother playing tug-of-war with your attacker," he tells me, giving my wrists a gentle pull to emphasize how little force is really needed to throw me off-balance like this. "Instead, use the weight of your body to check his." North exhales and I feel the breeze from his swishing tail against my bare ankle. "Push your ass out *hard* and slam into him with everything you have. As you do that, bend your elbows and lift your hands as high as you can. Shoot your arms out in front of you and take a step forward, following along with the momentum. Then swing your leg around and turn to face him."

"Can we try it?" I ask, heart pounding, nostrils flaring.

"We can try it," North says, releasing me and taking a step back.

This time, he doesn't ask if I'm ready, he just steps forward, this violent force at my back, his warm hands grasping my wrists and pinning them against me. I don't think. Instead, I react, throwing my weight back like North asked, slamming my ass into his crotch. I don't *think* it's supposed to be an erotic move, but it feels like one and my breath hisses out as I bend my elbows and then throw one back into his gut.

That wasn't part of the exercise, but it feels good, especially when he grunts in pain. But the move also throws me off-balance again and I fall backward, giving him easy access to shove me onto the floor and pin me with my cheek against the mat.

"That's why you want to throw your arms *forward*," North tells me, holding me down for just a moment and then letting me go, sitting down next to me as I push to my hands and knees, panting and shaking with adrenaline.

"Got it," I whisper, sweat dripping from my forehead and onto the black surface of the mat.

"It's all about energy and flow—it doesn't matter how big or small you are. For example, if you're grabbed around the mouth or neck, throw your bodyweight forward and you can flip the bloody wanker over your back and onto *his*."

Sitting up, I shove a few rainbow colored strands of hair from my forehead.

"Where did you learn all this stuff?" I ask and the savage duke smiles.

"The hard way," he tells me, one knee propped up, elbow resting against it. He's so sweaty and brilliant and beautiful. But I don't know a damn thing about him as a person. You know, except for the fact that he turns into a jabberwock. "Would you like to try again?"

"Let's do it," I say, but when we both stand up, I find myself too close to the much taller man, gazing up at his face, hardly able to breathe, let alone fight. North stares at me for a long moment and then shakes his horned head, moving around behind me and then clamping his hand across my mouth so suddenly that I almost scream for real.

Pulse pounding, I bend my body in half like he told me and feel his weight shifting forward … and then yanking back. North lets go of my mouth and grabs my wrists instead, like an enemy might if they were anticipating the move. This time, I let him pull me back, my body slamming into his and then I thrust my hands forward, breaking from his grip and spinning at the last moment.

The Vorpal Blade is nowhere near me, but I throw two fingers out in a sharp arc, just like Lar did and see North's hair and clothing rustling in a violent breeze. He resists it, squinting and pushing through the spell or whatever the fuck you want to call it, lunging at me and grabbing me by the upper arms.

I twist to the side and dislodge him briefly, throwing a knee into his junk and listening to the satisfying sound of his groan. We break apart and I finally have some space to defend myself.

"Better," he growls, "*much* better."

North comes at me again, and I throw out another spell, using that strange quaking energy inside of me that I swear was never there before. It must've … I don't know, taken over me when I entered Underland.

'Just as the sun will rise tomorrow, so too are you the only Alice we'll ever have.'

I wonder if this power has something to do with that?

North lashes out with his tail, putting up some sort of barrier that I can't see and then uses the muscular appendage to wrap around my waist and drag me close, towering over me with his gold eyes and devil horns.

"Got you," he snarls, and then he's tucking two fingers under my chin and lifting my face up to his. His mouth crashes into mine as my fingers curl against his sweaty chest. I don't even think about pulling away, rising on my tiptoes and letting him bury his tongue inside my mouth. His tail wraps even tighter around my waist, making me gasp as we kiss like animals in the throes of heat, ready to mate and …

Mate?!

The fuck?!

Shoving with both palms against his chest, I put some distance between my mouth and the duke's, my body quivering and throbbing in all the right places.

"You don't want me?" he asks, looking confused as hell. I push at his tail with my hands and he releases me, standing there looking pissed and horny as hell.

"I …" I start, but I'm eighteen years old for Christ's sake, and I just screwed the twins and I … don't know who I am or what I'm even doing here.

"The king will let you take eight other husbands besides himself, you know. It's in the prophecy." North licks his lower lip, like he's trying to clear away the taste of my mouth—or savor it.

"Oh? And you just thought you'd write yourself into one of the slots? Thanks, but no thanks."

"I thought you liked me?" the duke asks, but this time he's smirking at me. "What's the matter? Cat got your tongue?"

"Boo," says Chesh, appearing on the rim of an elaborate piece of wood molding that runs along the wall. He leans his head over, gazing at me with gray eyes and grinning that rictus grin, his white and black striped tail swishing against his leather pants.

"I'm going to bed," I say, taking a few steps back and wondering what their deal is, the duke and the cat. "I'll see you in the morning."

I spin away and head upstairs, finding—as Tee predicted—one twin asleep and the other writing in his journal. He looks at me, but all I do is crawl into bed beside Dee and wait for him to join us. I don't want to have sex with the twins when I'm thinking about North.

Or the cat.

That might be the way *this* world works, but I'm not used to it yet.

Yet?

Did I just say yet?

Tee crawls into bed behind me and curls up against my back, crushing me between his warm body and that of his twin's.

There's not a single place in that world or any other I'd rather be.

Several hours later, I wake from another one of my usual nightmares, soaked in sweat and trying not to think too hard about my part in Frederick's murder. I guess even training with the duke wasn't enough—the demons are in my skull and they don't seem at all inclined to leave.

If I hadn't dated Liam ... If I hadn't broken up with him ... If I hadn't gone to that party to tell him off.

But I know none of those things are my fault—Liam and his scummy friends are the ones to blame. For the rest of my life, though, I'll have to live with the awful knowledge that my mom's in jail because she was the only one willing to make the punishment fit the crime.

Throwing my feet over the edge of the bed, I crawl out from between the twins, the two of them facing in opposite directions, their tattooed backs pressed close together as I vacate the narrow space. For a moment, I just look at them, their handsome faces soft in sleep, and I consider waking them up. Hell, I consider climbing between them again and trying to fall back asleep.

But let's be honest here—I don't know these fuckers from Adam.

With a sigh, I dig my *Alice's Adventures in Wonderland* book from my satchel and quietly let myself into the hallway. A few torches burn on the walls, enough to light my way but not enough to banish the shadows in the duke's manor. It's a beautiful house, but at night ... with its bloodred walls and checkerboard floor, its crooked paintings, and grinning stone statues? It's a little creepy.

At some point during dinner, North started bragging about his library again but for the life of me, I can't remember where it is for shit. The only place I think I can safely navigate to and from is the solarium.

Heading down the stairs, I snag a short, fat candle from a nearby table and let myself into the dampness of the glass-walled room. I'm going to sit here and try my best to read as much of this damn book as I can. And then tomorrow, I'll let Tee and Dee recite the prophecy for me—but for intellectual reasons only, of course. Because as soon as I get to that goddamn Looking-Glass, I'm going home.

I find a bench buried in the foliage and wedge the candle into a nook of a nearby tree, turning and leaning my back against its trunk, the dancing orange flame just enough light to read by. The first few pages alone are enlightening—and eerily similar to what I've been through since falling down the Rabbit-Hole.

Running a thumb across one of John Tenniel's illustrations, I take a deep breath and lean my head back, closing my eyes for a moment and trying to remember how to breathe.

Oh come on, shock, you can't set in now, I think, *not after I've fucked two of these men who shouldn't rightfully exist.* That'd be *really* weird, wouldn't it? Waking up and finding out that what happened between me and the twins was all a figment of my imagination? Well, it's not so much the idea of a sex dream or a fantasy that weirds me out—I have those all the time—it's the idea that these guys that … I kind of *like,* enough to say the word *crush* deep inside the recesses of my own mind … could be fake.

There's no way.

I sigh and close the book, listening to the rain batter the glass walls and ceiling.

It takes me a moment to figure out what it is that's bothering me, but when I do, I find myself frowning and setting the book aside, my heart starting to race inside my chest.

The rain sounds a little different now than it did before, like … there's a window open somewhere.

Grabbing the stub of red candle from the tree, I make my way over to the wall and pause in front of a sea of shattered glass and water, a breeze from outside blowing into the room and making me shiver.

I'm not stupid enough to stand there and wonder what it could be—there's so much about this world I don't know. It could be fucking *anything.* Hell, it could be another jubjub bird or a wild bandersnatch female come to steal Rab away in the night. Not that I'd mind that last one so much. The guy's a right proper asshole, for real.

Turning toward the bridge, I start to run when the damn candle goes out and plunges me into blackness. Cursing, I dig the match out from behind my ear—practice makes perfect, so I've decided to start carrying one with me at all times while I'm here—and try to light it by striking it against the rough wood of the railing.

Before I can get it lit, lightning flashes outside and highlights a man standing not two feet in front of me.

Before I can open my mouth to scream, a hand clamps over my face, the palm warm and dry, the voice at my ear making me shiver.

"Hello, Alice," the second man says as the lightning flashes again and I get a good look at the other guy. He has ears like Rab, only his are brown, his eyes indistinguishable shadows in the dark. "If I let you go, you'll need to give me your most *sincere* fucking promise not to scream."

Fuck, I just practiced this, I think as I bend suddenly at the waist and toss the asshole behind me over my shoulder, sending him crashing into the rabbit-eared stranger. The move works, too, knocking them both down and giving me a precious few seconds to run for the door.

But … whoever this person is, they're not human.

Not even close.

In a blink and a blur, the man is standing in front of me again and I hear the distinct clicking sound of a hammer, the metal barrel of a gun coming to rest against my temple.

"I'd hate to have to blow the savior's pretty blonde head clean off. Wouldn't that be a terrific shame, March?"

"Terrific, yes. A shame, not so much," the rabbit-eared man says, coming to stand beside me and pausing at the sound of the solarium doors swinging open. "That you, Dor?" he asks just before a third man comes into view, dragging a body.

In the next flicker of white-hot light outside, I see North being dragged across the floor, a red trail of blood, thick and viscous and sticky behind him. I'm about ninety-five percent certain that he's fucking dead. The side of his head, right above his horn … is missing a *chunk*.

My stomach twists and bile fills my throat as I glance up and study the hulking beast of the man with the gun, covered in tattoos and wearing a massive top hat. It lilts to one side like it's diseased.

"Night to meet you, Alice," he says, lifting his gun up to his head and tapping at his own temple with the barrel. I don't need the light outside to know who these men are. Dor is the Dormouse, the man with the ears is the March Hare, and this … this is the Mad Matter.

Raiden Walker.

If he *was* from my world once upon a time, he isn't anymore.

He grins at me, teeth flashing white in the darkness.

"You ready to take a little trip to see the King of Clubs?" he asks, but I can't respond. I don't respond. I doubt he'll be taking a simple *no* as an answer.

But underneath my dressing gown, tucked into the leather sheath that North gave me, is the Vorpal Blade.

I might be ignorant of this world, but I'm not stupid.

"Good," he says, reaching for me with a tattooed arm and pulling me against the hard warmth of his body. The Mad Hatter leans down and puts his lips against my ear, making me shiver. "Because it's time for a tea party, Alice, and you … are the guest of honor."

XII
XI
X
IX
VIII
VII
VI

2
ALLISON
and the TORRID
TEA PARTY

Alice of Violent Wild Magic

Alice of violent wild magic
And loyal men who follow!
Though time be fleet, and truly tragic
The future is not hollow.
Thy mighty power will soon prevail
Turn nightmares into fairy-tales.

Underland soaked in haunting pain,
Topside goes burning after:
No other Alice sheds these chains
Spurred by her carnal rapture—
Blood shall spill when devils burn bright
Winning her the fucking fight.

A tale begun in other days,
When magic girls were glowing—
A simple time, that served divine
Before the Riving went a'sowing—
Dark echoes live in memory, yes,
Though greedy bastards say "forget".

Come, hearken then, ere voice of dead,
The Anti-Alice haven,
Shall summon to unwelcome dread
A melancholy maiden!
We are but wily soldiers, friend,
Who fret to find our homeland's end.

Without the magic, blinding power,
The storm-wind's moody madness—
Within Torrid Tea Party's tower,
A nest of lust and heat, true madness.
These magic words shall save us last:
All must love their warring badass.

And, through the shadow of a sigh
Her men push through the story,
For 'happy future days' come high,
And vanish'd bloody glory—
They shall not touch, with hands of hate,
The Pleasance of our Heart'd gate.

Chapter One

An Even Madder Tea Party

He's going to die, isn't he?

I sit in the back of a carriage made of fucking *porcelain* and stare at North's comatose form, blood leaking from his head at an alarming rate. In a way, that's a good sign, I guess, because if he's bleeding then that means his heart is still pumping, so he's still alive.

Dead things don't bleed.

"If you don't give him medical attention, he'll die before you make it to wherever it is that we're going," I say, staring up at the three men sitting in the back of the carriage with me. They're all situated on the floor in a semi-circle, sipping *tea*. Like, laced-with-drugs, seriously-going-to-mess-them-up tea. And then what? North will lie there and bleed to death, and I'll sit here, shackled to the wood floor, forced to watch.

"Oh, well, wouldn't that be a shame," the Mad Hatter says, his hat lilting to one side, this disheveled dishabille that he wears so well. And those eyes, the color of marmalade, this honeyed orange shade that I've never seen before. But hell, why should *that* surprise me? After everything I've seen in Underland so far, it's hardly the weirdest.

The man holds his teacup in hands dripping with ink, tattoos crawling out from beneath the black jacket he's wearing, over his knuckles, along his fingers. He's so dainty about it, too, like he's actually got some manners in that crazy head of his.

"You don't care if he dies then?" I continue as the three of them continue to lounge in the back of the jostling carriage. It's a big round, white thing that looks like a fucking teapot on the outside. The driver's sitting on a platform perched on the top of the spout, and the handle was used to open the massive door I was shoved through; there's not a single window in the whole damn thing, but I can see flashes of lightning through a circle in the roof, where I'm assuming there's some sort of 'lid'.

The screech of a jabberwock echoes outside the carriage, but nobody inside of it seems bothered except for me. Leaning back against the wall, I put my hands over my ears as the three men pass around a pot of tea like it's a bottle of whiskey. Only difference here is they pour it into a teacup before they sling it back like a shot.

"We're going to drop him off close to a musking female jabberwock nest and see what happens," the March Hare says, twitching his velveteen ears and crossing his legs at the ankle. The look he gives me is downright lascivious, but I think, rather than checking *me* out, he's fantasizing about North being ripped apart by an angry dragon.

"What the fuck does musking mean?" I ask, adjusting myself slightly and listening to the awful clank of my chains. We've been in this carriage for the better part of an hour and frankly, I haven't been able to brainstorm a way out of this one. Some part of me wonders if the twins'll come for me, but I'm also not into the whole *being-saved-by-a-prince* routine. Err, prince*s* in this case, I suppose. But still. I have to just assume that I'm alone here and try to find some way out of this mess.

"Musking," the Mad Hatter replies with this awful curve of a smile transforming his face. "That's just a dirty science word for *horny as hell*." He takes another sip of his tea and then tosses the cup aside, letting it shatter against the back wall of the carriage before crawling toward me, his honey-orange eyes bright, his skin as pale as moonlight. When he smiles, doves cry. That's how scary this motherfucker is. "We're going to leave him out there, helpless and prone, and see if there're any takers."

"You're sick in the head," I snap back at him as he reaches out and curls some of my blonde hair around his fingers, pulling it to his face for a sniff. Seriously? What a pervert. When I jerk back, all I end up doing is yanking my hair painfully; the Mad Hatter does *not* let go. "What's the point of all that anyway, taking a hostage only to watch him die? What purpose does that serve?!"

"Who says it serves a purpose," the Mad Hatter—Raiden Walker, I guess, is his name—purrs, using the handful of my hair to pull me toward his face. "The Duke of Northumbria is a supporter of the King of Hearts—and a hefty giver of tithes to the crown—so we figured, we came all the way out here to nab *you*, why not grab him at the same time?"

"Cruelty for cruelty's sake," I retort, but the pale—and admittedly handsome—man in front of me just grins bigger and snaps his fingers. *Bingo,* I guess, *I've figured it all out.* He lets go of my hair and then sits back, propping one knee and throwing his arm casually across it. The strangely beautiful color of his eyes drifts down to my neck, watching my pulse hum and throb beneath my skin.

"Cruelty is in the eye of the beholder," he says, just as vague and weird as everyone else that lives here. They can blame all their strangeness on the Riving if they want, but I blame it on testosterone poisoning. Clearly, with a ratio of ten men to one woman, that must be it. The air is thick with it. My guess? The Duke and this guy, Raiden, they have some sort of pissing war going on. "Tell you what?" he says after a minute, just when my eyes begin to stray over to the March Hare and the Dormouse. I turn my attention back to him and our gazes lock. "Answer me a riddle and I'll let the Duke go."

"Ask me a riddle and if I get it right, you give him medical attention and keep him *alive*. You don't even have to let him go; he can stay with me." The Mad Hatter raises two dark brows, his black hair curling out from under his hat in a defiant sort of way. I figure beggars can't be choosers and it'd be better if North were alive and being held prisoner than lying half-dead and free in the middle of the forest.

"You're an interesting one, aren't you?" Raiden glances over his shoulder at the March Hare, still slowly sipping his tea and watching us with eyes the color of dark chocolate, bitter and sweet at the same time. On his other side, the massive hulk of the Dormouse is sprawled and sleeping, teacup clenched in his huge hand.

"Smart, too," I quip, crossing my arms over my chest and hating the feel of the cold chains against my skin. I'm still wearing my dressing gown, and really, it doesn't provide a lot of coverage. In the darkest depths of my mind, I realize what could so easily happen to a girl like me, dressed in a nightie and kidnapped like this. The awful, awful fate I avoided that night at the hands of Liam and his friends—the salvation that cost my brother his *life* and my mother her freedom—that could all be revisited on me here.

But these men, they seem … well, *mad.* And if I can just keep them talking, maybe I can hold them off from trying anything else, buy myself time to escape. The Vorpal Blade is still there, resting against my thigh. I can practically *feel* it pulsing against my skin, begging me to spill blood. Or maybe that's just because I'm pissed off and hating these guys right about now?

A bit of crimson warmth from North's head wound soaks into the edge of my nightgown and I glance down, touching my fingertips to it and holding them up in a quick flash of lightning that briefly illuminates the dark interior of the carriage.

My blue eyes lift up to the Mad Hatter's orange ones.

"Ask me the damn riddle," I growl, dropping my hand into my lap. I'd scoot out of the way of the blood, but there's nowhere for me to go. I'm chained down; North is chained down. I can't even put his head in my lap or stroke the side of his face with my fingers. Seeing him like this, I wish I'd gone all the way during training and had sex with him.

What if he dies? What if I'm sitting here and he takes one, last shuddering breath? The thought makes my insides churn with anxiety, like a swarm of moths pulling apart an old blanket, leaving it riddled with holes. I can feel their tiny mouths nibbling away at me as I sit there and stare my captor down.

"Okay then," he starts, his voice this ice-cold lilt that somehow has me leaning forward to listen as he taps a tattooed finger against his lips. In my heart of hearts, I'm hoping that *this* time, life stays true to the prophecy, to the original book. Because if so, I've got an answer for the riddle I so desperately want him to ask. "Why … is a raven like a writing-desk?"

Fuck. Yes.

I try not to smile too much when I hear those words, the riddle from the classic novel *and* the same one used in the Disney adaption with Johnny Depp.

Oh, come on, this is almost too easy!

"Assuming you have no real answer in mind," I begin, because Lewis Carroll was once quoted as saying that it was originally intended that the Hatter's riddle had no answer. Later on though, about thirty years after the book was published, he made one up. "I'll give you one: because it can produce a few notes, though they are very flat; and it is nev*ar*"—I spell this part out because the word *never* is intentionally misspelled to read *raven* backwards—"put with the wrong end in front."

I sit back against the wall of the carriage and wait while the man stares at me for some time and then gives me this *slow* ass fucking smile that flashes me two sharp white canines in his mouth. Not like a cat, not like Chesh, but like … a *vampire*. The dude looks like a fucking bloodsucker.

"You're a clever little Alice, aren't you?" he asks and then tosses me a key. "Go ahead," he continues, reaching up to adjust the hat on his head. It's huge, at least a foot and a half tall, and slightly wider on the top than the bottom. "Free yourself, and him."

Even though I'm skeptical as fuck, I unlock the chains, my eyes drifting back to the March Hare as he sits there, stoic and unblinking, bathed in shadows. I have no idea what to make of him, but as long as he doesn't move, I'm okay with his creepy weirdness.

"North," I whisper, unlocking the chains and praying that maybe, just maybe, the man is playing dead. You know, like an exit strategy or something. But he doesn't move as I unshackle him. How could he? With a hole in the side of his head like that.

Raiden leans over next to me and grabs North by the horn, yanking him across the carriage and into his lap. My entire body goes stiff as the Mad Hatter flicks his orange gaze up to mine and smirks. He's fucking terrifying, this guy, and how the hell do I know he's going to help the Duke and not just slit his throat? I answered a riddle, so what? Bad guys never keep their promises, right?

"I do love riddles. I'll have to come up with another. Maybe if you answer the next one, I'll let you go?"

I snort.

"And why would you do that?" I ask as he lifts his wrist to his mouth … and *bites* it. Blood wells around his teeth, staining his tattooed skin before dripping onto North's pallid face. The poor jabberwock man is completely out, his pulse so light that I can't make it out, not even in a flash of lightning. He seriously looks like he's dead, like I'll never see those golden eyes again, feel that tail wrap around my ankle …

You just met this guy, so who cares? I try to tell myself, but it doesn't matter. I just met him, but I like him. A lot. He's charismatic and interesting, took the time to teach me, gave me the Vorpal Blade. He didn't *have* to do any of those things.

"Because," Raiden continues, pulling his mouth away from his arm and then placing his wrist at the Duke's pale lips. "I'm a mercenary. I do whatever I want, whenever I want. The King of Clubs paid me to kidnap you … but, for example, if I decide I like you, I just keep you for myself."

He presses his wrist against North's mouth, but the man is so out of it that blood just puddles on his tongue and spills out the sides. Raiden lowers his gaze to the comatose guy in his lap, removes his wrist, and then places it at his *own* mouth, sucking out the blood until his mouth is full.

With his lips pressed tight, he leans down again and places his mouth to North's, parting the Duke's lips with his tongue and *kissing* him, forcing him to drink all of that blood. My cheeks heat, and I can't decide whether to be pissed off, turned on, or … what.

"What are you doing?" I manage to choke out, but the Mad Hatter just lifts his orange eyes to mine and locks our gazes. He continues to kiss North until the Duke is shifting and groaning, dressed in a pair of cream silk pajama pants and nothing else. They're stained with blood, just like his golden hair and sun-kissed chest.

The Mad Hatter ignores me until North is shoving him back and surging up with a gasping, choking sound, almost bumping his head against our captor's forehead.

"What in the bloody fuck?" the Savage Duke growls, and my heart swells with relief. *Holy fucking shit.* I hadn't even realized until that moment how goddamn stressed I was. Without giving myself even a second to question my luck, I throw my arms around North's neck and … *kiss him?!*

Oh, well, whatever.

I tongued him in the training room and that was just pure lust.

This is so much more important than that … And even though it takes me a moment to remember that he just sucked down some dude's blood, I don't care. I pull back and put my forehead against his, my skin erupting in little goose bumps as he clamps his hands on my hips and squeezes *tight*, claws digging into the thin silk as he lets out this animalistic snarl and curls his tail around my ankle.

"Welcome back to the world of the living," Raiden says as North's gold eyes light on my face and then flick over my shoulder to look at the … well, actual fucking vampire dude?! I don't bother to turn around, reaching up and spreading North's hair to look for the missing chunk of skull and flesh that I saw earlier.

It's gone.

All closed up. Just smooth skin and gold hair and hard bone underneath it all.

"What on earth are you up to, Hatter?" North asks in that crisp British-but-can't-be-British accent of his. He pulls me even closer against him, squashing my breasts to his chest. There's not a lot of fabric between us, and I'm not wearing underwear so … I wish we weren't being kidnapped by a maniacal vampire mercenary.

"Oh, you know me, my loyalty goes out to the highest bidder," Raiden says from behind us, his voice casual despite the fact that both North and I are now free. He's not worried about being attacked? If he really is that powerful, we're fucked. If he's just that cocky, we might be okay. "Nothing personal, really."

"Please," North says, curling his arms around me and holding me so close I feel like I might choke. But he's so damn warm, and I'm so glad to see him alive. Plus, I'm riding the high of being shackled and then set free. "You've never liked me." The smirk that crawls over his face morphs rapidly into a wide grin, his teeth white in his bronze, bloodied face. "Especially not now that I have the love of the Alice."

"Love?" I ask, but it's hard to want to argue, trapped in the back of the carriage like this. I push back from North, but he only lets me go enough to turn around and sit on his lap, my back to his front. Does not make the position any less sexual. Between my legs, a throbbing starts up that I do my absolute best to quell. Now is hardly the time for thoughts of thick cocks and wet cunts and all that nonsense.

The Mad Hatter leans forward as I swipe some long, blonde tendrils out of my face.

"Your hair wants cutting," he remarks, those orange eyes glowing in a flash of lightning. Between bouts, it's almost pitch-dark in here, just a few stray shafts of moonlight cutting through the ice-cold drops of rain leaking in through the ceiling.

"You should learn not to make personal remarks," I snap, narrowing my eyes at him and tucking my hair behind my ears. "It's fucking rude."

He just smiles at me and then pauses when the carriage comes to a stop.

"And here we were planning on leaving you out for the female jabberwocky to pick apart," Raiden says with a small sigh, nodding his head to indicate something to the March Hare. The other man taps his palm against the wall twice and the carriage begins to rattle onward. "I was hoping they'd rape you, steal your seed, and leave a corpse."

My jaw drops open, but the Mad Hatter is already turning around and crawling back over to the teapot that's on the floor near the March Hare. There's not a lot of standing room back here, so he leaves himself completely open and vulnerable as he moves back to his original spot.

Turning my head into North's arm, I whisper as quietly as I can, "I have the Vorpal Blade with me." He tightens up, but it's too late. I've already made a mistake. As soon as Raiden turns around and slumps back against the wall next to his companions, he's smiling.

"You think I'm stupid enough to miss a blade? Also, I should warn you, having been bitten and turned into one of the undead has given me *spectacular* hearing. If I were you, I'd keep all my secrets to myself."

He picks up the teapot and pours himself a new cup. So far, I haven't noticed the Mad Hatter showing any signs of that light, ethereal nonsense I experienced when I was high on tea, but maybe he's just a heavyweight? A little patience might be called for in this scenario.

"Don't attack him," North tells me, his arms wrapped tight around my middle, just under my breasts. "Not with magic, not with the Blade. Just let it be." He squeezes me a little harder and I grunt. "And thank you for saving me."

"I'm not even sure how you're alive right now," I whisper back, but, of course, Raiden Walker, Vampire Extraordinaire, hears me and decides to comment.

"Vampire blood has incredible healing properties, doesn't it, North?"

"You may call me the Duke of Northumbria, my right and proper bloody title." The Duke leans back against the wall, taking me with him. I'm sitting there wondering why he isn't shifting and tearing this place apart when I feel his pulse thundering against my back, his breath coming in short, sharp bursts. He's physically healed from his wound, but his body is still recovering, damn it.

Still, shouldn't a massive black dragon be more than enough to bring down this house of cards, so to speak?

But the rules of this game, of Underland, they're all still a mystery to me. I'll just have to follow North's lead and hope he knows what he's doing. He seems pretty interested in not only delivering me to the king, but also becoming one of my … *gulp* … husbands. Anyway, I figure I can safely assume he's on my side.

"Well, *Duke of Northumbria*," Raiden drawls, tapping his fingers against his knees and smiling at us with his long, thin, beautiful mouth. I couldn't get that image of him French kissing North out of my brain if I tried—and I don't much want to try. "I was going to kill you, but seeing as the Alice answered my riddle fair and square, I figure we can bargain instead. How much to take you both safely to the King of Hearts?"

"What?" I ask, blinking stupidly in his direction. "Are you trying to *buy* your way out of a contract you already signed?"

"We don't sign contracts," the March Hare says, speaking up for the first time in a while. He leans forward, his dark brown eyes the perfect match for his brown ears and brown skin. But all three parts of him are different shades, giving him this earthy sort of look. He'd be hot if he wasn't kidnapping me, but what's new? Basically every man in Underland is hot as fuck. "People give us money and pray that they're not outbid. Think of it … like a silent auction or something." He glances down at the Dormouse and then both he and the Mad Hatter reach down and pinch the big man from both sides at once. "Wake up, Dor!"

The Dormouse slowly opens his eyes.

"I wasn't asleep," he says in a hoarse, feeble voice, "I heard every word you fellows were saying."

March snorts and gives the hulking man a scathing look.

"Bullshit," he says with a curl of his full, generous mouth. "You narcoleptic fuck."

"Ten thousand coins," North inserts as I watch the Dormouse sit up and stretch his tree trunk-sized arms over his head. He's just as attractive as his companions, but in a different way, not my style or type. He's got that bulky bodybuilder look that's a tad too much for me. And his face is a little Neanderthal, like *I-drag-you-to-cave-by-hair* alpha male-esque.

"Oh, please," the Mad Hatter says with a roll of his eyes, pouring himself another cup of tea and then turning his attention in my direction, an earnest sort of look on his face. "Take some more tea, Alice?"

"I've had nothing yet," I reply in an offended tone: "so I can't take more."

"Ah, you mean you can't take *less*," says the Hatter: "it's very easy to take *more* than nothing."

"Nobody asked *your* fucking opinion," I snap back, and he smiles at me in a way that makes me wonder how dark and how brutal this negotiation is heading. He doesn't just want money, does he?

"Who's making personal remarks now?" Raiden quips triumphantly.

"Thirty thousand," the Duke says, his voice this low, humming growl that vibrates through his body and straight into mine. It feels so good that I have to resist the urge to wiggle on his lap. Not here, not in front of these three assholes. "And you *know* the King will match whatever I spend."

"I quite imagine the King wants the Alice far more than he values sixty thousand measly coins," Raiden continues, glancing across Dor's lap and over to March. "Don't you think our friend here would've gladly *paid* sixty thousand coins to see the Savage Duke raped by jabberwocky?"

"One hundred thousand," North snarls, uncurling his tail from around me and slamming the long, black scaled length against the floor in frustration, quite like my cat Dinah does when she's having a fit.

"Let me bash his head in again, sir," the Dormouse growls right back, leaning his massive form toward us. In a flash of lightning, I catch the ragged stripes of scars across his face, and the small round ears sticking up from his tousled brown hair. "I'll give you my wages for the next ten years to take the privilege."

"You're starting to annoy Dor," March says, his voice crisp with a 'British' accent similar to North's. But there's something else to it, too, like maybe a bit of Irish? *Fuck, this guy looks* and *sounds like Rob Evans!* The sexual selection happening in Underland is seriously *insane*, like there are so many men they have to be hot as hell to have any chance of finding a mate. Makes sense from a scientific level, right? "And if you're starting to annoy Dor, then you're starting to annoy me, too."

"Five hundred thousand," the Duke spits, his arms tightening around my waist. "You bloody twat. Crook. Fearmonger."

"Five hundred thousand, doubled by the King of Hearts," the Mad Hatter continues, sipping his tea. "I like that. Oh, and also, I want to marry the Alice. Political power suits me, don't you think? I'd make a fine husband."

"Marry you?!" I blurt and then let out the most caustic, scathing laugh imaginable. "I don't think—"

"Then you shouldn't talk," the Mad Hatter inserts, causing me to grit my teeth and clench my fists in anger.

"If I get out of here, I'm going to make it my personal life mission to dump your body down a well," I snap back at him and he grins, flashing me those vampire fangs of his.

"A water-well or a treacle-well?" he purrs, and both men beside him let out these deep belly laughs, like that's the greatest joke they've ever heard. Me, I don't get it. I know treacle is like, syrup or molasses or something, but a well of it? I guess this world *is* weird enough for something like that. Still …

"Where would they draw the treacle from?" I snap back at him, even though I know it's totally stupid and a complete waste of my time. These idiots are obviously talking in riddles—like Tee and Dee—so why am I justifying their stupidity?

"You can draw water out of a water-well," says the piece of shit Hatter, "so I should think you could draw treacle out of a treacle-well—eh, stupid?"

I surge forward, intending to tackle this back talking a-hole, but North holds me still, his muscular arms like bands of steel around my waist.

"A million coins," he grinds out, but the Mad Hatter and the March Hare just exchange a look across the lap of the Dormouse.

"Five hundred thousand from you, and five hundred thousand from the king, and this girl's hand in marriage," Raiden continues, staring me straight in the face. "Or else we take you to the King of Clubs, as planned. *He* has already promised me a spot as one of your husbands, Alice."

"Alli*son*," I correct, but really, why bother? The people in this place are clearly deranged; they can barely seem to keep their heads on straight, so how on earth can I expect them to listen when I tell them my name. "So what you're saying is, accept this offer and pretend I'm making my own choice about taking you as a husband or else you'll sell me to the next highest bidder and then, what, rape me in our marital bed after the forced wedding?"

"Whoever said I needed to have sex with you to gain the political prestige of being married to the Alice?" he asks with a tilt of his head, his top hat falling to one side but still managing to stay atop his head of dark, wavy hair. "Let's make a deal: the promised coins, your hand in marriage, but I won't fuck you until you beg."

"Oh, please," I snort, with a sneer worthy of my little sister, Edy. "You're fucking delusional."

"Delusions are just illusions without any truth behind them," Raiden says, and it's such a stupid, useless riddle that I just count my lucky stars that he really *did* follow along with the prophecy and use the raven/writing-desk one in our bargain. If not, who the fuck knows what would've happened to North?

"Fine," I say before the dragon … err, jabberwock … behind me can protest. "It's a deal."

The Mad Hatter reaches out and grabs my hand in a tight shake before the Duke can stop us, squeezing my hand tight and then lifting his knuckles to my lips for a kiss that's too hot, too intriguing for a villain.

"Excellent," he murmurs as March smirks at me and the Dormouse scowls. But the way he stretches out those three syllables … it feels like the mark of a dark promise.

What the hell have I just gotten myself into?!

A few hours later, after dozing in the protective circle of North's arms, the carriage stops.

The sudden lack of movement churns my stomach, and I realize as I crack open my eyes how goddamn hungry I really am. There's a brief moment there where I don't *want* to wake up, where I want to sit with my nose pressed to North's bare skin, breathing in that sweet, musky masculine scent of his.

But then I realize that the back door of the carriage is open and there's sunlight streaming through. Outside, I see puddles reflecting back a blue sky dotted with shrunken gray clouds, like the rain's reminding us it's still there, that it's only taking a quick break to recharge.

With a groan, I sit up and stretch my arms above my head, wishing I could've been kidnapped in something besides a purple silk nightgown with lace accents. Leather boots, breeches, a jacket, now *that* is proper kidnapping material. At least the Duke is shirtless and in blood-soaked pj pants, so I'm not the only person here who looks a hot mess.

"You weren't kidding about the Hatter, were you?" I whisper to North as I sit up, adjusting myself so that I'm straddling his lap. He meets my eyes with his gold ones, dark horns curving out of his blonde hair. "He's fucking *insane*."

"Yes, well," the Duke breathes with a sigh, "I can only offer my sincerest apologies, Miss Liddell, and admit my surprise at being attacked *in my own home*." His voice drops down to an animalistic growl that rumbles us both. "But I can't say I'm not at all shocked at this turn of events. As soon as the Hatter found out the Alice was in Underland, he was bound to seek your company—whatever the price."

"Can't you just go jabberwock on his ass?" I ask as North scoots me off his lap and sits up, getting onto all fours and stretching like a cat, bowing the front part of his body low and lifting his tight, hard butt up into the air for me to stare at, his tail twitching all the while.

"There's no guarantee that I'd win a fight with Raiden Walker," the Duke says, scooting over to the edge of the carriage and dropping into a puddle, sunlit gold water splashing as he lands. He turns and lifts his chin, ever the picture of royalty, sophistication, and bestial beauty all wrapped in one. North offers me his hand and I take it, hopping down beside him and wondering what the *fuck* this Raiden guy must really be like if he has a goddamn *dragon* nervous to face-off against him.

"Good morning," March says, leaning against a tree and carving an apple with a knife. He braces his muscular shoulder against the rough bark, his fingers handling the blade with a precision that makes me wonder what else those hands can do. I mean, not to me, I'm not interested. I just mean in *general.* His brown eyes are flecked through with red and orange, like an autumn skyline, and his mouth is full and luscious, even as he wears it in a stupid, little smirk. The red apple peel comes off in one, perfect strip and then falls to the ground near his feet. In an instant, there are a half-dozen little flies dropping down to feast on it, their wings a shimmering iridescent turquoise, their bodies … in the shape of wooden rocking horses.

Fucking rocking-horse flies.

Fantastic.

I blink a few times and shake my head to clear it, putting my fingers to my temples.

"Good morning," North replies with a civil coolness, his tail splashing through puddles as he swishes it in frustration. "Shall we get on then? What's the delay?"

"No delay," the Mad Hatter says, appearing out of the trees with the Dormouse on his heels. They're carrying large chunks of soft, spongy flesh—*mushroom* flesh. That reminds me … I have a bit of the mushroom meat tucked in my sheath along with the Vorpal Blade! Well, fudge on a fucking stick. If I'd just remembered that a few hours ago, maybe I could've gone house-sized and kicked this son of a bitch's ass?! "I'll call Twinkle, and we'll be on our way."

"Twinkle?" I ask as Raiden adjusts his top hat, decorated with a little white slip under the orange-red ribbon that reads *In This Style 10/6*. He catches me looking at it and points up at his head. "Are you interested in this, darling? Because for my future bride, no price is too high for a hat." He pulls it off his head and underneath, there's *another* friggin' top hat, this one white with a black ribbon. Raiden moves over to me and reaches out to put the first hat on my head, but I slap his hand away.

"What does the tag mean anyway?" I ask as he smirks and drops it back over his head, covering up the white hat underneath once again.

"Costs ten and one sixth coins," he explains as I roll my eyes and the man puts two fingers up to his lips, letting out a shrill whistle that echoes through the towering forest of trees and mushrooms. I thought the King of Hearts literally killed people who fucked with his mushrooms? But none of the three assholes here seem to care as the Dormouse shoves the massive hunks of multi-colored mushroom meat into the back of the carriage, slams the door shut, and slaps his palm against the side of the oversized teapot.

The carriage takes off, the horses' hooves splashing rainwater as they gallop off. I remember North telling me that in a wild magic storm, a horse is as likely to be a pumpkin as it is an equine. But the Mad Hatter's horses are all wearing raincoats, little hats, and boots, and they seem just fine. Huh. Glancing down, I realize that my legs are now wet with this supposedly horrid magic rainwater.

"The wild magic moved on hours ago," North tells me as Raiden continues to whistle, "and the regular rain washed most of the power away. Don't worry." He reaches down and takes my hand in his, squeezing me so hard that his talons dig into my skin, these shiny black hooks of claw that I actually find sort of … sexy?

The Mad Hatter pauses in his whistling to sing a ridiculous little doozy of a tune, his voice this low, icy creepy sound that both fascinates and frustrates me to no end. His accent—because supposedly, he's from my world, right?—is definitely a West Coast USA sort of sound, but heightened, elevated, like he's a bit older than I think he is.

"*Twinkle, Twinkle, little bat! How I wonder what you're at? Up above the world you fly, like a tea-tray in the sky. Twinkle, Twinkle—*"

When he sings, I get chills. When he stops singing, cut off by the sudden sound of flapping wings above us, I feel the blood drain from my face.

What. The. *Fuck.* Is. That?!

My mouth hangs open as a massive bat swoops down low and drops two long ropes from its hooked back feet. With a skip and a hop, Raiden Walkers steps onto a metal bar attached to the rope and then curls his arm around my waist, snatching me from North's grip. Dor does the same, taking hold of the March Hare and the second rope at the same moment.

The dinosaur-sized fucking bat changes course on a dime, rising into the sky with huge, long flaps of its leathery wings. As dumbfounded as I am by the size and sudden appearance of yet *another* weird ass creature, I don't miss the fact that we've just left North behind.

"Wait!" I scream as the air rushes past me and the ground … gets farther and farther away. My stomach lurches and like, I have a fucking *thing* about heights. Remember that *C* I got in gym because I refused to climb the damn rope? Well, now I'm on a rope with nothing to cling to except a vampire/mercenary asshole who wants to marry me.

And the ground … the ground is so very far away.

Turning my head, I bury my face in the hollow of Raiden's throat and throw my arms around his neck. I even wrap my legs around him and hang on for dear life, my heart thundering in my throat, my eyes closed so tight they hurt. I bet the view is amazing. Hell, I'm sure it's *spectacular*. I just don't want to see it.

A roar sounds from behind us, this bone-shattering, eardrum-bursting screech that I somehow recognize as being North's. Well, at least that answers that. He's shifted and is following us via jabberwock wing. Good for him. Hope no horny females pop out of the trees and attack. How ironic, is it, that in this world, it's the *men* who have to live with a low-grade anxiety at all times, wondering if a woman might pop out of nowhere and sexually assault them?

All those stories Tee and Dee told me about the Riving, and about my world—Topside—affecting Underland make so much sense when I think about it from North's point of view. He's living the life of a human woman … as an Underland male.

"I'm going to puke all the hell over you and this bat thing that's carrying us," I choke out, but the Mad Hatter just chuckles and wraps his arms around me, holding me tight. We move through cool, misty morning air, beams of yellow sunshine warming our icy skin. My dressing gown sticks to my body like plastic wrap, whipping in the wind along with my hair.

Fortunately, the ride only lasts maybe an hour, but to me, it feels like *weeks*. Weeks in the goddamn sky, hanging above a forest made of old-growth trees and mushrooms. By the time we land, I'm shaking, brimming with adrenaline, and the last person in either world anyone should mess with.

The bat drops us off in a copse of trees, undistinguishable from the rest of the forest, and then flaps patiently above us as March and Raiden re-tie the ropes around its feet. Looking up at it, it doesn't look any different from the bats back home. Same piggish little nose and giant ears, leathery wings, black fur, hooked claws. Just … all in *gargantuan* proportions. Of course, it only looks that way until North lands behind it, a sinuous curve of black scales and horns and claws.

He hisses at the bat creature, and it hisses right back at him.

"Best control your male before he makes a fool out of himself," Dor barks, but I'm not in the mood to take shit.

"Maybe you best control *yourself* because you're already acting a damn fool!" I snap, storming over to the massive form of the black goddamn dragon sharing the copse with us. He's a jabberwock, fine, okay, but he *looks* like a dragon to me, this lizard/cat/dog hybrid with big webbed wings, claws, and a long sinuous tail cutting ruts into the undergrowth. He smashes mushrooms and wildflowers that explode with poofs of bright dust and glitter.

Hope none of that's poisonous because it sure as fuck looks it.

"Hey," I say, putting my hands on one of his massive front feet. "Shift back for me, would you? I could use someone to talk—" Before I can even finish speaking, North's wrapped me up in his massive tail and lifted me off my feet. He's so large that even though it's just the tip—get it?—that he's using, I'm completely wrapped up in thick muscle and smooth, black scales.

The Duke's eyes flash gold as he pushes his way through the trees and over to a spot of dewy nine-leaf clovers. I wasn't even *aware* there were such things as nine-leaf clovers, but he lays me down in them, still holding me with his tail, and proceeds to *sniff* me from head to toe. His breath is hot as he snorts from his massive nostrils and then slowly, shrinks back down to size.

That sun-kissed bronze body is now hovering above me, every muscle taut, cock swollen and erect, horns curved and deadly. The wings are the last things to go, shifting off of his back as his tail unwinds from around my waist. The smell of man, musk, and arousal is unmistakable in the air.

The Savage Duke indeed, I think, as he pins my arms down and sniffs the side of my neck again. I wiggle, bringing my silken nightie riding up my thighs.

"Mate with me?" North asks, his voice barely above the level of a growl. My heart is racing, and I so desperately want to fuck this guy, take the beast out of him, and bring him down to a more manageable level. What's hotter than that? Taking a wild animal like the Duke and making him feel human again. Something about that appeals to me.

We're both basically naked, so the question of condoms is out; clearly he doesn't have any.

"I don't want a baby *or* a disease," I choke out, even though it's the hardest thing in the world for me to say. There's nothing more I want to do right now than have sex with the Duke of Northumbria.

"Jabberwock," he snaps out at me, dropping his forehead to mine and then *nuzzling* the side of my face and neck with this rumbling growl that does all the right things to my body. My core is already slick and throbbing, my nipples pebbled and tight. "No diseases. Can't get a human pregnant." His teeth are clenched tight and he looks about two seconds away from tearing out of here and destroying everything in sight.

Putting my hand to North's chest, I try to use my magic to invade his mind the way I did Dee. Doesn't work though. All it does is encourage him to press closer, running his tongue up the side of my neck. He pushes his pelvis into me, the only thing separating us the thin layer of my silken nightgown. But I can feel the hard tip of him push into my body, just a little.

My breath rushes out and I arch my back, dragging that nightgown out of the way just enough that there's now *nothing* between us anymore. North drives into me and I groan, wrapping my legs around him as he fills up every empty part of me. My body contracts, gripping him tight, and he makes this *sound* in my ear that isn't at all human.

His tail, that stupid tail that I've been fighting off for days, wraps around the top of my nightgown and yanks the lace out of the way, curling around my breast and squeezing it tight, the tip flicking across the hard pink point of my nipple.

My fingers dig into North's hair, threading through the silken gold strands and then taking firm hold of both curved, wicked horns, holding on tight to him as he fucks me into the dewy clovers. My back is all wet from the foliage, and my *core* is all wet from my arousal and the Duke's deep, wild thrusts.

Our mating is a little … well, like a *mating* and not much like any other sex I've had. It's fast and wild and quick, but the Duke knows exactly what to do, dropping his tail between us and teasing my clit with the very tip. He keeps us going until my body locks around him and holds tight, my spine bowing in an intense, animalistic little orgasm. I claw at the Duke's hair, yank his head close to me, and kiss him with tongue and teeth until I feel him tense up, exploding inside of me with a snarl that catches between our joined lips.

When I collapse back into the clovers, the Duke collapses onto *me* and just lies there, panting hard, breathing frantic. His tail twitches absently against the wet leaves of the plants.

"So much easier to come down from my other form with a mate," he grumbles, and then pushes up, looking down at me with gold eyes and a satisfied smirk that both excites and infuriates me at the same time. I shove him off and sit up, the Vorpal Blade still strapped to my thigh, my heart thundering faster than the bread-and-butterfly's wings as it sits on a flower not ten feet from me.

I know what the damn thing is because I remember reading about it, an insect with wings of bread and butter, the body of crust, and the head a lump of sugar. Mostly, it looks like its head is actually made up of two multi-faceted pearl-white eyes, similar to what a dragonfly's back home would be. But I only stare at it for a moment because all three of our captors are coming through the trees, and I'm tugging my nightgown back down my thighs.

"Excellent," Raiden Walker says, adjusting his hat as he grins at me with two sharp canines. The March Hare is still lazily eating his apple, cutting slices from it with his knife and then stabbing them. He sucks the bit of fruit right off the end of the blade. The Dormouse, on the other hand, just glares at North and me like he's fantasizing about bashing both our heads in this time. "You've soothed the jabberwock, and now we see the king."

He removes a small, golden key from the front pocket of his jacket, steps over to a large tree and bends down, unlocking a tiny little door.

"For the future Queen of Hearts," March says, reaching into *his* jacket and pulling out a pair of bottles, both labelled *FUCKING DRINK ME!* I take them both, my heart contracting at the thought of the twins and what they might be thinking about my sudden disappearance. Without looking at the Duke, I pass over one of the bottles, our fingers tangling together and sending warm little thrills through my body.

Oh, what the hell? I can't help myself. I flick my gaze his way and pop the cork on my bottle. He does the same, and we toast each other.

"Bottoms up," I murmur, and then chug the sweet liquid in a single gulp.

Chapter Two

The King's Croquet-Ground

There are simple rules in life that everyone knows: such as, always smoke pot first and binge on booze after, the pullout method doesn't really work, and if you drink from a bottle marked 'poison', it's almost certain to disagree with you, sooner or later.

However, this bottle's marked FUCKING DRINK ME so like, I'm pretty sure it's not arsenic. Anyway, it's bubbly and reminds of champagne. It has, in fact, a sort of mixed flavor profile. And by mixed flavor profile, I mean this is some effed up Willy Wonka type shit. The taste on my tongue morphs from cherry-tart to custard, from pineapple to toffee, and then cycles through roasted freaking turkey and hot buttered toast. It takes me all of one gulp to finish it off, downed like a shot of vodka.

"What a … *curious* feeling," I grind out, blinking as my head swims and the Duke reaches out to steady me with a hand on my elbow. I can feel the whorls of his fingertips pressing against my skin, and a warm flutter takes over my tummy. Either I have a massive crush on him (hard enough to make *diamonds*) or this drink is not sitting well with me.

"Are you alright?" North growls, his tail curling around my ankle as I blink furiously through a flood of adrenaline. It sends my heart racing as I stumble into his big, beautiful bronze body. My fingers curl around his shoulders as an earthquake starts up beneath our feet, and I let out a high-pitched squeak.

"What the hell is going on?" I choke as the ground roils and the trees sway in a supernatural breeze. Or ... wait. Am I the one moving and they're all standing still? I squeeze my eyes shut as my stomach lurches up and into my throat. You know that first hill on a roller coaster, the one you roll up with an ominous *click-click-click* sound from the tracks? And then you hit the top and there's one peaceful moment before all hell breaks loose?

Yeah, well, there's no peace here, just that horrific feeling of my stomach being left behind while the rest of my body hurdles through space.

When I flick my eyes open, I'm standing in front of the little door that's not so little anymore. And when I turn back to look at the trees … they make the sequoias back home look like playthings. My brain swims as I blink frantically and try to make all of this strangeness work within the confines of my logicality.

There's a leaf next to me that's bigger than my ex's fucking car. That's a hard pill to swallow.

"What happens if I drink more of that while I'm this small?" I ask, and the Duke cocks a golden brow.

"Most certainly," he says in that crisp accent of his, looking down at me with serious bedroom eyes, "you'd go out altogether, like a candle. I wonder what you should be like then? What is the flame of a candle like after it's been blown out? Simply smoke, I'd say."

Carefully, I extract myself from North's grip, trying not to let what just happened between us take over my thoughts completely.

But oh, we're close. So close. I've got giddy girl thoughts for *days*.

Eep! Just look at him! My lady parts sing, staring at his chiseled muscles, wide shoulders, and … well, his entire package is still on full-display. Now, that, that is a *man*.

Crinkling up my nose, I turn back to the Mad Hatter as he lifts his hat and draws out a decorative black cane from underneath it. It shouldn't rightfully fit in there, but of course, it magically does anyway. As soon as North sees Raiden's new toy, he curls the edge of his lip up in a snarl, claws extending from his fingers.

It's made of the same material as the hilt of my Vorpal Blade … so, jabberwock horn? No wonder North is pissed.

"Shall we?" Raiden purrs, smirking at us before swinging his cane in a circle and taking off through the now open door and into bright-ass sunshine. Wherever we're headed is a hell of a lot less cloudy than the forest.

"I thought there was only one door into the king's garden?" I ask. "Or rather, one door that leads anywhere close to the castle-grounds at all." See, I do sometimes listen when Tee and Dee talk. *Tee and Dee … I bet they're freaking all the way out right now.* If I'd woken up and found them gone, I know I would be.

"There *is* only one permanent door," the March Hare says, smoothing his hands down the front of his black trench coat. Yeah, did I mention that yet? That he's gone total villain cliché with a trench, a *velvet* trench at that? Looks stupid good on him though, the bastard. "We just made this. Now, if you'd kindly step through before Dor gets fussy, that would be highly advisable."

March blinks big, brown eyes in my direction, and the ears on the top of his head swivel to listen to a distant sound, the cracking of a twig and the rustling of leaves.

Uh.

It sounds like something's stalking us.

I don't need to be told twice. I might not like taking orders, but I also don't like being hunted and eaten by things with names I can barely pronounce. Can you imagine, being masticated by a *mome rath*? Now try putting that on a headstone: *Allison Liddell, eighteen years of age, gobbled up by mome raths.*

Reaching down, I snatch North's hand and drag him through the door. Maybe I just want an excuse to touch him again? Maybe I just need to hold onto something that feels strong and solid? I have no idea. But he squeezes my hand with his just hard enough to pierce me with his claws. Doesn't hurt really. I almost like it.

No, no, I *do* like it. I should start being honest with myself. Then again, I often give myself pretty good fucking advice although I very seldom follow it. Probably why I've gotten into so much damn trouble in my short eighteen-year span on earth and … well, Underland.

A large rose-tree stands near the entrance of the garden; the roses growing on it are white, but there are three gardeners at it, busily painting them red. *Curiouser and fucking curiouser,* I think as we step through the small door into the royal grounds I saw on my very first day here.

Everything—including the flowers—towers above us, masking for just a split-second the rancid scent of blood in the air. My gaze drifts back to the gardeners, and I realize with a start that their red *paint* is actually blood.

"Jabberwock, bandersnatch, jubjub, and so on and so forth," North whispers, naked and standing too close to me. I can feel his heat, clenching my thighs tight and trying not to think so much about how wet I am between them. "That's their blood, mixed up and painted around the gardens to keep them away from the castle. It's *nauseating*." He wrinkles up his nose with a wicked little growl, sending a sharp surge of adrenaline through my body.

"Makes some sort of perverted sense," I say as Raiden Walker strides down a small dirt path that winds through a path of daffodils, as bright and cheerful as the morning sunshine. "But aren't we going to, uh, nibble some *FUCKING EAT ME* cakes and get big again?" I can't help it; my eyes find the gardeners again, as large to me now as North was to me in his jabberwock form.

"Not until we get into the castle," March tells me, tossing his apple core onto the ground … and then receiving a middle finger from one of the *flowers*. He flips it off right back as my mouth hangs open and I stick close to the Duke's side. I figure if someone comes close to stepping on us, he could shift into his jabberwock form and he'd be at least the size of a small dog, right? "If any of the guards see us here now, they'll probably stick us all full of arrows before we get a chance to explain."

"Oh, well, *that* makes me feel better," I snarl as Dor takes up the rear and we trudge on through the garden. At this rate, it feels like it'll take *days* to get to the castle. Shit, it probably will. And my thighs are wet, and I'm wearing a flimsy, damp nightgown. The Duke is naked, and neither of us is wearing shoes.

"You'll see, when you meet the King," North says, drawing my attention over to him. "Becoming the Queen of Hearts, that'll heal all of Underland." I narrow my eyes on him, trying not to think *too* hard about the wild, angry mating session we just had. That's a problem for later. Right now, I just want to get into the castle, shower, and put some damn clothes on.

I don't bother to tell the Duke that first chance I get, I'm bailing through the Looking-Glass. And not just because I'm afraid he'll try to stop me. No, it's more than that. I don't even *know* if I want to go back anymore. I make a rough, low sound in my throat and put my hands up to my face.

The Duke doesn't say anything else for a while, but he *does* curl his tail around my ankle. I let him do it, too, even though I grit my teeth. I guess seeing him comatose with a hunk lopped off the side of his head endeared the asshole to me more than I care to admit.

We walk like that for several hours, beneath the lush jungle-like folds of … a well-manicured flower garden. But from down here, it all seems so wild and untamed, so dangerous. The rocking-horse flies and bread-and-butterflies look like fucking monsters. They don't seem interested in us though, and North stays fairly calm as we walk, so I decide to relax my shoulders a bit and just marvel at the idea that I *am* this tiny. How cool is that? Besides, if I really need to, I have that mushroom meat stuffed in the Vorpal Blade sheath. I can pull it out at any time and return to my normal size.

For the next few hours, we walk in silence, the sunshine filtering through the leaves.

Occasionally, I hear Dor mumble something rude and violent behind us, but I ignore him. Seems like Raiden and March have him on a pretty short leash anyway.

Sometime later, just before we reach the edge of a white gravel pathway—a full-sized one that looks like a hundred mile stretch of white desert at this height—I hear the thundering of footsteps. It's like a herd of elephants barreling down on us, and I shrink back, unintentionally putting myself against the Duke's naked front. He's half-hard, too, and stabbing me in the lower back with his dick.

First come ten soldiers carrying swords; they're all dressed in red, black, and white livery decorated with hearts, their faces severe, mouths in tight, thin lines. Next, ten courtiers: they're all ornamented in dresses and jewels and fine shoes, cloaks billowing out behind them. I've never even seen such a prissy, spoiled looking group of people.

Oh. Wait.

An old memory of Ellie Arkley—showing up to the first day of school in a stretch Hummer limo, dressed in a pair of ten thousand dollar shoes and an outfit that could purchase a homeless family a decent place to live—springs to mind like a weed. I remember her glittering diamond earrings, plastic surgery smile, and eight hundred dollar haircut, and almost puke.

Yep.

That's what these people remind me of, privilege and unchecked wealth and greed.

I'll see when I meet the King, huh? Yeah right. If these are just the courtiers, then I'm sure the King is a nightmare. And how could I *ever* like a man who treats the twins the way he does? No, no matter what happens with the Looking-Glass and the prophecy and my staying here … this King and I are *never* going to get along.

After that horrid procession moves by, I finally catch sight of him.

The King of Hearts … *and* beside him, the White Rabbit.

"Rab!" I shout, tearing from North's arms and stumbling out onto the white gravel. He doesn't seem to notice *or* hear me, so I shove the silken folds of my dressing gown out of the way, flip open the small leather pouch on the side of the sheath and take out a bit of mushroom meat. I used my fingernail to carve a 'B' into one and an 'S' into the other—for big and small.

Taking a small nibble from the 'B' side—I learned a lot from reading the original Alice books, and I know not to take too much, too fast—I feel myself rise up into the air, like I'm on the rope dangling from Twinkle the Bat's massive hooked claws. My stomach lurches, and I almost scream, but then everything is snapping into place and I'm staring into Rab's red eyes.

"Miss Alice," he whispers, his ears twitching on his head.

I don't even get a moment to breathe before the *King* is putting a blade to my neck with so much force that I feel a drop of hot, red blood leak down my throat and chest.

"Your Majesty," Rab growls, putting up his white-gloved hands in a placating gesture. "Please, calm yourself. This is *the* Alice."

"My name is Alli*son*, so please Your Majesty," I snarl out between clenched teeth, my eyes meeting the dark irises of the King of Hearts. His hair is blood-red, his scar ragged and white in the sunlight. I've never *seen* such a handsome face, but my God, what a complete and total prick. Even though his advisor is standing right there, telling him who I am—the girl he *supposedly* wants to marry—he holds his blade in place for so long that I start to sweat, beads of moisture mixing with the blood leaking from my throat.

When he finally pulls back, he turns his mouth into this disgustingly triumphant smirk, sheathing his blade at his waist and planting his hands on his hips. He gives me a very slow, very unnecessary once-over and then nods, like I'm a bit of horseflesh that's met his stern and calculating approval.

This guy … he can go fuck himself with his royal scepter for all I care, shove it right up his ass to join the stick that's already clearly wedged there.

"The Alice," the King breathes, ignoring my previous proclamation. Eh, so what's new? Not a single person here has listened to me about my name … except for Tee.

Speaking of … Behind the King and Rab, just off to the right and down another white gravel path, a set of double doors swings open and there they are, my twins.

My twins?

Uh-oh.

"Allison-who-isn't-Alice!" Dee shouts, taking off across the gravel and grabbing me before I can take two steps toward *him*. He wraps his arms around me and squeezes me so tight and close that my feet come right off the ground. His wings are nowhere in sight—they couldn't possibly be, since I wasn't around to free them—but he's smiling so big and wide that I can't help but smile back. "Oh, you gave us quite the scare."

"Quite the scare," Tee chokes out from beside his brother, his amethyst eyes locked on mine, the sun catching on his purple-streaked black hair. His brother kisses me before I can get another word out, burying his tongue in my mouth and making me groan. He isn't shy about his hands either, groping my ass in two tight handfuls. I encourage it by leaning into him, rubbing up against his body and lifting my nightie a bit on the process. *Enjoy* that *show, you assholes,* I think, smirking as I continue my kiss with the angel prince.

I don't think Dee's intention is to break the curse—his kiss is too pure—but that's what happens anyway. In two brilliant bursts of sapphire light, Dee's wings explode from his back, pushing up his trench coat and tearing through his black and white striped shirt. There's a collective gasp from the courtiers waiting up ahead on the path, hiding like the little blue-blooded bitches they are behind a row of guards.

Oh. They don't like seeing how princely and perfect their slave really is, do they? Too damn bad.

I pretend not to notice the genteel gasps and mutters, pulling away from the kiss with a laugh dancing in my heart and tingling on my lips. I even take a moment to brush some blue and black strands of hair from Dee's forehead. The tension is thick enough to cut with a knife, but I make sure I look him in the eyes to let him know that to me, he matters. His expression is equal parts worry and fear, but he still manages a smile.

"You son of a bitch," I breathe, pushing him back a little, so I can get some air. He lets me go, and then his brother and I stand there awkwardly for a moment before I embrace Tee, too. It surprises me how happy I am to see him, and I find myself rubbing my cheek against his chest as he curls his fingers around the back of my head and pulls me close.

"I'm glad you're safe, Allison," he whispers, pressing a kiss to the crown of my head. His hot breath stirs my hair, and I shiver slightly. "And I'm sorry that we failed to keep you safe …"

"Oh, cheer up, would you?" an ice-cold voice says from behind me, and I whirl around to see the Mad Hatter rising up from the edge of the flowerbed. The King goes to put his sword to the man's throat, same way he did me, but Raiden just laughs and knocks it aside, throwing up some sort of magic shield to catch a good two-dozen arrows aimed for his back.

Soldiers rush up and surround him as I dive forward and just narrowly manage to protect the Duke from being trampled. My reward is to get kicked in the face, have my leg stepped on, and end up almost getting killed myself when a jumpy soldier shoots an arrow at *my* back.

"Enough!" the King screams, throwing his arm wide and sending the soldiers scurrying back. Most of them drop to one knee. All of them except one, tall, blonde woman with a serious fucking attitude problem. Her eyes catch mine for just the *briefest* of moments before I hear Raiden Walker chuckling behind me.

I glance back over my shoulder and find that it was him who snatched the projectile that was aimed for my back out of mid-air, his other hand held up and brimming with a magic shield to keep Rab and the twins back.

"Relax, relax, everyone," he purrs as I scoop the Duke into my hand and leave the March Hare and Dormouse on the ground. I also inadvertently saved them, too, but North is the only one I care about. I tuck him to my chest and then offer up the bit of mushroom flesh still clutched in my left hand. I forgot I was holding it, and it's a bit squished now, but it works. "You see, *the* Alice, why I didn't want to make such a fuss? Now you've ruined my grand entrance."

The Duke of Northumbria gives the mushroom a lick, and then he's toppling into me, knocking me onto my back and giving me a very vivid reminder of the sex we just had. We exchange a long, languid look before he finally stands up and pulls me along with him.

"What the fuck are you doing here?" Tee snaps before the King gives him a look. Tee curls his lip up in a snarl, but he steps back … even though his eyes go straight to mine and his hand hovers at the knife on his hip. I feel a little guilty, having had sex with North. I should tell Tee and Dee, first chance I get.

"Me?" Raiden says with a smirk and a cocky little head tilt. "I'm just delivering both the Alice *and* your precious Duke." A moment later, the March Hare and Dormouse sprout to life behind the Mad Hatter's shield. In fact, all five of us are trapped inside of it.

"Explain yourselves," the King says in a surprisingly level voice. His dark eyes are as cool and even as granite, his shoulders relaxed. While everyone else looks like they're about to turn this into a brawl, he looks like he's about to take tea. Well, maybe not boosted tea, but like tea back home. Normal fucking tea. "What do you want Hatter?"

"Your pet Duke here," Raiden begins, letting his marmalade orange gaze slide over to North. "He guaranteed me you'd match his generous donation of say … five hundred thousand coins, *and* the Alice here—*the* Alice, mind you—has also promised me her hand in marriage." He turns back to the King, but there's still no emotion brewing in the man's eyes.

"Bargains made under duress are no bargain at all," Tee snaps as Dee curls his lip in agreement, reaching up to adjust the peaked cap on his head. His wings cast beautiful shadows on the pavement in front of his feet.

"No bargain at all," he agrees, his sapphire eyes lighting on mine. I don't know what the hell this magic shield is that's separating us, but nobody seems willing to approach it, so I don't either. Instead, I hang back and wait to see how these politics play themselves out.

No chance in fucking fuck that I'm going to marry the Mad Hatter, but I'm also not going to tell *him* that while I'm standing inside some magic spell he's just cast.

"I can leave right now?" Raiden asks, pulling off one top hat, and then another, and then *another*. He tousles his dark wavy hair with his fingers, but just keeps smiling, like he knows he's already got this one in the bag. "Leave the Duke with a musking jabberwock, and turn the Alice into the King of Clubs like I'd originally planned."

"Stand down," the King says, lifting a gloved hand in the air. It's covered in rings that sparkle with an unnatural light, like there's so much more going on here than first appears. I feel a sigh come over the courtyard as the courtiers stop tittering, and the soldiers rise to their feet to put their bows away. A quick glance up at the walls and the turrets shows me dozens of other soldiers relaxing their postures—pretty much all of them are women, by the way.

The monarch licks his lips and then flicks his eyes down my front before turning back to Raiden.

"I'll have a page show you to a guest room. Clean up. Have something to eat. Join me on the lawn for croquet—*both* of you. Duke, with me, if you please."

The King gives me one last look, his dark eyes meeting my blue ones, before he spins away in a sea of red and black robes, Rab catching my attention before he moves off after him, dressed in a waistcoat and pinstripe slacks.

The shield around us comes down, and nobody tries to stop North and me when we move out of that bubble and over to the twins. Dee puts his arm around my waist in a semi-possessive but also comforting sort of way.

"Let's get you some food," he says as my tummy rumbles, and I put a palm over the front of my nightgown. Dee rubs his coat sleeve against my throat to clean off the blood from the King's knife as I glance briefly at North, still gloriously naked and not giving two flying fucks about any of it. He meets my eyes, and I find myself biting my lower lip in a flirtatious sort of way. Gross. Edith would make so much fun of me if she could see me in my current state—panty-less and making come-hither faces at a dragon.

"I suppose I should tend to the King," North says, but the way he looks at me makes me think he'd rather be tending to *me*. I shiver and Dee cocks a dark eyebrow in my direction. Ah. Clearly I have some explaining to do. "Take your time and fetch yourself a pair of knickers." He flashes a sharp grin at me as my cheeks heat and I narrow my eyes on him. "I'll keep the wanker occupied and be waiting for you when you come down." He reaches out with the long, muscular length of his tail, tucking my hair behind my ear with the tip before he turns and moves down the path in the direction of some rolling green lawns.

"Something's changed between you," Tee says, drawing my attention back to him. He doesn't sound upset though, just … curious. And relieved. God, if I could bottle up his relief and sell it, I'd be a millionaire back home.

The thought makes me smile.

"Food sounds good," I say, finally responding to Dee's statement, "but I'd prefer a shower and some fresh clothes first, if you've got any."

"Your wish is my command," Dee says, keeping his arm around me but affecting a little half-bow as he sweeps his hat off his head. The feathers of his wing brush against my bare back and make me shiver as he stands up straight and folds them tightly together.

As we walk away, I look back and see the Mad Hatter, watching me with a smirk on his face and a wink at the ready.

He gives it to me nice and slow, theatrical, and then we turn the corner to head inside and he disappears from view.

"I was so fucking worried about you," Dee says, hugging me close and making me go all warm and fuzzy inside. The feel of his hard muscles pressing against the thin fabric of my nightie is nice in so many ways. I missed him, weird as that sounds. I mean, we were only separated for a day. Not even, really. But it feels like an eternity. I guess the thought that I might be raped and killed has sort of … *shifted* my priorities.

"*We* were so fucking worried about you," Tee says, standing straight and tall and proud on my other side. He's looking dead ahead, toward a set of double wood doors that are standing wide open. On the outside, he's all calm, quiet strength; on the inside, I can see him fuming. When he flicks his aubergine eyes in my direction, I can tell he's scared shitless, too—or *was*.

For me.

Tee was scared for me.

"Worried, anxious, distraught, broken, twisted …" Dee pauses and adjusts his hat with his left hand, shifting his wings around in the process. Before I can think better of it, I reach out and ruffle the feathers, making him shiver. He casts me a lascivious little wink and tosses a smile my way that's only slightly tainted by worry. My disappearance really messed with their heads, didn't it? *Just like you're starting to care about them, they're starting to care about you,* I think and then shake my head to clear it.

How can I really care about someone I just met? How can they care about me? And yet … I study Dee's blue military jacket, the silver heart buttons, the tight black denim jeans, and the leather belt with his knife hanging off it. His mouth is pinched just a little too much, his eyes are just a tad too hooded.

Yep.

For whatever reason, he cared that I was gone; he cared a whole fucking lot.

"Were you really?" I ask, feeling my heart thunder in my chest. Just before we head inside, I glance out at the lawn once more and see North standing next to the King, gazing after me with heavy-lidded eyes. He blinks them twice then smiles. Guess he's not worried about this whole effed-up situation. He is, after all, a 'hefty giver of tithes to the crown' anyway. These dudes all seem pretty serious about this prophecy thing, and about dating me, so maybe the Duke'll keep me safe against the King?

If he can.

I give North a wave, he salaciously rubs his hand up one of his horns, and then I turn back around just in time to see the black and white checkered marble floors of the palace. We're not two feet into the place before things start to get weird.

The arched ceilings are covered in faceted mirrors, lending this eerie funhouse quality to the ostentatious beauty of the palace. There are intricate gold arches sweeping above us, a match to the gilded frames on the walls featuring various members of the royal family in frilly gowns or furred cloaks—essentially all of them are female.

"I take it there aren't often kings that aren't attached to queens?" I ask, and Tee makes a slight, soft sound in his throat. Almost a scoff, but not quite. His amethyst eyes are focused straight ahead, but I direct my stare toward him, let it burn until he finally flicks them my way and blinks like he's coming out of a coma.

"It's your world, reversed. So no, there aren't many unattached kings." Tee rubs his hands down his face, flashing some of the tattooed skin on the backs of his arms, and sighs again, like he's exhaling the stress of the last twenty-four hours. "The court expects him to be married as soon as possible."

"As soon as possible," Dee repeats, his voice a much more chipper version of his brother's. "To you, of course." He fluffs his wings, almost like he's just checking to make sure they're still there. I see Tee's eyes go straight to them, and I'm tempted to free his, too, right here where any asshole could see. And yet, there's something about the idea of kissing Tee that makes my cheeks go bright-red. I think it's his intensity. While Dee is light and fluffy and fun, like a beam of sunshine on the skin, Tee is as fleeting and rare as moonlight.

"I'm not marrying the King," I say, and those aren't empty words. My brother died because he was protecting my right to decide what to do with my own body. He shouldn't have had to, but he did. And I bet marriage in this world carries similar expectations to that in mine. If you're not catching my drift here, I'm talking about sex. "I'm not fucking that prick of a king," I say aloud, grinding my teeth. "If I have to, I'll make a run for it, straight through the damn Looking-Glass."

Tee turns me suddenly toward him, cups my face in his hands, and kisses the ever-loving shit out of me. His tongue slides against mine in this passionate, frenzied tangle. There's fear in that kiss, or maybe panic, I'm not sure. Either way, his wings burst from his back, rending his shirt, and spreading like rain clouds across a desert sun, bringing shadow and wetness where there was none. I feel *drenched*, and I mean metaphorically speaking, not just between my thighs.

"Don't talk about it," Tee whispers, his lips pressed close to mine. I open my eyes and all I can see is him. His face is too close to my own, there are too many shades of purple in his irises, and his mouth is too full and beautiful. My knees start to quiver, and if he didn't have his hands on my waist, I might've hit the floor. "Not here."

"Won't the King flip out if he hears you were tonguing his future bride?" I whisper, my hands trembling and curling into unconscious fists in my nightie. I can feel a single bead of sweat working its way down my spine, a warm heat blossoming low in my belly.

"We belong to you," Tee says curtly, releasing me and stepping back. But I don't miss that last, lingering look he gives me, his eyes as purple as summer grapes. Dee makes a sound from behind me, and we all pause as a pair of *playing cards* with arms and legs scurry past us. They're the size of small children with faces printed on their fronts, frozen in expressions of terror, like they died screaming.

And they're fucking terrifying.

"What the hell are those?" I ask, stumbling back and slamming into Tee's broad chest. He puts his hands on my shoulders and squeezes as the pair of animated cards walks past with silver trays on their outstretched palms. The creepiest part is how human their appendages are, with skin tones in shades of cream and cocoa. Not to mention they each have scabs and scars and *hair* decorating their limbs.

"House servants," Dee says, snapping his fingers. One of the cards, the one with a female face, makes her way over to us, a pair of black Mary Janes on her feet and little frilly white socks poofing around her ankles. "Can we get three meals brought up to the Penthouse Suit, please?"

"Penthouse *Suite*," I correct, but Dee just raises a dark eyebrow at me.

"Not Suite, although it is very *sweet*, but Suit. Penthouse Suit, like Suit of Cards. Although it's just the difference of a single 'e', now isn't it?"

"Make that *four* meals, you crooked little tidbit of dark magic, you," a voice purrs —quite literally—in my ear. In the span of an instant, I've got a heavy weight on my left shoulder, and a fucking cat rubbing against my cheek. "I'm quite *fur-amished.*" I narrow my eyes at the admittedly terrible pun, and reach up to give Chesh a small scratch on the head. There is a distinct possibility he's looking down my top, so I should probably punch him, but I'm too much of a crazy cat lady at heart. Even lecherous pussies deserve love.

"Are you even allowed to be here?" Tee asks, crossing his arms and lifting his chin in the direction of the guards posed against the opposite wall. These, at least, are human, even if their red suits of armor are a bit strange. They reek of blood, too, this coppery scent that stings my nostrils and makes my eyes water. If the blood is supposed to repel things like jabberwocky, then how is North putting up with it?

"Can a person really be allowed or disallowed from being in a certain place or time?" Chesh slides off my shoulder, shifting as he goes, like a cloud of smoke moving from one place to the next. When he materializes, he's dressed in tight, leather pants, a silver chain belt, and nothing else. It's hot as hell, especially when he licks his tattooed right arm and slides it over his head, crushing one of his striped ears against his dark hair as he cleans himself. "Only gods have the right to do that, and gods do not exist." Chesh flicks his tail and narrows his gray eyes on the three of us. "How was your date with the Hatter?"

"Maybe we should head up to the room before we discuss this?" Tee snaps, and Chesh lifts his gaze lazily up in the twin's direction. He looks downright bored—like most cats. I still can't figure out his position in all of this. There's the King, the King's servants, the King's bloody Duke, and the King's, uh, spiritual advisor, as well as the King's enemy-plus-sidekick, and then there's … this guy. With no relation to the King whatsoever. I'd been guessing he was the Duke's servant, yet he seems a tad … removed from the situation.

But standing here under a mirrored ceiling, with fucking playing cards sweeping past us with their creepy little legs and silently screaming faces, is not really the place to get into it.

"I could use a bath," I say, feeling a slight heat suffuse my cheeks. There's still *evidence* down there of my rumble with North. And yeah, by evidence, I mean cum—his and mine. "And a dress that doesn't show my nipples."

Dee snorts as Chesh smirks lazily at me, his mouth stretching wider than it rightfully should, all sharp, white teeth and sass.

"I like a dress that shows your nipples," he says, disappearing from view until there's nothing left but that smile.

"Mind your manners," Tee snaps, brushing strands of hair from his forehead as Dee gives him a quizzical sort of look. I think Tee carries more stress on his shoulders than his brother realizes. I'm starting to wonder what time they realized I was missing last night, and if they got any real sleep. Tee has dark purple bags under his eyes. "You may come *only* if Allison gives you permission."

"Allison, is it?" Chesh purrs, his eyes and striped cat ears fading back into view. "Oh, he calls her *Allison*. How charming. But her cat—and we all know there's no higher authority on Topside above or Underland below that's more prudent—calls her

The Midnight Knicker Dancer." I choke on my own spit and Dee has to pat my back to help me breathe again.

"What the hell did you just say?" I ask, feeling my cheeks go beet red as I think about dancing in my panties at home in front of my little black cat, Dinah.

"Your *pussy*," Chesh purrs, reappearing fully and then rubbing his whole damn body against mine, "calls you The Midnight Knicker Dancer. It's written all over your face and ankles." He pauses in front of me and points to my head and then my feet with a sharp-nailed finger before leaning in and rubbing his cheek against mine. "Cats have scent marking glands in their face, didn't you know?"

"Yeah, I *did* know," I say, pushing him away from me as Tee scoffs and Dee raises both eyebrows. "What does that have to do with a stupid nickname you just made up?"

"Made up?" Chesh asks, putting one hand on his bare chest and drawing my attention to his myriad black and gray tattoos. "If I were going to make up a nickname for you, it most certainly wouldn't be *that*." He licks his lips, his two little feline fangs sticking out in the most adorable way. "Your cat left it written in your scent, as bright as the fireworks on coronation night. She quite literally *rubbed* you the wrong way, didn't she?"

"You learned all that by smelling me?" I ask, getting sassy and cocking a hip out as I cross my arms over my chest. As soon as the question leaves my lips, I regret it. *Oh God, my tumble with the Savage Duke!*

"That's not *all* I smell," Chesh purrs as Tee shoves him to the side and grabs my arm.

"Let's head upstairs. You don't want your first meeting with the King to be when he's in a mood." Tee scowls, tossing a glance over his shoulder that's pure poison. I'm not sure yet if he hates the Mad Hatter or the King of Hearts more.

"*Head* is right," Dee says with a small grimace, drawing a line across his throat with his finger, reminding me of the King's scar. "Because heads *will* roll if we piss him off." Dee takes up a position on my other side as Chesh shifts again and hops into my arms. I grab him out of habit, but give out a little growl of my own when his head gets too close to my boob.

If he 'scent-marks' that with his cheek, there'll be hell to pay.

"Lead on," I tell the twins, and they do, away from Raiden Walker and the King of Hearts and all of their bullshit.

At least … for now.

But peace, true peace, doesn't last long in Underland.

The Penthouse Suit of Hearts is basically an entire floor that encompasses a bedroom, sitting room, library, and bathroom all in one. Only downside is that the bathroom has no door, just a sheer curtain on a circular metal loop that I can pull closed. I decide I don't care enough for modesty to be bothered by it, and sink into the hot water. It was piped in here, just like it was at Rab's. This world is both medieval and modern. Total fucking mind trip.

"So what happened?" Tee asks, just outside the curtain, leaning against one of the curved, white walls with his boots crossed at the ankles. It's like he's afraid to walk away from me, like I might disappear if he does. Hell, maybe I would? In this place, it's hard to find anything that's an impossibility.

"You mean when I was kidnapped?" I ask, feeling the deliciously scalding water surge over me, cupping the sweet soreness between my thighs, buoying my breasts. Have you ever noticed that? That breasts float? Like … sexy pool toys or something. "Because I was about to ask you the same thing. You said I was safe on the Duke's estate."

"I thought you were," Tee chokes, his voice much rougher than it was before. I think he feels like he failed me. Not in my book though. I get the idea that the Mad Hatter and Company are pretty badass. He's a fucking vampire for Christ's sake. "Although that doesn't excuse our behavior."

"Off with our heads," Dee quips playfully, trying to lighten the mood as he lounges on my new heart-shaped bed. There's a knock at the door, and I watch as his shadow rises to its feet and makes its way over to answer it. Guess our food is here. And it's been delivered by creepy little card people with macabre expressions of torture and terror etched into their fronts. I'm sure dinner will be downright goddamn delectable.

"Did the king order you beheaded?" I ask, narrowing my eyes. I've read the book; I've seen the movie. Isn't that what the Queen of Hearts always says? Off with their heads?

"He said it, but he doesn't mean it," Tee growls as Dee wheels in a cart and heels the door closed with his boot. "He likes our pain and suffering too much to end it."

"Well, if North was captured by the Mad Hatter and the March Hare, there wasn't really much hope for me, was there?" I say, picking up a red bar of soap. It's, unsurprisingly, also in the shape of a heart. They're really big about themes around here. I lather up and start soaping my armpits. Hate to admit it, but I could really use a razor. "They were waiting downstairs with North's head bashed in. I had the Vorpal Blade, but no chance to use it."

Running the soap down both arms, I take a surreptitious glance at the decorative table next to the tub. It's plied with all sorts of different toiletries, but I've only got my eye out for one thing. I spot a straight razor next to a bottle of glowing perfume that says *FUCKING SPRAY ME!* which is like, never going to happen. If EAT MEs turn me into a house and DRINK MEs shrink me into a mouse, what the crap does that thing do?! Grow me some slimy green tentacle arms?! I snatch the razor up, flip it open, and try to figure out how to shave my pits without filleting all my skin off.

Yes, I am a very classy girl. Cue eye roll.

"How on earth did the Duke manage to survive that particular encounter?" Chesh purrs, curled up on the massive continent they call a bed. Clearly, it was made for like … hmm, let's say *ten people.* Yeah, I really could fit nine suitors into that thing. Huh. They really do take that fucking prophecy seriously. "It's no secret that the Hatter and the Hare are not exactly fans of the Heart."

"I made a bet and won it," I say, letting my mind wander to that glorious kiss between Raiden and North. Now, that made the whole experience almost worth it. Almost. I mean, other than the threat of being sold to the King of Clubs, forced marriage, and/or death. "Raiden gave him some blood and voila, he was healed."

"Raiden gave North blood? Because of a bet?" Tee pauses and exhales. "Sounds about right. He's fucking insane."

"Mad really," Dee says, pushing aside the curtain and making me squeak. I'm covered in bubbles, but still, the invasion of privacy annoys me. Sure, we had sex, but that doesn't mean I want him watching me shave my armpits with a too-sharp razor. My anger is mollified though when he hands me a chocolate cupcake with sparkly heart candies on the top. "Can I get you a towel, Allison-who-isn't-Alice? Or a kiss? A hand job perhaps?"

Never mind. My anger is not mollified. I'm still irritated, but also … I think he's cute, too. Damn my girlish hormones.

"A towel, yes. The rest: not a fucking chance," I say, tearing the wrapper off the cupcake and shoving half of the dessert in my mouth. Dee complies, fetching a red towel and robe from the cabinet and draping it over the little side table. He slides the gauzy red curtain back into place, giving me that extra second I need to finish shaving.

And why are you so concerned with shaving, Allison? I think as I examine my calves for any stray hairs. *Because you plan on rubbing up naked against a pair of fallen angel princes?* With a sigh, I drop my leg back into the water and realize that I've sort of given up on fighting this whole Underland experience. It's happening; I'm here; I'm going to make the most of it.

"The King was serious about us joining him downstairs?" I ask as I splash my face with water and fight off a crippling wave of fatigue. When my head finally does hit those (obviously heart-shaped) pillows, I'm a goner. "Because I could really use a nap."

"A cat nap?" Chesh purrs, but I ignore him.

"The King is always serious," Tee says, and the melancholy in his voice makes me want to wrap him up in a hug. It was the current king's father who sent soldiers after the twins' people, right? I can't be bothered remembering the whole history of Underland; I'll ask questions later, when Chesh isn't around to eavesdrop. Speaking of the prior king … those soldiers in Dee's memory, they looked like cards, too, didn't they? What's up with that? "The Duke will keep him occupied for a while, but we shouldn't push our luck."

"Speaking of the Duke," I start, wishing I could sink into this bathtub and drown my embarrassment, "we sort of … mated."

Hearts above, why did I just use the m-word?! What the crap is wrong with me?!

"With that arrogant look on his face," Dee muses, rooting around on the food cart, "there was no doubt." All I can see through the curtain is shadow, but his voice sounds light enough. There's not even a hint of jealousy in there.

"No doubt, nohow," Tee repeats softly, and I wish fervently that I could see *his* face. I pop a soap bubble with my finger. "And no surprise: there's not a soul in Underland who didn't think the Alice would fall in love with the Savage Duke."

"I'm not in love with him," I blurt, but does it really matter? I slept with him; I like him. I guess that makes him one of their supposed nine? "But, uh, aren't I supposed to ask the primary if he can … join the harem?"

"Oh, harem, I like that word," Dee says licking something off the tip of his finger. It's hot, even if all I can see is his shadow.

"Can I join your harem then?" Chesh asks, tail flicking anxiously. "Because I didn't just bring you mice—I brought you *rats*. That's a worthy gift, don't you think?"

"Make Tee the primary," Dee says, ignoring the cat. His voice is still all light and fluffy, but I can see right through him. He cares about his brother, and he's trying to make him happy. My heart grows three sizes like the damn Grinch's, and I shift in the bathtub, my bare butt cheeks squeaking against the porcelain. "And ask him."

"I don't need to be the primary, Dee," Tee says, and his brother snorts, turning and leaning against the food cart. I need to get out of this damn bath, so I can see facial expressions.

"Contrariwise," Dee snorts as I stand up and dry off (well, in a half-assed sort of way—there's still some bubble bath in my crack). "You're the older twin, so you should be the primary. Technically, *you* were the crown prince back home." I wrap the fluffy white robe around myself and step out of the bathroom, trailing bubbles behind me. Both twins and Chesh turn to look at me with varying expressions on their handsome faces. "Don't argue with me: you know I always win."

"Fine," Tee says, giving in surprisingly easy. My guess? He didn't *want* to win this particular argument. "Then I accept the Duke, but not you."

"Ouch," Dee hisses, cringing and then winking at me as I pause next to the smorgasbord of … totally weird shit. It *looks* like food, but who knows for sure? I drop the cupcake wrapper off and trade it out for, well, I *think* it's a sandwich. There's a dark brown roll (did you guess that it was heart-shaped? if not, you fail, because it is) that smells like sourdough, and it's piled high with meat and veggies. What sort of meat, I just don't want to know at this point. Probably freaking jubjub bird again. "So awfully cruel, brother."

"And what about the *cat*?" Chesh insists, pulling out a pack of cigarettes and lighting up. "Or has he not courted Midnight Knicker Dancer for long enough?"

"If you call me Midnight Knicker Dancer again, not only will you not be welcome in my harem, you won't be welcome in my room, or even my good graces." I sit down heavily on the edge of the bed with my food and try not to sigh with bliss. It's beyond soft. The King of Hearts really knows how to live. It takes every ounce of willpower I have to resist the urge to lie down and go to sleep. Back home, it's my favorite activity. In this world, it's a rare treat. I rub my hand down my face. "Let's pick up this discussion later, when I'm running on more than just fumes. What do I wear to this croquet thing anyway?" My lids are heavy, and my lashes feel as if they're coated in sandpaper and sitting heavy on my cheeks. "And do I really have to play the game with a flamingo as a mallet and a hedgehog as a ball?"

"Even more proof that you *are* the Alice," Dee says, swinging back a heavy red velvet curtain on one wall and revealing a hidden closet. It's about, I'd say, three to four times the size of my bedroom at home. There's a crooked chaise lounge, no less beautiful because of its wonky shape, and a chandelier made out of skulls that are just a bit too human for my liking. The clothes inside, however, are exquisite: velvet, furs, brocade, leather, embroidery, silk, and more jewels than one girl could wear in a lifetime.

I miss jeans and t-shirts.

"How is that proof that I'm the Alice?" I ask, taking a bite of my sandwich and sighing with relief when it actually tastes good. I force my tired body off the bed with a groan and move to stand in the entrance to the closet. It's too big, too grand; I don't know what to do with it. As nice as it is, it can't last. Nothing good ever really does. "I'm too tired for riddles."

"You just know the prophecy oh so well," Dee says, hip-bumping me out of the way and moving across the thick white rugs piled high on the closet floor. He opens one of the cabinet drawers on the far wall, digs around a bit, and pulls out a pair of black suede slacks, a peaked cap similar to his own, red leather riding boots, and a black and white checkered blouse. "You've even got it memorized."

"So … there are flamingos and hedgehogs then?" I ask as Dee presents me with the clothes, and cocks his head to one side.

"What's a hedgehog?" he asks, but my brain is too tired to deal with nonsense. I just push him out the closet door and kick it closed, so I can change in peace. I keep telling myself that in this castle somewhere is the Looking-Glass, my ticket home. I'll get to see my dad and my sister again, my cat, Dinah. Somehow none of that provides me much motivation, not when I know the fate I'd be leaving Tee and Dee to. And then there's North … and *his* cat. Fucking Cheshire Puss.

Ugh.

This is why I don't sleep with guys on a first date. Things get complicated; things are *already* complicated.

"How do I look?" I ask after I slip out of the robe and into my new outfit, throwing the closet door open with a dramatic flourish. Dee ruffles up his hair with long fingers and gives me a slow, calculating once-over.

"Like a queen," he says, and then I'm sorry I even asked. How can I be a queen of anything when I can barely take care of my own life? Back home, all I do is read, sleep, and eat. Rinse, repeat. That's my entire life; I can't be expected to run anyone else's.

"You look beautiful," Tee adds as I exhale and pick my robe up off the floor. Maybe there are servants who do that sort of thing here, but having morbid little card creatures doing my laundry is not an idea that appeals to me.

"Good enough to *eat*," Chesh purrs, arching his back and digging his nails into the bedspread. He hops off the bed and swaggers his leather-pant-wearing ass over to a tall, carpeted sculpture in the corner.

Oh. It's a cat tree, as in a play structure made specifically for cats.

"Who are you anyway?" I ask, glaring at Chesh as he climbs up and then lounges on said cat tree—in full human form, I might add. His leather pants are too low slung, and there's a tantalizing trail of dark hair below his belly button. Normally, I'd try not to stare, but this is Underland, and I'm tired, and there's a vampire and a king waiting downstairs for me. So I just look at him until he reaches down, unzips his leather pants, and then— "Please don't lick your crotch while I'm in the same room as you."

"Would you rather lick it for me?" Chesh growls, mouth spreading into a cat's grin. I flip him off and take a red wool military jacket from Dee's hands, our fingers brushing together for a moment. He purposely tangles his with mine and pulls my hand close, giving my knuckles a long, lingering kiss with his hot mouth.

"I'm glad you're safe," he whispers, going down to one knee in front of me. Our eyes lock, and I feel this little quiver of excitement sizzle through me. I can't forget the feel of his wings on my skin, the warm slide of his body inside of mine. "I'm really glad." Dee gives my hand a kiss and a squeeze, and stands up, stepping back to give me some room. Tee hands over the thigh-sheath with the Vorpal Blade in it next, *and* the Queenmaker tucked in a gorgeous red leather waist holster with tooled black hearts.

"Thanks," I say, licking my lips and glancing down at the black hearts on the toes of my new boots for a moment. There's an awkward silence that follows that I'm so desperate to fill, I turn back to Chesh again. "Anyway, you ignored my question: who *are* you?" I repeat, focusing on the asshole's pierced septum and wondering if I sound too much like Lar. Speaking of, where is that cheeky butterfly?

"Why, I'm the cat," Chesh purrs, sweeping his black and white tail around in a curious little wave. "The *Cheshire Cat*."

"I'm well-aware," I say, struggling and failing to put the new belt around my waist. Tee steps close to help, his body heat seeping into mine, his serious stare a welcome bit of steel in this crumbling world of rainbow madness. "What I meant was, who are you in relation to the hierarchy here? Are you the Duke's servant?"

Chesh blinks huge, gray eyes at me, and then yawns, flashing his bright pink tongue.

"Servant? You know as well as I that a cat serves no one but himself." Chesh sits up and leans over, his beautiful stomach muscles bunching up, my eyes drawn right back to that line of dark hair all over again. "I'm the Duke's friend. Don't you have any friends, Alice?"

"Alli*son*," I say out of habit, sweeping back wet strands of hair from my forehead. "And that's it? You're just a friend?"

"Just a friend?" Chesh asks, cocking one triangular ear back. "Friends are rarer than diamonds and twice as precious. Are you quite mad?"

"Apparently," I say, shrugging into the wool coat and taking a deep breath. *I'm about to play croquet with a bunch of mentally insane psychopaths; this is a new low, even for me*. I hadn't had much of a plan before I got to the palace, and I'm starting to feel like I'm even more out of my league than I first realized. "We're all mad here. I'm mad, you're mad …" I trail off as Chesh howls with laughter, run my suddenly sweaty palms down the front of my new jacket, and get ready to face off against the King of Hearts.

The March Hare is waiting just outside the gargantuan double doors that lead from the palace to the royal gardens. He's got a carrot in his hand which should be funny, considering his brown rabbit ears and all, but really, it's almost sexual the way he eats it. He sucks the tip into his mouth, swirls his tongue around the orange flesh, and then gives me this easy, one-sided smirk.

"The Boss wants me to keep a close eye on you," he says, his voice laced through with an English accent. It's much less formal than North's, but it has this quiet, lilting quality, like I'm hearing his words inside of a dream.

"Does he now?" Tee snaps, his teeth clenched tight. "Seems to me that your *boss* best defer to the King when it comes to the Alice."

"Oh?" March asks, tipping his top hat forward to shade the velvet brown color of his eyes. "You think the King of Hearts has any influence over the Hatter? That's a unique perspective."

"You think one mercenary asshole has the power to topple an entire kingdom?" Tee asks, stepping forward and putting the toes of his boots against March's. It gives me a little thrill, watching him stand up for me like that. Not that I can't stand up for myself, but it's always nice to have allies.

The look on the March Hare's face is demented. Deliciously demented, but still, it gives me pause. He runs his fingers along his chin and twitches one brown ear.

"Ask the Queen of Clubs," he drawls, and then sets off toward the grassy area on our left. I've never seen such a curious croquet-ground in all my life. Hell, I'm not sure that I've *ever* seen a croquet-ground in my life. It's all ridges and furrows; the croquet balls look like ivory lumps, and the mallets shimmer in the sun like bone.

The wickets are made up of the little card people, their grotesque faces twisted into silent screams. Just looking at them, with their human legs and arms bent into unnatural positions, makes me want to puke. Sure, the garden is beautiful, and the flowers smell like honey and sugar, but there's a tension in the air that I don't like. It snaps against my face with each gust of wind, stinging my lips and tangling my white-blonde hair into snarls.

It also brings with it the metallic scent of blood.

"What the fuck is that?" I ask, but I'm well-aware of what I'm looking it, shimmering in the sunlight across the courtyard.

It's a guillotine.

Not sure how I missed it before.

It's impossible to miss now, considering the fact that it's spattered with blood, and there's a guard dragging a body away. For a moment there, my chest fills with panic when I see a pair of limp, butterfly wings on the back of the dead man. But then Lar is standing right beside me with a deep-set frown etched into his face. Relief pours over me in a wave.

"What's going on here?" I ask him as he studies me with eyes like chips of ice, his pale blonde hair tinted with the slightest drop of blue. It goes well with his pale skin and provides a nice contrast against the vibrant sweep of his blue, black, and gold wings. He has the most mild of expressions on his face, too, like nothing in the world bothers him. His hands though, I can see them curling into loose fists.

“It’s nice to see you’re still alive, Sunshine,” he says, eyes going half-lidded as he smiles at me. The wind picks up strands of his shoulder-length hair and sends his sapphire earrings dancing. Light refracts through them and casts a blue glow on the white squares of my checkered top. When he finally lifts his head to look in the direction of the guillotine, his smiles fades to a thin line. "The King likes to kill decoys to vent his anger, when he can't be bothered to rid himself of the real thing."

"He's killing a decoy of you?" I ask, studying Lar's white jacket, tossed casually over his shoulders. I still can't get over how similar he is to the character of Howl from the movie *Howl's Moving Castle.* Kills me every time. I find myself subconsciously running my tongue over my lower lip. Hard to maintain a flirty moment though, knowing some innocent dude was killed because he *looks* like the Caterpillar. "Why?!"

"We failed the king by losing you," Tee whispers, voice low and dark. He won't look at me now, especially not when he sees my gaze swing over to the trail of blood that mars the perfection of the white gravel pathway. At the end of it, there's a whole sea of familiar corpses, wearing hats that match the twins, one with a tail that matches the Duke's.

I know then and there that I am always, *always,* going to hate the King of Hearts.

"We failed the King, but he fails himself if he loses us," Dee riddles, adjusting his hat to protect his eyes from the sun. I notice that most everyone out on the croquet-ground is wearing a peaked cap of some kind. Guess it’s in fashion around here. Even the King—can't miss that handsome face, not even from a hundred yards away—is now wearing slacks, a jacket, and a hat, too.

“Oh, but he’d kill *me* if he could,” Chesh says, curling his furry little cat body around Dee’s neck and staring at me from eyes like two full moons in his black and white striped face. “You’ll see no by-proxy murder of this pussycat. The King hates me with a violent passion. Not a cat person, but I suppose there’s no accounting for taste.” Chesh waves his tail across his body and disappears behind it, like he’s erasing himself from existence. The only sign that he’s still there is the faintest whisper of a purr.

“This can’t be happening,” I whisper as I shake myself out and rub at my temples with two fingers. There’s no one actively being shoved onto the guillotine, but I’ll be damned if I stand by and watch an innocent person die. “I can’t let this happen.”

“Tread with care, Sunshine,” Lar whispers, tugging on one of his sapphire earrings and giving the twins’ angel wings a slow once-over. “The King is already displeased with the lot of us.”

“Yeah? Well I’m displeased at his execution factory over here,” I grind out, gesturing wildly in the direction of the bodies. There are multi-colored crows pecking at the corpses, their feathers a sea of rainbow colors that reminds me of the dyed strands in my own hair. Just over the castle wall, perching in a tree, is a row of vultures with eyes like shards of obsidian.

I shiver and straighten my coat out, starting across the too-green grass with my metaphorical hackles raised, the men trailing along behind me. The March Hare is waiting along the way, falling into step beside us, but I ignore him, cutting a path straight to the King, the Duke, and the Hatter. I do not, however, miss the mischievous little smile March tosses my way. He's eating again—a big ripe peach this time. I wonder if he ever stops?

"Well, well, so lovely to see you again," Raiden says, the orange-color of his eyes obscured by heavy lids and thick lashes. There are two card servants nearby, holding up frilly parasols covered in hearts. They shade Raiden's pale skin from the relentless rays of the late afternoon sun. "And so soon."

The Duke snarls under his breath, claws curling from his fingertips as he whaps his tail against the lawn, creating little divots. He's dressed in a loose white top, fully unbuttoned and flashing bronzed skin, as well as tight brown leather pants and black boots with red hearts on the toes. His gold eyes glare daggers at the Mad Hatter before sweeping my way with a heat that's twice as powerful as the sun's rays. Now I feel like *I* might need a parasol.

"You're dressing people up like your servants and then having them slaughtered?" I blurt as the King turns slowly toward me, his face drawn into this expression of intentional neutrality that scares the crap out of me. He's not scared of anyone, not intimidated by anything—not the Duke, not the Hatter, and most especially not me. "The great wonder is, that there's anyone left alive."

Glancing around, I notice that the entire entourage that was parading through the garden earlier is seated and watching … and they're all fucking staring at me.

"Here," says the King, his dark eyes sparkling in the sun. He passes over a mallet which, unsurprisingly, is a petrified skeleton. It looks like a flamingo, you know, except for the sharp teeth in the fossilized little beak. "Take a mallet, hit a ball, Alice."

"It's Allison," I correct, watching the dark shadows flit over the King's face—both physically and metaphorically.

"Well, *Alice*," he says, purposely putting emphasis on the name and tapping the skull of his mallet against the soft ground. He's tall, towering over me and enjoying looking down his perfect nose, I bet. It really is a perfect nose, too. It offsets his full mouth beautifully, the scar just barely noticeable on the right corner of his lips, trailing down his chin, and slicing across his throat. His blood-red hair ruffles in the breeze, and I'd almost find him handsome if he wasn't such a horrible human being. Or … is he human? I don't even know. "Why don't you play a game with me? Winner can decide when the killing stops." He lifts his hand and the human guards in their red and white suits of armor drag one of the card people over to the guillotine, cutting the creature in half with the wicked metal blade before I can even think to utter a protest.

Blood sprays everywhere, and the scream that spills from its dying throat will haunt my nightmares for years to come. My hand drops to the Queenmaker, and I have to fight really goddamn hard not to blow this arrogant asshole's head right off.

"Careful, Miss Alice," an icy voice whispers in my ear, just before Rab appears on my right side, holding out a mallet and a ball. His red eyes meet mine, and he raises his brows as if to say *you have no idea what you're messing with here.* "The King is as vindictive as he is handsome."

I snatch the equipment from Rab as the King smirks and twists his white-gloved hand around the base of his mallet. The way he's looking at me makes my blood boil, like he's a farmer inspecting his cattle and finding one of his beasts sorely lacking. My nostrils flare as I struggle to hold in my temper and do my best not to think about all the eyes on me. I've never been much for public displays; I'd rather sit in a corner and read.

"You're on," I say, dropping my ball to the grass and putting my foot on it. It takes me a moment to realize it's a *skull*. Yet another fossil in this maelstrom of hell. Not sure if this one's human or not. If it is, it must've belonged to a child. Bile rises in my throat as my stomach roils. "I win, and you stop beheading people without my permission."

"Your permission?" the King asks, his voice low and dangerous, like the whistle of a far-off wind, one that promises future storms. "How interesting. It's a deal then: you beat me in a game of croquet, and I'll let you stay my executions." His mouth curves up into a cruel smile, pulling at the ragged scar etched into his skin.

I take a deep breath and shrug my shoulders, loosening my joints.

No fucking way I'm losing this match.

"And if I win," the King continues, moving closer to me. When he glances over at Rab, the rabbit-eared man takes several steps back. I meet the Duke's narrowed eyes over the monarch's shoulder and at least get the feeling that he'd fight to defend me if needed. That doesn't do much to comfort me though because I'm not at all certain he could take the King down. "You'll kiss me in front of the entire court."

"Are you insane?" I ask, but the arrogant male triumph on his says he most definitely is *not*. Piece of shit. "Fine, bring it on, bitch." The King raises his brows at my name-calling, but tosses his skull into the air and then rolls it onto the grass next to a red and white stake.

Oh, wait. It's not a stake—it's a bone with blood spatter on it.

"How intriguing," says the Hatter, adjusting his black top hat and grinning with two sharp canines. "Mind if I excuse myself to make some bets? Where there's a challenge, there's always money to be made." He moves off to join the March Hare near the white lawn chairs where the audience sits, and starts to smoke a cigarette in a gold holder with lazy drags.

My eyes lock onto the King's dark ones, but they're impossible to read. I've never seen someone so closed-off before. It's terrifying. Kissing this guy must be like swallowing a mouthful of ash and hate. *You're only thinking that because you're disturbingly intrigued by him,* my mind whispers, but I ignore it.

"So, what are the rules?" I ask, because like, I've clearly never played fucking croquet before. Even if I had, I doubt the rules in Underland would be anything like they are back home. "Who goes first?"

"The blood-spattered ball *always* goes first," the King says, turning his skull ball with his foot so I can see the red stains on the front. "And the rules … are exactly what I want them to be." He lines up a shot with his macabre mallet while the grotesque little card creatures shiver and shake, their painted faces twisted into expressions of horror. Without even bothering to aim for the wickets, the King knocks his bloody ball into the fray, and the cards shuffle to accommodate him. "Four points," he calls out after the ball passes underneath several arches. "And four extra swings." I watch as he works his way around the heart-shaped court. I think in traditional croquet, the wickets and stakes are supposed to be in a double diamond shape. But, of course, there's nothing traditional about Underland. "Your turn, Alice," he mocks as the nick on my neck throbs and smarts. I won't forget that he held a blade to my throat anytime soon.

"Son of a bitch," I snarl as I kick my own ball into place, trying to ignore the entourage behind me. Tee, Dee, Lar, and … I have no idea where Chesh went, maybe rubbing his invisible self against the Duke's legs. Rab is standing off to the side, arms crossed in front of him, one of his white ears twitching. It's impossible to miss the grimace that crosses his face.

He turns one of his arms over and shows me the watch tattooed there, ticking down to something ominous, no doubt. Probably my inevitable loss in this game.

As I ready my shot—because I have to at least try—I notice something strange shimmering in the air near the slave-card wickets. It weirds me the fuck out until I realize that what I'm looking at is a grin.

"How are you getting on?" says the cat, as soon as there's enough mouth for him to speak with. It's no use talking to him until his ears are there, or at least one of them. In less than a minute, there's a cat's head floating in the air not six feet in front of my face.

"I don't think they play at all fairly," I growl, gritting my teeth and glancing back over at the King. He's staring at the cat with a mixture of rage and frustration. Oh. I like that. So there *is* something that can shake the unshakeable. Good to know. "There don't seem to be any rules in particular; at least, if there are, nobody fucking attends to them."

"How do you like the King?" says the cat in a low voice. Clearly, he's trying to pick a fight. Not sure how smart of an idea that is. The rest of the guys seem pretty freaked-out by the King of Hearts. Understandably so, considering he kills random strangers to vent his anger.

"Not at all," I say. "He's so extremely"—I pause when I notice how close the King is behind me—"likely to win, that it's hardly worthwhile finishing the game."

The King smiles, but it's not a very pretty expression.

"I see you're back again," he says, resting his hands on the end of his mallet, the skull dug firmly into the grassy earth near his boots. "After last time, I'd think to find you more intelligent than all that." Chesh smiles, his eyes twinkling, a disembodied tail fluffing around behind him. "I don't like the look of you at all. However, you may kiss my hand if you like."

"I'd rather not," the cat remarks, and just like that, all of that cool, easy calm leaves the King in a violent flood. I can see the muscles in his jaw ticking with rage.

"I'd fetch the executioner myself," he growls out, "if you had a body that I could remove your head from."

"What a pity, what a *shaaaame*," the cat purrs, its head twisting around until it's looking at us upside down. "So there *is* something the precocious King of Hearts can't attend to?"

"Whatever am I going to do with you?" the King grinds out as Chesh tosses me a little wink, licks his lips, and promptly disappears from view.

"He belongs to the Duke; you'd better ask him about it." And then I crack my mallet on the ugly little skull and send it flying. The card wickets try to shuffle out of my way, but a little shimmer and a swipe of some nearly invisible claws keeps them in just the right place for my ball to fly right on through.

"*Five* points," I mock as I stand up straight and give the King a triumphant look that, had these idiots not completely bought into the prophecy thing, probably would've gotten *my* head lopped off.

The King's gloved hands squeak as he tightens them around the handle of his mallet.

"Very well then," he says, curling the edge of his lip up and meeting my eyes dead-on. The crown perched atop his head slides to one side, this lazy little dip that's too sexy for words. But it doesn't fall off, like it's defying gravity just for him. "I'll play you fair, Alice." The King stands up and spins his mallet in a circle, cracking the skull side against the ground before he takes off to meet his ball, the empty eyes of the hollow skull staring up at a blue, blue sky.

"Don't even *try* to win, Allison," Tee whispers, grabbing my arm. I glance back at him, and whatever he sees on my face must convince him that I'm doing this whether he likes it or not. "Fuck, you're going to get yourself killed." With a growl and clenched teeth, he releases me, watching as I follow along after the King.

The asshole's next shot is damn near perfect, and even without cheating, he manages to knock his ball through three more wickets. Not sure how many of those arches are *supposed* to be in the game, but here in Underland, there are hundreds, maybe thousands. It almost looks like a graveyard, all these silent faces staring up at an unyielding sky.

"I've got your baaaack, so to say," Chesh purrs in my ear. I can't see him, but at least when I hit my ball, all the cards stay in place. I miss the next wicket and don't get any points, while on the King's next turn, he hits my ball with his own, calls a 'roquet', and then smashes my ball into kingdom come with his next swing. I finger the Queenmaker as I grind my teeth. *Bet this baby could turn the dickhead to mush,* I think as I stretch my neck and give a deep sigh.

The audience may as well be made up of corpses for all the noise they make, sitting quiet and still as a storm cloud rolls in, covering up the sun and casting strange shadows on the field.

"You should know better," the King says, his voice even-keeled and wicked all over again. The way he looks at me, I just want to turn and run, stumble through the castle until I find the Looking-Glass and forget I was ever here. There's something in his stare that promises I might do things I never thought I'd do—and that I might *like it.* "Challenging me."

"I've seen bigger bullies than you," I snort. If I hadn't met the Mad Hatter all of say, oh, twenty-four hours ago, that might not be the case. I can't help but glance over at the man in question, wondering not only how he came to be in this world, but also how he became a vampire. "Now if it will please Your Majesty …" I can't help an eyeroll to punctuate my words as I gesture at the King with my mallet. He glances down at the lump of bone near his feet, folds his arms across his chest, and stays put. With a small snarl, I stalk over to him and stand far too close for comfort.

He smells just as good as his garden, but with a solid note of thyme and rosemary that hits the back of my tongue when I breathe in, something savory to balance out all the sweet.

"You know what *would* please his majesty," he whispers, his breath far too near my ear for comfort.

"No," I say firmly, cracking my ball and managing to just barely sneak it through the right wicket. "And I don't think I want to know."

"I will have you, Alice," he says, his dark eyes glittering like a starry sky. "You've always been destined to be mine."

"I'd rather marry the Mad Hatter," I grind out, and the King's full mouth twists into a severe frown.

"That's part of the arrangement. At first, I was upset. But I've decided this can only bring prosperity to the Kingdom of Hearts. If the most powerful mercenary on the continent is tied to the crown, think of the possibilities."

"I think that my heart and my vagina aren't bargaining tools," I snap as the King purposely brushes past me, his fingers curling around my wrist. When I glance up, I get caught in his eyes. Fuck, I practically fall into them. It's like I'm tumbling down the Rabbit-Hole all over again, getting twisted up in glitter and bones.

"And *I* think that your fate is to belong to me." The King grabs my chin in tight fingers, but my reaction commands are on point. I smack his hand away and stumble back, stepping on one of the poor cards by accident. The sound it makes … it's like I've taken all its breath away. A gasping choke tears from the poor creature's throat as I jerk back, tripping over and crushing my ball before falling right on my ass.

The card person thrashes and chokes, sitting up and turning its silent screaming face toward me. It reaches its too-human hands up and claws at its neck, like it's choking. I back away, even though I know I shouldn't, even though I know I should feel pity and sympathy instead of horror and fear.

"It's a curse they brought on themselves," the King says, smashing the end of his mallet into the card's face. A tear of blood escapes its frozen eye before it collapses to the ground, shudders … and dies. "You're wasting your sympathy."

I look up at him with this expression of horror plastered across my face. When he sees the way I'm staring at him, something flickers in his gaze that I can't quite read, like a shooting star cutting across all that darkness. But he turns away too quickly for me to get a good read on it.

"Your Majesty," Rab is saying, his red eyes flickering briefly to me and then back to the King's. "The Mocking Turtle and the Gryphon … they're at the gates."

I wish I could explain the expression of rage that crosses the King's face then … and the look of terror.

Chapter Three

The Mocking Turtle's ... Scary As Fuck

"Who won the game?" I ask North as we follow the King's entourage through the palace, trying my hardest not to think about the dead card servant that was just dragged across the lawn outside. If I think too much about what just happened, I'll get dizzy and this fatigue headache I've been nursing will finally win over and knock me on my ass. The Duke's long, black tail slashes across the checkered floor like a scythe, but the expression in his gold eyes is pure, unadulterated *excitement*.

And I think that excitement might be for me.

Oops.

I wonder if mating with him really was a good idea? Or maybe his lack of mating was what made him savage in the first place?

"Clearly, the bloody King," he says, and despite his expression, his words are a bit clipped, gold gaze swinging over to the grand front entrance of Castle Heart. We come to a stop in an area that's roughly five times the size of my school's gymnasium—and this, this is apparently the *foyer*. "Although I suspect he'll wait awhile to collect on his prize." North flicks his attention back to me and smiles lasciviously. "I doubt he wants to share your first kiss the same day you experienced the most wonderful lovemak—"

"Ooookay," I say, interrupting him before he can get started regaling the others about our tryst in the woods. If the twins really want to know, I'll tell them later. Right now, I want answers. Well, I would if the Duke's shirt weren't unbuttoned, a stretch of bronze chest exposed. I can see all the hard lines of his muscles as he turns toward me and leans in, breath hot against my ear.

"You're thinking about something, my dear, and that makes you forget to talk." North nibbles the edge of my earlobe, and I slap him away, coming to like I've been splashed with cold water. I really need to figure out how to function with hot guys swarming around my hormone-addled body all the time. "I dare say you're wondering why I don't put my arm around your waist?"

I decide to ignore the Duke and focus on Lar instead. He looks like an intelligent enough man. And those eyes, they're like soft blue sea glass. They pierce straight through me.

"Who are the Mocking Turtle and the Gryphon, and why did everyone shit their pants when their names were mentioned?" I ask, my cheeks warming slightly as Lar smiles at me and reaches out to push a few loose rainbow strands of hair back from my face. I feel like Tee notices my barely-there blush, but that's not a surprise: Tee notices everything.

"I have an unfortunate inkling that you'll soon find out for yourself," Lar says, holding his jacket over one shoulder, his ice-blue shirt unbuttoned just enough that I can see the keys pierced through his nipples. As I watch, he reaches inside his top and unhooks one, passing it over to that blonde woman I saw this morning, the one with the nasty frown who keeps *staring* at me like she expects me to sprout a second head.

She's tall, thin, and that sort of dangerous pretty that makes grown men weep. I'm surprised *she* doesn't have an entourage of dudes drooling after her. Dressed in a full suit of white armor and carrying a lance, she looks like she could take on a jabberwock. That is, until she trips over a potted plant and lands face-first on the rug in front of the gilded gold doors.

"Take those nonsensical things off and answer the damn door," the Duke calls out as the woman finds her feet and whips around to glare at him, smacking him in the face with her waist-length hair in the process. At first I'm not sure what the hell he's talking about, but then I notice the strange metal fins feathering around her feet. Ah, no wonder she tripped. I was too busy being jealous of her boobs to notice her weird shoes.

"These are *ankle shields* to guard against the bites of sharks—it's an invention of my own. I don't see *you* inventing anything new." The woman sniffs and lifts her chin haughtily, clutching Lar's key in one hand, and flicking her lavender eyes over to mine. She stares at me a moment, taking in my state of dress, and then sighs. "You'll hardly be able to defend against these assholes wearing this."

I'm still wondering why the hell she thinks she needs to guard against sharks on dry land when she reaches up and flicks two buckles open, one on either shoulder. Her white breastplate comes right off and she moves over to fasten it on me.

"This, it's an invention of my own," she tells me as I sag underneath the metal armor. How the fuck am I supposed to stand up while wearing this?! It weighs about a million pounds. "I don't have a name for it yet, but I will."

"Do spare my mate the idiocy of your inventions," the Duke says with a little growl, his gaze focused only on me. It's like he doesn't even *see* the gorgeous blonde standing beside me. And I like that. And I also feel a bit like a misogynistic prick for thinking that way.

"He might bite," Chesh says, appearing out of thin air on my left, still dressed in leather pants and nothing else. "Either you or the Alice, I'm not sure." North weaves his arm through my right while the Cheshire Cat does the same to my left. "But if he bites you, White Knight, it won't be for pleasure."

"My job is to protect the Kingdom of Hearts, and that includes keeping the Alice safe. Stand down and let me do my job." She turns on her heel and heads back to the throng of guards near the front gate, unlocking the double doors, and gesturing for the card servants to open them with long ropes.

"I do quite like a little nibble every now and again," the Duke growls, tightening his grip on my arm as Tee rolls his eyes and Dee grins. But in the next minute, all their faces fall, Lar's included, and I glance up to find the King standing there in front of us, arms folded, frowning like a thunderstorm. Rab's standing just behind and to the right of him, one tattooed hand holding a cigarette, the other swinging a pocket watch around on a gold chain. He smirks at me when he sees me looking, and I flip him off.

"A fine day, Your Majesty," the Duke says, his voice high and threaded through with a growl. He sounds annoyed, but I'm not sure if it's with the King or with the Mocking Turtle and the Gryphon, whoever the fuck they are. All I know about them is what I read in the original story; they scared the shit out of me in those old Tenniel drawings. Gross. "How can we be of service?"

"They want to meet the Alice," the King says, lifting his cell phone and reminding me that they *do* in fact have phones here. That they never use because their network is 'compromised'. I guess when you're talking to the enemy anyway, it doesn't matter if they've tapped the phone lines. I notice Tee and Dee exchange a worried look.

"They want to rape and kill the Alice," Dee growls out, surprising me. He's generally a jovial person. To see him so angry is disconcerting. I *really* don't like it—especially when he reaches out and puts his fingers on my hip, just above the Queenmaker, like he's reminding me it's still there. Nobody here seems concerned about giving me a gun in the presence of a king I already hate. I can't decide if it just means the Castle Heart security is poor, or if the King is such a badass that me having a weapon in my hands doesn't matter much.

My bet's on the latter.

"Tell them no and send them on their way. Better yet, carve their flesh like a holiday ham and mail their corpses back to the Walrus and the Carpenter," the Duke says, curling the corner of his lip up in a snarl, curved horns catching the light above us. I'm sure as soon as I have a moment to myself, I'll start thinking about our wild rut in the woods in graphic detail, probably masturbating to it, too. For now, I sort of need to compartmentalize it.

Did I just hear rape and kill?

"If I could, I most certainly would," the King says, tilting his head to one side. The gold crown he wears catches the light as he narrows his eyes on me. "But they're Recitations, obviously. We could obliterate them, but what good would that do? We may as well get as much information from them as we can."

"What's a Recitation?" I ask, scrubbing my hands down my face. I don't even want to *speak* with the King, particularly after watching him kill the card servant earlier, but I also need to know who—or *what*—is trying to kill me. I mean, rule one of survival: know your enemies.

"A Recitation is a copy of a person's image, with no person waiting behind it." Lar pulls—no joke—a glass pipe from the pocket of his white slacks, and lights up. Clearly, he's not smoking tobacco. Is it too much to hope that there's a little pot in there? Rab flicks his cigarette butt on the floor, and a card servant promptly cleans it up. The two men each take a drag on the pipe before Rab finishes Lar's thought.

"It's a mirage," he says, smoothing his hand down one of his ears and smiling at me in a way that I can only describe as half horror movie/half romantic comedy. Looking at his ears makes me think of the March Hare and the Mad Hatter. They disappeared at the mention of the Gryphon and the Mocking Turtle, and I haven't seen them since. Coincidence, much?

"A mirage that can spy and report back to the Walrus and the Carpenter." A shiver chases down my spine when Tee says those two names. They should be ridiculous—I mean the *Mocking Turtle* for fuck's sake—but there's something eerily ominous about them, and I can't help but think of the prophecy. Just what do these guys have to do with all the bullshit befalling Underland? When Tee murmurs another stanza under his breath, I get this horrific sense of déjà vu, like I've been here, done this all before.

"The eldest angel sneered at them,
And many a word he said:
The stubborn monarch closed his eyes,
And said she won't be dead—
They had to let the Alice think
Else his Queen would soon bleed red."

The King lets him finish and then turns to me with his ebon eyes as Dee whistles under his breath.

"You have to admit, Highness, that's hardly coincidental. Lar?" Dee glances over at the Caterpillar, but all he does is tug on one of his earrings and shrug his shoulders in a noncommittal sort of way before taking his pipe back from Rab.

"I deliver prophecy—I don't interpret it." Lar folds his wings together behind his back at the same moment Dee drops his feathered appendages to the floor, and Tee curls his protectively around his shoulders. I notice the King of Hearts keeps his gaze entirely focused on me.

"Well?" he asks, and there's this challenge in his voice that just gets me. He thinks I'm going to say no. He must, the way he's quietly smirking at me. But then, he doesn't know Allison Pleasance Liddell, does he? I never back down from a challenge.

"I want to see them," I say, feeling the muscles in my lower belly tighten. The King tosses some red hair off his forehead … arrogantly. How one can toss hair arrogantly is beyond me, but he manages to pull it off without looking like a total twat. "Where are they?"

"Come," the asshole says, turning in a billow of his heavy white and red coat. Without waiting to see if I'll follow, he moves with long strides across the checkered marble floor, Rab and a female guard flanking either side of him, and soldiers trailing in two lines behind. With both North's and Chesh's arms tucked in mine, I move to stand behind him and notice that the large, gilded gold doors have opened up to reveal … two wooden doors that are painted red.

When the King waves his hand, these, too, are opened. And behind door number two? More fucking doors. As the servants continue to open them, I notice that the entrance is getting smaller and smaller. On the ceiling above, there are remnants of all the previous doors in layers, like a fucking cake.

"I don't suppose that disappearing act of yours is contagious?" I ask the cat as he rubs his cheek against my shoulder. He seems almost above all this hierarchal bullshit. Which, of course, makes complete sense if you know anything at all about cats.

"Perhaps it's sexually transmitted?" he purrs, flashing me a bit of canine. "Maybe we should test the theory?"

"Don't be crude," North drawls, but he's hardly paying attention to my exchange with his pussycat. No, his gaze is focused on a small set of metal doors no bigger than my front doors back home. They're silver and inlaid with a massive anatomical heart. It splits in half in a crooked, jagged shape, like a broken heart in a child's drawing, revealing a long, dark stone walkway … that leads to nowhere.

It protrudes past a cliff's edge, over a vast valley shadowed by the clouds overhead. For miles, all I can see are trees and mushrooms and the blue snakes of raging rivers. There's no discernible way for a person to get up here, other than the pair of red doors on a floating island at the end of the path.

Another portal then?

"I'll be here if you need me," the White Knight says, moving to stand beside Rab and the King. She taps her chest with a gloved fist, like she's trying to remind me that I've got her breastplate on. I suppose it helps boost my courage a *little*, although it is heavy as hell.

"And I won't be," Lar says, flapping his wings softly. They glow a gentle blue-gold as he gifts me with the briefest of smiles and tugs on one of his earrings again. "Can't risk stumbling into any visions or prophecies with that lot around. Good luck, Sunshine." With another flap of his wings and a puff of glitter and dust … the Caterpillar is gone and there's a butterfly drifting lazily through the air in his place.

Um. The hell did I just witness?!

I blink a few times and then turn to North, but he's focused on that walkway and whatever's at the end of it. One glance and I can already tell what's caught his attention: there are two men waiting just in front of the red doors. My nostrils flare and this … this *feeling* shoots through me, like a shooting star made of acid, burning its way into the depths of my soul. The Vorpal Blade on my thigh tingles, and the Queenmaker just begs me to wrap my fingers around the grip and fire.

They might look like men, but the creatures I'm staring at are fucking monsters.

Without meaning to, I step outside and then pause on the stone walkway, sliding my arms out of Chesh's and North's grips. The Duke immediately curls his tail around my ankle, but I'm too focused to care. The only time in my life I've ever felt this way about another person was when I was damn close to being raped. Those boys that attacked me, that subsequently killed my brother, they had the same aura as these men. Now, I'm not sure if I believe in such basic concepts as good and evil, but there are checks and balances in every facet of nature. On one end of the spectrum, there are cuddly kittens and puppies licking faces and batting balls of yarn … on the other end, are these guys.

Pure pond scum.

"What fun!" says the man on the right, the one with a massive pair of eagle wings protruding from his back. They should be pretty, like Tee's or Dee's, but instead, they're scraggly and scarred, casting strange shadows over the man's beak-like nose and too-full lips. He's 'handsome' enough, I suppose, following the unwritten rules of this world that every dude needs to be attractive, but there's a slimy quality to him that puts me immediately on edge.

"What *is* the fun?" I grind out as the King steps aside, his entourage parting like the Red Sea. He crosses his arms over his chest and looks right at me with eyes as dark as a starless night. His lashes are so goddamn long though, sweeping up and framing his expression of disdain with just the right amount of pretty.

"Why, *he* is," says the winged guy who I'm guessing must be the Gryphon. He nods his pointed chin in the direction of the King of Hearts. "It's all his fancy that: he never executes nobody worth executing, you know. Come on, have a stroll down here so we can have a look at you."

"Everybody says 'come on' here," I growl as I plant my feet firmly on the walkway and mimic the King's pose, crossing my arms under my breasts and lifting my chin in defiance. No way in hell I'm taking a single step closer to these men. "I never was so ordered about before in all my fucking life." Scowling, I spit and try not to look too closely at the other man. If the Gryphon scares the piss outta me, the Mocking Turtle is what makes up *his* personal nightmares. "Never. And I'm not about to start obeying orders now."

The Gryphon smirks, running his hand over his slicked-back brunette hair. It reminds me of John Travolta in *Grease*, just … way less attractive. Disturbing, really. It's hard to explain, but it's the very mundane blandness of this man that's scaring me. He's so unremarkable as to be remarkable, like a sterile white waiting room in a hospital with squeaky clean floors and the scent of iodine. Only, beneath it all, you can still smell the blood.

"Don't let them pull you in," Tee whispers from behind me, his calm, inner strength seeping into me when he puts a firm hand on one of my shoulders. "Don't let them get to you; that's what they're here to do."

"I can see why the guy on the right is called the Gryphon, but where did the name *Mocking Turtle* come from?" I whisper as Dee rests his chin on my right shoulder. The twins' clean mountain air scent wraps around me like a shield, calming my frantic heartbeat just a tad.

"Legend goes that he can bring any person to tears with a single word, and send them to the grave with a short story. He quite literally *mocks* his enemies to death." I'd laugh at Dee's words if I wasn't already starting to wonder if they were true. Turtle-Dick hasn't said a word yet, and I've already got the chills. *Click, click, click* go his fingernails as he clacks the pointed black tips together.

"And the Turtle part?" I breathe, just before I finally catch sight of his face and see the hooked shape of his upper lip. He smacks his jaws at me with a disturbing amount of force, and I notice that he hasn't got any damn teeth.

"Legend goes," Dee starts again, standing back up and putting his palm on my lower back for comfort, "that he bites like a snapping turtle."

"Oh? Is that all? Fantastic," I grind out as the two men start forward in disturbingly perfect unison, pausing only when Rab moves to cut them off. But they're close enough that I can *smell* them. There's the sharp, bitter scent of fresh soap with the underlying choke of rot, like roadkill left in the hot, hot sun. It makes me gag, which of course only makes them both smile.

When the Gryphon smiles, doves cry. When the Mocking Turtle smiles … angels die.

He looks at me with large eyes, as dark as the King's but without a hint of soul in them. There's just nothing there, like an endless void that leads to nowhere. Just staring into them makes me sick to my stomach, like I'm falling down that Rabbit-Hole all over again, only I'll never find a place to land. I step forward and put one of my hands on Rab's tattooed muscular forearm, remembering the feel of him catching me when I fell. Maybe, metaphorically, he's doing the same thing now? When he glances down at me and I see that ironclad calm, I know I'm in good hands. I guess I might forgive him for shooting Brandon. Maybe.

"This here young lady," says the Gryphon, glancing over at his bald-headed companion, "she wants to know your bloody history, I believe."

"I'll tell it to her," the Mocking Turtle replies in a deep, hollow tone, "so long as she doesn't speak a word till I've finished." He licks his gross lips with a thick, slimy tongue. "*Frederick*."

"Fuck you," I growl out, putting my hand on the Queenmaker. I saw what it did to the jubjub bird. I bet it could blow these men to bacon bits. How *dare* he bring up my brother's name. Even bigger question: how did he know it in the first place?!

"They're not really here," North says, squeezing my ankle even tighter with his muscular tail. I thought I hated the feel of it on me before, but now I think I'm starting to like it. That's what a surge of sex hormones will do to a person, I guess. "They're Recitations, just ghosts of their true selves."

"Well, I'd still like to blow them to queendom come," I say, whipping the pistol off my belt and using a flick of my right arm to open the chamber. With my left hand, I open one of the leather pouches on my belt and remove a fuse, metal ball, and a couple of fresh matches. One of these I strike, just so I can see it burn, smell the scent of sulfur. The other, I tuck behind my ear before I load the weapon and snap it closed. "I don't care about your bullshit; I just want to know what you're after."

"Hold your tongue," snarls the Gryphon, before I can finish telling him to fuck off. "Clearly you've missed a few classes at finishing school. When a person talks, it's only polite to listen. Can't you see he has a story to tell?"

"Now where was I?" the Mocking Turtle asks, glancing over at his companion. "Was I discussing Tweedledum and Tweedledee's dead family?" Both Dee and Tee stiffen up behind me, but they don't say anything. Good on them. I could practically spit I'm so fucking mad.

"No, I don't believe so," the Gryphon continues, rubbing at his chin thoughtfully. "Were you talking about that time the *former* King of Hearts tried to kill his own son? Or that *other* time the former King of Hearts cut up the White Rabbit's pet mouse and fed it to him?" My eyes dart over to the men in question, but neither of them reacts. Rab, actually, looks quite happy smoking a fresh cigarette.

The Mocking Turtle snaps his fingers as I grit my teeth in anger. There are so many revelations running through my mind right now, but I have to pick them apart later. Now is not the time.

"Oh, *that's* right," the Mocking Turtle says, turning to glance up at the very last bit of sun showing above the navy mountains. Very soon, it'll be full dark. At least there are two moons here, right? More silver moonbeams to cut through the horror of this meeting. "I was discussing her dead brother Frederick and how he had to die because the Alice is a whore."

"You son of a bitch," I snarl, snatching the match from behind my ear. I'd have lit it, too, if Rab hadn't curled his gloved fingers around my own. "Say that again and we'll see how well the Vorpal Blade can perform a castration."

"No, she's certainly never been to finishing school, a crude cunt like her," the Mocking Turtle says, adjusting his tie. Yes, he's wearing a suit. Both of these crazy men are. Unlike the Gryphon, I don't suppose the Mocking Turtle would be considered handsome by anyone. He's tall and muscular, but almost *too* muscular, like some kind of pre-human caveman species. That, and he has the most grotesque mouth I've ever seen with those hooked lips, toothless gums, and thick grimy tongue. "I'd like to put her into a class at the school of Reeling and Writhing, and then run her through the different branches of arithmetic: Addiction, Dissection, Mutilation, and Derision."

I remember this play on words in the original Lewis Carroll book, the Mock Turtle's strange twist on *addition, subtraction, multiplication, and division.* Only … you know, it wasn't so macabre. And compared to *this* turtle, that one wasn't so scary after all. Their lyrical nonsense doesn't frighten me though, no way, no how.

"Stop with the riddles and the bullshit. What do you want, and why do you give two shits about me?" My men—err, the hot Underland dudes I've been hanging out with—wait quietly behind me, providing a wall of support at my back.

"You *are* a simpleton, aren't you?" the Gryphon mocks, lifting his wings high up on his back. I wonder what species he is, as he's the only person I've seen with feathered wings other than Tee and Dee. But they were very clear: they're the only angels left alive in Underland. So what is this guy?

"If you insult the Alice again," North snarls, his accent clipped and sharp. Black, scaled wings explode from his shoulders, and his tail tightens around my ankle, squeezing to the point of pain. "Well, *nobody* insults a jabberwock's mate and lives to tell the tale."

"Shut your mouth," the Gryphon says, and I have to hold North back by grabbing his tail *tight* in my fist. "The last thing we need is the opinion of another useless, cursed male. We're here to speak to that slut of an Alice." The Duke crouches low and punches his fist into the stone walkway, leaving a crack and a mini crater in his wake. I'd try to comfort him, but I'm too busy watching the way the Gryphon and the Mocking Turtle watch *me*, like they're soaking me up, like they have sponges for eyes. My stomach twists in my gut, and bile rises in my throat.

Maybe Tee was right and this wasn't such a good idea?

"The Alice is like the sun that blasts away the shadows," the Turtle says, twisting his hand in a small half-circle. He summons darkness to his fingers, just like that. "But there's always an eclipse to look forward to, isn't there?"

"Eat shit," I say, whipping another match from the pouch on my belt, striking it, and lighting the pistol's fuse. The Turtle begins to laugh, head tilted back, his Adam's apple bobbing with the chortle. The Queenmaker launches my little cannonball into the air, and sends it right through the Turtle's apparition. It falls over the edge of the cliff, and explodes in a sea of fire that reaches the sky. "If you didn't come here to talk, then what is it that you want?"

"To state our intentions," the Turtle says. Just like I thought originally, he's clearly the leader of the two. "And let you know that there's only one future queen of Underland." His mouth stretches wide, flashing swathes of empty pink gums.

"There's a future queen of *Wonderland*," the King of Hearts says, but almost like he's bored. Apparently, their intimidation tactics don't work for shit on diagnosed socio or psychopaths. Oddly enough, I'd almost like the guy if I hadn't seen him murder one of the poor card servants earlier. "Underland won't last long."

The Mocking Turtle—let's call him M.T.—stretches his mouth into a grin, and I watch as he bends down and picks something up in his hand. I can't see anything until his fingers are curled around the creature. Only then do I realize he's holding a lobster, an animal unfortunate enough to actually be in the same plane as that nutjob which, in turn, makes me really glad that I'm *not*. I will take a Recitation any day, thank you.

The lobster's clearly still alive, claws waving around as the Turtle lifts it up to his face, opens his mouth so wide it looks like his jaw is coming unhinged, and then bites the thing's head clean off.

It might 'just' be a lobster, but I get the idea that M.T. would enjoy it just as much—or more—if it were a kitten or a puppy … or a human baby.

"Tastes like the sweet flesh of an angel infant," he says, licking his fingers as the Gryphon crows with laughter. Both Tee and Dee move around me, tearing their knives from their belts. But this meeting is done; we all know it.

"Get the fuck out of my kingdom," the King says, his voice like a sonic boom, just as powerful as the blast of the Queenmaker. With a snap of his fingers, he dismisses the two Recitations like fog in the wind. Their see-through visages shimmer and fade, ripped back through those red doors on the floating island. They slam shut, forming the shape of a heart and leaving nothing but the scent of rot and blood in their wake.

When the King turns back to look at me, bloodred hair dripping onto his forehead, I feel like I can see the hint of a cruel smile on his face.

"How do you feel about staying in Underland now, Alice?" he mocks, before waving his hand for Rab, the White Knight, and the soldiers to follow after him. The King of Hearts disappears inside the castle, and me, I disappear all the way up to my room.

"You have no idea how good it feels to lie down," I say, turning my head slightly to the right to look at Dee. His blue and black hair is rumpled, and his smile is sweet, but there's a shadow lingering across his face that mimics the darkness eating away at his brother's.

"We're only going to get a second alone," Tee says, pacing at the end of the bed, his boots shuffling against the shaggy white carpet. It's a very similar, err, rug to the one that Rab had in his house: white with purple spots—i.e., something's *skin*. Tee lifts his amethyst eyes to mine, sending a small shock through me. He's just so damn pretty, this fallen angel prince. "Whatever you do, don't mention the Looking-Glass. If we get a chance … no … *when* we get a chance, I'll take you through it. Allison, I'll take you home."

"Give me a few more days," Dee pleads, sitting up all of a sudden and running his fingers through his hair. "Give me a chance to show you what you can *do* here, all the changes you can make. Allison-who-isn't-Alice, you can turn Underland into Wonderland again, undo a hundred plus years of pain and suffering. You can fix it *all*."

Dee wiggles closer to me, sliding one of his wings underneath my body and making me shiver. What he doesn't know is that I've already sort of, kind of decided to stay. The night Tee and I first made love, he looked at me like I was changing his mind about Underland, too. How can I throw that away? And how can I possibly leave this place in the hands of the Red King, the Mad Hatter, and that freaking Turtle-Dick? What kind of person would I be? It'd be worse than handing Underland over to Henry VII (the shitty king who murdered all his wives). An uncontrollable shudder overtakes me.

Tee and I exchange a glance, and I swear, it's like he's reading my mind. His mouth twitches up at one corner.

"Who's this queen those assholes were talking about?" I ask, running my hands down my face. It's been … what? … a week and a half since I got here? And yet it feels like months. Years, even. But not in a terribly bad way. I mean, the Gryphon and the Mocking Turtle weren't particularly pleasant, but all they've really done is incentivize me to fight back.

"The Alice is the one, true queen of Wonderland," Tee says, his voice pitching low. From the look on his face, I can see right away that this isn't a subject he particularly wants to talk about. And yet … why? He's been nothing but forthright the entire time I've been here. What's so bad about this chick? "But if you liked the status quo … no, if you wanted things to get *worse*, how would you fight against a queen?" Tee blinks his dark-lined eyes nice and slow. "Only a queen can battle a queen."

"It's like a game of chess," Dee says, opening his azure eyes to look at me. "The king wants to be protected by a queen because in all reality, he's worthless." I prop my head up on a hand, breathing in nice and deep, past the sweet smell of sun-dried linens and soap, and pulling in two deep lungfuls of the twins' shared scent. "So the other three kings, they'll want to go toe-to-toe with us."

"The other kings?" I ask as Dee sits up and takes his shirt off, getting it tangled in his wings and then simply *tearing* the fabric off like some romance novel MMA fighter. My heart starts beating like crazy because I just *know* that I'll have to free his wings for him again tonight. In fact, I've been fantasizing about what *else* that magic kiss might lead to since I saw the twins in the garden this morning. "I thought those two psychos worked for the Walrus and the Carpenter?"

"The Carpenter and the Walrus," Tee growls, reversing my order, "aka the King of Clubs and his brother." He's scowling so violently his face looks like it might split in half. "The Carpenter currently wears the crown. But don't worry: I'm sure they'll take over the Kingdom of Diamonds or the Kingdom of Spades next, and then they'll *both* wear jewels on their filthy heads."

"Did somebody say jewels?" a voice asks, just before a bag appears out of thin air, turning over and spilling a sea of diamonds onto the carpet. "Because I've brought more presents." The Cheshire Cat's kitty head appears upside down, grinning wildly at me. "I've made all of this, you know. With just my love for you."

"You're not in love with me," I say, crossing my arms over my breasts, and over the silky soft perfection of my new sleeping gown. I was going to go all modern and wear a tank and panties—because they do have that shit here—but hot damn. How could any girl resist a nightie like this? Edith drools over crap like this in the Frederick's of Hollywood window all the time. Wait, though. Does that make this lingerie? Am I wearing lingerie right now?!

"Am so," the cat says, spinning his head around. His body appears next, like an ink drawing being traced into the warm air of the room. Outside, storm clouds have rolled over the castle grounds, and there's that same electric charge in the air from the other night. Wild magic, free magic, tainting and eating away at the landscape. I can't help but think how all of that power used to reside in the bodies of this world's women. Now, it's just a plague, like acid rain rolling across the landscape and poisoning everything in its path.

Is it any wonder that this whole world's gone mad?

"You are not," I say, throwing my feet over the edge of the bed and tucking them into fuzzy slippers with hearts on the toes. The King certainly has a thing for branding; all of his soldiers have sleeves of heart tattoos. Yeah. Not *one* heart tattoo, whole sleeves of red and black and gray. Or so Dee says. Hard to tell with all of that armor they wear. "And put those diamonds back where they came from. The last thing I want is to have my head lopped off for harboring stolen goods."

"Oh, the King would never lop *your* head off. Perhaps a stand-in dressed in blue and white. But never you, oh beautiful Alice." Chesh shifts in mid-air into his human form, and lands barefooted and quiet as a pussycat on the carpet. The look Tee throws him is one of supreme annoyance, but not outright hatred the way he looks at the King. Good sign, right?

"He may very well take *your* head then," I say, wondering if the cat is checking out my nipples again, and debating how hard I may or may not want to punch him in the nuts.

"Have you ever heard of taking a head when there's nothing but a head to take?" Chesh's body disappears for a moment before flickering back into place. "It just simply doesn't make sense."

"Do you just exist outside of this whole hierarchy then?" I ask, moving over to a small table near the door. There are tiny cakes and pies, a pot of hot water, and plenty of tea. There's a small part of me that considers drinking it, but then I remember where I am and what's at stake.

Somewhere in this castle, there's a Looking-Glass that leads to home. To Edith, to Dad, to … sort of Mom. And on the other side of these walls, there's a pair of mercenaries-for-hire and a mad king who wants to marry me. Either way, getting high on boosted tea is not a good idea. I pull open the door to a tiny cabinet that sits on the back of the table and find it full of FUCKING DRINK ME bottles and FUCKING EAT ME cakes. Hmm. I push it closed again and leave the small key in the lock where I found it.

"You mean why am I such an insolent little prick?" Chesh asks, coming up behind me and taking a bit of my hair in his hand. He sniffs it, and I reach back to slap him away. As soon as our skin brushes though … ugh, I'm done for. I can feel the chemistry between us brewing like a witch's cauldron. If I drank that shit, I'd probably turn into a frog. "The answer to that is simple, Alice."

"Is it now?" I ask, piling a plate high with sweets. I'll go on a diet when I get back home. Or not. Turning around, I eye the tall, lanky frame of the cat with a discerning gaze. I'm desperately trying to find *something* wrong with him. Like, if he had a huge, bulbous red nose with tons of pores and pimples then maybe I could pretend I don't find him attractive. But he doesn't. No, of course he has a small, triangular nose above his full, wide mouth. His striped ears twitch in his ebon dark hair, and his silver piercings catch the dancing flames from the fireplace. He's got a piercing in the center of his nose—a *septum* piercing—as well as one on either side of his lips, and hoops lining both his cat *and* human ears. "So what is the answer to your stupid riddle?"

"I'm a cat, of course." Chesh shrugs his muscular shoulders and then scratches at the line of dark hair below his belly button with long inked fingers tipped in pointed black nails. He swishes his tail as he grins at me, and I roll my eyes. I figure he followed the Duke here: he seems pretty overprotective of North. So why then is he in *my* room?

The doors to my bedroom fly open and in struts North, still dressed to the nines in his stupidly tight leather pants. His white shirt is still unbuttoned and flashing bronze skin, and his golden hair is shiny and straight, highlighting the wicked darkness of his horns. He flicks his tail and smashes it into the wall, rolling up his shirtsleeves as he does.

And right behind him is the Mad Hatter, the March Hare, and the Dormouse.

"This is a ridiculous violation of my rights," the Duke says, and he sounds *savage* all over again. My skin heats up, and his eyes whip over to mine, the corner of his mouth raising up in a small snarl. He thrashes his tail again, knocking a sugar dish to the floor and breaking it, then crosses his arms over his chest. "This bloodsucking demon is demanding a room in the Suit of Hearts—one of the *Suit*or's Rooms, to be specific."

"You're telling me," the Mad Hatter starts, tilting his lazy top hat in my direction, "that I'm asking too much? The Alice *is* my future bride, after all." His orange eyes flash as he smirks at me, taking in my nightgown with a very discerning edge. There's no doubt that *he* is checking out a whole lot more than just my nipples.

"You're a real piece of work, aren't you?" I ask as March helps himself to a heap of pink heart cookies from my table. He nibbles one and twitches a single brown ear in my direction, his dark eyes flicking to each of the twins and then over to the cat. I get the idea that the Mad Hatter is the brain of this operation, the Dormouse is the muscle, and the March Hare is the eyes, ears, and nose. He twitches his like he's scenting for something. "Like I didn't notice you disappeared the *second* the Gryphon and the Mocking Turtle showed up?"

"Calm down and have some wine, Alice," March says, blinking big brown eyes at me.

I grit my teeth and curl my hands into fists.

"I don't see any wine," I choke out as March tilts his head to one side.

"There isn't any," he says as Raiden chuckles. The Mad Hatter pulls his cane out from beneath his hat, tapping it on the floor as he makes his way over to one of the leaded glass windows next to my bed. He stops to gaze out at the pouring rain like it has all the answers.

"Then it wasn't very civil of you to offer it," I snap, raking my fingers through my tangled hair. It's time for bed—like *way* past time—and here I am with an entire harem of men in my room.

"It wasn't very civil of you to accept the Hatter's hand in marriage if you weren't going to let him stay in your Suit. A Suitor does belong in a Suit, after all, you must agree," March drawls lazily, snapping a heart cookie in half. The Dormouse grunts from behind him, and I see this quick flash of annoyance on March's face as he turns to look at the much bigger man. Dor has a Neanderthal's thick head, and arms that are hairier than the Cheshire Cat's fluffy tail. Gross.

"This girl don't look like much to me," Dor grumbles, shaking his head and ruffling up his brown hair with thick fingers. "Don't see why we're even bothering. Let's kill her and the jabberwock and be done with it."

"You are most certainly not qualified to comment on muchness," March growls with a dramatic roll of his eyes, finishing his last cookie and taking up a cupcake next. "You're not much in the way of muchness, yourself." Dor narrows his eyes like this is the worst insult he's ever heard in his life while I'm standing there trying to puzzle out what their fucking conversation is even about.

"Certainly it's standard for a Suitor to live in the Suit," North interrupts, digging his dragon nails into his palm and making himself bleed. I start to move over to stop him when Chesh rubs his cheek against the Duke's shoulder and lets out a fierce purr. After a moment, the Duke of Northumbria stops and gives Chesh a scratch behind the ears, visibly less upset than he was a moment ago. "But Miss Liddell has only just arrived, and it's custom for the primary to assign each man his Suit."

"Tee is my primary," I blurt, and all the men turn to look in the twin's direction.

"The King is the primary, surely," North starts, but I'm already shaking my head and waving my arms.

"No, no, nope. No fucking way. You tell that asshole if he wants to play ball" —I pause because that reference is clearly lost on these guys— "metaphorical croquet with me, he'll listen to my demands. The first is that Tee and Dee stay with me at all times." My throat clogs up, and I have to force the next words past my lips. "And the Duke."

Oh, and the look he gives me … it's so savage.

"Well, then," March says, drawing a key out of the front pocket of his velvet trench, "you'll be wanting this then."

"The Queen's Key," Dee chokes out, and he looks like he's about to have a heart attack. "Where did you get that?!"

"I pinched it, of course. The King should take better care of his things, don't you think?" He flicks the key in my direction, and I just barely manage to snatch it out of the air, uncurling my fingers to find a gold key with a heart on both ends, one big and one small. When I look up, March gives me this slow, dangerous little smile before pointing over to one of the paintings on the wall.

I follow along and glance over at the framed art piece. It's an intricately rendered oil painting based on John Tenniel's—the original illustrator of the Alice books—illustrations. Or … is it the other way around? This particular painting is of the Mad Hatter, mouth open as he sings *Twinkle, Twinkle Little Bat* to Alice. The only difference between this piece of art and the original, is the small gold lock in the center of the Hatter's bow tie.

"Oh for fuck's sake," I whisper as I shuffle across the carpet, the men's eyes following my every move. As soon as I lift up the key and touch it to the painting, it slides into the lock and turns. The entire frame swings forward as I step back and find myself looking into a long stone hallway dotted with torches in the shape of top hats.

My eyes narrow as I turn to look at Raiden Walker, vampire-mercenary extraordinaire.

"Remember when I agreed not to leave the Duke naked in jabberwocky territory?" the Mad Hatter asks, twisting his hat around on his head. It keeps spinning long after it should've stopped. "This is all I asked for in currency. Well, this and a million coins." He flashes a vampire grin, strides up to me, and leans down to whisper in my ear. "Remember: not until you *beg*." He stands up and just laughs when I punch him as hard as I can in the arm.

"You can sleep in there with the door *locked*," I grind out, pausing to glance over my shoulder at the March Hare and the Dormouse. "But they have to go." The look Dor throws me in that moment is pure hatred. If the Hatter let him off his leash, he'd probably tear me into little pieces and lap up the blood.

"Dor will go; March stays." Raiden turns to go and then pauses, nose twitching as he glances back at the twins. He studies them for a long, agonizing moment, and then smiles. It's not a very nice fucking smile, I must say. "I thought I smelled angels. Interesting." With an exaggerated wink, he saunters down the red runner that covers the hallway's stone floor.

"Boss!" the Dormouse calls out, but March is already chucking his cupcake wrapper in the big man's face.

"Stay, *pet*," he drawls with a sneer, pausing to turn and bow for me. *Technically*, he's being respectful, but I sense this nibble of mischief eating its way into his smile as he stands up, steals a few small pies from my table, and heads for the hallway.

Tee shoves the painting closed behind him, and I hear the very distinct click of a lock sliding into place.

"You know where the exit is," he snaps at the Dormouse, and it looks like the big man is seconds away from tearing Tee's wings off his back. As if on cue, the grandfather clock in the corner of my room chimes, and the twins' wings fold back into their body with the sound of clanging chains. The look of anguish on Tee's face makes Dor grin.

"Cursed fuck," he grumbles, putting his meaty hand on the doorknob and turning it.

"Woman-less prick," Dee calls out, and I see Dor's shoulders tightens as he rips the door open, storms out, and slams it closed behind him. Some of the tension clears from the air as I finger the gold key in my hand.

"Why would Raiden be interested in angels?" I ask, because it feels like I might be missing something here. That statement, it wasn't at all random.

"Angel blood sends vampires into Frenzies," Chesh says, pouring himself some cream in a chipped tea cup. He doesn't actually add any tea, just licks the cream out and purrs again. It's kind of hot, actually—probably because the hand holding the tea cup is covered in tattoos.

"Frenzies?" I ask as Tee scowls and takes his cap off, reaching out to drop it on a hook near the door. As he extends his arm, the gold hook stretches out and takes the hat from him. It's fucking creepy as hell. *Note to self: have that shit removed in the morning.*

"Doesn't matter," Tee says as he starts to unbutton his coat. "There are only two angels left in Underland, and he won't be drinking from either of them."

"Either of *us*," Dee says with a roll of his blue eyes. "Only crazy people talk about themselves in the third person."

"Contrariwise," Tee says as he shrugs out of his military jacket *and* his shirt. I try my best not to drool. "I'm the only sane person here besides Allison; I make the rules." Dee grins and slumps back into the pillows, watching me carefully as I pick up and nibble on a pink star cookie with little sprinkles in the shape, size, and color of pearls.

"So, are there nine suites … I mean *Suits* in here?"

"Sure are," Dee says, fluffing his pillow and snuggling into it. It doesn't look like he has any intention of moving off my bed. "*Nine big cocks.*"

"They didn't all have to be big, you know. The Alice is bound to get exhausted. A few medium-sized ones would've been appreciated." Chesh and Dee both laugh, Tee's cheeks look a tad pink, and North's eyes sweep me in my nightgown appreciatively.

"Sorry I can't help with that last request," he growls out, and I grind my teeth.

"So … what happened between you two anyway? I mean, other than sex," Dee asks, and he doesn't sound at all upset by that. What a weird change from back home. In my world, these two guys would be beating the shit out of each other, squirting testosterone all over the damn room. Gross. I like this better.

"I had to tame the beast," I say with a loose shrug of my shoulders. "It was a stressful morning." Just *thinking* about that giant bat is giving me the heebie-jeebies. Not because of the bat though, just the height. Ugh. Next time, I'm riding North.

Heh.

Riding North. Get it?

"Thank fuck for that," Chesh says, sliding his tongue in a circle around his full mouth to clean off the cream. His tongue is longer than a normal person's. Can't decide if it creeps me out … or if I'm sort of curious to see what he could do with it. "It's been quite a long time since the Savage Duke has had anyone in his bed. I should know; I usually sleep at the end of it."

He flashes a fang when the Duke reaches out and absently scratches Chesh on the top of the head.

"Are you two lovers or something?" I ask, tilting my head to one side, white-blonde hair sliding over my shoulder. The rainbow streaks are still there. If anything, they seem even brighter than when I left. Not the weirdest thing I've seen since I got here, so who gives a shit?

"Lovers?!" North asks, completely and utterly aghast. He even puffs out his chest in indignation. At first I think he's about to go on an anti-gay rant, and I get my feathers all ruffled. "Are you quite serious? The Cheshire Cat is my *pet*."

"Meow," Chesh says with a grin, curling his hand into a little paw and then teasing me with it, like a cat batting at some yarn. "You hear that: his *pet*."

"Where are the rest of your people?" I ask, because he can't possibly be the only cat person in the entire world.

Wrong question to ask apparently.

Chesh shuts down and looks away at the same time Tee sighs. We exchange a look and the expression on his face tells me all I need to know.

Maybe Chesh *is* the last of his people?

"How did you two meet?" I ask as Chesh moves over to my bed and crawls onto the end of it, stretching the full length of his body out on the red comforter. His tail twitches lazily and his right ear swivels in my direction to listen.

"He showed up bloody and soaked to the bone on my doorstep," North says, looking at me with a very serious expression in his gold eyes. "How else does one acquire a *pussy*?" This last part just oozes out of his mouth, dripping with carnal decadence.

Getting a straight answer out of these people is damn near impossible.

There's another knock on the door, and I sigh, reaching out to open it. I'm fearing the worst, expecting the King of Hearts and his ostentatious entourage. Instead, it's Rab and Lar, waiting with torches in hand.

"I thought we'd never get out of there," Rab says, his white ears twitching on the top of his head. He blinks red-red eyes at me and then tilts his head to the side. "Well, aren't you going to invite us in?"

With another sigh, I step back and welcome the two men into the room.

We've got a full house in here now, but I don't really mind. I'll be going home eventually and … then I'll be all alone again. See? Doesn't it make more sense for me to stay here? I'm starting to truly believe it does.

Sucking in a sharp breath, I run my hand down my face. I'm no idiot. It's pretty clear all *these* idiots think they're sleeping in here tonight. Not sure why. Even if I *were* inclined to take nine lovers, it'd be nice if I got some say in the matter.

Lar unfurls his butterfly wings, that blue and gold shimmer reflecting the light from the fire. I wonder if he's got another prophecy? If he does, I'm not sure if I want to see it. If I'm going to get eaten by a giant bird tonight, I'd at least like to sleep first. But all he does is relax his wings until they're dragging on the floor.

"The King likes to work us until we can't stand up anymore," Rab says with a sigh, sitting down hard in an upholstered chair and letting his head fall back. "Prick." He crosses his legs at the ankle, his feet bare, like he's already dressed for bed. The long-sleeved black nightshirt and black and white striped sweats add to the ambiance of comfort. I doubt he was assassinating people for the King of Hearts dressed in that.

"These walls do talk," Lar says, playing with the gold bracelets on his arm. He lets his ice-blue eyes slide over to mine, catching my gaze. There's so much emotion packed in there, I can't even begin to unwrap it, so I look away. "Even in the Alice's room."

"No," Rab says, lifting his head for a moment. His voice is like the howl of the winter wind, chilling and intriguing all at once. "The King certainly isn't *that* stupid, bugging little Sonny over here? Does he know what a praying mantis does after it mates?"

"Are you insinuating that I'm going to fuck the King or that I'm going to eat his face off … or both? I'm not sure which of those things is more offensive." I take my plate of sweets and my tea over to the bed. It says it's chamomile. I've changed my mind about drinking it; I figure even if it's boosted, it oughta put me to sleep, right?

"All I'm saying is that you have the power to kill the King." Rab shrugs, and then smiles, the expression making it painfully obvious that he is, indeed, a psychopath. Only a true crazy person can smile like that, like a knife cutting its way across the face. I half-expect to see blood spill. "I'm glad to see you alive though. Quite the surprising treat."

"Why, thank you," I quip as Lar shrugs out of his jacket. Tee watches him for a moment before heading to one of the dressers and pulling out a pair of pajamas for both himself and his brother. Doesn't surprise me that their pj's are already in 'my' room. This is what the King's been expecting this whole time, for me to show up here. "I'm also quite glad to be alive."

Rolling my eyes, I settle into the pillows again and start to deconstruct one of the fancy little toadstool cupcakes. The top is covered in some sort of red modeling chocolate with little white spots. It really does look like a mushroom. Underneath the cap though, there's a creamy fudge filling that tastes a bit like hazelnuts.

"My prophecies tonight …" Lar starts, making up a cup of tea. "They were quite disturbing." I notice his shoulder-length hair dancing in a magical breeze. It teases the strands and stirs the white fabric of his shirt, but it doesn't touch anything else. He's brimming with power; I can practically smell it. I'd hate to see what happens when the Caterpillar gets pissed.

"Flames and blood, the stench of death. It was like the post-Riving all over again." Rab accepts the cup from Lar's long, pale fingers, and takes a sip, closing his eyes with a small groan. "The Walrus and the Carpenter were unmistakably present."

"They want to put their own queen on the throne," I repeat, staring into my own tea cup. I remember Lar saying he could read tea leaves. I'd like to see that sometime. That is some straight-up *Harry Potter* shit right there. "And then do what?"

"Dismantle the four kingdoms, make them one again," Lar says as Tee disappears behind the bathroom curtain and starts to strip. I can't help but watch his shadow as he undresses. Crap. What am I going to do with these guys? I've got to take them home with me, right? I mean that's what Tee wants. Dee, I'm not so sure about. If I did leave, and I took his brother with me, would he come or would he stay? "Except, they don't want to restore order; they want to maintain ironclad control. They're both sociopaths, the Walrus and the Carpenter. Lewis Carroll used to be their soothsayer, you know?"

"How is that possible?" I ask, putting my tea cup down on the saucer so loudly that the clink makes me cringe. "That'd make them both over a hundred and fifty years old."

"Time is relative to some," Rab says, lifting up his shirt to show off the ticking clock in the center of his chest. "They're both—*relatively*—immortal."

"If they're immortal, then how am I supposed to kill them?" I ask, lifting an eyebrow.

"I said immortal, not invincible," Rab replies, his voice like an icy breeze on the back of my neck. It makes all the hairs on my arms stand on end … and heats up a warm pool in my lower belly. Told ya I was attracted to crazy people. I must be damaged, but I suppose that's okay—I'm pretty sure everyone else here is, too. "They can still be killed; that's your job, Sonny."

"Marry the King. Kill the bad guys. Save the world." I keep my gaze focused on my tea for a moment, and then chug the rest of it in a single sip. "Sounds easy enough." Just a few days ago, I would've taken this shit in stride because I wouldn't have planned on doing any of it. Hell no. I was ready to run home like a rabbit down its hole.

But not anymore.

Now I'm freaked the fuck out.

Because I'm pretty sure I'm *not* going home until I make some positive change here in Underland.

"Now get the fuck out of my room, so I can go to sleep." I poke the Cheshire Cat with my toe as North moves over to stand beside me. My heart starts to pump, and I can't help but lift my head to look up at him. He smells like sandalwood and musk, and it's making me feel a little dizzy.

"I have my own wing here," he says, bending down next to me and taking a knee. His gold hair feathers across his forehead, and I have the strangest urge to brush it away with my fingertips. Instead, I bite my lip and pretend my nipples aren't so hard they hurt. "But I'd be honored if you'd give me access to one of your Suits. After all, as your future husband, it only makes sense."

"Listen buddy," I start, but he's got such a sincere look in his gold eyes … plus, you know, that bloody beautiful accent. I just shrug and gesture at the other paintings on the wall. There are nine, now that I think to count them. "Be my guest."

"Wonderful," North declares, rising to his booted feet before leaning down and capturing my lips with his. My first response is to stiffen up and punch him in the nuts. Instead, I end up groaning and leaning into the kiss, enjoying the feel of his tongue sliding against mine. He tastes like a good chai latte, nice and spicy and sweet all at the same time. When he pulls away, I'm breathless and wanting, a boat adrift without an anchor. I almost reach for him, but end up curling both hands into fists. "The moral of the story is: if you need me, you have but to call." He steps back and gives me this hungry, half-lidded look that undoes me completely. "*Oh, 'tis love, 'tis love, that makes the world go round!*"

North sings this last bit as he rises to his feet and snaps his fingers. With a growl, the Cheshire Cat shifts back into furry form and lets the Duke pick him up, stroking his back with long, sure fingers.

"I will see you in the morning for practice," he says with a sharp nod. "It wouldn't do to have an Alice who can't fight."

North pulls a ring of keys from his pocket, removes one, and leaves the rest on the bench at the end of the bed. He approaches another painting, this one of a jabberwock, and uses the key to unlock the door that the giant black dragon's just busted through. With a salute, he passes inside and closes it behind him.

"You may as well help yourself to some keys," I say, gesturing at Lar and Rab. "Because I get the feeling you're not going to leave me alone until I give you each one." Setting my food aside, I crawl into the blankets to wait them out. Maybe if I pretend to be asleep, I'll be left alone? I'm just *so fucking tired* right now.

Besides, I figure after Rab and Lar leave, I'll kiss the twins to free their wings. And maybe … something else, too.

I'm asleep before Tee finishes tucking me in.

The night is as dark as velvet when I wake next, studded with stars that twinkle like fine diamonds. Both Tee and Dee are asleep on either side of me, but they look exhausted, so I do my best not to wake them up. I feel bad that I conked out before I could free their wings, but I suppose there's time for that later. Instead, I kick the covers back and slide carefully off the edge of the mattress. Tee stirs and blinks his eyes open for a moment, but when he sees me slip behind the bathroom curtain, he closes them again.

I make sure to pee before I try anything else; I have a feeling Tee and Dee are going to be more cautious with me from now on. Last time I snuck out, I was kidnapped by the Mad Hatter. Maybe not the best idea in the world to sneak out again, but I want to see a bit of the castle without an entourage. I could wake the twins and ask them to show me the place, but I need a minute alone to think. But only a minute. Alone and lonely are two entirely different things, but back home, I was alone so much that I *became* lonely. I really do prefer the company of these men—even if they're all mad.

Slipping on a furred crimson robe, I tiptoe to the door and let myself out into the hallway. The stones are cold beneath my feet, but the torches on the walls seem to give off an unnatural amount of heat and light.

This place is huge, at least four or five times the size of the Duke's place and that was a fucking palace to me. Padding softly across the stone floors of the upper level, I just start checking doors. Most of them are locked which frustrates the hell out of me. Of *course* they're locked. The few that open lead to empty bedrooms or sitting rooms. I feel like Belle, exploring the Beast's castle, looking for the forbidden wing. Now, if the furniture starts talking, I'll have really seen it all.

"If you're in search of the Looking-Glass," a voice says from the shadows, "then rest assured: it's well-guarded. The Walrus will never find his way into your world."

"It's not the Walrus I'm worried about," I say, curling my hands into fists as the King steps out of the shadows. He's dressed in a *suit* this time. Yes, a suit. A black suit with a black undershirt, well-pressed slacks, and shiny white loafers with hearts on the toes. His tie is even covered in hearts.

He moves forward to stand beside me, looking even older than he did outside on the croquet-ground, like he's in his late twenties, possibly early thirties. Or maybe it's just the suit?

"It's me. I need to be able to go home when I'm ready." I cross my arms over my chest. Even if I was just caught snooping, I'll remain obstinate. It's one of my better traits.

"Home? You are home, Alice. Your bloodline descends from Wonderland." The King pushes gloved fingers through his bloodred hair as I examine the scar on his neck. It reminds me of his guillotine, and the pile of headless bodies bleeding next to it. The Gryphon mentioned something about the former King of Hearts trying to kill his own son; is the King's scar related to that? My guess would be *yes*. No wonder the guy's a cranky asshole.

"Yeah, but *I* don't. I'm not from here. And I have a sister, a dad … and a mother back home that need me." There's not a single doubt in my mind that that's true. They all might treat me like I don't exist, like I'm not important, like I don't matter. But they all lost Fred, and I know that if they lost me, too, then his death would seem like it was for nothing at all. I can't do that to them, even if the more selfish parts of me would rather stay here in Underland forever. I'll stay *awhile*, and then I'll go home. That makes sense, right?

"There's an entire world that needs you here," the King says, his voice full of quiet, commanding strength. "Stop being so selfish." His lips turn down in a frown as his ebon eyes sweep over me. He exhales a long, tired sigh and shakes his head. "I've never put that much faith in the prophecy *or* the Alice, but really, you're still a disappointment."

My blood boils, and I step forward, into a shaft of silver moonlight. I can feel that strange tingling in my fingertips again, the power collecting in my hands. Guess beheading would be a real possibility if I accidentally, like, zapped the King, right?

"You're one to talk," I snap, feeling anger overtake me in a crimson wave. "You killed that poor card for no reason." When I close my eyes, I can still see its silently screaming face. And all that blood …

The King just smirks at me, a perfect twist of the lips that would have any girl swooning.

But I'm not just any girl—I'm a cynical asshole. We're a special breed.

"Good. Just continue to deny your destiny. It'll give me more fodder when I put you on trial and have you deported. Oh, you'll get to home for sure—but on my terms. Trust me Alice: getting rid of you is now my number one priority." The King turns to leave, but I stop him with a hand on his arm. I half-expect to have my ass handed to me by the palace guards, but there don't seem to be any around right now.

We're well and truly alone.

"Why did you bring me here if you're just planning on sending me home anyway?" I ask, hearing my voice crack with frustration. If I didn't know better … I'd say I hurt the prick's feelings? But no, that can't possibly be it. The King's hair glints in the moonlight, as red as fresh blood from an open wound.

"I will have you, Alice. You've always been destined to be mine." Why did he say that if he wanted to get rid of me all along anyway? It doesn't make any sense. No, I smell a bruised ego. I bet he thought I'd stumble into the castle, fall all over him, simper my undying love … Ew.

"There are still idiots who believe in the prophecy," he says, looking down at me. No, he towers over me, *lords* over me like he owns the fucking place. I mean, I guess technically he does, but I've always had a problem with authority, so screw him. "Like Tweedledee for example. And if I can't appease the simpletons, I could very well have a riot on my hands. But don't worry, Alice. All I needed was for you to fail, and you're doing an excellent job at that already."

The King starts moving as my fingers loosen on his arm, his footsteps loud as he heads down the dark hallway in the opposite direction from my room. I wait until he's out of sight and then lean my back against the stone wall, sinking to the floor with my robe and nightgown billowing around me.

I never asked for any of this.

So why the hell do I feel so goddamn bad about it all?

It's not my responsibility. What should I care if the King makes a fool of me before he sends me home? It's what I want anyway. I should be *happy* about it.

And yet … I'm not.

Not at all.

I feel like crying, like the original Alice from the storybook, shedding so many tears that I flood the entire castle. But I don't cry anymore, remember?

Brushing a small bit of liquid off my face, I stand up and shake the feelings off before I make a liar out of myself.

Instead of crying, or running away … I'll just have to prove the King of Hearts *wrong*.

Chapter Four

Lost in a Quintrille

"Rise and shine, Allison-who-isn't-Alice," Dee says, stroking a finger down the length of my nose. "We've got a busy day today. Breakfast with the King, training with the Duke, and your dress fitting for the ball."

"A ball?" I ask with a groan, pushing Dee's hand away from my face. "How cliché is this place?"

"Clichés are simply repeated patterns," Dee says, grabbing the pillow I've just chucked over my face and prying it from my sleepy fingers. "They couldn't even be clichés unless we repeated them. A princess arrives at the castle, and we have a ball. It all fits the story, you see."

"All I want to see are the backs of my own eyelids," I say, but my blankets are being thrown off and onto the floor. Dee is already dressed in his usual outfit: painted on black denim jeans, a button-up shirt, and his blue and black military coat. He's even got his peaked cap nestled onto his blue-streaked black hair.

"Breakfast is always served in the garden," he says, setting a stack of clothes on the bed next to me. I recognize Edith's dress right away and my heart catches in my chest. When I'm home, I hate her. Now that I'm here, I miss her terribly. "And lunch today will be served in the solarium. Training with the Duke will take place in the athletic facility between meals, and your fitting will be later this afternoon."

"Where's Tee?" I ask groggily, rubbing at my face as Dee brings over a cup of tea and carefully places it on the intricately carved nightstand next to the bed. The top is made out of a piece of red quartz in the shape of a heart. Back home, I'd have flipped my lid to own furniture even half this nice—or this cool. No boring oak shit here. No, everything I look at is a piece of art, something different. Sometimes it's kooky, sometimes it's ugly, but it's always interesting.

Can't say that about home.

"He's with the King; they all are," Dee says, nodding his head at the paintings on the wall. "But he shouldn't be long. We're yours now. We'll be spending all our time with you." Dee lifts his chin in the direction of my tea. "Drink up. It has a light energy boost in it, that's it. It won't fuck you up." He winks at me, claps his heavy steel-toed boots together, and offers up a salute. "Soldier's honor, miss."

"Can I wear something else?" I ask, rubbing the white apron of the dress between my fingers. This dress represents the conundrum inside my head and heart; I don't want to wear it right now.

"You can wear whatever you like," Dee says, opening the closet door and moving over to a row with dozens … maybe *hundreds* of outfits in glittering high-def.

Jesus.

Edith would shit her pants for this. Maybe she should've been the Alice? We were at the same party after all. In fact, she had to *beg* me to go. What if this is all some sort of mistake, and I'm stealing my little sister's destiny? I watch Dee walk back toward me, thinking that maybe he should've been hers.

That thought *infuriates* me.

I push the stack of clothes aside and stand up suddenly, throwing my arms around Dee's neck and pressing my lips to his. As soon as I do, I feel it, that power exchange between us. The air smells fresh and crisp, a mountain high that swirls around us. Dee's jacket explodes outward to make room for his wings, the fabric billowing in the rush of magic.

We have a bright citrus-y kiss, like spring and lemonade. I smell flowers and an easy breeze, my tongue tangling with Dee's as he wraps his arms around me and lifts me off my feet. Only my toes are touching now, and just barely. The fingers of my right hand tangle in his hair, while I use my left to shove the chains from his wings.

They hit the floor in a clanging heap, echoing around the circular bedroom.

"The King will be furious," Dee whispers against my mouth after a moment. But I don't care. If the twins are supposed to belong to me, then I'll damn well do with them what I want. And what I want are their wings, free and clear. Not that I mind kissing them every day, but I want to find the witch that cursed them and get rid of this spell. Whoever she is, she's going to be sorry when I get my hands on her.

Dee wraps his wings around us like a cocoon, cutting us off from the outside world. I love that, feeling safe inside his feathers. His breath stirs my hair as I look up into his sapphire eyes, sliding my hands over his shoulders to tickle his feathers.

You just met this dude, my brain continues, ever the persistent optimist. And yet, I can't bring myself to care. I *like* being around Dee, more than I ever liked being around Brandon or … Liam. Especially Liam. And the sex is better, too. If Liam weren't already dead, I'd go back home with the Vorpal Blade and the Queenmaker, and I'd kill him myself.

"You let me worry about the King," I say, stepping back and enjoying the soft brush of Dee's feathers against my bare arms and shoulders. After last night, I'm more determined than ever to piss the asshole monarch off. After all, who was the focus of the prophecy? Not him. *I* am the one who's supposed to save Underland, so who the fuck does he think he is? You know, besides the ruler of an entire country.

It's virtually impossible for me to leave an asshole that smug, that arrogant alone. Nah, it's my job in life to bring him down a notch or two.

"By the way," I start, making my way over to the row of clothes and putting my hands on my hips. "What's the King's name?"

"It's Brennin," Dee says, pausing next to me and reaching out to finger an outfit that's eerily similar to his own that's hanging on the rack next to the one with all the dresses. "Brennin Red."

"Red, huh?" I ask, grabbing the outfit Dee's touching off the rack and taking it from the hanger. The jacket and button-up are basically identical to his, save the color which, of course, is *red*. There are no jeans though, just a pleated red skirt. I like it though. Boots and pleated skirts are sort of my thing. Drives Edith nuts. "You people like to keep things themed, huh?" I move over to one of the stands in the center of the room, the top encased in glass with a black velvet cushion beneath, laden with jewels. There are drawers down the side of it where undergarments are kept. Shocker: all the panties are white with red hearts on them. Bras, too.

I drop my nightgown to the ground and glance over my shoulder to find Dee watching me, his eyes half-lidded and burning. When he flicks his gaze up from my ass to my face, a slow smile takes over his mouth.

"The King likes to keep things branded," he says, his voice husky as I turn away with a chuckle and get dressed, slipping into the skirt which hits at mid-thigh, my new bra, and the button-up shirt. I leave the panties for last and then decide to tuck them into the front pocket of Dee's jacket instead. The look he gives me is freaking priceless. He cups his palm over the pocket and smiles lasciviously. "He's a very controlling individual, as if you couldn't tell."

"Well then." I shrug into the red and black military coat, sweep my hair out from under the collar, and step into a pair of boots before turning around to throw a feisty smirk Dee's way. "Let's go get breakfast with Brennin *Red* then. If that piece of shit thinks I'm going to call him *Your Majesty,* then he's got another thing coming."

As soon as we step into the back garden, I start to hear voices.

Panic surges through me and for the briefest of moments, I wonder if I really am crazy, if I've dreamt this whole thing up. They say schizophrenia sets in during puberty, right? I mean, I'm way past puberty—I started my period at age twelve—but there's still a chance, isn't there?

"I can see right up your skirt, and you're not wearing any skivvies," a matronly voice says from near my right ankle. With a squeak, I jump and slap my hands over my ass, glancing back to glare at Dee. I'm expecting a servant—maybe a human one this time—but instead, I don't see anything but the handsome man with the azure eyes looking at me curiously. "And if you're not going to wear skivvies, could you at least have manicured down there?" the voice continues from somewhere in the cluster of daffodils.

On closer inspection … I realize that the voice isn't coming from inside the cluster. No, the daffodils are fucking talking.

I did not see any of this shit when I was mini and creeping through the small garden door. Think I would've noticed if the local flora had nasty, judgmental attitudes.

"What the fuck …?" I start as the flower scoffs at me. "You can talk?!"

"We *can* talk—provided there's anyone worth talking to," replies a tiger-lily from the next garden bed. They're laid out in color coordinated rows, creating a beautiful waving rainbow effect from where we stand, all the way out to the exterior walls where the roses drip with blood. I can smell it from here, the metallic copper bite mixed with the sweet cloying smell of rot.

"Soon as I saw you," the daffodil continues, tugging at the lace of my boot with one of her leaves, "I said to the others, 'Her face has got *some* sense in it, though it's not a clever one!'"

The flowers chortle in unison, waving in the breeze.

"If you don't hold your tongues, I'll pick you," Dee says, putting his boot dreadfully close to the face of the bitchy daffodil. When I bend down and squint, I can just make out her tiny eyes. She's most definitely glaring at me. And then, as we stand there, she lifts her leaves up and makes a gesture that I'm pretty sure is meant to convey a staunch *fuck off* message.

"Talking flowers," I say to Dee as I stand up. "I never thought of that before."

"It's *my* opinion that you never think *at all*," the red rose says.

"I never saw anybody that looked stupider," a violet chimes in, just before Dee bends down and plucks several of the flowers up by their stems. My mouth hangs open in shock as he lifts up the bouquet—now containing a daffodil, tiger-lily, rose, and violet—and hands it over to me. Blood drips from the stems, and I feel bile rise in my throat.

"What have you done?" I choke out as I feel leaves pummeling my calves.

"He's just plucked my prettiest blossom," the matronly voice says, coming from a different daffodil. "What a foul, lazy, useless beast. It's no wonder that his people went extinct!"

Dee plucks another daffodil and adds it to the bunch.

"The flowers are inhabited by pixie spirits," Dee says, pushing the bouquet closer to me. The blood has mostly stopped dripping, though there are spatters of it all across the white gravel. "If you pick one flower, they just move onto another."

"Eat shit," one of the roses says, ruffling up its petals. I carefully extract the bouquet from Dee's hand, feeling our fingers brush together in the process. Heat suffuses my cheeks, and I try to pretend that I don't see the majority of the men sitting at a table under a gazebo, watching us.

Dee lifts his wings for a moment, shading my face from the sun before he leans in and puts his lips close to my ear.

"I'm afraid," he says, but I just turn my face and kiss him again, lifting up my right hand to push his wing out of the way so that everyone can see. *Fuck you, Brennin Red. You might be* a *king, but you're not* my *king*. I'm an American, goddamn it. We don't respond well to authority.

"Don't be; I've got you."

I turn and follow the winding path through the garden over to the table where the King sits front and center, his arms crossed over his chest, his ebon eyes sliding over my shoulder to glare at Dee.

But … he doesn't say anything.

Lucky him.

When Brennin looks back at me, I can see the smallest hint of a smile on his face. It's not a pleasant expression though, not even close.

"Good morning, *Alice*," he says, putting such a strong emphasis on my name that I know it's on purpose. He gestures for me to take a seat opposite him, opposite all the men really. On the opposite side of this table, there are nine seats.

And just me on this side.

Dee makes his way around me and sits on the far end, opposite his brother. I can feel Tee watching him, watching me, taking in the situation. His wings are next, preferably if I can kiss him in front of both the King and the Hatter.

Just taking in the row of male specimens, I can sense it: two supreme alpha assholes.

"Well, well, aren't we looking lovely this morning?" Raiden Walker oozes, his purple velvet top hat sliding forward on his head, the brim casting the most perfect of shadows across his marmalade colored eyes.

"Eat shit, asshole," I say, turning to the King. "This man tried to kill your Duke, tried to sell me to the King of Clubs, and blackmailed his way into the castle. And you're going to sit here and have breakfast with this piece of crap?"

The Mad Hatter throws his head back and laughs at me, flashing fang.

"You're one very brave woman," Raiden says as the King's mouth lifts up at the edge again. He's wearing the same suit from last night. Would not have surprised me if he wore it all night and never slept. Do villains really need to sleep? Or do they just run off evil batteries? He probably charges them by kicking puppies and burning books.

"Not really," I say with a sneer, sitting down and popping my bloody bouquet into a glass of ice water. "I just don't like you." I tap my nails on the table and let my gaze drift to North, sitting on the King's left. Chesh is next, then Lar, with Dee on the end. On the opposite side, the Hatter sits next to March, Rab, and Tee. Behind Raiden and March, there's a host of palace guards … and Dor.

I really, really, really don't like Dor.

The way he's looking at the back of North's head is scaring the skirt off me. The dragon … err, jabberwock … seems to know he's being hunted though. His tail is thrashing violently against the white and red stone patio, and he keeps looking over his shoulder. I wonder how Dor caught him off guard in the first place? He's not a man easily taken advantage of.

"You don't like me?" the Hatter asks, taking off his purple hat and revealing a marmalade colored one underneath that matches his eyes. Instead of *In the Style of 10/6* on the tag, this one reads *In The Spirit of 10.* It's probably a reference to the nine men in the prophecy, plus me. See, I'm not stupid. What I am is frustrated. "But we had such a lovely trip together?"

"You are not part of my nine," I say with a snarl. Maybe I'm getting too involved in this prophecy shit, but I can't help it. "None of you are unless I say it." I pause and wet my lower lip. I've always been a fan of the underdog … "And Tee and Dee most certainly are."

One of Rab's white ears swivels in my direction and he smiles. It's almost pleasant. Almost. If his smile wasn't as icy as his voice, I might think he was enjoying the moment.

"And …" *I feel like I might regret this later.* "North." My voice catches in my throat, and I stuff a scone in my mouth to cut off the sound. Pretty sure I got lucky with my choice of food though. As I chew, I notice that the breakfast assortment this morning is, how should I say, *eclectic*. Some of the boys have colored drinks with crickets for garnishes. I'm pretty sure Tee is drinking out of a large blue flower—a real one.

"Quite bloody right," North says, giving me a look across the table. His gold eyes meet mine just before he snakes his tail underneath and wraps my ankle. I even let it go this time.

"I thought just last night you told me you wanted to go home?" the King asks loudly, loudly enough that I'm sure all the guards and a couple dozen bitchy flowers probably heard him. There are human servants tending to our table. Maybe even old Red finds the silent, screaming cards creepy?

"If I'm the Alice, I can claim nine men, and I'm claiming those three." I pick through the crumbs of my scone, checking for insects. Fortunately, there aren't any. There *is* a candied honey bee on the cupcake I grab next though. I carefully pluck it off and set it aside. "Does it matter what I said or didn't say last night? Because if I did say it, I certainly didn't mean it. And if I didn't say it, then I'm most certainly not at fault, am I?"

Look asswads, I can riddle, too!

"Cute," drawls Brennin, but I'm pretty sure I just pissed him off. "But to answer your previous question: these men are here because you brought them. There are no package deals here. Only the Alice knows who the true nine are." The King taps his fingers on the table while somewhere off in the distance, there's that horrible whistling sound of the guillotine. When I glance over, I see a body with two big angel wings, twitching while blood spills across the pavement.

Cold chills break over my body, and I find it suddenly hard to swallow. It's obvious even from here that the wings are fake, but the gesture has its intended effect. Both Tee and Dee pale, and I can feel my heart thundering wildly.

Brennin Red just smiles.

"Listen *Brennin,*" I say, putting a huge amount of emphasis on the prick's name. "If you don't stop executing people left and right, we're going to have problems."

"Are we now?" the King asks. He puts his head on one white-gloved hand and leans his elbow on the table like he's bored. "And what, exactly, are you going to do about it?" I squeeze my hands into fists on my thighs as anger roils hot and wild inside of me. What am I going to do about it? Against the King and his million guards? All I have is a knife, a gun, and a few loyal allies. But would the Duke really stand up against the King for me? I wouldn't want to test that theory.

Brennin waves his hand in the direction of the guillotine. I glance over my shoulder just in time to see a girl in a blue and white dress being dragged toward the bloody red edge of the blade.

"What the fuck?!" I snarl as I stand up, knocking my chair over in the process. "Don't you dare." Now I'm shaking, my fingers curling into fists on the white tablecloth. "Don't." This last word is whispered, my eyes locked onto the King's ebony ones.

The way he smirks at me … I know I'm in for some trouble.

He gives a slight nod of his head, and the girl is brought forward, shoved to her knees, her neck put on the wooden part of the guillotine.

"I said *don't,*" I repeat, feeling that strange energy spiral up and through me. Magic. *My* magic. And I'm not afraid to use it—even on a King. Lar's blue eyes widen, his earrings and hair dancing in the breeze, while the March Hare raises one arched brow at me. They're the only ones who seem to notice that's something going really wrong inside of me.

"Or what?" Brennin taunts, standing up from the table. He stares me down for a long moment before tilting his head just slightly. The guards pull the rope and the menacing blade of the guillotine rushes down toward the girl's neck.

Something wild floods through me, like electricity coming from inside my heart, trying its best to find a way out. Without thinking, I fling my arm up in the direction of the execution, and energy shoots through me, tearing across my chest and making me scream. It feels like I'm being ripped to pieces from the inside.

"Allison, don't!" Tee screams, shoving up from his seat and leaping the table in a single vault. He's at my side, grabbing me before I can hit the ground. My body spasms like I'm having a seizure, but even with all of that, I don't miss the fact that the guillotine explodes into a million pieces. Even the blade shatters, sending shards like knives throughout the garden. "Allison!" Tee shouts, putting his fingers into my mouth.

I don't realize how hard I'm biting my tongue until he gives me relief from it. Pain explodes like starbursts behind my eyes as I bite down on his fingers instead. He grits his teeth, but doesn't pull back, keeping my airway clear as the power finishes its wild ride through my body.

"It's okay, Allison-who-isn't-Alice," Dee whispers, kneeling on my other side. He spreads his wings and then dips one underneath me. Tee lets his brother pull me up and into an embrace, taking his fingers from my mouth only when he's certain I won't choke on my tongue … or bite it off.

I'm panting now, eyes rolling back into my head.

"Well now," the King says, pausing beside Tee in his stupid suit. The Hatter stands next to him, his decorative cane held underneath two carefully folded hands, tapping gently against the stones beneath his feet. "That sure was stupid, wasn't it?"

North slides between us, tail smashing the stones beneath his feet.

"You know I'll do whatever it takes to protect my mate," he snarls, and the King nods.

"At least now I know she's not entirely useless," Brennin says, looking down at me like a tool he's just found a use for. "So the magic *does* still sleep inside of you?" The King smiles and leans down, getting in my face. "By the way, I prefer to be called *Red*, rather than Brennin. Maybe I'll call you Allison instead of Alice if you return the favor?" The King stands up with that awful smirk still on his face, and then saunters off in the direction of the castle. I can hear the flowers chuckling at me from their beds. *Butt waffles.*

"Are you alright?" Dee whispers as I shake and shiver in his arms. I can't even describe what I'm experiencing; it's too intense. My thoughts feel like electric sparks pinging around inside my skull. I don't even feel human right now. All I can think about is the Riving. If my weak-ass magic just fucked me up that bad, then what was it like to be torn apart by it? To be changed into a man and stripped of all that power?

Because even though I feel like it just killed me, I want it back.

No, not just back.

I want more of it.

As much as I can fucking get.

♦ ♥ ♣ ♠ ♣ ♥ ♦

The Duke sits on the end of my bed, the long black lengths of his talons digging into his pants. I can see tiny of beads of blood welling up through the pierced leather breeches. That's nice, and very prophetic—the first thing I see when waking up from my short nap is blood. I reach out and grab the pocket watch that's sitting on my nightstand—pretty sure it belongs to Rab—and check the time.

"No training today?" I manage to choke out. Three hours and a nap later, and I've just now gotten my voice back. Sort of. I sound like a frog with strep throat.

"Are you taking the piss with me?" North asks, looking over his shoulder and blinking big gold eyes. He *did* stand up for me out there, didn't he? The thought warms my heart, and I lick my lips as I struggle to sit up. "I've already cancelled lunch and dinner; our meals will be sent up to the room."

The Cheshire Cat stands up—in cat form—and stretches his front paws out in a little bow, kneading at my sheets and snagging the fine fabric. He doesn't seem to give two shits, and neither do I. I hope he fucks up all the King's nicest linens *and* pisses on his pillows. Because that's what cats do when they're mad: they pee all over your favorite stuff.

"The King was going to execute that girl," I cough, picking up the strange pink drink on my nightstand. My hands shake, and I end up sloshing half of it onto the bed. But when Dee approaches to help, I wave him away. I've got this. Even if the drink is glittery and has gold sparkles around the rim of the glass, I'm too thirsty to care. "Because she looks like me."

"Miss Liddell," North starts, and then pauses. He turns more fully to face me, tail swishing gently as Chesh bumps his furry head against my elbow. "That girl is dead anyway."

"No," I say, starting to shake my head, but that doesn't change reality, does it? I screamed and cried and wished and prayed away my brother's death, my mother's incarceration. It didn't change anything. No, I lost my family to toxic masculinity and nothing can bring them back, no matter how hard I protest.

"The King only kills convicted criminals," Tee says softly, but with a voice laden with anger. I don't think he's trying to defend Brennin; he's trying to protect me. "He just wanted to hurt you, make you think it was your … *our* fault. But it's not. He just dresses them up like that to screw with our heads. Those people are all murderers—or worse."

"Underland is not a pretty place," Dee adds, crawling onto the opposite side of the bed and making his way over to me. There's more than enough room for his wings, at least, on a bed this big. "I promise you, if they were innocent, we wouldn't let the King execute them like that."

"It's still fucked up," I say, scrubbing at my face with one hand while I hold my drink with the other. It tastes like strawberries and sunshine. Honestly, it tastes a little bit like Dee himself, like I'm kissing him every time I take a sip. I take three more. "Psychological torture. And how do you *know* they're guilty?"

"A simple curseworker incantation can turn a person's hands red if they're guilty of murder," Tee says, reminding me of the King's gloves. He's *always* wearing gloves. Why is that, I wonder?

"Discussions of capital punishment aside," I begin, sipping the sweet glittery drink. Despite the dead butterfly garnishment on the side of my glass, it's actually pretty miraculous. With every sip, I feel the fiery pain in my throat easing a little. "What the hell happened out there?"

"You called on the magic," North says, lifting his head up, like he's scenting the air. He pauses after a moment and looks back at me. "The Alice is special because she isn't limited to the power inside of her; she can draw on the world's energy like it's on tap. *That*, my dear mate, is why the world either wants you … or wants you dead. There's no one you can't defeat, if you learn how to use that skill."

"Except for the anti-Alice," Chesh says, shifting back into place with his head on my lap. Dirty, sneaky little trick. I shove him off, but I can't resist pinching and rubbing one of those fuzzy little ears first. He bats at me with his fist curled up like a paw.

"What's the anti-Alice?" I ask, feeling this ominous shadow creep over me. The ice cubes clink in my glass, and I realize my hand is shaking. Whatever I did out there, it really and truly messed me up. I'm not sure if I've ever felt this weak *and* this powerful, all at the same time.

"The Walrus and the Carpenter, their queen," Tee says on the end of an exhale, his amethyst eyes glittering with anger. "She can quite literally suck the magic out of anything and everything. She can't use it, but she can absorb it. It's why training with the Vorpal Blade, and with the Queenmaker, with North … why it's so important. If you're going to destroy her, you're not going to be able to use magic."

"Not that I can use magic now," I say on the end of an exhale, but my lids are already feeling heavy and I'm too tired to argue. Everything on me hurts, *everything.* I feel like I'm having period cramps in every part of my body, that's how bad it is. And ladies, you *know* that's real pain.

"We'll get there," North says, watching me as my eyelids slip closed. Dee reaches out at the last second and grabs my drink, sliding his fingers gently against mine just before I pass out. It's nice, having them all there.

Even after the crap-tastic day I've had, I'm starting to *like* it here.

What the fuck is wrong with me?

"Can I get sick every day that I'm here?" I ask as Dee places a tray on my lap the next morning. His wings are gone, and poor Tee never got to have his out yesterday. But that couldn't be helped: I slept through the afternoon, the night, and into the early rays of dawn. Once, when I opened my eyes, I could've sworn I saw Lar drawing some sort of magical symbol in the air in front of my face. Then again, there's also a good chance I hallucinated that, too. "Then I won't have to see the Hatter or the King. Frankly, I'd take about a hundred of those magical shocks to stay *out* of their company."

"I also brought you breakfast, if you prefer a raw food diet," Chesh interrupts as he drops an armload of rodents on my floor, most of them in various states of decapitation. Off with their heads, right? He grins at me, and then crawls up to sit on the top shelf of the carpeted cat tree in the corner. Pretty sure it was intended for him in cat form, but he doesn't seem to care, leaning his elbows on his leather covered thighs and peering at me with curious gray eyes.

"Uh, thanks," I say, lifting the silver lid on my tray and finding porridge with edible flowers. I wonder if some of them were talking a few minutes prior to my meal? Oh well. They all seem like assholes anyway. It brings me some sadistic pleasure to crush their pretty petals between my teeth. "But as much as I enjoy cat-spit covered, dead rodents, I'll stick with the porridge."

"We'll need to continue with your training today," North says, standing with his arms crossed at the end of the bed. He seems awfully eager to get back into it. Maybe he just wants to rub his sweaty, muscular body all over me again? Perv. Or am I the perv for looking forward to it? "You'll also need to learn about the quintrille."

"What the fuck is a *quintrille*?" I ask as I dig around in my food. The flowers have a bright, sharp sweet taste that melds perfectly with the strawberries and blueberries mixed into the porridge. Truth: I'm just making sure there aren't any insects hidden in there.

"It's like a quadrille, only different," Dee supplies, smiling brightly in my direction. I cock a brow at him.

"Thank you, oh so helpful seer. And a quadrille is … what, exactly?"

"It's a card game," he quips, teasing my arm with the tips of his fingers. I like it too much to stop him.

"Or a dance," Tee adds.

"But never both at the same time." Dee crosses his arms behind his head as he watches me eat. If I knew having this many boyfriends would essentially give me free slave labor, I'd have started my little harem up months ago. I wonder if they write scholarship essays, too? Because my parents used up Fred's college fund on his funeral, and mine and Edith's on a lawyer for Mom. If I want to go to college—maybe I don't anyway—then I'll need some serious help paying for it.

Then again, maybe I'd just rather stay in Underland for the rest of my life?

"And which version will I be learning?" I ask as I wonder where the White Rabbit and the Caterpillar are. Brennin Red the Royal Prick seems to 'need' their services on a regular basis. Not that I need or want them around anyway, but … what if I did, huh?

"The dance," Chesh purrs from his perch. "But certainly the Savage Duke won't be teaching you. He's a Hearts-awful dancer, aren't you, North?" The Duke ignores his cat, narrowing his gold eyes, his horns ridiculously tantalizing to my achy fingers, like they're just begging to be touched. If I ran my fingertips up the hard, curved lengths and touched the tips, would I bleed?

"Lar will teach her," Tee interjects with a small sigh, raking his fingers through his purple-streaked black hair.

"Why not you?" North asks, tilting his head quizzically. "You and Lar, you're the only ones who dance the quintrille with any skill or grace." He pauses for dramatic effect. "Well, besides, Red."

Red, huh?

'By the way, I prefer to be called Red, *rather than Brennin.'* Puh-lease.

"I've got errands to run today," Tee says, and I catch his gaze for just long enough to know he's talking about the Looking-Glass. He wants to find it for me, even as he's starting to believe I might be able to make a difference here. I don't stop him though, even if I'm beginning to believe the same thing. Having a steady, reliable way to get back and forth between Topside and Underland is vital. "Lar's a good teacher though. He'll make sure you know it well enough to dance at the ball."

"The Ball of Broken Hearts and Stolen Tarts," Dee singsongs with a sigh, folding some laundry and moving into the closet to put it away. He doesn't seem to be bothered that he went from prince to pauper in a relatively short period of time.

"The Ball of Broken Hearts and Stolen Tarts?" I ask, because what the *fuck* is wrong with that name? It's a rhetorical question, so nobody bothers to answer me. "What's the point of this thing anyway?"

"To introduce the Alice to the Court of Hearts," Tee says, exchanging a glance with the Duke. "Although I don't know how good of an idea this is. We'll need to be on top of security at all times. Assassination attempts are likely."

"Oh, well, great," I say with more than just a little sarcasm. Sunlight streams in through the massive windows on either side of my bed, casting gold bars across the thick furs covering my legs. There's a knock at the door, and I watch as Tee moves over to answer it. "Now I've got assassins chasing after me?"

"You had assassins chasing after you already," Rab says, sweeping in the door as Tee opens it. "Remember? *I* so gallantly protected you." He swipes his gloved hands down the front of his red and black striped vest and pulls out a watch from his front pocket. The white ears on the top of his head twitch. "The King of Clubs—the Carpenter—he sent that Rabbit after you."

Rab pauses near the refreshments table. It's always fully stocked with goodies although I never see anyone tend to it. I'm pretty sure it's the terrifying little card people, but frankly, I don't want to know. Maybe it's just Dee?

The White Rabbit pours himself a glass of lemon-infused sparkling water, and then makes his way over to stand near the bed. Having him this close to me, I can feel the tension between us, as taught as a bowstring. Let it snap and an arrow's bound to fly. The question is: exactly whose heart will be pierced by the wicked tip? "I'll be on patrol during the party, so don't worry." The look he flashes me is built of both confidence and violence as he taps a single tattooed finger against the side of his glass, lifting it carefully to his full, smirking lips for a drink.

"In bandersnatch form?" I ask, fishing for information. Supposedly, all Rabbits have three alternate forms, but I have yet to see more than one of Rab's. Considering Rabbits have to *eat* the meat of all their other forms, I just hope he doesn't turn into a kitten or a puppy. Shudder. Although I do suspect he can turn into a mouse. M.T. and the Gryphon basically said as much.

"We'll see," Rab says, his voice low and slow and dangerous. No wonder he's the King's personal go-to guy; he's terrifying. He blinks those red eyes at me, and I have to resist the urge to squirm as he snaps his pocket watch closed and tucks it into his pocket. His sleeves are rolled up, so I can see his tattoos, tick-tick-ticking away. "It depends on how … interesting the night gets."

"Hopefully not too interesting," Tee says with a small sigh. He takes a small step back, and when I reach for his hand, he takes another one, putting himself out of my reach. I raise an eyebrow. "Wings might … make my chores take longer today," he says, giving me another look. Ah. Gotcha. It's a bit harder to sneak around with a thirty-foot wingspan, huh? I nod and let him go, waiting until the door closes before I set my food aside. All of a sudden, I've got butterflies.

What if Tee comes back in an hour and says he's found the Looking-Glass? What will I do then? Take the twins with me and leave the others behind? Leave Underland to the King of Hearts and the Mad Hatter and the Anti-Alice?

Shit.

Since when did I grow a conscience?

"So," I start, swinging my legs out of bed and feeling this prickly rush of sensation race through me. "Should we get started with training?"

"Only if you think you're up for it," North says as I rise to my feet and close my eyes against a sudden wave of dizziness. I slept so hard and so long that I didn't realize it was morning when I first woke up; I still thought it was the previous afternoon. Fail.

"I'm up for it," I say, opening my eyes and locking gazes with the jabberwock. "Let's go downstairs, so you can kick my ass."

Or cup it, pound it, or otherwise touch it some way ... That part I only add inside my mind.

Yep, I am the pervy one here. No doubt about that.

The Vorpal Blade reflects the light from the chandelier above my head, the one made of black and red glass in the shape of little hearts. It's quite beautiful, if out of place for a gym. But this is no regular gym. The floors are a sleek, shiny black, the walls are striped, and the ceiling is mirrored.

It's disconcerting, to see my own sweaty face staring at me when I'm flat on my back on the mat.

I wonder what else I could be doing on my back on this mat?

"Focus," the Duke growls, circling around me with quick steps. "The Anti-Alice will have trained her entire life for this moment. You ... may get months at most, more likely weeks." He pauses and ruffles up his golden hair. "Hopefully not bloody days."

"Days?" I ask, feeling my throat get tight. I can't imagine fighting a combat trained woman in my current state. Whatever happened with that magic, it's still affecting me. I don't *feel* right, and I imagine it's going to be several days before I'm back to normal. But this ball bullshit, it's at the end of the week.

That doesn't give me a lot of time to prepare.

"What happens if I stab her with this?" I ask, flashing the blade. The Duke gives me a savage smile and steps close, bringing that warm, masculine scent with him. He reaches out one bronzed finger and traces it down the length of the blade, drawing blood.

"The Vorpal Blade is part of a Looking-Glass, pure magic. If you manage to penetrate the Anti-Alice with it, she'll try to absorb the power in it."

"And ..." I start as blood drips down the length of the blade, hot and warm against my skin. I still don't understand who this Anti-Alice is exactly, and why she's called the Anti-Alice, but I'm learning as I go. It's hard to get a straight answer out of these people on the best of days anyway. If I were to sit down and ask them to lay everything out for me, they'd probably just confuse me with stupid riddles.

"Well, just as you can only channel so much magic without feeling the effects, it's the same with her. She'll pull endless amounts of energy through that blade ... and she'll die."

"I've never killed anyone before," I say as North wraps his fingers around my bloody wrist and pulls me close, so close that my breasts brush against his chest when I breathe. His stare is so intense, I swear I can feel it cracking my soul in half.

"You'll do just fine," he says as Chesh moves up to stand beside us, flicking his fluffy, black and white striped tail. He's supposed to be my sparring partner while North corrects my form. So far the only thing he's done since coming down here is nap. "There are two sides to every coin; you can't always flip for heads."

"That doesn't make any sense," I say, stepping back from North. If I let myself, I could get all wrapped up in the Savage Duke. Hell, I'd *love* to be wrapped up in the Savage Duke, tangled up in blankets, his hot, sweaty skin pressing against mine … Yeah, opening my sexual floodgate was maybe not the best idea. Now it feels like *all* I can think about is sex. "Not a lot does in this world."

"Maybe it's your world that makes no sense?" Chesh purrs, sheathing and unsheathing his claws. "Have you ever thought of it that way?" He circles around me like, well, a cat circling a mouse. Only, this bitch is no mouse.

North adjusts my grip on the Vorpal Blade's black hilt and then turns me to face the Cheshire Cat. He's wearing a loose leather vest over his bare, tattooed form, along with tight leather pants, and no shoes. I'm properly dressed in the full 'twin' outfit: black denim, button-up shirt, and boots. I started off in the coat, but I'm already soaked in sweat. I shed that shit a while ago. And yeah, there was no way I was wearing a skirt to train in. Can you imagine? It would get beyond carnal in here.

I did, however, put on Lory's corset with all the little hidden knives tucked into it. Figured that could very well come in handy.

"Put *him* on his bloody back," North growls, shaking himself out and then reaching up to tap at the pointed tip of one of his horns. "I already know you're good on yours."

"Oh fuck off," I snarl as I widen my legs in a fighting stance … and Chesh yawns, stretching his arms up over his head. Clearly, he's not concerned. "Are you gonna fight me? Or you gonna lick your crotch again?"

"I'd much rather have *you* lick my crotch," Chesh says as he flashes a grin at me, showing off just enough fang to be cute. His eyes are wrapped in liner, and he's wearing a fucking collar. It even has tags on it—with *my* name on them. Well, Alice's name anyway. And I guess I am the Alice. Mistake or not, I'm the one that's here.

"Make me," I say, but Chesh just yawns and scratches at his fuzzy little kitty ears. Bastard.

"I'd rather just wait. That's what cats do, you know, stalk their prey. Don't you ever just sit and converse with your pussy?"

"Dinah doesn't exactly talk much," I say, ignoring his innuendo, and then I lunge forward, swinging the Vorpal Blade like North taught me. I hold it tight and low, thrusting forward as I pivot on my feet. I may as well have tried to shoot a slingshot at a fly.

Chesh leaps nimbly out of the way and lands in a crouch, smirking at me.

I shove my hair off my face, sending rainbow strands fluttering as I feign left and then sprint right. Chesh just flops onto his side and rolls out of the way, tail flicking as he laughs at me.

"Come at me, Alice," he purrs, all four limbs sporting claws. He looks like Dinah does when she meets a new cat or dog, lying on her back with all five of her weapons exposed—two front paws, two back, and a mouth full of teeth. Dogs might be surrendering when they show their belly, but cats … they're getting ready to whoop some ass.

"You son of a bitch," I growl as North circles around us, watching Chesh twist up like an acrobat and land on his feet. When I come at him again, he grabs my wrist and uses my own momentum to flip me over and onto my back.

All I can say for myself is that I manage to keep the knife.

Using my left foot, I kick out at Chesh's right knee, and watch as he jumps and sails right over it, landing with a foot on either side of my pelvis. I see that he's going for a pin, and pull both legs back, doing this awkward somersault thing that gives Chesh the perfect moment to go for my throat.

His fingers dig into the back of my neck, claws drawing blood. I cry out, but I don't stop, using my full bodyweight to pull back. This time, I stumble, but I don't fall. Warm rivulets of blood drip down the sides of my neck as I fling my head back just in time to see Chesh coming at me again. Instead of throwing a punch, he shifts into his cat form, slips between my legs, and comes up behind me.

"In Underland, there's always another trick or two up your opponent's sleeve," he growls as he wraps an arm around the front of my neck, pulls back, and lifts me clear off my feet. Without thinking, I stab the Vorpal Blade down and back.

I really don't expect to hit him.

Blood explodes hot and warm around my fingers as Chesh screams and releases me with a hiss, stumbling back and collapsing to his knees. This time, he really does take the blade with him.

"Fuck!" I curse spinning and falling into a crouch next to Chesh. He's pulling the Vorpal Blade out with a snarl and tossing it aside. The mirrored weapon spins across the floor, leaving a trail of red in its wake as Chesh puts his hands over his wound and curls up in serious pain.

"Let me see it," North snaps, trying to pry his … uh, cat's … hands off the wound. There's blood everywhere, so much fucking blood. I feel woozy for a moment as I remember my brother, Fred, lying in a pool of the stuff. Dead. Cold. Gone forever.

My throat closes up, and I feel the hot, uneasy waves of panic washing over me.

"I didn't think I'd hit him," I choke as North forces Chesh's hands away from his stomach and takes a look at the injury. "I didn't know I *could* hit him."

"Never apologize for improvement," North says, but he's frowning *hard,* sweating, too. "Get the Mad Hatter," he tells me, flicking his gold gaze up in my direction. I look from his sweaty bronzed face to the Cheshire Cat's pale one, and I realize how much trouble we're really in.

Without hesitating, I stand up and take off for the door that leads back into the main hall. I have no idea where to find Raiden Walker, but I'll figure it out. I'll choke a dozen card servants if I have to.

Instead, I run into March.

He's waiting just outside the athletic facility doors, checking the cylinder of a revolver. Might be gold-plated, but I don't hold that against it. Everything in this world is deceiving.

"Where's Raiden?" I ask, and one brown rabbit ear swivels to face me. Or is it a hare's ear? I have no idea.

"He's in conference with the King," he says, noticing the blood on my hands, and reaching out to touch his fingers to mine. I jerk back, but all that does is make the asshole smile. "Why? Have you finally decided you can't live without him?"

"Just get him for me!" I scream, and I swear to God, the entire palace shakes around me. "Get him *please*," I correct, but the March Hare is already smirking at me. He closes the cylinder on his revolver, slides it into a holster under his jacket, and nods briskly. "I live to serve," he drawls, but I get the idea that I'm being mocked. Doesn't matter, as long as he's getting the damn vampire mercenary asshole for me.

Well, it doesn't matter *right now.*

Later, I may very well punch him in the nuts.

March moves down the hallway, leading me to a small, quiet study at the opposite end of the palace. I swear, it takes forever for us to get there. I want to run or scream, but I have the feeling that if I do, he'll take longer, just to see me sweat.

When we finally do get to the room, the guards let us in without question, and I burst inside, all dramatic and shit.

"Hatter, I need you," I say, hating the words even as they come out of my mouth. They feel like sand, scraping past my tongue. When he lifts his head to look up at me, there's already blood on his mouth. And there's red on the King's neck. That bastard Brennin Red just *smiles* at me, like he doesn't care that I've just caught him red … uh, necked? No, that sounds too much like hillbillies. Red-throated? Fuck, red-*handed* it is then.

"You do?" Raiden asks, his dark hair feathering around his face. He looks like a metalcore star, some guy who screams onstage in a five-piece band and makes millions for doing drugs and banging chicks. I hate him. "That didn't take long, did it?"

"The Cheshire Cat," I start, and I swear to fuck, the King actually smiles, like he looks *happy*. His crown slides forward on his head, obscuring one of his stupidly beautiful eyes. "I need you to heal him the way you did the Duke."

"The Cheshire Cat is dying?" Brennin asks, so interested it's almost creepy. The one eye of his that I can see is literally sparkling with magic. It really does look like a galaxy, filled with endless possibility and stars. At the same time, the expression on his face is most certainly malevolent. "Excellent. Let the little bastard bleed out."

"If you let him die," I start, curling my hands into fists, "you'll wish you'd never brought me back to your palace."

"Is that so?" Red asks, standing up from his massive desk and tilting his head to look at me. "And you have the power to back that up, *Alice*? Because yesterday, it seemed to have laid you flat."

I can feel those knives burning a hole in my corset. If this asshole keeps pushing …

"Hatter," I start again, focusing my attention on the man sitting at the King's right. He pulls a white handkerchief with red hearts on it out of his pocket and dabs at the blood on his lips. "Please."

"There's a price for every occasion, Alice," he says, standing up from his chair. From the shelves, I hear strange whispers, like the books are talking. I don't have time to deal with that shit right now, so I file it away for later. "What are you willing to pay?"

I'm shaking so bad right now that it feels like I'm having another seizure.

"Save the Cheshire Cat and prove to me you're not a complete waste of breath," I snarl as Raiden rises from his seat, picks up his cane, and makes his way over to stand beside me. His orange eyes are locked on mine. I feel trapped, like I can't look away. I wonder for a moment if he's trying to like, fucking hypnotize me or some shit. "And if you ask me to answer another riddle, I'll stab you with your own cane."

Turning away, I start back toward the doors, the Mad Hatter following along at my heels. The March Hare is waiting just outside for us, but doesn't bother to move as we pass him by.

"Leave the cat to die," Red says, moving into the hall behind us. "That's an order."

Without thinking, I spin around and stalk back toward him. The guards bristle a bit, but the King holds them off with a wave of his gloved hand. Guess he isn't afraid of me. He should be though. Tenacity goes a long way for making up for lack of physical strength.

I open my mouth to start off on a rampage, but the Mad Hatter beats me to it.

"If you think you can order me around—even on a good day—you've got another thing coming," Raiden says, reaching out and taking me by the wrist. The King is lucky, really. I might've stabbed him.

I can practically *feel* Brennin radiating anger from behind me as Raiden pulls me down the hallway, our boots loud against the marble floors.

"You're lucky, little Alice," the Mad Hatter says as we move in the direction of the athletic center. I'm so stressed right now that I can barely think straight. The thought of the Cheshire Cat dying at my hands is making me sick to my stomach. "Because I don't take orders from any king."

We step into the gym and move over to Chesh, lying on his back in a pool of blood. His face is ashen, and even the sturdy Duke looks concerned.

"What price is this going to come at?" North snarls as Raiden kneels down beside him, unconcerned by the blood soaking into the knees of his pants. I wonder what he was doing in there with the King, but I don't have time to analyze that at the moment. Another issue for future-Alice to tackle.

"Only your dignity," Raiden says as he bites hard on his wrist and opens his veins. Chesh is awake and breathing heavily, eyes half-lidded. "I just hope you'll remember this next time *I* need a favor."

"You're insufferable," Chesh manages to choke out before the Hatter puts his wrist to the man's lips. The cat laps it up with a grimace while I look on fascinated. There's something about all of this that interests me. Maybe it's because I've been a bookworm my whole life and now, I'm finally the character in the story. Isn't that what every reader wants? To discover their own adventure?

"Insufferably vital," Raiden purrs as Chesh reaches up and digs his claws into the Hatter's arm—with his claws out. The exchange only lasts a moment, but when Raiden pulls his arm back, Chesh's face is already warming up, pink returning to his cheeks. He sits up and adjusts his vest, giving me a sly look.

"Nice shot, Alice." He winks at me as he rises to his feet. There's blood literally everywhere, but nobody seems to mind. In fact, I'm pretty sure I'm the only one freaking out. Before my nervous heart can catch up with my brain, I'm flinging my arms around the cat's neck and giving him a massive hug.

He hesitates for a moment, but then his arms go around me. You can tell a lot about a man by the way he hugs. Chesh is strong, and he squeezes me tight, but not too tight. His breath feathers my hair near my ear, but he doesn't press his luck or turn the moment into anything weird.

As I pull back, I reach up and give him a pat on the head and a scratch behind the ear. He doesn't look offended by it; I even get a little purr out of him.

"I'm really sorry," I say as North picks up the blade, swings it around in a circle with a single flick of his hand, and then offers it up to me. I hate to say it, but I'm pretty sure that look on his face is *relief.* "I let you both down."

"Down?" the cat asks, swishing his tail. "You just stabbed me. And if you can stab me, you can stab the Anti-Alice. I must say, I'm quite proud."

"If anything, it was my fault as your teacher," North says, and he's flicking his tail, too. They look like tail twins, these two men. It's kinda funny, really. "But now that I know you've moved past the *fatal flop* stage and onto a new level, I'll be more vigilant." North glances briefly in the Hatter's direction, sneers, and then grinds out a forced, "*thank you.*"

"Don't thank me, thank the King," the Hatter says, dipping a finger in the blood and lifting it to his lips. He sucks the red off while staring right at me, and then grins. "If I didn't hate him quite so much, your pussy here might just be dead."

He stands up and leaves the three of us staring after him.

"Grab a mop," North says, gesturing with his horned head in the direction of a supply closet. "Clean this up, and let's get going again. There's certainly no rest for the wicked."

My next lesson of the day is with Lar in the ballroom.

I *thought* I was prepared to see the grandeur of that room.

I was nowhere near it.

As soon as I step into the domed room, I'm reminded of *Beauty and the Beast,* of Belle dancing under that chandelier in a yellow dress.

"Shocked shitless?" Dee asks, holding the door open for me. The ballroom is in the shape of a heart—no surprise there—but the architecture is to die for, reminiscent of gothic revival but ten times as intricate. There are arches carved with roses and faces of happy, dancing couples, their clothing flowing in a non-existent breeze. Above us, the ceiling is made entirely of glass, revealing the setting sun and washing the red walls with rays of gold. Several chandeliers drip from the ceiling, heavy with black and red crystals, giving off flickering light that adds to the ambience.

In the center of it all, Lar's waiting in a pale blue shirt that matches his eyes, his sky blue/blonde hair falling just below the level of his chin. When he brushes some loose strands back from his forehead, his sapphire earrings dance, and his ice-blue gaze locks onto my own.

"I hear there was drama with the Cheshire Cat," he says, his voice like a calm breeze. It's a refreshing change from North's savagery, Chesh's cattiness (pun intended), and Tee's direct honesty. I find myself exhaling for the first time in hours, reaching up to rub at my sweaty forehead. I tried to find time between training and dancing for a shower or bath, but Dee grabbed my elbow straight after lunch and brought me here.

"Yeah, well, I accidentally stabbed him in the kidney and almost killed him." I shrug my shoulders loosely as the scent of blueberries and fresh-cut flowers fills my nostrils. Jesus. Every dude in Underland smells good enough to eat and looks it, too. No wonder I can't keep my hands to myself. "Okay, so I don't know if I actually stabbed his kidney, but it sounds more dramatic that way, right?"

Dee chuckles beside me as Lar raises a pale brow, tilting his head to one side as he studies me.

"Getting the Hatter under your thumb so quickly, I'm impressed," Lar breathes, his white and gold jacket draped loosely over his shoulders. He folds his stained-glass wings together behind his back.

"Gossip travels quickly around here, doesn't it?" I ask, unable to pull my attention from Lar's gaze. As glorious as the ballroom is, it doesn't compare to the beauty of his face. He has high, fine cheekbones, a gloriously full lower lip, and long lashes framing his pale eyes. There's something about the way he holds his mouth, lips just slightly parted, that intrigues me. It's like he's always on the edge of asking a question, like there's a question mark resting on the tip of his tongue. "Although I'd dare say the March Hare is the one you should watch out for. Sometimes, he's not just the Hatter's right hand—he *is* the Hatter."

"He's …" I start, and then realize what Lar's saying. My eyes fly wide, and the Caterpillar chuckles softly, pulling out a small glass pipe in the shape of a toadstool. He snaps his fingers and then lifts his pointer finger in the air, a small flame dancing on the tip. He uses that to light his pipe, the grassy scent of marijuana quickly taking over the room. It's not quite right though, like pot mixed with a bit of rosewater, some crushed lavender, and just a hint of chai tea spice. "He *ate* some of Raiden's flesh?!"

"What do you think?" Lar replies in a low, cool tone that helps soothe away some of my anxiety. He takes a long drag before passing the pipe my way, exhaling beautiful blue smoke from between his lips. I'm about to tell him no, because as much as I want to get high, I have a feeling that could also get me killed in this palace of hell. "Just a little bit goes on a long way," he tells me, the edge of his mouth twitching in a smile. "I can't properly teach you to dance if you don't take any."

"What is this?" I ask as I glance over at Dee, but he's shaking his head and putting his hands up.

"Just a bit of *whiting*," Dee says as I raise an eyebrow. "But I can't have any. I have to keep both feet firmly on the ground, so I can play the piano for you."

"On the ground?" I ask as I glance back at Lar, and finally take the pipe from his outstretched fingers. Our fingertips brush together, and a warmth fills me, traveling down my arm and into my chest, making my heart beat. I jerk my hand back and cradle the pipe in my palm. "Isn't a whiting a type of fish? You know, like salmon or trout."

"Just like a quadrille can be a card game or a dance, so can a whiting be a fish or a magical plant." Lar taps the side of the glass pipe with a fingernail. "Take a hit, Sunshine, and I'll show you what it means to join the dance."

"Good luck," Dee says, leaning in to give me a kiss on the cheek. His mouth lingers, turning the relatively chaste moment into something so much more. His wing dips down and brushes along my bare arm, making me shiver, before he finally retreats, moving over to a massive red and white grand piano in the corner. Dee stretches his fingers *and* his wings out as he sits down to play.

"Good luck?" I ask Lar, turning back to him as I lift the pipe to my mouth and inhale. I close my eyes as I do it, feeling the hot smoke curl its way into my lungs, the taste of lavender and chai clinging to my lips. As soon as I breathe out, I feel it hit me, this lightheaded, airy sensation that makes me feel like I'm floating. "What's he talking about?"

The Caterpillar just smiles at me, takes the pipe, and sets it on a small glass table next to a gramophone. When he holds out his hand, I hesitate to take it.

"I haven't forgotten about Raiden and March," I say, and Lar's smile turns into a confident smirk, like I've taken the bait. Exhaling sharply, I put my hand in his and watch his pale fingers curl around my own. It's enough to make a girl swoon—if I were the swooning type, that is. I am most definitely *not*.

"I mentioned that little tidbit all of two minutes ago," Lar says as he leads me into the center of the room. "I wouldn't have expected you to have forgotten already." I roll my eyes because he knows what I mean. What a dick.

As I pause beneath the largest of the five chandeliers in the room, I wish suddenly that I'd worn a dress. Dee suggested it, but nooooo, I had to be a rebel. Damn it.

"Sunshine," Lar says, releasing my hand, and then taking a bow. When he stands up, he whips his jacket off his shoulders, revealing a short-sleeved sky blue tunic underneath. He then shakes it out and tosses it behind him, spreading his wings briefly like he's trying to hide the garment from me. I never see it hit the floor; when Lar folds his wings together again, the jacket is gone. Magic. It's everywhere in Underland. "Tell me: do you know how to waltz?"

"I don't know how to dance for shit," I reply, feeling my cheeks warm slightly. I've never been much of a dancer, not even a social dancer. But I *have* read about a million books with characters who attend balls and dance their asses off with noble princes. Does that count?

Dee starts to play some sad, slow sort of song, his fingers dancing across the ivory keys as a card servant I hadn't noticed before begins to pluck at a harp with its too-human fingers. I can't look at its face, no freaking way. If I do, I'll get too creeped out and leave before my lesson has even begun.

"Just follow along and don't worry about it for now," Lar says, placing one warm hand on my hip and curling the fingers of the other through my own. I find myself licking my lips and avoiding any sort of eye contact. We're standing far too close for that. Besides, he smells like tobacco and blueberries, a toxic sort of combination that makes my heart flutter. "You're thinking too hard," he tells me as we start to sway, and I end up stepping on his foot.

"Oops, sorry," I say as I cringe and struggle with where to place my left hand. Lar sweeps his right up my side, making me shiver, and takes hold of it, placing it on his right shoulder. He just smiles at me, earrings swaying with the motion of our bodies. He holds his wings just high enough that the curled tips brush the ground. "I'm sort of a dance-virgin."

Lar smirks at me, his eyes going half-lidded as the chandeliers flare to life, brightening up the room before the sky is completely dark outside.

"Don't apologize for being inexperienced, only for refusing to learn. Seems to me like you're trying plenty hard." He spins me around as Dee picks up the pace on the piano, giving us a bouncier tune than I'd expected. I have no idea what one dances a quadrille or a quintrille to, but I suppose I'll soon figure that shit out.

"There's certainly a lot to, uh, take in," I say as Lar picks up our speed. He's right though: when I'm not focusing on what I'm doing, I have no problem keeping up. As soon as I let myself get laser-focused on his feet, and my feet, and that yummy smell of his … that's when shit gets fucked up.

"Don't think too hard," Lar whispers, moving his hand from my hip to tap at my chin. I lift my face up to look at him as we make our way around the dance floor. "And don't think too little, either. Just enough to point yourself in the right direction. Once you've done that, you have to learn to trust yourself."

"So you're a seer *and* a wiseman?" I ask as the Caterpillar starts to guide my feet with his own, pushing me back with his shoe, or to the side, or beckoning me forward by hooking my ankle. It's a little unorthodox, I have to admit, but I'm not really thinking about dancing anymore. I'm just looking at him. He has big, round eyes, but they seem to be in a near perpetual half-lidded state. His mouth is generous and full, lips pink, skin pale, and that hair … it's blonde, but when you look at it just right, it tints blue. I wonder if he really is a faerie?

"I'm a slave," he says with a loose shrug of his shoulders, spinning me around again. If I had a dress on, the fabric would swish around my calves right now. Damn it. I should've just worn the fucking dress. That easy, fantastical high I felt when I took a drag on the pipe amplifies with each movement we make, promising that I'm in for a serious trip. "I'm whatever the King wants me to be."

"You're a prisoner, too, huh? Who isn't?"

"The damn cat," Lar says in a soft voice. It's not weak, just … quiet. Like he expects the world to shush up and listen to *him*. Considering his talents, I don't think that's much of a request. "And the Duke. I think he actually *likes* Red."

"Anyone else?" I ask, thinking of Tee and Dee. They are most certainly prisoners. Slaves, actually.

"You know Rab hasn't much of a choice either. Although I think he likes his place in the palace now. There are bets out there to decide if he was crazy before or only after the King made him a Rabbit."

"Psychopath? Or sociopath?" I ask as the music slows, stops, and then starts up again. Lar doesn't skip a beat, keeping us moving before I can trip on my own feet.

"Both?" he asks with a lift of one, pale brow. There's something soothing about his hand on my hip, this guiding presence that makes me feel like I'm being taken care of. But, like, not in a creepy way. "Rab is an easy man to get along with, but a terrible man to cross."

"He shot my schoolmate in the face," I say, looking past Lar and feeling my eyes blur with the memory. God, that feels like it happened ages ago. When was it really? A week and a half ago? For fuck's sake.

A week and a half back home without me … Dad and Edith are probably frantic. I just hope they haven't told Mom. Being trapped in jail with no way to look for me, that very well might kill her.

"King's orders," Lar says simply, shrugging his shoulders. After meeting the royal prick, I guess I can see why they're so eager to do what he says: he's not insane, he's just evil.

Our steps get more elaborate as we go, until I feel like I'm really and truly dancing for the first time in my life. My hair billows out behind me in a blonde and rainbow wave as we make another turn on the dance floor.

"This is easier than I thought," I say, just before I trip over Lar's foot and end up stumbling into him. He catches me and helps me upright, my face ridiculously close to his. His breath is sweet, fanning against my lips. I have to swallow hard to get past the sudden lump in my throat.

"Nothing is so hard you couldn't figure it out, mighty Alice," Lar says, folding his wings together and then opening them slowly, like he's putting on a show. I'm not sure that he even realizes he's doing it though.

"Well, most things anyway," I say as I right myself, brush my sweaty palms down the front of my red button-up shirt, and take a deep breath. Lar and I get into position again as Dee starts up a new song, this fast-paced piano solo that makes me want to move.

"I've never met a problem I couldn't solve," he says as I cock an eyebrow.

"The King of Hearts?" I hazard, but Lar just shakes his head, long blue-blonde strands of hair falling across his forehead. His earrings catch the light as he moves, too, and I can't help but admire them. He has a fine-boned look to his face, this aristocratic air that begs attention. Jewelry suits him.

"He's not a problem," he says with a long sigh, blinking pale lashes at me. "The King of Hearts is the *best* ruler Underland has right now. Compared to the King of Spades, and the King of Clubs, he's practically a saint. I'll serve him without resistance," Lar starts, leaning in and putting his lips against my ear, his breath tickling my skin, "until I find someone better."

I feel weightless, with the Caterpillar this close to my face. It's quite obvious to my body right now that a slight turn of my face would put my lips to his. We could kiss right now. My tingling lips tell me it's the right thing to do, that I should try. After all, when am I ever going to feel like this again, like I'm floating across the dance floor?

Lar chuckles, like he can sense what I'm feeling. When I do turn my head and kiss him, it's with laughter dancing on both our lips. My mouth presses softly against his, and he doesn't press the moment, letting me come to him. My fingers squeeze his right shoulder, curl around his left hand. His tightens on my hip, letting me know that he's enjoying the moment as much as I am.

Barely spoke ten sentences to the guy, and you're shoving your tongue down his throat, my brain quips, but I'm not listening to her. When am I ever going to get this chance again? I'm surrounded by attractive men that want me, that think I'm the literal answer to all their prayers. Am I supposed to keep fighting this? Am I supposed to hate it?

I don't.

Lar teases the tip of my tongue with his own before pulling back and leaving me breathless. My chest aches as his wings open wide, a gold, black, and blue backdrop to … the sky? I blink a few times and look down.

I shouldn't have looked down.

With a squeak, I realize we're floating far above the dance floor, our heads just a foot or so from the domed glass ceiling of the ballroom.

"Lar," I choke out, but he doesn't seem concerned, twirling me around as easily up here as he did on the marble floor below. My feet continue to follow his, mimicking the steps of the dance as best I can. I'm afraid to stop. What if I fall? "I have a thing about heights."

"Will you, won't you join the dance?" the Caterpillar whispers, tugging on one of his earrings. The blue jewel lights up, and then dozens of wall sconces burst into brilliant flame, casting beautiful shadows across the walls and floor. "When the King asks you that at the ball, you take a curtsy and reply '*What matters it how far we go?*'"

My eyes get caught on Lar's as we twirl through the air, dancing on the wind as easily as if it were the earth beneath our feet. Next time these people ask me to smoke a pipe, I won't question it. Prophetic visions and magical air dances? Sign me up.

As we move, Lar's wings sparkle, the colors in the center shifting and adjusting until I'm looking at something … *carnal.* There are two naked people in this image, playing out like a porno inside the confines of his beautiful wings. Just like last time, I can see, hear, smell, almost *taste* that vision. It's so real that I have to shake my head to remind myself that it isn't actually happening.

No, I'm just *watching* two people fuck.

"A prophecy," I start as I squint and … realize that the two figures in the image are me and Lar. I squeak and jerk back, slipping from Lar's arms. Almost immediately, I begin to fall, tumbling through the air like I'm on my way down the damn Rabbit-Hole again. Lar tucks his wings in tight, dives down, and snatches me from midair, setting us both gently down on the marble floor.

When our eyes meet, I feel my cheeks heat.

Lar looks at me for a long moment before raising his head and narrowing his eyes at something over my shoulder while Dee finishes up the music and turns on his bench seat to follow the other man's gaze. There's a tingling between my shoulder blades, and it takes me a moment to realize that's because there are eyes boring into my back.

When I glance over my shoulder, I find Brennin Red watching me with cold, dark eyes.

"I'm starting to get the feeling you don't like me," I call out, putting my hands on my hips and staring the asshole down.

"You're a deplorable dancer; the court will notice." He runs a finger absently along the scar at the corner of his lip. "Oh well. Nobody expects the Alice to be … cultured. I suppose it'll have to do. We don't have a lot of time."

"Is your stupid ball that important?" I ask, moving across the marble floors toward him. I get the idea that this is a guy that thrives on manipulation and intimidation, and I refuse to play into his hand.

"The Ball of Broken Hearts and Stolen Tarts is a send-off for my soldiers, the people who inhabit this world that means nothing to you. The Walrus and the Carpenter are mobilizing an army on our border. You wouldn't want to see what they'd do if given free rein to terrorize the kingdom. *You* might be interested in disappearing through the Looking-Glass, but the rest of us are stuck here, *Alice*."

"I'm not responsible for the pain of an entire world!" I shout as Brennin—or Red or whatever his stupid name is—turns and leaves the room with an entourage of guards swarming after him. The White Knight is with him, but at least *she* gives me a sympathetic look as she follows the King out. He's wearing that stupid suit again. I'm guessing it's his version of casual wear. Prick. He probably sleeps with a stick shoved up his ass.

"I don't think Red likes you, Allison-who-isn't-Alice," Dee says, moving up to stand beside me. He puts his hat back on and pulls it down firmly over his mussy hair. With Lar on one side and Dee on the other, their beautiful wings resting behind them, I feel pretty plain and boring. At home, I was the weirdo. Here, I'm the beige house with the white picket fence.

"Good, because *I* really don't like him," I say as Tee strides in the open door and makes his way straight over to us. He pauses for a moment as he glances at the Caterpillar.

"Continue your plotting," Lar drawls, reaching down to play with his gold bracelets. "I already know what you're up to. Don't worry: I won't tell."

Tee narrows his amethyst eyes before looking over at me. I can't believe I had sex with him. What was I thinking? Now I'm invested in what happens to the guy. Life must be a hell of a lot easier for assholes like the King and the Hatter.

"The Looking-Glass," he starts, giving Lar another skeptical look. With a scoff and a shake of his head, Tee turns back to me. "It's inside a Game."

"Fuuuuuuuck," Dee says, sliding his hands down either side of his face. "How the hell are we supposed to deal with that?!"

"Uhh, what's a Game?" I ask, crinkling my brows up. Lar is whistling, so I'm going to guess that this shit is bad. I've already flown over the forest hanging from a giant bat, so I don't think they're going to be able to say much to surprise me.

"It's enchanted by a curseworker," Tee says, putting his hands on his hips and looking at the floor.

"And what is *it*?" I ask as Dee runs the tip of one finger along the leather brim of his hat.

"A Game can be … a lot of things," he says with a loose shrug of his shoulders. "But in the King's case, it's probably chess." He lifts his blue eyes up to the glass ceiling above us as the giant bat passes by overhead with a screech that cuts straight into my brain. Speak of the devil …

Twinkle, twinkle little bat, my ass.

"A chess game with life-size pieces," the Caterpillar adds, looking at my mouth for much longer than is really appropriate. His stare makes my lips tingle, and I shift unconsciously, doing my best not to think about that vision in his wings, the one that just showed me making love to the guy. "And life-size appetites."

"In short, they're armed, alive, and very, very angry," Tee adds as I look between the three men.

"An entire set of aggressive, people-size chess pieces?" I ask as I raise my eyebrows. "And what idiot curseworker was responsible for that shit?"

"I was," a voice says from near the door. I look up and find a beautiful woman cloaked in flowing red robes with a big frilly white collar around her neck. The way she smiles at me, I can tell we're not going to be friends.

"Who's that?" I ask, feeling a small spark of fear. This is only the *second* woman I've spoken to since I got to Castle Heart.

And I don't like her.

Ugh, I'm trying not to act on my patriarchal-blessed internal misogyny, but all of a sudden, I'm nervous. Like, *really* fucking nervous. A bunch of alpha dude assholes, I can deal with. But women are smart, creative, and logical. That scares the crap outta me.

"The Knave of Hearts," Tee says, curling his hands into fists at his sides.

"A knave is a jack, right?" I ask, and I feel like I should get serious points for that. Doubt Edith would've known the answer. And Fred … I wonder if Fred could've been the Alice?

"She's like, a second-in-command, as Underland doesn't consider males intelligent or rational enough to run kingdoms, yet at the same time shuns anyone who isn't of royal blood," Dee adds. "All the kingdoms have male rulers now with no queens, so the Knaves act as backup. They can veto any decision the King makes."

Oh … dear.

The Knave sweeps into the room with a pair of men on either side of her. One is dressed in gold with a thick brown-gold beard, sideburns, and mustache, while the other has long white hair scooped into a bun on the back of his head. He doesn't look old though, maybe thirty at most. They stick to her like glue as she makes her way across the empty marble dance floor toward us.

"Those are her husbands, the Lion and the Unicorn," Tee growls out, and I can already tell he doesn't like this woman any better than I do. I stare at her, her silky brunette hair hanging nearly to the floor, her spring green eyes focused on mine.

"Why are they called the Lion and the Unicorn?" I whisper, but then, I'm standing next to a dude named Caterpillar, and a pair of twins named Tweedledee and Tweedledum, soooo … Stupid question much?

"The Lion has all that facial hair," Dee says with a chuckle, catching my eye and winking, "and the Unicorn, well, it's not because his horn is on his forehead, if you catch my drift." I clamp a hand over my mouth to stifle a chuckle, and the Knave narrows her eyes on me. I'm wracking my brain trying to remember any of these characters from the original books.

The Knave … pretty sure he was accused of stealing the Queen of Hearts' freshly baked tarts. He was a minor character though. And the Lion and the Unicorn? They must be from *Through the Looking-Glass, and What Alice Found There*. I'll have to check in that copy Tee gave me. There's no such thing as being too prepared here.

"Aren't you pretty?" the Knave says as she pauses next to me, a good half a foot shorter than me *at least*. Her husbands, however, are huge. I have to look up to meet the cold, silver eyes of the Unicorn and the equally drab rust-red of the Lion. "These are my husbands, Rook and Knight." She gestures at the Lion first, and then the Unicorn. But considering the Mad Hatter's name is Raiden, the King is Brennin, and the freaking Duke's name is North, I'm not surprised. Normal names, weird nicknames. It works with the Underland vibe.

In fact … I sense a chess reference. Isn't the entire second Alice book just one big chess game? My chest feels tight suddenly, like a queen on a black and white board. Fuck. Is Tee sure the Looking-Glass is trapped in a Game? Because it feels like *I* am already one of the players.

"I could say the same for you," I reply, smiling tightly. I *could* say the same, but I'm not going to. I'm hoping the Knave will miss my play on words, but nobody here ever does, do they?

"The King doesn't seem to like you," the Knave quips bluntly, stepping back so she can look me over. "You are a bit scruffy, and awfully uncouth. Although it's not a surprise why the Hatter is interested."

"A mercenary powerful enough to topple kingdoms? That's an offensive thing to say," I blurt, knowing that I shouldn't start shit with a person I just met. Who knows? Maybe we could be friends? Lord knows I don't have many back home. Before the Knave can speak again, I exhale and hold out a hand. "Name's Allison Liddell. And you are …"

"Ines Fripon," she says, looking at my hand like it's diseased. She lifts her green eyes up to mine, and I see it right there in her beautiful irises: she's jealous of me. Guess it makes sense, considering I'm supposedly the next Queen of Hearts. I get this little mean girl thrill out of the moment, and then shove it down.

No, that's something Edith would do, use this woman's insecurities against her. I'm not like that; I don't want to be like that.

"Nice to meet you," I say, forcing a genuine smile. It almost hurts my mouth. Guess I'm still a cynical asshole at heart. Dee looks at me like I've sprouted a second head—something I feel could easily happen here in Underland—while Tee frowns hard. Lar brushes some of his pale hair behind one ear, showing off his silver hoops at the top of his ear. He appears contemplative, looking between the two of us like he's got money riding on our interaction.

"We came to see if you needed any further assistance with the quintrille? It's a very important dance, you know," the Unicorn, err *Knight*, says. Think that *I* might go mad trying to memorize all these fucking weird-ass names. "It's vital for building alliances and friendships within the court."

He smiles at me, and I swear, he's got big, horsey front teeth. Maybe *that's* why he got the nickname Unicorn? Just so long as he doesn't ask me to start believing in him, we're good.

"Allison is a quick learner," Lar says, lifting both brows. "I think she'll make a fine dance partner."

"Well, we'll see," the Knave of Hearts says with a little titter of a laugh. She looks over at Dee like she's just seeing him for the first time, and her lips curl up at the sight of his wings. As soon as he sees her looking, I notice his shoulders stiffening up. "Glad to see you and your brother are getting along now." Her sneer changes to a smile as she flicks her eyes up and down my boys. "Because I'd *hate* to see what I might do the second time around."

The Knave turns and leaves, gesturing for her husbands to follow after.

"Wait," I start, looking between the twins. "Is that …"

"The witch that cursed us?" Tee asks in a low voice. "Yes."

Oh.

Well.

No wonder I hated the cunt from moment one. Never mind all that shit I said about the benefit of the doubt and whatnot. Bitch is going *down*.

CHAPTER FIVE

Tweedledee, Tweedledum, and the Alice's Harem

"You didn't think to tell me about the Knave?" I ask Tee and Dee as we sit on these ridiculously comfortable red chairs in a fitting room so draped in fabric, I feel like I'm crouching inside a tent. *Hoarders: Underland Edition,* anyone? There's so much fabric in here, I could easily drown in it.

"She's not important," Tee says, watching Rab as he checks his pocket watch for the thirtieth time.

"He's late," the White Rabbit grumbles, rolling his red eyes. His gaze comes to rest on March, and I see the corner of his mouth curl up into a sneer. "He's late, and you're not welcome. What do you want with a dress fitting anyhow, you stupid fuck?"

"Oh, I'm the stupid fuck, now am I?" March asks, reaching out to finger a pink dress on a headless mannequin. Heh. Hope that one's not for me. I am *not* a fan of the color pink. "I'm not the one who broke the FUCKING DRINK MEs and left the Alice behind. You know, if you hadn't done that, it's doubtful that Raiden and I would even be here."

Rab scowls, snapping his pocket watch closed with a finality that promises violence. So far as I know, all 'Rabbits', that is, servants to the Kings and Queens of Underland, have bandersnatch forms. That's what *makes* them Rabbits. As for their other two forms … I intend to ask March about his Raiden form at some point.

"It feels like you're here simply to irritate me," Rab grinds out, swiveling one ear back in March's direction. When he glances over his shoulder with those bloodred eyes of his, I get chills. "And you know I don't fucking like to be irritated."

"Are you going to fight me in here while the Alice watches?" March teases, his panty-melting accent dripping with disdain. "I'd bloody love to see you try."

The White Rabbit turns around slowly, this cool, calculating look tracing its way over his features. I would not want to be on the receiving end of that look. He glances down at his vest and then slowly, oh so slowly, unbuttons it. Once his bare chest is revealed, he seeks out a clock and taps his finger against the tattoo.

"Damn, it's not quite your time to die," he says with a false moue of disappointment. "Shame, that. I was looking forward to hastening your demise."

March just laughs and shrugs out of his velvet trench coat, tossing it onto the pink-dress wearing mannequin before striding forward in his massive combat boots. When he stands next to me, I realize how fucking tall the guy really is. I hear he's some sort of master thief, but how the fuck does he get any sneaking around done with that big, muscular body of his?

"If you'd like, *the Alice*, I could challenge Rab to a cock-race, and you could see which Rabbit fares best in a brawl."

"Thanks, but no thanks," I say, still feeling slightly lightheaded from my dance with the Caterpillar. I hate heights, but I have to say, that was one of the most miraculous things I've ever done. I'm suddenly desperate to do it again. How long do I have until the ball? A week? And I have lessons with Lar every day until then.

Fantastic.

My mind conjures up that moment when our mouths connected … and then dives straight into the dark, carnal delights of that vision.

I shake my head to clear it, and reach my fingers up to rub at my temples.

"After this, we'll go back to the room," Tee murmurs under his breath, giving March a dirty look, like he doesn't appreciate him standing so close. "I'll have dinner brought up."

"By one of those creepy card servants?" I say, because I still can't stop thinking about the King and how he killed one of them in cold blood. Nor can I possibly forget that he won a *kiss* from me—a kiss in front of the entire court.

I imagine he'll collect at the ball. Why wouldn't he? Fucking prick. I hate him.

"At least you know they're all given fair chance to defend themselves at the Trial," Dee says, lounging back in his chair and tapping his fingers against the red leather arm. I can see about two inches of the chair's actual fabric peeking out beneath the mounds of cloth draped over it. This entire place is just swimming.

"*The* Trial?" I ask as March leans against a decorative column, keeping his brown eyes locked on me. It feels like he's searching for something intangible, something I can't name, but want to keep hidden. Maybe I'm just imagining it? Does not hurt to be paranoid in a place like this. "Like, there's only one?"

"The King holds the Trial once a week," Rab says, pausing in front of me and smiling in that cruel way of his, a slash across the face, sharp as a knife. "The accusers are tested with magic to determine their, shall we say, *veracity*. Some are selected for servitude … and others for execution. Rapists, murderers, traffickers, that sort of thing."

"I feel like you're trying to make me hate the King less. FYI, it's not working." I cross my arms over my chest and try not to sigh. Whoever this tailor person is, I'm getting mighty irritated. All I want to do is crawl up the stairs and flop into bed. Of course, now that I've fucked North, Tee, and Dee, it's like sex is on the plate with all of them—it's an option. I *could* go back to the room and invite them into bed with me.

Oh, it's tempting …

"I would never try to sway your opinion," Tee says, looking up from under the leather brim of his peaked cap. My mouth is aching to kiss his, to free those gorgeous wings from his back, but again, it feels weird to do it in front of these other men. Not because I'm ashamed or embarrassed, but because it feels like special moments with Tee should be private. "I just want to reiterate: if any of those people were innocent, Dee and I would've made a stand a long time ago."

Exhaling, I lean back in my chair and close my eyes, crossing my legs at the ankle. With the twins around, I feel safe. Maybe I shouldn't, considering I *did* get kidnapped out of North's house, but I do anyway. Since the biggest, baddest mercenary in all the land is now supposedly engaged to my ass, I may as well relax.

The sound of a curtain swishing back draws my attention, and I crack my eyes to see Rab slipping out of his vest, and slipping into … another vest.

"What are you doing?" I ask him as he picks up a pair of wire-rimmed spectacles from a side table and perches them on the end of his nose, peering at me over the top of them.

"I've just received a text from the King," Rab says, shaking his phone in my direction. Every freaking time I see one of these weirdos holding what looks like the newest iPhone, I have a mini heart attack. It's just too weird to be sitting in a castle, being fitted for a ball, and seeing the King's servant holding something that looks like it could be browsing social media or looking up porn. "The tailor was executed this morning, so I'll be acting tailor until we can find a new one."

"Do you know anything at all about sewing clothes?" I ask as Rab buttons up his new brown leather vest and rolls up his sleeves to reveal a sea of glorious ink. It feels like every time I look at him, I notice something new. My eyes catch on a sea of ghosts drifting up from a graveyard toward a full moon. Very pretty, very me. I would totally get something like that tattooed on my body.

"I've sewn flesh before, does that count?" Rab asks, which is not a particularly comforting sentiment.

"Flesh?" I ask as he holds out a tattooed hand, gesturing for me to step up on a round dais surrounded by mirrors. There are a lot of fucking mirrors here. I wonder if Brennin Red has one above his bed?

Aaaand, why am I thinking about Brennin Red's bed anyway?

"You know, battle wounds and all that," Rab replies, but his voice is too smooth and practiced. He's lying to me. And the sad part is, I don't actually want to know the truth anyway.

"Since when have you ever sewn up a wound, mate?" March asks, trailing along behind me as I stand up and head for the dais, shrugging out of my coat and boots. Reluctantly, I also set the Queenmaker and the Vorpal Blade aside. "Usually you're the one making them."

"I've been known to show compassion," Rab says as he grins at me, white ears twitching atop his head. I can smell him from here, this musty, earthy scent mixed with the copper reek of blood. I shouldn't find it appealing, but I do. My nipples pebble beneath my shirt, and I curse under my breath.

Great.

He's going to measure me, and I've got my headlights turned on bright.

Fan-fucking-tastic.

Tee and Dee flank either side of the dais, arms crossed over their chests in identical positions. One has wings, and one doesn't. That makes me sad somehow.

"You? Compassion?" I ask as Rab slides a cloth measuring tape from a hook, winding it around his hand as he watches me with those red, red eyes of his. He manages to make the motion sexy, wrapping it around two fingers and suggestively licking his lower lip.

I roll my eyes.

Hey, I can't help it: I'm a fucking young adult. It's in our DNA to do annoying shit.

"Sorry, but I can't see it," I say as Rab steps closer and March circles around behind the dais, balancing a knife on the tip of his finger. "You being compassionate, I mean. Isn't that against the very nature of a sociopath?"

I'm smirking when Rab comes around in front of me, but that quickly dies when he leans in and wraps the measuring tape around my waist, tugging it tight and stealing my breath away. His mouth is disturbingly close to my nipple.

"Psychopath, you mean," Rab whispers, taking note of the numbers on the measuring tape and calling them out to March, of all people. The brown-eared Rabbit takes the knife in his hand and carves the measurements into the wooden stand of a dress form. "And you're right: I have no compassion. What was I thinking?"

He slides the measuring tape up in the back and then cocks a dark brow at me.

"Well? Do I have permission to touch the Alice's luscious breasts?" Rab doesn't look ashamed to be asking. Nor does he look professional, as a tailor should. Instead, he's just … lascivious. I hate him. Okay, not really. I hate the King and the Hatter maybe, but not the White Rabbit, not even if he shot Brandon in the head right in front of me.

After all, it led me here.

And I'm starting to *like* it.

"Provided you act a gentleman," I say, lifting my chin as Rab pulls the measuring tape up and over my breasts … *riiiiiight* over the pert points of my nipples. It feels good, even through the shirt and the knife-filled corset underneath it.

"I never act a gentleman," Rab purrs, his voice like a frost-covered branch collapsing under the weight of fresh snow. It's like he's having as much trouble touching my boobs as I am having them touched.

"How long is this going to take?" Tee snaps, flicking his attention between March and Rab. Clearly, he's not much of a fan of either Rabbit.

"The more times you ask that, the longer it takes," Rab purrs, squeezing the measuring tape around my breasts and forcing a sharp exhale between my lips. I feel almost as lightheaded now as I did when I was dancing with Lar in the ballroom. But … at least my situation's a *why choose* moment, right? I can't imagine having to pick between these men. That'd kill me.

"The Alice needs her sleep," Tee grinds out, grabbing the lapels on his jacket and forcefully straightening out the fabric with a sharp snap. "So save your dirty flirtations for another day."

Rab ignores him, moving down to measure my ass next. I've never been measured for clothing before—ever heard of Target, anyone?—so I'm not sure how orthodox any of this is, but I *like* it.

"Don't you dare cop a feel," I whisper, and Rab pauses to look up at me. He's so gloriously sexy, dripping in ink, his hair black as black, his eyes as vibrant and piercing as his tattoos. "You may measure my ass, but *be a gentleman.*"

"How boring," Rab drawls with a sigh, but even though he's a psycho murderer, he keeps it respectful as he wraps me in the measuring tape again. "Like I said, most definitely *not* a Mary Sue."

I almost smile, because I can hear the teasing note in his voice, and I like that, too. But then something occurs to me.

"How do you know what a Mary Sue is anyway? That's a term coined Topside." I like the way I refer to my own world as Topside now, like it's as easy as breathing. Something about that makes me happy. Clearly, I've gone mad.

"I spend a lot of time Topside, Sonny." Rab stands up and reaches for one of my arms, pushing my sleeves up and making my skin pebble with pleasure, like he's petting me or something. "I know what a Mary Sue is, I prefer Pepsi to Coke, and I do *looove* to read manga."

"Manga?" I ask as Rab measures my leg, my foot, my … ear? And then lastly, my head. I suppose that makes sense, seeing as I could be getting a custom hat. But my ear? Sigh. "You read manga, like Japanese comics?"

"Exactly that," Rab says as he finishes up and steps back, looking me up and down with a sly smile. "Surprised?"

"Honestly, no," I say, sensing that we're done, and hopping down from the dais. "It suits you." I pause and glance down at my button-up shirt, fingering the fabric as I narrow my eyes. "Wait a minute. When I got here, there was a closet full of clothes, all in my size. Actually, I've never had clothes that fit better than the ones that are in my room upstairs." I raise both eyebrows and glance between the four men. "So what is this fitting all about?"

"We're not measuring your body, you cheeky twat, just taking your mettle." March pauses next to me and grins, grabbing his velvet trench off the mannequin and fishing out a small note. "Here."

"What is this?" I ask, as he pulls out a small green vial, flashes me a sharp grin, and then tosses the small glass item on the floor to shatter. Smoke billows out, smelling like sour green apples and sugar, and when I blink through it, the March Hare is gone.

I unfold the note as Tee steps forward to explain.

"This isn't about body measurements—we need your *mettle*, that is, how resistant you are to magic. Your dress for the ball is going to have spells woven into it." I glance down at the note—there's a location and a time scribbled on it—and then back up at Tee.

"And who's going to cast those spells?" I ask, already fearing the answer.

"The Knave …" Tee says, and then pauses, glancing over at his brother. They both turn to look at me as Rab pockets his borrowed wire spectacles. "We're not happy about it either, but … King's orders."

"Well, clearly the King wants me dead because I don't trust the Knave for shit." I stare at the note again. *Tomorrow, same time. Ask where the dungeon is.*

Oh, the dungeon, huh? That sounds promising.

I crumple the note up and chuck it toward a half-full trash can. Tee intercepts it in mid-air, and opens it to read it, scowling as he goes about it.

"She cursed you both, and you want me to wear a dress with her magic in it? No way, no how." I cross my arms over my chest as Tee passes the note to Dee. The twins exchange a look.

"I'll be with you the whole time, Miss Alice," Rab says, grinning maniacally at me. "I wouldn't worry about the Knave. As much as she dislikes you, she quite likes the King … and she also likes keeping her head. Besides, you'll have an ace in the pocket, so to speak." As I watch, Rab's ears shrink toward his head, becoming rounder the smaller they get. At the same time, his body folds inward, and bright white fur sprouts up over his skin and clothes.

Before my mind can even register what's happening, there's a tiny mouse clawing his way up my pants and clinging to the hem of my button-up shirt.

Wish I could say I was shocked. Instead, I just scoop the mouse up and hand him over to Tee, so I can put my jacket back on. As soon as I do, I pop the Rab-mouse into my pocket.

"I will be your eyes and ears at the ball," he says, tiny pink nose twitching. It's fucking weird as fuck, but the mouse-Rab has tattoos on his naked little rodent feet. One of them is tick-tick-ticking away. *"As well as your teeth and claws."*

Oddly enough, I do feel better.

"After the Knave spells your dress, Dee and I will check it out, don't worry." Tee reaches out and squeezes my hand, and I nod.

But I have a funny feeling about the Knave.

And a woman should always trust her instincts.

♦ ♠ ♣ ♥ ♣ ♠ ♦

Dinner is turtle soup which sort of creeps me the fuck out.

"*Beautiful soup, so rich and green, waiting in a hot tureen,*" Dee singsongs as he ladles me a bowl and passes it over. I take it, but only begrudgingly, and only because I'm starving and tired. Snatching a bit of cheese from the refreshments table, I pass it down to Rab who's been transferred from my jacket pocket to my pj's pocket.

Chesh watches him hungrily from his perch on the cat tree.

"Put the little mouse down, and we'll have some fun," he says, pupils dilated, tongue sliding across his lower lip. "Play a little game of cat and mouse."

"How about a little game of cat and bandersnatch?" Rab says, his icy voice the same in his mouse form as it is in his … human? is he a human? … anyway, same as in his human form. It's a tad disconcerting.

"That doesn't sound nearly as fun," Chesh purrs, stretching and then wincing slightly. He reaches down and touches his side. There's no blood there, just a phantom pain, but according to the Duke, it takes a while for the Vorpal Blade's magic to run its course. Poor Chesh really is still hurting, despite the Mad Hatter's intervention.

I sit down on the bed, and Tee moves forward to fluff my pillows for me.

"You don't have to do that, you know," I say, feeling a slight blush color my cheeks. And I am not a girl who blushes easily. It's not that I don't like being fawned over, but I just sort of feel bad when Tee does it. He's too princely, too regal.

"I don't have to; I want to," he whispers, making me comfortable before retreating to grab his own bowl.

My room is bustling, far from the quiet little sanctuary I thought it was going to be.

Every one of my wannabe lovers save Red, Raiden, and March are here.

"Was I dreaming or did you cast some sort of spell on me while I was sleeping?" I ask Lar, looking at the green soup on my spoon and seriously debating if I'd rather live off cupcakes and candied honeybees for the rest of my stay here. There's even a plate of brightly colored mushrooms that each taste like a different fruit. How desperate am I for a hot meal right now?

"I cast a spell," he says, eating his own soup in a way that's undeniably sexy. He puts the metal spoon into his mouth, sucks on it, twists it around, and pulls it out oh so slowly. "Just to give your body a small reprieve from the pain."

"You knocked me out?" I give him a look that says that sort of pisses me off. Although, to be fair, I'm glad I slept through most of the day yesterday. That agony I felt when I used my magic was almost incomprehensible.

"No, I cut a small hole in your natural aura, so the extra magic would bleed out." Lar lets his wings hang loosely over the arms of the chair, like two glorious glittering tapestries.

"The Caterpillar isn't just a soothsayer," North purrs, lounging on the chaise at the end of the bed, black tail curled around the bedpost. "He's a fine curseworker in his own right."

"You flatter me," Lar says, putting his spoon down and setting his bowl aside. He crosses his legs and steeples his fingers atop his knee. Some men might look ridiculous in blue and white pinstriped pj's, but not him. He's a fucking enigma, and I love it. "But the Knave is better."

"Is there a difference between witches and curseworkers?" I ask, because I've heard the men use them interchangeably. Closing my eyes, I take a quick bite of my soup and pray to whatever goddesses rule over Underland that it won't taste so bad I puke.

Ohmyfuckinggod, that's good!

Turtle tastes like … veal.

And the broth is spicy and flavorful, a punch to the tongue that reminds me of Fred's favorite Indian restaurant. But then I swallow, and the yummy flavor leaves my mouth, making room for melancholy. When Fred was alive, we fought like cats and dogs. Now that he's gone, I miss him so much that I feel like I'm having period cramps even when I'm not.

I take another bite of soup to ward off the agony of missing my brother.

"Synonyms," Dee says, flopping down on the bed and somehow managing not to spill a single drop of soup. His wings are gone, disappeared in a flash at midnight, but since he's shirtless, I can see the beautiful tattoos they make along his back. Drool-worthy. "But the Knave is the highest ranking curseworker in the Kingdom of Hearts, which means she can throttle the power of other curseworkers." He takes a few bites of soup, blue-black hair falling across his forehead.

"She has you on a leash?" I ask, and I can see Lar's mouth tighten at the corners. Maybe that wasn't the best way to phrase things?

"Only the King holds my reins," the Caterpillar says, taking out a small pipe and fingering it for a moment. As soon as I see it, I'm reminded of his prophecy in the ballroom: we're supposedly going to have sex one day.

Wish I were shocked by that.

But then it's like he doesn't have the strength to see anything else today and pockets the pipe instead, pulling out a cigarette and smoking that while Rab's mousy nose twitches. Without thinking, I reach down and stroke the mouse's tiny head. *I'm stroking the tattooed asshole assassin,* I realize, but I don't stop doing it either.

"I'm just not *permitted* to use magic beyond a certain extent," Lar says, flicking his tongue across his lower lip and gently fanning his wings. He taps his cigarette ash into a gold tray shaped like a mouth, and I swear to fuck, it *burps* afterward.

"So you can't spell my dress?" I ask, still unsure how I feel about the Knave putting her stupid cursing fingers on it. She messed with the twins, violated them in a way I'm not even sure I understand; she took away their wings. I'm not okay with any of that.

"No, but I'll check it over—we all will. Sunshine, we won't let anyone or anything rain on your parade." Lar flaps his wings hard, sending glitter and brilliant blue-gold dust into the room. In his place, there's a small butterfly that flits over to one of the flowers from Dee's bouquet and rests gently on a white petal.

I have a feeling that Lar is not a shifter like Rab; he's gone to his room or wherever else. The butterfly is just that, just a beautiful insect.

"I want to sleep in here tonight," Chesh purrs, melting into his cat form and giving me a very dramatic stretch with his tail straight up in the air.

"Agreed," North says as I pull the Rab-mouse from my pocket, and set him on the end of the bed. "I say, banish those that aren't in the Alice's harem and leave the rest of us."

"Right little bugger," Rab growls as he grows in size, his fur sucking back into his skin, his ears elongating into a rabbit's, and his clothes falling neatly back into place. So Dee claims that North's clothes don't shift because he was cursed into becoming a jabberwock, while Rab was born a shifter and gets to keep his. Makes about as much sense as anything else I've learned here. "Nice trick, but the cat can't stay either, now can he?"

The White Rabbit slides off of my bed then turns to face me, looking down at me with a lascivious little smirk. He pushes his shirt sleeves up, flashing brightly colored tattoos.

"Tell me I'm a part of your harem, and I'll stay. I'll even fuck if you want."

I smile sweetly back at him.

"Get the hell out of my room," I sneer, and he grins, sliding the gold key from his pocket and heading for—surprise, surprise—the painting that features the infamous Tenniel image of the white rabbit checking his pocket watch.

I wait until he leaves before I take the last bite of my soup and set the bowl aside.

"Please tell me I can join your harem?" Chesh begs, padding across the air toward me, leaving little glowing paw prints floating behind him for a brief moment. He hops onto the bed and bats at my bare feet. "Ask your primary if I can join. I promise I'll be good." The Cheshire cat climbs up my legs to sit in my lap, looking up at me with big, round gray eyes, like two full moons in a night sky.

"Go to your room," I tell him, whittling down the men in my bedchamber to the ones I've fucked. Not sure if that's a good idea or if I'm just crazy.

Chesh shifts into human form, still sitting in my lap, and all of a sudden, it's not so cute or cuddly anymore. The tags on his collar jingle as he leans in toward me, one tiny fang peeking up over the edge of his lip. He's glorious, covered in tattoos, his vest gaping open to reveal the hard muscles underneath.

"I'll purr for you," he says, putting his mouth close to my ear. Chesh curls his fingers around my upper arm, and then licks my ear. I reach up and give his silver hoops a tug. He has them on both his kitty ears and his human ears.

"I'm glad you're not dead," I tell him as he pulls back just enough that his mouth is near mine. I can smell sweet cream and cupcakes on his breath, and I wish I could kiss him. But I've already kissed one stranger today, and that's enough. "Go to sleep, and we'll talk later."

"About me joining your harem?" he presses, and I flick him in the ear. I'd be mad if I thought Chesh was pushing at me like a typical misogynistic a-hole. He's not though. He's just lonely. If he really is the last of his kind, I can't blame him.

"Bed, now," North says, waving his hand lazily in the direction of the jabberwock painting. There's another one next to it though, one with a big smiling Cheshire Cat on it. I open the nightstand drawer, take out a key, and hand it to Chesh.

He curls his fingers around it, and meets my eyes with a much more serious expression on his handsome face.

"Thank you, Allison."

It's the first time he's ever called me by my real name.

Chesh curls his tail around my wrist as he turns, sliding the silky fur across my skin before he wanders off, unlocks his door, and leaves the room.

There's a certain finality to it when it closes.

"If I'd … sucked Tee off and swallowed, would you have had to eat some of his jizz, too?" I blurt at Dee, and I really wonder why the fuck I chose that moment to ask that question. He blinks big blue eyes at me. "I mean, when we first met, and you wanted me to go through the garden door …"

Dee lays back in the pillows and laughs while Tee flushes and turns down the lights.

The look he throws North is not particularly pleasant.

"I wouldn't have sucked my brother off if that's what you're asking," Dee chortles, chest heaving with laughter. "Just a little lick or a taste would've worked fine. I could've kissed you after and gotten enough to make the change, I'd think."

"I could've just … tasted some and gotten small?" I ask, wondering how a blow job would work with these guys. If I got even a little bit of cum on my lips, I'd grow or shrink depending on the twin? Sounds inconvenient. Yep, I am definitely going to break this curse. "Still gross, and I wouldn't have done it," I say, wondering what might've happened if Rab hadn't broken those bottles. Where would I be now? Home? The thought makes me uncomfortable. Would I still be here, lying in a half-dark room with these three men? Or sitting alone in my parents' quiet, broken home? "But really?"

"You have to swallow a certain amount for it to work, but basically, yes." Tee collects the empty soup bowls and spoons, setting them all on the refreshments table where I assume a card servant will come to collect them.

I lay back in the pillows and try not to seriously love the way all the linens smell here, like sunshine and wind. Back home, I had to do my own laundry, so let's be honest: my sheets did not smell even half this good, more like old Victoria's secret perfume and sweat.

"Enough about angel jizz," North growls, peeping his head up over the footboard to stare at me from narrowed, gold eyes. "You wanted us in here for a reason."

"Maybe she wants to discuss the nine?" Tee asks with a sigh, picking up my jacket from the floor and hanging it on one of the creepy, moving hooks.

"Maybe she wants to hear the rest of the prophecy?" Dee inserts, humming a tune under his breath.

"But nine young suitors hurried up,
All eager for their treat:
Their hair was brushed, their faces washed,
Their clothes were clean and neat—
And this was good, because, you know,
To date the Alice was a feat."

He starts reciting it, but North cuts him off, growling out another verse as he waves his hand dismissively.

"For all the monsters followed her,
They craved her bloody corpse;
So thick and fast the hordes attacked,
Just more, and more, and more—
All hoping for a bite or two,
Her men must prevent gore."

"There, you've heard quite enough of that nonsense," he says, climbing up over the footboard and crouching like a beast on the end of the bed. Tee moves over and sits beside me, crossing his arms over his chest. "Let's talk *shop*."

"There is no shop," I snort. "My vagina is not an open garage."

"A garage?" North asks, thinking hard on the word. "I'm not sure I know what that is. What I do know is that I am particularly interested in your *vagina*, for lack of a better word."

With a groan, I flop back into the pillows and cover my eyes with my arm.

"Please don't say vagina," I moan, feeling awkward tingles trace over my skin. I'm hot and achy inside, and I don't know what to say or do. I'm totally flubbing this moment up. Wait, flubbing? Where did that word come from? "I just … want to let you guys know that I'm not planning on running out and leaving you here." I move my arm off my eyes and pick at the edge of my blanket as Dee leans in close to me, pushing some rainbow strands of hair back from my forehead.

"You want to stay?" he whispers, and I shrug loosely.

"I want to help you," I continue, "for as long as it takes. I might … even want to stay. That doesn't mean I don't need to go home." I look up and find Tee watching me. "Because I do, but I want to be able to go back and forth, like Rab."

"Do you want me to show you?" Tee asks, tucking his hands into the pockets of his black linen pajama pants. He's wearing a tank top that shows off the muscles in his arms, and the purple and black feathers on the back of them. I swear on some Underland goddess' tits that if Edith and I had been watching a movie with Tee and Dee in it, I would've ended the film with my chest covered in drool.

"The Looking-Glass?"

I glance between the three men, and then back to Tee; he nods.

"Oh bloody hell," North growls out, but he stands up, too. "If Red finds us slinking around the Looking-Glass, he'll be furious." He taps a clawed finger against his lips and then shrugs those massive shoulders of his. "Oh well, I suppose it can't be helped. Were he to act a gentleman, he'd have offered the Alice use of it already."

"I understand not wanting to leave the portal open for the Walrus and his ilk, but I agree." Tee looks into my eyes, and I feel a shiver trace down my spine. He's got an old soul, that one. "You deserve a chance to see your family."

"You never realize how important they are until you lose them," Dee chokes out, standing up from the bed and grabbing his peaked cap off the nightstand. He tucks it over his blue and black hair, and then spins it around with a finger on the brim. "Let's go see the Looking-Glass, Allison-who-isn't-Alice."

My heart thunders in my chest, and I realize suddenly that I'm afraid.

And not of the King or the Hatter, not even of the Walrus and the Carpenter.

I'm afraid of going home.

Sometimes, our greatest fears are not our most obvious. Sometimes, our darkest terrors hide in plain sight.

"So," I whisper as we walk down the dark hallways, a shirtless dragon on my left, and twin fallen angel princes on my right. "Do the card servants …" I trail off and lick my lips. I understand that they're just cursed convicts, but they do bear an awful resemblance to the soldiers in Dee's vision-memory thing.

But then, I haven't told him that I saw that, so how do I even go about asking?

"They're just cursed souls, don't worry about them," Tee says while Dee grabs a torch off the wall as we pass. There are tapestries everywhere in here, and I swear to fuck, it feels like some of them are watching me.

"If the King can enchant them to be servants, then couldn't he make soldiers, too?" I hedge, hoping I'm not pushing too hard. I don't want to make the boys relive their trauma, but I'm dying to know.

"It's not the King that enchants them, though he could," Dee says, his face paling slightly as he taps a finger against the brim of his hat. He's trying to be casual, but I can see right through that facade to the pain underneath. "It's the Knave that spells them. And yes, when the previous King of Hearts ruled Underland, he did order her to create soldiers."

"But not anymore?" I ask, and the twins exchange a look.

"Brennin Red doesn't need or want those sorts of soldiers in his army," North growls, slamming his tail against the stone floor as we walk. "He's nothing like his father."

"So you say," Tee snaps back, raking his fingers through his hair. "And yet, we're still slaves. Underland stills suffers. The guillotine runs non-stop."

"He's *different*," North snarls back, and I start to wonder if I might have to insert myself between the two men. "And he's only been on the throne for three years. Try cutting him a break, hmm?"

"It would take two seconds for him to free us," Dee whispers, reaching over his shoulder to touch his tattoo. He looks over at North who grits his teeth.

"The Knave won't allow him to do it; he's tried."

"Bullshit," Tee quips, but then we're all standing before a massive red door in the shape of—you will never guess this shit—a *heart.* Le gasp.

"This is it?" I ask, glancing over my shoulder and down the long stone hallway we just traversed. A dozen hallways and who knows how many staircases later, and we're here. I was almost hoping we'd have to, I don't know, cross a moat or something. Some part of me wants the Looking-Glass as far away from me possible.

Who knew I had such trauma?

I clutch the front of my pj's in a fist as Tee pulls a chain out from beneath his shirt, a pair of keys hanging from the end of it. One of them is the key I gave him to access a Suit in my room, but the other is twice as big and made of solid iron.

"Keeps the pixies from pinching it," Dee explains with a sharp nod, like that makes all the sense in the world. Right. An iron key keeps magical flower-possessing pixies from stealing it. Sounds good.

Tee unlocks the door and steps inside, holding out a hand for mine. I take his in one, and Dee's in the other, moving slowly into the room and pausing on a ledge with a gold banister separating us from the rest of the room.

Down below … there's a giant chessboard in black and white.

"Holy butt waffles," I choke out, making Dee chuckle.

As we watch, one of the giant chess pieces—easily as tall as North if not taller—slides across the board into a new space. It's the red king, moving out of a "check" by the black knight.

The pieces seem to be made of some solid stone, like granite or marble, their faces frozen and silent, but menacing nonetheless. What would happen if I went down there and joined the Game?

"To get through to the Looking-Glass, you'll have to win against the black pieces," Dee explains, leaning his elbows on the gold banister and waiting for red to make their move. The red queen slides across the board, and a shiver travels down my spine.

"Don't get too close to the edge," Tee says, reaching out to grab a handful of his brother's shirt. "You've seen what those things can do if you piss them off."

"If you're not standing on edge, then you're taking up too much space," North says, crossing his arms over his bare, bronzed chest, and watching the Game play out below us. On the other side of the room, there's a mirror leaning against the wall.

It doesn't appear to be anything but a mirror from over here. I can even see the reflection of the chessboard and pieces in its silver surface. That's not to say it isn't gorgeous—it really is—with big gilded gold edges, a filigreed pattern etched into the swirling bits of metal. The frame reminds me of a winter-dead tree, its spindly branches reaching out to the edge of the world. If I saw that online back home, I'd order it. If I could afford it, that is.

"That's the Looking-Glass?" I ask, and both Tee and Dee reply at the same time.

"It is."

Curling my fingers around Tee's, I struggle to keep my feet in place.

I want to run.

Because going back home means facing all the unspoken issues I left behind. It means remembering that Dad is never home anymore, that Mom is *never* coming home, that Edith is drifting further and further away from the girl she used to be.

"If I win the Game, I can cross through the Looking-Glass?" I repeat, and North nods.

"But nobody has ever won the Game without the King's permission to play; it's rigged. You cannot win without Red's say-so." The jabberwock shifter glances over his shoulder at the sound of skittering feet out in the hallway. "Card servants," he explains before he looks back at us, "probably collecting information for the Knave. We should be going before she sends her ridiculous husbands after us."

"We'll figure out a way to get you home," Tee says, the conviction in his voice warming my insides. Before, I think he wanted to send me home for my own sake, but now I think he's just desperate to make sure I get a chance to reconnect with my family.

I love him for that.

Love him?!

Ew. No. No, I do not fucking love him. What is this, some young adult romance novel?! Gross.

"Let's go upstairs," I say, feeling that hot heat between my thighs start to pulse. Just the idea of taking the three of them to my room turns me on. It's persistent, that throbbing, desperate need, when I'm around these guys.

All three men turn to look at me.

Oh yes.

That invitation, it's as lascivious as it sounds.

"Are there any lions or tigers about here?" I ask as Tee unlocks the door to my chambers and pushes it open just enough that I hear a rumble from inside.

"It's only the Red King snoring," Dee says with a chuckle, pushing the door open the rest of the way and revealing a dark bedroom bathed in moonlight and shadows from the dying fire.

"Isn't he a *lovely* sight?" Tee says with clenched teeth, moving into the room to stand beside my bed.

I couldn't say honestly that he is. He has a tall, red night-cap on, with a tassel, and he's lying crumpled into a sort of untidy heap, snoring loudly.

Wow.

Talk about … total shock.

This man looks about as far from the dignified dickhead I've been dealing with as anything I've ever seen. He may as well have shape-shifted into a baby kitten.

"He's dreaming now," North says, cocking his head to one side. "What do you suppose he's dreaming about? The Alice's creamy thighs?"

"You're disgusting," I choke out, feeling like the King's just doused my hot, summer—wait, what season is it in Underland?—night in ice water. "What is he doing in my bed anyway?"

"That's an excellent question," Tee growls as Dee fills a small glass with water and moves over to stand next to Brennin Red's face. I notice that even in his sleep, he still wears gloves.

"If you try to wake him up by touching him …" Dee starts with a shrug, drawing his thumb across his throat. I get it: off with his head. So, much to my horror and chagrin, the younger twin tosses cold water onto the King's sleeping face.

He comes to like a wild animal disturbed in its den, eyes snapping open, one hand reaching for his glove. It's half off, and he's off the bed before I can even register what's going on. I catch a glimpse of a red palm before he realizes it's just us, and tucks his fingers back into the white fabric.

"A simple curseworker incantation can turn a person's hands red if they're guilty of murder." Tee's words ring in my head as I raise an eyebrow.

"What are you doing in my room?" I query, crossing my arms over my chest.

"And how did you even get in?" North asks, tilting his head to one side. His gold hair slides around his dark horns. "Only the Alice or one of her Suitors can let someone into the Suit of Hearts."

"Rab allowed me in," Brennin says, lifting his chin and still managing to look like some entitled asshole CEO with a bad attitude, even in his stupid night-cap. "I needed a place to rest my head tonight that might allow me to keep it." The way he says that, biting off the words, it sort of scares the shit out of me.

What the fuck does that even mean?

Is the King afraid in his own castle? If so, how the hell am I supposed to feel safe here?

"Don't you have your own chambers?" I snort, and Red narrows those ebon eyes on me.

"Nowhere in Castle Heart is as safe as the Alice's chambers. I was going to head to my own room, but my keys seem to have been misplaced." As Brennin talks, his teeth clench even tighter, and his jaw tightens to the point where I swear it may very well just fall off. "Rab let me in, and then I started to wonder where you all *went*." He gives North a look, like he's disappointed in him. "Sneaking around the castle in the middle of the night, tsk-tsk, *Savage Duke*."

"The Alice wants to use the Looking-Glass," North says, and Brennin scowls, tearing the cap off his head and tossing it aside. I swear to fuck, I see it glow. "She has a right, certainly, considering she hails from Topside."

"She has no right," Red snarls, giving me a look over his shoulder that could curdle milk. "Any use of the Looking-Glass leaves us open to assault from both Underland and Topside. It isn't happening, not until I get things under control." The King turns back to the window and watches the rain pour down the glass. "And then don't worry: I'll ship the Alice back to where she belongs."

"I don't—" Tee starts, but I put a hand on his chest to stop him, storming up to the King and getting in his face.

"You don't know anything about me, and you haven't bothered to try to learn. I don't want to go back home *forever*, I just want to see my family and let them know I'm alright. I'm committed to this shit now, okay? I'm in. For fuck's sake, if you're going to make accusations, at least get the facts straight first."

The King whirls on me, and I can see in his eyes that he's not used to being defied.

He raises a finger in my face.

"And you don't know *anything* about this world or its problems. You are not the savior, just a piece on a board to be moved. So, *Alice*, just go where I tell you and do what I say. And what I say is: don't bother wondering around the fucking castle unless you want to lose your head."

Brennin reaches down and into the pocket on my nightgown where I've stashed the keys to the Suits. I keep them on a ring with the master key when I leave the room, just in case. He takes one of the keys off, and then throws the others on the floor, moving to a painting of the King of Hearts, sitting on his throne and holding a heart-topped scepter.

That fucker ...

I follow after him because I'm not about to be disrespected like that. I let Liam treat me like shit for so long; I will never let another man walk all over me.

"Listen up, *buddy*," I snap as I step into the dark hallway, and the painting swings shut behind me, trapping me inside with the King. He turns around to look me, completely aghast that I've dared follow him.

Dickhead.

"You need to learn to control your temper." Brennin steps up close to me, but I'm not afraid of him. I've faced the worst in life; this is nothing. "If you want my help—no, if you need it, and I think you really do—then you have to tell me what's going on."

The King just stares down at me, a muscle in his jaw ticking as he clenches his teeth, his fists curled tight, his breathing coming in hard, angry pants. I'm breathing fast, too, and sweating profusely. My fight or flight instinct has kicked in, and I am so done with this man's shit.

"Just show up at the ball, and do what you're told," he snaps, and I reach up to grab the front of his robes without meaning to.

"Don't boss me around like I'm a fucking *dog*!" I shout, and then … something just snaps between us. One minute I'm grabbing the King and getting ready to shake him to death, and the next, my back is pressed to the stone wall, my arms are around his neck, and his mouth is on mine.

The first hot press of his tongue between my lips drags a groan from my throat that echoes down the dark stone hallway. The throbbing warmth between my thighs floods with wetness, and before I know it, I'm letting the King lift me up and press me against the wall. Our bodies grind together in this hot, sweaty tangle, our mouths feeding at one another. It's like for a split-second there, I'm not even human anymore.

With a gasp, I shove the King back, and he stumbles, dropping me to the floor. I manage to catch myself on the wall, my knees weak and shaky beneath me. My eyes are wide, and I'm just staring at the floor like I can't figure myself out.

"My Queen of Hearts," the King says, and there's this break in his voice that tells me all I need to know. I was right: I bruised his ego. He fucking wants me, doesn't he? "I told you that you were meant to be mine."

He takes off down the hall before I can figure out a retort.

Doesn't matter anyway, because all I can think to say is: *no, you were meant to be* mine.

"I'm sorry about last night," I say as the twins walk me to the athletic center, one on either side. North and Chesh were gone when I woke up, but Rab and Lar joined me for breakfast. So did March, but I chose to ignore him. It's pretty obvious the Hatter is sending him to keep an eye on me.

I don't trust that fucker as far as I can throw him.

"You don't have to apologize," Tee says, but the way he keeps his eyes on the floor makes me wonder if I should. I wanted last night to get lascivious … and I suppose it did, just not with the right guy. Or guys, rather.

"The King has a powerful presence," Dee says, looking up at the ceiling. We pass by several empty sitting rooms as we head down the stairs, take a sharp right, and then another hard left. One more right to get to the gym. At least it seems I'm starting to get the layout of Castle Heart down.

"I wanted to spend the night with you," I whisper, drawing both twins' attention my way. Dee opens his mouth to say something else, but when we come around the next corner, we stumble on the Knave and her creepy husbands. They're all dressed in black, with tiny pops of red hearts.

"Good morning, the Alice," the Knave says, looking me over and then flicking her eyes to either twin with this awful, smug sort of expression, probably enjoying the fact their wings are not out.

"It'd be a better morning if this curse were broken," I say, pointing opposite hands at either twin so that my arms make a cross in front of my chest. "We're all on the same side here, so what say you?"

"I say your friends still have a lot to learn," she says, her brunette hair swept into a perfect bun, her tiny crown sitting pretty on top of her head. Her green eyes bore into me, and I know for a fact that this fancy dress she's spelling for the ball, we'll have to check it very carefully. The Knave wants me gone; I can see that plain as day. "Once I feel they've learned their lesson, I'll remove the spell."

"You mean once we bow down and kiss both your feet, and the King's?" Tee snaps, curling his lip up in a snarl. "I'll keep the curse."

"Suit yourself," the Knave purrs, giving us a venomous little smile. "Your people were offered two choices: come to heel, or die. They chose the latter. I see stupidity runs in your veins. Now, if you'll excuse—"

"Are you looking for the King?" I ask, taking a step closer to her and noticing that both the Unicorn and the Lion are watching me with predator's eyes. Fuck, I don't like a single person in the Knave's little family. "Because after he kissed me, and we nearly fucked last night, he went to bed in my chambers." I smile, but the Knave's expression doesn't change. I do see a bit of the skin around her eyes tightening though.

I've pissed her off.

"He might still be in bed." I smirk and then turn to Dee first, wrapping my arms around his neck and kissing him hard. His wings unfold from his back in glorious swathes of black and blue feathers, the chains falling to the stone floor with the loud clang of metal. I feel something else, too, something I never noticed before: an loosening, an unleashing, an unraveling of power that explodes from Dee's body along with his wings.

His magic.

Without giving the Knave and her men a chance to walk away, I turn to Tee and I kiss him hard and fast in front of them, freeing his wings and his power to the scoffing dismay of the witch.

"I'm shocked the King lets you get away with such behavior," Ines clucks as I lean back and look into Tee's eyes, the lust and want and need playing out there making my toes curl inside my boots. "I doubt the Court of Hearts will allow you such trivialities."

She pushes between me and Tee, her lackeys … I mean *husbands* trailing along behind her.

"Fucking"—I start, looking for an insult that isn't inherently misogynistic—"butt waffle nipple licking asswad."

Tee raises an eyebrow at me, and then folds his wings around my body, holding me close.

"That was a creative insult," he says as Dee pushes his way between Tee's wings, and slides his arms around my waist from behind. Being sandwiched between the two boys is a serious fucking turn-on for me, and I feel myself struggling to swallow past a surge of emotion.

"She deserves a creative ass-kicking," I whisper as the twins step back just enough to give me some space. And yet, the last thing I want to do is move out from between them.

"She does indeed," Dee says.

"Indeed," Tee repeats, but the way he's looking at me, I'm pretty damn sure he isn't thinking about the Knave anymore. Fuck her, right? I'm the Alice, so I should be able to (eventually) break the curse on the twins by myself.

"Why is the Alice called … well, the Alice?" I whisper, doing my best to change the subject. If I focus too much on the twins, and their glorious wings, their jewel-tone eyes, or their shockingly different but still amazing personalities, I'll probably collapse into a puddle on the floor.

"Because …" Tee chokes a little and takes another step back from me, like he doesn't know what might happen between us if he stands too close. "It stands for *All Living Individuals Can Escape*. You are their escape from Underland, from the madness, from the remnants of the Riving." He turns his head and looks away for a moment.

"And you are *the* only one. You are not just Alice, or an Alice, you are *the* Alice." Dee puts his hands on my shoulders and kneads my flesh, sending warm tingles throughout my body.

It's not just because his touch makes my heart thunder—it's because I feel like he's right. Edith could've been the Alice, maybe, but now I *am* the Alice. This is *my* job.

Leaning forward, I let my breasts press against Tee's chest, and thread my arms around his neck.

"Allison," he says, almost like he's trying to warn me.

"What's in that room right there?" I whisper, pointing to the door behind him. Dee doesn't waste a single second in hurrying over to open it, letting us into a small library filled with the scent of paper and ink, that delicious old book smell that could turn me on even if I were soaking wet and on my period.

Add in the gorgeous twins with their beautiful wings?

I'm a goner.

The sound of whispering fills the room as Dee heels the door shut behind us.

"Do the books talk?" I ask, and I can't help it: I whisper, too. With my arms still threaded around Tee's neck, I lift my head up and gaze at the bookshelves soaring above us. They must be at least thirty feet tall, if not taller. The room we're in is small, and pentagonal, but there must be tens of thousands of books in here, at least.

"Don't judge a book by its cover," Dee says, picking one up and flipping it open. "Judge by its pitch."

"A tale of knights so bold, so brave, they not only looked death in the face, they bent him over and fucked him in the ass with their swords."

Dee snaps the book closed and smiles at me.

"Holy fuck," I breathe, blinking stupidly at him over my shoulder before I turn back to Tee. "I'd read that. How come my Alice book doesn't talk?"

"It came from your world," Tee explains. Ah, that's right. There's no magic Topside. Nothing there but pain and suffering and rapists who walk out of court with smirks on their faces.

I'm struggling to remember why I wanted to ever go home in the first place. I mean, besides briefly to see my family. I *have* to see my family, but once I let them know I'm okay, I may never leave Underland again.

"You've convinced me," I say, letting go of Tee just enough that I lean back into Dee when he slides up behind me again. Just in case I haven't made it clear, I repeat myself. "I want to stay, Dee. I want to change the world."

The sound he makes from behind me, it's fucking priceless.

Releasing Tee, I turn around and put my hands on either side of Dee's face, leaning up on my tiptoes to kiss him. He beats me to it, dropping his face until our mouths are brushing together, until I can smell his clean air scent, feel his breath on my lips.

Our kiss starts slow and easy, almost languorous, but it quickly picks up speed.

My fingers tangle in Dee's jacket, and I drag him over to the chaise lounge, pushing him down onto it, and straddling his lap. When I grind my hips against him, I can feel his erection through his slacks.

I've never been on birth control because, as a point, I don't feel it's all a woman's responsibility to take it. There are much easier ways to deal with that, without having synthetic hormones coursing through my body: condoms, pull-out method, *male* birth control (about half the side effects, people), etc. But at least here, I don't seem to need it, at least not with North, Tee, or Dee.

Thank fuck, right?

Dee tangles his fingers in my hair, and I do the same to him, kissing him with all the pent-up emotion that's been coursing through me for the past few days. I'm surrounded by gorgeous men, and I'm resisting them at every turn when what I really want is to give in and let myself get swept up in the fantasy that's become my reality.

"Tee," I whisper, reluctantly breaking from Dee's lips for a moment, the only noise in the room the whisper of the books and the combined sounds of our heavy breathing. I look up at the elder of the two twins, and see a book slide off the shelf and flutter around like a butterfly, leaving gold sparkles in its wake.

Talk about a turn-on.

For a second there, I think Tee's going to run, but then he takes a step forward. And another, and another.

Tee climbs onto the couch behind me, sliding his palms over my rib cage and making me groan. When his hands reach the front of my body, he slides them up, palming my breasts through the pale blue, ruffled button-up I picked out for today.

He squeezes them gently at first, and then firmly, like he's decided for sure that he's doing this.

I lean back into him as Dee takes me by the hips and encourages me to move, grinding our bodies together in a way that's ridiculously pleasant, even with our clothes still on. Sliding my palms over Dee's shoulders, I find his wings and give his glossy feathers a sharp tug as we kiss.

Tee continues to caress and squeeze my breasts, finding my nipples through the fabric and squeezing them until I stop making any sounds that are remotely human.

Why didn't I wear a skirt today?! I think as Tee's left hand comes down and starts to unbutton my pants. He makes an awkward sexual necessity into something sensual and exciting, sliding his hand inside and teasing the front of my heart-patterned panties.

"Three lovers entwined together in a weird, weird world," one of the books whispers as it crashes to the floor and opens onto a lewd ink drawing of a threesome.

How appropriate.

Dee moves his hands to my shirt, tearing open the fabric and sending buttons flying. He goes for my breasts next, popping the full, round mounds over the top of my corset and sliding his thumbs over my aching nipples.

I do the same to him, tearing his shirt open and teasing *his* nipples, making him buck his hips up against me while Tee utilizes his wings to brush and tease my now bare shoulders. Dee sweeps his up and around his brother, trapping the three of us in a feather cocoon.

Our hands and mouths explore and tease, work our bodies into wild frenzies. I can feel Tee hard and wanting behind me, grinding his hips into my ass as he teases my clit with his fingers, making me squirm and groan.

A book flutters past me as I sit up and start to shimmy out of my pants. I just want them off *now*.

Tee and Dee help me out, removing one leg first, and then the other. It's not the most acrobatic or sensual thing, and I certainly don't belong in a porno, but my awkward fumble ends with my pants *and* my underwear on the floor, and me feeling a hell of a lot happier about my current situation.

I scoot back slightly and help Dee out of his black denim jeans, freeing his cock from the confines of the fabric and taking him into my hand. My fingers curl around his shaft as he bucks up into my grip.

"Allison," Tee says in my left ear, "how do you want us?"

I'm not sure if I've ever heard a sexier question in my whole life. North's *"Mate with me?"* comes pretty close, but that's the only thing in the running.

I have to think for a moment because I've never been in a position quite like this before.

Two beautiful men, two glorious shafts.

Just … what do I do with them?

I've only tried anal sex once, and I hated it, but that was with Liam. Tee and Dee are different—and not just because they're fallen angels. No, these are *real* men. They care about how I feel, what I want, how they can pleasure me and not just themselves.

"I'd like to try …" I start, licking my lower lip. *Oh hell, Allison, if you can't even say it, you don't deserve to be having it.* "Having both of you at once."

There's a sound that Tee makes that travels straight to my core and floods me with vibrant waves of lust. He can't make that sound in my ear and not expect me to go crazy.

I lift myself up on my knees and gasp when Tee takes my hips, helping me guide his brother to my opening. I'm moaning and crying with pleasure before I've even taken all of him, putting my face in the crook of Dee's neck and breathing in his scent. His wings sweep around us again, this cocoon of safety that I just can't get over. It's too much, too amazing to be held in their wings like this.

Behind me, Tee kisses his way down the side of my neck, pausing to nibble at my shoulder. I get the weirdest thought then, of how I'd like to get each of them tattooed on my arm, an entire sleeve of Underland's most beautiful men.

Ink dreams aside, I settle down until Dee is fully sheathed inside of me, filling up all that empty space in my heart at the same time he fills my body. I feel happy and complete here with him and Tee; I trust them implicitly.

I know I shouldn't because I've only known them for two short weeks, but that doesn't matter. I'm riding the sex high in that moment, and I'm getting these waves of affection and feeling toward them that I've never experienced before.

"Touch me," I whisper as my eyes water. I'm not actually crying, but it just feels so damn good that my eyes are tearing up. "All over." The boys comply as I stare into Dee's half-lidded sapphire eyes and see his lips curve up in a cocky little smile.

"Your wish is our command," he purrs out, his voice this mix of playful and confident that I find irresistible. He's one of those people who's so full of emotion, they need to be unpacked on a regular basis. I feel an empathetic pang as I lean down to kiss him again, and he caresses the back of my neck with his fingers.

"Ditto," Tee whispers, sweeping hair off the side of my throat, so he can kiss me there again.

"Ditto, ditto," Dee growls as his brother fumbles with something behind me. When I look back, I see that he has some sort of lube bottle in his pocket, and raise my eyebrow.

"I—" Tee stutters, flushing red and then flattening his mouth out into a severe line. The expression is much less intimidating than it should be, considering he's got his cock in his hand. "This isn't what you think."

"Sure it's not," I say, but I don't care where he got lubricant or why.

I turn back to Dee, kissing him until his brother is ready, teasing a lubed finger down my ass crack and then stroking my opening. He caresses and plays with me until I'm warmed up and writhing, biting Dee's lower lip and wishing Tee would just put it in already.

When he does, there's this tiny, brief moment of pain where I'm convinced this position isn't going to work. But Tee is so gentle and so careful that he works me up again, going nice and slow as I slide up and down on Dee's shaft.

"More," I grind out, sweating all over the poor boys and wondering if I still look sexy with blonde and rainbow strands of hair stuck to my forehead and cheeks. Dee reaches up and carefully peels some of it away, cupping the side of my face in his hand.

He locks eyes with me as his brother introduces a second finger, teasing that wall of flesh between my ass and my cunt. It feels *so fucking good.* I can barely even breathe.

"Allison-who-isn't-Alice," Dee breathes out, running his thumb over my lip. "Beautiful girl to change the world."

"Intelligent woman to win the war," Tee singsongs back, pulling his fingers out and putting the head of his shaft up against me. I wiggle back into him, but both he and Dee hold me in place and force me to keep it slow.

"Glorious angels to defend the queen," I say, and they both make these noises of acknowledgement. We're a team now, we got this.

Tee presses up against me, and then eases his shaft into my ass as my back arches, and I struggle to keep myself together.

I'm breaking apart in the most beautiful way; I'm coming unhinged in glorious madness.

And all I want is more. More, more, more.

Once Tee is settled, there's this moment of perfect peace where both boys are sheathed inside of me, their cocks pressed tightly together with the thin wall of my flesh between them, a glorious twin sandwich that reminds me of my favorite books: The Kit Davenport series by Tate James.

Kit gets a twin sandwich and now, so do I.

"Fuck me?" I ask, but the twins respond in unison in the most twin-ly way possible.

"Fuck us?" they repeat in unison.

My body begins to move, but the twins can't seem to help themselves. They quickly take over, their fingers intertwined over my hips, their own hips thrusting in unison. Their shafts press tight against that sensitive bit of flesh I didn't even really know I had. I mean, logically, I always knew it was there, but who knew that pressure on either side of my vaginal wall would feel as good as a clitoral orgasm?

Dee takes over my breasts, leaving Tee to guide our movements as a group, thrusting hard against me. I can feel the strength in his hands and arms as he holds me and fucks me at the same time. These boys might be young, but they are fucking *strong*—physically and metaphysically.

I can't wait to see them kick some ass.

Dee's wings spread up and back all of a sudden, jostling all three of us. He arches his back and groans, squeezing my breasts so hard I might get bruises, but I don't think he means it. No, he just comes hard and fast, groaning and writhing with the pleasure as he spills himself inside of me.

My pussy is throbbing, my nipples hurt, and my brain feels like it might just explode if I don't get some release. It's like Tee can sense what I need—he always seems to—and his fingers find my clit, rubbing and teasing it with both my wetness and his brother's, making me come just as violently beautiful as Dee.

My fingernails dig into Dee's shoulders as I throw my head back, both twins sweeping their wings around me until I'm wrapped up in feathers and bliss, orgasming with a scream that echoes around the quiet, whispering library. I even drag Tee with me, making him grunt and pound harder until he finishes inside of my still throbbing body, the aftershocks squeezing my muscles around both twins' shafts until they can't take it anymore.

Tee rolls off and onto the floor while Dee very gently pushes me off of him.

For several moments, we just lie there and breathe.

There's—for lack of a better word—*fluid* all over the place, running down my thighs when I stand up.

"Do you think North will forgive us for being late?" I ask, but at that moment, I'm too happy to care.

"I think he'll have no choice," Tee says, and even though he's lying on his back on the floor, he looks haughty and sexy as fuck. "*I* am the primary, so he better get used to it."

I grin, and press a kiss to Dee's lips first, and then Tee's.

Bring on the training, bring on the Knave, bring on the ball.

I'm Allison Liddell, and I have fucking got this.

♦ ♠ ♣ ♥ ♣ ♠ ♦

"My mate," North mutters as he opens a pistol of his own and loads it up with a small metal ball. It looks like a Kingmaker to me. I love that it's smaller and less impressive than a Queenmaker. In the human world, anything labeled queen is usually smaller and less important than the king version: beds, chess pieces, etc.

Underland is weird as hell, but it's refreshing, too.

"Mine," he growls, tail thrashing as he grits his teeth and turns to me. The White Knight is there, too, and she gives him a very unimpressed look.

"Your strange jabberwock possessiveness is entirely unappealing," she says with a sniff, lifting her chin and then glancing over at me. "And this is why I don't keep husbands. Too much work."

"It's simply in my nature to want the Alice to be mine," North says, flicking blonde hair off his forehead in a very dramatic and Duke-ly way. He takes his station very seriously, prancing around with his nose in the air and his gold eyes full of disdain. I sort of love him for it.

"Well, get over it," Chesh purrs, lying on the rafter above us, one arm hanging down, his finger drawing glowing gold designs in the air that disappear like fireflies in the wind. "Everyone knows a cat owns everything he sees."

"I thought Underland men were supposed to be different than Topside men? You all belong to *me*," I say, aiming the Queenmaker at the targets in the far distance. We're standing just outside the athletic facility, the back doors wide open, facing a stretch of beautiful green field as far as the eye can see.

There's a floral border on either side of the grass, separating this part of the royal gardens from the rest of the grounds. I can hear the flowers bitching about me right now.

"As likely to blow 'er head off as the Carpenter's," one says, her accent reminding me of every generic peasant character I've ever seen in a cheap budget fantasy movie. *"Maybe she should aim for the Walrus', eh? At least he's got more to shoot at!"*

"Won't last a minute against the Anti-Alice," a lily replies, flicking her leaves in my direction. *"We're liable to lose the Kingdom of Hearts to the clubs."* I turn and point the Queenmaker in her direction. I would blow us all to kingdom come if I were to shoot at this close a range, but at least I see the stupid flower quiver, and the pixie spirit jumps to a blossom several feet away from me.

Another one of the stupid things tries to pull my room key from my pocket, and I slap it away, watching its translucent wings as it flitters over to a daisy and slips inside. This is my first time actually seeing the pixies, and I'm surprised to find that they really do look like fucking Tinkerbell or some shit, albeit with brightly hued skin in every color of the rainbow.

They are also naked as fuck, and I swear I've seen enough pixie pussy in the last five minutes to last me a lifetime.

"The Queenmaker uses your magic," Tee explains as Chesh shifts into cat form and hops off the wooden beam under the awning and onto my head. About two hundred yards out, there are nine silver bowls gleaming in the sunlight. North and the twins claim they'll help absorb the blasts from the Queenmaker, so I don't destroy the entire castle while I'm still learning. "That's what makes it so powerful; it's more than just gunpowder and sulfur."

"How did I just randomly pick this off a shelf in the Rabbit-Hole?" I ask, but nobody bothers to answer me with actual words.

Instead, Dee claps his heels together, salutes, and recites another verse from the prophecy that never ends. How many fucking stanzas is this thing?! My guess, based on personal experience here in Underland, is that it has eighteen, just like the original *The Walrus and the Carpenter* poem.

"The Gryphon and the Mock Turtle
Watched on from perches far,
And then they contemplated hell
On kingdoms so bizarre:
The Queenmaker their only hope
Against a ragged scar."

Dee finishes with a little bow, and a grin.

"Prophecy, Allison-who-isn't-Alice-but-whom-I-quite-adore." He winks at me as I flush and turn back to the targets, watching as the White Knight loads up a gun that matches her armor. It looks like a flintlock pistol as well, but it's all white, like it's been carved of marble or something.

Apparently, it's called a *Knightmaker.* Very creative, huh? I do appreciate the theme, however.

"So I was destined to hold this weapon in my hands?" I ask, teasing my fingers along the gold designs on the side. I lift my eyes to look up at Dee, and he smiles softly.

"You were destined," he says, but I don't fully believe him. I think people can create their own destinies. Then again, maybe there's magic at work here, as a guiding hand or something? I can't help but think how I was compelled to follow the White Rabbit down the hole, or how I keep saying things that are straight out of the original book without even meaning to. It's like there's some grand storyteller in the sky, trying to guide my fate.

If there is, she better fuck off, because I have ideas of my own.

"What's your name?" I ask the White Knight, because everyone here seems to have a nickname, even me. In fact, I have several: the Alice, Allison-who-isn't-Alice, Sonny, Sunshine, Miss Alice, Miss Liddell, and so on and so forth.

"My name?" the White Knight repeats, blinking pretty lavender eyes at me. She tosses some blonde hair over her shoulder, and it shimmers in the sunshine like it’s spun gold. Seriously, she must be the most beautiful woman I've ever seen in my life. "Chevalier." She smiles at me like she thinks I have no idea what that means in French. It means *knight*, by the way. I took like two years of classes at my high school.

"Is your last name *Blanc*?" I question with a raised brow, and the White Knight grins. So the White Knight's name … is literally *Chevalier Blanc,* aka White Knight in French. Very creative, almost as creative as calling the Cheshire Cat, Chesh.

"The King wants to make sure you're actually learning something down here," she states in crisp, clear tones, no judgement, just fact. "And he knows I'm the best woman for the job."

"You're an inventor?" I ask as North steps up close behind me, and makes my entire body tingle as he adjusts my grip on the gun, putting my fingers in the same place that Dee did. Having a second teacher repeat the same lessons I learned before is helpful in cementing them into my brain.

"That's right," the White Knight says, lifting up her gun with one hand and putting on a very dramatic sideways pose with her left arm outstretched. She fires off a shot that lobs up toward the sky and then falls perfectly down into the center of one of the metal bowls, slamming into the bull's-eye with a horrific wave of fire and heat. "Bam," she growls, lifting her pistol to her lips and blowing on it. "I'm a knight by day, inventor by night. Ironic, isn't it? It feels as if I should be a knight by night, and inventor by day perhaps?" She tilts her head to one side in that weird Underland way.

More nonsensical logic.

Fantastic.

"How are you enjoying your breastplate of courage?" she asks, making me feel a little warm and fuzzy inside. You know when you read a book, and the female main character only has meaningful relationships with men, and you're left wondering why the fuck all her interactions with women are hateful and gross?

Yeah, I despise that shit.

I just want to … go get my nails done with the White Knight or something.

I *like* her.

"Breastplate of Courage?" I ask, lifting a brow as North steps to the right of me, takes aim and fires his own shot off. He, too, hits the silver target, but not the bull's-eye. The White Knight grins and he growls at her, thrashing his tail around wildly.

"I didn't just invent those easy-on/easy-off buckles," Chevalier declares proudly, tapping at her shoulders. "I imbued the armor with courage. If you put it on, you'll feel like a wolf amongst sheep."

"Huh," I say, taking aim with the Queenmaker and doing my best to hold her steady in both hands. "Do you think I can wear it to the ball over my dress? Because dragons that make my ears bleed and birds that shoot spider silk are okay, but dancing in front of other people sounds like pure hell."

"I think wearing it would be a great idea," Tee says, the warm sound of his voice making me tremble just enough that when I fire, the metal projectile goes wide, a miniature cannonball flinging through the air toward the row of flowers.

Pixies scream and flee their garden as North waves his hand, and with a bit of magic, sends the projectile into one of the targets where it explodes with enough force to singe the hairs on my arm.

Holy fucking hearts.

Dee moves over to a small table near the wall where a gramophone sits, spins the handle on the side, and then carefully removes a record from a sleeve sitting on a shelf full of others. He places the needle carefully onto it, and then steps back as it begins to crackle.

Some vintage, twenties sounding song starts to garble out.

One thing I would miss living here: fucking Spotify and iTunes.

I still have my cellphone … somewhere. I should dig it out and see if I can't get it to play some modern day music for these boys.

"Sorry, I was distracted," I say as Chesh weaves between my legs, rubbing on my ankles as the White Knight moves over to help me reload the Queenmaker.

"The sound of your lover's voice," she begins, and I blush. I'm still a tad sore downstairs, and every movement I make reminds me of my threesome with the twins. I won't soon forget. "Is nothing compared to the chaos that will ensue during battle."

The Cheshire cat shifts back into his human form beside me, as gloriously half-dressed as always, and stares at me from big, gray eyes.

"If you need to keep your calm during battle, simply repeat this mantra inside your head. It'll keep you focused," he purrs as Chevalier once again fixes my grip. I will get this, eventually. I'm not doing too shabby considering I've never shot a vintage, magical flintlock pistol before last week, right? "Ahem." The Cheshire cat clears his throat, licks his paw, and runs it over his dark hair and his striped ears, making the silver hoops in them jingle merrily. "As it goes:

'Twas brillig, and the slithy toves
Did gyre and gimble in the wabe:
All mimsy were the borogoves,
And the mome raths outgrabe."

Chesh pauses for a moment and smiles at me with that feral cat grin of his.

"Beware the Jabberwock, my girl!
The jaws that bite, the claws that catch!
Beware the Jubjub bird, and shun,
The frumious Bandersnatch!"

I raise my eyebrows as North growls from behind me, and I hear an icy voice at my back.

"Frumious?" Rab drawls, smoking a cigarette and swinging a pocket watch at his side. He's dressed in red and white today, no black. It makes his red eyes and dark hair pop even more. "How *daaare* you?"

Rab pauses next to me, and nods with his chin in the direction of the targets.

"You're already late for your dancing lessons with the Caterpillar," he says, that cold voice doing more to warm up my insides than it rightfully should. "So let's see what you can do with that thing and get going."

"I've barely gotten time to practice," I grumble, but I suppose that's my own fault. Mine and the twins', that is.

I glance over at Rab, his eyes ringed in dark liner, his smile a dangerous sort of pretty that kills happy hearts and makes them wish they had a million lives so they could die over and over again.

So not a guy I should be going after.

And yet …

Rab is so freaking distracting that I have to tear my eyes away from him and actually start to mumble the cat's stupid, catchy little *Jabberwocky* poem.

"Twas brillig, and the slithy toves," I grumble.

I smirk, take aim, and fire off a second shot.

This time, I hit the center target … *and* the bull's-eye.

♦ ♠ ♣ ♥ ♣ ♠ ♦

When I leave the athletic facility and head for the ballroom, I realize that I'm actually looking forward to my lessons with Lar.

"I get an entourage today?" I ask, because Chesh, Rab, North, and the twins are all with me right now.

"You get an entourage the rest of the week," Rab says, glancing over at the Duke like they know something nobody else does. We pass under glass ceilings and glorious arches, past huge doorways that lead to Hearts only knows where. Card servants are everywhere, scurrying around like ants. I can barely stand to look at them, and based on the twins' reactions, I think they feel the same. "The castle is restless. Everyone wants to meet you. And, to be quite frank, several of them want to murder you. Personally, I'll settle for fucking you. What do you say?"

"I say … eat a dick?" I reply with saccharine sweetness as I flip him off.

When we head into the ballroom, the Caterpillar is already waiting for us, sitting on a big blue velvet pillow in the center of the room. He has his white jacket with the gold epaulettes resting on his shoulders, but there's no shirt underneath, showing off his glorious chest and those two key piercings through his nipples.

Don't think about the sex prophecy he showed you, I warn myself. *Don't think about it, Alice. Don't, don't, don't.*

Aaaaanndddd, now I'm thinking about it.

In detail.

Glorious, glorious detail.

"Welcome," Lar says, his eyes half-lidded, the color of a summer sky. He gestures for us to take seats on the colored pillows surrounding his, passing the hookah he's smoking over to me.

"Are we going to dance in the air again?" I ask, and I get this lazy, confident smile in return.

"We're going to dance the quintrille," he says, which is not really an answer to my question. "Although … we're a bit short on dancers."

I notice there are more pillows on the ground than people.

As in, say, ten total pillows including the one I'm sitting on.

Hmm.

The ballroom doors swing open, and I glance over my shoulder to find the Mad Hatter and the March Hare sauntering into the room with Dor on their heels.

"Oh *heeeeelllllll* no," I say, letting go of the hookah and standing up. The air is perfumed with the sweet scent of blueberries and tobacco, but as much as I want to experience that glorious feeling of floating and dancing, I will not put up with the Dormouse.

I mean, Raiden Walker and March are bad enough, but the Dormouse dick basically clobbered a chunk of North's skull out—and he'd happily do it again.

"I will not dance with him," I say as the big, ugly man scowls at me and scratches as his tiny, stupid mouse ears. They're so little and they blend in with his brown hair, I can't even remember if I've seen them before.

"Fortunately for you," the Mad Hatter says, whipping off his hat. A swarm of bats—yes, you heard me, a *swarm of bats*—explodes out from underneath, swirling in the air around him and then taking off for the domed glass ceiling, chittering as they go. "You won't be dancing with Dor tonight."

Raiden pulls his cane out, and taps it against the floor before replacing his hat and smiling at me with sharp, white vampire fangs. I'm too freaking dumbfounded to speak. Bats. Fucking bats. Now I really *have* seen it all.

"Then who's taking the place of this last pillow?" I ask indignantly, pointing down at the red velvet cushion on the floor.

"Me." The serene calm in that voice draws my attention over to Brennin Red, standing in the doorway to the ballroom with the White Knight on one side, and the Knave on the other. *Grrreeaaat,* exactly the woman I wanted to see. She has her two weird husbands behind her, too, and I'm pretty sure all three of them are glaring at me.

Red walks his supreme asshole-ish-ness over to me, his dark eyes hard, his crown drooping lazily over his forehead. His white gloves squeak as he reaches up and adjusts the gold hook and eye clasp that holds his voluminous white and red robes in place.

"You'll be expected to dance with me at the ball, so we may as well see what clumsiness we can iron out today."

"I'd rather dance with Dor," I say, but I don't mean it. My palms are sweating, and I can't take my eyes off the King's. He makes my throat feel tight and sticky and sore, my heart thunder, my fingers twitch. I want him dead, but I also want to leap into bed with him. I've never been so confused about my own feelings before.

"Is that so?" Brennin asks coolly, eyeing me up and down like a steak served too well-done. He'd rather just send me back and get a new slab of fresh meat for his plate. "Well, too bad. That brainless thug isn't the ruler of an entire kingdom—*I am*. And as my future queen, the court will want to see you dance with me."

"I am not your future queen," I snap back, hating myself for having made out with this guy. Shit, more than made out: I practically fucked him. I turn away and run my fingers through my hair, making eye contact with March.

He sucks on a very … shall we say *phallic*-shaped lollipop, and gives me this dirty half-smile that promises awful, awful things.

"Lackey piece of shit," I grumble as I sit back down on the velvet pillow and take the hookah from Lar, letting his pale fingers tangle with mine, just so I can feel that little thrill between us. "Whatever. I don't have time to argue. Let's just get this over with, shall we? After the ball, we'll figure out how to deal with each other."

I can *feel* the King staring at me from behind. His eyes are like lasers, making me squirm with their heat. Fucker.

Deep down, there's some part of me that's *thrilled* at the idea of being the Queen of Hearts. What little girl wouldn't jump at the thought of not only visiting their favorite childhood storybook world, but *ruling it*.

"Maybe we can get married, and just not talk?" I glance over my shoulder and find Brennin Red still staring at me. The Knave's mouth is turned down at both corners, and I just know I'm going to trip and fall on my ass because she's here staring at me. Thus, the story of my life. "Then I can be the Queen of Hearts, your little prophecy will be fulfilled, and then we can just never speak again?"

"Mm," Lar murmurs, and when I glance over at him, I catch him watching me with that half-lidded stare. I get the feeling there's something he's not telling me. Another prophecy? I wouldn't be surprised.

"Your lack of interest in our glorious King of Hearts is disturbing to me," the Knave purrs, her voice like velvet and sandpaper. There's a painful softness to it that makes my teeth hurt. "And what's disturbing to me is disturbing to the court."

"That's quite enough of that," the King says, and when I glance over my shoulder again, I get caught in that ebon stare, and find it impossible to take another breath. "You were invited to observe, not to talk."

The look on the Knave's face is *priceless.* The Lion—I can't remember if he's Rook or Knight—takes a step forward, but Ines reaches out and puts a hand on his shoulder. The three of them move over to a seating area filled with tufted chairs in red and white, sitting their black-clad asses down on the cushions. They look like they're on their way to a freaking funeral.

I turn back to Lar and accept the hookah again, pulling in a long, smoky breath of tobacco and flowers, teased through with the fruity freshness of blueberries. Already, I can feel that lightness in my skull, as if I'm starting to float.

"Let's get to this, shall we?" March says, his accent thick and sexy as hell. He looks like a model, lounging there in an unbuttoned white shirt, the sleeves pushed up, a small top hat on his own head. He's still eating—do I ever see him *not* eating?—sucking the lollipop between his lips in a very suggestive sort of way. "The Alice and I have an appointment in the dungeon."

"And you're already late," Rab says, checking one of his tattoos. "I don't see how we're going to be ready for the ball. If everything went smoothly—and I mean *everything*—we'll be lucky to get out of there with a disdainful approval from the court. But I can hardly imagine getting through the evening without bloodshed and substantial crimson splatter."

"Why is it you sound so fucking excited about that?" I ask, passing the hookah around the circle. Brennin Red finally sits down on the side opposite the Hatter, two titans in one room. I have this feeling they're being civil for *now.* But their relationship is like a powder keg ready to explode. I'm desperate to know what they were up to in the study, with that blood on the King's neck and Raiden's mouth. Clearly, the vampire was drinking from the King, but why? And why did Red let him?

"Oh, I love blood and bones," Rab says, rolling his head in a circle and blinking those disturbingly beautiful eyes at me. "Snacking on assholes feeds my soul."

"You'll get a chance to eat at the ball, I'm most certain," the King says, his voice that disturbing eerie calm I was so awed by when we first met. I've seen his temper though, and it's mighty. I've also seen his self-control crumble away, when he pinned me to the wall and kissed the fuck out of me.

The way he's staring at the floor though, I get that there's something else going on inside these castle walls. Internal politics. Gross. I've never liked politics. As far as I'm concerned, republicans and democrats … douchebags and turd sandwiches.

"Well, I hope so," March says, drawing Rab's attention over to him. "Because it's been a while since I've popped someone's head from their shoulders. It comes right off, just like a bloody grape."

"Don't you dare steal my kills, or I shan't ever fucking forgive you," Rab says, as Tee rolls his eyes, meeting mine from across the circle.

"Can we get on with this?" Chesh purrs, sitting with one knee propped up, his elbow resting atop it. "I've got rodents to kill, a hairball to choke up, and an Alice to woo."

"Please don't put *hairball* and *woo* into the same sentence," I say as the hookah finally makes its way back to the Caterpillar.

"*Purrrr-lease* make me part of your harem, Alice?" Chesh yowls, flopping onto his side and pawing at the air with tattooed hands.

"Insufferable beast," the King grinds out, as North slaps his tail against the floor and then grabs Chesh by the collar, making him sit upright like the rest of us.

What a ragtag group of men, I think as I glance from Raiden Walker to Tweedledee. *What am I going to do with them all?*

"So," Lar says, his quiet, commanding voice drawing a close to all of the nonsense. "The quintrille. Alice, do you know why it's called that?"

"Uh, no clue," I say as he gives me this calm, easy sort of smile. He draws designs in the air with his fingers, and the blue-gray smoke from the hookah forms into a little, smiling crocodile.

"Because it requires five couples," he explains. "As opposed to the quadrille which requires four."

"Quint and quad, got it," I say, giving him a salute without even thinking about it. My cheeks flush and Dee grins at me from across the circle, his wings framing his beautiful face. I've been around the guy for a handful of weeks and already, I'm picking up his habits. "Five couples, ten people, the prophecy?" I continue, cocking a brow.

Everything in this damn world revolves around the prophecy.

"Ten people," Lar says, standing up and handing off the hookah to a card servant. There are a few of them scattered around the room, staring at us with dead, ink-drawn eyes. A few others approach as the men stand up, removing the pillows as Lar slowly unfolds his right arm, holding his hand out to me. "Five couples. Come, Sunshine, and we will dance."

I take his hand as the boys pair up around me.

Tee and Dee; Chesh and North; March and Raiden; the King and Rab.

Lar leads us into the center of the ballroom, positioning us over a gold medallion inscribed with small designs. They make a story around the circle, with a much larger design in the center. I don't have time to examine it at the moment, but it looks interesting.

The Caterpillar leans in, putting his mouth against my ear, overwhelming me with his scent.

"Pretend I'm the King," he says, but I'd rather not. I get that I'll be dancing with Brennin Red at the ball, but I'd much rather dance with Lar right now. "You'll start in the center of the room, with everyone else around you."

He places my hand on his shoulder, and curls his fingers around my other. We stand tall and straight and proud, staring into one another's eyes.

"The other couples will approach the circle, turn to one another, bow." Lar nods his chin, and one of the card servants starts up the gramophone. "And then they'll turn to their right, and bow again."

The music gurgles out of the old machine, a cheery marching band sort of sound with trumpets and a piano.

Lar and I wait, poised like statues as the King and Rab waltz forward to meet March and Raiden, weaving around us and clasping hands as they pass. When they get to the opposite side of the circle, the King puts his hand on Rab's lower back and they spin in a circle, coming to face us again. They do the same moves one more time before clasping arms and parading around us.

I'm happy standing right here, not doing any of the actual dancing.

"How long does this part take?" I whisper as the same two pairs move forward and switch partners; the Hatter ends up with the King, while March and Rab wind up together.

Oh.

The plot thickens.

"You'll see," Lar says, tilting his head to the side, his beautiful hair feathering across his face, his earrings dancing in that strange supernatural wind that seems to follow him around. He, too, has an aristocratic air, and I can't help but wonder if he's some sort of fae prince. It would only stand to reason, considering Tee and Dee. But who knows? In Underland, anything is possible.

The other two couples switch partners as well, and then repeat the first set of movements, doing what the King and Co. did in reverse.

"Now, we dance," the Caterpillar says, turning us in a circle, sliding his hand to my lower back, and then galloping us around the circle of men. I can feel all their eyes on me, watching me, studying me. I've never had so many guys interested in me before; it's fucking weird.

Some part of me can't be happy about it though, because it feels like most of them are after the Alice and most definitely *not* Allison.

Except … not the twins, or North, maybe not even the cat.

Lar, he's hard to read. I study his face as we weave in and out of the four other couples, our feet slowly rising off the ground as we go. My heart stutters a bit, half from fear, half from excitement as the ballroom slowly falls away.

My dance partner opens his wings, these two glorious glittering swathes of color and magic. They glow blue, the edges ruffling in the breeze. It jangles the bracelets on his arms, his earrings, teases his nipple piercings. The coat, despite not actually being on his arms, sits pretty on his shoulders, the gold fringe and epaulettes catching the wind.

God, I hate heights, but holy shit I love this, I think as we dance, Lar adjusting our arms until they're hooked at the elbow, and spinning us in a circle. What girl doesn't want to fly, after all.

The other men are floating, too, but not as high as we are, not until Lar spins me one more time and releases me. He pauses for a brief moment, wings flapping softly, as he adjusts my arms so that one is behind my back, the other held to the side, bent at the elbow, with my palm up.

He bows and sinks down a few feet, switching places with the Hatter.

Fantastic.

"Hello, *Alice*," he says, grabbing my outstretched hand and bringing it to his lips for a kiss. I shiver, but not in an unpleasant way, letting him parade me around in a circle.

The sky outside is darkening, but I do not miss that giant ass bat landing on an arch and peering in at us with eyes as dark as the King's.

"Your pet is staring at us," I say as Raiden raises an eyebrow and marches us around in the air. A small bat peeks out from under his hat and takes off, perching itself upside down from a decorative rose carved into the golden arches of the ballroom.

"Is that so?" he asks, not even bothering to look in the creature's direction. "Does she bother you?"

"No," I say, feeling far less comfortable all the way up here with Raiden than I did with Lar. Not only does the Caterpillar have wings, but he's just generally a much nicer guy. "I don't like heights, that's it. I don't have a problem with bats."

I stumble over my own foot, an odd sensation floating that high up in the air, but the Mad Hatter catches me and keeps me upright, his tattooed fingers curled around my arms. His marmalade colored eyes are so intense, all I want to do is look away. And yet, I can't bring myself to do it.

"How did you get here anyway?" I ask, licking my lower lip and trying my best to keep my gaze neutral and focused. "To Underland, I mean. You're from Topside, aren't you?"

"Not everyone that falls down the Rabbit-Hole is an Alice," he breathes, spinning me around and then stepping back. Before I get a chance to probe him further, the King is taking his place, and I groan.

"Try not to act so thrilled," Brennin grinds out, his stupid crown reflecting back the chandeliers' lights as they flicker and dance along with us.

"Don't worry: that shouldn't be hard," I quip as the music changes to this slow, strange drawling song with a heavy bass and a chorus of snapping fingers, like some jazz lounge special performance.

"What's all this talk of marriage?" he says, his eyes like shards of onyx. "I thought you wanted to go home?"

"You clearly don't listen to a damn thing I say: I want to be able to go home and come back at will. That's what I want. Free will. Ever heard of it?"

Brennin tightens his lips at my words, but he doesn't stop dancing. I realize that North and Tee were right: he's as good as Lar. Raiden was a decent dancer, but I had to think about the steps with him. With the King, it comes naturally.

We stop talking then, and with the arrival of silence comes that awful, aching tension.

My body *wants* the goddamn King, and I don't know how to make it stop.

"Your Majesty." A female voice rings out, and I glance down to find the Knave with her head tilted in our direction, the White Knight at her side. "We have a problem."

With a growl, Brennin Red scoops me up in his arms. I let out a small squeak, but I'm all the way up in the fucking air, so I thread my fingers together against the back of his neck as we drift toward the floor. Without meaning to, I play with the fine red hairs at the base of his scalp, and feel my heart skip a few beats.

"What is it?" he asks, setting me down and stepping away in a swirl of robes.

The White Knight cups her hand around the King's ear, and I see him stiffen.

He glances back at me, slides his eyes down my body and makes me feel like I've just been dipped in warm honey. When they flick back to my face, I know I'm in serious trouble.

This thing between Brennin Red and me, it's going to come to a head at some point.

"Continue with the lessons," Red says, snapping his fingers. The White Knight steps forward and offers me a cheeky smile and a little bow, stepping in to take the King's place. I wish I wasn't sorry to see him go.

But I am.

Fuck.

He moves across the marble floors with the Knave and her minions falling into step behind him.

"Interesting," Raiden purrs, exchanging a look with March. "Very interesting."

"Keep your filthy nose out of the King's business," North snarls, getting between the two mercenaries and his ruler's retreating back.

"The King's business?" Raiden asks, tapping the brim of his hat in thought. "But the King's business is now my business. We're soon-to-be husbands-at-arms."

"Over my dead body," I grumble, but I'm not about to get into it with them right now. I cross my arms over my chest as the Duke stares down the Hatter. Near the ballroom entrance, the Dormouse stirs, cracking his knuckles and stretching his neck from side to side in a particularly menacing way.

If he goes for North, I swear, I'll unleash some of my special Alice magic on his ass.

"Boys," I say, stepping between them before things can heat up. The last thing I need is a jabberwocky/vampire battle in the ballroom. "When am I going to start training to use my magic?"

"Once we've dealt with the Anti-Alice," North says, but my change of subject isn't working. He's not even looking at me.

"After the Torrid Tea Party," the Mad Hatter says, finally turning to look at me. "I'll show you how to use your magic."

"The Torrid Tea Party?" I ask, blinking stupidly as the other men gather around us. "Is this one of the 'Hatter's famous parties'?" I make little quotes with my fingers.

I get a saucy vampire smile in response.

"Oh, most certainly."

"And when is this supposed party taking place?" I ask as March lifts up his top hat and extracts a new lollipop, this one in the shape of a knife.

"The night before the ball," Raiden says, smirking and looking stupidly delicious as he goes about it. Bad guys are not supposed to be attractive. They're supposed to wear dark robes, smell like old cheese, and cackle from the shadows. "I have to know who I can trust."

"And how would a tea party help with that?" I ask as Dor moves up to stand beside his boss in a very threatening sort of way. North reacts, black scaly wings exploding from his back as he takes a step forward.

I leap between the two of them and put my hands on the sides of his face, kissing him hard and fierce, a tangle of tongues that he accepts with carnal desperation. His hands are all over me, his wings wrapped around us, his tail squeezing my ankle.

"If I weren't a civilized monster …" he snarls against my mouth, and I find myself melting against him. "I'd throw you to the floor and fuck you right here in front of the rest of these morons."

"Oh god, don't say that," I breathe, my body throbbing in response to his words. "I might just take you up on that."

"When I get agitated, I need to mate," he growls, nuzzling at my hair. I wrap my arms around him and sigh, knowing that everyone else is staring at us. Frankly, I just don't give two fucks. "It calms me down."

"Oh, I see how it is," I whisper, but North tucks his wings back behind him and looks me over.

"I can wait though," he says with this devilish expression on his face, his big black horns curving wickedly up from his gold hair. "Tonight, we'll mate in the Suit of Hearts."

"Thank you for announcing that to the whole world," I say, feeling a blush color my cheeks as the White Knight chuckles at me, and the Dormouse scowls. I hope he gets hit by a brick and dies. Freak accidents happen, you know.

"Shall we continue?" Lar says, appearing beside us and holding out a hand.

"We shall," March replies from behind me. "Enjoy your dancing, because in about, oh, an hour or so … I'm going to fucking poison you."

The dungeon is as clichéd as my future ball.

It's down a spiral stone staircase, and it's cold, damp, and scary as shit.

"This is beyond creepy," I say as the twins escort me past flickering torches and down into the bowels of Underland. The March Hare is walking just ahead of us, but I can see his brown ears swiveling to listen to our conversation.

"The former King of Hearts used to keep prisoners down here," Tee says, and there's something incredibly melancholic about the way he phrases that. I wonder if any angels were locked up here previously? "The current king just curses them into card servants or sends them to the guillotine."

Tee pushes purple-streaked black hair off his forehead and casts his jewel-toned eyes in my direction. I can't tell if he's relieved or upset by what he's just said.

"They say the stones have absorbed the screams of the wicked over the years," Dee whispers, keeping his wings tucked in close and refusing to touch the stone walls if he can help himself.

"Nonsense," Tee scoffs, and Dee rolls his eyes.

"Contrariwise, it makes perfect sense. Locations absorb trauma, that's common knowledge."

"It's common nonsense," his brother quips back, and I smile. I love their interactions. It makes me miss Fred a little, but in a good way, floods me with happy memories. Oh, Fred. Being here in Underland, that trauma seems so far away, but I know I'm not over it, not even close. Does a person ever really get over losing a loved one? Or does the pain just crouch deep inside the soul, waiting for the worst possible moment to pop out and shout *peekaboo!*

"I've set up a little *la-bohr-uh-tory* for myself down here," March drawls, stretching out the word laboratory while he sucks on his knife-shaped lollipop. He pushes open a door at the bottom of the stairs and welcomes us in with a flourish.

"What did you mean about poisoning me?" I ask as I step inside and notice the various jars filled with colored fluids, the beakers, the tiny pots with handwritten labels.

"I'm going to start you on a series of poison-pricks, so we can build your immunity to the most common ones." March moves over to a table covered in knives and picks through them, setting one aside. It has a purple edge that glows faintly, warming up the dark space with each pulse of light.

Creepy.

"I don't like this at all," Tee growls as Dee exhales and rolls up his sleeves.

"Which is why I'm going to test the poison *first*," Dee says as his brother raises his brows. "Dear brother, you are the heir to our people's throne. And she"—he casts me a sly look—"she is the Alice. Please, allow me." Dee sits down on one of the stools as March shrugs out of his velvet trench coat, turning to face us. I can't help but stare at the bare expanse of mocha colored skin showing between the two unbuttoned sides of his white shirt.

He, too, rolls up his sleeves, revealing two, thick muscular arms.

Thief, poison expert, Hatter's lackey, shapeshifter.

That's all I know about the March Hare—stupid facts. I have no idea who he actually is as a person, and I'm not sure I care to. He and the Hatter are, for lack of a better word, dickheads.

"Eventually we'll move onto mixing poisons, but this'll do for now."

"What are your other forms?" I ask, crossing my arms over my chest and glancing around at the old prison cells on either side of us. They still have their rusted gates, separating off these tiny cubicles that I can't imagine could even fit a twin bed inside. The people that were kept here, they suffered—*greatly*. "If you're going to poke and prod and stab me, I have a right to know a little more about you."

"Oh, Alice-Doll," March says, his chocolate-colored hair cut short into a neat, polished style, like a model. The longer hair on the top of his scalp is slicked back and hidden partially beneath his purple top hat. I notice he never wears a larger hat than his boss. "I imagine when we bed each other, it'll be a lot less violent than all that. Nobody wants to be poked or prodded or stabbed with a cock. It's all about the thrust."

"I meant the needles ," I snarl, narrowing my eyes as I point at the collection of shiny, sharp objects on the table beside me. Apparently, this is going to be like those allergy tests at the doctor, the ones where they poke your skin with tiny needles tipped in allergens. Hopefully, I don't die down here. That'd suck. "You know what I meant. I know you can shift into a bandersnatch. What else?"

"You're a pushy little Alice, aren't you?" he murmurs, his brown eyes twinkling.

"Can we just get this over with, so we can move on?" Tee snaps. "If the King hadn't personally ordered us down here, we wouldn't be here. And if anything—and I mean *anything*—happens to Allison, I'll kill you myself."

"Oh?" March asks, and then he throws back his head with a chortling laugh. His ears, on either side of his top hat, twitch. "Glorious. I'd love to see which of us would win in a fight. I might bet against myself, to be quite honest with you." March stands up and moves next to me, a good foot fucking taller. I have to crane my neck to look up at him. "Would you believe me if I told you I could shape-change into a *slithy tove*?"

"What the fuck is a *slithy tove*?" I snort, vaguely recognizing the words from the original *Jabberwocky* poem, the one that Chesh recited for me earlier to keep my head calm. I've been sing-songing it in the back of my mind all day now. I'm not sure how calming it is, but it's certainly catchy.

"A tove is a … sort of like a Pegasus," Tee explains as my eyes open wide in disbelief.

"Okay, sure …" I start, but March is already laughing at me, and I can't decide if he's telling the truth or not. "So can you really turn into the Mad Hatter?"

Well, now, *that* stops him dead.

He pauses with his hands on a bottle marked … well, *Poison* before turning to look at me. He tries to hide his surprise with a smarmy smirk, but I can see it. I've well and truly shocked him.

"Where would you get a ridiculous idea like that?" he says, but his voice is too casual while his shoulders are too tense.

The Caterpillar was right.

I smirk back, because even if I have no idea if he's telling the truth about the *tove*, I know at least this much is true.

"None of your damn business," I ooze, enjoying my temporary feeling of superiority and smugness. It's not often one gets the jump on a mercenary bastard asshole. "How many poisons are we testing today?" I ask as I take a seat on the stool next to Dee; he immediately starts up a game of footsie with me. Cheeky bastard. It lightens the mood in that dreary dungeon with its long hallway, its straw-filled cells, and the light but persistent reek of sweat and urine.

"Just a handful," March says, dipping a tiny needle into the bottle, and then turning to face me. "Don't want to overwhelm your fragile system, Doll. Now, arm." He gestures with his fingers, and I sigh, removing my red and black military coat and pushing up the sleeve of my button-up.

The Vorpal Blade is strapped to my thigh, the Queenmaker is on my hip, and I'm wearing the corset filled with knives. I have to say, I feel like kind of a badass.

"Me first," Dee says, gesturing with his own arm.

March obliges him, cleaning Dee's skin with alcohol, and then poking just the tiniest prick into the pale flesh of Dee's underarm. He tosses the needle and readies a new one while the twins and I wait in tense silence. I think we're all half-convinced that Dee's going to keel over at any given moment.

Fortunately, several pass and nothing happens.

"Oh give me some credit where credit is due," March says as Tee very carefully watches him poison a new needle. "Killing the Alice in the King's castle with two angels to face off against, knowing my boss is eventually going to hunt me down and kill me, while I've already pissed off the King of Clubs with no way to go running back. Must think I'm bloody daft, eh?"

He moves over to me, running his fingers up my arm. I swallow hard, but I refuse to let him see that he's having any effect on me. March carefully pushes my sleeve up a little further, running his thumb over the pulse in my elbow. He swabs my arm in slow, lazy circles with a cotton swab, the sharp sting of alcohol teasing my nostrils. And when I say alcohol, I don't mean rubbing alcohol—I mean, like, fucking *whiskey.*

"You look like Rob Evans," I blurt, and March raises an eyebrow just before he pricks me. There's something weirdly intimate about that moment that I don't like, and I jerk my arm out of his grip, cradling it against my chest.

"Who?" he quips, sounding a bit like an owl.

"A model from Topside," I murmur, rubbing at the sore spot. I feel a little tingle there, and start to panic, but it fades as quickly as it came. I've had worse wasp bites or bee stings.

"A model, huh?" he asks, as I refuse to look at how tight his pants are over his firm ass. Underland is turning me into a freaking nymphomaniac. "You think I'm that pretty, do you?" He grabs up a banana from a bowl of fruit, peels it, and stuffs half in his mouth while he readies the next needle.

"Hardly," I say, but I'm probably the only person in that room who believes what I'm saying. Even then, it's questionable.

"We're going to work our way through these poisons," March continues, flattening his rabbit ears against his skull as he struggles with a corked bottle. "And then I'm going to give you a test kit to keep with you. At any time you suspect something is poisoned—food, clothing, even a fucking handrail—you take the swab out and test it. If the liquid turns cloudy, it's poison." He turns back around and moves to prick Dee with a second needle.

"Cloudy, huh," I murmur, thinking how ingenious that would be, to poison say, a doorknob or a banister. Something innocuous and unexpected.

"It'll test for ninety of the most common poisons." March murmurs after he's finally sucked the rest of the banana into his mouth and eaten it all. Impressive. Bet he could give good blow jobs with that gag reflex. Speaking of … I've sort of been wondering if he has a thing with the Mad Hatter?

Wouldn't surprise me.

"And if you leave it for about a week," he continues, taking care with what he's doing to Dee. That makes me happy, to see that he actually does give a shit about this poison stuff. It's the first time I've seen him really show off his own personality, aside from being the Mad Hatter's second-in-command. "You can test for another nine."

"Ninety-nine poisons, huh?" I ask as March steps up next to me again. When he gets close enough, the stale reek of the dungeon fades away, and I get a hint of gardenia and the musky bitterness of dark tea on the back of my tongue. He smells like a tea party in a garden, this giant dude with all the needles and knives. "Can we test the Knave's dress? I don't trust her for shit."

The March Hare smiles at me and looks up, meeting my eyes.

"Can I tell you a secret?" He leans in and puts his lips disturbingly close to my ear, stirring my hair against my overheated skin. "Neither do I."

I shiver as he grabs hold of my arm, rubbing my pulse with his thumb, and then pricks me—all while staring into my eyes. Those shifting flecks of color in his gaze remind me of fall again, of pumpkins and changing leaves and apple cider. The March Hare has all of the colors.

"You know what," he says, taking a step back, his eyes twinkling with mischief. "Take this." March reaches behind his back and pulls the glowing purple knife off the table, balancing the hilt on his fingertip for a moment before he flicks it up in the air, lets it spin, and then catches it again. He grabs a leather sheath off the table and slips it inside before offering it up to me. "Just don't stab yourself with it, love, or you are *f-u-c-k-e-d*. Up bloody shit creek with no paddle."

He winks at me as he hands over the knife, tangling our fingers together in a very purposeful way. I notice then that his fingers are covered in rings, and I have to wonder if it's just for looks … or for beating people up. Hmm. Considering the way he flanks Raiden Walker, like some movie bad boy bodyguard, I'm guessing the latter.

"Why?" I ask, sliding the knife out and gazing at the glowing poison. Not particularly subtle, but I don't think this is meant to be. No, a weapon like this is a *threat*, a warning, like a caterpillar patterned in bright colors. Fuck off, jubjub bird. "There's no antidote?"

"Just my cum," he says with a bright grin, and I swear on Hearts and Diamonds, I almost stab him with his own blade.

Why does everything in this world have to do with drinking semen?!

"Well, shit, if that isn't motivation to take care …" I use the leather straps on the back of my new sheath to hook it to my thigh holster, putting the poisoned weapon right next to the Vorpal Blade.

Look at me: I am a veritable freaking badass.

"If you get into any trouble at the ball," March says, leaning his tight ass against the table and crossing his huge arms over his chest. His grin is cheeky as fuck, white-white teeth in a face cloaked in shadow. "Stab the cocksucker with that, and I'll know exactly where you are."

I glance over at Tee and Dee, both of them watching my interaction with March with interest.

I turn back to him and smile, touching my fingers to the knife.

"Thank you," I tell him, and both brows go up. Pretty sure he expected some witty banter.

He'll get that … later. For now, I'm just trying to be nice.

"You're welcome?" he says, almost like it's a question, tilting his head to one side as a single one of his ears flattens back against his skull. Aha. He doesn't know quite what to make of me, and I love it. "Now, shall we prick you again, Doll?"

Doll.

Fantastic.

Another goddamn nickname.

North is naked on my bed when I get upstairs.

"Oh for fuck's sake," I whisper, but I'm actually seriously turned on when I find him there with nothing but a scrap of blanket over his erect dick. "Look at you, jumping the gun like that." I fill a plate with goodies from the refreshments table as Tee goes about preparing cups of chamomile tea for Dee and me. I've learned from conversations with the twins that it's boosted with a drug that makes you go to sleep fast, and sleep well. That, I can handle. It's just, like, melatonin or something.

"I'm just making myself available," the Duke drawls as I sit down on the bed and accept the cup of tea from the angel prince's fingers. Tee gives me a tight smile as he does the same for his brother, and then sits down at the desk to pull out his journal.

We both like to write down our thoughts, me and Tee. It makes me like him more. *If I do get to go back home, I should grab my diary while I'm there.* I'd even start a new one tonight if I felt I had the energy. But after the sex, the shooting, the dancing, and the poison … I have nothing left.

"If you're too tired to change into pajamas," the cat purrs, curled up in a black and white ball on his cat tree," you could certainly sleep in the nude."

I kick my boots off onto the floor and give him a look.

"Sorry, dude, not tonight. You're just going to have to use your imagination if you want to see my boobs." I give him a tight smile, flip him off, and then take a sip of my tea.

"Imagination is the only weapon in the war against reality," Chesh purrs, shifting into human form as he leaps off the cat tree and lands on all fours on my bed. His collar jangles as he slides up between North and me. "Jules de Gaultier."

"How do you know who Jules de Gaultier is?" I ask. I mean, you have to admit, it's weird as hell that the Cheshire Cat knows a quote from an obscure French philosopher.

"He used to live in Underland, before he traveled Topside after the Riving," Chesh says, grinning widely at me. "Don't you love how full of useless information I am? All cats are, you know. We're keepers of knowledge."

I snort in response, picking through the banana bread on my plate as I look for insects or flowers or whatever other weird shit might be in it. Working off a random thought, I pull one of the March Hare's test bottles from my pocket, unscrew the top, and swab my food. I put it back into the liquid, put the top back on, and shake it up as instructed.

"Not poisoned," I say as the liquid stays clear. March had said it would turn cloudy right away if there was even a trace of poison.

"Likely not," Chesh purrs, kneading the pillows next to me with his black painted fingernails. "The card servants test all your food before they put it down. If it were poisoned, you'd see their corpses littering the floor around the table."

"Thank you for that image," I say as I eat my food, smiling when Dee begins to snore.

"You're quite welcome," the cat replies, pillowing his head on his arms and swishing his tail as he closes his eyes.

The door to the room opens, and Lar and Rab walk in, completing our little evening routine. To be quite honest, I'm starting to enjoy it. I'm glad we have a few days before the ball. There's a weird feeling in my gut, like everything's going to change after that. So even though I know it won't last, I want to enjoy this peace for a few more days.

"Evening, Miss Alice," Rab says, taking off his shoes near the door and getting comfortable in one of my chairs. The Duke makes an annoyed sound, but he doesn't bother moving from his position on my bed to put any clothes on. I'm quite enjoying the bronze expanse of his chest, so I appreciate that.

Besides, I never said I'd changed my mind about, uh, *mating*.

"Sunshine," Lar says, sweeping his jacket off his shoulders and hanging it up.

"Evening to you both." I set my empty plate and cup aside, unstrapping the Vorpal Blade from my thigh and setting it on the nightstand. North had originally said the blade was owed to him. I wonder why? But that's a question for another day. I'm too tired to delve into it tonight.

"How was your appointment with the March Hare?" Lar asks, lips twitching as he spreads his wings open wide and stands with his back to the fire. Based on the cheeky expression on his face, I think he already knows.

"You dropped that information about his Raiden-form on purpose." I don't even phrase it as a question; I know it's true.

"He liked that, did he?" Lar pushes his hair back from his face and uses a gold hairband he pulls from his pocket to tie it back. "I know all sorts of things about the Mad Hatter and the March Hare that would, well, not drive them mad since they're already mad, but perhaps *madder* still."

"He told me his third form was a *slithy tove*," I say, and several of the men laugh. Tee ignores it all, scribbling things down in his journal. The clock strikes twelve as he's writing, and he gasps, his wings folding into his back and leaving the glossy sheen of feather tattoos on the backs of his arms.

Note to self: break that fucking curse!

I care about the twins now, and I want to see them freed. Plus, I'm a smug bitch. I would *love* to see the Knave's face after I fuck up her spell. That'd be priceless.

"He is a tove, I believe, yes," Lar replies, surprising me. "It's a useful form, I'd think."

"It's a throwaway," Rab growls, looking toward the painting on the wall that depicts the March Hare sitting at a tea party. It has not escaped my knowledge that the nine men I'm now surrounded by are all featured in these paintings. Or that I find them all physically attractive, even if their attitudes stink.

Fucking prophecy.

"What's your final form?" I look Rab straight in the face when he turns to stare at me, his gaze as icy as his voice. I feel like I must be getting frost on the tips of my eyelashes.

"State secret," he says, and I groan in frustration, flopping back into the pillows.

If there's a polite way to ask the rest of the men in the room to vacate so I can fuck a dragon, please point me in the right direction because I don't know how to go about doing it.

"Come to my room," North whispers in my ear, making me shiver. Chesh lays between us, but he doesn't seem bothered much by North's naked body leaning over him. I guess as the Duke's pet, he's probably seen worse. I wonder how many women he's seen North take to his bed? For whatever reason, that thought pisses me the hell off. "I'll fuck you into my mattress, and make us both scream."

"Oh lord," I choke out, but I'm opening my eyes and sliding them over to look at the jabberwock painting on the wall.

"Go," Chesh says, nuzzling against my arm. "If he doesn't get mated, the Duke will be rather savage."

"I …" I start, but nobody is looking at me, nobody's judging. And I *am* curious as to what the Suits look like down those long hallways. "I'll at least go and take a look at your room."

Chesh chuckles, like he's calling my bluff and I smack him, standing up to follow North into his chambers. His bare bronze ass when he stands up is *glorious*.

Don't drool, Allison, I think as he pads over and unlocks the painting for me, letting it swing aside so I can step into the hallway. Gotta wonder where he was keeping that key though. Clenched between his firm, bronzed buttocks perhaps?

Buttocks.

I snort and then slap my hand over my mouth to cut off the sound.

"Do you know," the Duke continues as he follows along, the door swinging shut behind us. "That in a siege, your attackers must fight their way through all nine chambers before they get to yours. That main door is spelled; anyone without a key must be let in by someone inside."

"That's … pretty fucking cool actually," I say, sweat dripping down the back of my neck. It does not help me calm down much when North reaches out and tickles my skin with his claws. No, pretty sure my dripping sweat becomes a monsoon. It's like I'm nervous or something, a blushing virgin on her way to the honeymoon suite. Cue eyeroll.

I follow the hall to its natural end, pausing to glance into a glorious marble bathroom on the right before I step into the bedroom.

It's small, but cozy, shaped like a heart with a bed situated in the point opposite us. There's a dresser on either side of me, both of them wilting and wonky, like they're melting. The ceiling is draped with red fabric, the floor with rugs, and there are chaises and chairs scattered all around. Also, I'm pretty sure the Alice statue on the opposite side of the room just waved at me.

"My sweet mate," North growls into my hair, wrapping his arms around me from behind. "Every day that I don't touch you is torture."

"We fucked once; that doesn't make me your mate," I whisper, but the words sound weak, like even I don't believe them. That's been happening a lot to me lately; it's like maybe I don't know myself at all. Or maybe I just stopped trying after Fred died. I changed after everything that happened, and I changed into someone I didn't want to know. Perhaps it's time for me to try? If I do, I might find that I don't hate myself as much as I thought I did.

"That's what it means to me," North says, pushing me forward. I stumble a bit, putting my palms flat on the surface of the bed to catch myself. I'm fairly certain that's exactly the position he wants me in, bent over with my ass sticking out.

Instead, I stand up and spin around before he can grab me.

I look up and meet gold eyes shimmering with lust.

"Slow down, would you?" I say, putting my hands on his flat stomach. Liam was not sexy like this, not even close. He was a boy, and North is most certainly a man. It's like I'm not even sure where to put my hands; I just want to touch all of him.

"How can I slow down when all I want is to ravage you?" the Duke whispers back, his voice hoarse, his tail thrashing. I reach up and give a tug on one of his horns. I could never take him back home; he wouldn't last a day in Topside. Of course, the horns and tail are dead giveaways. I imagine he can probably shift them off the way he does his wings, but his temper would eventually get the better of him.

"Ravage, huh?" I ask, sliding my fingers down his body. He's already sweaty, that musky, masculine scent of his driving me up the wall. "That's a strong word."

"I have strong emotions," he says, curling his tail around my waist and yanking me even closer to him, so close that his erect cock is trapped between our bodies. With a snap of his fingers, he lights the flickering candles in the room and dims the chandelier at the same time. Magic. I can't wait to be able to use my magic.

"I can see that," I whisper, pushing him back with my hands on his chest.

North obliges and moves back. Let's be honest: if he didn't want to move, I would not be able to make him. He's huge and built like a truck. Plus, you know, he can turn into a dragon. Maybe my Alice magic could blow him to bits if I really tried, but I'm sort of fond of the guy now.

Slowly, I drop to my knees with the Savage Duke standing above me.

When I look up and meet his gold eyes, they're practically molten, dripping with lust. His horns cast wicked shadows on the ceiling and walls, making him look like a monster. A beautiful monster, but a monster nonetheless.

I wrap the fingers of my right hand around his bronze shaft and give it a squeeze, just to test his sensitivity. North exhales, tangling clawed fingers in my hair. He's dominant, but not cruel, and a definite change of pace from the twins. Dee is loving and cheerful, Tee is reserved but intense, and North is … savage.

He's fucking *primal*.

Licking my lips, I put my mouth up to the head of his cock and gently kiss his hot flesh, working my way down his shaft to his balls. My tongue runs along that seam of flesh in the middle as my fingers tease the soft skin.

"Allison Liddell," he grinds out, his hips moving up to meet my face. "You're going to break my black, little heart, aren't you?"

I just smile and keep going, licking and teasing him until his breathing is ragged. Then I oblige his desires and put my mouth over the head of his cock, just enough that he can feel the warm, wet heat of my tongue, but gets no satisfaction from it.

My right hand works his dick like a corkscrew, twisting around his shaft and making him growl in frustration.

"I want to fuck your mouth right now," he snarls, but he doesn't move. He just sits there and lets me pleasure him, working salty pre-cum from the tip. *I can't believe I'm sucking off a dragon,* I think, and seeing as my jaw is already starting to ache, I know the prophecy is right about one thing.

Nine big cocks.

"Aren't you glad we're taking our time?" I whisper, making sure my lips move against his shaft when I speak. Once I've got him all lubed up with saliva, I breathe against the shiny wetness on his cock, and he snarls at me.

"I can't quite decide at this precise moment," he grinds out, and I grin. I open my mouth and lightly tease him with my teeth before sliding my lips over the head, taking as much of him in as I can.

I slide my mouth up and down North's shaft like a porn star, and then hold him deep in my throat. That's when I start to hum. As soon as the sound vibrates from my mouth and into his shaft, the Savage Duke fucking loses it.

He slides his cock from my lips, picks me up off the floor, and tosses me onto the bed.

He's crawling on top of me before I can even catch my breath.

The Duke of Northumbria pins me to the black fur comforter on his bed, his strong hands holding my wrists with a firm but controlling intensity that makes my heart flutter. I both love it, and find that it scares me.

"I …" I start, thinking of Liam and his friends, struggling to pin me down. I don't want to have flashbacks like that with the Duke, but I can't help it. There's so much trauma inside my chest that I've never dealt with, and I can't keep pushing it back. I know that as soon as I cross that Looking-Glass, it'll come rushing back, a tsunami of pain and frustration. I'm from a world that doesn't care or respect me, and now I'm in one where everyone wants a piece.

I don't even know what to do with myself.

"Relax, Miss Liddell," North whispers, putting his mouth to the side of my neck and kissing me. "You're quite tense all of a sudden."

"I had something happen to me," I say, but I don't want to go into it. There's no point in ruining this moment. To be honest, I just want to get fucked by a dragon and not think about any of it. But maybe if I say it aloud, some of the pressure will go away?

North stiffens up, releasing his grip on my wrists. I put my palms up against his chest, over the hard points of his nipples.

"Someone hurt my mate?" he asks through gritted teeth, gold hair falling across his face and getting stuck to his sweaty brow. "I'll fucking tear their cocks off, and melt their faces with fire." He exhales and little puffs of smoke escape his nostrils. He leans down to rub against the side of my face.

"They didn't get to go through with what they were planning," I say, licking my lips and noticing that North sits up and takes notice, his eyes following the path of my tongue like a man possessed. "Although the incident did ruin my life. Is it wrong for me to want to start a new one?" He shakes his head and looks at me with this undeniable certainty.

"No."

Fucking kiss me then, I think, and either he's a mind reader or else he's just good with body language.

The Duke drops his face to mine, capturing my lips with a delicious fervor that reignites the passion in my blood. Later, I'll tell him more about what happened. Right now, I just want him to touch me … all … fucking … over.

North cups the back of my head with one hand, cradling my skull in his huge palm while he kisses me, paying special attention to my lower lip. He sucks it in between his teeth and then nibbles on it, making me writhe. His musky male and sandalwood smell is like a perfumed cloud, taking over my body and drowning my senses, making it hard for me to believe there's anything else left in the universe.

He's so much taller than me, so much bigger, and I love it, especially when he uses his tail to reach up and unbutton my pants. The muscular tip slips inside and strokes my already damp panties, just before he uses it to start pulling my pants and underwear down.

"I want to be consumed by you," he growls, and I swear, even as my clothing comes off, I giggle.

"You just want me because I'm the Alice," I say with a roll of my eyes, and North goes completely still.

"Lies," he hisses, and there's literal fire on his breath. "It was your *scent* that got me. A jabberwock chooses its mate by scent. You smelled like mine from moment one."

"I thought female jabberwocky picked their mates?" I ask, suddenly breathless again, and North snarls, biting my lower lip.

"Sometimes they do, sometimes they rape the males, sometimes it's a mutual attraction. Allison Liddell, our attraction is mutual, is it not?"

He sits up and yanks my pants aside, chucking them onto the floor, and then tearing my shirt off next. The fabric rends as he tosses it away like it's somehow personally offended him, and then he goes for the corset next.

"It's mutual," I whisper as his bronze fingers slow, and he carefully undoes the hook and eye clasps, unwrapping my sweaty, aching body from the corset like he's just gotten the most amazing Christmas present.

"Look at how beautiful you are, *Allison*," he snarls, and then he flips me over and puts my ass in the air, holding onto my hips as he positions himself at my opening.

We're both naked, both sweaty, and I can tell this is going to be just as wild and animalistic as our first time.

"Fuck me, Savage Duke," I whisper, and that's all it takes. He drives himself into me hard, his pelvis hitting my ass with an audible smack. His hips move with a wild frenzy as I dig my fingers into the fuzzy bedspread and hold on for dear life.

There's something so freeing, so wild about that moment, and yet all I can think about is what he just said to me: *It was your* scent *that got me.*

My scent.

I find that wildly sexy.

North squeezes my pelvic bone with his fingers and curls his tail around my waist to help hold me in place as he pounds into me, his balls hitting my clit and teasing just the right spot to make me groan.

I don't feel like a lost, restless young idiot in that moment; there's something about taking control of my sexuality like this that makes me feel like a strong, capable adult. I know it's just fucking, but … I like it. And I like knowing that I do.

The Duke isn't gentle with me, taking me hard and fast, just like I wanted.

Surprisingly, he gets *me* to finish first, my body collapsing onto the bed, the only thing holding me in place his muscular tail.

My muscles spasm around him as he readjusts his pace, transitioning to slow, steady thrusts that make me feel like I'm sobbing. It almost feels *too* good, too intense. I don't even know where to begin.

North pulls out and flips me onto my back, holding his slick cock in his hand and staring down at me with his metallic eyes as he works himself with confident, sure strokes.

I bite my lower lip and wait, absorbing this moment and filing it away for later. Surely, there will be some shitty times in my life, and this will be one of those split-seconds in time that I hold onto and dream about later.

The Duke lets his head fall back, his glorious golden hair feathering against his dark horns, and then he comes with a sharp buck of his hips, spilling his seed all over my belly.

When he collapses onto all fours, I think we're done, and I try to decide if we're going to snuggle in here or if I should shower and rejoin the twins or … or what. There is no Google here for me to look up *when in a polyamorous relationship, should I stay in bed with guy three while guys one and two are waiting back in my room?*

Wouldn't that be nice if there was an easy answer to that question?

But then North's mouth is on my belly, making my stomach muscles flutter as he kisses and licks the sticky semen from my skin. My fingers tangle in his hair and then slowly creep toward his shiny, black horns, taking hold of him and steering him to my aching clit.

His tongue finds the sensitive, swollen bit of flesh, swirling around it and working it into a stiff, desperate frenzy. It's that pleasure on the edge of pain, that line that both wants to be crossed and abhors it. It's that moment in the bedroom where you're not even sure you know your own body anymore.

I let mine take control, thrusting my hips up against North's face as he takes hold of my pelvis, his claws pricking my skin, drawing tiny beads of blood. He licks these off, too, and then moves to my opening, loving me with his tongue before he uses his long black tail to slide into me.

I'm not sure at first if I love it … or hate it.

But then he crooks the tip and teases the sensitive flesh just inside my opening, and I'm done for yet again.

I yank the Duke up toward my face by tugging on his horns, and then I kiss him, tasting a mixture of his seed and my own on his lips.

"You've got the Duke on your side now, the Alice," he whispers, kissing his way along my jaw. "So tell me, what will you do with me?"

"Well," I whisper, panting and tingling and enjoying the aftershocks of my double orgasm, "I think … I'm going to turn Underland into Wonderland again."

Chapter Six

In Which Allison Liddell Attends a Torrid Tea Party

"Lurid, sordid, a bacchanalian affair," Dee says, twirling his hat around on the top of his head. He's dressed in red and white today, like everyone else here. The uh, matchy-matchy thing is starting to get ridiculous. Although I do have to admit he looks damn good in the red military coat with the gold buttons, the tight red and white striped shirt, and the black slacks. "*That* is what a Torrid Tea Party is."

"This is a real thing?" I ask, squinting in his direction. "Like the cock-race? This is an actual *thang*?" I'm sitting at the edge of the training room with a spread of toadstool cupcakes, *actual* toadstools that glitter, and huge stacks of bread with butter. Tea is always served, and I always refuse, but this time there's also floral infused water with little edible blossoms floating on the surface.

There *is* a chance these things were alive and flipping people off not three hours ago, but I try my best not to think that. No point in it. The flowers are dickheads anyway.

I poke at one with my finger and try to bottle up some of this weird, gushing joy that's poisoning my body. There's no way happiness like this can be caged or contained. No, it always flutters away on broken wings.

"The Torrid Tea Party is a real event," Lar explains, his wings outstretched and drooping lazily on the floor. His key-shaped nipple rings keep catching the sunlight streaming through the glass ceiling panels, and I feel the urge to ask about them perching on the edge of my tongue. I saw the White Knight open the front gates with one, but why? Why is the most important key in the Kingdom of Hearts pierced through some guy's nipple? "The Mad Hatter is famous for it."

"So what makes this different than a *mad* tea party?" I ask, looking into Lar's blue eyes and thinking how much brighter they are than Dee's. The twin's eyes are an azure shadow, a rich jewel tone that gives his happy face a slightly darker note. Lar's eyes are almost Caribbean, light in color but heavy in saturation. In the sunlight, I'd almost call them *aqua* or *teal* or whatever the fuck that tropical blue-green color is. Sorry, but I played with black Sharpies instead of crayons as a kid. My parents were always too busy to remember to bring any when they took me to work with them. It was just me and Fred and yellow legal pads and Sharpies.

Fucking Fred …

"All tea parties are mad, of course," the cat says, slinking up beside me and putting his head in my lap—his very *human* head with the double lip piercing, the septum ring, and the silver stud in his eyebrow. Asswad. I shove him off, and he groans when his skull hits the red and white striped blanket underneath us.

Yeah, even picnic paraphernalia is themed here.

The King of Hearts has a big ego … among other things.

Piece of shit, I hate him, I think, even as I get this uncomfortable throbbing between my legs. Thinking about Brennin Red turns me on. And it shouldn't. And yet it undeniably does.

"All tea parties are mad?" I ask, trying to see if I can get clarification. It seems like, in Underland, that all of the nonsense really does have some sense to it which I suppose *makes* sense because the word sense is the root of the word nonsense. Sensibly, of course.

Oh God.

What the fuck did I just think?!

"All tea parties are mad, but there are even madder tea parties which is to say, that the Torrid Tea Party is really the maddest party of all," Dee starts, looking up toward the ceiling as he muses and taps a single finger against his chin. "Seems strange then, to wonder why it isn't simply called the Maddest Tea Party? Since it *is* mad, and the Mad Hatter is undeniably mad, and the March Hare may very well be the maddest of the mad—"

"Dee," I interrupt, reaching out to put my hand on the back of his. "Thank you." I force a smile that quickly turns real when he flashes one of his happy grins at me. I don't actually mind his riddling nonsense anymore. It's growing on me. Maybe it's growing on me like a tumor, but that's okay. I accept it.

"Why, thank you for such a glowing compliment," March says, snapping the end off a white chocolate bar with little red berries in it. See what I mean? All done up in the kingdom's colors yet again. I'm pretty sure he's always eating. In fact, I'd be hard-pressed to think of a single moment where he hasn't had *something* in his mouth.

Once again I can't help but wonder if he's had Raiden's *something* in his mouth, too. Like, are they lovers or just companions? And how does the Dormouse factor into all of this? I hope he's not at the Torrid Tea Party; he gives me the fucking heebie-jeebies.

"Explain to me exactly what goes on at these things again?" I continue, pushing some stray strands of hair off my sweaty face. The rest of it is gathered up in a high ponytail on the back of my head. North yanks on it during training, but I refuse to cut it off. Guess I do have some vanity, huh? Maybe the whole world does? Err, both worlds I mean.

"The room falls dark," Dee whispers, walking in a half-circle around us while he spreads his arms wide, palms out like he's miming the shape of this imaginary room. "The curtains are drawn, the candles are lit, and the tea is served piping hot." He squats down across from me, next to his brother, eyes glittering. "Tarts are served. Tarts are always served, preferably with gooseberries or cloudberries."

"And fresh cream," the Cheshire cat adds, still lying on his back and lifting a single black-nailed finger, his black and white striped ears twitching in his raven-dark hair.

"The tea is boosted with twice the usual magic," Tee says with a small sigh, pushing some of his purple-black hair away from his handsome face. The twins have such big, round eyes and long lashes, it feels impossible to look away from their faces sometimes. They're this perfect mix of pretty and masculine, this dichotomous contrast that makes my lady parts titter in the best way possible. "And steeped in truth herbs. Whoever it is that you're trying to vet—because a Torrid Tea Party is always about uncovering enemies or vetting allies—sits in a circle and drinks one cup per round."

"What's a round entail?" I ask, examining a glittering pink mushroom as North steps back in from the hallway, and my heart starts to skitter and jump. He's so … *much*. I mean, he must be exuding like alpha male beast pheromones or something because I don't act right when he's around. My cheeks flush with heat and I stuff the mushroom in my mouth. It's all crystalized with sugar, and it crunches when I chew. The taste of bubblegum fills my mouth, and I almost choke. Not because it's bad, but holy shit, that's weird as fuck.

"A round …" the Duke starts, making his way haughtily over to us and sitting cross-legged on my right, his chin raised defiantly. I'm starting to realize he's one of the *only* people in the kingdom that can or will stand up to the King of Hearts. I wonder what they were talking about out there? When Ol' Red popped his head into the training room and asked to play a quick round of croquet with the Duke, I figured something must be up. More internal politics maybe? "Consists of one question and one answer." He flicks his gold eyes over to mine and then sneaks his tail around my ankle. I let him do it, too, and I *like* it. Ugh, I really, really like it.

It's really starting to grow on me, this idea of being queen and dating all these guys. I mean, who wouldn't want that? The only obstacle is the King. Because he's a piece of shit and I hate him.

Oh and also … my family.

I can't leave my family with more questions than answers, especially not after Fred.

I lift my face up to meet Tee's gaze. It feels like he can sense when I'm thinking about my family. Maybe because he lost his, he's more empathetic or something? We stare at each other across the circle of food before I look away and pick up a toadstool cupcake. One bite and I can already tell I'm going to like it: it tastes like vanilla ice cream and hot fudge.

"One question and one answer?" I ask around a mouthful of cupcake. Oops. I have bad manners, sorry. Sometimes I talk while I chew. Guess we all have shit to work on, huh?

"Sometimes the question is a quest which is interesting because quest is the root of question," Chesh says, sitting up and stretching as he also surreptitiously goes to curl his tail around my other ankle. I grab it first, and give it a squeeze which turns his face into a leering grin.

"May as well just stroke my cock then?" he purrs, sitting up and then rubbing his cheek against my bare shoulder. He nips me and I yelp, causing a stir of chuckling around the circle. I'm still getting used to the idea of these guys *not* being jealous of one another.

"Get stuffed," I tell him, bringing the floral water to my lips, so I don't have to say anything else. Because the idea of touching Chesh's cock is pretty enticing. It's like I'm sitting in front of more than just a food-laden smorgasbord. There's a buffet of men here for me to choose from, and I can have any one of them I want. Or all of them. And that's the best part. Why choose?

"So, a quest or a question?" I ask and then snap my fingers. "Truth or dare?"

"That's a silly name, isn't it?" Lar asks, blinking long blonde lashes in my direction. "Quest or question makes much more sense."

"And how do you figure that?" I ask as he shrugs his jacket off his bare shoulders and leaves his muscular arms open to investigation from my wandering gaze. And boy does it wander. Being eighteen and perpetually horny never looked or felt so damn good.

"Because a quest implies a goal while a dare implies nothing but cheekiness," Lar continues, looking at me like he's staring into my soul. I notice he's finished his cup of tea, and as I watch, he leans in and pokes around the tea leaves at the bottom of his chipped, wonky little mug. "This tea party tonight," he says with a nod of his head, blonde-blue hair falling over his forehead, "it'll give us answers." He lifts his face again and smiles in a way that promises there's something else that he's not saying.

And from the look of him? I'd say it was something truly lascivious.

"How humdrum dull and boring," Rab drawls as he rolls his red eyes. His right ear flops in half and he reaches up to straighten it. He's dressed in a black vest with his pocket watch chain hanging from one pocket. There's no undershirt this time, just rippling muscles dressed in tattoos. "Just pick a dress and be done with it. We're already late." He taps the clock on his right forearm and then saunters over to stand behind me.

When I glance back at him, I see that his slacks are hanging way too low again. There's this delicious strip of skin between his vest and his pants that's making it hard to concentrate. I wonder if he's finding it as difficult to focus with me wearing nothing but a pair of red lacy panties and a matching bra? Did I mention that there's a heart cutout on the back of the undies, flashing a delicious amount of crack?

"We could make it more interesting, however," he starts, his warm breath stirring my hair. It's interesting, how cold his voice is in contrast. He smells like the forest after a good rain, like wet earth and the softness of decaying leaves.

"And how might we do that?" I ask, digging through the massive closet and trying not to be creeped out that everything fits. Have you ever had that before, an entire closet of clothes *made* for you? Even stuff that doesn't look like it'll fit ends up stretching or laying just right. There are items in that closet that I never would've picked up before, big poof-y things that remind me of Edy's dress.

"I think *naked* is more interesting than *dressed-up*, don't you?" Rab comes around to stand in front of me, leaning against the wall near the door and looking me up and down with slow, decadent menace that turns my insides to mush. Asshole. He's a serious asshole. Most of these guys are. Maybe they have to be to survive in Underland? It's fucking brutal here.

"What makes you think you deserve to see me naked?" I ask as I flip through dress after dress after dress. This event has a dress code: black. And although my closet is made up of rainbow colors, it's a rainbow that's heavily skewed toward red and white.

"I'll fight in a cock-race for you," he whispers, red eyes focused on me, white ears twitching. When I look at him, I can't help but think of his bandersnatch form. But what is his third one? What other meat did he get forced down his throat at the Inaugural Feast? "I'll whip my dick out, and swordfight the King's prick if I have to."

"You'd fight the King?" I ask with a chuckle and a roll of my eyes. Imagining Rab and Brennin slapping their erect dicks together is about ninety-percent *hilarious* and maybe like ten percent sexy. Maybe eleven or twelve percent. "Please. You're his lackey, through and through." I pull a skintight black dress off the hook and hold it up to examine it. I would *never* wear anything like this back home. It's sort of … grown-up and sexy, and I want it all over my body right now. Besides, it has bat shapes cut out of the midsection, leaving these sexy little gothic peepholes. The back is low-cut, and sewn to look like the top of a bat's wings. "King's orders," I mimic in Rab's cold voice, miming shooting a gun at Brandon's head.

Brandon.

Well, fuck.

Now that I've been here and I've seen what I've seen, I believe Rab. Which, of course, means that the Rabbit who was parading around as Brandon … had to have *eaten* the real Brandon's flesh at some point.

Gross.

"You're still upset about me blowing your crush's brains out?" he asks, licking his lips as I step into the dress and wiggle it up my body. It has cap sleeves and a soft lining on the inside that makes my skin tingle. If I pair it with the black pirate boots I got from Lory, I will look fucking dope.

"It was a hard thing to witness," I admit, glancing at Rab and watching as his ears twitch like antennae on the top of his head. They're so expressive. I can see everything he's thinking. "But I … guess I'm glad it happened."

"Oh?" Rab asks as I scoot around him and pause for a moment in front of the mirrored dressing table to the right of my bed. It has little clawed feet on the bottom and I swear, it wiggles its toes every now and again. "You *like* it here, do you Miss Liddell? Fitting, since you'll be the ruler of Underland-turned-Wonderland for one hundred and twenty-seven years, give or take a decade or two."

"Nobody lives to be a hundred and twenty-seven," I start, and then pause. Or do they? After all, we don't have any angels or Rabbits or cat shifters back home.

"You will be, if you live long enough to save Underland. It's in one of Lar's prophecies."

"Well, don't believe everything you read in tea leaves, I always say," I joke as I lean over the table and apply red-red lipstick and too much black liner. The lipstick smells like berries, and the liner has a sweet, smoky sort of scent. Hey, I bet it's all natural, right? Probably organic. Most likely *not* vegan. This world is so fucked-up, I would not be surprised if my lip color was made from the blood of baby lambs or some shit.

"It was in his wings, I saw it," Rab growls, and there's something fiercely protective in his voice that draws me around to look at him. His reflection isn't enough; I need to see his face. He's looking down at me with this determined set to his features. I almost want to reach up and touch his cheek. Almost. Instead, I drop my arms to my sides and glance away, toward the door.

Everyone is already at the party. Even Tee and Dee went early to set it up. It's just me and Rab they're waiting for.

"We should go," I say, but when I try to move away, Rab reaches out and curls his fingers around my arm, drawing me close to him.

"There's only a thirty-five percent chance," he whispers, mouth slightly parted, red eyes ringed in liner and flooded with shadows, "but it's a chance worth fighting for." Rab touches the side of my face with his tattooed fingers, running his warm fingertips from my cheekbone to my chin, cradling my head in his hand.

We just look at each other for a long, quiet moment before Rab uses his other hand to brush the hair from my forehead.

"Can I kiss you, Alice?" he asks me, his voice like the quiet, cool shadows of a cave. I want to crawl into it and curl up, sleep in the circle of his muscular arms. *Eww, what the fuck?!* I must be getting soft.

"Yes." It's the only word that can make it past my already parted lips.

Rab slides his right hand back to cup my head, pulling me close and breathing against my mouth. I can already tell what his is going to taste like, this refreshing mix of peppermint and lavender that makes me wet my lips with anticipation.

The asshole takes his sweet time coming to me, teasing my bottom lip with his tongue, tasting me and making me groan. I rise up on my tiptoes and lean into him, pressing my breasts against his vest. It's not enough fabric to disguise the flat, chiseled expanse of muscles underneath, and my nipples pebble into hard points.

My right hand slides up and over his shoulder and doesn't stop until I'm running my fingers up the soft, fuzzy length of his ear.

"Oooh," he growls, moving his hand from my face so he can wrap an arm around me instead. "*Harder*." He pushes his lips against mine, his tongue invading my mouth. It's the sort of first kiss you don't forget and yet, one where you can't remember all the details because it's nothing but a wild, ardent blur.

Rab lifts me up and sets me on the edge of the dressing table, knocking makeup and FUCKING DRINK ME bottles onto the floor. He presses in close, grinding our pelvises together and pushing my dress up in the process. I can feel him hard and wanting through his slacks as he presses against me, and I squeeze him tight between my thighs.

My hands play with his ears while one of his plays with my breasts, kneading and massaging the tender flesh until I'm breathless and wanting, near desperate for it. Rab drops his grip to my ass, squeezing me and pulling me even closer to him.

"If we didn't have an appointment with the King …" he growls against my mouth, and I turn my face away, these breathy gasps for air passing between my lips as I close my eyes and try to pull myself together.

"You said you'd fight the King for me," I whisper as Rab lowers his mouth to my neck and licks me, from shoulder to ear. My entire body flushes white-hot and I rub my pelvis against Rab's without meaning to.

"I can challenge him to a cock-race, if you want. But there'd be substantially more blood and substantially less cock than I might've promised." *He* is the one to break us up, stepping back and sighing as he smooths his palms down the front of his vest. He's still sporting a boner, but I don't think anyone in this nightmare fest gives a shit.

"No, I don't want that," I say with a sigh, running my fingers through my hair. "Besides, what would be the point? It's not like I'd fuck the King even if he *did* win." With a smirk, I hop off the dressing table and shove my skirt down my hips, heading for the door without waiting to see what the expression on Rab's face—or ears—is like.

Nope, I don't want to know.

And yet, my cheeks are warm and I know for a fact that there's a smile on my face I can't wipe off.

The Torrid Tea Party is being held in a tower because like, of course it is, since this is a fairy tale on crack.

In the Disney version, there'd be a glittering pink wonderland in that tower where I'd wait for nine shining princes with white-toothed smiles and shimmery gold hair to come and save me.

In the Grimm version, I'd have a sleep spell cast on me and wake up giving birth after being raped. Yep. Did you know that's how the *real* Sleeping Beauty tale goes? Yeah, it's fucked-up beyond all reason.

In this version, there's a winding staircase with flickering torches and stone stairs worn down in the center to little dips that threaten to trip me with each step I take. At the top, there's a heavy wood door with a gold handle in the shape of a heart.

How shocking. More heart paraphernalia.

I reach out to open it, and the door swings inward on its own, propelled by the long, graceful fingers of the Mad Hatter.

"Hello Miss Alice," he whispers as he gives me a vampire grin and steps back to welcome me into the dark, hazy interior of the tower room. The incense is thick and smoky, and it smells like sandalwood and roses.

I can't see much of what's going on inside, but I can hear Dee chuckling from the shadows. I ignore Raiden and step into the darkness, feeling it close around me. It's not as stifling as I thought though, more like a warm blanket being wrapped around my shoulders. As I stand there, trying to take it all in, my eyes adjust to the flickering candles and I start to see familiar faces sitting at a table in the center of the room.

My eyes catch Tee's first, then Dee's, Chesh's, Lar's, North's … and the King's. I narrow my eyes on him, but he barely acknowledges me, leaning back in a black-on-black suit and looking like he's fucking bored out of his skull. On the opposite side of the table, March waits with a shiny *black* apple in his hand, yet another fairy-tale trope that scares the shit out of me. Sorry, but thanks, no thanks. He can keep it.

I sit down at the head of the table (or is it the foot?), so I can be next to Tee, staring at the other men across a small pile of warm rocks with a kettle resting above them. It has two spouts and no handle which is weird as shit, but I'm still all twisted up over my encounter with Rab. I'm like a soda bottle that's been shaken, all fizzy and threatening to bubble over the top.

Rab flops down on my left, purposely pushing his shoulder into mine as he passes.

"I can't believe you're letting these mercenary fucks put us through the wringer," I tell the King, wondering what the hell his motivations are. I half-expect to see the Knave and her husbands lurking at the dark edges of the room with Dor. I'm pleasantly surprised to find them all absent.

"When one is entrenched in shadows, one doesn't simply turn on a light." The King sits up and stares at me from across the glowing embers. They cast strange shadows on his face, highlighting the perfection that is Brennin Red, the King of Hearts. He has high, defined cheekbones, and a mouth that won't quit. That little scar on the corner of his mouth just emphasizes how gorgeous he really is.

"What *does* one do?" I mimic, fluttering my hands near my face. "Trip on a pile of dirty clothes and break one's toe?"

"Speaking from experience?" Dee asks with a bright grin. His wings cast beautiful shadows on the wall behind him, and I have to hold back a malicious grin when I see Ol' Red cast a frustrated glance in the twins' direction.

"Maybe," I quip with a small shrug. "One of my toes is a little crooked. You make your own assumptions."

"Assumptions …" Dee starts, but then pauses when he notices the dark-eyed gaze of the King sweeping over him. With a sneer, Brennin turns back to look at me as the Mad Hatter carries over a tray of chipped little tea cups.

"Aren't you a clever one?" Brennin purrs cruelly, tugging at the white gloves on his hands. It's driving me up the *wall* trying to figure out why he never takes them off. Like, maybe because he's a murderer with red palms? "Look at you with your puns, *Your Majesty*." The King sits up straight, crown sliding lazily across his bloodred hair. The heart-shaped jewels seems to glow in the ominous half-light. "I'm sure that'll make for exceptional pillow talk."

"Go eat a dick," I say smartly, smirking and flipping him off as I get comfortable and glance over at Rab. He's pulling a pipe from the pocket on his slacks and glancing over at me with eyes the color of a smoky moon. Last year, there were so many forest fires in California that the smoke tainted the sky for days, and the moon … the moon was as red as blood.

"You thought I was poking you with something else?" he asks as I snort and shake my head.

"If your pipe is capable of growing when aroused, and caps out at … six inches," I start with a loose shrug of my shoulders. I'm a little bit full of shit though because I'm pretty sure it was longer than that. His dick, I mean, not his pipe.

"Such a clever little Alice," Rab says, lighting up and holding the smoke in his lungs for an inordinate amount of time. When he exhales, it all comes out through his nose, like a dragon billowing smoke.

Speaking of dragons …

My eyes meet North's gold ones from across the circle, and he smiles at me, reaching up to slick some of his hair back. As he does, he runs his fingers over one of his horns. Pretty sure that's, like, a come-on. It's working, too.

"Welcome all," March says, waving his hands dramatically over the flames. He flicks water into the coals, and pink steam rises up from the warm rocks. I have no idea *why* the steam is pink, but at this point, if I asked questions about *every* little idiosyncrasy in Underland, I wouldn't get a single other word out. "To the Torrid Tea Party."

He stands up and claps his hands, casting a dark gaze around the table. There are sky-high silver trays filled with cookies, cakes, tarts, sliced fruit, and unidentifiable little pastries covered in raisins. Dee *and* March are already eating, so I just help myself.

"Before we begin," March says, adjusting his own top hat. It's not *quite* as top-hattish as the Mad Hatter's, but that's to be expected, isn't it? Clearly, we all know who the boss is here. "I'd just like to acknowledge a very merry un-birthday to both Alice and the King."

"Oh fuck my life," I groan, putting my face in one hand. "Here we go with the nonsense."

"So you can see they're a perfectly matched pair," March continues, whisking a teacup off the tray and spinning it in his hand. With a brisk flick of the wrist, he pushes it down the length of the table. It twirls and dances until it comes to a stop directly in front of me. At first I think he's given me three cups stacked together, but when I move to pull them apart, I realize it's all one piece.

"We mustn't waste China," Chesh purrs, tapping at the side of my cup with a nail. "It's on the other side of the world, you know. To get there, we must dig a very great hole." He winks at me, and I'm not sure if he knows how ridiculous that sounds. I'm about fifty-fifty on that one.

"Before I was so rudely interrupted," March continues, and Chesh puts his ears flat against his head.

"I was *un*-rudely interrupting," he corrects, and March pauses like that's actually a valid point.

"Righto, my apologies," he says, lifting his hat and pulling out another small tea cup. "I should pay more attention. I just get so … *excited* when we host these parties."

At the word *excited*, March reaches down and cups his junk. I fling a pastry in his direction and he catches it with his *mouth*. "As I was saying, clearly the Alice and the King are meant to be together as they share the same un-birthday. What a coincidence."

"We *all* share the same un-birthday," I growl out because a girl can only take so much nonsense before she snaps. I grab another raisin-covered pastry and bite into it. The inside is savory and spicy, filled with some sort of meat and vegetable paste. It's actually fucking delicious, although the *source* of the meat is a questionable thing.

"So we do …" March continues in his drawling English accent. "Bloody brilliant observation. So, we all share the same un-birthday—except for Dor. Today *is* his actual birthday."

"And you've locked him out of the party?" I ask with a roll of my eyes. "Some friends you are." Although I'm seriously fucking thrilled that nutbag was not invited. I'd be more likely to put my life in the hands of the wisteria blossoms outside my bedroom window (although one of them did call me a whore today which is most certainly *not* appreciated) than trust the Dormouse.

"We are *not* friends," March says as Raiden leans back in his chair and crosses his booted feet at the ankle. "Friends are as rare as diamonds and twice as precious. The only person with a friend in this room is the goddamn Savage Duke."

"I have *three* friends," North growls, squeezing my ankle with his tail. "The Cheshire Cat, Brennin Red, and Sonny Liddell." He ticks the names off his fingers with a little growl. "I may very well be the richest man in the Kingdom of Hearts."

"Second richest, as I've just taken a large sum of your money," Raiden corrects, pulling his top hat low and shading his orange eyes from view. He's unbelievably gorgeous, dressed in a black and white striped suit jacket with a frilly white undershirt and a big orange bow-tie. The only part of his face I can see right now is his smile, twisted to the side and sharp as the slash from a knife.

Good thing I remembered to strap *my* knives to my thigh before I left; I've got my trusty ol' Queenmaker on my hip, too. Allison Pleasance Liddell, totally rad badass extraordinaire … in training. Can't forget the in training part.

The Duke just growls as March spins a second tea cup over to his boss. I can *hear* the King's white-gloved hands curling into squeaky fists. I get a kick out of that and decide I don't *quite* hate the March Hare as much as I thought I did—although he does give Red his cup next.

"So it seems we're *all* celebrating a special day today," March continues, locking eyes with me as he passes out the Duke's cup, then his own, Rab's, Lar's, Chesh's … and then Dee's and *then* Tee's.

Clearly, he's the least favorite of the twins. This is not the first time I've noticed.

Tee clenches his hand tight around his mug, his nostrils flared, a muscle in his jaw ticking. I also notice he fluffs his wings dramatically, drawing the attention of the entire room.

"He's a prince, too," I say, looking into my cup. "They both are."

"They're servants, little more than slaves," the King says, and I slam my cup down so hard that it breaks it half.

"They're *mine*, you gave them to me," I snarl, even as Tee reaches over to put a hand on my arm.

"Allison, don't," he whispers, voice tight and ragged.

"So I did. It doesn't change the fact that that's what they are." The King lifts his gaze to mine, and there's this unyielding defiance in them that makes me crazy. For the first time in my life, I want to *break* someone's spirit, watch them collapse into a heap on the floor covered in tears and snot.

I hate the King.

I fucking *hate* him.

"Your idiot father did this to them. He slaughtered an entire *race*." I stand up from my chair, knocking it to the floor. Brennin follows me up, leaning his palms on the table and *staring* at me like he's feeling the same damn way, like he wants to break me.

Well, all I have to say to that is *good fucking luck, buddy.*

"My *father*," the King says, sliding a gloved finger along the scar that bisects his throat. "Did *this* to me. My *father*," he continues, stepping back. I notice that he manages to keep his chair upright. "Murdered my mother and my sisters, and he tried to murder me." He comes around the table to lord the fuck over me, and I just curl the corner of my lip up in a snarl.

"So you're going to continue his legacy by treating the twins like garbage?" I ask, my voice low and dangerous. Swear to God, I am *this* close to stabbing the man with the Vorpal Blade. Wonder if I could do it?

"What do you suggest I do with them?" he growls out, and I lift my face to look into his.

"Let them go. Release their chains, remove their curse, and admit that *your* father made a mistake." I cross my arms over my chest as the King stares at me. He looks like he wants to strangle me. Instead, he turns away with a flutter of his black cloak, and returns to his seat—the biggest, nicest chair of the whole bunch. He might not be sitting at the head of the table, but he's damn well made sure we *all* know who he is.

"Continue, and let's get this nonsense over with," Brennin says with a wave of his hand.

I resist the urge to chuck my broken tea cup in his direction as Tee helps me right my chair, pushing me back in before he whispers in my ear.

"No one has ever stood up for us like that before," he whispers, curling his fingers around my upper arms and giving me a long, lingering kiss on the cheek. Dee is watching us, his mouth half-stuffed with cupcake. He stops chewing as he gazes in my direction. There's too much there, in Tee's whispered words and Dee's longing stare.

I glance away sharply.

What can I say? I have intimacy issues.

March lifts up his hat again, sliding it up and over his ears, so he can grab another tea cup. He gives it a little spin and sends it my way.

"Once I pour the tea, we all drink, and then we switch places," March says as he picks up one of the twenty-plus teapots on the table. This one is painted to look like a jabberwock's scales. I wonder if all jabberwocky are black? Seeing as I've only *seen* one, I have no idea.

"Why would we switch places?" I ask, and I get several *are you serious?* looks from the men.

"To have a clean cup, of course," March says as he walks around the table and starts by pouring me a steaming cup of black tea. He pours in the same order he passed out the cups, and I swear it takes a *massive* amount of effort for me to hold my tongue on this one.

Once March is seated again, he lifts his cup up for a toast and everyone else follows suit.

I'm the last one to raise mine up.

"To a very torrid tea party," March says, and the other men repeat after him.

"To a very torrid tea party," I say, lifting the cup to my nose for a sniff. I'm getting hints of molasses and a subtle milkiness, even though I've yet to add any cream. When I peer a little closer, it looks like the liquid inside my cup is redder than I first thought.

Oh, and also, there are little jars filled with *needles* on the table that I failed to notice before. The men each grab one and start pricking their fingers, kneading tiny drops of blood into their cups.

"To activate the magic," North explains when he catches me staring at him.

Oh, well, of *course* we'd add blood to our tea. Nothing less would make sense. With a sigh, I do the same, wincing as I stab my finger and watch a tiny crimson drop well up. I shake it into my cup and try really hard not to think much more about it.

"What sort of tea is this?" I ask as a few of the men add varying amounts of sugar and cream to their cups.

"It's quite tippy," the Mad Hatter says, cocking his head to one side. I still can't see his eyes with the brim of his hat pulled so low. "Large golden buds, delicately twisted leaves. There's a copper finish to it, wouldn't you agree, March?"

"This here blend is a Golden Shower Black Tea," March says, sipping his cup with a single pinky outstretched. There's a pretty wicked looking ring on it, too, and I get the idea that maybe the motion isn't just for show.

"Pardon, what?" I ask, blinking stupidly through the shadows at him.

"Your pardon is granted," he says, but he doesn't bother to answer my question. I narrow my eyes at him and try to resist the urge to throw hot tea in his face. I'll show *him* what a scalding hot golden shower can do.

"Golden Shower means the tea was watered *only* by rain coming down when the sun is out." Tee adds two scoops of sugar with one dash of cream, staring at his drink like he's already dreading taking a sip.

"So what do they do the rest of the time when it rains?" I ask as Dee fills his cup with cream and about ten scoops of sugar.

"They cover the field with a tarp," he says, downing his own drink in a single gulp.

"A golden shower back home—" I start, when Rab interrupts me.

"Is hot piss in the face during sex? We know that, Alice." Rab smokes his cig, glances to his right and takes a good, long look at the Mad Hatter sitting next to him. "We're all moving one space to the left, am I right?"

"Most assuredly," Raiden growls, one sharp fang showing over the edge of his lip. He watches as Rab taps his cigarette ash into the tea cup. "How clever are you? Perhaps I'll leave a wad of warm jizz in your cup next time I serve you?"

"Wouldn't be anything I hadn't tasted before," Rab says as Lar extends his pale hand across the table and takes the cigarette from Rab's fingers. The light from the fireplace filters through the Caterpillar's wings, turning them into stained glass windows that paint the faces of the men on the right side of the table a brilliant blue.

"You've tasted jizz before?" I ask, but the Cheshire Cat is already tapping at my glass with the tip of his tail.

"Drink, Alice, drink," he says, his pupils dilated to the point that I can't even see his gray irises anymore. I can't tell if that's because of the dark … or the drugs. Maybe both. "You and your angel prince."

I look around and realize that Tee and I are the only ones yet to take a drink.

"Are you okay?" I ask him, noticing the tightness around his eyes and the hard lines next to his even harder frown. He takes his peaked cap off and rakes his fingers through his hair.

"Tee used to be a tea addict," Dee says, rhyming the words in that silly singsongy way of his. "He was drunk more often than he was sober."

"You don't have to do this if you don't want to," I say, but Tee is already shaking his head. I can see small beads of sweat on his forehead, and I pick my red cloth napkin up to wipe them away.

"He can't leave, not now," March says, twitching his brown ears. Rab's white ones seem to twitch in response, and the two men turn to glare at each other. They're both the same species, aren't they? And they're both cronies for corrupt kings. They're rivals when really, they should be besties.

"Why not?" I ask, narrowing my eyes and then tilting my head as I hear the lock on the door slide closed. My mouth drops open and I flick my eyes in that direction.

"Once a Torrid Tea Party's started, it's impossible to get out the door," March says with a shrug, and the Mad Hatter tsk-tsks, wagging a finger in his direction.

"Not impossible, simply *impassable*—nothing's impossible." He lifts his hat up and flashes those marmalade orange eyes in my direction.

"If he leaves, he's out," the King says, in that same bored, no-nonsense voice of his. "You cannot marry him." I flip Brennin off and turn to Tee, reaching out to put my hand across the back of his.

"If you don't drink, neither do I," I whisper, and he lifts his amethyst eyes to look into mine. There's a quiet pleading there, but also an inner strength that I feel resonating in the very depths of my soul. We're peas in a pod, me and Tweedledum. Heh. Tweedledum … I like his nickname better.

"I'll drink," he says, looking straight into my eyes, "for you."

He lifts his cup and downs the whole thing before I can even take another breath.

I watch his hands shake as he puts the cup down and runs his arm across his mouth, gasping as he shakes his head and yanks his cap back down on his head.

If Tee can do it, then so can I.

But also … I want to know more about his time as an addict later.

"Cheers," I mumble under my breath, and then down the sweet-smelling tea, feeling the hot liquid burn its way down my throat.

As soon as it hits my stomach, I can feel the effects.

"That was delicious," I blurt without meaning to.

"Truth herbs," Lar says, crossing one arm over his chest and resting his head in the hand of the other. "It makes you say and do things you never would otherwise."

"I want to fuck the Alice," the King says, and then he smirks at me and I get the idea that maybe that *wasn't* an accidental little quip.

"I want to kill the King," I say, crossing my arms over my chest and then shrugging, sticking my tongue out in a silly, stupid way, like Dee always does. "Oops. Guess the effects of the herbs are already setting in."

"I don't want to become an addict again," Tee whispers, and then closes his eyes and covers his mouth like he didn't mean to say that.

"Shall we begin the torrid bit of our illustrious tea party?" March asks, lifting his finger and motioning for us all to switch. Like we're playing a game of musical chairs, we all stand and shift places, moving one spot to the left. I get the idea that it'd be *really* easy to poison someone like this. I should've used one of my test kits. Epic fail.

"Has anyone poisoned these cups?" I ask, and I get several blurted *no's* in response.

From everyone but the King and the Hatter.

"Sadly, no," Raiden says after a moment. Spinning his top hat around on his head, he flicks his attention in the direction of the King of Hearts. "And you, dear friend?"

"He knows that if he poisoned you, I'd blow his head off," March clarifies as he gestures absently in Red's direction.

"I didn't poison anyone," Red says with a cruel smile that stretches the scar on the edge of his mouth. "If I wanted someone dead, I'd simply take their head." He adjusts his crown and then lifts his chin. "So *Your Majesty,* please pick a man and start the questioning."

"I start?" I ask and several of the men nod, like that's the obvious route. "Okay, then … Red." I turn to look at the King and try not to scowl. "Did you really bring me here with the sole purpose of showing the court how useless I am?"

"Yes," he answers without hesitating, sitting up and crossing his arms over his broad chest. I can hear Tee growling from beside me. "I don't like you, and I think you're a useless figment of the past. The Alice you might be, but I don't need your help to right Underland's wrongs."

"I suggest you watch your tongue when you speak to my bloody mate," North growls, skin rippling like he's having a physical reaction to watching me be disrespected. "You know I can't handle that."

"My turn," the King says, ignoring the Duke *and* the order in which March passed out the cups; he looks straight at me as Raiden snarls some very creative curse words in the background. Like I said, battle of the alpha titan assholes. "If I were to give you the key to the Looking-Glass right now, would you leave? Would you *run*?"

"I'd go, but I'd come back," I blurt, digging my nails into my thighs to stop myself from elaborating on that. But I guess those truth herbs are *really* fucking strong, and I can't seem to hold myself back. "I can't leave my family not knowing. I also don't think I can abandon Underland, not anymore."

The King's mouth flattens into a thin line.

"Sorry, not sorry to disappoint you," I spit out, and I don't even try to fight the herbs on that one.

"The Knave wants you dead," he says, and then he cringes slightly as I raise my brows.

Well.

Now I don't feel so bad about hating the bitch.

"Why would the Knave want the Alice dead?" North says, slapping his heavy, muscular tail against the stone floor in a rhythmic pattern. "She wants your dick, doesn't she, Red?"

"She wants to be the Queen of Hearts," the King says, which is virtually the same thing. "I'm not sure if she wants to kill me or fuck me."

"She can't be queen," North growls, his nails lengthening at the end of his fingertips. "She isn't the Alice. The prophecy most *specifically* mentions the Alice. And you, you should be ashamed of yourself for trying to get rid of her. Fucking wanker." The Duke leans back in his chair with the gilded gold frame. He just sort of *melts* into it, draping his body elegantly across the navy blue velvet cushions.

"I should have you beheaded," Red says, but then the truth herbs kick in and he adds, "but I never will."

"No, you shouldn't. I hear a jabberwock can still bite with its head cut off." North taps his nails against the table and then scowls. "And now the Mad Hatter may have one question."

"I have a quest, not a question," Raiden Walker says, his mouth curling into a cheeky little smile. "For the Alice."

"Shocker," I say with a roll of my eyes. "What do you want?"

"I want you to let me drink your blood—and I *dare* you to enjoy it." The Mad Hatter lets his smile eat up his entire face, shadows from the fireplace dancing across his pale skin.

"Those are two separate things," I mumble, but I can already feel my cheeks heating.

Avid reader, remember? Like I've never fantasized about what it would feel like to be bitten by a vampire … Fuck.

Fuck, fuck, fuck.

I'm going to enjoy this *too* damn much, aren't I?

"I'm only asking you to let me as a quest," Raiden says, running his tongue over his lower lip. "Whether you enjoy it or not, that's up to you."

"What happens if I refuse the dare—err, quest?" I ask, not because I really want to, but because I feel like I need to make *some* sort of motion to pretend I'm not as eager as I am.

"Then you're out," Lar explains, folding his wings behind him. "You don't get to ask anymore questions although you must answer them."

"And if I refuse to answer?" I ask, and several of the guys chuckle at me.

"The herbs won't let you refuse." Lar smiles, gold bangles dangling on his arms as he leans back in his chair.

"Well, there's no way in fuck I'm letting myself lose this game," I say, standing up from my seat, and throwing some rainbow and blonde hair back from my face. I move over to the Mad Hatter and sit down on his lap before I can stop myself.

And oh.

Holy shit, that feels nice.

He wraps his arms around me and pulls me closer, filling my nose with that metallic, bloody scent of his, making my heart flutter strangely in my chest. I reach up to take his top hat off and hear several of the men make sounds behind me. Guessing it's taboo to touch the Mad Hatter's hat?

Still, he lets me take it off. And the next one. And the next one. The fourth hat is a small white one with the name *Alice* in gold cursive on the tag. It has red hearts, a big black feather, and black lace on it.

It's unspoken that it's supposed to be mine.

"A gift," Raiden says as I take the top hat and put it on my head. I can almost feel it *sealing* to my skull and let out a little yelp. "A spell to keep it on your head," he explains as I experimentally lift it up and set it back down again. Weird, but useful, I suppose. "It's got a little extra magic in there, too, just in case."

He sweeps my hair over my shoulder with long fingers, making me shiver as I close my eyes tight.

"This might hurt, at first," he whispers, kissing the side of my neck and sending hot, excited little thrills zinging through my blood.

"This is sexual, Alice," Tee says, his voice rife with worry. "If you don't want him to touch you like that, just refuse the quest. I'll ask your questions for you." His offer makes me smile, but I'm not backing down from this.

Not only will my stubborn side not allow it, but it … feels really freaking good, too.

Raiden licks his way over to the throbbing pulse point in my throat, putting his lips to it and tasting me as I struggle to hold back a groan, wiggling on his lap and feeling his cock hardening beneath my ass.

His teeth graze my skin, lighting every nerve-ending I have on fire.

When Raiden bites me, sinking his fangs into my neck, there's this white-hot burst of pain behind my eyelids that makes me cringe. I'm about to shove him back and pull away when a delicious heat spreads through me, invading my blood, poisoning me from head to toe. I let out a little whimper and sag against him as his arms tighten around me, and he growls against my throat.

I swear there's a string between that bite and my clit, yanking and pulling on it, making it throb. Like I wasn't already hot and bothered from what happened between Rab and me. But this, this is overwhelming. I feel like I'm drowning in my own pleasure.

Raiden takes his sweet time, sucking and licking, twirling his tongue around each of the teeth marks on my neck before he bites me again. And again. And again. Leaving his mark on my neck.

His arms tighten around me and I can't help but wiggle on his lap, eliciting a sharp groan from his throat. The sound weaves around and through me, almost like a drug, and I find myself melting into him.

"That's enough of that," the King says, and there's a strange tightness in his voice that's either jealousy or longing or *both*.

I pull away from Raiden, slamming into the table and knocking over several ceramic tea pots. One rolls to the floor and shatters, but I'm too dizzy and disoriented to care. My head is spinning and I'm not sure if it's from the bite or the tea or what.

"Holy crap," I groan, using the table to feel my way back toward my chair. I end up in Dee's lap instead, and he helps steady me. "Is that … the bite or the tea?"

"Both," Raiden says, and he sounds … *explosive*. Not at all like the cool, calm psychopath he's been presenting himself as. "It's fucking both."

He's panting heavily, a bit of blood smeared across his mouth. When I lift my fingers to touch the bite, it feels too good and I let out a small groan of pleasure. My fingers are stained with red when I stand up, smearing across the surface of the table as I do my best to make it back to my chair.

As soon as I slump into it, I know I'm not going to make it very long.

We have to drink a fresh cup of tea after each round? You've got to be fucking kidding me.

"North," the March Hare says, ears twitching as he grins, his teeth white in his dark face. "Your turn."

"My question is for the Cheshire Cat," he says, surprising me. I sort of figured almost all of the guys would go for me. Egotistical much? The Duke turns toward his friend and leans in close. Chesh does the same until they're nose to nose, tails twitching in a similar rhythm.

"Do you like the Alice? Or are you simply after her because she's my mate?" His accent flows over me like water and invades my brain. I am so high, y'all. Like, higher than a goddamn kite. My head lolls against the back of the chair as I blink through a foggy haze and start to sway to imaginary music.

"Maybe a little bit of both?" Chesh says, triangular ears swiveling on the top of his head. He flattens one back against his dark hair and then glances over at me. "She's growing on me, you know. And she seems to like princes. Must be part of the prophecy?"

"You're a prince, too?" I ask, just barely managing to swing my gaze over to him.

"I'm a *cat*," he says, flashing me pointed little kitty teeth. "All cats are princes."

What a non-answer. But I'm too high to question it.

"Looks like I'm next," March says, rubbing his hands together and then plucking up a sugar cookie in the shape of a pink bat. He bites into it and then gestures at me. "Okay, Doll," he says, and even though I'm feeling out of it, I roll my eyes at that. "Are you afraid?"

"Am I afraid?" I ask, and the question gives me cold chills.

Because the answer … is yes.

After meeting the Mocking Turtle and the Gryphon, after seeing the King so callously kill one of his card servants, after hearing the Mad Hatter tell me he'd like the

Duke to be raped and killed … How am I supposed to tell who the bad guys are anyway?

"Yes," I say, because I'm just an eighteen year old girl from nowhere … but the question is, am I destined for somewhere? Am I really meant to be something? Prophecy or no prophecy, it's really up to me, isn't it? Only I can decide.

"True fear is fine," March says as he looks at me with eyes the color of coffee with cream. I want to drink them up, savor them against my tongue. Aaaand how high did that shit sound just now? Jesus. "It's how brave you are in the face of it that matters."

"Excellent question," Rab says, smoking his cigarette with this easiness that invades every action he takes. He's just so damn confident, but also a little bit scary. I think about him holding me over that pile of bones beneath the Rabbit-Hole, and I can hardly match the memory to my current reality. It's no use going back to yesterday; I was a different person then. "But mine's better. Mine isn't simply a quest*ion* but a quest which is funny because question is actually longer than quest, but I suppose spelling doesn't much matter tonight?"

"Just get on with it," Tee grumbles, slipping out of his jacket and using his napkin to wipe sweat from his neck and chest.

"My quest is for you to *let me prick you, Miss Alice.*" Rab taps his cigarette ash onto the floor and then flicks the butt across the table and into the fireplace. Pretty impressive. But I'm still sitting there fucked off my ass on boosted tea and trying to figure out what he's *really* saying.

"You want to give me a tattoo?" I ask, because if he wanted to sleep with me, he'd just come out and say it. Well, I'm sure he *does* want to sleep with me, but I feel like there must be an unspoken rule *not* to ask for sex during the Torrid Tea Party. Although the word *torrid* means ardent or passionate, right?

"Exactly that," the White Rabbit says, leaning forward in his chair and steepling his fingers beneath his chin. "So do you accept my quest, Sonny Liddell?"

"I've always wanted a tattoo." The words burst from my lips before I can stop them. Fucking truth plants or whatever the hell they are. There must be a cooler name than *truth herbs,* right? Everything else here has weird names. "Okay."

"Allison," Tee says, and I get the idea that maybe I've agreed to something I don't quite understand.

"Come here," Rab says, leaning back and patting his knee. It takes a *lot* of effort for me to stand up, pushing my bat dress down my thighs because it keeps riding up. No wonder I only wear jeans at home. That's one thing I'm really starting to miss. Note to self: if I ever do go back through the Looking-Glass, I need to snatch my favorite denim to bring back with me.

Back with me?

Wow. Look at that. I've already committed myself to coming back to this crazy place.

Because … I can't just let Underland descend into madness, now can I?

Steadying myself with my palms on the table, I make my way over to Rab, using the backs of Tee's and Dee's chairs to keep myself upright until I reach him. And then I tumble right into his lap, same way I did to the Hatter.

"Where do you want me … I mean *it*, Miss Sonny Liddell," he whispers, tucking some loose hair behind my ear.

"Where do I want it?" I ask, looking down at my bare thighs. I tap the left one as the blood sloshes around in my head like waves in a storm. I'm so fucked up right now, but I also figure that I've always wanted a tattoo. How could I possibly regret this?

Sounds like something a drunk person would say, huh?

Rab reaches out and pulls one of the tea pots close to him, lifting the lid and … removing a tattoo machine full of gears and cogs?! What in the ever-loving fuck?

"Who puts a tattoo gun in a teapot?" I slur, even though I've been told by several different tattoo enthusiasts that it's rude to call it a gun. It's a *machine*.

"Someone who's mad," the White Rabbit says, setting the machine aside and then tapping his fingers against the sheathed Vorpal Blade. "May I borrow your knife, Sonny?" He whispers my nickname against my ear and I shiver.

"For what?" I ask, but Rab's already ripping the sheath open and sliding his fingers along my thigh. My breath catches, and I feel that pulsing heat between my legs like it's shouting at me via vagina-megaphone.

Rab slides the knife out and then tugs a small China creamer over. He empties the cream out into his empty tea cup then cuts his wrist, bleeding a profuse amount into the pink and white harlequin patterned China.

I watch mesmerized as he massages ruby red droplets from his wrist, grabbing yet another teapot and adding some steaming hot tea to his bloody concoction.

I'm weirded the fuck out, but nobody else seems bothered by what Rab's doing, so I just wait. I've seen a man turn into a cat, prophecies played out on faerie wings come to life, and a living card have its neck snapped. I may never be shocked by anything ever again.

"And a little sweetness, just for you, Sonny," Rab says, adding a bit of sugar to the mixture and stirring it up with a teaspoon. He sets it aside and goes for the Vorpal Blade again, stuffing a cloth napkin into his mouth and biting down on it before he lowers the blade to his arm … and starts to cut into his skin.

My lips part in shock, but it feels like I'm moving in slow motion when I reach out to stop him. The Mad Hatter leans over my shoulder and pulls my hands away.

"Let him finish," he whispers into my ear, and I wait as Rab filets his pocket watch tattoo off and peels his skin away from his arm. My tummy rumbles with nausea, and if I weren't high, I might make a fucking run for it.

"What the hell is going on?" I ask, my voice slurring like I've had way too many bottles of Dad's top-shelf brandy. He used to have a small glass every Friday, Saturday, and Sunday night, sitting in the living room with a fire blazing and some hard-boiled crime show on that he'd watch with Mom.

Guess he didn't realize he'd be starring in a real life version of one, huh?

Rab pulls the tattoo off his body as I shriek like a banshee. When he puts it on my leg, I almost faint.

"Can I get a heal?" he grinds out as he picks up the tattoo machine, and pulls a … a needle and fucking *thread* from the end of it?! It's a literal goddamn sewing needle and piece of string.

The Mad Hatter releases my hand and bites his wrist, lifting it up to Rab's mouth. The White Rabbit licks him as he makes eye contact with me, stirring my hormones into a frenzy. I can't stop myself from thinking about what I walked in on, with the Mad Hatter's mouth on the King's neck.

If drinking blood can be sexual then what the hell were they doing in there?

As I sit there and watch, Rab's arm heals over. The tattoo is gone, but his skin is unblemished and whole. I run my fingers over it, and he shudders.

Of course, there's still a bit of his skin sitting on my leg.

Rab takes the needle and thread, and then bites my earlobe, making me shiver.

"Hold still," he breathes in his bones-and-ice voice. He dips the needle into the blood and tea mixture, then threads it into my skin, making me yelp. As I sit there trembling, he 'sews' the edges of his tattoo to my skin. As he goes, not only does he tattoo a lacey design onto my flesh, but he melds his tattoo into my leg, to the point where I can't see where his skin ends and mine begins.

When I poke at the design with a fingernail, it hurts.

It's not Rab's skin anymore, it's *mine*.

When he finishes and removes the needle, snapping the thread with his teeth, the seconds hand on the clock begins to tick.

"What is this a countdown to?" I ask as I rub my thumbprint over the design. There's a tiny calendar on the open face of the pocket watch, and I can see that we've got quite some time until this one hits its target.

"This is a pivotal point," the White Rabbit says, wiping some of the blood from my leg. It hurts, but it's also riding that fine edge of pleasure and pain. "We probably won't know what it means until it happens. Could be this is the moment you either save Underland … or destroy it." Gently, he pushes me off of his lap and pulls his white ears down to cover his eyes. "Now get the fuck off my lap before I come in my slacks."

"Charming," I groan as I look down at my new tattoo and wonder how long I'm going to last before I pass out … or what I might think when I wake up. I manage to make it back to my chair, but just barely.

"Now," March says, grinning and then biting down hard on a pastry. Red filling squirts out of the end like blood, making me feel dizzy. My leg, it still hurts like hell, too. "My turn." He watches me for a moment, and then turns to the Mad Hatter. "My quest for you … is to kiss the King."

"Really?" Raiden says, looking irritated. He pops an elbow on the table, cradles his hand in it, and sighs. "I suppose if I must."

"Really." March shoves the rest of the pastry in his mouth and then delicately wipes off his fingers with a cloth napkin. "That's my quest: kiss the goddamn King on the *mouth*."

"As opposed to where?" Raiden asks, tilting his head to the side and giving March a pissy little look.

"I'm sorry, but … *if you must*?" Brennin drawls, looking bored out of his fucking skull. I'm not sure what March is up to with this game, but I'm intrigued to see how it plays out. That is, if I can keep my eyes open. Twice the boost, they say. More like ten times. I remember how I felt dancing at The Pool; it wasn't nearly as psychedelic as this. "You'd only be so lucky."

Raiden stands up and straightens his bowtie with a sigh, letting his gaze slide over to mine. Now I'm thinking about his mouth on the King's neck which, of course, makes my own neck tingle and throb. I put my fingers against it, smearing blood everywhere, and find myself letting out the most embarrassing fucking moan known to man.

I sound like a dying cow or a birthing giraffe, maybe some combination thereof.

"Why were you sucking on the King the other day?" I drawl, flopped over my chair like one of Salvador Dalí's melting clocks.

"Royal blood has a certain …" the Mad Hatter pauses and adjusts his velvet top hat. "*Je ne sais quoi.* The King knows how to win over a mercenary's shaky loyalty."

"What a non-answer," I drawl, rolling my eyes as Raiden makes a show of rounding the table. The King acts like a kiss with a blackmailing rival mercenary male means nothing to him, leaning back in his chair and waving a gloved hand around dismissively.

"Let's get this over with, shall we?" He scoots his chair back, and then gets this super fucking annoyed expression on his too-handsome face when Raiden steps between him and the table, leaning down and putting his palms on either of the chair's arms. The Mad Hatter is pinning the King of Hearts into his seat and getting ready to kiss him.

Somebody pinch me please.

"I knew you'd like this, the Alice," March drawls, eyes sparkling like maybe I'm not the only one who's enjoying the show. I can't decide if he's into the guy-on-guy thing or if he just likes teasing his boss and seeing the King suffer.

Raiden Walker stares Brennin Red down, his top hat sliding forward to shield his eyes from view. Yet I can tell from here that they're both staring at one another. The Mad Hatter holds that position for an inordinate amount of time, letting the crackle of the fire be the only sound in the room.

"Well?" Red demands, reaching up to adjust his crown. He just sits there with his stupidly stoic face until the Mad Hatter finally grins, flashing fang. Raiden closes the distance between them slowly, languorously, his mouth hovering above the King's scowl for an uneasy moment. I almost wonder if Brennin is going to shove him away and put an end to the Torrid Tea Party.

Instead, at the last moment, Raiden Walker rips his hat off—his *last* fucking hat!—and Brennin Red tilts his head slightly to the side. Their lips meet, and their mouths part. There is clearly tongue at play here.

My jaw drops, and I find myself leaning forward in my chair to gape at them.

The kiss doesn't last long—a few seconds maybe—but it's one of the most beautiful things I've ever seen. Not only do both men look like experts in the field of making out, they execute it with movie-style perfection, a single take that falls together in perfect unison.

When they part, there's this thin string of saliva that connects them for half a second before the King shoves his gloved hand across his mouth, and the Hatter lets out a raucous laugh.

"Now, that was fun, wasn't it?" he asks, standing back up and swiping his palms down the front of his jacket to straighten out imaginary wrinkles in the fabric. Of course, there are none because the Mad Hatter is perfection incarnate.

He returns to his seat, as the King sighs dramatically and rubs at his temples.

"White Rabbit, if you'd please. I have other business to attend to tonight."

"Well, don't let my torrid little party interfere with your busy work schedule," the Mad Hatter says, putting his fingers to his chest in a very mocking way. He rolls his marmalade colored eyes and replaces his hat.

"Is that an order to hurry my ass up?" Rab asks, checking his pocket watch and sighing dramatically. "Oh my ears and whiskers, how late it's getting." He tucks the watch into his vest and sighs. "What do you wish me to ask, Your Majesty?"

"Wait, what?" I snap, getting just a hint of mental clarity back. "It's your turn: you pick the quest or question."

"I live to serve," Rab drawls, propping his head on his knuckles and staring at the King with a rather disrespectful expression. Brennin ignores him, sitting up in his seat and raking his gloved fingers through his red hair.

"Ask the room if anyone has been involved with the tampering of our network as related to the King of Clubs." Brennin pours himself a cup of tea from a red pot—I'm assuming this is just regular boosted, drugged tea as opposed to truth herb tea—and takes a sip. Seems to me like he's throwing a bit of shade.

"We all heard the question," I mumble, but Rab repeats it anyway.

"Is anyone in this room involved with the tampering of our network as related to the King of Clubs?" Rab touches his fingertip to the flickering flame of a taper candle. His eyes shift around the circle, waiting for the truth herbs to kick in and kick our asses.

"No." There's perfect unison from the twins, a grin from the cat, and me rolling my eyes as I answer.

"Intriguing question and good use of our time," the Mad Hatter says, watching the King carefully. "Well-played. And no, no I am not involved."

"Nor me." March moves onto his third or fourth cupcake—I've lost count at this point—and flattens his ears against his head.

"I would never." Lar fans his wings softly and takes up smoking a cigarette on a long, decorative gold holder, blowing blue smoke rings into the hazy darkness.

"And we all know I'm clear. I kill things; I don't network." Rab smiles sharply and unbuttons his vest, like … *it's getting hot in here, so take off all your clothes* sort of a thing.

"You'll ask the Mad Hatter and the March Hare how the Clubs knew the Alice was with us on such short notice," the King says, looking to Lar next. "I mean, unless it was pure unhappy coincidence that the Mocking Turtle and the Gryphon showed up like they were summoned."

"That's a low blow, coming from someone like you," Raiden says, but the way he's grinning at the King says he likes the way this is going. There's violence and sex in the air here, and I feel like I'm drowning in it.

My body likes it though. As if I weren't wet enough from my encounter with Rab, from the Mad Hatter's mouth on my neck, his kiss with Brennin Red, the drugs also seem to have an arduous effect on my cunt. My panties are soaked, and my nipples hurt from staying pebbled for so long.

"Where did the Clubs happen to come across information that might lead them to believe the Alice was in our care?" Lar repeats, leaning back in his chair and using his finger to draw dog-and-caterpillars in the air next to him. Ya know, bugs with cat and dog heads? I'm assuming they exist somewhere in this nightmare.

"I haven't the faintest idea," the Hatter says, glancing over at his right-hand man. "March?"

"My only guess is that they were keeping a pretty close eye on us, tracking our movements. I can't imagine the King of Clubs trusts us much. After all, we do have reputations, don't we Hatter?"

"Oh March, we most certainly do. And so undeserved, too!" Hatter replies, spinning his hat around on his head.

March winks at me from across the table, and I cock a brow. Right. Undeserved. I shift in my seat because my pussy is so damn swollen, it almost hurts. March notices. Like I said, eyes, ears, and nose of the operation.

The rest of us mutter our thoughts on the matter, or lack thereof. It's quite clear this is a chess match between the Hatter and the King. Nobody else matters much.

"And now it's the damn cat's turn," the King snarls. "Horrid beast. I found hairs all over my finest robes this morning. How do you think they got there? I don't keep *cats*; I prefer *dogs*."

"No accounting for taste," Chesh repeats, disappearing from view, and then reappearing as an upside down white smile. His grin is as big as his head. "Though I suppose with the truth herbs I can't outright lie to you. All I can say is that I quite enjoyed urinating in your shoes." The Cheshire cat laughs as I sway in my seat and notice that the darkness in the room has now begun to take on multi-colored hues. Oh dear. I'm quite high, aren't I? "For my turn, I'd like to offer up a quest for the Alice."

"Of course you do," I ooze, barely aware of my own lips moving. "And what's that? A blow job? Because I'm not into perpetuating rape culture. A little bit high over here."

"A blow job?" Chesh's smile asks, turning back around the proper way. "Not at all. I was going to ask if you might scratch me behind the ear?"

The King sets his mouth into an ugly snarl, and sneers at the poor cat in a way that makes me furious. I stand up so quickly, my chair almost topples over, and Tee has to reach out to steady my swaying ass.

"You, sir, are a *prick*," I say before I head over to Chesh's spot, throwing my arms around his neck before he even really has one. His human body fades into view and he starts to purr. I rub my cheek against his, feeling this white-hot heat flare between us. Oh, this is so much more than a simple pet; it feels like a mating ritual.

My fingers stroke over his silky black and white ears, teasing the silver hoops, and noticing that there's a very distinct bulge in his lap that was not there before. His tail hooks around my ankle, and he makes this growling/mewling sound that has my panties all twisted in a knot.

"We'll be explosive pussy partners, don't you think?" he asks as I stumble and end up falling into his lap. I don't bother to move because, well, is there a better seat in the house? That, and I'm not sure I'll make it back to my own chair.

"Piss in my shoes again and you'll see the meaning of explosive," the King snaps, looking up as I chuck a teacup in his direction. He knocks it aside at the last moment with a gloved hand, and it explodes in the fireplace, sending bits of China all over the old stone floors. "That was not a particularly smart decision, *Your Majesty*."

"The cat is mine; he belongs to me. Leave him alone." I rub my cheek against Chesh's as his grin grows to gargantuan proportions, like it may very well fall off of his face. "You're mine now, Cheshire Puss. I'll hug you and love you and snuggle you as if you were my very own Dinah."

"Oh dear," Dee says, gritting his teeth from beside me. "You are quite out of it, aren't you Allison-who-isn't-Alice?"

"She won't make it a second round," Tee says, but I'm barely listening. I'm too busy snuggling the Cheshire Cat. Never snuggled a cat with an eight inch erection in his leather pants, but hey, there's a first time for everything! "Dee, make this count."

The chipper angel prince nods his head and offers up a salute, shifting in his chair to look at me, the feathers on his wings rustling.

"Allison-who-isn't-Alice," he coos, reaching out to run a finger down the bridge of my nose. "I need to ask you a question, my little Mary Sue." I grin and try to smack his hand away, but it looks like it's flickering in about a million different colors, and I find myself simply staring. "Can you look at me?" He taps my chin, and I lift my gaze to those glorious blue eyes of his. Like oceans, I could swim in them.

We stare at each other for what feels like eons, and I know in that crazy drug-induced moment that it will never be long enough. I want to stare at Dee forever.

My hand lifts up and seems to cup the side of his face of its own accord; Dee leans into my touch.

"Allison," he says, using my real name for once, "what should I ask?"

I blink my eyes at him, and it takes a good twenty seconds for the question to sink in. Lar and Rab still defer to the King, but the twins … are mine.

"What's Rab's third form?" I blurt, which is really a waste of a question, but I'm entirely *wasted*, so what does it matter? I reach over the table and snag a cupcake from one of the tiered silver trays. It has a crystallized butterfly on the top, which I eat in one bite. It tastes like marmalade and butter on toast.

"Rab," Dee singsongs as the bandersnatch assassin rolls his red eyes, "what's your third form?"

"It is a literal state secret that I've sworn on my life not to reveal without the King's permission," Rab says, looking like he's about to choke on his tea. The Duke grins and passes over a jug of ice water with tiny flowers dancing on the top.

"Two magical oaths warring against one another," North says, smiling and teasing the tip of one of his horns with a finger. "Whatever shall you do?"

"Your Majesty?" Rab chokes out, giving the King a look. But Brennin simply sits stone-still and says nothing at all. "Fuck." Sweat pours down the sides of his face as he leans over and curls his fingertips into the wood of the table. "May I simply say that my third form is a royal and be done with it?" After the words leave his lips, there's a visible loosening of the tight skin around his eyes and forehead. "Oh for Heart's sake, that was awfully cruel."

Rab exhales and leans back in his chair, my curiosity peaked to high hell. A royal, huh? Perhaps his third form is the King, like March's is the Mad Hatter? It wouldn't surprise me.

"An intriguingly insightful question," North says, glancing over at the King. Brennin returns his look and they hold each other's gazes for the longest fucking time. Or maybe I'm just high on boosted tea? Either way, that look is sketch as fuck. Makes me wonder if Rab's third form is actually something worse? What … if he's got the King's father's form in him or something?

"Surprisingly so," Tee replies, narrowing his eyes slightly. He doesn't trust North, and I know it's because of the Duke's close relationship with the King. But I think—*think*—that North is on my side now, or at least leaning that direction. "I won't waste your time because I can see Allison isn't faring well. Lar." He turns to the Caterpillar who's still lazily smoking his cigarette. "In any of your visions, did you see us as being the Alice's nine?"

Oh.

Damn.

Tweedledum does not fuck around.

Lar smiles slow and easy, tilting his head to one side, earrings swaying with the motion. His jacket is black today, to match the dress code, but the epaulettes and fringe are still gold, rustling in that supernatural breeze of his. When he opens his mouth to speak, smoke escapes and begins to dance in the air with fantastical shapes.

"How doth the Alice prophesied
Improve her all-male harem,
She dates assassins, kings that bleed
princes, angels, dragons!

How cheerfully her kitty grins,
How neatly shifts her rabbit,
She welcomes winged seer men in
While dating thieves is habit!"

The Caterpillar fans his wings as he recites and then executes a very small bow from his seated position.

"That's about all I know," he replies cheekily, a saucy smile taking over his lips. "Make of it what you will."

"That's not at all subtle," I drone, trying to push up from Chesh's lap. I don't believe in destiny or prophecy anyway; if these guys are interested in being one of my nine, they better show me their true colors and let me decide if they're worthy of my time. "Is it time to drink and switches places again? I could very well use a clean cup." I try to grab a teacup half-filled with tea, but Dee extracts it from my wobbly grip.

"Nah ah, Allison-who-isn't-Alice, you must wait for the official pouring and the blood prick to drink."

"But I'm thirsty," I whine, throwing my arms around Dee's neck. I end up tumbling out of Chesh's lap and straight into his. He collects me in his arms and holds me close.

"No more extra tea for you," he starts and then pauses suddenly, like he's seen a ghost. Slowly, I crane my head around to see what he's looking at.

It's Lar, bent over his empty teacup with a severe frown in place on those perfect pink lips.

"Oh, dear," he says, as the King glances into the cup alongside him. "Well, this certainly isn't any good." Ah, he's reading the tea leaves. I'm both fascinated and terrified to find out what it is that's caught his interest—doubly so, considering my intoxicated state. "We need some whiting, and promptly."

Rab scrambles up and out of his seat, moving to a cabinet in a dark corner. All I can see of him as he digs around in it are his white ears. When he returns to the table, he has a hookah, and he quickly readies it to be smoked.

"What does it say?" the King asks, gesturing at the chipped tea cup in the Caterpillar's hands. "Don't be coy, Lar, spill the tea, please."

The Caterpillar sighs and tugs on one of his earrings.

"The cup spells danger, clear and immediate danger." Lar snaps his fingers and the White Rabbit passes over the hookah. He takes a drag, exhaling blue-gray smoke, and then passes it around the table, starting with the King.

We all take turns breathing in the sweet scents of tobacco and blueberries. The high hits me like a ton of bricks, compounding on the two cups of boosted fucking tea that I drank.

I hope I'm awake long enough to see Lar's premonition, let alone act on it.

He stands up and pushes his chair to the side, spreading his wings wide behind him. They're bigger than the fireplace, blocking out the flicker of flames, and turning into this hazy dreamland that I can't seem to look away from.

Images flicker to life within the black-gold edges, sucking me into the dark gardens of the castle and beyond the wall. It's like I'm inside the head of whatever's watching us, staring up at the tower from the safety of the woods.

There's a long moment of silence, broken only by the melodic sound of an insect that vaguely—and only vaguely—reminds me of a cricket. Vultures in every color of the rainbow sit perched on a heavy tree limb, watching and waiting.

"Oh, I do believe we're being spied on, old chap," the Gryphon says, lounging next to the vultures like he's one of them. Now that I think about it, his face does vaguely remind me of one of the ugly scavenger birds. His wings, too.

"I believe you're right," the Mocking Turtle says, smacking his pointed and deadly mouth with a grotesque, wet smack. "But no prophecies will be held here today. This is a warning to hand over the Alice, not a chance at espionage."

The Mocking Turtle glances up from his position at the base of the tree and waves his hand, cracking the vision in the Caterpillar's wings and making Lar cry out. Blue, gold, and black dust explodes outward, coating everything.

Lar collapses, but the King is there to catch him, hoisting the other man up and then laying him on the tabletop with the Duke's help. Cups and teapots scatter everywhere, rolling to the floor and cracking into pieces.

"We need to get out there," Rab snarls, and he doesn't wait for the King to give him an order of any kind. Instead, he shifts into the massive, hulking form of the bandersnatch, his thick white coat spotted with black, his tail fluffed, the hair along his spine raised. He noses open a set of black shutters I hadn't noticed before, so buried in the shadows were they.

Silver light from the double moons shines into the room in thick beams, ruining the Torrid Tea Party's ambiance. Tee moves up beside Rab and opens the massive windows for him, throwing them out and into the night air before he makes room for the angry bandersnatch.

I try to head for the window, too, but Dee holds me back.

"Oh hell no," he says, shaking his head and wrapping me up in his wings. "They're here because they want to see you—if not snatch you. You're not going out there."

"But I'm *the* Alice," I slur, drunk as fuck on boosted tea. I manage to somehow get the Queenmaker off my belt and into my hands, but Dee curls his fingers around my grip and shakes his head. "I'm the …" I stop and sit down heavily in Tee's vacated chair.

My head is *swimming*.

The King and North manage to tie Lar down by borrowing both the Hatter's and the Hare's belts, stuffing a cloth napkin between his lips to keep him from biting his own tongue. The fit he's having looks awfully similar to the one I had.

Magic is afoot again.

I stand up and put the palm of my hand against Lar's forehead, glancing over my shoulder to find that Tee has also disappeared from the room. The Mad Hatter and the March Hare are conferring in the corner, and the Duke is already on his way out.

"Kisses, love," he says, putting his mouth to my cheek. "I won't shift unless I have to, but if I do …" He winks at me as I blink big, stupid eyes up at him. "I'll be quite savage, and I'll need my mate." He tousles my hair and then heads for the window, climbing out onto the roof before shifting his jabberwock wings.

"Well, you wanted a part of my kingdom. Are you planning on defending it?" Brennin growls at the pair of mercenaries. Chesh simply shifts into cat form and hops onto my shoulders. I'm not sure how useful he is in a fight. I mean, he could very well throw up his hand, shout '*Moon prism power!*' and change into a magical girl for all I know. Anyway, he takes up residence on my shoulders, prepared to watch the power exchange taking place in front of us.

"That depends," Raiden says as March balances a butter knife on his fingertip. "I want the Alice to tell me how she plans on weaseling out of our little marriage deal—while she's high on herbs. In fact, have her drink the second round cup and tell me."

"If she drinks another cup, she'll pass out," Dee snaps, losing his cheerful attitude to defend me. "Fuck you, vampire dick."

Raiden raises an eyebrow and shrugs his shoulders. I can hear shouting outside, the crash of stone, the crack of a tree limb. I race over to the window with Dee on my heels and peer out, finding Rab scrambling to his feet in a tangle of broken branches, blood dripping from his wolf-y jaws.

He flattens his rabbit ears against his skull and circles the pair of disturbingly calm men.

As if they can sense me, they both look up in unison and meet my eyes. A shock travels through me, and I stumble back and away from the open window again.

"Those are not Recitations," I whisper, feeling my body start to shake. It's involuntary, that shaking. I can't control my emotions right now; I can barely control my own feet. "They're really here."

"If they're willing to approach Castle Heart, they're not afraid," the King says, moving to stand beside me. "That's not good at all." I have the Queenmaker still clutched in my hand, but as I stand there, I find my fingers inching toward the Vorpal Blade. "Don't touch it," Red snaps, grabbing my wrist. The cat hisses at him and scratches out with a paw, but it's all for show. He knows better than to make the King bleed. "They're trying to get a read on your magic, so they can summon the Anti-Alice. The Vorpal Blade is power incarnate; activate it, and the Anti-Alice will come running. I can smell her out there in the woods, like dusty coffins and death."

My eyes widen, and I choke back a small sound of terror. This tea is making me paranoid *as fuck*.

"Can they get in?" I whisper, watching North stalk along the top of the wall. There's a huge fucking hole in it, but neither the Gryphon nor the Mocking Turtle seem inclined to cross that invisible barrier.

"*They shall not touch, with hands of hate, the Pleasance of our Heart'd gate*," the King says, and clearly he's reciting some poem or prophecy or something. He turns ebon eyes to me, the silver moonlight turning his red hair into fire. "They can't get in, but the Anti-Alice can … *if* you fuck with the Vorpal Blade while the wall is down. And anyway, even if those two can't get in, it doesn't mean they can't hurt you, Allison Liddell. If I were you, I'd leave. Now."

"If you'd fucked Liam and his friends, your brother would still be alive," the Mocking Turtle calls out, and my entire body goes cold. I turn my head slowly to look at him and find those cold, dead eyes watching me with interest. I have a feeling he's not the only audience in that macabre stare; someone else is looking at me through his face.

And, if possible, they're even more terrifying than the Mocking Turtle himself.

"If you'd just relaxed and let it happen, your family would be whole. How does that make you feel?" I just stare at him because there's bile in my throat and a horrid, righteous anger clawing its way through my heart. If I lose my temper now, while drunk and confused, I'll regret it later.

So I say nothing.

Because there's nothing bullies hate more than being ignored.

I back up and leave the raucous outside to the men … for now.

One day, I'll kill those bastards.

Tonight is not that night.

"Here," Raiden says, handing me a teacup and a needle when I turn around. "Do me a favor, and I'll end the chaos outside." I look down at the tea and then up at his face. He really is gorgeous, like a movie star or something. His eyeliner is flawless, his lips full, his smirk just arrogant enough to be attractive.

But I don't need magic tea to deal with him.

"I won't fuck someone I don't love—not ever again. If you want to try to win my heart, go for it. Otherwise, I'll marry you as a political move and nothing more. You can have your slice of the kingdom I'm going to turn around." I push the teacup aside and lift my chin while Chesh nibbles my ear and lets out a wild purr. "So, help those men outside or don't. Your choice."

The Mad Hatter lets the teacup go, letting it crash to the floor in a sea of boiling liquid and shattered China. He looks at me for a long moment, smirks, and then reaches out to tap the brim of my new top hat.

"I knew I liked you, little Alice." With a jerk of his head, the Hatter moves toward the window with March trailing behind him. As his boss jumps out the window and into the garden, March turns back to look at me with eyes like wet earth, brown and endless and deep.

"Good choice, Alice-Doll. You make smart moves with your pieces." He wiggles his ringed-fingers, and then starts to shift into a bandersnatch, brown fur sprouting up through his clothes, the sides of his muscular body marbled like a Bengal cat.

The March Hare shakes out his coat, and then hops down next to the Mad Hatter.

"Party's over, my friends," Raiden says, slow-clapping as he approaches the wall. "Nothing to see here, move on."

"You, sir, are a right bloody traitor," the Gryphon replies, shifting his ragged, ugly wings as Rab pants and watches M.T. and the Gryphon like he'd rather enjoy biting their heads off. Tee is standing on the wall opposite North, flanking the giant hole in the stone.

In the distance, I hear the scream of a jabberwock and blood begins to trickle down my ears. North stiffens up, so I figure it's a female, but he's safe inside the castle walls, right? The King seemed to think the Anti-Alice's ability to get in was unique.

"What can I say?" the Hatter asks with a shrug as Dor makes his way out of the castle to stand beside his boss, on the side opposite the March Hare. The Dormouse crosses his arms like a Hollywood bodyguard, holding his wrists in front of his junk. "I received an offer I couldn't refuse. Send the King of Clubs my apologies. Oh, and let him know my army will be joining the King of Hearts' on the borders of this illustrious kingdom."

The Gryphon visibly bristles, but the Mocking Turtle does not take his eyes off of me.

"Untie me, please," Lar chokes out, and I whip my head around to find him lying there with his wings curled inward, like he's in a serious amount of pain. "You and me,

Sunshine, we need to get out of here. You don't want to be on the end of the Mocking Turtle's stare."

"Why not?" I ask as Dee helps me stumble over to the table. He very gently pushes me into a chair while Chesh shifts back into human form and helps untie Lar. The Caterpillar sits up, chucking aside the saliva soaked red napkin he's just spit out.

"He can sense your mettle. That's something we want to keep as secret as possible." Lar stands up on shaky legs and holds his hand out for me.

"Let's get you back to your room," Dee says, peering into my eyes and brushing some hair from my forehead. "They've got this, I promise you. Nobody can cross onto the castle grounds without permission from the King." He pauses and grits his teeth. "Well, nobody but the Anti-Alice."

"Or the Knave?" I ask, but Dee shakes his head, and I let out a sigh of relief.

"Just the King," he says, and then pauses. "Or the Queen."

The way he looks at me, I know there's no doubt in his mind that one day, I *will* be the Queen of Hearts.

♦ ♣ ♣ ♦

Dee tucks me into bed next to Lar when we get back, but try as I might, I cannot stay awake.

Guess I'm a boosted tea lightweight, huh?

The only time I wake up that night is to check on my men.

"Everyone's okay," Tee whispers, kneeling next to my bed and stroking hair from my forehead when I wake up in a blind panic, thrashing around and tangling the sheets up in the process. I have a full bed tonight, too, with the Caterpillar, the Cheshire Cat, the White Rabbit, Dee, and North.

The bed is plenty big, at least.

"You're sure?" I ask, panting and trying not to think about finding Fred in that dark alley, dead and bloody and alone. I'm not sure I'd survive that a second time.

"Positive," he says, bathed in yellow and orange from the dying fire. His journal is open on the desk, so I figure he probably came back, showered, and starting writing—all without waking me up. "They left; it's over."

"For now," I say, trying to figure out why those pieces of trash showed up in the first place. But my head is too full of sleep, and my hands are still shaky from my boosted tea. "But they must've come for a reason; they weren't just stopping in for tea."

"Definitely not." Tee smiles at me and then moves to close the gap between us, kissing me with this soft, gentle sweetness that curls my toes. His wings unfold from his back in glorious folds, the dark feathers catching the moonlight, the chains falling to the floor. Waking my prince at midnight. It'd be like a fairy tale, if everything weren't drenched in blood. "A distraction, maybe?"

He sighs as I lean back in the pillows and scoot to make some room on the edge of the bed, patting the mattress to invite him to lie next to me.

After a second's hesitation, he climbs up, dressed in pajama pants and nothing else.

I'm still wearing my bat dress, but it's ridden up to my hips, and it only takes a minute to kick my panties off.

"What are you doing?" Tee whispers, but I just smile and roll onto my back, encouraging him to follow after me, so that he's on top.

Before you can say *o frabjous day!*, he's sliding into me and we're making love by moonlight.

Chapter Seven

The Ball of Broken Hearts and Stolen Tarts

I wake the morning of the ball to find a pirate standing over my bed.

"Lory?" I choke out, scrambling to sit up and swiping the drool from my face. My increasingly bright rainbow hair is stuck to the corner of my mouth. Oh, I must *really* look like the future Queen of Hearts now, huh? I'm hungover, slightly confused as to where I am or what's going on, and now sporting a brand new tattoo on my freaking thigh—a tattoo made of *skin*. "What are you doing here?!"

"I invited her to the ball," Dee says, sitting up, his hair scruffy but somehow still cute. Wish I could wake up with a playful pink in my cheeks and a mischievous grin hovering around my full, delicious mouth … fuck. I've been up all of two seconds and I'm ogling Dee again. Before I forget, I lean over and give him a quick kiss on the lips, freeing his wings from their cursed prison. He grins at me as I sit back, refocusing on Lory and blinking to clear the sleepy cobwebs from my vision. "Anyone from the Kingdom of Hearts is allowed to attend anyway."

"They wouldn't give me a visa for Eaglet," Lory says with a loose shrug of her shoulders, and I remember vaguely the bandanna covered in diamonds he was wearing on The Long Tale. "Border control is tight right now." Lory adjusts her black tricorne hat—that's what a pirate hat is called, you know—and then plants her hands on her hips.

Tee is standing behind and to the right of her, so I figure he's the one that let her in. Stretching, I lift my arms above my head, and curl my toes against a soft, fuzzy pillow tucked under the blankets. Wait.

"Chesh!" I admonish, lifting up the covers to find the black and white striped cat purring and kneading the sheets near my toes. Before I can escape his reach, he flicks his little pink tongue out and licks my toes. "Shoo," I growl, pretending he's Dinah and grabbing his scruff. My little black asshole cat likes to sleep in my blankets and then attack me when I climb into bed. I'm used to this maneuver.

I pull Chesh out by the scruff, but he shifts back into human form just as I'm dragging him from the blankets, landing on top of me with all of his beautiful muscles and that delicious fresh honey and black tea scent of his.

"What the …" I start, but I find the words stuck in my throat, heart thundering like a herd of wild bandersnatch. That is, if bandersnatch even run in herds? I have no fucking clue. "Get off of me," I breathe, but the words don't come as bitchy or forceful as I intend them to. I haven't forgotten that I almost killed this guy a few days ago. Or that last night was a serious clusterfuck.

"Yes, mistress," he purrs, the tags on his collar jangling as he leans in and licks the side of my face.

"Should I go wait in the hall?" Lory asks, flicking some of her brunette braids over one shoulder. "You about to get it on in here?"

"No, no," I snarl, scrambling out of bed and rubbing at my sleepy face with the heel of one hand. Looking around, I notice most of the men are missing. It's just me, Chesh, and the twins left now. I suppose they're all out preparing for the ball. I'd almost forgotten that tonight's the night. "What time is it?"

"Time to be up and about," she declares, dressed in brown breeches, a red peasant blouse, and black boots. Reminds me … I move over to my satchel, hanging on the hook near the door, and reluctantly pull out the outfit she lent me: corset and knives and all. "You lazy assholes better start getting ready. Guests are already arriving."

"Here," I offer up my borrowed clothes, but Lory waves them away with a hand covered in gold rings. They make a pretty contrast against her ebony skin.

"Keep 'em. We got paid handsomely by the King to bring the best tea in the kingdom down the river. I can afford new ones." She grins at me with white-white teeth. "Plus, I got an in with the Queen. That makes me pretty special, don't you think?"

"I'm not the Queen just yet. I won't ever be if I have to spend much time around Brennin Red. I'm as liable to murder as marry him," I start as Tee offers up a cup of coffee and a muffin. Our hands brush together and we exchange a look. It very clearly says *I know what you did in the dark*, and I smile. If I close my eyes, I can still feel him sliding inside of me last night. Other than that, the night is pretty much a blur.

"*Yet*," Lory repeats, turning, her long hair swaying against the backs of her calves. She moves over to the refreshments table and gets herself an EAT ME cookie, tucking it into her belt. There's a small wooden cabinet there as well that she opens, revealing several tiny glass bottles with FUCKING DRINK ME tags dangling off of them. Lory pockets two, and then turns back to face me, leaning her butt on the edge of the table. "You're not the Queen yet, but you will be."

"So you already know I'm the …" I stop talking and she throws her head back with a raucous laugh. It's nice though, to hear someone so free and unrestrained. Sitting in this palace, I'm starting to feel fucking stifled.

"The whole kingdom knows you're the Alice now," she says as Dee stumbles out of bed and knocks over a table with his wings. I don't think he's quite used to having them out all the time. Our eyes meet across the room as he flushes and does his best to fix it. Too bad the legs are broken into several pieces. I just smile, thinking of last night, the way he oh so carefully tucked me into bed.

Lory snaps her fingers in front of my face, and I groan. I'm doing it again, the stupid teenager daydreaming thing. After last night's nightmare, don't I deserve it though?

"Although I suspected when I first met you. Why do you think I had you come down to the ship so early? Coulda let y'all sleep in while we loaded cargo, but I wanted to get a good look at ya." She grins at me, pulls a knife from her belt, and promptly picks her teeth with it. "So, where's your dress then?"

"My dress?" I ask, because in the excitement of the last few days, I realize I haven't actually seen the damn thing. Got measured and fondled and caressed by Rab, but I never picked out fabric or anything. I don't even know what style of dress it is that I'll be getting. My bet is … that it's gonna be red which is fine by me. Just so long as it's not pink. "Good question."

"The dress will be delivered in …" Rab starts, stepping out of the painting on my right, the one with a white rabbit wearing a waistcoat. He's shirtless again, running his hands down his body in a way that just can't be accidental. He points to one of his clock tats. "About two minutes."

"Perfect," Lory says, settling herself into a wingback chair in the corner. "I'll wait and you can try it on for me."

"We'll have a fashion show," I say with a smile, sitting down on the bench at the end of the bed to eat my muffin and drink my coffee. "I'll show you mine; you show me yours."

"Bloody can't stand dresses," Lory says, shaking her head and sending her braids flying. "Makes me sick to my stomach; I'll be wearing my military uniform. You're more likely to see Dodo in a dress than me." She slides her knife back in its sheath and grabs a muffin. "Hear you lot got into trouble last night."

"And who's spreading that rumor?" Tee asks, hanging up a pair of identical outfits on a hook. Must be for him and his brother. Really, they're just nicer, more frilly versions of what they usually wear. Red military style coats, white button-ups, ruffled cravats, and black boots. The matching hats have giant red feathers sticking out of them.

"It's all over the castle. Nobody's stupid enough to miss the card servants scurrying to the hole in the back wall." Lory glances over at Rab as he lays out the stack of clothes draped over his arm on my rumpled bedspread. Chesh leans over to sniff the items and wrinkles his nose. He doesn't appear to have any intention of dressing up for the ball.

Fuck, I don't even know if he's invited.

Then again, he did practice dancing the quintrille with us, so maybe the King isn't as stupid as he pretends to be? If he excludes Chesh, I'll be pissed.

"Yes, well, we had some late-night visitors," Rab says, popping behind the bathroom curtain and stripping down. Lory barely glances his direction, grabbing an apple and peeling it with her knife. The motion of her hand on the blade reminds of me of March, of the two Rabbits shifting into bandersnatch form to face the enemy. "But that's been taken care of."

"The Knave looks to have her knickers in a wad this morning," Lory says as Dee picks candied insects off the pastry selection on the refreshments table. "Guess she's finally realized she's never getting Brennin Red's dick, eh?"

"That's about right," Dee says with a yawn, turning around to see me scratching at my new tattoo with a chipped fingernail. When Rab comes out from behind the curtain, running a gloved hand over his white ears and dark hair, he pauses and grins at me.

"You like what you see, Sonny?" he purrs, and I raise an eyebrow. This is some gorgeous ink, but I cannot get over how it came to be. I look at the empty spot on Rab's arm, and then back down at the lacey cameo of my new tattoo.

"Getting this … was one of the weirdest experiences of my life," I say, tapping my fingertips against the tattoo and making a mental note to myself: *during visits home, I need to cover my moving clock tattoo with pants or a long skirt.* Not sure how I'd explain this fresh ink to my father.

Not sure how I'll explain my two week long absence either.

My throat gets tight, and I push that thought aside. I just need to get through this stupid ball, and this stupid dance, and then I'll figure out how to get into the Looking-Glass. Lord knows I'm no chess champion. Fuck, I barely know the names of the damn pieces.

"I'm so glad you enjoyed yourself," Rab purrs as I stuff the rest of the muffin in my mouth. He moves over to stand beside me, cracks his knuckles, twitches his ears. His body starts to shrink, his ears get round, his nose flushes pink. Within a few seconds, Rab is sitting on the carpet in his mouse form, looking up at me with red eyes. *"I'll be with you the entire night,"* he promises, climbing up the leg of the bench to sit beside me.

"Oh, how delicious," Chesh purrs, clawing at the air above Rab's head. "I could just eat you right up."

"Do, and see what happens when I become a bandersnatch in your belly," Rab teases, whiskers twitching. I will not forget what he said last night, twisted up into a magic induced conundrum. Royal blood, huh? I need to know what this third form is; it's killing me.

"Put some nice clothes on; you're dancing the quintrille tonight in front of the whole court." Tee lays out an outfit for Chesh, too, and the cat's ears go back in frustration. He obliges, stripping down and changing right there in front of Lory. She raises her eyebrows but doesn't ogle. Guess she knows cat's don't give a shit about nudity; they will literally put their buttholes right in your face while asking for pets. Thankfully, Chesh hasn't done that to me … yet.

There's a knock on the door, and we all pause. Dee moves to open it, accepting a big red garment bag and four different sized boxes from a card servant's creepy human hands. He slams the door in its face, and spins around, the bag dangling from his fingers. He hands off the towering stack of boxes to his brother.

"Excited, Allison-who-isn't-Alice?" he asks, smiling from ear to ear.

"More like terrified out of my fucking mind." I put my coffee aside and stand up, unzipping the bag and trying not to cringe at the amount of poof and lace that explodes out. “Oh dear,” I mumble, pushing the garment bag back to get a good look at what’s inside.

There’s a dress, a short coat, and a corset. And from the looks of the boxes in Tee’s arms, I would guess jewelry, hat, shoes, and … undergarments.

“Hmm.” I pull the items out, handing the coat and corset to Chesh while I lift the dress up for examination.

It’s a red ball gown with a satin bodice and a heavy skirt comprised of yards of flouncy, lacy fabric. It literally bounces when I shake it, and I narrow my eyes. I was hoping for something more modern, like the bat dress I wore last night.

“This is positively medieval,” I murmur, and Dee chuckles. The dress has off-the-shoulder sleeves, a heart-shaped neckline, and a deep V where the satin bodice dips into the skirt. I hang it up on another hook, cringing a bit when the hook reaches out to assist me, scooping up the wooden hanger from my hands. I take the black and white striped corset with the gold buttons out next and hold it up, imagining it layered over the dress.

Things are starting to look up.

“Okay, I can work with this,” I say as I take the velvet coat and add that to the ensemble. It has three-quarter length sleeves, epaulettes, fringe, and long coattails in the back. The front of the jacket should hit me at about mid-waist.

Tee sets the boxes down on the bench and removes my coffee cup before it gets a chance to spill.

Dee's like a kid at Christmas, tearing open the top box and pulling out a garter belt and thigh-highs.

"Oh Hearts on a card," he groans, rubbing the garments against his cheek. I snatch them from his hand and sigh.

"I'm not wearing these," I say, chucking them onto the bed where Chesh bats at them playfully. "I'll wear plain cotton panties, thank you very much." I shove the lingerie box aside and check out the hat box instead.

Inside, there's a crown.

A fucking crown.

It looks like the King's, gold with big red diamonds, sharp points pricking my fingers as I run a fingertip along the top rim. The bottom is padded with white fur speckled with black spots, big roses—*real* roses—clustered on one side.

When I place it on my head, I feel it seal to my scalp the way the Mad Hatter's top hat did last night. A spell. Which reminds me …

I take the crown off and hand it over to Tee.

"Take a look at this," I tell him, wondering where Lar is. I could use his help checking over the spells in my new clothing. Like I said, I'm not stupid: I don't trust the Knave for shit. Moving over to the nightstand on the left side of the bed, I pull out a wooden box filled with the March Hare's test kits.

I'm going to use every single one of them.

The door to the room opens and I feel a huge shock of relief when the Caterpillar waltzes in, dressed in red and looking fucking scrumptious in his new outfit. Of course, he's wearing a half-shirt under his red jacket which is a little weird, but I can see his beautifully taut stomach muscles, so I'm not complaining.

"You're here," I say, glad to see that Lar's recovered fairly well after last night. When the vision in his wings shattered, and that dust went floating everywhere … fuck, I was worried. He smiles at me from across the room, his red earrings catching the light.

"I wouldn't miss your dress delivery, Sunshine," he says, turning to the red monstrosity and drawing a sigil in glowing gold over it. I move up beside him and open the first kit. I'm going to test several spots on this damn thing, just to be sure. "How are you feeling this morning?"

"Like total crap. Yourself?" Lar smiles, but he doesn't respond for a minute, drawing the same sigil over the corset and then the jacket. Nothing happens, and he doesn't say anything, so I'm assuming there's nothing wrong with the outfit.

When my first few test kits come up clean, I start to get annoyed.

I was almost hoping the idiot Knave would do something like poison or spell my dress, just so we could catch her embroiled in bullshit. My instincts are still screaming that something is wrong with that woman. You don't just lust after a position of power your whole life, and then roll over and take it when someone steals it from you.

No freaking way.

"Sleeping next to you, that revived me," Lar says, and I can't tell if he's joking, flirting, or being totally serious. He turns to glance at Lory, giving her a small nod of acknowledgement before he tests my new high-heeled boots, my jewelry, and even my stupid lingerie. "It's all clean," he says, but he defers to Tee for a moment. "Look it over yourself, too, see if there's anything I might've missed."

"Who are we distrustful of?" Lory asks as Tee touches the clothing with his fingers, rubbing the fabric together between like he's searching for residue or something. I don't know anything about angel powers, so I have to assume he knows what he's doing. Then again, assumptions make an ass out of you and shins, and …

Jesus Christ.

I'm mad, completely and utterly mad—and loving it.

"The Knave," I say with tight lips, and Lory nods her head.

"Good on you. I wouldn't trust that crazy bitch for nothing. She was the one who vetoed the King when he wanted to send food down the river. She let whole cities starve and then burn."

Well.

That's new information.

I wait for Tee to finish his inspection, and then raise an eyebrow.

"Everything looks legitimate," he tells me, trying for a smile. "But that doesn't surprise me. The Knave is smart. If she were to try something, it'd be more subtle than tampering with your dress."

"You're probably right," I say with a sigh, rubbing at my forehead. "This world is just making me paranoid."

"This world makes everyone paranoid," Chesh purrs, lying on his back and looking at me from eyes the color of a wild storm. I take the dress off the hanger and give it a long, lingering look. "Well, I suppose I could do worse for my first official ball. I wore jeans and a wifebeater to junior prom. This'll be a new experience."

I whisk myself off into the bathroom to shower and change into my outfit—which, of course, just has to include the white breastplate gifted to me from the White Knight. It's supposed to give me courage, right? And tonight, I am going to need that shit in spades. Err, in hearts? Anyway, you know what I mean.

Tonight, Allison and the Alice, they'll be one in the same.

Wonder how the Knave will like *that*?

♦ ♠ ♣ ♥ ♣ ♠ ♦

The ballroom looks completely different with the double doors thrown open, hordes of people moving between the foyer and the dance floor. Their outfits create a sea of shimmering red, white, and black, the fabrics shining under the flickering flames of the chandeliers.

I feel completely fine with the way the day is going until I'm standing outside those doors, starting to notice the ripple in the crowd as people turn to stare at me. This breastplate is supposed to give me courage? I call bullshit. I feel like the Cowardly Lion.

"We've got you," Dee whispers, giving my hand a squeeze. He's got his elbow through mine while Tee takes up a similar position on my other side. The cat is on my shoulders, lounging and probably napping, while Rab-mouse sits in the pocket of my velvet jacket. My makeup is done thanks to Tee because I have little to no makeup skills of my own; my rainbow hair is coiffed, this time thanks to Dee because … well, you get the drift. Lar stands just behind and to the left of me, like I really am a Queen and in need of an escort. Hell, maybe I do because the White Knight stands opposite him, flanking me.

Wonder if someone will try to kill me tonight?

My panties are dry, my weapons are strapped in place, and my heart is pounding like I've just run a triathlon.

"I can't do this," I whisper as my throat closes up and I find that my feet have ceased to move. "I don't want to do this."

"Do crowds frighten you so?" a cool voice asks from behind me.

I don't need to turn around to know that it's the King.

Fuck.

I steel myself and glance casually over my shoulder, like I just can't be bothered.

But oh. Oh. Ooooooh.

The King looks good, wearing his lazy crown, his red and white robes framing his lean but muscular frame, a decorative sword hanging at his hip. He's got a huge, furred cloak on, too, and I get the weirdest urge to wrap myself up in it. Or … let the King wrap me up in it. When he moves, I notice the pants beneath his robes are black and white striped, very matchy-matchy to the corset beneath my breastplate.

Ugh.

"I'm fine," I say, turning back to look at the sea of unfamiliar faces. "I just don't care for parties."

"Oh, you don't?" Red drawls, swaggering up to stand beside me. "That's too bad. You'll just have to suffer through this one." He snaps his fingers and several very human guards clear the crowds away from the doors, unrolling a red runner and sprinkling it with bloodied rose petals.

Like, really?

We're going to do the whole song and dance routine?

A Rabbit wearing the Castle Heart emblem—a broken heart intersected by a sword—on his surcoat, runs up the aisle with a trumpet. When he puts it to his lips and blows, every single person in that room goes silent.

"I hope you weren't thinking to make an entrance without us?" Raiden asks, appearing on my other side. While the King is dressed in luscious red and white robes, Raiden is drenched in black, save the single rose decorating his massive, wilting velvet top hat. He's got on a pair of leather pants, a ruffled top, and a white tie covered in black bats. The March Hare is dressed similarly, except his tie has little brown rabbits all over it and his shirt is white. He's also wearing a much smaller hat … and eating a pear. Plus, he's got a whole series of glowing vials around his neck that I can only guess contain poison of some sort.

He flicks an ear in my direction as he takes a bite of the fruit, spattering his beautiful lips with juice.

I look away, toward the ballroom.

There's a set of steps that lead inside, and at the bottom of them, I see the Knave and her husbands waiting.

Fantastic.

Usually we enter the ballroom from the downstairs entrance, so I've never actually come in this way. Maybe that's why I never really noticed how fucking cavernous this place is? I mean, I knew it was big, but standing up at the top of these steps, it looks like a football stadium, full of judgmental courtiers and women dressed in military uniforms decorated in badges. Each of them is surrounded by clouds of men, and none of them look very happy to see me.

The general population, however, people like Dodo and Lory who are waving at me from the center of the room, seemed thrilled.

"I'm going to puke," I whisper, no longer giving a shit that the King is standing right next to Tee. The elder twin grudgingly steps aside, ruffling his feathers in annoyance, so that Brennin Red can take my arm, pulling me ahead of Dee and giving the cat a glare so intense, I swear it makes *me* sweat. Or maybe that's the three hundred pounds of lace and tulle I'm dragging around? Or perhaps it's the thousands upon thousands of stares from the Court of Hearts?

"Please wait until after the quintrille, then you can be sick all you want in the privacy of your own room." Brennin pauses as the Duke strides up to us, wearing red breeches, a white shirt with tiny heart buttons, and the most ridiculous hat known to man. When he pauses next to me, he sweeps the hat off from between his dark horns and takes a ridiculous bow, tail thrashing behind him.

"My mate, the gorgeous Allison Pleasance Liddell, the Duke of Northumbria awaits to accompany you to the ball." I smile as North stands up straight and replaces his stupid hat with the giant cluster of feathers. His gold eyes sparkle as he takes me in and licks his lips appreciatively. The King simply rolls his eyes at our exchange.

"Fashionably late, as usual, North," he says, letting the Duke take up on my other side. "Thank you *so* fucking much for joining us."

"Anytime, *Your Majesty,*" he purrs as the King parades us over to the top of the stairs where the trumpet-wielding Rabbit is waiting. He lifts the instrument to his lips, gives three sharp blasts, and then unrolls a parchment scroll to read from.

"His Majesty, the King of Hearts, would like to formally present his future Queen of Hearts, the Alice, to the court. Make your judgments, state your intents, and if you should protest, now's the fucking time. For tonight only, all executions are stayed!"

The crowd cheers as I go pale and give the King a scathing look.

"Awfully presumptuous of you, isn't it?" I snarl. "Introducing me as your queen already?"

"You said it yourself: marriage for political gain. I've accepted it." Brennin ignores me as we start down the stairs to cheers and whispers and gasps. I'm sure I've been the topic of polite conversation all week.

So what do these people think of me, this little blonde girl with rainbow streaks in her hair?

I feel like a fraud.

"Alice, you're going to change the whole world, aren't you?" Dee's words ring in my head, and I close my eyes, taking a deep breath and trying to gather my courage together.

I tumbled down the Rabbit-Hole, fired a flintlock pistol at a giant monster bird, haggled my way out of a kidnapping by Underland's most infamous mercenary, and learned to fight with my hands. I have magic, a sharp tongue, and the will to make things better. I … survived an abusive relationship, found my brother's body, watched my mom get convicted in court.

This crowd, or the Knave, or the Hatter or the King … how can I let them intimidate me now?

The answer is: I *won't.*

I open my eyes as we pause next to the Knave, the Lion, and the Unicorn.

"Good evening, Alice," she says, her strange voice ruffling my metaphorical feathers. A quick glance at Dee shows me she does quite literally ruffle his *actual* feathers.

"Ines," I reply coolly, using her name instead of her title on purpose. Now whose feathers are ruffled?

The King quickly sweeps us past her, taking us down a row of glittering aristocrats and military personnel. There's no way I'll remember any of their names, so I don't bother to try. Instead, I focus on keeping my chin up, my shoulders back, my steps slow and confident. The Duke takes care of all polite conversation for me, thank God.

We make several rounds through the ballroom before Brennin finally releases me, letting go of my arm and watching me like he thinks I'm going to make a run for it.

The only thing I make a run for is the table piled with food. What can I say? I'm a comfort eater.

It's all the usual weirdness I'm starting to love about Underland: candied flowers, bowls of crickets covered in chocolate sauce, slabs of purple meat, and salads that are as colorful as a spring rainbow. There are toadstools, cupcakes, lollipops, and plenty of tea.

So much fucking tea.

I pick through the food, reaching absently into my pocket to stroke Rab's tiny head.

"If you're going to eat something," March says from beside me, sliding a test kit from the pocket of his leather pants. "Please test it first."

"I tested my dress," I whisper as he moves up to stand shoulder to shoulder with me. Well, arm to shoulder, I guess. I'm not nearly tall enough to reach his. I'm not the only one people are staring at. The Mad Hatter and the March Hare have quite the audience as well. "There's no poison."

"Nothing that shows up immediately," he drawls which, of course, makes me paranoid.

"You're a dick," I say as the March Hare tests some fizzy grapefruit infused water, and then passes it over to me. "Are you sure I should drink this? Or am I going to drop dead later from one of the nine less common poisons?"

"Guess we'll know by next week if the vial changes color, won't we?" he drawls, giving me a saucy little look as I sip my drink.

"You're awfully concerned about poison," the King says, still standing far too close to me for comfort. I half-expected him to wander off into the crowd, but it looks like he plans on shadowing me instead. How lucky am I?

I grab a fruit tart off a tray. After all, this *is* the Ball of Broken Hearts and Stolen Tarts, right? In the original book, it was the Knave that was suspected of stealing the Queen's tarts. Tonight, the Knave isn't stealing anything from me, not if I can help it.

The music tonight is played by a live orchestra, situated in the corner of the room and made up entirely of card servants. They're quite good actually, and I have to wonder how it's possible that the King managed to find an entire orchestra worth of criminals to curse.

I glance over at the Knave, still watching me from across the room. She's not subtle about it either. It could've been her, couldn't it? She's the official curseworker for the Kingdom of Hearts, right? I would not put it past someone like that to frame a horde of musicians for her own amusement.

"I couldn't get a read on anything else regarding tonight," Lar whispers, and I'm not sure if he's talking to the King or to me. Maybe both of us? "The Mocking Turtle ripped me in half, metaphysically speaking. I'm still healing." He sets an empty teacup down hard on the table, and I notice the tea leaves sitting on the bottom. "You're on your own tonight, Your Majesty."

"No matter," Brennin says, but his dark eyes won't stop scanning the room. It's as if I'm not the only one looking for trouble tonight … He notices me watching him and lifts his chin haughtily, turning away in a swirl of robes.

"Sorry to say," I tell Chevalier as she stands guard beside me, "but your Breastplate of Courage doesn't seem to be working. I'm scared out of my mind." The White Knight just smiles at me, and I notice she's wearing her shark shields or whatever the fuck they're called. Maybe she is just a kook?

"It's working," she says, still smiling at me. I quirk an eyebrow, but I'm not about to argue. If it is working, then it's not working very well. I mean, I'm putting on a good show, but I'll be relieved as fuck when this is over. "Just give it time."

"Her inventions never work; she's a nutcase," North says with a sniff, and clearly, he's also on edge tonight. It's either because of last night, or because of whatever's been going on inside the castle. For the most part, these men, as nonsensical as they are, have been pretty open with me. The only thing they seem to be holding back on is who or what they're nervous of inside the palace walls.

I wonder why?

"You'll see," the White Knight repeats, entirely unaffected by the Duke's insult. She sweeps long, blonde hair over her shoulder and maintains vigil on the room.

Unfortunately, when the Knave approaches from behind, nobody stops her. After all, she's a good guy, right? About as pure and innocent as Jafar from the movie *Aladdin*. I just hope she's not the King's 'most trusted advisor'.

"*The Queen of Hearts, she made some tarts, all on a summer day; the Knave of Hearts, she stole those tarts, and took them quite away!*" I turn around to meet the Knave's green-eyed stare as she chuckles politely with her hand over her mouth. I see that she's donned a gown of her own for the occasion, one that's made up of yards of black satin and lace. A half-veil covers her pretty face as she looks me over with disdain. "Have you heard that one before, the Alice?"

"What do you suppose *that* means?" I ask her as the twins move up close on either side of me. At least I know their wings are out, and that each rustle of those beautiful feathers is like a stab to her broken, shriveled little heart.

"I've never been much for interpreting prophecy," she says, glancing over at Lar for a moment. "What do you think, soothsayer, what does it mean?" The Caterpillar gives her a bored stare right back, removing a pipe from the pocket on his red coat and lighting up. He smokes it for a moment and then shrugs his shoulders.

"I only repeat prophecies; I don't claim to understand them."

The Knave's husbands remain behind her, as stoic as statues, their gazes focused on me. I have no idea what their purpose is in this game, but I get the idea that they haven't made their moves yet—not even close. This is a disaster waiting to happen.

"How … useful," she says, moving past Dee and purposely hitting him with her shoulder.

Very mature.

"I hope she trips and breaks her face," I grumble, and notice Lar smiling at me from behind his pipe. He passes it over to me, and I take a hit, recognizing the very distinct scent of the whiting, like lavender and chai tea. Aaaand, now I'm starting to wonder why I didn't follow my own advice and put on plain cotton knickers like I'd planned. When we start floating during the quintrille, the whole court's going to get an eyeful of my lingerie. I *knew* I shouldn't have worn it! Damn my weak, curious little heart.

"She'll get hers one day." The Duke waves his hand lazily before taking the pipe from me, looking far more excited than any sane person ought to at a function like this. I get the idea that he enjoys politics and intrigue. That's sort of his thing. "Besides, seeing us dance the quintrille is likely to ruin the rest of the evening for her. She's always dreamed of being center stage in court."

"It is?" I ask, perking up substantially. "She has?" The cat bats at one of my earrings with a furred paw, and I swat him away. "Shall we dance it now then?"

"It's generally polite to make conversation with the courtiers first," the King says, but I'm already rolling my eyes. I pull the Rab-mouse from my pocket and set him on the table. The Cheshire cat gets put on the floor, and I hook my arm with the King's. I notice the Knave watching me again, and throw her this horribly triumphant look. It stinks of smug, but I just can't seem to help myself. I'm petty sometimes, so sue me; we all have our faults.

Brennin's eyes widen in surprise as I drag him toward the center of the room, and the gold medallion design on the floor that I was admiring the other day. This time, I can see it's the quintrille, laid out step by step around the outer circle. In the center, a King and Queen dance the night away. How fitting.

As soon as our feet hit that medallion, the music stops briefly and a hush falls over the crowd.

"This is entirely unorthodox; the quintrille requires an announcement." I put the King's hand on my hip, and his fingers tighten around me, making me gasp. His black eyes gaze down at me from that severe but handsome face of his. He's a dark horse, this King of Hearts.

"And you're the King. Try setting the rules instead of following them." His mouth twitches as the other men slowly gather around us, just like we practiced. The card servant orchestra starts up again with the dark, haunting notes of a cello. Above us, the lights dim until we've got nothing but moonlight to see by.

I put my hand on the King's shoulder, underneath the folds of his cloak, and I try not to notice how warm his body is, how intense his stare. If I let myself, I bet I could drown in his darkness. I would die with wetness in my lungs, but intrigue in my heart.

"Will you, won't you join the dance?" the King asks, his voice booming above the music, echoing around the ballroom. It's loud enough to project above the cello's desperate moans.

"What matters it how far we go?" I whisper, just before the other men begin to move, dancing around us, like river water around rocks.

There is nothing we have to say to one another, so the King and I simply stand there, staring at each other. There's an intensity to that stare, and it makes me want to fidget. Or run. Instead, I meet him dead-on, waiting for our turn.

As I'd thought, when we begin to move, my dress swishes around my legs, the fabric as bright as the King's hair, as red as blood.

Our feet begin to lift off the floor, carrying us above the crowd.

I swear though, I don't see anything but Brennin Red in that moment. It's as if he's put me under a spell. The way his hair falls over his brow, the slight gap in the buttons of his robes and the peek of his white shirt beneath them … I literally cannot stop staring. That is, until the pace of the music changes and he breaks his grip on my hand.

"You seem awfully interested," the Duke purrs as he switches places with the King, twirling me around in the air and teasing my ankle with his tail. I won't soon forget that he recently fucked me with it. Or that I loved it. Or that I'll do it again first chance I get. "Decided you like the King now?"

"I never said that," I whisper back as the music intensifies, the viola singing her notes in a high-pitched wail that brings goose bumps up on my skin.

"No, you never did," the Duke replies, "but I can see it in your eyes."

"Bullshit," I snort, frowning as he kisses me on the cheek, finishing our round before he switches with the Mad Hatter. Of course, they're both good dancers, but they're nothing like Lar or the King. I decide to tell Raiden Walker that, and see what happens.

"The King's a better dancer," I tease as he holds me in strong arms and manages to catch me before I mess up one of the steps. "What do you think about that?"

"Credit where credit is due, I always say," he purrs, flashing fang. My neck throbs and aches, but I refuse to touch it. When I showered this morning and went to scrub some of the crusted blood off, I almost fucking came. "Such as last night, when you stood up to me. I liked that." He leans down and puts his mouth near my right ear. "Although I still plan on making you beg."

"Fat chance of that ever happening." I break away from him, falling into Rab's arms next and loving the way he tosses a challenging glance in the March Hare's direction. There's something about their rivalry that interests me. Two Rabbits, two sidekicks to two powerful men. But they're both much more than just sidekicks. It's not impossible for me to think of them overcoming the rulers they're supposed to serve.

"What are you all watching out for?" I ask as his cold hand embraces mine, sparking an intense heat.

"What ever do you mean?" Rab drawls, not even bothering to hide his wicked smile. "You don't think you're the only one who's worried about the Knave, do you?"

My mouth tightens into a thin line.

"If you're all so worried about her, why doesn't the King lock her up? Have her questioned at his famous weekly Trial?" I raise a brow, but the White Rabbit doesn't look like he has any intention of answering me, marching us in a circle around the other men and trading me off to my next partner.

The quintrille … it's a lot of fucking work.

"Well, hello there, Doll," March says, sweeping me rather close to him. Much closer than the steps in the dance call for. "Did you miss me?"

"How can I miss you when first off, I don't even like you. And second, you never go away?" The March Hare laughs at me, flattening his brown ears against his head and causing his small top hat to slide forward until it's leaning at a rather precarious angle.

"Admit it: you don't *want* me to leave." He smirks at me, but I'm not about to dignify that response with an answer. No point in it anyway because he's soon handing me off to Tee. This dance, when performed at its proper pace, is breakneck. I feel like I can barely breathe, like I'm as high as I was last night, the edges of the room flickering in psychedelically brilliant hues.

Our eyes lock as we come together in the center of the room, the literal freaking center of the room, halfway between the floor and the domed glass ceiling. In the silver moonlight, the purple streaks in Tee's hair are twice as bright. I reach up to finger a stray strand and he smiles at me.

"Wondering how I managed to move up from last place?" he asks as I lean into him, breathing in that fresh mountain air scent of his.

"You drew straws?"

I can feel Tee smile against my hair as he spreads his wings wide, letting the full thirty-foot length of his wingspan shine its glory for the entire crowd. And it is fucking *magnificent*. The purple feathers catch the light the same way his hair does. I can just imagine the Knave, standing down there in the crowd and fuming.

"We drew sugar cubes," Tee says, and I lift my head away from his chest to give him a questioning look. Of course, then we're switching partners yet again, and I end up with Dee, grinning his magnanimous grin at me.

"What does drawing sugar cubes entail?" I ask, and he laughs, throwing his head back. The sound echoes around the room, this joyously infectious chortle that makes me smile.

"You pick a cube from the sugar dish, and whoever has the most granules goes first. The person with the least goes last, and everyone else in between."

"How do you know how many granules are in each cube?" I ask, and Dee squints at me.

"You count them, silly." Oh, right, of course. Excuse me.

"Does the King have the power to investigate the Knave? Have her locked up or something?" Dee's smile fades slightly and he tucks his wings in tight, like just the mention of the cursed witch is upsetting to him.

"Not at all," he says, licking his lower lip and then looking away from me. "Not unless there's a Queen of Hearts on the throne who agrees to the same punishment. You'll have to have an official wedding ceremony with the King first, but we can only hold that once the Knave approves."

"Which will be never?" I manage to grind out between my teeth. This bitch is becoming a silent thorn in my side. I've barely spoken a handful of sentences to her and yet, she seems to be around every metaphorical corner I turn.

"She's only allowed to delay the King's proposed date twice, and even then only by sixty days. He, of course, proposed you get married either the day you arrived or the day after."

Shocker.

Dee smiles at me one last time and then spins me to face the Cheshire Cat, looking ridiculously debonair in the suit that Tee picked out for him. It's a full ensemble—coat, tie, cufflinks in the shape of paw prints. I'm surprised the angel prince actually convinced him to wear it. Since I first met the fucker, he's been shoeless, mostly shirtless, painted into leather pants.

"I look a fool, don't I?" he says, flattening his ears against his skull and stumbling over the steps of the dance twice as badly as I am. We must make quite a pair, me and him. Actually, I don't remember him being as bad of a dancer as this when we practiced. "I feel so constrained, like I can barely move."

I chuckle at his melancholy expression, remembering the last Halloween before Fred died, when we dressed Dinah up in a tiny hot dog costume. She collapsed to the floor and acted like she couldn't possibly walk around in it. Oh, cats sure are amusing creatures, aren't they?

"You look stupid handsome," I say, giving his collar a tug. He's still wearing it, along with the tag that has my name on it. He's got all his piercings in, too, which gives a nice contrast with the crispness of the suit. "If I found you as a stray, I'd most certainly take you home with me."

One black and white striped ear perks up, but then we both stumble again, and Lar is there to catch us. He steps in a few seconds early and helps correct my form, passing the cat off to the Duke to watch over.

His pale blue-blonde hair makes a nice contrast against the red of his suit jacket.

He's definitely the best dancer of the group, hands down, even when paired against the King.

"Keep your eyes out tonight," he whispers, putting his mouth against my ear and making me shiver. "The only prophecy I've seen since last night was a broken image in the bathtub. And it was of you, covered head to toe in blood."

Lar leans back and for just a split second, the confidence in his face is gone, replaced with concern and just a hint of fear.

No wonder everyone's acting so sketchy.

Before I can think of how to respond to that statement, Lar is cupping my face with his hand and leaning in toward me. He leaves the moment up to me, lets me decide if I want to close that gap or not. I decide to go for it, lifting up on my toes to kiss the Caterpillar's full mouth.

That asshole of a king interrupts me, cutting into our sequence far before it's his turn again.

"What the hell was that for?!" I ask, giving him a little shove and hoping like hell he tumbles out of the air and breaks a leg. Instead his hand tightens around mine, his fingers digging into my hip possessively. The look on his face is pure, carnal hell.

"I won a bet during our croquet game, remember?" he growls, and my cheeks flush with a mixture of frustration, embarrassment … and lust. The music comes to an end, and Brennin Red tucks his gloved fingers under my chin, lifting my face toward his. *I knew it! I just knew it! He would wait until this moment to collect, wouldn't he?!*

My eyes slide closed of their own accord, just before I feel the hot heat of his lips on mine. His tongue isn't far behind, invading my mouth and drawing a groan from me that echoes around the quiet ballroom. I'm not even sure if I'm still floating at that point, or if our feet have finally made contact with the floor.

The King does one better and sweeps me up in his arms, crushing me against his much larger frame, holding me like I really am his queen.

My arms go around his neck, and I find myself on my tiptoes, straining for more, desperate for it.

"So it's true: you're a whore in both worlds."

That voice … it shatters my blissful little cocoon, and I end up breaking away from the King and stumbling. I spin around, trying to find the source of the voice. It sounds like the Mocking Turtle, but it can't possibly be, right?

"What is it?" Brennin asks, and in less than a second I'm literally surrounded by all nine men *and* the White Knight.

"If you'd just done what you did with the King, with Liam and his friends, your mother would be free. Your father wouldn't be broken. And your sister, Edith ... oh, what a delicious little tart she is."

"You leave my sister alone!" I snap, putting my hands on the sides of my heads. How can I hear the Mocking Turtle if he's not even here? He can't get inside the walls, remember?

"The Turtle," Tee says, taking one look at me and catching onto the problem. Perceptive, as usual. He would've made an amazing king to his own people. "You shouldn't have let her look at him so long."

"Me?" Dee asks, but he's busy looking around the room as the rest of the men whisper.

"He's not doing this on his own," March says, tapping a knife against the palm of one hand. "If she's hearing him in her head, then he's got an accomplice in here somewhere."

My eyes fall on the Knave, frowning at me from the edges of the crowd.

"I'm going to go after Edith, and I'm going to have a little taste—the same sort of taste that Liam wanted." I fucking snap when I hear that, shoving past Chesh and Lar and moving over to the Knave. I don't even bother to be nice about it. I just grab her by the front of her dress and get in her face.

"You're doing this, aren't you?" I choke out, feeling like my skull's about to explode. "You brought him in here somehow."

"I don't have the faintest idea what you're talking about," Ines says, lifting up a hand when her husbands move forward to disengage me. What she does do is smile, which only pisses me off more. "But please, continue. Show the entire court what a useless waste of life you are."

"Oh, please do. Then they'll lock you up, and Edith will be all mine to snack on." The Mocking Turtle's voice drives me up the bloody fucking wall, like nails on a chalkboard, that screeching sound trapped inside my skull where nobody else can hear, nobody else can take the burden off of his awful words.

Shoving my skirt up, I whip the Vorpal Blade out of its sheath and press the mirrored blade against the Knave's neck. It's at that point when she actually has the grace to look scared.

Whispers break out amongst the crowd as they all peer at my weapon in wonder.

The Lion is there an instant, swinging his fist right at my goddamn face. To be fair, I do have a knife to his wife's throat, but I honestly don't expect it. Brennin Red moves in the flash of an instant, getting between us, but he does end up taking a fist to the face.

The court lets out a collective gasp as blood drips from the King's mouth, and he reaches up white-gloved fingers to touch the blood, staring at his fingertips for a moment before he gives the Lion a look that the other man won't soon forget. Me, I'm still standing there holding the Vorpal Blade and wondering what it is that I've just gone and done.

"You fool," the King hisses, turning around and snatching my wrist before tearing the weapon from my hand. He slips the blade back into the sheath, yanks me in the direction of a small door, and charges forward as the crowd parts for him like the Red fucking Sea.

The King of Hearts drags me down a hallway, his white-gloved hand squeezing too tightly on my tender wrist. He throws me against the wall and then slams his palm into the stones near my head.

"Are you an idiot?!" he snarls out, his teeth gritted in anger, a muscle ticking in his jaw. He's panting, his chest rising and falling, speckles of blood decorating his cheeks and lips. There's just enough light from a flickering torch for me to see the scar that runs from the right corner of his lip and down, slicing right across his throat.

His father ... he actively tried to behead him.

Those words echo in my mind as I swallow hard and squeeze my left hand tighter around the hilt of the Vorpal Blade. I shouldn't have taken it out here; the King warned me as much last night. But I just … got so goddamn pissed. The Mocking Turtle is digging up my worst fears and spattering them around inside my skull like so much carnage. That, and last night was such a blur, it slipped my mind and …

"Do you want to meet the Anti-Alice today?" he growls, his ebon eyes flashing as he turns away from me with a scowl. It's awfully dark back here, and the King smells awfully good. I hate how much I like it, and I hate how I can even notice something like that at a time like this. But I know logically that the Mocking Turtle cannot get to Edith; she's safe on the other side of the Looking-Glass. I won't let his words get to me. "You just risked everything, and for what?"

"My pride and dignity," I grind out, sniffling and then reaching up with my left hand to rub away some of the King's blood from my face. I hadn't realized so much had spattered when he took that punch. "I figured at least *you* would understand that?"

"Some things are more important," he snaps at me, slamming his gloved palm into the wall again for emphasis. I'm just suddenly desperate to know what's under there. What's he hiding anyway? Brennin leans in and puts his mouth deliciously close to my ear, his breath warm against my skin. "Like the fate of Underland. Not that you give a *shit*."

"You don't know that!" I snap back at him, turning my face so fast that our mouths brush together.

There's this … weird, tense moment between us. It stretches hot and strange, our hatred boiling out and over, tainting the air with pretty poison.

Red's mouth slams into mine, his hands going to my waist and pushing me back against the wall. He crushes me to it with his body, his gloved hands squeezing my corseted waist tight as he slips them beneath my breastplate. With our matching clothes, and this frightening level of passion, it really does feel like I could be his Queen of Hearts.

He bites my lower lip, sucking it into his mouth, and stealing a groan from my throat at the same time. I think this man is a piece of human garbage, but oh my ears and whiskers, as Rab might say, this is too much. It feels too good, burns too hot, sears my inhibitions away along with my rationality.

The fingers of my right hand fist in his bloodred hair as our mouths work to fire up these sparks into a raging flame. I'm making sounds right now I didn't even know I was capable of, curling my left hand around the nape of the King's neck. He's already soaked in sweat, and I love it. Pretty sure his mouth is dripping blood all over my dress, but it's already red so who would know? Besides, in that moment, I can't find it in myself to care about anything but this ardent heat. I need to seek it out to its natural end.

Brennin Red tangles his hands in my full skirts, pushing them up and out of his way. His fingers brush the Vorpal Blade's sheath as he slides his palm up my inner thigh, over the thigh-highs and garter belt I said I wasn't going to wear but did anyway. When his fingers brush over the dampness on the front of my panties, my knees buckle and the King puts one of his between them to keep me standing upright.

My only wish right now … is that he keeps his fucking mouth shut.

I keep kissing him with the sole intention of making that happen. Yeah, uh, no, I'm not at all interested in kissing the bastard for any reason other than this. The stupid crown on my head tilts to one side, but doesn't fall off. Guess that is a useful spell, even if the Knave did cast it.

I move my right hand from Red's hair to the clasps on the front of his pants, buried underneath his robes. These are not freaking jeans, people. There are way too many buttons, so many that I end up tearing them just to get access to what's inside.

My fingers slip into Red's pants and … brush across a hard, metal object.

"The hell is …" I start, pushing him back just a bit so I can see what it is that I'm groping. I was aiming for dick and ended up with a bejeweled codpiece?! "What on earth …"

"These are in fashion," the King snaps at me, just before he rips his codpiece off and chucks it aside. In case you were wondering what, exactly, a codpiece is, I'll tell you. It's a fancy dick cup that was worn by men in the fifteenth and sixteenth centuries because ladies, dick measuring contests have been around since the dawn of time.

My next kiss cuts off whatever else he was going to say. Frankly, I don't care. If he keeps talking, I'll stop wanting to fuck him. And right now, that's all I want to do.

At least underneath the codpiece is nothing but warm, velvety skin. My fingers curl around the slick length of him, using his sweat as lube. Red growls against my mouth and kisses his way across my jaw and over to my ear, biting my lobe as he teases my clit through my panties. I want them inside now, but I also don't want to speed the moment along. No, I want to enjoy it. For just a minute, I want to pretend that I am going to marry the King of Hearts and be his Queen, take nine husbands and rule over Underland.

But … why can't I?

What's stopping me?

I can just let myself stay here, see if I can finally find out what happiness feels like, tastes like, fucks like.

But back home, I have Edy and Dad and Mom waiting for me.

My heart stutters and cracks, and I open my mouth to ask the King about the Looking-Glass. If I can jump back and forth, then … then this could work. Surely, he'd be willing to compromise?

But then his gloved fingers slip under the fabric of my panties, pushing into the hot slickness of my core and teasing me with crooked motions. He knows all the right places to press to turn my body to jelly.

In response, I tighten my hand on Red's cock, squeezing hard enough that he makes some accidental noises of his own, too close to animal sounds to be faked. I love it. Running my thumb over the tip of his cock, I feel his hips buck against my hand.

The King moves his mouth back to mine, hovering his lips just out of reach. I try though, leaning up on my tiptoes for his kiss. Because he might be a total fucking prick, but he's an amazing kisser.

"My Queen," he says, thrusting his fingers deeper inside of me at the same moment he leans down and starts to kiss and lick and nip at my throat. Oh Hearts and Diamonds, I curse inside my own head. Because there's just no way in hell I can talk aloud right now. The only noises that seem able to escape past the torrid confines of my lips are groans, moans, and whimpers. "My Alice."

Brennin sucks on my skin hard enough that I just know I'm going to have a major hickey, but also just hard enough that I don't give a shit. With my left arm, I pull him closer, encouraging him to push this up a notch, join our bodies, break this tension.

Guess the King of Hearts is no idiot because he gets the hint, removing his hand from my panties as I extract my own from his pants. He lifts me up against the wall with one arm, my legs automatically wrapping his waist. There's so much skirt fluff, but he shoves it out of our way with a growl, locking his ebon-dark eyes on my pale blue ones.

There's nothing to be said, so neither of us bothers.

Instead, the King uses his right hand to push aside my panties, and guides himself to the throbbing heat between my thighs.

Keeping our gazes locked, he thrusts inside of me so hard that I let out a small scream. It feels so good, but he's so big, and the sensation of him is so foreign. When I try to bury my face in his neck to stifle my sounds of pleasure, he cups my face with one gloved hand and forces me to keep looking at him, pumping his hips in a hard, fast, frenzy. It's so quiet down this hallway, with just the two of us, that all I can hear is the wet sound of our joining.

My eyes get half-lidded, and my mouth parts for his, letting him slide his tongue in against mine, letting him claim me and loving every second of it. This is so different from North's animal instincts, from Dee's loving nature, Tee's reserved confidence. This is … probably seriously fucking unhealthy. And yet, I've never felt such a rush before.

I'm completely flooded by passionate hate, and craving ardent ire.

"I hate you so much," I manage to choke out, and the King makes a sound, kissing me hard enough to bruise. He fucks my ass into that wall so roughly that I know I'm going to be scratched and bruised, and yet, I find myself losing control, my muscles clamping down around him. I'm freaking coming before he does, wiggling and fighting against his movements as pleasure destroys me.

The King comes with this angry, frustrated sound that soon finds its way to this horrid superiority and triumph that I so desperately want to punch off of his face. He finishes inside of me and then collapses against the wall, crushing our bodies together.

What. The. Fuck. Have I just done?

"Your majesty," Tee says from the end of the hallway. As soon as I hear his voice, strained and tense, it's like a bucket of cold water's been thrown over my face. The King separates us and fixes his pants before setting me down.

I'm panting and soaked in sweat, but suddenly ice-cold.

I push my skirts down and turn to face Tee with guilt riding heavy on my shoulders. I'm supposed to ask the other members of my, uh, harem before taking a new guy, right? Did I just … cheat? God, I have no idea how this whole thing works.

"Yes?" the King asks, his voice that deep, annoying know-it-all baritone that made me want to stab him with the Vorpal Blade the first moment I met him. But the way he looks at Tee, it's not like a King looking at his servant. It's an alpha male sizing up a threat.

"We have two dead guards in the kitchen, and no idea what or who is in the castle with us. The White Rabbit says he doesn't sense anything else out of the ordinary, but clearly, something's going on." Tee bites this last part off the end of his tongue, flicking his amethyst eyes to one side. He's not mad at me … he's fucking terrified.

I listen for the Mocking Turtle's voice inside my head, but it's gone. At least for right now. Or maybe I just couldn't hear it over our furious grunting and groaning? Gross. A hot flush fills my face. There's a strange silence in the hallway, broken only by the music from the ballroom which is still playing. Surely, if something nefarious was going on, the music would stop?

"Bring me the Du—" Red starts, cutting off abruptly and yanking what I thought was a decorative sword from his belt. He spins just in time to intercept the Gryphon's blade, looking boss as hell even with his robes gaping open and several buttons missing on the front of his pants. The King raises a boot and kicks his opponent in the stomach, knocking him back several feet.

Tee's at my side, tearing out the Vorpal Blade and putting it back in my hand.

I give him a look, but he just shakes his head.

"It's too late now; come with me," he says, but the Gryphon is using the tight space to his advantage, filling the hallway with his wings and using the extra appendages to attack the King. Now, I'm not sure I even like the prick, but he's one of the few threads holding Underland together. Snap that, and everything falls apart.

I break away from Tee's grip and head for the battle, intending to step in with the Vorpal Blade … or maybe a little bit of magic, and turn the tide. But I'm not faster than a fallen angel prince. He cuts me off by thrusting one of his wings in front of me and yanking me back.

"We need to go now," he snaps, gritting his teeth and pleading at me with his eyes to listen. "Where do you think all the guards are? Clearly not on their way here. The Mocking Turtle must be in the castle somewhere." He yanks me back and I stumble, watching as he moves his black and blue feathers out of the way to reveal the King struggling in his fight with the Gryphon. It looks like the two men are pretty evenly matched. If this were to play out to the finish line, well, I wouldn't be making bets on a winner.

We need to get help for the King, but I see Tee's point.

If I die, there's not just a paltry thirty-five percent chance to save Underland … there's nothing at all.

I let Tee pull me down the hallway, but when we reach a T-shaped intersection, both sides are littered with the bodies of card servants, and the Mocking Turtle is waiting for us.

"Hello Alice," he says, whistling a tune under his breath as he leans against the wall, hands tucked into his pockets. He lifts his dark eyes to mine, their murky, swampy color making my stomach churn. "You really have saved a lot of lives today—we were going to slaughter everyone inside the ballroom to get to you. But popping down to the catacombs for a fuck? Brilliant."

Tee puts me behind him, spreading his wings to block off the hallway, as he removes his knife from his belt. I push his feathers out of my way, so I can see what's happening. Behind me, the King continues to struggle with the Gryphon, the clank of their blades echoing against the stone.

Whipping my attention back to M.T., I catch sight of his eyes flicking briefly up to the ceiling and then back down to Tee just a split-second before he launches an attack, yanking out a knife of his own.

But it's that quick flick of the eyes that saves me.

I spin around just in time to see a girl fall from the ceiling.

She doesn't come from a secret hatch in the wall though, no, it looks like she was simply clinging to the stone like a spider.

When she does land, she twists her body in a way that I just know isn't natural. If I were to move like that, my spine would break.

I adjust my grip on the Vorpal Blade and take a deep breath, waiting for the girl to lift her face and look at me. She smells like death, but not the sickly sweetness of fresh death, more like cobwebs and dust and forgotten tombs. When she lifts her head, I recognize her and almost choke.

"Edy?" I whisper, because for the briefest of moments, the woman—if you can even call her a woman—looks just like my little sister. Or me. Fuck, she looks like me. But this is no dark version of Allison Liddell; this is someone else entirely. And this is a someone else I feel I should recognize, but don't.

Her mouth is black, her skin gray, her hair as white as bones, but her eyes are as blue as my own.

I take a step back, an icy shiver working its way through my blood. Moments ago, I was gettin' hot and sweaty with the King of Hearts. Now, I'm staring at something that could very well be my own corpse.

The Anti-Alice.

This is the Anti-Alice.

I move my feet apart into a fighting stance. Because I know for fucking sure I'm going to have to fight right now; there's no way around it. All those lessons with North, I hold them close to my heart and take a deep breath. If I'm good at anything, it's reacting well to a stressful situation. Well, at least good at *reacting*. Like how I chased Rab after he shot Brandon. I mean, it's better than freezing up, right? Even if I do make mistakes.

The Anti-Alice is wearing a ratty pink bow on her head. It's rotted away at the ends and riddled with holes, but somehow seems important. It's the only thing on her entire body that's in color. She's literally a color study in black, gray, and white. And she's wearing a dress that's eerily similar to the one Edith gifted me, with a skirt that goes to the knees, short sleeves, and a dirty white apron. It's black and white striped, like an old prison uniform, but it's pretty, in a morbid dishabille sort of way.

Well, okay, so I lied about the pink ribbon being the only color on her body … that white apron is spattered in blood.

She stares me down for what feels like hours, but what I know can only be seconds.

There are wounds all over her body, rough and scarred over but clearly visible against the ashy gray of her skin. Her nails are black and chipped at the ends, but far too long and sharp for any normal person. I can't take my eyes off of them as they curl around a curved sickle blade that looks like it's made of bone.

She doesn't say anything, but the way she looks at me says it all: *I'm going to consume you, Alice.*

There's a—how should I put this—lack of energy in the air around her, like she's sucking the color from the world. I can feel her disturbing lack of power as strongly as I can sense the blood flowing through my veins. Whatever she … *it* … is, it isn't human.

When the girl runs her black tongue over her lower lip, I know I'm in trouble.

This is going to hurt, I think, seconds before she throws herself at me like a rag doll or a zombie, like she has no bones and exists as simply as ashes in the wind. I barely manage to stumble out of the way of her weapon. It crashes into the wall next to my face, shattering the stone into pieces. Shards rain down on the back of my head as I roll out of the way, narrowly avoiding a second blow that slams into the floor inches from my face. Some rainbow strands of hair flutter away as they're sliced off.

Holy shit, holy shit, holy shit, I think as I struggle and fail to get to my feet, slipping on the shards of debris and thanking whatever spirits or gods are listening that I'm wearing thick-soled boots instead of regular heels.

My skirts wrap around my legs as I fall on my ass with a grunt, keeping my hand wrapped around the hilt of the Vorpal Blade only with serious effort on my part. All I have to do is stab her, but there's no chance for it. She's on top of me before I can even think about lifting up the blade. Her sickle sword comes down at me with a speed that'll probably sever my head from my neck.

I have just long enough to recognize that fact, but not enough time to do a damn thing about it.

The Mad Hatter's cane whips down and deflects the blade, sparing my head. Arms go under my pits and drag me to my feet—it's March—and then haul me out of harm's way, trading places with Raiden Walker.

He flips off his black top hat with his cane, and pulls out a revolver from underneath it, leveling it on the undead girl's face and pulling the trigger. Instead of sparks and gunpowder, the weapon releases a net that drags the Anti-Alice to the ground with a wicked screech. It's ten fucking times worse than the jabberwocky noises, and I feel hot crimson liquid draining from my ears.

"Let's go," March says, hoisting me up and holding me in his arms like a baby. Not my favorite position, but I'll take this over decapitation.

"Tee!" I scream because the Anti-Alice is already clawing her way out of the net, and the Hatter is already on his way back over to us, leaving the angel prince alone with two enemies instead of one.

The King is still fighting the Gryphon, but now there are men in black armor, decorated with clubs. Soldiers sent by the King of Clubs, aka the Carpenter. Fuck. Brennin's outnumbered almost ten to one.

"Oh, get on with it, would you, Your Majesty?" Raiden rumbles, but even he sounds stressed.

The vampire mercenary badass that the fucking dragon doesn't think he can beat … is nervous.

As I watch, the King rips off one of his gloves and reveals a palm as red as his outfit. He slams it into the chest of the nearest man. The effect is instantaneous. Blood begins to pour from the guard's mouth, nose, eyes, and ears. And his screams, they echo like nightmares in the skulls of the insane.

The guard's head twists around in a circle … and then his neck splits, decapitating him.

What. The. Fuck?!

Red does the same to the next guard, and the next, and the next.

There's so much fucking blood. No wonder his name is friggin' Red—he's painting the roses red, that's for sure.

"We have to save Tee," I scream, fighting my way from March's arms, so that I'm standing on the stone floor again. I'm penned in between him and the Hatter, and neither of them look all that interested in giving into my request.

Actually, they're not looking at me at all.

"Do we take her to the Looking-Glass?" Raiden asks, staring instead at the King. Red manages to take out the guards, but the Gryphon is another matter entirely. I notice Red doesn't even try his magic hand technique on his sparring partner.

"The entire palace is overrun with Clubs," March says, looking up. His ears twitch and he bares his teeth in a snarl. As if in response to his statement, the sounds of pounding boots echoes from overhead.

"Are they here?" the Hatter asks, his question sharp and jagged as it rolls off of his tongue. *They?* Who's they? The Gryphon and the Mocking Turtle are already here. He doesn't mean … the Walrus and the Carpenter, does he?

"If the Anti-Alice is here, it's safe to assume they're nearby," March says, turning at the sound of shattering stone behind us. The wall caves in from the right and a jabberwock head snakes through with a hiss.

And this jabberwock is not the Duke of Northumbria, I can tell you that.

The face is all wrong, and the eyes are black, not gold. It screams at us and continues to dig and scrabble at the stone. If we don't hurry, it'll block our way completely and we'll be trapped in here.

While Raiden and March are distracted, I turn and run in Tee's direction.

The Anti-Alice is already coming at me, her skirts catching on her legs as she sprints full-tilt down the hallway, shattering the glass sconces on the wall as she passes. She doesn't even have to touch anything to bring destruction.

I stop suddenly, my full skirts billowing around me as I feel the tingle of my own magic. I can't use it on her, but I can make an assist, right? Using what little power I can summon on short notice, I chuck the Vorpal Blade as hard as I can. It embeds itself in the Anti-Alice's throat, and she stops dead in her tracks, choking on blood. It pours out of her mouth and down her throat in a crimson waterfall. But I'm already running again, shoving past her and pulling out the knife March gave me. The poison sparkles on the edge like glitter.

"Tee!" I scream, but he's too locked up in the fight to turn and face me. Doesn't matter. I can't leave him here to die. There are Club soldiers streaming down the halls on both sides. Tee's holding his own against M.T., but it's only a matter of time before he's overrun.

I move up beside him and stab the small blade into the Mocking Turtle's shoulder. Because of their violent struggle, it's the only place I can aim for that I know I won't hit the angel, too.

The Mocking Turtle barely acknowledges that I've stabbed him, not at first. But then I figure the poison must be setting in because he's shoving Tee away and stumbling back into the onslaught of soldiers.

I snatch Tee's hand and take off.

"What a stupid move," Raiden says, but he picks me up and throws me over his shoulder while Tee follows along behind us. On our way past the King, Raiden tosses his gun to March, and the man fires off another net, pinning the Gryphon just long enough for Brennin to join us.

I notice then that the Vorpal Blade is in March's other hand, and the Anti-Alice is nowhere to be seen. So where the fuck did she go?!

Now we're all running down the hallway, slipping past the jabberwock before she—because this just has to be a she—cuts off our exit completely.

Red leads the way, taking us up a set of narrow stairs and into what I'm assuming is a servant's hallway.

This is where Tee showed me the Looking-Glass, I think as we round the corner and run straight into Dee. He's holding his cell phone in his hand and smiling tightly.

"Thanks for the text," he says, blood spattered across the front of his new shirt. It's sticky and glossy, making the fabric cling to the hard planes of his chest. "I might've gone down the main hall and gotten myself killed."

Dee pushes past us, opens up the main screen on his phone … and hits the bomb icon.

With a whistle, he chucks it back in the direction we came. It lands on the floor with the sound of shattering glass, cogs and wheels scattering across the stones.

"Go!" Dee screams as our ragtag little group pushes around the corner seconds before the jabberwock scrambles up the hall behind us. There's the distinct smell of sulfur in the air and then … *boom.*

The phone explodes with so much force that we're thrown forward. The Mad Hatter manages to keep me in his arms as he rolls, shielding me from any injury. When he stands up, he sets me down and then steps aside for the King, watching as the man unlocks the door with a simple wave of his hand. He doesn't even *need* the key that Tee stole.

"What about North?" I ask, panting and choking on the smell of smoke. There are spatters of blood and gore on the walls behind us, the heat of the flames chasing along the tapestries and carpets in our direction. "Lar? Chesh? Rab?"

"Not our problem," Raiden grinds out as Brennin opens the door and steps aside to let us in.

"Not *your* problem, you mean," I scream, shoving him away from me, feeling this frantic energy clawing at the inside of my throat. I put my palm against my chest, feeling my heartbeat fighting to escape my skin. "The prophecy says the Alice has nine husbands, right? So what happens if four of them die here today?!"

Ugh, I'm overreaching like crazy, I think as the five men in the room stare at me like I've completely and utterly lost the plot, as North might say.

Sapphire, amethyst, ebon, chocolate, and marmalade. Those are the colors blinking back at me with disbelief and anger and frustration. And like, there's no way in hell I'm committing to all these guys, but I'm also too invested in them to let them die. Lory's in there, too, somewhere with Dodo and Eaglet, and if I can, I'll find her, too. Oh, fuck, and the White Knight! I can't leave them all behind.

I move to the leave the room, and the King steps in front of me, looking down at me with this wild expression on his face that both turns me on and infuriates me at the same time.

"Get in the Looking-Glass, Alice," he whispers, low and dangerous. I glare at him as the March Hare slides up beside me and forcibly curls my fingers around the hilt of the Vorpal Blade.

"Go to *hell*," I growl out, but Red is grabbing me by the arm so hard that I let out a small scream. He shoves me back and into Tee and Dee and *they* wrap their arms around either one of mine. "Fucking traitors!" I scream, thrashing against their grips.

With another wave of his red palm, the King orders the giant chess pieces aside as if they're as harmless as puppies.

"Take her Topside and don't come back until I send for you," Red says, moving toward the door and pausing to put his glove back on. Now that I know what he can do with his hands—in more ways than one—I'm even more terrified and turned-on by him. Not a healthy combination, is it?

As he moves away, he gives me a dark look, curses under his breath and slams the door behind him. I hear several locks slide into place.

Is he going back for the others?

There's no way to find out because the twins are turning me around and leaving me to face my own reflection. Now that the mirror's magic has been … enabled, or whatever, it's as wild as a storm. The silver surface stirs up my image, creating a disturbing mess of color that's supposed to be me.

The gold and silver nightmare leans against the wall, like a wonky melted caricature of a real mirror. The edges are inlaid with carvings of all four suits, and there's a single red heart at the top. It'd be a pretty mirror, if I had time to fucking admire such things.

As it were, Tee's putting his mouth close to my ear and whispering in a tense, low voice, "I'm sorry, Allison," and then he and Dee are shoving me forward and into my own messy reflection. There's no time for me to scream or wonder if this is going to work. I slip straight through the liquid silver, my hands and arms blurring to a bright silvery mist as I start to fall. Much like the Rabbit-Hole, there's this sense that I've reached a new reality, like I'll just be falling forever and ever and I should get used to it.

This fall, however, doesn't last nearly as long.

For a few seconds there, I'm suspended in a silver liquid, falling and drowning at the same time. In the next instant, I'm tumbling out of the mirror above the living room fireplace and landing in a messy heap on the carpet.

Dinah arches her back, hissing at me, while my little sister Edith rises to her feet … and starts to scream.

Chapter 8

Looking-Glass House of Hell

Edith darts past me and grabs the metal poker from next to the fireplace. I'd be proud of her for defending herself is she hadn't started beating me with it.

"Fuck!" she screams randomly, hitting me in the legs with the weapon. I roll onto my back between swings and use my lessons with North to bring the Vorpal Blade up, connecting with her next blow. Our eyes meet and everything goes still—even Dinah stops hissing.

"Son … Sonny?" Edith whispers, her eyes widening as I lower the blade and wait for her to put her own weapon down. Instead, she just stands there with it hanging in the air above my head.

I'm too busy shaking and lying there in a pool of silver goo to do much but freak the fuck out inside.

I've been fighting to get home for *weeks* and now that I am home … I want to go back.

This isn't right, I think, sitting up suddenly and leaning my head over my bloodied skirts. I feel like I might throw up. I *just* had sex with the King, and how I'm sitting in Dad's living room?

The mundane normalcy of my old life crashes into me with the force of a freight train, and I find myself gagging. Mostly on the mirror goo, but also … I'm suddenly *desperate* for the wicked depravity of Underland and the crazy men that I said I hated but maybe actually liked.

"This can't be happening," I whisper as Edith drops the poker onto the floor and stumbles back, falling onto the smaller sofa like her bones have just turned to Jell-O. "This can't be happening," I say again, pushing up to my feet and stumbling into the fireplace. There's a roaring flame burning, and it singes the edges of my skirts, but I don't care. I'm too busy putting my palms on the surface of the mirror and choking on my own doubts and fears.

Did I imagine all of that? Surely not, right? I mean, I *am* still wearing a bloody ballgown and holding a knife.

The Rabbit-Hole. If I have to, I can just go back to that house we were at the night of the party …

"Allison, is that you?" Edy whispers from behind me. I look at myself in the mirror, my ice-blue eyes so vibrant that even *I* have to wonder if I'm wearing contacts. The rainbow streaks in my hair have spread, their color twice … no, *three* times as bright as it was the day I put it into my white-blonde hair. My lips are full and swollen from Red's kisses, and there is most definitely a hickey on the side of my pale throat.

Plus, there's blood *everywhere*.

I didn't imagine a damn thing.

"Edy," I start, turning to look at her just before my fingers slip into the warm, liquid softness of the mirror. My head whips around just in time to see Dee tumble from the glass and straight into me, knocking me on my back on the floor. He ends up straddling me which is kinda nice, but then Edith picks up her poker and whaps him in the back with it.

"Aren't *you* a lovely sight?" Dee grumbles, grabbing the poker and yanking it from my sister's hands before he looks back down at me with his beautiful sapphire eyes, three shades darker than mine and twice as pretty. If I were liable to cry, I'd weep until the whole house was flooded with tears. "Are you okay, Allison-who-isn't-Alice?" he asks me, and I just barely manage a nod. "Good," Dee says, rolling off of me and taking me with him.

We move out of the way about three seconds before Tee slides through the Looking-Glass, landing on his boots like a boss, military jacket billowing out behind him. He steps aside and looks straight into my face.

"I'm so sorry Allison," he repeats, but my emotions are too twisted for me to process his words. I'm excited to see him, but now that he's here and my fears of Underland being a dream or a fit of madness are banished, I'm freaking out about the people we left behind.

"What's going to happen to the castle?" I ask, panting and holding the Vorpal Blade so tight that my fingers start to cramp. What I'm really asking is *what's going to happen to the ones we left?*

The Mad Hatter hops from the portal while Edith gapes at us like she's about to burst a blood vessel in her brain. Seeing her sitting there with her blonde hair in a braid, her pink Under Armour shirt with *Break the Ceiling* scribbled across it, I feel like *she* is the weird one in this room.

How twisted is that?

Once March arrives—also gracefully, so I guess Dee and I are the clumsy ones—he takes the mirror off the mantle, wraps it up in his velvet trench coat, and tucks it under his arm. His ears twitch as he glances down at my sister.

"Rob Evans?" she chokes which would be pretty funny if the circumstances were any different.

"Put that back!" I say, pushing past the twins to stand next to March. I'm still panting and sweating, and I wish I had time to lie back on a bed and daydream of my time with the King. Buuuut, I don't. "The others might be on their way soon."

"*If* they come through," he says, handing the Mad Hatter back his revolver, "then surely a coat won't be enough to stop them?" He shakes out his free hand, spattering the ground with goo. Not that it matters: we're all covered in it. "Do you happen to have a shower available in this hovel?"

"This is a *nice* five bed, three bath in a good neighborhood," I growl out at him, lifting up my skirts and tucking the Vorpal Blade away in my thigh sheath. I hold out my arms like I expect him to give me the Looking-Glass … and he does, plops it right down. I almost fucking drop it.

"If you break that, there's *no other way through*," March says, locking his brown eyes on mine. "Do you understand what I'm saying, Allison? If the Looking-Glass breaks"—he points at it for emphasis—"then Underland and Topside are parted forever."

"What about the Rabbit-Hole?" I ask. It only goes one way, but at least I could get back … well, not *home* but …

"The Rabbit-Hole is like a stream off a river," the Mad Hatter says, adjusting his top hat and glancing down at my sister like he's just seen her. She's shaking now, her eyes so wide they look liable to roll right out of her face. "This is the river," Raiden says, caressing the edge of the mirror suggestively.

He turns and looks around the living room like it's been a while. He's from Topside, right? *Did you just think of home as Topside?* I think, and I almost roll my eyes. If the situation were any less dire …

The mirror in my arms suddenly seems to weigh a ton, and I feel sick to my stomach.

If I drop this, it's all over.

"Here," Tee says, and when he offers to take the Looking-Glass, I pass it over. I trust him not to break it a hundred times more than I trust myself. "And don't worry about the others: they're all capable men, I promise."

"What about Lory and The Long Tale crew?" I ask, wringing my hands in the fluffy folds of my dress. I should probably address Edith, but … she feels like a stranger, sitting there on Dad's white couch. I don't even know what to say to her.

"They're pirates, remember," Tee says with a small smile, and I have to blink several times to adjust to the idea of him standing in my living room. It's surreal as *fuck*. "They'll be okay. Once the castle's secured, the King will send for us."

I nod, but I can't tell if Tee's just trying to humor me, or if he really means what he says.

"Who's this?" Dee asks, looking down at my little sister with his hands on his hips. "Mini-Allison-who-isn't-Alice?"

"This is Edith," I say as I move over to the couch and sit down next to her in a puff of skirts. I'm probably getting blood everywhere, but it hardly matters now, does it? I'm also coated in mirror goo, just like everyone else.

"There *is* a shower, thank my paws and fucking whiskers," March growls, slamming the door to the downstairs bathroom closed. The sound of the water running in the guest bath blurs into the normal background noises of my childhood home: the running of the refrigerator, the clink of fresh ice from the ice maker, the bubbling of a coffee pot.

"Edith," I start, reaching out a hand to touch her knee. She jerks back from me and swallows hard, sitting like a deranged crab on the back corner of the couch. "Calm down for a sec and talk to me," I coo, doing my best to stay calm. I did just hate-fuck a king, fight an undead girl, and run from a dragon, so that's a wee bit difficult at the moment, but I'm trying. Fuck, I'm trying. But now my teenager-senses are kicking off and I'm thinking about the mess of silver goo on the floor, the spatters of blood on the couch, and … me.

Back home after two weeks.

With four strange men.

Two have wings. One has rabbit ears. And the other has orange eyes and vampire teeth.

Oh I'm *sure* Dad is going to love this. Aaaaaaand, I doubt he's going to believe my story of a White Rabbit leading me down a magic hole. Oh no. I bet Brandon's murder was all over the news, connected with my disappearance. How am I going to explain any of this?!

"You … you … *you*," she chokes out, slipping her phone from her pocket and frantically hitting the emergency call button on the bottom. I snatch it from her hand and hold it out of reach. "You … you … you," she repeats, starting to shake.

Hey, I get it: her missing sister just fell out of the living room mirror followed by four incredibly hot but really weird guys. That, and this weird ass silver shit is on *everything.* It's like that shiny silver oil paint I used on my dresser last year. I dribbled a little on my carpet and ended up having to cut the fibers off. That shit would not come out.

I hope this isn't like that since it's on everything, including Mom's favorite rug.

Not that she'll ever get to see it again. She's in prison for life, remember?

"Where is Dad?" I ask, looking into her face. I need her to snap out of it and talk to me.

"You … where … I didn't drop any acid," she chokes out, reaching into her pocket and pulling out a blunt and a lighter. "I swear, I didn't."

"Edy, this isn't an acid trip," I growl, reaching out to snatch the pot paraphernalia from her hands. This time, she manages to dance out of my way, and then Tee grabs it from over her shoulder for me, making my sister scream.

"This isn't happening," she whispers, curling up into a ball and starting to sob.

Scratch what I thought before. Now that I'm sitting here and looking at her, I know for a fact that she could not have been the Alice.

"This *is* happening," I say, getting on the floor in front of her and taking her hands in mine, just like I did the night Fred died. I held her hands and I told her through the thickest of tears that it wasn't a dream or a nightmare—it was real. This is … surprisingly, much less stressful. "But I'm here, and I'm safe."

"Brandon's dead," she sobs, letting me hold her hands. "I found his body." Gritting my teeth, I squeeze her hands and curse Rab out in my head, while simultaneously wishing with every molecule in my body that he's still alive. "And you were … I saved your book." She sniffles and lifts her head up to look at me. Tears drag her eyeliner down her face in two dark stripes, and my heart stutters a little. If I stay in Underland, I'll be leaving Edith behind. Can I really do that?

"Hey," Dee says, kneeling down next to me. When I look at him, I get a different sort of stutter in my chest, like my heart is doing happy somersaults in the hot, hot sun. Warm, wild, a little messy … "Are there cleaning supplies around? Tee and I will work on fixing this place up."

"I … uh, next to the fridge," I start and they both cock their heads in unison.

Ooookay.

Right.

They have cell phones and revolvers in Underland, but not refrigerators. Gotcha.

"In the kitchen," I say, pointing in that general direction and refocusing my attention on Edy. The Mad Hatter walks in a slow, lazy circle, pausing next to the front window to peep out the curtains. "How long have I been gone?" I ask, because although I'm pretty damn sure time works the same in both worlds, I have to check.

"thirteen days, four hours, and eleven minutes from the last time I saw you," Edith whispers, looking at me with fresh tears dripping from her blue eyes. The fact that she's been counting down the literal minutes makes me feel like a shit sister. "Where …" she starts and then pushes her blonde braid over one shoulder, lifting her fake eyelashes to peer up at the Mad Hatter.

He's standing behind me now, arms crossed over his chest.

"Where the fuck were you?" she chokes out, swallowing hard and running her tongue over too-red lips. Edith looks like she's about to go out to a bar. She's sixteen fucking years old.

"I was …" *Jesus, how do I respond to this?* "I'll explain later. You need to tell me where Dad is."

"Search party in the woods behind Brandon's house," she says, and I get goose bumps all over my skin. What if someone stumbles across the Rabbit-Hole? What then? "He'll be home in a few hours." She pauses and blinks stupidly at me. "Do you want me to call him?"

"No!" I snap, harsher and louder than I mean to. I'm just wound all the fuck up right now, rising to my feet and glancing back at Raiden. He meets my eyes with his orange ones, and smirks at me. "No, not yet. Are there police here?"

"There were for the first week. But … not anymore." Edith stands up and I realize she's wearing my leather jacket on her small shoulders. "Everyone thinks you were raped and killed, Allison. They've been trolling me on every social media platform known to man …" She trails off, and I wonder if she's just realized she's making this about herself—as usual. But then, I'm just happy to see that she's okay. "Sonny, what the fuck is going on?"

"It doesn't matter," I say as I stand up and look at the mess in the living room. There's silver goo all over the damn place. Plus, the broken bits of the coffee table I smashed into when I landed. That, and I've smeared blood on the edge of the couch. "Let's get everything cleaned up and—"

"It doesn't matter?!" Edith asks, standing up and breathing hard. "You've been missing for weeks! I thought you were dead, Sonny. So did Dad. And Mom … How could you do this to us?" she screams, like I had any choice in the matter.

I just look at her, and I'm at a complete loss for words. There's too much turmoil inside of me. I can't stop thinking about North, Chesh, Lar, Rab … the King. And then Lory and her men, the White Knight, all the innocent bystanders at the ball … I need to get back to Underland, but to do that, I have to smooth things over here first.

"You have the Liddell blood as well, do you?" the Mad Hatter asks, cocking his head to one side as he studies my sister. She jumps when she notices that it's her he's talking to, and then her cheeks get red. "Share some with me, would you? Your sister is *such* a tease." He moves up beside me as I curl my lip in a little snarl. "Did I mention she's my fiancée?"

"Wha … what?" Edith asks as I mentally stab the Mad Hatter with the Vorpal Blade.

Tee and Dee come back into the room with a mop and a broom and not much else. I don't blame them; cleaning supplies in Underland probably look a hell of a lot different than they do here.

"You were kidnapped … and then engaged … Or were you kidnapped?" Edith asks, trailing after me into the kitchen. I'm tempted to wrap her in a hug and tell her everything's going to be okay, but we've always had intimacy issues in our family, issues that only got *worse* after Fred passed away. "Some people said it was *you* who killed Brandon."

"Me?!" I choke as I grab paper towels, Windex, and garbage bags from under the sink. I stand up and turn around to look at Edith to see if she's fucking joking. There's no way any idiot in their right mind could think I shot Brandon. With what weapon? With what *motive*?! "Please tell me you don't believe that."

"I …" Edith steps toward me, lowering her voice to a husky whisper. "You just fell out of a mirror followed by four weird-ass looking dudes. What should I believe, Sonny? Hmm?" She trails along behind me as I dump the cleaning supplies on the floor and Dee lifts up the paper towel roll to his eyes like a telescope. It'd be cute and funny under different circumstances.

"We have to clean all of this up before my dad gets home." I shove rainbow and blonde strands of hair from my face as I use the dust pan to scoop up some of the silver goo. It's glittery and extremely viscous, like molasses or something. Or blood. Yeah, maybe it's more like blood, warm and sticky. "Our brother Fred was a big guy. And my parents haven't touched his room since he … passed. Go in there and change into some of his shit." I yank a huge clump of paper towels from the roll and go at the carpet with some fucking OxiClean. Of course, the stupid things flake all over the place and get caught in the fibers.

"You can't give them Fred's clothes!" Edy yells, standing way to close to me, her shoes stuck to the carpet. The twins both have their wings out, and I'm not quite sure *what* to do about that. Edith hasn't really said anything, but maybe she thinks they're fake? I have no clue. I just figure she's probably in as much shock as I was when I fell down the Rabbit-Hole. Maybe more. "Who the hell are these guys anyway? And what are—" She reaches out to grab Tee's wing, and his hand flies up, slapping my sister away.

"Please don't touch my wings," he says, folding them tightly against his back as my sister gapes in horror.

"They're not real though," she chokes out, stumbling back and sitting down hard on the edge of the couch at the same moment the bathroom door opens and March steps out in my father's black robe. "They're not real, they're not real, they're not real."

I ignore Edith for a moment and focus on March instead.

"It's doubtful you have any servants, in a house this small," he says, and I swear to God, I would punch him in the junk if I were close enough. Rab has servants and his house is about the same size. So what's that about? Being a dick for dick's sake. "So who does the washing?"

"A machine," I snap as I gesture with my chin toward the bathroom. "Raiden, you're next. I'll bring some clothes down in a minute." I scrub the carpet harder, almost furiously, my hands shaking.

I'm all shook up; I'm freaking out; I'm home and I feel like I'm on Mars.

"Why don't you go shower and get us all fresh clothes," Tee says, reaching out and taking my wrist. He rubs his thumb along the sensitive flesh, tracing a purple vein underneath. I can feel our pulses thumping against one another. "We'll get this cleaned up and then take our turns washing."

We look at each other over the shredded lump of paper towels, and I realize I just want to throw myself into his arms and have a hug. Maybe these weird dudes are helping with my intimacy issues just a little?

"Okay," I say, because I'm too tired to argue, and I just *need* a minute.

"Can I come, too?" Edith asks, and when I look over at her, her eyes are just a little too big and weepy for me to say no.

"You can sit on the toilet," I tell her as I stand up and look around at the mess in my living room.

I'm finally home.

And ironically enough, it's the last place in the world I want to be.

♦ ♠ ♣ ♥ ♣ ♠ ♦

The stupid fish-patterned shower curtain is see-through, so I just know Edith is staring at me as I uncoil what's left of my fancy hairdo, and squeeze some of her hibiscus-bamboo shampoo into my hands.

I'd like to clean my *whole* body, if you catch my drift, but I can't very well wash off evidence of my tryst with the King while my little sister's eyes are on me.

"Could you stare at the wall or something?" I ask as I lather up and rinse, feeling all the bumps and bruises on my body. Suddenly, I'm just *tired*, and I can't think of anything better than a nap. It's doubtful I'll be getting one anytime soon.

"I just can't believe you're here," Edith says, wrapping her arms around herself and staring at the red and black heap of my dress and jacket on the floor. "Mom, Dad, and me … we all thought you were dead."

My throat tightens up and I turn away, staring at a drip of water as it runs down the white plastic shower surround.

"You're not going to believe where I've been, but I hope you at least believe that I didn't run away by choice. And I came back as soon as I could." I grab the conditioner next, soaking my hair in it and rubbing a few colored strands between my fingers.

"Who are all those guys?" she asks me quietly, the bathroom fan almost drowning out the sound of her words. But I'm on hyper-alert right now. I feel like I could hear my sister from a thousand miles away if she screamed for me.

"Friends," I say, because I am *not* addressing that fiancée comment right now. Raiden Walker, that prick. "From … where I was staying."

"They're all cosplayers?" Edith asks, and I mean, that's as good a guess as any. "Those wings look so *real.* They must've cost a fortune." Swiping soap from my eyes, I glance over at her through the wavy plastic of the shower curtain and see her picking at the hole on the knee of her jeans. "Where did you guys come from? It … looked like you fell through the mirror."

"We … there's a secret door in the fireplace mantle," I say, which is so fucking stupid and lame that I can't believe I even said it aloud. But Edith's in shock, and she's never really been into fantasy—unless you count *Vampire Diaries*—so her mind isn't quite as open as my own.

She believes it as soon as I say it because it's the safe thing to believe, that somehow there's a useless door secretly hidden in the fireplace.

"We had some paint for our, uh, costumes," I continue, hating myself for lying and knowing I don't have a lot of other good options. If I were to tell her what really happened, she wouldn't believe me anyway. "I spilled it everywhere when I came in the door."

"How do you get in the door anyway?" she asks, her voice sounding tinny and far away. Yep, she's definitely in shock.

"The attic," I say, because she's never been up there in her life. Too scared of spiders.

"You were in the attic?" Edith continues, and I realize I'm about to get these questions and more from my dad, mom, and probably the police. I need to come up with a story about Brandon's murder and quick.

"I climbed the trellis in the back, snuck in my room, and went to the attic." I bite my tongue and shake my head. Such a stupid lie, but if she buys it, fine. "Just don't tell Dad about that. Let me tell my own story, okay?"

"Why were you cosplaying when you knew we'd be worried about you?" she whispers, and I feel my entire stupid story fall to pieces. I don't know what to do or say; there is no rule book for this shit. For the first time since I fell down the Rabbit-Hole, I feel my age. Eighteen-years young and shaking under the hot water blasting from the shower head.

"Edith, just … believe what I'm saying and let it go, okay? I don't ask a lot out of you. But, just this once, *please*."

There's a long period of silence as I finish washing and then turn off the water, wrapping the fluffy pink towel around myself.

There's a knock on the door before it bursts inward, and I see Tee and Dee waiting in the hallway.

"We have a problem," he says, just before I hear my name shouted from downstairs.

It's my dad.

"Allison!" he screams, his voice so raw and shattered that I feel like I've just been dipped in a vat of broken glass.

I rush out of the bathroom, slamming the door in Edith's face. I don't mean to be rude, but I need a minute to get a handle on this situation. Grabbing the twins by their hands, I drag them to my room and lock us in.

"Is there a way to put your wings back?" I ask, looking between the two of them. "Reactivate the curse? Just for a little while," I correct when I see dual expressions of disappointment on both their faces.

"If you can control your magic, you can do anything," Tee says, and then before I can even ask, adds, "even here in Topside." He looks at me with such a genuine expression on his face that I feel weak in the knees again. The King brought about that emotion with passion, and Tee … brings it out in affection. Without further explanation, he reaches out and cups the side of my face, bringing my lips to his for a kiss.

"We belong to you. There's nothing you can't see if you don't want to." Dee's words sound loudly inside my tired skull, and I put a palm up to Tee's chest the way I did to his brother's the first night we made love. Closing my eyes, I let myself flow into him, catching on the edge of a memory and pushing it away. If I get sucked down that Rabbit-Hole—pun intended—I won't have enough time to get the twins into proper shape to meet my dad.

Oh God.

It finally hits me.

The Mad Hatter is in the living room with my father.

I'm sure this'll turn out *great*.

Dad, meet my vampire boyfriend. He has a pet bat that's bigger than your SUV.

I shove those emotions aside, putting my hands on Tee's shoulders and kissing him with this theatrical reverence, rising up onto my toes. My towel falls off and he curls his arms around my naked body. We've been here, done this before. I'm more than happy to let him hold me, even if I get silver goo on my freshly washed skin.

With our tongues dancing together, I reach into Tee with my power and find the curse, that ugly black heart stamped onto his soul, sizzling and burning him with every thump of his pulse. One day, I'll crush it completely, dragging it kicking and screaming out of him and toss it right back at the witch-bitch who cast it in the first place. For now, I nudge it with my magic and feel it tugging on Tee's soul.

His lips break from mine, and with a groan, he collapses to his knees, taking me with him. His wings fold inward with a burst of black light and the sound of metal on metal.

"Allison!" I can hear my dad screaming from the top of the stairs now.

Fuck.

"Dee," I whisper as he squats next to me, his lips twisted in a soft smile.

"You've got this, Allison-who-isn't-Alice." When he leans in to kiss me, I realize that he tastes different than his brother. Tee tastes like rainwater and sunshine breaking through storm clouds. Dee tastes like blackberry honey and mint. I tangle my fingers in his hair and do the same to him as I did to his brother, feeling like a traitor all the while. But there's no way in fuck I can convince my dad these wings are fake the same way I did my sister, especially not if the cops get involved.

Dee's wings light up with that same eerie black light before collapsing inward like a telescope.

It's at that moment that my father kicks in my door, tearing off the locks, and finds me kneeling, naked, and kissing a boy covered in silver goo.

How the fuck am I going to explain this one?

Chapter 9

The Garden of Lies and Cowards

Henry George Liddell stands in my doorway with his brown eyes wide, and his dark hair tousled and messy. He looks like he hasn't slept in days, and his glasses are crooked and sitting on the tip of his pointed nose. Edith and I both look like little Mom clones, while Fred was always a spitting image of dad.

Right now, however, he just looks like a demon risen from the depths of hell.

"Allison," he breathes as I gather up my towel and rise to my feet.

I have to admit, I'm terrified.

There are only three times in my life that I've been more scared than I am right now.

The night I was almost raped.

The night Fred was killed.

The day my mother was sentenced in prison.

"Dad," I choke out as he puts his arm against the doorjamb and leans so heavily into it that he looks like he might collapse altogether. His eyes take me in like I'm the second coming of Jesus before he flicks them to Dee, and then Tee, and then back to me again.

"Allison," he repeats, stumbling into the room … and giving me a hug?

I haven't had a hug from my dad in months. Honestly, I was starting to wonder if he even gave two fucks about me at all anymore.

"I can't believe you're here," he whispers, and I feel hot, salty tears falling on my bare shoulder. It's weird, to hug my dad wearing nothing but a towel, and yet I can't seem to find it in myself to move away from him.

Edith watches from over his shoulders, arms folded across her chest, eyes watching me and Dad like this scene is as shocking—or even *more* shocking—than the five of us tumbling out of the Looking-Glass.

Dad pulls back and then levels this *look* on Tee and Dee that I haven't seen since the trial against Liam and his friends, the one where they were acquitted of Fred's murder.

"What the hell is going on?" he demands, wrinkling his nose up at the sight of the two nineteen-year olds covered in goo. If he only knew I'd just screwed a twenty-eight year old king against the wall of his castle. Of … what could easily be *my* castle.

I don't really feel like a queen though, standing in front of my much taller father dressed only in a pink towel and a cloak of shame. Not for the kissing or the sex or anything like that, but because I already know that in my heart, I've abandoned my family.

I want to go back to Underland. And Lord willing and the creek don't rise, I *will*.

"Give me a minute to get dressed," I start slowly, pitching my voice like I'm talking to a scared and cornered dog. Dad looks like he might either piss himself, or attack. Not really sure which would be worse. "I'll come down and—"

"Get out," he tells Tee and Dee, and I could almost swear there's smoke leaking from his nose. The boys exchange a look and then check with me. I give the briefest of nods and they remove themselves to the hallway with my father. He, on the other hand, sends Edith into my room. "I'll be waiting," Henry tells me, reluctantly closing the door. Well, *mostly* closing the door.

"What were you doing in here?" Edith asks me, looking at the towel and then my face like she's never seen me before.

But … that's an excellent question.

I'm sure my dad will have a similar one.

Moving over to my dresser, I pull a drawer out and just … *stare*. It's been so long since I've worn my favorite jeans that I'm practically salivating. Ignoring Edith's penetrating stare, I drop my towel, yank on some cotton panties, and then slip into my jeans and a loose tank. I grab the Queenmaker and the Vorpal Blade next—I told Edith they were cosplay props and had her hide them in my nightstand drawer while I showered. But I need to hurry: if I leave my dad out there long enough, he might start shit with the boys.

Even though I know I'm going to catch crap for this, a girl can't be too careful. I strap the thigh sheath on as well as the gun holster, even as Edith stares at me like I'm a crazy person. Sorry, not sorry for trying to protect myself though. Besides, I have that mushroom flesh tucked in a side pocket that's strapped next to the Vorpal Blade. It's so small, and it's already attached to the thigh holster anyway, that I sometimes forget that it's there.

I slip my feet into fuzzy kitty slippers and can't help but think of the Cheshire Cat.

As much as I would hate to explain men popping out of mirrors to my dad, I'd like to see him. All of them. Fuck, I just want to know that Castle Heart is still standing.

"Come on, Edy," I mumble, moving past her and stepping into the most awkward moment of my life.

"Can we have … coffee downstairs?" I ask as I flick my gaze from my dad and over to Dee. His features, his smile, his eyes, they somehow seem more familiar to me than my own father's.

"Coffee …" Dad starts, like he's not even sure what that word means. "Right, right, coffee." He's looking at me like he's about ten seconds away from bursting into tears. And after all this horrid apathy he's been showering us with since Mom's sentencing? I don't even know what to make of it. "I should call your mother."

He turns away from me, shaking his head, and starts down the stairs. As he descends, he keeps casting glances over his shoulder, as if he's checking to make sure I'm really there.

The Mad Hatter and the March Hare—who must've shifted because he's sans ears—are sitting on the sofa side by side, watching us all descend like they're taking in their favorite scene from a play. They look bemused, interested, but not off their asses scared shitless like they could be.

They don't know the wrath of a parent.

Dad moves into the kitchen, but I notice that he scoots the coffee pot over so he can stare at me through the doorway while he makes up our mugs.

"What do you want us to say or do?" Tee whispers.

"Because you know we're with you, through and through," Dee adds, and their stupid rhyming makes me smile.

Edy is watching us from across the room, but I don't think she can hear us. At least, I hope not.

"No clue," I whisper, because my mind is still churning and trying to figure out a way to explain what just happened to my dad.

"Let me do the talking," Tee says as Dad reappears with three steaming mugs. One's for me, one's for Edy, and one's for himself. No way in shit he's going to make any coffee for the four weird men I brought home with me.

"If he'll let you," I mumble as my dad sits in his favorite chair. I can see that his hands are shaking, and I figure he's probably in shock. Can't really blame him, now can I? He lost one son to murder already. With a sigh, I take a sip of my coffee and notice the old family portrait of my parents with Fred and … my older sister Rhoda. She only lived for five days outside of the hospital, and passed away years before I was born, so I forget about her sometimes. But my parents lost a child to SIDS. That's two of their four babies gone.

How the *fuck* could I have forgotten that?

A cold chill creeps down my spine, but I ignore it. Rhoda has nothing to do with any of this.

"Allison," my dad says, and the way his voice falls so softly, I know he's more than just angry, he's happy that I'm home. "Where have you been?"

Where have I been?

Well, let's see.

I fell down the Rabbit-Hole, watched a bandersnatch and a jabberwock fight a jubjub bird, played croquet with a king, learned to wield a sword, and used a mirror to travel between worlds. I've *been* in Underland. But I can't exactly tell him that.

"You wouldn't believe me if I told you," I start, and my dad's hand tightens around the handle on his mug. He lifts his brown eyes to mine, accusation glaring and hot bright, like a spotlight searing my skin and turning my flesh to ash.

"Allison, don't do this to me. If you have something to tell me, you can say it." He swallows hard and glances away sharply. "You're eighteen years old. You're an adult now." Dad seriously chokes on those words, like he can't believe he's even having to say them. "If there's something you've done, or somewhere you want to go, I can't stop you." He lifts his head to look at me, an emotional plea hanging on his gaze.

"I didn't kill Brandon," I say, because I can feel that accusation tainting the air in the living room. It's making it hard to breathe. "But I *did* follow the murderer; I chased him. And I ended up … somewhere I never could've imagined in my wildest dreams."

My dad opens his mouth to say something, pausing when a knock sounds at the door.

"Eureka police," a voice booms, and I feel my heart plummet to my feet.

"Police?" Dee asks, blinking a few times, like he's trying to put together what that means with reality.

"Well, damn," Raiden says, rising to his feet as my dad moves over to the door to answer it. There's a bit of mumbled conversation as my heart thunders in my chest and makes it hard to hear anything above the screaming of my rapid pulse.

Dad steps back to let the police enter, and I drop my mug on the carpet that Tee and Dee never got a chance to finish cleaning.

The Mocking Turtle and the Gryphon are standing on my fucking doorstep.

For a moment there, I question myself. They *look* like M.T. and the Gryphon, but they're missing all of their, how might you say, *idiosyncrasies*. The sharp lips, the toothless gums, the wings. But as I watch, they shift right back into place.

They're wearing uniforms, but their faces are unmistakable now.

"Allison!" Tee shouts, grabbing and throwing me out of the way as something explodes from the mirror in a wild, screaming mess.

It's a giant fucking cat, as big as a lion, with black and white striped fur, and eyes the color of rain clouds.

Chesh.

Dee barely has time to pull me out of the way before he crashes into one of the policemen, knocking Mom's side table to the floor and cracking both the legs in half. Edith starts to scream, but my dad, ever the cool and calm one in the family, manages to stand up and set his coffee aside. He doesn't spill a single goddamn drop.

"Alice, the Vorpal Blade!" a voice calls from behind me, just seconds before a shot goes off. I swing around to find the March Hare with a pair of twin revolvers pointed up at the ceiling.

At the Anti-Alice.

She drops from the ceiling in a flutter of skirts and comes up swinging, ignoring the blood dribbling down the front of her face from a set of gunshot wounds through her forehead. March's aim is dead-on. Unfortunately, I think the Anti-Alice might be dead, too.

I leap back and drag the Vorpal Blade from my thigh sheath, throwing it up just in time to counteract the scythe she's swinging my way.

Her blade hits mine with a horrible fucking crack, and I realize with a burst of white-hot fear that that sound … is my *arm* breaking. Shock takes over, and I don't feel a damn thing. I also can't seem to keep my feet, falling on my ass and using my left hand to push the Vorpal Blade forward and defend myself. My right arm flops uselessly at my side, broken by the impact of the Anti-Alice's swing.

Holy. Shit.

And I thought I was ready after training with the Duke? I might be ten times stronger than I was when I fell through the Rabbit-Hole into Underland, I might be a hundred times stronger, but it's not enough. Not by a long shot.

"You're *the* Alice!" Dee screams at me from across the room, shoving Edy behind himself as he holds up his knife and just *barely* manages to avoid being cut in half by his opponent. The Gryphon is swinging that same sword I saw him use on the King, but without Dee's wings, the angel doesn't have much of a chance of standing up to him. "Use your *magic*."

The smell of rot and bone taints the air around me, making my nose burn and my throat close up tight. The Anti-Alice has eyes like dark pools, the endless depths of forgotten wells. I feel like I could tumble right down them, and my body would never be found. Besides, I *can't* use my magic against her, right? Isn't that the whole point.

But then I remember how I threw the Vorpal Blade at her. I don't need to actually touch her with my powers; I just need to manipulate physical objects.

The Anti-Alice presses in hard, draining every ounce of physical energy that I have as I try to hold her back. With a sudden jerk, she pulls away and then swings again. I throw the Vorpal Blade up, but not with the intention of deflecting her blade, but with every ounce of power I have. It vibrates every molecule in my body, turns my soul into a restless mess.

Energy surges up and swirls around me, throwing furniture at the Anti-Alice, knocking her across the room and into my father's antique record player.

The Mad Hatter is there, helping me to my feet, and offering up his bloodied wrist at the same moment. Even though my dad's looking, and Edith's screaming, I take hold of it and drink as deeply as I can, the coppery sweet taste of his blood tainting my lips.

There's an immediate relief in my arm, but no relief in the battle.

Something *else* is coming through the Looking-Glass, and it's not one of my boys.

Two thick arms claw their way through, followed by a bulbous body and a face with horns protruding from the lips. The thing crawls through and shakes its blubbery, brown body out.

Doesn't take a genius to recognize the Walrus.

He looks like a goddamn ogre, with a massive underbite and tiny, beady little eyes.

And here I was, thinking everyone in Underland was attractive. My bad.

"Alice, don't," the Mad Hatter says, grabbing and jerking me back before the man finds his feet and grins at me, tipping a tall, vinyl top hat in our direction.

"So we finally meet the Alice," he growls in this guttural Scottish accent. "Plucky little thing, ain't she? I'd like to throw her over my knee and give her a good spanking." He smacks his big lips at me as the Mad Hatter curses under his breath. "And you," he says as the sound of a struggle echoes from just outside the front door. When I glance over my shoulder, I don't see Tee, March, or the Mocking Turtle, and that scares the shit out of me. My head whips around as the Walrus takes a step toward us, smelling like the rotten crabs my mom bought for Christmas dinner one year and then forgot in the trunk of her car. Death, rot, and crusted sea salt. That's what the Walrus smells like. "You made a bargain with the King of Clubs, and you broke it. You won't get that chance again."

The Mad Hatter grabs me and moves me just in time to avoid the slither of a massive head through the Looking-Glass.

It's a jabberwock, but it *isn't* North.

No, and it's not alone either.

On top of its massive skull sits a man that's all skin and bones, with sunken cheeks, and a wooden leg. He has a fucking axe cradled in his scrawny arms.

The Carpenter.

"Oh shit," I whisper as the Mad Hatter inserts himself between me and the jabberwock. It seems to get stuck on the other side of the mirror, one arm in the living room, smashing furniture as it struggles to crawl through.

"Oh shit is right," Raiden says, his pupils dilating as the Carpenter climbs off the dragon's head, and it retreats back through Looking-Glass. I'm just standing there staring, and all I can think is *I need to get that mirror before something breaks it.* Because … because … if I get separated from Underland, I will break. I will shatter into nothing and float away on the wind.

The Anti-Alice is pushing to her feet, pink bow fluttering in the breeze from the open door. It's then that I see the photo hanging on the wall beside her, of Rhoda cradled in my mother's arms at the hospital. And … she's wearing a pink bow on her head.

Bile fills my mouth and I almost throw up.

The Anti-Alice … is my sister?!

I shove the Vorpal Blade inside its sheath at the same time that I dive forward to grab the Looking-Glass, struggling with its weight as I do my best to stand up and beat a hasty retreat.

I'm about ninety-nine percent certain I'd have died right there if the March Hare didn't lift the Looking-Glass up and over my head, and kick my legs out from under me at the same moment. The Anti-Alice's bone scythe lands, and buries itself in his chest as he stumbles back, blood spurting from the wound.

I struggle to stand up, slipping and sliding in the hot crimson flood as the Mad Hatter takes the Looking-Glass from March and carefully sets it in my father's favorite chair. In the same breath, he catches the March Hare as he falls, and thrusts his wrist against the Rabbit's mouth.

"Well, now, this looks like a whole heap of fun, wouldn't you say, brother?" the Walrus chortles, his blubber jiggling as he laughs, his whisker-covered cheeks reddening. "There's nothing I love more than blood, death, and a screaming woman trapped beneath me."

Swear to fuck, I puke a little. I don't mean to; it just happens.

I back up next to the Mad Hatter and the March Hare as the latter finally seems to find his feet, standing up and shifting all in one breath. In the span of an instant, I have my hand on the bloody, furred flank of a bandersnatch.

Yet somehow, I'm still worried.

"Focus on the Anti-Alice, no matter what," Raiden says, his mouth twisted into a severe frown. I don't like that look. That look says *we might not win this*. Holy hearts and diamonds, what the fuck?!

"Rhoda?" my dad steps forward, forgotten and standing by the bay window. His expression is rife with pain as he moves toward the undead monster that used to be my sister. Without thinking, I snatch the Vorpal Blade up and move between the two of them.

I don't see Dee, Edith, or the Cheshire Cat anymore, and I'm starting to panic.

One thing at a time, Allison, I tell myself.

"Free up one of the twins for me," Raiden growls, and the March Hare goes trotting out the front door. My dad barely looks at the giant, fantastical beast in his living room. He only seems to have eyes for the Anti-Alice.

"You're going to face off against us alone?" the Walrus asks, glancing over at his brother. "Who knew this would be so bloody easy?" With a roar, the Walrus' body ripples, his fat ballooning until he's almost too big to fit inside the house. He has a tail instead of legs, and by some stretch of the imagination, I can see why he's nicknamed the Walrus. He almost, *almost*, looks like one.

Another scream tears from his throat as he thunders toward the Mad Hatter, at stark contrast with the skinny, creepy little Carpenter who's still standing there and watching *me*. He reaches down and strokes the bulge in his pants, making me sick to my stomach.

We are outclassed, outmatched.

Without more help, we are *fucked*.

And yet, the Looking-Glass is quiet, the walls are spattered in blood, and I have no idea what I'm doing here.

We are so screwed.

Holy fucking hearts, please help me.

XII
XI
X
IX
VIII
VII
VI

3
ALLISON shatters the LOOKING-GLASS

A Blade Beneath A Stormy Sky

A blade beneath a stormy sky,
Fighting just this one last time,
Alice drowning, black and red tide—

Men of nine that fight so near,
Eager and above all fear,
Terrified this tale to hear—

Long had darkened sunny skies:
Echoes fade, memories die.
Shadowed frosts have slain good guys.

Still she haunts me, phantomwise,
Alice battling under bloody skies
Never seen by waking eyes.

Citizens yet, the tale to hear,
Wide, wide eyes and bleeding ears,
Terrified they wrestle fears.

In an Underland they die,
Dreaming for bound wings to fly,
Wishing for a Wonderland gone by:

Ever drifting down the stream—
Lingering in prophecy's gleam—
Life, what is it but a dream?

CHAPTER ONE

Looking-Glass Instincts

Everything smells like blood.

I'm choking on it, that metallic burn that tastes like pennies on the back of my tongue.

My dad is standing behind me, but I don't recognize him right now. He looks like a fucking zombie, the way he's staring at the Anti-Alice. How he recognizes her as Rhoda is beyond me. Hell, maybe I'm crazy, too? How could that undead monster be the daughter my parents lost so many years ago?

The Walrus—who's now about ten times his previous size—is barreling across the living room toward the Mad Hatter, knocking aside what's left of the furniture. Raiden Walker moves out of the way at the last second, taking the Looking-Glass with him and using whatever vampire voodoo bullshit he's got up his sleeve to reappear outside the bay window.

Doesn't stop the Walrus though. He just smashes right through the wall and ends up in our front yard.

And Dad used to be concerned about the neighbors' opinions on his choice of lawn ornaments.

Well, pretty sure *this* is going to get my parents in trouble with the HOA.

I suck in a deep breath, my gaze locked onto the too-blue eyes of the Anti-Alice, like shards of summer sky in her undead face.

It's my job to fight her off; it's my job to kill her.

I'm the only one who can do it.

"Okay, bitch," I say, hating the way my voice shakes. "Come and get me."

Oh, I'm such a badass in my ripped skinny jeans and uni-freaking-corn tank top, I think with a roll of my eyes. How am I supposed to beat the Anti-Alice with no shoes (just kitty slippers), no real-world fighting experience, and no courage? I'm fucking terrified.

You would be, too, in my position; don't judge.

The Anti-Alice cracks her neck to one side, and her gray skin tears, ruby red blood spilling from the wound in a foul-smelling wave. My nose wrinkles as I widen my legs in a fighting stance, the Vorpal Blade held out on my right side.

"Allison," Dad whispers from behind me, and there's something so wrong with his voice that I feel myself falter. He recently lost a son, so what's going to happen if he watches his daughter kill the reincarnation of his other dead kid?

Or … *be* killed by her.

Cursing under my breath, I turn and grab Dad's arm, shoving him into the open bathroom door and then pushing my back against it to close it. The Anti-Alice is already on me, swinging her scythe and smashing it into the closed bathroom door when I duck.

Her black and white striped skirts swirl as she spins to face me, yanking the bone scythe out of the door with an explosion of shards. I'm doing my best to stand up, but I can't seem to get my feet under me, and end up on my ass.

"Allison!" I hear Tee scream my name just seconds before the March Hare slams into the Anti-Alice from the side, knocking her back against the bathroom door. My dad was just starting to open it, too. Now the door is cracked in half but wedged in the doorframe; I'm not sure he'll even be able to get it open.

March grabs the Anti-Alice by the arm and then gives her a death shake, snapping the bone, and sending her scythe flying across the room.

I can do this! I think, feeling a rush of adrenaline pump through my veins. I've got an opening, and I've got the Vorpal Blade and—

There's a sharp shock of pain as my head is snapped back; some asshole is yanking on my hair.

When my head hits the floor, I look up and see the Carpenter standing over me, his big bulbous nose obscuring the two tiny pinpricks of his eyes.

"C'mere bitch," he says, dragging me across the floor and throwing me against the wall next to the kitchen entrance. My back hits the drywall so hard that it cracks, and a picture falls from the wall to the ground, shattering to pieces.

For one brief second, I have a clear view of the destroyed living room and the yard outside.

Edith is on the back of the Cheshire Cat monster, this glorious beast in black and white, with silver hoops in its ears, and a collar around its neck. It's almost as big as the goddamn bandersnatch, and it's bleeding profusely, all over the fucking street.

Neighbors are standing in their yards, gawping at the scene of carnage in front of them.

In minutes, the police will be here; I can already hear the sirens.

"I likes the look o' you," the Carpenter says, swinging his long, thin tongue over his lower lip. He's tall and gaunt and reedy, and his fingers are spindly and knobby. When he reaches out for me, I instinctively swing the Vorpal Blade at him.

He grabs my wrist so hard, I hear bones break.

Pain shoots through me, this electric burn that buckles my knees, and I find myself hanging by my injured arm like a rag doll. It happens so quickly that I'm not sure how to react. Fortunately, I'm not alone.

Tee drops to his knees next to me, grabs my face between his hands, and kisses me hard on the mouth. His wings explode from his back just before he uses one to knock the Carpenter's arm up and away. The creep's long fingers release me, letting my pain-riddled body crumple into Tee's arms.

"I've got you, I've got you," he whispers, hoisting me up against his chest. I've somehow managed to maintain my grip on the Vorpal Blade which, really, is my only saving grace. I guess getting knocked around the training floor by North, Chesh, and the twins really did teach me something. "We need to get to the Mad Hatter, and quick."

My mind is only half there, broken up into shards by the pain, but I nod my assent as Tee carries me across the remains of my parents' living room, and toward the front door.

"Why do I feel like we're going to lose this?" I whisper, realizing that there's a bit of bone protruding from my wrist. Tee doesn't answer me, but I see his lips purse. Not a very promising facial expression.

He vaults over what's left of the broken half-wall, and onto the lawn.

The Walrus monster is halfway down the street, and he's got something … no, he's got *someone* in his fucking mouth.

That someone is flung toward us, their broken body smashing into the side of my father's SUV and *knocking it over.* Do you understand the force required for that to happen?!

And yet, the Mad Hatter is up within a few seconds, bleeding everywhere, clothing torn, but somehow still in one piece. He glances over as Tee runs up to him, gives me his wrist, and puts his mouth against the angel prince's neck all in one go.

"Angel blood sends vampires into Frenzies."

I can hear Chesh's words as I suck down yet another mouthful of vampire blood. Hey, I'm starting to get accustomed to the taste. Slather some of that on toast for me next time I stub my toe, okay?

Raiden's hand grasps the back of Tee's dark head, nails digging into his scalp as he drinks. When his eyes open, I can see that the marmalade color has brightened to a wild, glowing pumpkin orange. That, and his teeth look bigger, longer, scarier as he pulls back and slides his arm across his mouth, smearing blood.

"Oh, well, now *that* was delicious."

The Mad Hatter breaks into a dozen pieces, shattering like a broken window, and becoming a flock of bats. Their eyes glow as they take off toward the Walrus in a swarm, surrounding the creature's head and then reforming into a single entity.

Raiden Walker materializes on top of the Walrus' blunt skull, whipping off his hat and pulling out his cane. Without sparing a single second, he unscrews the skull at the end of it, revealing a blade that he promptly stabs down into the Walrus' brain.

The blubbery creature roars in pain, towering over the bystanders on the street and, when the first cop car comes around the corner, he sends it flying with one of his front flippers. The car eats a hole through our neighbors' garage door and destroys the brand-new motorcycle Mr. Jones was just bragging about.

"Holy fuckballs," I groan as my wrist knits together, and Tee sets me back on my feet. "They're going to send in the army!"

"Your ruler will send his army for this?" Tee asks, and although he's adorable as shit, I don't have time to explain that yeah, the National Guard will probably be here within a few hours. Or hell, if my neighbors are streaming this shit on social media, we're already screwed.

"We need to end this—quick. I don't even care if we win: can we just get these fuckers *back* into the Looking-Glass?!"

Tee looks at me like I'm mad, which, considering the situation I now find myself in, is bound to become even more accurate by the minute.

"Allison," Tee says, nodding his head to redirect my attention. "We're not going anywhere unless we get the Looking-Glass *back*."

"Back?!" I choke, whipping around to find the Gryphon taking off with ... *the Looking-Glass in his fucking hands?!* "No! Tee, go!" I scream, but he shoves me behind him and intercepts a ... tongue?

Oh holy hearts, diamonds, clubs, and spades. Oh, fuck the whole damn deck!

The Mocking Turtle whips his tongue in Tee's direction, and the prince catches it around his knife. When M.T. sucks it back in, Tee goes with it, still clinging to his weapon. At least Dee isn't far behind, sliding up next to me with blood pouring down the side of his head.

"Love you, need it, gotta go," he whispers, kissing me with bloodied lips, and pulling away as his wings explode into existence, unfolding from his back like an origami project. The chains are still dangling off of them as he makes a run for it, taking off into the air with a flap of those powerful appendages, heading after the Gryphon.

A gush of wind explodes out behind Dee, ruffling up my hair as I heft the Vorpal Blade up and watch the Anti-Alice crawling over the half-wall with the jagged shards of glass. She doesn't seem to mind as they rip and tear her flesh apart. No, she just spider-crawls out of the house and then looks at me with bloody, white hair hanging in her face.

"Mistress," Chesh growls, padding up next to me just before his front legs collapse and he ends up kneeling like a horse, his massive feline body swaying as he tries to keep the rest of himself upright for Edith.

"Allison," she wails, but she's sobbing so hard, nothing else comes out. When Chesh lets out a groan and finally falls onto his side, she almost goes with him. I grab her hands just in time to yank her off before he lands on the cement with a yowl of agony. "I'm so fucking scared."

Edy throws herself at me, but I'm already pushing past her to check on Chesh. There's just so much damn blood that I almost slip as I kneel down next to his massive head. He's three times bigger than the tigers at the local zoo, with massive paws, and a pair of gray eyes clouded with pain.

"I'm sorry, *Midnight Knicker Dancer*," he breathes, and my eyes fill with tears. I whip my head around to see the Anti-Alice swaggering toward us with her scythe. I don't have time to sit here and watch Chesh die.

"Shit," I snarl, standing up and whipping out the Queenmaker. I have matches, gunpowder, and musket balls in the third pouch of my Vorpal Blade holster, but not a lot of time to fumble around with them.

One shot might be all I get.

I whip a match out, only to realize that I have something else up my sleeve: the mushroom flesh.

I snap the pouch closed, scrape the match on the bottom of the Queenmaker, and light her up.

The Anti-Alice starts to run at me as I take aim—and *fire*.

The metal ball lobs up and away, smashing into the cement just behind the Anti-Alice. The flames and the heat chuck her like an undead Autumn leaf, sending her right over my head and onto the Smith's roof.

Heh.

And Mr. Smith is always bitching that my parents don't address the moss issue on theirs. Now who's got a 'dangerous growth' on their roof, huh?

Joking aside, Edith and I are also thrown back, right into Chesh's fuzzy, muscular kitty belly. The orange and red explosion from the Queenmaker makes a mini-mushroom cloud in the middle of our suburban street.

Edith refuses to get up, curling into Chesh's side and burying her face in his fur. He might be dying, but I know he'll protect her to his last breath. Me, I need to get the Mad Hatter over here, and I need to do it fucking fast.

Stumbling to my feet, I put the Queenmaker back in her holster, and pull out a bit of mushroom meat.

Looking down at the spongy, white flesh, I praise my own foresight: I carved a 'B' with my fingernail for house-big, and an 'S' for mouse-small into the pieces. Also, I curse myself because the mushroom tidbits have been bouncing around in the holster pouch, and the messy 'B' looks just the same as the 'S'. Or is it the 'S' that looks like the 'B'?

"Shit on a Saltine," I curse, letting my head fall back. Oh well. If I just take a nibble, that should answer the question for me, right?

I keep my eyes on the Anti-Alice as she struggles to get to her feet, her hair and clothes burning as she locks gazes with me and hops straight from the roof toward me.

Fuck.

I take a quick bite of the mushroom—and my stomach gets ripped right out from under me. That roller-coaster feeling is back, and within just a few seconds, I'm looking up, up, up as the Anti-Alice sails right over the top of me.

Her scythe destroys the pavement just behind me, and I realize how goddamn lucky I am that I ate the 'wrong' mushroom. Stuffing the bit of extra fungi flesh into my pocket, I turn around, take a few steps back, and bite off a huge chunk of the other side.

My head whips back as I sprout straight up, like the blackberry seedlings in the backyard that Mom used to curse at. You know, before she got put in prison for murdering the rapists that slaughtered my brother.

I scream—can't help it—as I shoot into the air like a firework, my limbs lengthening to the size of small trees, my voice booming like a tornado warning.

In the span of an instant, I'm dizzy and stumbling, but towering over my parents' house—*and* the Walrus.

Raiden Walker is still battling the monster, but now, I'm much bigger than that blubbery piece of shit. As I reach for him, I see the Carpenter first, striding out of the house with blood all over his body and a smile on his grotesque, bony face.

I redirect my focus to him, snatching that motherfucker up in one of my giant fists and *squeezing* as hard as I can. It's disturbing, to say the least, feeling a man's body burst in my hand like a grape.

Blood and bits spatter everywhere, a meaty sack falling to the pavement as I release my grip. I almost puke, but then, at this height, it would drown the entire neighborhood.

This is the most surreal shit I've ever done! I think as my mind scrambles to get away from the fallout of my violent act. I cannot think about it, or I will fall apart. And right now, I can't afford to do that.

I start to turn back to the Walrus when I notice that the Carpenter's bits … are sliding back together, the flesh and blood slurping into his meat sack until he's standing right in front of me again, completely and utterly unharmed.

"What the …?" I curse, and the words echo around the neighborhood as the next cop car screams into view. And then another, and another, and another. Before I can even remotely figure out how to handle this problem, the men in blue are out and pointing their weapons at the Walrus.

They fire off dozens of shots that stick in the monster's blubber and do … absolutely nothing at all.

What. A. Clusterfuck.

A sharp pain digs into my ankle, and I scream, glancing down to see the Anti-Alice with her scythe buried in the fabric of my jeans and the flesh underneath. At first, it's just a pinprick, and I figure I'll grab her and squash her next. But then, I feel this horrible suction, like there's a void just outside of my wound, eating up every ounce of warmth I have inside of me.

Tee lands on my shoulder, startling me out of my shock.

"She's sucking all your magic out! Just like you need to hit her with the Vorpal Blade and *hold it*, so she has to do the same to you with her weapon!" I just stand there, my heart pounding, darkness creeping into my vision. And then I feel another sharp pain in my leg, glancing down to see that Chesh has just crawled several feet over to bite me.

The warm seep of blood from my left ankle snaps me out of it completely, and I kick the Anti-Alice away, dislodging her scythe in the process. She lands in the bushes near my parents' ruined house, but she doesn't stay down for long.

"Tee, what do I do?" I ask as he flaps his wings and moves over to my other shoulder, pointing down at the car-sized Vorpal Blade in my hand.

"Hit her with *that*," he growls, and I get this *aha* moment going on.

Giant blade … absorbs more magic than small blade?

Riiiight?

I drop down to my knees, shaking the street, and I swing the Vorpal Blade in the Anti-Alice's direction. Her pink ribbon flutters from the breeze of my movement, and her midsection severs right in half.

Oh my god, more blood.

Blood, blood, blood—it's *everywhere.*

The Anti-Alice stands stone-still for a split-second, and then falls apart, collapsing to the ground in *pieces*. And yet, she is most definitely not dead. Not by a long shot.

The Walrus barrels into my knees, knocking me back as he's chased by a swarm of bats. As I stumble, he moves over to the Anti-Alice, picking up *both* halves of her in his mouth before he takes off with the Carpenter clinging to his side.

The Mocking Turtle is on the Walrus' back, riding him like a goddamn blubbery dragon.

They smash through the fence between our house and the next one over, heading for the empty field and the forest.

"I can't find the Looking-Glass!" Dee wails, landing on my other shoulder. "The Gryphon is fucking gone! They must have Topside allies."

"Topside allies?!" I ask, but then I feel this sickening lurch inside of me, and I realize that I'm swaying a little, like I'm all of two seconds from passing out. Crap. I lift the massive lump of mushroom meat to my lips and take a bite, stumbling as my stomach lurches, and I start to feel like I'm falling.

The twins take off from my shoulders before my body's too small to stand on, but the sudden rush of the ground coming at me, the wound on my leg, and the magic that's been sucked out of me … promptly sends me falling over my feet into a face-plant.

The last thing I see of the battle is the awful gray of cracked cement.

My dreams are so beyond fucked, they make Underland look like Wonderland. I thrash and sweat, tangling myself up so badly in the sheets that when I do wake, I'm convinced I've been kidnapped by the Walrus and the Carpenter, that they're holding me down like Liam and his friends, that—

"Allison," Chesh whispers, sitting by me in cat form. He's got Dinah next to him, staring at him like he's the second coming of Christ. I jerk upright, fighting tooth and nail to get the sheets off of me, when the door opens and my dad walks in.

"You passed out," he says, brow knitted with worry as he shoos the cats out of his way and sits on the edge of the bed. "Here, I brought you some of Mom's famous chicken noodle soup."

"Mom made this?' I ask, which is a stupid question because, of course she didn't. She's in prison. Motherfucking, cocksucking prison. "I mean, you used Mom's recipe?"

Dad nods as I take the tray, all the while trying to figure out how he's so damn calm when our house is destroyed, he saw his dead daughter reincarnated as a monster, and his other daughter just reappeared after two weeks of radio silence.

"The police are here; they want to talk to you," he says softly, looking down at his lap, his glasses sliding to the tip of his nose.

Of *course* the police want to talk to me: the entire street looks like a war zone.

"How's Edith?" I manage to choke out, taking a spoonful of the yellow broth and letting it dribble back into the bowl. I can't even look at my father right now, and I have no idea how I'm going to face my sister. She was so scared, she pissed herself. How do I apologize for bringing all of that back with me?

"Angry, happy, confused." Dad looks away from me, toward a poster I have on my wall. It's from the *Alice's Adventures in Wonderland* exhibit at the local museum, and it features one of John Tenniel's illustrations.

Heh.

Bet that one doesn't open into a dark hallway with torches, or lead into a heart-shaped bedroom where a gorgeous Duke …

The door flies open, and there he is: the Savage Duke, staring down at me with gold eyes. His blonde-gold hair hangs over his brow, but his horns, and his tail, they're gone.

"Allison Liddell," North says in that booming voice of his, commanding everyone in the room to stop and look at him.

Pretty sure my dad leaps right out of his skin.

"I said all cops downstairs!" Henry barks, standing up off the bed and puffing his chest out. The Duke's is already inflated, so it's almost, sort of, kind of funny to see them having a stand-off in my bedroom door.

"I, good sir, am not—" North starts, as I push the chicken noodle soup aside, and fling myself out of bed, inserting myself between the two warring men.

"I'm sure this detective just wants a statement," I start, pushing North back and into the hallway before taking him by the hand and dragging him toward Mom's old office. I'm about to shove him in and lock the door when I look down the stairs.

And see the fucking King.

He's wearing a suit and gloves, but his hair is as red as blood, and his frown is sharp enough to cut cheese.

"What …" I start, because I can very clearly see the living room, and nothing's been destroyed. Everything is as it was when I first tumbled out of the Looking-Glass. "No way, no fucking way," I murmur, stumbling down the first few steps and then just *staring* at the unblemished perfection of the house.

The front wall is still there, the window is whole, the couch is clean and white.

The only 'off' thing I notice is a lamp that seems to be glued *underneath* the side table, rather than sitting on top of it. Oh, and there's the breakfast table from the front nook, resting on the ceiling and fully set for tea with place settings, napkins, even a teapot.

I sway a bit, but the Duke catches me by the elbow, and I realize then that I'm probably just having another dream. I mean, how else do you explain the sudden appearance of the Duke and the King? The reincarnation of the living room? The lack of SWAT members in my house?

"Hello, Sonny," the White Rabbit says, appearing from the direction of the kitchen with a stopwatch in his right hand. He presses a knob on the side and my dad, who was halfway out of my bedroom door, freezes in place.

Like, he quite literally *freezes,* and I find myself looking at a statue version of the man named Henry George Liddell.

"What in the ever-loving fuck?" I whisper, trying to pinch myself awake.

Doesn't work.

All I get are tiny welts on the inside of my arm.

"Just relax and listen: I can't hold this long without passing out myself," Rab says, his voice like shadows over ice. Beautiful, but cold, lonely. I kind of want to warm him up. I also sort of want to slap him, because … what the hell is going on here?!

"We've repaired the damage to your house," Lar says, wingless and yet still ethereally beautiful with his blue-blonde hair and his summer sky eyes. He's standing near the front door, and I was so perplexed by the transformation of the living room that I didn't notice at first. Looking at him now, I can't imagine how I missed him. He's too beautiful, too perfect, to be looked over. "And for the moment, your sister and father don't remember what happened. But they will. No memory stays hidden forever."

"How did you guys do this?!" I gasp, and Rab grins at me with big, white teeth, no rabbit ears in sight on the top of his head. I already find that I miss them greatly.

"Magic," Rab says, lifting up his stopwatch. "But it won't last, and it isn't limitless. I only have so much in me before I die."

"Die?" I ask and he grits his teeth, nodding sharply.

"Die. Each second that I freeze time takes an hour off of my life."

"What?!" I snap, storming down the stairs and snatching the watch from his hand. The thought of losing so much time with him is— Well, I barely like the guy, but … but it's infuriating! "Stop using it then," I growl out as my dad starts to move again, blinking abruptly at finding me suddenly standing at the bottom of the stairs with the four men I didn't think made it through the Looking-Glass.

But I can't ask now. Later, though.

As soon as I get my wits together enough to really pay attention, I see that Lar and Rab are both dressed in black police uniforms. The King and the Duke have suits on, like they're FBI or some shit.

"Now, I asked for patience and respect with my daughter," Henry snarls, already in papa dragon mode. Wonder what would happen if he faced off against a real dragon? Err, sorry, jabberwock. "I can already see you guys diving in for the kill."

"Dear Sir, if I *were* 'diving in for the kill', as you so eloquently put it, then *you would know*," the Savage Duke growls this last part out which confuses the fuck out of my father as he seems to be under the impression that the man standing in front of him is some sort of detective or something.

"Okay, okay," I say, running up the stairs and realizing that holy *fuck*, my leg still hurts, and Jesus H., this is going to be a difficult day to get through. "I'm sure the nice man is just trying to do his job, right *Detective North*?"

The Duke gives me this … I want to say, *aggressive, carnal* sort of look, and Dad's eyes widen. Pretty sure when North's beautiful lips part to say something, the first word on the tip of his tongue is *mate.* Okay, so maybe the first word was *my*, but mate was a close second.

"Well, I find his conduct inappropriate," Dad says, grabbing me by the shoulder and pushing me aside. "And I really don't like the way he's looking at you. Now, I have no problem with the Eureka Police, but I will soon if you don't get out of my house."

"He was just leaving anyway," I say, giving North a *please, dear God, just go!* sort of a look. I feel a little squeeze around my ankle and realize that the Duke has his goddamn tail out. "So, go, bye."

I push my dad away, and wait for North to descend the steps.

It takes him an awkward amount of time to stop staring at me before he finally goes, sliding his hand down the banister, chin raised like he's still back in Underland in his fancy-pants palace.

He pauses at the bottom, next to Brennin Red, and then glances back at me.

Now, all four men are staring.

The King and his entourage.

So where are the rest of my … I mean *the* guys?

"When you get a minute," Brennin says, his voice like charcoal and smoke, "please send a messenger with an invitation for croquet."

Ehhhh?!

"A messenger?" Dad asks, looking completely and utterly baffled.

"Or. I. will. call. you. on. your. *cellphone*," I snarl, pointing at the front door.

"My phone doesn't work Topside," the King says, lazily waving a gloved hand in the air. He flicks his bloodred hair off of his forehead as I clench my teeth and do my best not to scream.

"He has bad service," I tell my dad, "Sprint."

"You had time to discuss cell service?" Dad asks, but then he looks down at me, and something just breaks inside of him.

We are still not over my being back, not even close.

"We left your *things* next to the *cat*," Lar says, giving me a small wave as the four of them make their way to the front door, and let themselves outside.

I miss them already.

I feel like I'm being left behind.

And then a soft, furry body rubs up against my ankles, and I glance down to find Chesh leaping up against my calves. Somehow, I'm dressed in an old nightgown with no memory of changing clothes. I bet one of the guys did it; they better not have copped a feel. That's assault, you know, just in case you were unaware.

"Allison," Dad says softly, shards of his broken heart fluttering in the air with his voice. "Just because you showed up last night, and it's now morning, that doesn't change anything. We have a lot to talk about."

"I know," I say, feeling so guilty I can barely stand it. "But is it okay if I shower first?"

Dad nods as Edith's door cracks open, and I see her sleepy face staring at me. She used to do that all the time when we were little, prop her door open and watch me in the living room, or on my way to the bathroom, in my room when I occasionally left my door open. I hated it back then … not so much anymore.

"Shower?" Dad asks, staring at me in a daze. He adjusts his glasses and smooths his hands over the front of his wrinkled white button-down. I'm used to my dad looking perfect: he's a university professor, after all. But right now, with coffee stains all over his chest, his belt missing a loop, and two left shoes on his feet … I hardly recognize him. "Yeah, of course, but … leave the door cracked."

"Dad!" I admonish, falling back into old habits. It startles him for a second, but then there's this awkward silence between us, like he doesn't even know me. "I'll just shower, and get dressed, and …"

"Aren't we going to see Mom today?" Edith asks, pushing her door open the rest of the way. She's already caked in makeup, her hair curled, dressed in a white undershirt and short-shorts.

"We'll go see Mom," Dad says, just staring at me as I retreat back into my room and close the door behind me. I put my ear against the wood and listen for a minute to see if Edy and Dad are still out there, but it seems quiet enough.

Chesh is sitting on my bed next to Dinah. She won't stop rubbing her head against him, which I find adorable but which I'm pretty sure he does *not*. I pat him on the head and then pause next to my desk to start up my iPod.

White Rabbit by Egypt Central starts up, and I raise an eyebrow. That's … a strangely appropriate song.

"Okay, talk to me," I say, sitting down on the edge of the bed next to the two cats. I pull Dinah into my lap, stroking my fingers down the sleek, black fur of her back. Chesh is looking at me like he wishes I'd stroke him instead.

Just … maybe not his back.

"Talk to you?" he purrs, standing up and stretching. I fully expect him to stay in kitty form because my dad or sister could quite easily walk in at any moment, but … why should I expect sensibleness from these Underland men anyway? "I'm supposing you want to know where the others have gone?"

He shifts into his human form, still dressed in that suit I last saw him in during the Ball of Broken Hearts and Stolen Tarts. Makes me wonder where the Duke and the Hatter got *their* suits from.

Chesh throws his arms around my neck, and nuzzles into my throat, making my heart pitter-patter as I feel his warmth press against my back.

"I was so worried when you left with the King," he murmurs, nibbling my earlobe. It feels so damn good, that it's almost physically painful to pull him off. "As soon as you did, there was a commotion. The White Knight and the Knave got into a bit of a tussle."

"Really?" I ask, imagining Chevalier going toe-to-toe with Ines and her two creepy husbands.

"And then someone found dead guards in the kitchen, yada yada." Chesh yawns, letting go of me, so he can arch his back and scratch his nails on my bedspread. Dinah lets out a tiny mewl, and bats at him, but he hisses at her and she backs off. "It was simply a clusterfuck-fuckity-fuck-fuck-fuck."

"Very descriptive," I say, realizing that dried blood has flaked off of Chesh's arm and onto my own. Which, of course, reminds me that when I last saw the Cheshire Cat, he was bleeding to death. "How are you still alive?" I ask, spinning around to face him.

He takes my face between clawed fingers and then leans in toward my lips.

"Perhaps bringing the vampire mercenary into the Kingdom of Hearts was not the worst idea in the world," he purrs, licking my bottom lip, his black and white striped tail swaying lazily behind him.

One of Chesh's kitty ears quirks in the direction of my door, and then he's rolling away from me and onto the carpet next to my bed.

Edith pops in a moment later and gives me a look.

"Who were you talking to?" she asks, slipping inside and closing it behind her. A split-second later, Chesh in kitty form hops up onto my bed and stretches. Edy gives him a weird look.

"Where'd this cat come from anyway? I tried to put it outside, but it bit me and then sprayed my bathrobe."

"I, uh, I found him on the street, soaked to the bone. How else does one acquire a cat?" I smile as I quote the Duke's words, crossing my arms over my chest and trying not to get frustrated with Edy. She doesn't know I'm dealing with otherworldly politics. All she knows is that her sister disappeared for two weeks, and now she's back.

"Don't think I've forgotten what happened yesterday," she says, and the hair on the back of my neck stands up straight. Chesh's, too. I stroke him to soothe his fur back into place. "You and the cosplaying weirdos. Where are they now?"

Oh, that.

She remembers us tumbling through the Looking-Glass; that's all she remembers, I hope.

"Do you remember having coffee with Dad?" I ask, and Edith raises an eyebrow.

"Yeah, and uh, how is that important compared to you, and your silver paint, and hugging some guy we've never met buck fucking naked?"

"What happened after coffee?" I ask, because I am getting curiouser and fucking curiouser by the second.

"After coffee, you passed out and Dad carried you upstairs. Jesus, you must really be out of it. How many drugs *did* you do while you were gone?"

I have to really think about that one for a moment.

I smoked a lot of pot, err, *whiting*, and I definitely drank some boosted tea.

"I need to shower," I say, collecting a fresh pair of jeans, a tank that says *They Can't Burn Us All* with a pentagram trapped in a Venus symbol, and some undergarments. I scoop up Chesh in my other arm and head for the bathroom.

"Running out on me won't make me forget," she whispers as I pass, but since I have no clue *what* to say to her, I just slip into the bathroom and close the door behind me.

Once the water and the fan are running to give Chesh and me a little privacy, I give him a look.

"Can I have a moment to change?" I ask, and he cocks his head to the side like he's thinking, tail twitching behind him. He licks his shoulder and then looks back up at me.

"You may have two moments and thirty-some odd seconds," he says, but then he just keeps staring up at me with those gorgeous gray eyes of his. With a roll of my own eyes, I grab him by the scruff, stuff him in the cabinet under the sink and change as quickly as I can.

Fortunately, there's a window in the shower, this old eighties one with frosted glass that my father thinks is lewd, and my mother loves because it lets sunshine in while she showers. Um, showered, I guess, since she's never getting out of prison to come back here.

I let Chesh out and climb right through it, leaving the water on as I go. If Dad or Edith somehow figures out that I'm gone, I'll just tell them I stepped out for air or something while they weren't looking. If they *are* watching the door, well, I already disappeared for two weeks, so sneaking out the window for ten minutes shouldn't matter much, right?

Crawling across the roof tiles, I take my tried-and-true route to the backyard, hop down onto the hot tub lid, and raise an eyebrow as Chesh shifts in mid-air on his way down after me. He lands with about a hundred times more grace than me, popping his bow tie off and chucking it into Mom's tulip bed.

She planted them into a heart shape, so every year, they die and then grow back in that same shape. Gotta love flowering bulbs. Well, in the spring anyway. It's just a patch of bare dirt right now.

"I assume you know where we're going?" I ask, and then I hear a familiar voice from the bushes on my left.

"Assumptions make an ass out of you and shins—two of which we all have." Dee steps out of the arborvitae and gives me a little wave, his black and blue hair rumpled and matted with old blood. "Unless of course you're an amputee which then you could have one shin or none shin and then the only person that's an ass is you."

"Oh, wow, thank you for that," I whisper, but I can't seem to stop myself from crossing the lawn in a half-jog. I throw my arms around his neck as he laughs, and give him a quick kiss on the cheek—can't risk one on the mouth at the moment because, you know, wings and all. "I'm glad you're okay."

"We're all fine," he whispers, "but if the King and Company hadn't come out of the Looking-Glass when they did, we'd all be dead."

"Then the Looking-Glass—" I start and Dee gives me this tight-lipped expression that speaks volumes.

We don't have it.

"We can go back down the Rabbit-Hole," I start, but he's already shaking his head.

"We can't go anywhere until we get the Looking-Glass back," Dee says, but in my heart, I already know that. Whoever holds the Looking-Glass holds the power, don't they? I mean, to be able to travel between worlds is monumental.

"It's not broken is it?" I ask, but Dee's already shaking his head and raking his fingers through black hair streaked with blue. His wings are gone, but for now, that's for the best. Explaining a thirty-foot wingspan to every Tom, Dick, and Harry doesn't exactly sound like a good time.

"The Walrus and the Carpenter are as concerned with keeping the Looking-Glass whole as we are." Dee pauses and glances over his shoulder, into the dark shadows of the woods. "Come on. There's something I think you need to see."

Dee takes my hand and pulls me after him while the cat shifts and pads along in the leaves next to us, collar jangling as he walks.

As we move, I notice tiny toadstools popping up from the wet dirt, sparkling and glittering in unnatural colors. That's … not normal for Topside. I should know: I grew up in this boring, dull, and humdrum world.

"Dee," I start, but the woods are so fucking quiet, unnaturally so. I don't hear birds or insects, just the crisp crunch of leaves beneath our feet. He looks at me, but I just shake my head. Later, I'll ask later. Right now, I've got butterflies from his cryptic statement. Something I need to see? Nobody drops a statement like that unless something bad is going on.

We weave through the woods, drenched in shadows and dripping in evergreen boughs. Tiny, frozen droplets of water kiss my nose and lips as I look up.

"Perhaps you should warn her?" Chesh says after a while, shifting back into human form and swishing his tail back and forth. He looks over at Dee with eyes that match the sky: a dark, stormy gray.

"Perhaps," Dee says, pausing when we hear the sharp snap of teeth, and smell the pungent reek of blood.

"The Mocking Turtle?" I ask, but Dee shakes his head again, reaching down to scratch at his belly through his t-shirt. Pretty sure I recognize that shirt—it's Fred's. And now that I think about it, those suits the King and the Duke were wearing were Fred's, too. I'm surprised Dad didn't notice? Or maybe he did, and they just used some of their Underland voodoo on him?

"It's the Mad Hatter," Dee tells me, looking down at the ground and then back up at my face. "He's … pretty fucked-up. I'm not sure how else to put it."

"He's in a Frenzy," Tee says, stepping out from between two trees. My heart leaps when I see him, that curiously stern look on his face that makes him look a decade older than his twin brother. He rubs the palm of his right hand down his left, flashing me the glorious feather tattoos on the backs of his arms. "And we don't know how to snap him out of it."

I move past Tee and around a tight cluster of birch, finding myself face-to-face with the Mad Hatter.

Or … what used to be the Mad Hatter.

"Holy fucking hearts," I curse, slapping my hand over my mouth when those wild eyes of his turn to look at me.

Raiden Walker is chained to a massive redwood tree; his ankles are locked tight together with thick, heavy links of metal, and his arms are up and out to the sides. The expression on his face is not at all human. Fuck, he *looks* like a goddamn vampire right now. His marmalade-colored eyes are neon orange and glowing, and his teeth are twice as long and sharp as they were before. He's snapping at the air like a rabid dog, and snarling, slaver and blood dripping from his lips.

The March Hare is leaning against the side of the tree next to him, bleeding profusely from his neck. It doesn't just look like Raiden bit him, more like he tore a *chunk* out of his friend.

"What the …?" I start as March reaches up with a big hand and rubs at his bleeding wound. Well, really, it's more like raw, ragged flesh, but if I look too closely at it, I might be sick. I'll just keep my gaze elsewhere. Like on the Mad Hatter, and his too-white skin, his dilated pupils, and the bulging veins in his arm muscles as he struggles to escape his confinement. "This is what a Frenzy looks like?"

"This is what a Frenzy looks like if it goes unchecked," March snarls, dropping his head. This time, his top hat actually falls off and hits the forest floor. All sorts of things fall out of it: twin revolvers, several knives, poison vials … lubricant? "I tried to feed him before he lost the goddamn plot, but he's lost his fuckin' *shite*." March slams his fist back into the tree, cracking the bark and drawing the Mad Hatter's attention over to him.

Raiden bites at the air, rattling the chains and making the links creak. I'm seriously concerned he's going to escape.

"It's his fault we lost the fucking Looking-Glass, mercenary scum," Red snarls, standing there wearing my brother's suit, and looking completely out of place in the dark shadows of the forest.

"Hey," March says, snatching his hat up from the ground and shoving all his goodies back into it. "Without that *mercenary scum*, your Alice would be dead." March stands back up and tucks his hat on his head, blood soaking his shirt and sticking it to his chest. Looks like he also borrowed some of Fred's clothing. We'll have to be careful; my dad might've been too out of it to notice this morning, but if he catches me with nine dudes all wearing my dead brother's clothing, we're going to have problems.

"True point," Tee says, giving the King a look. "And you know I'm no fan of the Hatter's. But if he hadn't gone into a Frenzy, the Walrus and the Carpenter would've killed us all, and you know it."

"Well, if he'd managed to hold his Frenzy back just a fraction of an inch, we might've been able to take the Looking-Glass. Instead, we spent our time trying to make sure he didn't murder us or any unsuspecting Topsiders who, by the way, are *moronic.*" Rab looks around the forest with his red eyes, like he's searching for eavesdroppers. "However did you survive eighteen years here? What a nightmare."

I raise an eyebrow because … come on. Underland is *fucked,* but then, so is Topside. When I first got to Underland, all I wanted was to come home. Now that I'm here, all I want is to go back.

"There's as much magic here as there is back home," Lar says, wingless and looking miserable for it. He plays with one of his red earrings and sighs. "It's just … trapped."

"Under a layer of toxic masculinity, divisive two-party politics, and bullshit?" I ask, but nobody gets the joke and anyway, I don't think I could find much funny with the Mad Hatter snarling and biting the air like that. "Can't he just turn into a flock of bats and escape those chains?"

"A colony of bats," the March Hare corrects, as the Duke scowls and stirs up fallen leaves with his tail. "It's called a colony of bats, and yes, he could. It's why we're watching him particularly close. If he does, and we catch even one, we can keep him from reforming. Even in this wild state of his, he knows that. He'll be cautious about what he does."

"So how do we fix this?" I ask, taking a few steps closer. My movement draws the Mad Hatter's attention again, and I pause, nervous titters taking over my belly.

"Blood," March says, but even he looks a bit … freaked-the-fuck out. "But he's so out of it at this point that I wouldn't advise offering your neck."

"What do you usually do with him when he's like this?" Dee asks, cocking his head to one side and studying the Mad Hatter with sapphire eyes.

"Usually? Because there are so many angels for him to feed from?" March asks, and then sighs, like he isn't purposely being a dick for once. He takes his hat off, digs around in it, and pulls out a lollipop in the shape of a … well, a top hat. He sticks it in his mouth and sighs again. "I'm bloody stumped. Sex, perhaps, could help?"

He looks right at me when he says that.

"Sex?" I choke out, and flush when all nine guys turn to look at me. That's a lot of um, big dicks, to satisfy. Fucking prophecy. Have I ever mentioned that I hate prophecies? "I'm not having sex with him; he'd bite my vagina off."

"Sex to soothe a beast?" the Savage Duke asks, and I notice the tiniest points of horns sticking out of his golden hair. The King reaches over and puts a palm over one, pushing it back into place as North snarls at him. "Is that what you're saying?"

"I'm saying, I have no fucking clue what to do. This is Raiden's first time in a frenzy. He's only twenty-eight years old, you know. Just a baby vampire." March leans back against the tree, sucking on his lollipop and playing with the brightly colored vials around his neck.

"He's twenty-eight?" I ask. *The same age as the King.* Not that old in reality, but … like, I'm eighteen, sooo … "When did he leave Topside for Underland?"

The Mad Hatter snarls and snaps, spattering blood all over me. It takes me a minute to realize where the blood is coming from: he's bitten his own tongue and lips. Ouch.

"Fifteen years ago," March says, raising a brow. "Why?"

"Just … never mind." I stand there for a moment, running my tongue across my lower lip. "So, what do we do?"

"You're the future Queen of Hearts," Red says, his face as stupidly arrogant as it always is. I still can't decide if I hate him, or if I'm fucking obsessed with him. "You tell us. We need the Looking-Glass back, we need to get home, and we need the Mad Hatter to cease his destructive behavior."

"*And*, I need to spend some time with my family." I give the Duke a *look.* "Also, please don't interact with my father or sister without expressly consulting me first. I already have enough shit to deal with regarding my two week absence."

"We were covert this morning, I felt," Lar says, his blue-blonde hair tousled by a supernatural breeze. Even here, in Topside, he has magic all around him. "The spell I cast on them should keep them from remembering too much at once. By the time it hits them and they remember all they've seen, we'll be gone." He pauses, soft blue eyes sliding to the side, like he can see something lurking in the forest. "Hopefully."

"My family's importance doesn't end when I go back to Underland." I give Brennin Red a hard look, meeting his dark eyes dead-on. "I want full access to the Looking-Glass."

"And look how well that went yesterday," he says, narrowing his eyes at me.

"This is a deal breaker for me," I snap, and I realize that I'm being way too fucking loud. We're in the woods, sure, but there are houses all along the edge of this park. Plus hikers, teenagers looking for places to fuck or make out, homeless people. We could be stumbled upon at any moment, and I have a man literally foaming at the mouth that I need to fix somehow. "I'll give the Hatter my blood."

"Allison!" Tee snaps, biting his bottom lip. He tucks his fingers into the front pockets of his borrowed jeans. Even with his purple eyes, and those gorgeous wing tattoos, he looks like a normal kid right now. To me, he's just as sexy like this as he was when he was channeling his angel prince side. "He'll fucking *kill* you if he gets the chance."

"Well, we can't just leave him like this," I say, taking a step closer to the Mad Hatter, wondering not for the first time who he used to be, where he came from. He must have a family out there somewhere, right? Somehow, in my mind, I'd imagined him as some old ass vampire from like two hundred years ago, someone whose family was dead and gone.

He might still have a mother out there looking for him, a father, siblings.

I reach my hands up, jerking back when Raiden snaps at me. His top hat is still on, lilting lazily to one side, and he's wearing the same clothes from the ball, only they're torn to bits and splattered in blood.

"Hey," I say, peering carefully at his face, "I know you're in there somewhere, the antagonistic, blackmailing prick that I met just last week." Sucking in a deep breath, I reach out and tap the side of his face while he acts like a feral cat and tries to bite me. I wonder briefly if I should offer up a wrist or something, but then I have the very real fear that I'll get my hand bitten off.

I trail my fingers down the Mad Hatter's cheeks, being careful to keep them out of reach of his teeth. When I slide them up and into his silky, black hair, I see his entire body go stiff.

"We need your help," I tell him, because I saw how fucking close we came to getting our asses handed to us already. And if the Walrus and the Carpenter have the Looking-Glass, they could be bringing even *more* reinforcements through. There is no way in hell we'll get it back without Raiden Walker.

"Be careful," Dee whispers, standing fairly close behind me. I'm guessing he's getting ready to yank me out of the way in case something bad happens. That's probably a good idea, too, because I'm still fumbling my way through this.

I have no idea what I'm doing here.

"Give him a blow job, and see what happens," March suggests, and I cast him a narrow-eyed glare. He just keeps sucking on his lollipop, a meaty chunk missing from his neck. I can barely stand to look at it, and I figure it must hurt like *hell*. We have to get Raiden up and running again before it can be healed though.

"I'm not giving him a blow—" I jerk back when Raiden bites at me again, blood and saliva flecking across my face. *Gross.* I swallow hard and put my hands on the Hatter's shoulders, kneading his flesh. It calms him down—but only a little. I run my palms up the back of his neck, tangling my fingers in his hair again. I give it a little jerk, and he snarls at me, but it's a different kind of snarl.

Fuck.

"He needs to be mated," the Duke says with a long sigh, cracking his knuckles. "Wild beasts, sated by violence, blood, and sex. That's what vampires and jabberwocky have in common. March, perhaps you'd like to take this on?"

March shrugs, swirling his tongue around his sucker and then running the sticky candy across his lower lip.

"You want *me* to suck his cock, do you?" he asks, and I turn to glance in the March Hare's direction.

"Have you done it before?" I raise a brow, but March just shrugs his massive shoulders. I have to say, he looks fan-fucking-tastic in that tight t-shirt. Fred used to wear it as a sleeping shirt, but March barely fits into it. It stretches across the wide expanse of his chest and shoulders. That, paired with the huge biceps hanging out of the shirtsleeves? Ugh. I can't even right now.

"This is your gig now, Doll." He stands up and moves away from the tree, letting the white stick of the lollipop hang out of his mouth. March holds his hand out, like he's presenting me with the Mad Hatter.

"Thanks for the non-answer," I mumble, pushing blonde and rainbow-streaked hair back from my face. I put my palms back on the sides of Raiden's face as he continues to snap and snarl. "Come on, Hatter." I pull in a deep breath and close my eyes, trying to summon up a little of that crazy energy I know I have inside of me.

"Miss Liddell," North warns, but I have to at least *try* this, right?

The power bubbles up from my lower belly like warm currents in a hot spring, spreading to my fingers and toes. I haven't tried to do anything with it yet, but it's there, just waiting for me to take hold of it.

"That's enough," Dee whispers, putting his hand on my right shoulder. I open my eyes and glance over to find him smiling at me, that angelic little half-smile that hides so much pain. "You're the Alice; there's no limit to your magic. If you take too much in, you'll have an episode like you did last time."

I exhale, and stop trying to seek the magic, instead focusing on letting it … I don't know, *percolate* through my fingertips and into the Mad Hatter.

"*Twas brillig, and the slithy toves, did gyre and gimble in the wabe.*" I hear Chesh purr when I start to recite his poem. Well, I guess it's not technically *his* poem; it was in the original book. But it does help, all of that nonsensical rhyming.

The Mad Hatter's pupils become slightly less dilated, and he makes this gasping sound that's unlike any of the noises he made before.

"Allison Liddell," he chokes out, blood leaking from the corner of his mouth. Raiden lets his head fall back against the tree, closing his eyes and breathing in short, harsh pants. "I need to be grounded."

"How do we do that?" I ask, reaching fingers up to touch the side of my neck.

"This doesn't seem like a particularly sound idea," Rab drawls, pulling out a cigarette to smoke. He looks at me with eyes that are far too bright, much too red, to be natural. But I guess contacts provide an easy explanation, right? I read this book once, called *Pack Ebon Red*, and there were a bunch of werewolves with unnaturally colored eyes. Anyway, they used the colored contacts excuse, and it seemed to work for them.

Real life is stranger than fiction though, right?

I clear my hair from my neck, and then lean in toward the Hatter, just as the Duke *and* Tee move forward to stop me.

With a wild growl, the Hatter's head pops up, eyes going wide, mouth going even wider. He latches onto my throat, making me cry out.

"Allison!" Tee screams, but the March Hare steps between us, whipping his lollipop from his mouth like a weapon, and pointing it at the angel prince.

"Back off, mate, and let nature take its course, yeah?"

Tee barrels into him, and the two of them end up having a scuffle on the ground near my feet.

I don't see much of it though, because my brain is flooded with a rush of blinding pain as Raiden's teeth penetrate my skin, just inches away from where he bit me last time.

"Don't," I whisper to North, holding up a palm as the Duke puts a hand on my shoulder. "Leave us alone for a minute." Grudgingly, he takes a step back, snarling all the while.

I whimper as the Mad Hatter bites down harder, making my knees weak with agony. I can feel him drinking both my blood *and* my magic, and at first, I'm pretty sure I'll pass out from the excruciation. But then his tongue begins to lap at the wound, and the pain slowly begins to fade to pleasure.

I bite my lower lip to stifle a groan, leaning into the bite and loving every moment of it.

More, more, more, God, MORE! I think as the Hatter takes and takes and takes, making me feel dizzy. He's groaning now, too, licking at my neck as much as he's sucking. The hot heat of his mouth against my skin feels too good, and I squeeze my thighs against a rush of pleasure, bumping into Raiden's body and feeling him thick and hard through his black leather pants.

My right hand drops down and caresses him through the fabric, drawing a wild sound from his throat that's nowhere near sane. But when Raiden finally lets go of my neck, I turn and meet his lips with my own, tasting blood but not caring. We kiss in a wild frenzy, my left arm sliding around his neck, my right squeezing his cock.

Our mouths work at each other, tongues tangling. His teeth nick me here and there, but it doesn't bother me; I love it.

My nipples get hard, and I wish suddenly that I'd worn that comfy t-shirt bra. As it is now, with no bra at all, I can feel them scraping against the cotton fabric, and it's turning me on. *Although I wish it were Raiden's fingers on my breasts instead.*

Eep! Did I just think that?!

But it's too late to stop it, this flood of violent heat and hormones, my lust unfolding like the petals of a dahlia. My need is thick and relentless and irresistible.

I unzip the Hatter's pants, slipping my hand inside and finding the thick, warm length of him. I take him in my palm, rubbing my thumb over the head of his shaft and finding him slick with pre-ejac.

Thank you again, Mrs. Davenport for teaching us about pre-cum. I guess there's a reason our school district has the lowest rate of teen pregnancy in the state of California. Sexual education, people. It's effective as fuck.

My fingers work Raiden up, his hips pumping against my hand as we kiss. And yet, he's definitely still in a Frenzy. When I pull back, his pupils are so big, they obliterate his orange irises.

My lips are swollen and sore, but tingling, as is my neck. I can taste blood on the back of my tongue, and I'm pretty sure we have an audience.

The Mad Hatter stares at me, his top hat hanging forward and partially obscuring his right eye, his black hair disheveled and sticking up. He's covered in red splatters, and his veins are bulging as he strains his muscles for escape. And what he might do if he *did* escape both scares and fascinates me.

I lick my lips and kneel down, my jeans soaking up the moisture from the wet dirt, and I curl my fingers around the base of Raiden Walker's cock.

My tongue flicks across the tip, but that only seems to enrage him. He bucks his hips and snarls, making the chains creak and groan as he strains with every ounce of his strength. I'm honestly shocked they're holding him in place. Maybe they're made of some sort of material that's like Kryptonite to vampires or something?

Doesn't matter.

All that matters is the salty taste of Raiden's cock as I wrap my mouth around him, pleasuring him with swirls of my tongue and pumps of my hand. I try to work him hard and fast, hoping an orgasm will be enough to cure him of his Frenzied state.

Note to self: next time you feed the vampire, angel blood, make sure you're ready for the fallout.

The delicious, delicious fallout.

Raiden moans and thrashes, scraping the chains against the bark of the poor old tree, thrusting in time with the movement of my hand.

With a screech of metal, he tears one arm loose, shackles hanging from his wrist as he grabs me by the hair and pulls me to my feet, making me gasp. Our mouths clash as he drops his hand down to my hip, squeezes me hard, and then slides his palm up to grasp my breast. The rough whorls of his thumb scrape across my nipple, making me moan in the most embarrassing way possible.

Hey hikers, bikers, and any potential wandering bums: I'm about to have sex in a public park! How exciting is that?!

But then, I also have a pretty impressive audience of *eight* other dudes who want to be my lovers or *are* my lovers, so there's that, too.

Raiden moves his hand from my breast to my jeans, unbuttoning and unzipping them before he starts to peel them down my hip. The shock of cold air on my ass is almost—and I repeat *almost*—enough to snap me out of my own frenzy, but then Raiden is thrusting two fingers into my hot cunt, and I'm just done for.

I shove my own pants down as he fingers me, struggling to maintain control in the rush of pleasure. Briefly, the Mad Hatter withdraws his fingers, so I can kick my pants down to one leg, and then, he sort of cups my ass and pulls me to him, propping my left thigh up with his right arm.

It's up to me to position our bodies, using my own hand to guide Raiden where I want him to go. I have a brief thought as to STDs and pregnancy—thank you yet again, Mrs. Davenport—but then I'm also young, and people make mistakes, so I move my hips forward and slide myself down Raiden's shaft.

We connect with a deep groan from both parties, and then his mouth is on my neck again, and my hips are working overtime. I thrust because he can't move much with the chains, working my pelvis against his body with wild, harried motions. It just feels too good, and I can't stop.

I don't even see the men around me, my eyes closed in bliss as Raiden feeds on my blood and we fuck at the same time. My shirt is caught up over my bare breast, so my hard nipple presses against his chest, rubbing against his skin through a hole in the black, frilly shirt he wore to the ball.

My orgasm starts the same way as my magic, like warm bubbles coming up from my lower belly, filling my limbs, making my head seem light and fuzzy. I whimper, feeling my body tighten up in pleasure, ripples of it pulsating down between my thighs, squeezing and caressing the Mad Hatter as I go.

It happens too fast for me; I want to keep on going. But then I'm coming hard, grinding into Raiden as fast and wild as I can. He latches hard onto my neck and then thrusts as best he can while chained, losing himself inside of me with a snarl, his right hand clamping onto my ass so tight, I bet he leaves fingerprints.

For a few moments, we just sit there, his mouth still on my neck, his body still sheathed inside of mine, and we just breathe.

"You back to normal, boss?" March asks after a little while, and I feel this hot flush creep up the back of my neck and burn my cheeks—the ones on my face. The ones on my ass are freezing cold from the winter breeze, and I pull away from Raiden with a groan, stumbling on the one pant leg that's still on, and finding myself held up by the cat's hand on my elbow.

"Steady there, Midnight Knicker Dancer," he purrs as I blush and furiously try to dress myself.

"Quite so, March," the Hatter says as he fixes his pants with his one free hand. Without having to be asked, March goes about unchaining him while the rest of the men stand silent and brooding. Well, most of them are brooding. Tee looks pissed; the King is full of quiet fury; the Duke is growling.

Sigh.

I fix my jeans and my shirt, and then start to wonder how long I've been out here, and if my dad and sister are looking for me yet.

"I need to get back to the house," I start, looking at anything but the faces around me. I end up focusing on a knot in a nearby tree.

"You can't leave," the King says, playing with his gloves. I have not forgotten what he can do when he removes them. He can literally fucking decapitate people with a *touch*. A goddamn touch. "We need to formulate a plan to retrieve the Looking-Glass."

"You're either deaf or dumb or most probably both," Chesh says, disappearing from view and reappearing as nothing but a big, white smile in the darkness. "She says she has *family* issues to sort through, you twat."

His smile disappears, and I feel a heavy but manageable weight on my shoulders before the Cheshire Cat fades back into view, licking his furry paw.

"One day, I'll remove your head from your body, and toss your corpse into the river," the King says, but I don't have time to listen to their bullshit.

"I have to go, but I'll be back. Do *not* come to the house unless I come and get you first, understood?" I give the men a look, but there's a lot of skepticism, even from Tee and Dee.

"We don't know where the Walrus and the Carpenter are," Dee says.

"Nor the Anti-Alice, the Gryphon, or the Mocking Turtle," Tee adds.

"Our only goal is to keep you safe," they both say in unison. Dee adds a heel clack and a salute on top of it.

"'The time has come,' the Walrus said,
'To talk of many things:
Of pain—and bones—and murdering—
The Alice and her kings—
And how her blood is boiling hot—
And tearing angels' wings.'"

For once, Tee actually takes Dee up on the bait and adds another stanza.

"'Don't wait a bit,' the monsters cried,
'Before we have our snack;
For some of us are starved to death,
And all of us are mad!'
'Yes, hurry!' said the Carpenter.
They thanked him much for that."

Tee pauses and bites his lower lip.

"We're not trying to rush you, Allison," he adds, rolling his shoulders like he's seriously missing his wings. "But it's life or death. Can we at least wait out on the sidewalk?"

"Make a perimeter, if you want," I say, tucking my hair back and feeling that uncomfortable wetness between my thighs, "just don't let anyone see you."

I turn away, but the Mad Hatter grabs my arm. I give him the briefest of glances over my shoulder and find those marmalade colored eyes watching me.

"I'll be nearby, if you need me," he says, but since we just fucked, and I don't know what to do with myself, I tear my arm from his grasp and head toward the backyard at a jog, the damn cat hitching a ride on my shoulders.

Women don't owe men sex—*ever*. And I certainly didn't *owe* the Mad Hatter anything, but I liked being his savior. What kind of fucked-up sex fantasy is that?

"It's okay to have fantasies, Allison," I murmur as I squeeze back between the dewy arborvitae. These fucking plants are *coated* in spiders; I mean it's spider heaven back here. Edith used to call them spider hotels when we were kids.

"We all have fantasies, Knicker Dancer," Chesh purrs as I sneak past my dad's koi pond, check to see if the back door is unlocked, and peep inside. I don't see anyone. "And we all have dark fantasies we don't wish anyone to know."

"Shh," I whisper, sneaking down the short length of hall to the staircase. I run up it and dig a bobby pin out of my pocket that I'd tucked away earlier, inserting it into the lock and slipping inside while praising gods above and below that I *made it.*

Of course, the water is ice-cold now, but I strip down and shove Chesh in the cabinet again, leaping in the shower and scrubbing my vagina, my armpits, my scalp.

The doorknob jiggles, and in just a few seconds, Edith is slipping into the bathroom and flinging the curtain back.

"Dad says I should leave you alone, because we don't know what trauma you experienced while you were gone, but I just fucking came in here and you were gone *again*." She puts a hand on her hip and gives me this saucy look, like she owns the damn world. Her fear and elation at my disappearance and eventual return are gone, and they're starting to be replaced with anger. "So what the fuck, Sonny? Were you out meeting your new boyfriend?"

"Can you get out and let me finish showering?" I snap, leaning back into the freezing water to rinse my hair. I don't care how bad my teeth are chattering or how intense my goose bumps are, I'm getting clean.

I turn around and Edith lets out a squeal, clamping her hand over her mouth and pointing at my ass.

Oh.

Oh, fuck!

I glance over my shoulder and find fingerprint-shaped bruises.

She flicks her eyes up to mine, and we lock gazes.

"Just don't," I snap as she sits down on the toilet and just stares at me. "You have no idea what's going on."

"All I know is that you don't seem very traumatized. In fact, you look better and happier than I've ever seen you before. You found time to get a new tattoo, and you're clearly getting some hot ass, so what's the deal? You just got tired of this shit hole?" She glances away, her blonde hair falling to obscure her face like a curtain. "Because I do, too. Sometimes, I think about running away like you did. Thing is, I never plan on coming back."

"Edy," I start, just before Dad knocks on the door.

"Are you girls okay in there?" he says, and I can still hear that tight strain in his voice. I'm hurting him, and he's already been hurt enough. *His infant daughter somehow showed up as a full-grown undead monster. As soon as he remembers that, he'll be in pieces.*

I shake my head to clear it, turn the water off, and grab my towel.

"We'll be out in a minute!" I glance over at Edith, who's still staring at me, and I try to figure out what to say. Clearly, we're having a moment, but all of my wisdom is Underland wisdom which isn't really all that wise at all. "We need to talk," I tell her, but she just shrugs her shoulders and looks away from me.

There are lines in her face that I swear were never there before; she looks hollow, sad, and broken.

And that makes me feel hollow, sad, and broken.

"Whatever," she says, standing up, but I grab her arm.

"No, we *are* going to talk later," I say, but she shrugs me off and leaves the bathroom before I can think up any insightful, sisterly shit to say.

And this is why I can't just run back to Underland, and leave my problems behind me.

I love those problems too much to let them go.

♦ ♠ ♣ ♥ ♣ ♠ ♦

Walking down the stairs to meet Dad … *terrifying*.

I'm literally fucking shaking, my palm squeaking as it slides down the banister.

"I'll be here for moral, emotional, or sexual support," Chesh whispers in my ear, giving it a little lick as I hit the bottom of the steps and then just *stand* there, like I'm a stranger in my own home

My dad is sitting on the ground with the side table next to him, trying to pry the lamp off the bottom of it.

"I don't think these sorts of pranks are funny," he snaps, finally freeing the lamp from the wood, but leaving a weird burn mark in its place. "And I'm tired of it, Edith."

"I didn't do it!" she shrieks, gesturing up at the ceiling and the fully set table hanging from it. "How do you think I'd even get up there?"

"I don't know, Edy, with a *ladder*?" Dad shoves the table back up, and rises to his feet, slamming the lamp down on top of it.

"It was probably Allison and her weird friends," Edith snaps, gesturing randomly in my direction. If looks could kill, the one she throws me … would *slay*. "One of her four new, stupid cosplaying boyfriends."

She storms over to the front door, throws it open so hard that it cracks the drywall, and runs out, leaving it open behind her.

"Should I go after her?" I ask, but Dad shakes his head, pushing his glasses up his nose with a single finger.

"She won't go far; we're leaving to visit your mother in an hour."

"We're … what?!" I ask, and my entire body goes cold. Visiting Mom is … it's hard and exhilarating both at once. It's like, I feel so many things when I see her that it's as if there are little explosions going off inside my heart and brain. She makes me happy, sad, angry, proud, but she also makes me feel guilty without even meaning to.

Because if I hadn't started dating Liam, the bad boy douche with the motorcycle, then none of this would've happened. But then, I know logically it's not my fault that he chose to victimize me, it's not my fault that he then chose to victimize Fred, and it's not okay that the courts let him and his cronies walk with no punishment.

I never asked my mom to kill them although I have to admit, I was happy when she did.

But she made her own choices, and now, I have to make mine.

Something occurs to me, this little *click* in the back of my mind that dries the words in my throat. *I have a dragon, I have a Rabbit with time magic, I have a vampire.* Could we not, then, feasibly break my mother out of prison?!

Could I not take her back to Underland with me?!

My skin goes cold and then hot, and I start to shake.

"Your mother was as worried about you as Edy and I were. Just because she's in prison, doesn't mean she doesn't care." Dad sighs and runs his fingers through his dark brown hair, making it stick up in all sorts of weird ways. "Knowing you were gone, and knowing there was nothing she could do about it, that almost killed her."

I feel that disgusting, white-hot wave of guilt wash over me, and reach my fingers up to pet the cat. Clearly, it's a little weird that I have a black and white striped cat on my shoulder that my father has never seen before, so I probably shouldn't be drawing anyone's attention to him, but I can't help myself.

Chesh rubs his furry face against my own, and I swear on a deck of cards, I hear him whisper a few words of that damn poem.

"*She took her Vorpal Blade in hand:*
Long time the manxome foe she sought—
So rested she by the Tumtum tree,
And stood awhile in thought."

I flush as my dad squints in the cat's direction.

"I didn't mean to leave, and I didn't mean to stay gone," I whisper, but the words come out all cracked and weird. Henry George Liddell just stares at me with brown eyes, blinking at me like he barely recognizes me.

"Where did you go, Allison?" he asks, his voice soft and understanding. He *wants* me to confide in him, but how can I? What can I really say? If I tell him the truth, he won't believe me. *Maybe I should just ask Chesh to shapeshift right now, and see what happens?*

Also, though, I'm a little scared of my dad having a heart attack.

"Dad, I just need you to believe me. Can you do that?" I sort of want to step toward him, but I stay standing still. He just stares at me. I don't think he knows what to do here, how to handle this.

"I believe you. You're my baby; I'll always believe you." But I'm not sure that he does. Instead, he turns away and stares up at the table on the ceiling. "Your sister's been acting out quite a bit lately. I don't know what to do with her anymore." He drops his gaze back to me, and there's a pleading in it. "Please, don't leave again. If you do, I'll lose you *and* your sister, I know I will."

Well, fuck.

Fuck, fuck, fuck.

"I …" I just stand there and stare at my dad. "I need a soda."

I head into the kitchen, grab a can from the fridge, and then escape into the backyard, sitting on the bench at the end of the deck near the koi pond. Rab purposely rustles the bushes to draw my attention over to him.

"We're going to see my mom," I whisper, cracking the can open with a hiss and just staring at the aluminum top. "So we'll be driving. I take it you guys don't have access to a vehicle?"

"We can boost one," he says, smiling coldly at me from between the leaves. "Once, I stole a billionaire's Bugatti."

"That's … really weird." I glance over my shoulder and find my dad pretending not to stare at me out the window while he washes dishes. I'll have to make sure to keep my voice low. "You don't have to steal a car; take Fred's."

"You want us to take your dead brother's car?" Rab repeats, his voice as cold as the air outside. But not emotionless, not cruel. He's just … wired differently, the White Rabbit is. "Where are the keys?"

"They're still hanging on the key rack near the front door. Car's parked in the garage. It's a 1991 Acura NSX in red that my brother *begged* for. It was his dream car." I put the soda down and run both hands over my hair. Just thinking about Fred's face when he got the keys … I want to break down and scream. "Just make sure you get back and park it before *we* get home. Also, it only seats two, so … draw sugar cubes or something."

"Just make sure you leave the King behind," Chesh says, licking his paw. "He always causes trouble."

"Two of us won't be enough to stop the Walrus and the Carpenter if they decide to come after you again; we all need to go." Rab pauses and glances out toward the street. "I'll find a different vehicle; don't you worry."

"Please don't use your time magic," I say, scrubbing at my forehead. I'm a tangled ball of emotions right now, and it *blows.* I'm not the best with feelings on a good day. Toss in the undead reincarnation of my sister, nine weird supernatural boyfriends, and my parents … and it's not really even an okay sort of a day. "An hour per second is not a good deal. You never know how much time you have left in life, and when the end does come too soon, you'd give anything for an extra hour with the ones you love."

"That's profound, Sonny," Rab says, tapping at his lower lip. He's wearing a black t-shirt and dark jeans with combat boots that, actually, I think are mine. Sometimes I buy them three sizes too big, so they look extra clunky with my pleated skirts. "But I doubt anyone would miss me if I were gone an hour or even a hundred hours earlier than the universe intends."

"See?" I say, grabbing my soda and standing up. "That's the sort of shit that pisses me off." I turn to head back into the house, but then Rab is just there, standing in front of me. "My dad …" I start, but then I notice that everything around me is frozen, even the leaves on the trees, even the damn cat. "Rab, don't."

He touches the side of my face with tattooed fingers, looking like, well, sort of a *kid* in his borrowed shirt and jeans.

"Why not?" he asks, running his thumb along the length of my jaw. "Does it bother you, the thought of me murdering myself with magic?"

"How old are you?" I ask, pushing his hand away. The thing is, once I've got hold of his arm, I don't let go. I just hold his wrist down by his side, teasing his pulse with my thumb. "I keep thinking you're all so much older than you are."

"We grow up fast in Underland." His breath feathers across my cheek as he leans in and puts his lips against my cool flesh. It's starting to sprinkle out here, a nice winter drizzle that I'd enjoy a lot more if I were inside with hot cocoa and a book.

"But in years …?" I start, and Rab chuckles.

"Twenty-six," he says, and even though he's a lot older than me, he looks like a sad, lost kid in that moment. He might be a bit of a psycho, but I'm also pretty sure he's lonely. I wish I could find out what his third form was; I wish that he could tell me. It's obvious he's under some sort of spell to keep him from saying anything. "Why?"

"You look sad to me." I let go of him and step back. "Now, make yourself scarce, and start time again. *Please* stop wasting your magic."

Rab steps forward and cups my face in both of his inked hands, wind tousling his dark hair. It must be more of that supernatural wind because nothing else is moving.

"Kiss me, and then maybe I won't be so sad anymore." He's joking, I think, when he says it, but not so much when he leans in toward me, brushing my mouth with his own. Heat sears between us, this flaming frenzy that burns my lips and tongue as we come together. For a man with such an ice-cold voice, Rab sure is hot to the touch. "Mm, Miss Liddell, you taste like cola, moonlight, and magic."

He pulls away from me, smirks, and then reaches up with his thumb to touch the corner of my mouth.

"Later, Sonny," he says, and then I blink and he's gone.

That fucker.

"Allison, are you ready to go?" Dad asks, opening the back door, a dish still clutched in his hand, like maybe he's afraid I'm going to take off again and never come back. *Shit.* I give my best smile, lift my soda to my lips, and hope to hearts that this meeting goes well.

Sitting in a quiet car with Dad and Edith? *Fucked.* Trying to explain why I think it's a good idea to bring a weird cat with gray eyes that's black and white striped like no natural creature on earth other than a zebra is … *lame.*

I keep glancing out the back window, trying to figure out where the guys are or what they're driving. It occurs to me that now would be a perfect time for the Walrus and friends to come after me. They could flip the car and kill me instantly. It really wouldn't take all that much effort. Hell, I bet the Anti-Alice could pick my dad's SUV up and chuck it down the highway.

Since I can’t very well carry a gun and a knife into the prison, I had to leave the Queenmaker and the Vorpal Blade with Tee. Makes me feel fucking naked, I’ll admit. *Please, please, please Underland foes, don’t start a brawl on Highway 101 today.*

"You talked to Mom on the phone, I'm guessing?" I ask, stroking my hand down Chesh's back. His nose is twitching and he keeps looking at the pocket on my rainbow hoodie like he’s on the hunt. Right. I feel something *move* inside the fabric and let out a little squeak.

"Of course I spoke with her," Dad starts as Edith glances over her shoulder to glare at me. I reach my hand inside my pocket and find a mouse. It nibbles the tip of my finger gently, and I purse my lips tight. I have no idea when Rab snuck in there; I wasn't wearing the damn sweater when I was outside.

And yet, I've got a mouse in my pocket now.

If he used that damn time magic again ...

"Why? Are you worried about something?" Henry glances at me in the rearview mirror as I wrap my fingers around the squirmy little mouse and give it a squeeze. His brown eyes are dark with stress, and I swear, there are new lines in his face that weren't there before.

Yes, Dad, I'm worried about seeing my mom who's currently incarcerated for murdering *a bunch of teenage rapists/murderers who tried to violate me and also killed my brother. And I'm nervous about having to explain to her why I disappeared for two weeks with no discernible reason, and no good explanation.*

That's what I'm worried about.

Nah, nah, not worried—fucking *terrified.*

"I'll get through it," I say as Edy scowls at me and turns back around.

"I've already got a cat and a mouse. Might as well have asked the March Hare to shift into a slithy tove, so he could come, too," I mumble when Edy flicks on the radio. She finds some grotesque pop song, and starts jamming in the front seat.

"Toves are enormous," Chesh purrs near my ear. "You could ride one, but you certainly couldn't put it in your pocket."

Rab-mouse pokes his head out of my hoodie, tiny pink nose going a million miles an hour. He looks around for a moment and then ducks back inside. I don't know what either of these guys thinks is going to happen: the prison does a pretty thorough check before you're allowed inside. I highly doubt I could sneak a mouse and a cat past security.

"Hey," I whisper, checking on Dad in the rearview mirror to make sure he's not staring at me. "Do you think we could break my mom out of prison and take her to Underland with us?"

"You have quite a few powerful men at your disposal," Chesh says on the tail end of a yawn—*tail*-end, hah. He curls himself around my neck and rubs cheeks with me. I think Dinah's in love with him. If she weren't spayed, I'd honestly be worried about her trying to steal him from me. How fucked-up is that? "All you'd have to do is … *ask*."

We pull into the parking lot, and Dad reaches to turn the radio off as he cruises, looking for a free space.

"I called your school while you were in the shower this morning." He's trying to be casual and failing miserably. "Your teachers have all agreed to provide you with make-up work, and the school has offered you an entire week to get everything back in order."

"Is that so?" Just the thought of going back to school … sucks. My senior year of high school … or Underland. There are bread-and-butterflies, toadstools as big as houses, and a kingdom that's falling apart—a kingdom that *I* can save. "Sounds good."

Now is not the best time to explain to my family that I want to leave again, but that I'll do my best to come back, too.

Fuuuuuuck.

I take off my seat belt and climb out, leaving Chesh on the back seat.

"Stay here until the coast is clear," I whisper, shutting the door and walking ahead of Dad and Edith, so I have a moment alone with Rab.

"If you're not driving the car, then who is? You, March, and Raiden are the only people that've been Topside, aren't you?" Rab pokes his white furry head out of my pocket and stares at me with red eyes.

"You worry too much, Miss Liddell." He sniffs the air, hops out of my pocket, and scurries underneath a parked car. I glance over my shoulder, but luckily Dad and Edith are too busy arguing to notice that I've just tossed a rodent out of my sweatshirt.

When they both flick their eyes in my direction, I get the idea that they're arguing about me.

A familiar minivan pulls into the parking lot and takes a handicap space not twenty feet from me. I pause for a moment, squinting through the window as I see our neighbor, Mrs. Jones.

"The fuck …" And then I notice the man sitting in the passenger seat. It's the goddamn Hatter. He tips his top hat at me, and winks those pretty marmalade eyes. *He was inside of you like, not even three hours ago.*

I choke on my own spit, and start walking faster, pausing near the door for my dad and sister to catch up.

"In a huge hurry or something?" Edy asks, purposely pulling out a pack of cigarettes and glaring at Dad, like she's challenging him to stop her from smoking one. "I forgot to leave these in the car. Mind if I smoke one before I put them back?"

Dad purses his lips, and then turns away, opening the door to the jail and stepping inside. Or is it a prison? Well, fuck if I know the difference. Anyway, so long as Mom is on good behavior, she gets to stay in low-security.

The building is as cold, sterile, and depressing as always.

I swear, as soon as my foot hits that concrete, those emotional fireworks start going off in my brain.

She can't even go into her dead son's room and smell his clothes or lay on his bed like you do sometimes. She is stuck here forever; you should've had the guts to do what she did before she did it.

We get in line at the desk, and I glance back at the tinted glass double doors that lead inside. They swing inward and I expect Edith, or perhaps a stranger, but instead … I get the Mad Hatter and the March Hare.

They don't even look at me as they sweep in, dressed in fresh clothes that I think might be Dad's. I mean, they could be Fred's, too. Dad seems to notice them as they walk by, and pauses.

"Isn't that my—" he starts as Raiden stops dead and turns to look at him, his eyes flashing bright.

"Nothing that either of us is wearing is recognizable to you," Raiden says, and then he smiles with sharp teeth, sweeps up the line with March following behind him, and cuts right to the front. The March Hare is snacking on a peach, juice making his lips and fingers sticky. He meets my eyes as I gape at the pair of them.

Raiden purrs something to the man at the front counter, and voila, he's heading toward the security check. He slips right in and disappears, leaving me to stand there gaping.

Fucking vampire voodoo bullshit, I think as Edith finally deigns to join us, smelling like tobacco and smirking like she owns the world. I literally cannot believe my dad is letting her get away with that. In the past, before Fred died, he would've taken her phone and laptop away, probably her makeup and shoes, too. There's no worse punishment for Edith than having to go to school wearing old ratty flip-flops or torn, stained sneakers.

Maybe Dad's just tired, because he simply hands over our IDs and then escorts us to security. After a totally fucked-up amount of groping from a female guard, I'm let into a small, carpeted room with vending machines and small, round tables that look like they belong in a junior high cafeteria.

Mom is sitting in the back of the room, arms folded across her orange jumpsuit, staring off into the distance like she's only half in this world. Maybe some part of her is wishing she were spirited away to, say, a place called Underland. After all, it's her family line, the Liddell line, that I got the Alice blood from.

I move across the patterned carpet slowly, trying to think about how it looks like hotel carpet, and not about how creased with worry my mother's forehead is.

She hears my shuffling feet and turns slowly to look at me, tears springing to her blue eyes. She looks just like me and Edith—blonde, blue-eyed, fair-skinned. We could be clones, the three of us.

"I don't know whether to hug you or slap you," she whispers, turning away for a moment. She squeezes her eyes shut tight, and counts to twenty. She's always had a pretty healthy way of dealing with stress. Used to drive Fred fucking nuts. He would scream and yell at her, and see if he couldn't break her out of her counting. Never worked.

I really miss Fred.

I sit down hard in the plastic chair next to her, only to be promptly enveloped in a tight hug. Two seconds in, and some asshole guard is already blowing a whistle and calling out her name.

"Hannah Reeve Liddell, hands to yourself, please." My mother sits back down in her chair and smiles at Edy and Dad as they approach, giving Edy's hand a squeeze and Dad's lips a kiss.

They sit down on the other side of me as my mother takes both of my hands between hers and looks me straight in the face.

"Where did you go, Allison?" she asks, as I hear a very familiar laugh, and flick my eyes to the right to see the March Hare sucking on a piece of licorice, twirling his tongue around the end of it, and *staring* right at me.

I purse my lips and resist the urge to flip him off as the Mad Hatter carries on a conversation with some old woman that's acting like she's known him for years.

My gaze swings back to Mom, and I realize that already, I'm starting to sweat.

"Underland," I whisper, and then I hate myself because I have no idea how that just slipped out. Mom stares at me, blinking pale lashes, and then sits back in her seat. She squeezes my hands again for reassurance, like she's simply waiting for me to explain.

I feel a little tug on my jeans and glance down to find Rab-mouse climbing my pants. He clings to the back of my calf, but doesn't move, hopefully out of sight of my family.

"Under-land," Mom says, trying out the word as two separate parts. "Is that a club? A … shelter? Allison, just help me out here."

My throat is so dry, I bet there are tumbleweeds in there. It makes me cough, and I take that as an excuse to buy myself some time.

"Could I have some money for the vending machines?"

"Seriously," Edith whines, rolling her eyes dramatically. "You were gone for like, a million years, and now you don't even have the decency to tell Mom where you went?"

Dad takes his wallet out and gives me a few dollars, and I stand up, my chair scraping across the carpet.

As I head toward the snack area, I can hear my family whispering about me.

"What are you going to tell them?" Rab asks, climbing up to sit on my shoulder. A visitor at a nearby table gives me a look, but I just pat the mouse's head and smile.

"He's a pet," I say, sweeping over to the machines. They're sort of sitting behind these giant, rusted cages. It's ridiculous, like the inmates would waste any of their precious visiting time to break into a stupid vending machine for an overpriced bottle of water.

I put my forehead against the metal, even though I know my family's probably staring at me.

"Well?" Rab asks, nibbling at my earlobe. "Don't you need a plan?"

"Plan?" I ask, as I stare down at a bottle of Mountain Dew Code Red.

Red.

Plan.

"Fuuuuuck." I bang my head against the metal a few times, and get a look from another prison guard. Err, correctional officer? Screw being politically correct anyway. "I had sex with Red and Raiden without protection."

"So?" Rab asks, giving my hair a tug.

"So, diseases? Pregnancy? Don't you have that sort of thing in Underland?"

"We have a sexually transmitted disease that turns a man's cock green with yellow spots. Women remain unaffected; the extra magic they carry protects them."

"That doesn't help me, Rab," I snap, and then notice the guard is taking a few extra steps in my direction. She probably thinks I'm talking to myself, that maybe I somehow slipped my orange jumpsuit and belong in this hellhole.

I shove the cash in the machine, grab my water bottle, and then head back toward the table.

"The King nor the Mad Hatter would have any diseases." It's funny how, even in this form, Rab's voice is ice-cold. "And that's not just me being optimistic: Raiden Walker is a vampire, therefore he's immune to disease. And the King, well, if he ever contracted anything, he has a curseworker on staff to cure him. Anyway, all of that is irrelevant as you most certainly consumed some of Raiden's blood during your little make-out session. His blood cures *everything*."

I squeeze my hands into fists, wishing I wasn't so pessimistic. I mean, I'm sure Rab is right, but how can I really know that?

"I Googled *Underland* on my phone," Edith smirks as I sit back down and unscrew the cap on my bottle. "The only thing that pops up is some weird reverse harem book. So, where the fuck were you?"

Reverse harem?

Right.

Like, say, me with all nine of my new fucking friends.

The atmosphere is tense and weird as I take a sip and look around at the three most familiar faces in the world to me. Well, in Topside anyway. I'm getting rather fond of Tee's and Dee's faces. Rab has crawled into the hood on my sweatshirt; I can feel him moving around as I suck down half the bottle in one go.

"I'm trying to be patient," Mom says, exhaling and counting to twenty again. "But I don't exactly have all day, Allison." She pauses and tugs at her orange sleeve, blue eyes watering again. "If you don't want to tell me, that's okay; I just … I'm glad you're safe." She glances up again. "And if there is something you want to tell me later—even if it's a *decade* from now—I'll believe you, baby."

"Mom, I wasn't raped." I scrub a hand over my face. "But thank you for trying to be understanding; I know you'd believe me." I drop my hand into my lap, and I just stare at her, listening to the Mad Hatter babble nonsense at a table three stations over.

Back when Liam and his friends attacked me, some people didn't believe me. They said I was a liar, a whore, that I wanted attention … or even worse. But my family believed me—and not just because Fred was there. They trusted me in my trauma, and I knew how precious it felt to be loved and believed by the people that were supposed to be there for me. It'd be a one in a billion girl who'd ever *want* attention from an assault accusation: people treat you like less than pond scum for it.

"You disappeared the same night a boy was murdered." Mom takes my hand in hers and rubs her thumb over my knuckles. "You're my daughter, too. Do you understand the implications of that?"

I just stare at her because, holy damn, she has a good point.

"I didn't kill him," I repeat, but what evidence is there to the contrary? I touched Brandon's body, was the last person seen with him, and the real culprit is a man who doesn't even exist in this world.

Wow.

I need to get the fuck out of here and … rarely, if ever, come back.

But I'm also not leaving my mom, not when I have a chance to save her from a life of imprisonment. Hell, I'll take Edy and Dad with me, and they can decide if they want to stay or go later.

"I know you didn't," Mom says, her voice soft and pleading, "but who did? Allison, you don't have to tell me or your father anything"—Dad makes a grunting sound but stays silent, pushing his glasses up his nose—"but if you don't tell the detectives *something*, then you might be in trouble."

"There were police at the house this morning," Dad adds, making me wonder how the guys got rid of the *real* cops in the first place. "And to tell you the truth, they were being entirely inappropriate: I asked them to leave."

Mom sighs and closes her eyes. She looks like she's about to have a nervous breakdown. I knew it; I fucking *knew* it. It's killing her to be trapped in here, locked behind iron bars, unable to help one of her kids.

My thoughts stray to the Anti-Alice, and I feel a sickness bubble up inside of me. I don't know how a deceased child becomes an undead monster, but that was Rhoda; I know it was. It makes sense, right? Someone of Liddell blood is going to take over Underland.

I just have to make sure that someone is me.

Dad is staring at Mom, watching her fall to pieces, but even though he's wearing an expression of sympathy, he doesn't look as bothered by it as I feel he should. The day Mom got sentenced, I thought he might kill himself. I've known since a young age that he loves her more than he loves me, and I'm okay with that. I think parents *should* love each other more; it gives the kids a foundation to stand on, and motivation for their own future.

But the way he's looking at her now, it's not enough. *I must be going mad*, I think as I shake my head and sigh. Dad glances my way, so casually that it's almost … not that casual at all. It's like he's studying me, gauging my reaction. Huh.

"I feel like I'm dying, day by day," Mom whispers suddenly, voice cracking. She sounds like shattered glass, just pieces of something beautiful that's now worth nothing. It kills me to hear her like that, but Dad … he just squeezes her hand like she's simply asked him for a tissue. There's no sparkle in his eyes, no violent starburst of love and affection glowing bright in his brown irises. "Henry, it gets worse every day."

"It'll be okay, Hannah. You'll get through this." *You'll get through this? Not 'We'll get through this'?* It's quite possible that I'm going mad, but something about that statement bugs me. And then, not three seconds later when I see my dad reach up and scratch his head, something occurs to me.

"How do you recognize a Rabbit?" I whisper, and I know that Rab can hear me.

"That's the special thing about us: you *don't*."

CHAPTER TWO

Whiskey and Water

As soon as we turn down our street, I see the detectives sitting in their car on the driveway.

It's not like I didn't know this moment was coming, but it *sucks*.

We pull in beside them, just as our neighbor, Mrs. Jones, parks in the driveway one over. The detectives are already climbing out, but so is the Mad Hatter, snapping his fingers and drawing their attention over to him.

"Ladies," he says, giving both women a sly smile, "you came here to interview Allison Pleasance Liddell and take her statement, but there's nothing worthwhile here. Wouldn't you agree?" He pauses and looks them both dead in the eyes.

That must be the trick, the eyes.

The detectives look at each other, and then back at me, while my dad blinks stupidly in the Mad Hatter's direction. The March Hare is right behind him, still fucking eating. He's always fucking eating. Guess it doesn't matter since he's as big as a Clydesdale and built like one too, all thick, rippling muscles and a nice white smile.

"Hello Allison," Raiden says as the King, the Duke, the twins, and Lar crawl out of the minivan. How the *fuck* they all managed to fit in there is beyond me, like some clown car type shit. *Underland* type shit. They all look rumpled, confused, and furious—in varying degrees. Except for Dee; Dee is always smiling. "Mr. Liddell."

Raiden looks right at my father, eyes flashing bright. He stares at him for a moment before turning to Edith, who's giving him this too-cool-for-school look with her mouth hanging half-open and one hand propped on her hip.

"Go up to your bedroom, and watch your favorite TV show with the volume turned up. Doesn't that sound nice?" Edith raises an eyebrow at him, and opens her mouth to give some sweet sass when Raiden steps forward and leans down, putting his mouth near her ear. His top hat slides to one side of his head as he tilts his face. "Please. For me?"

Edith blinks a few times, like she's as confused as the detectives. At about the same time they head for their car, so she goes for the front door and lets herself into the living room.

And then Raiden looks back at my dad.

"Would you like to go in and have a nice whiskey and water, perhaps?"

Rab-mouse leaps from my pocket, shifting as he moves; Chesh does the same.

That's … when I'm pretty sure I'm in some deep shit.

Lar draws a sigil in the air with his fingers, throwing up a shield between me and my father that glitters as pretty as his wings would if I could see them right now.

"Allison, what's going on?" Dad asks, turning to look at me with fear in his eyes. He meets my gaze through the layer of magic that makes up the shield, and I can see that whoever this is, he is really and truly afraid.

And even though it hurts my heart to see someone who *looks* like my father so scared, I know it's not him. I knew as soon as he looked at my mom. I fucking knew.

I take a step back, bumping into Tee's chest as Raiden grabs Rabbit-Dad, flipping his arm behind his back and slamming him into the car.

"We could rip you to pieces right now, feed you to the jabberwock." North gives a little snarl for emphasis as March puts his lips to Rabbit-Dad's ear and whispers. "Or you could tell us why you're still here, and what you want?"

"When I shot that little bitch cosplaying as Brandon," Rab says, appearing from behind me with a gun held up to his temple. He taps the barrel against his scalp a few times as he stares with red eyes into my not-father's frightened brown ones. "He said he needed more time. More time for what?"

"Please don't kill me here," the man whispers, staring right at me. "If my soul gets trapped Topside, I'll be eternally miserable." I wonder for a second if he knows something about souls and reincarnation that I don't, but then I see Rab rolling his eyes, and figure it's just conjecture.

Huh.

Well, he has a point anyway.

"Start spilling," Raiden says, stepping back and letting the man go. Rabbit-Dad's face shifts, like molding clay twisted by the hands of unseen gods. In just a few seconds, I'm looking at a completely different *woman.* She looks young, too, like … say, young enough to have just had her Inaugural Feast. Which, if she's changing into my dad …

"You ate my dad?!" I choke out, feeling my knees go weak. Chesh catches me around the waist and holds me up as I go ice-cold on the inside. Dad can't be dead. Just because this Rabbit *ate* some of his flesh doesn't mean he's dead, right? The Mad Hatter's still here and supposedly March can turn into him.

"Only a taste," the Rabbit says, cringing, her orange hair hanging in big ringlets on either side of her face. She couldn't look any less like my father if she tried, grabbing her fuzzy ears and pulling them down to cover her face. "I had a small nibble, a tidbit really, a *crumb.*"

The Mad Hatter slams his palm against the car window, making the Rabbit jump. Her ears are out, but considering we just had a guy cast a spell, hypnotized my neighbor, and saw my dad turn into a redheaded woman, I guess her black ears are the least of our concerns. If the HOA wants to write us a very sternly worded letter about the incident, they can fucking go for it.

I glance around, but our neighborhood is as vanilla and nine-to-five as it gets; everyone is at work or school it seems. I bet Edith was pissed to have to miss class today. Even though she's turning into a rebellious little fuck, she's obsessed with being the most popular, having the most friends.

"Where's my dad?" I whisper as the Rabbit's green eyes shift from side to side, looking for a way out. Unfortunately for her, she's surrounded by nine supernatural badasses … and me. I guess I'm a supernatural badass, too, in my own way? Of course, the Vorpal Blade and the Queenmaker are still with Tee; all I have is a massive well of magic that I can barely use without having a seizure.

"He's in Underland," the Rabbit says, twitching her nose.

"What nonsense is this?" the King asks, stepping forward and grabbing the Rabbit's skirt. He tears the fabric over her hip, and I swear, I'm about to punch *him* in the face. But then I see a string of diamonds tattooed on the girl's side. "You're working for the Clubs?"

"No! Never!" she gasps, slapping two gloved hands over her mouth. One of her black ears twitches and flops over her right eye as she repeats herself: "I'm *not* working for the Clubs."

"Then who?" the King drawls, gesturing with one gloved hand. When the Rabbit shows no signs of answering him, he very slowly and purposely begins to pick the fingers of one glove off, revealing his reddened palm. Hearts above, what he can do with that thing … "I don't ask questions twice, do I, Rab?"

"Once is just a drop in a teacup," he purrs, leaning in toward the girl and touching the side of her face with the barrel of his gun. "Twice is a whole damn pot. Answer the fucking question." Rab pulls back the hammer on his weapon and then brings the gun to his own lips, running his tongue around the tip of it.

Oh, for fuck's sake.

"I-I've been Topside for weeks. Months, really. Even longer before that, studying my subject." The Rabbit looks right at me. "I've come to care about you and your sister, Alice. Truly."

"Fuck you," I snap, pushing Chesh away, so I can take a step toward her. "Where is my fucking dad?"

"If you've been here that long," Rab starts, glancing over at the King. "Then I assume you came through when the Kingdom of Diamonds still had their Looking-Glass?"

"I did, and I left the real Henry George Liddell with your knight, you know. I assumed he'd be in good hands. Look, I know we'd all love to go back to murdering each other, but the King of Diamonds wants the Alice to succeed as much as anyone else. Not a single soul is interested in serving the Anti-Alice, the Walrus, and the Carpenter."

"My knight?" the King asks, clipping the two words off the end of his tongue. He closes his eyes for a moment and curses under his breath.

"I *told* you we shouldn't trust that saccharine sweet little kook," the White Rabbit says as Tee and Dee exchange a look.

"The White Knight has your father," the Rabbit-girl repeats. "I haven't the faintest what she's done with him."

"I knew they were both in on it, the Knave *and* the Knight," Tee snaps, and I feel like I'm missing something here. Is this the court gossip and inner politics they were all heavily hinting at? Why the King felt it was safer to sleep in the Suit of Hearts over his own chambers? "It's the entire fucking court I bet."

"Don't be pessimistic," Dee groans, rubbing both hands down his face. "It's just as likely to *not* be the entire court."

"Contrariwise," Tee snaps, but I'm too busy having my fucking mind blown to listen to their banter.

The White Knight.

Holy freaking shit.

Of course! Of *course!*

"We tested the dress, and we never touched the breastplate," I choke out, wondering how I could be so damn stupid. Chevalier Blanc and all her smiles, and she's a bad guy?! How?!

"You didn't, Doll. We bloody did," March says as Raiden grabs the Rabbit by the back of the neck and drags her back a few steps. He taps his fingernail against the pulse in her throat.

"What else?" he purrs. "Before I tear your throat out and bleed you dry?" The Mad Hatter flashes his sharp teeth, and my neck throbs. I can't resist reaching a hand up, pressing my palm against the spot where he bit me. The wound itself is gone, but I swear I feel a phantom throb of pleasure.

"I'm only here on reconnaissance, to watch over the Alice. I was here before she left, and I'm to remain until ordered otherwise." The Rabbit's black ears both fold down to cover her face. "Please, I was ordered to give my *life* for the Alice's. Surely, you can't fault me for that? My colleague—the Rabbit you call Brandon—he was a double agent. He was working for the White Knight as well."

"Ahh," Rab says, sounding very much like a crazy person. "*I just need more time for* … an explanation? More than likely, that's what he was going to say. Oh, and it's been bothering me for weeks, that rampant curiosity." The White Rabbit grins, but it's not a particularly pleasant sight. "Oops. I may have unnecessarily murdered someone then." He puts the gun back up to the Black Rabbit's head. "Wouldn't be the first time … or the last."

"It's an oops only if she's telling the truth. Could be lying. Off with her head," Brennin snaps, shoving his glove back into place and waving his hand. He starts off toward the house, but I grab onto his arm. His black eyes flick back to mine, and wild, violent heat surges between us. I feel like I'm choking on it.

"You are *not* going to kill her," I grind out, and Red sneers at me like I'm gum on the bottom of his perfect loafers. "I have more questions. And besides, she hasn't done anything to deserve death." I rub my forehead with the heel of my hand. *Not to mention the fact that we don't exactly have a guillotine handy in the garage.*

"You want to let her free? On the off-chance she's being truthful, on the slimmest knife's edge of possibility that she has your best interests in mind?" Red lifts his eyes to the sky and exhales. "I knew there'd be a learning curve, teaching you to be the Queen of Hearts, but my cards, Your Majesty. That is most certainly *not* an option."

He tears his arm from my grip, but doesn't make a move toward the house. Probably a good thing because I don't know how long that enchantment-hypno crap the Mad Hatter used is going to last on Edith; I hope it's a while because I really don't want to see her get into it with the King of Assholes and Hearts. *Dickhead.*

"I don't know about you," March says, snacking on some peanuts he's stored in his front pocket. I think he stole them from the prison. I think, believe it or not, he *did* steal them from the vending machine, metal cages be damned. Master Thief March, stealer of salted peanuts. "But I don't trust Rabbits." He looks pointedly at Rab.

"I don't much trust Rabbits either," he retorts, blinking red-red eyes. "But I do so wish to please the Alice. Perhaps, if the King and the Caterpillar will it, we could conjure up a truth spell?"

Lar rolls his eyes and reaches up to run pale fingers through his hair.

"If Sunshine and the King so wish it …" He catches my eyes as I lift my chin and square my shoulders. I don't want this woman dead. First off, even though I *know* that technically, she's a trained assassin, she looks scared out of her mind. Second, I've spent all day thinking she was my dad, and to be fair, she did an okay job of it. The only real thing she did wrong was not look at my mother with a lifetime of love in her eyes.

"I so wish it," I say as Brennin crosses his arms over his chest, narrowing his dark eyes, and staring right at me instead of the Rabbit.

Lar gives a small bow as Raiden steps aside, leaving the Black Rabbit standing in the middle of the driveway all by herself. She watches Lar wearily as he steps forward, looks her dead in the face, and then draws another one of his gold sigils in the air, flicking his wings forward in a violent motion and dousing the girl in gold, blue, and black glitter.

She sneezes several times, rubs at her eyes, and groans.

I move up to stand beside the Caterpillar.

"If we let you go, will you run?" I ask, but the Rabbit-girl is already shaking her head.

"My orders are—"

"Sure, sure, to keep the Alice alive at all costs. That's not what I asked." I cross my arms, mimicking the King's pose. "Will you run?"

"No," the Black Rabbit blurts, wrinkling her nose, like she didn't even make a conscious choice to respond. Reminds me of the Torrid Tea Party a bit.

"Are you working for the White Knight? Will you try to kill any of us?"

"Yes, and no," the Black Rabbit snaps, sneezing again. I notice as Lar stands beside me, fanning his wings, that they're not quite as bright and sparkly as they usually are. I wonder how many times he can cast that spell in a row, or if he has to wait for his wings to recover fully before he can do it a second time?

"Will you be a good sport and do your best not to make me want to kill you?" Rab interrupts, and I roll my eyes.

"Yes." The Black Rabbit's nose twitches. "And before you ask: no, I don't know what the White Knight is after. But I believe in her and her causes, and I serve *my* King with respect."

“Old Humphrey?” March chortles, like this is the most hilarious thing he’s heard all day. “You serve Old Humphrey with respect?! Thanks but no thanks, love—I’ll serve the Mad Hatter any day of the week.”

“The Mad Hatter is a nice second to serve, but I always choose winners first.” Rab and March stare each other down, and I swear to fuck I can feel energy crackling between them. I step forward, blocking them from glaring at one another.

There’s this heavy weight settling around my shoulders that makes me shiver. *Dad is missing, the White Knight is a traitor, and I stupidly wore that breastplate without questioning it.* Ugh. Tee notices the shift in my mood, coming to stand beside me and offering up the Vorpal Blade and the Queenmaker. I take them in my hands, squeezing the leather holsters tight. If I hadn't pulled the Vorpal Blade on the Knave, then … fuck, maybe I wouldn't be standing here right now?

I can't decide if that's a bad thing … or a good one.

Now I know my father—poor, boring Henry George Liddell—is trapped in Underland.

He must be having a goddamn heart attack.

"There were moments," I start, thinking of Edith's scolding this morning, "when you really did act like my father." I look up at the Rabbit's eyes, as green as fresh grass, and she smiles at me. She's nice, too nice. It makes me wary of her in a way I should've been wary of the White Knight all along.

"I studied him for a very long time," she whispers, eyes twinkling, nose twitching. "And any good Rabbit knows: once you take on a form, you take on *all* aspects of it." She reaches out a hand to cup the side of my face in a very … motherly, or should I say *fatherly*, sort of way.

I stumble back and into Chesh, his fingers curling around my shoulders and giving them a little squeeze.

"Shall we go inside, little Knicker Dancer?" he whispers, and I nod. I can't imagine standing outside with such an entourage is a good idea. Hypnotism and spells and bullshit will only go so far and then before we all know it, we'll be strapped down in a government laboratory while scientists cut us apart to see what makes us tick.

I'm sure the US government would *love* to get their hands on killing machines like the King, or the Duke, or the Hatter.

The Rabbit-girl pauses for a moment, and then follows along, holding the front door open and letting us all in before she locks it and watches as Lar casts a simple spell, drawing gold sigils across the wall with his fingers.

I can hear Edith's TV blaring from upstairs and let out a small sigh of relief as I collapse onto the couch, putting both hands over my face.

What a clusterfuck.

What a serious, goddamn clusterfuck.

"You don't think the White Knight would hurt my dad, do you?" I ask, glancing over at the King. He's sitting in my father's armchair like it's a throne, gloved fingers curled around the ends of the armrests.

"I haven't the slightest," he says, exhaling and closing *his* eyes, like he's the one who's about to have a panic attack.

Dinah trots into the room like nothing's at all amiss and starts to rub on Chesh's legs. I'm a bit pissed at her for, you know, marking me as the Midnight Knicker Dancer with cat-cheek pheromones, but I guess I'll get over it.

There's a part of me that wonders how much fun Chesh and I might get up to if we did a bit of midnight knicker dancing together …

"How did the Mocking Turtle and the Gryphon get Topside if they didn't have access to the Looking-Glass?" I ask, trying really hard not to look at the Mad Hatter. How did I just fuck that guy?! What the hell is wrong with me?

"Could be a Rabbit-Hole we don't know about?" the Duke says, perching on the bricks of the fireplace and crossing his legs like he's quite the delicious little gentleman. I miss his horns and … oh wait, his tail *is* out, slapping against the carpet in a rhythmic pattern and drawing my attention to the fact that this isn't actually my mom's rug at all. It's been replaced.

Guess even time magic can't help a bunch of dudes clean silver Looking-Glass goo out of a Persian rug, am I right?

"There are Rabbit-Holes that come Topside?" I ask, thinking about how I fell down the original hole. So, if I were in Underland, and I found one, would I still fall down? Or would I fall up? Because certainly one can't fall down to get to one place, and then fall down yet again to go back up?

"There used to be dozens," Dee says, sitting down so close to me on the couch that he has to drape one of his legs over my own. Can't say that I mind much. He's a bit of sunshine in all this Underland darkness. "But when the Kingdoms began to war after the Riving, most of them got wiped out along with the Looking-Glasses."

"A shard, perhaps?" March asks, moving into the kitchen and sniffing around until he finds the fridge. He opens it, and I can hear him mumbling under his breath about what a *bloody interesting machine* it is. When he comes back, unscrewing a jar of maraschino cherries, I give him a look.

"A shard? Like the Vorpal Blade?"

"Sure," he says, his ears sprouting from the top of his head like fuckin' daisies. As I glance around, I see the rest of the men *unfolding,* so to speak, bits of wonderful Wonderland-Underland nonsense unfolding from their bodies like, well, *magic*. "A shard can't be used to travel back and forth like a Looking-Glass, but, in the right hands, it can be manipulated."

"How so?" I ask, forcing myself to my feet with a groan. If the other men are going to, uh, hang with their junk out, so to speak, then Tee and Dee may as well. And I know that junk means *dick and balls,* but let's just lump in wings, horns, and tails, too, okay?

First though, I'm going to make some fucking coffee.

Delicious, delicious coffee, how I've missed you.

"You can sacrifice a shard to make a Rabbit-Hole, can't you?" Chesh purrs, taking off his jacket, unbuttoning his shirt, and sliding his body along the back of the couch cushions. Dinah follows him and curls into a tiny, black ball in the small of his back.

"So rumor has it, but it's never been confirmed," Lar says, standing there in his borrowed suit. I wish he were still wearing the red half-jacket from the ball. If everything works out, and we all get back to Underland and live … well, I don't think happily-ever-after really exists in Underland, so let's just say *live,* then I'm having a goddamn fashion show with these men.

They owe that much to me, to say the least.

"Well, thanks for telling me now," I joke with a roll of my eyes, "so then if it happens later, it's not a plot hole, am I right?" Dee and Chesh chuckle at my stupid joke, but everybody else looks at me like I'm insane. But also like they like that I'm insane, so I guess that's good.

As I pass into the kitchen, I see one of the two photos in the house that have Rhoda in them. I've walked by them so many times, it stopped occurring to me to even notice them. If I mentioned my deceased sister to anyone at school, they really *would* think she was a plot fucking hole.

I'm sorry, but I don't think about my dead baby sister all that often. It's not that I'm heartless or that I don't care, but she passed several years before I was born, died at just a few days old, and my parents never talk about her. Rhoda just doesn't cross my mind often enough.

"I can't believe you all knew," I say, but how can I be mad at them? I could tell when they talked about the Anti-Alice that something was wrong. Tee got so pained whenever he mentioned her; he was worried about hurting me. "You all *knew* that Rhoda was the fucking Anti-Alice."

"It had to be someone of Liddell blood," Tee pleads, almost like he's trying to apologize to me. He comes to stand near the entrance to the kitchen as I prep the coffee maker. "It had to be, and there was no one else."

"How did someone who died so young, like, *grow up*?" I ask, putting my hand on the side of the machine as it makes its familiar crackling and bubbling sounds. I grew up with the sound of fresh coffee being made every morning; I think most of us do. There's something about that smell, that sound, the tired half-smile on a parent's face as you come downstairs and they're dressed in a robe and holding a mug.

My heart spasms, and I close my eyes. I can't think about something happening to my dad or I won't be able to function.

When I open them again, I find myself staring at the stupid koi pond outside the window. Well, no wonder 'Dad' was so disconnected these past few weeks. It wasn't even Dad here at all.

"Necromancy," Tee says softly, coming into the kitchen to stand beside me. He gives the coffee maker a weird look, but doesn't say anything. "I don't know much about it. After the Riving, nobody really practices it anymore. Well, nobody but the Carpenter."

I move over to the cabinet, open it, and search around for Fred's favorite mug. It's white with a cartoon version of Britney Spears on the front of it. He wouldn't drink a hot beverage unless it was in this damn cup. And honestly, Fred was the original 'Midnight Knicker Dancer'. I would peep into his room and see him in his boxers, lip-synching *Oops! ... I Did It Again* into a pencil or a rolled-up piece of paper as his microphone.

God, I miss him.

I take the mug and slam the cabinet door. I'm taking this freaking cup back to Underland with me if it kills me.

And, considering our current situation, it very well might.

I pour myself a cup, add a generous dollop of *Pumpkin Spice* creamer—I'm a basic bitch and proud of it—and head back into the living room with Tee following behind me. I stare across the room at the Rabbit-Girl.

"How did *you* know the Anti-Alice was Rhoda?" I ask her, realizing that I haven't offered anyone coffee. I'm not exactly the consummate host. "Sorry, does anyone else want a cup?"

"Black, please, two sugars," Rab groans lying on his back in the middle of the room with his gun on his chest. "March, don't you drink coffee as well? Or, with your acidic personality, would you prefer drain cleaner?"

"Aren't you funny? I haven't spent near as much time fucking around Topside as you, but I'll have a coffee, please." He sniffs the air as he pops a bright, red cherry between his lips, sucks on it, and then uses his tongue to pull it into his mouth. "And I'll have some of that cinnamon-squash stuff you put in yours."

"Cinnamon-squash, huh?" I ask, staring down into my coffee. I guess if you really think about it, pumpkin *is* a squash, and surely there's cinnamon in there, too? Fucking weird, though. "Sure. What about you … uh, what's your name? Wait, wait, you probably have a nickname like … Orange Hair? Freckle Face? Something descriptive and weirdly obvious?"

"This is the Black Rabbit," Lar says, giving me a sardonic little smile. He finds this all amusing, good for him.

"Oh, the Black Rabbit, huh?" I study her dark ears and move into the kitchen to start pouring coffee. In my head, I was already calling her the Black Rabbit. Bully for me. "You want coffee, Black Rabbit?"

"Yes, please, just as your father likes it," she says, voice soft as she stares at me. "When you take on a form, you take on their attributes. I told you that. I knew Rhoda because … a parent knows their own child."

"Yes, well, and it's common knowledge in the Underland underground that the deceased Rhoda Caroline-Anne Liddell is the Anti-Alice. Don't forget that little tidbit of knowledge," Rab adds in his bones-and-ice voice.

I make the coffee, hand two of the cups to Tee, and take the third to the Black Rabbit.

She accepts it gratefully, staring at me with this odd happy-sad expression on her face. If only she'd started to fall in love with Mom, I'd have never known. Maybe the men already did? I have no idea.

"I'm glad you're safe," she tells me, but I just roll my eyes. If she's a Rabbit, surely she could've joined in the fight? Either she was too busy trying to keep her cover or else she inherited my father's general skittishness. I can't keep looking at her, thinking about her taking a bite out of my dad's body, chewing up his skin and flesh, and *swallowing* it.

I shiver.

"So what do we do now?" I sit back down on the couch, still purposely refusing to look at the Mad Hatter.

"We need you to either *track* or *attract* the Anti-Alice," Raiden says, adjusting his hat and fucking *staring* at me until I have no choice but to look right at him. A flush colors my cheeks, and I see this slow, wicked smile curve over his perfect lips. "Or would you like to go upstairs and have a repeat of this morning first?"

A mean smile takes over my mouth this time as I look at him, blue eyes staring into orange.

"Remember how you said you'd make me beg?" I quip with a sassy little tilt of my head. "Well, it was the *other way around*, bitch." I lean back into the cushions and sip my coffee as Raiden raises both brows, gives me a slow little clap, and then goes right back to smirking.

"I've always been into strong, capable women. You did not disappoint, Little Alice." He licks his lips as I sneer at him.

"You're a fucking perv," I growl, hiding my blush in Fred's mug. *If he's a perv, then I am for sure one, too.* I was the, uh, aggressor in that moment, wasn't I? I mean, the Hatter was chained to a freaking tree.

"A perv who knows how to track the Anti-Alice and the Looking-Glass," he says, perching on the edge of the chair where the March Hare has taken up residence. He has this look of pure bliss on his face when he sips his coffee. Must be the pumpkin spice creamer. Guess March is a basic bitch, too.

"We should set up some sort of perimeter," Lar says, stepping into the center of the room with his wings unfolded in all their glittering glory. It occurs to me that Edith could come down at any time, but I've got more to worry about than just a freaked-out little sister. Anyway, can't Raiden just vamp-hypnotize her again?

"A perimeter, and then a nap," Chesh says, rubbing against my shoulder.

I know he's just being a cat, but he has a good point.

"Let's get some rest," I say, scrubbing at my face. I feel emotionally *and* physically exhausted. "Can't kill the bad guys when you're falling asleep sitting up. Even the coffee isn't helping."

"Yes, get some sleep," Lar tells me, looking at me with those blue-blue eyes of his. "And we'll watch over the house, Sunshine."

"*Some* of us will watch over the house," North growls, standing up and offering me his hand. "We'll sleep in shifts."

I reach over Dee to set the mug on the side table, the one where the lamp was stuck upside down just a few hours ago. And then I take North's hand. I expect him to pull me to my feet. Instead, he yanks me up and then sweeps me into his arms like he's some sort of golden-haired prince charming. Only, my prince charming has horns and a tail.

"Maybe a shower first? I'm pretty wound-up; I don't think I'll be able to fall asleep yet," I say, but then … I don't even remember getting up the stairs.

The world was wrecked and withering,
wrecked and full of fright:
The Alice did her best to take ...
In the horrid sights—
But this was hard, because it was
The corruption of her life.

The moon was bathed in blood and hate,
It blotted out the sun
The kings had got no business there
Because their time was done—
'It's very rude of them,' she said,
'Slaughtering everyone!'

The blood was red as red could be,
The bones were dry as dry.
You could not see a star because
Gray clouds were in the sky:
No angels flying overhead—
There were none left to fly.

The Walrus and the Carpenter
Were stalking close at hand:
They grinned maniacally to see
The forming of her band:
'If this were only cleared away,'
They said, 'it would be grand!'

'If nine big men with nine big cocks
Presumed to hold her near,
Do you suppose,' the Walrus said,
'That we could get her clear?'
'I know it,' said the Carpenter,
And gave an awful leer.

'O Alice, come and walk with us!'
The Walrus did beseech
'A pleasant walk, a pleasant talk,
And mend this bloody breach:
We can still slaughter nine or more,

So say goodbye to each.'

The eldest angel sneered at them,
And many a word he said:
The stubborn monarch closed his eyes,
And said she won't be dead—
They had to let the Alice think
Else his Queen would soon bleed red.

But nine young suitors hurried up,
All eager for their treat:
Their hair was brushed, their faces washed,
Their clothes were clean and neat—
And this was good, because, you know,
To date the Alice was a feat.

For all the monsters followed her,
They craved her bloody corpse;
So thick and fast the hordes attacked,
Just more, and more, and more—
All hoping for a bite or two,
Her men must prevent gore.

The Gryphon and the Mock Turtle
Watched on from perches far,
And then they contemplated hell
On kingdoms so bizarre:
The Queenmaker their only hope
Against a ragged scar.

'The time has come,' the Walrus said,
'To talk of many things:
Of pain—and bones—and murdering—
The Alice and her kings—
And how her blood is boiling hot—
And tearing angels' wings.'

'Don't wait a bit,' the monsters cried,
'Before we have our snack;
For some of us are starved to death,
And all of us are mad!'
'Yes, hurry!' said the Carpenter.
They thanked him much for that.

'A bit of flesh,' the Walrus said,
'Is what we chiefly need:
The deaths of Alice's true nine
Are very good indeed—
Ready, my Anti-Alice, dear?
We can begin to feed.'

'Not on us!' Heart soldiers cried,
Lifting their weapons high,
'Oh, such madness, we can't let be
'else we will surely die!'
'That would be fine,' the Walrus sighed,
'Bloody corpses I do spy!'

'It was so kind of you to come!
You must taste very nice!'
Says Carpenter to Alice then,
'I'll cut another slice:
I wish you were not quite so live—
I'll have to kill you twice!'

'It seems a shame,' the Walrus said,
'All nine of them are dicks,
After fighting them so long,
We will not kill them quick!'
The Carpenter said nothing but
'My dolls just need a lick!'

'I weep for you,' the Alice said.
'I deeply sympathize.'
With head held high, she sorted out
The plan of their demise.
Holding Vorpal Blade in hand,
Before their widened eyes.

'I vanquish thee!' screamed Alice then.
'You've had a nasty run!'
She slaughtered all her enemies.
Then cheering there came tons—
And that was scarcely odd, because
She'd beaten every one.

I snap awake with a gasp, clawing at my throat, moonlight falling across my bed and turning the bedspread into a quilt of prison bars. It's like I'm sleeping under a cage of moonlight, and I don't like it. I scramble out from between the twins, waking Tee up in the process.

"Are you okay?" he asks, and I nod, picking up the cat off the end of the bed—well, one cat, sorry Dinah but you're staying here—and heading for my bedroom door.

"I'm fine, I just … I need to breathe." I head out onto the upstairs landing, pause to check on Edith—thank fuck, she's still sleeping—and then tromp down the steps like a galumphing troll. The Mad Hatter, the March Hare, and the King are sitting in the living room, staring at me while I descend.

I pause for a moment, watching them watching me.

Fucked two of the three, good for you, Allison. That thought draws my attention over to March, sitting there and fingering the colored vials around his neck while he sips some coffee. His poisoned knife saved my life, maybe Tee's, too. I should probably thank him. Instead, I can't stop repeating the verses of that damn prophecy in my head.

'The time has come,' the Walrus said,
'To talk of many things:
Of pain—and bones—and murdering—
The Alice and her kings—
And how her blood is boiling hot—
And tearing angels' wings.'

I shake my head as I walk, and then start to whisper the Jabberwocky poem aloud instead.

"Twas brillig, and the slithy toves
Did gyre and gimble in the wabe;
All mimsy were the borogoves,
And the mome raths outgrabe."

Chesh leaps from my arms, shifting in mid-air. He must've stripped down while I was sleeping because he's shoe-less and shirtless again, wearing nothing but unbuttoned black slacks. I can see his happy trail which kind of, uh, makes me happy, too.

"*Beware the Jabberwock, my girl!*" he hisses, making little clawed hands at me as he grins that kitty grin of his. "*The jaws that bite, the claws that catch!*" He curls his fingers around the back of my neck and gives me a little scratch on the back of my scalp that feels too good for words. "I told you it was catchy as fuck."

"It is pretty goddamn catchy," I murmur as I open the door to the back deck and find Lar sitting by himself on the steps, wings folded over his shoulders like a cloak. He glances back at us, blue-blonde hair dancing in a real breeze this time. The movement of his hair matches the sway of the orange and yellow leaves on the trees, autumn's last goodbye before winter inevitably wins. "Hey Caterpillar."

"Sunshine," he says, patting the wet deck next to him. I don't really care that it rained; I just need to get away from that dream and that prophecy. How I even dreamed it all without ever hearing the end is beyond me. "Are you alright?"

"I dreamed the rest of the prophecy," I say, staring out at the dewy grass as Chesh lays down beside me and puts his head in my lap, black and white striped ears twitching as he closes his eyes and starts to purr. I end up petting him without even meaning to do it. "But I don't see how that's possible when I've never heard it before."

Lar smiles, and I can't help but wonder if he had something to do with it. I decide there's no harm in asking.

"Did you infiltrate my dream or something? I have no idea what sorts of powers you actually have, so …"

"I'm simply a wise, misunderstood seer," he drawls, pulling a pipe out of his pocket and lighting up. He blows smoke into the dark air and swirls his finger around, making little shapes dance around. I see a walrus, and I see a skinny monster of a man that looks like the Carpenter.

"That's all you are, huh?" I shiver a little and wrap my arms around myself. A moment later, the Caterpillar tucks me under one of his wings and pulls me close. Despite their delicate, almost tissue paper-esque look, Lar's wings are remarkably strong. Warm, too. Tucked against him like this, I smell tobacco and blueberries, this comfortingly musky yet sweet scent that wraps around me and soothes the butterflies —pun intended—in my stomach.

He doesn't answer me, just keeps smoking and smiling as Chesh makes biscuits in the air, sheathing and unsheathing his claws. I can't believe he can turn into a housecat *and* a beast big enough to make a lion shit its pants.

"The prophecy never mentions *who* the Alice's nine are supposed to be. I mean, it vaguely mentions angels, for example. And the King, but it doesn't exactly tell me who I'm supposed to trust. The only foretelling that seems to mention them at all is the one you gave me, at the Torrid Tea Party."

"The prophecy was never meant to be an exact prediction of what's to come. The future is like … a river with tributaries and streams branching off into the infinite." Lar stares straight ahead, into the darkness of the woods where I fucked the Mad Hatter. His blue eyes are shadowed, but the porch light catches on his hair, turning it into a kaleidoscope of blue and gold. "All we can do is guess. So the prophecy doesn't mention the nine, because the nine have to be chosen by the Alice, and nobody *knew* who or when the Alice would appear."

"What about your little, uh, poem?" I ask, trying to remember the words. Lar's smile turns sultry as he glances down at me, taking another drag on his pipe, and then offering it up to me. I'm not sure that I want to see any visions if he comes up with them, but ignorance is never something to be proud of.

With a sigh, I take the pipe and pull in two big lungfuls of sweet-smelling smoke.

"*How doth the Alice prophesied,*" he begins, drawing designs in my exhaled smoke and making … well, *me.* "*Improve her all-male harem. She dates assassins, kings that bleed; princes, angels, dragons!*" As he quotes, he draws more of the shapes with his fingers. They're crude little art pieces, like animal crackers or something, only vaguely recognizable shapes, but I like them anyway. "*How cheerfully her kitty grins,*" he continues, drawing Chesh's big, white smile in the air as the cat himself gives a real-world replica. "*How neatly shifts her rabbit. She welcomes winged seer men in while dating thieves is habit!*"

Lar bats his left wing, sending the smoke figures dancing into oblivion.

"Yep, that one," I say with a slight smile, lifting up a finger and catching the very last twirl of the Alice smoke figure. "That spells you guys out pretty clearly, don't you think?"

"It's a prophecy based on you, specifically," Lar continues, glancing over at me, his red earrings catching the porch light and glittering like rubies. "But it's only a guess. Sunshine, you are free to choose your nine. We're only here because we want to be."

"You all want something from me," I say, but it's not a judgment or even a concern. It just … is. "Tee wants a partner; Dee wants a savior; the King wants a queen." I look down at Chesh, brushing my fingers through his dark hair and rubbing at the fuzzy tips of his ears. He cracks one gray eye to look up at me.

"We were the most likely to fall into place as your nine, but it's all up to you. Choose nine; choose one; choose none. You make your own destiny. We'll fight beside you, regardless. You'll have nine warriors, one way or another." Chesh purrs and winks at me before closing his eyes again, kneading the air in sheer bliss. Typical cat, only pops into the conversation to state their opinion.

I sigh and lean against Lar's shoulder, just because it's solid and comforting and he smells freaking delicious. I love the way he moves his hands and fingers, like he's always halfway to casting a spell. And his mouth, slightly parted, like he's this close to asking a cheeky question.

Lar takes the pipe back from me and continues to smoke it, pausing when the White Rabbit steps out onto the deck. I glance over my shoulder and see him standing there, dressed in pajamas he must've borrowed from Dad: plaid flannel pajama pants and a white top. What is it with straight dudes and plaid flannel pajamas? I swear, they all own a pair.

"Anything?" Rab asks, taking a few steps forward and peeling Lar's wing off my shoulder. He peers into the blue center, squinting hard. "Well, fuck my dick and call me *Rabbit*. Nothing at all, really?"

"Nothing yet," Lar replies, voice strained. I wonder if he's still hurting from whatever the Mocking Turtle did to him. Just so long as I don't have to hear that creep's voice spouting nonsense in my head, I'm calm. He threatened Edith; he tried to poison me with victim-blaming bullshit. "But if I were the Walrus, I would take my entourage back to Underland, and I would send an army back here to protect the Looking-Glass."

"We have to hope we have support in Underland then," Rab says, but he doesn't *sound* particularly hopeful. I keep staring at him as he pulls a pack of cigs from his pocket, lights up, and folds his bunny ears back like a pair of scissors. "If the Court can just keep more assholes from coming through …"

"Or prevent *these* assholes from going back," Lar says, nostrils flaring as he gives a sharp exhale. "If the Mocking Turtle and the Gryphon came through a Rabbit-Hole in

Underland, then they can certainly send reinforcements; that doesn't do a damn thing for them if they can't get back."

"Good point," Rab says, smoking his cigarette with a thoughtful expression on his cold features. '*Kiss me, and maybe I won't be so sad anymore.*' Ugh. Why'd he have to say that? Now I almost feel sorry for the guy. "I just keep hoping they come to us, on our terms."

"Mm." Lar makes a sound in his throat, but he doesn't seem convinced. "Why would they? They have the Looking-Glass which means they have the upper hand. They'll wait for us to come to them."

Nobody speaks for a while, the only sound an occasional hoot of an owl or the chitter of some far-off rodent being hunted.

That's what I feel like right now, a mouse scurrying around in the crunchy winter-dead leaves.

"Could I perchance try this coffee that you speak so highly of?" Lar asks with a little side smile.

"I want to try a *meow-ka*," Chesh says, grinning brightly, and I realize he's making a mocha pun. Laughter bubbles out from between my lips before I can stop it, and I grin, patting him on the head.

"How do you even know what a mocha is?"

"The Rabbits used to deliver goods from Topside," he explains, sitting up and yawning, flashing two sharp kitty fangs. His tail whisks back and forth, and he smiles so big it looks like it might just topple off and into the grass. Happiness fills my chest like helium in a balloon, making me feel light, like I'm floating.

A green and white toadstool pops up, and then a pink one. They sparkle and glitter, and the pink one's spots bloom into white roses.

"You're carrying around a lot of extra wild magic from Underland," Lar says, glancing at them and then up at me. "You must've picked up some free magic from the storms."

"Is that … good or bad?" I stare at the glowing toadstools and then look back to Lar, Rab, and Chesh. All three of them are smiling at me.

"Gooood," Chesh purrs, one tiny fang hanging over his bottom lip. "It's very fucking good."

"Blow the Walrus' dick off," Rab says, grinning and tossing me a wink. "That's what it's good *for*."

"Although it won't help against the Anti-Alice," Lar whispers, looking at me like he's not sure whether he should even let himself like me.

He's looking at me like he thinks I might soon be ... dead.

"The Anti-Alice," I repeat, feeling a cool breeze tease my hair. I stare out into the shadows for a moment before rising to my feet and offering each of the two men a hand. They both take one, and each other's too, so that when they stand up, we make a little circle. Rab steps close and inserts himself into the group. "Shall we make some coffee then? Raid the cabinets perhaps? I'm starving."

"Just so long as you're in bed before this clock strikes two," the White Rabbit purrs, touching a red clock on the back of his wrist.

"Deal," I say with a little smile.

I don't end up in bed until way, way, *way* after that.

Someone's erection is stabbing me in the back, but I feel warm and cuddled, and I don't particularly want to move.

It's Dee.

"Good morning, Allison-who-isn't-Alice," he murmurs against my hair. My head is tucked under his chin, and there's a furry black and white tail smacking me in the face as the Cheshire cat watches birds flittering about outside the window. "Did you sleep well?"

"I did, until your dick poked me in the spine and woke me up."

"Oops," Dee chuckles, pressing a kiss to the side of my neck that feels too damn good for words. He works his way up my shoulder to my throat, drawing a small moan from my lips that I'm too tired to suppress. I open my squinted, tired eyes the rest of the way and stare out at my childhood bedroom with equal mixtures of discomfort and relief.

I know where I am; this is where I've always belonged, where I've always felt comfortable. And yet, this is now one of the last places in the world I want to be. Everything is as it should: my laptop sits on my desk, my clothes hang in the closet, and the decorative Alice clock my mom got me when I was eight ticks away the seconds with a gentle *tock-tock-tock.*

Everything is normal, calm, usual, and yet nothing is.

My father is in Underland; my mother is in prison; my brother is dead; and the deceased big sister I'd nearly forgotten about is trying to kill me.

"I need to check on Edith," I grumble, but I lift my head up to see Tee standing near my dresser, folding clothes. Generally, I leave clean clothes on the floor in heaps or, if I'm feeling productive and responsible, I jam them into my dresser drawers and play a game to see if I can get them to shut without any bits of fabric sticking out.

"Already did," Tee says, putting a shirt that says *Stomp the Patriarchy!* with a unicorn on it into an overnight bag. "The Hatter gently asked her to go back to bed; she's safe."

I sit up and lean into the pillows, closing my eyes against the bright sunshine and doing my best to stop thinking about all the evil things M.T. said about Edith. I would rather die than let something bad happen to her.

"Are you packing me a suitcase?" I ask Tee and he pauses, looking down at the half-packed bag.

"I don't want to take liberties assuming I know what you might want to bring, but …"

"He's being optimistic," Dee says, nodding his chin at his brother and ruffling up his blue-streaked black hair with his fingers. "And he thrives on doing chores and accomplishing tasks; if he can't do that, he gets unbearably unbearable."

"You are unbearably unbearable, and I find your company insufferably insufferable."

Tee grabs another item out of the drawer … and ends up with a pair of lacy panties in his hands. They're crotch-less, too. I've never worn them; I lost a bet to Edith once and she dared me to purchase them when we were at the mall. She thought it'd embarrass the hell out of me, but it didn't.

I mean, it didn't *then*.

It's embarrassing the hell out of me now.

"Oh," Chesh says, shifting and snatching the underwear from Tee's hand before the poor, blushing angel can figure out what to do with them. "These are lovely! And so practical, too." He purrs and rubs his face on the lacy bits.

"You're a fucking perv," I growl, taking them back and balling them up in my fist. "Leave my knickers alone."

"Show me a midnight knicker dance *please*," Chesh yowls, falling back into the pillows and covering his face with inked hands. "I'll join in, too. I'll boogie with you, Alli Cat." He pulls his hands down and grins, teeth shining white in the sun. "Did you see what I did there? So *claw*-ver, am I. The claw-verest one of them. Alli Cat."

"Do not keep making up nicknames for me, please. For the love of Hearts." I take the panties with me and scoot to the end of the bed to look at Tee. He's stopped packing, and is now simply standing there and staring at me. "Why are you packing me a bag? Are we in a hurry?"

"We might be," Tee says softly, looking at me with tired purple eyes. "I just … in case we have to do something drastic, I wanted you to have some items from this life. I know what it's like for everything to change in an instant. I'd give an arm just to have the bag of marbles I played with as a kid, or my favorite hunting knife, or … anything really."

I push up to my feet and open the bag, looking inside to find a strange assortment of items.

There's my diary, a tiny glass cat figurine, a few t-shirts, a hairbrush, Fred's Britney mug, Edith's earrings, Dad's watch, and one of Mom's scarves.

"I tried to get one item from each family member," Tee says as I look up at him and find his amethyst eyes focused on the window and not on my face. I look back down at the bag and keep digging, finding a few family photos on the bottom. Most of them have me, Edith, Fred, Dad, and Mom in them. One of them has my parents … and Rhoda.

I look up again.

"Thank you, Tee." He nods as I zip the bag up, patting the side of it with my palm. I glance up and find my own reflection staring back at me. If something living climbed out of it, I'd sure as fuck notice. "If the Looking-Glass was in my living room all along, how did Rabbits pass through without anyone noticing?"

"Well," he begins as Dee scoots up to join us, and the Cheshire cat bats at strands of my hair with a paw … err, a hand. A tattooed hand with *claws.* "Until recently, there were several Looking-Glasses scattered around Underland. Not anymore."

"The Kingdom of Diamonds *and* the Kingdom of Hearts each had their own, but Brennin Red made a deal with the Diamonds to use their mirror. The other half was held in a museum basement; we had connections there." Tee pauses and Dee takes over, their voices so similar and yet so different. One man is sunshine, the other rain; the earth needs both to thrive.

"The Hearts have always kept their Looking-Glass under lock and key." Dee smiles at me. "We needed to see who the Alice was going to be; we couldn't chance influencing it in any way by coming over here and snatching or disturbing a Liddell. Nobody else knew your family had the other half of the Hearts' Looking-Glass."

"What happened to the others?" I ask, glancing between the twins. They exchange a long look, blinking in unison before they both flick their gazes down to stare at me.

"They were shattered," Tee says, his voice thick with melancholy. "To prevent the Walrus and the Carpenter from getting Topside."

"And yet, somehow they got Topside anyway?" I ask with a long sigh. Chesh sits and puts one of his legs on either side of me, sweeping up my hair in his fingers and combing it with his claws. After a moment, he starts to braid, and I get all these jittery butterflies in my tummy.

"Remember how we said the Riving happened because there was such an imbalance in your world?" Dee asks, blinking big sapphire eyes at me. "Topside is thick with toxic masculinity; that sort of evil and hatred fuels the Walrus and his followers. He's a big, ignorant, mindless idiot who feeds off pain and suffering. He *thrives* on the dissent, infighting, and mass suffering in your world."

"Keeping him from coming here was Underland's number one priority. For once, the four kingdoms weren't at war with each other," Tee adds as Chesh finishes braiding my hair, snapping his fingers and pointing with a single claw at my dresser. Tee picks up a rainbow-colored hair tie and hands it over. "If he gets a foothold in this world, he'll use the imbalance here to his advantage; men have all the power. He can purposely set off a Riving on this side of the Looking-Glass."

"But we don't have magic the same way you do in Underland," I say, feeling myself start to sweat. Tee nods, and Dee takes my hand in his.

"No, you don't. That's why I tried to warn you: if it affects Underland, it affects Topside and vice versa. In Underland, the women had all the magic, and the Riving destroyed us. Here, men have all the power; it'll destroy your world just as surely. Maybe in a different way, but that's what the Walrus wants. Upset the balance on this side, and we feel ripples down below. He wants to weaken the remaining three kingdoms, so he can get his hands on them."

I lean back into Chesh and try not to puke.

What a way to wake up.

"Even if we do get the Looking-Glass," the King says, surprising me by stepping into the room dressed in his clothes from the ball. Just seeing that stupid red and white outfit makes me think of the jeweled codpiece that was underneath it. "And we pass through it, we'll have to hope we still have enough support on the other side to keep it safe."

He blinks his dark eyes at me, and I feel my throat starting to close up.

"*My queen, my Alice.*"

Eek.

Did he really say that shit to me?!

"Can I talk to you for a minute?" I ask, standing up and pausing. I need to talk to Brennin, but … also, wings. If we get attacked, I need both twins at full strength. "One sec," I say with a snappy little hip pop. I turn back to Tee and put my hands on his shoulders, looking up at his too-serious face, his dark eyes, that almost perpetual half-frown. His lids get heavy as I lean up on my tiptoes, pressing my mouth against his.

He tenses up, but only for a moment. When he puts his palms on my hips, and squeezes, I feel a wild *thump-thump-thump* in my chest. My body leans naturally into his, and I find that we just fit together, like two pieces of a very complicated puzzle. My whole life, I've felt like a square peg being forced into a round hole. When I'm with the twins, I feel like I'm with my tribe.

Tee's wings unfold from his back with a rush of energy and heat, the chains falling to my bedroom floor in a useless lump. Now that I'm aware of the magic emanating from him, I feel like I could just bask in it, like Dinah sunbathing on my bedroom windowsill.

Our tongues touch, tentatively at first, and then we're just kissing each other as fast and hard as we can. Tee wraps me fully in his arms, tugs me closer, and then wraps me in his big, beautiful wings with their black and purple feathers.

As we pull back from one another, a single amethyst feather floats gently down between our faces.

"Can I tell you a secret?" he whispers, leaning down to put his mouth near my ear. His warm breath makes me shiver, and I can feel a very distinct bulge in his borrowed jeans. Have I mentioned how delicious Tee and Dee look in jeans, by the way? And did I mention that the ones Tee's wearing today are not Fred's: they are mine.

Boys in girls' pants. One of my biggest fucking turn-ons.

"Tell me," I whisper back, putting my ear against his chest and breathing in his scent. He smells like crisp autumn air after a rainstorm, like standing on the top of a mountain after a blizzard's just passed but the sun has yet to come out.

"I do—" he chokes out, voice cracking. He has to clear his throat to speak again. "I do get jealous sometimes, Allison." I lift my head up, but Tee is already pulling back, pressing a kiss to my forehead and stepping away. He folds his wings together behind him and just watches me.

We make eye contact, and Tee smiles.

I don't think he has any idea how much he's just turned me on with that statement.

"For the love of Hearts," the King snarls, but I ignore him, moving over to Dee and straddling his lap. He groans and covers his face for a moment with his hands, flashing the tattoos on the backs of his arms.

"I can't fight the Carpenter with a boner," he groans, but I peel his hands away and throw my arms around his neck, kissing him on the mouth with all of the passion that's swirling around inside of me. I don't have to work Dee up into being hot and bothered: he's already there. I feel his cock beneath me, hidden inside some borrowed pajama pants—also mine, black with little red hearts—and nibble his lower lip as his wings burst forth and scare the shit out of poor Dinah.

She takes off out the door with her tail fluffed behind her.

"Can we stay like this forever?" Dee asks, nuzzling me. I give *him* a kiss on the forehead, and then stand up, only to see the Cheshire Cat watching me with big, gray eyes.

"Where's my kiss?" he asks, flattening one ear back against his head and giving me a look that reminds me of Puss in Boots in the movie *Shrek 2*. Only this time, the look is coming from a pierced, tattooed, shirtless Adonis in the flesh.

"Don't you dare kiss that filthy cat," Brennin says, which, obviously, only makes me want to do it more.

I climb over Dee and onto the bed, covering Chesh with my body. My knees are on either side of his hips, my palms on either side of his face. He looks up at me without blinking, and then grins, teasing one of his lip piercings with his tongue.

"Cheshire Puss," I whisper, leaning down toward him. His tail curls around my waist and tugs me closer, drawing an oomph from me as our bodies come together. And holy *shit*, Chesh feels good pressed against me like that, every inch of my body sandwiched with his.

"Knicker Dancer," he whispers back, and then I'm slanting my mouth to his, tasting him, running my tongue against his tiny fangs. His tail strokes along my back and down to my ass, cupping and squeezing me, making me chuckle in the same breath as I moan.

His hands slide from my back, nails raking my skin gently through my clothes, and since I know the King is watching and hating every moment, I wiggle against Chesh and make him groan. My left hand sneaks up, my palm scraping over his nipple.

There's something about the way he tastes that reminds me of cherry tarts, and he smells like pine forests and soft earth, with just a hint of wood smoke. He's an expert kisser, too, this Cheshire Cat. I bet he ties cherry stems into bows and all that.

When I pull away from him, he catches onto my lower lip and gives it a quick nibble.

"I told you I could perform, Alli Cat," he says, purring the last word as he strokes right down my ass crack and along my, well, *other* crack with his tail. It feels good, too, so good that I almost don't have the strength to stand up.

If we were alone right now …

But alas, we're not.

I push up and scramble away from him, sliding off the bed and giving the King a very triumphant sort of look. He stares down at me like he couldn't give a fuck less, but there's this twinkle in his obsidian eyes that tells me otherwise.

"Three men with hard-ons, and you with wet pajama pants. Am I supposed to be impressed?" he asks as I flush and frown, and grind my fucking teeth. "Come." He turns and sweeps from the room like he's back at Castle Heart instead of parading around Suburbia, USA.

Brennin Red actually lets himself into my mom's study and then holds his arm out like he's ushering me into his personal chambers, reaching up to adjust his lazy crown.

Cue the eye roll.

He moves to shut the door, but I put a palm on it, curse myself out under my breath, and call out down the stairs.

"Raiden!"

There's a brief moment of silence, and then I see the Mad Hatter step out of the kitchen, balancing his palms on his cane. His hat droops over his right eye.

"Yes, my dear?" he drawls, the one eye that I *can* see sparkling brightly.

"Could you come upstairs, please?"

He takes the steps at a gentleman's pace. And by gentleman's pace, I mean slow as fuck. When he finally does deign to step into the study, I almost slam the door in his face, just for good measure.

March is at the bottom of the stairs, snapping the end off of a chocolate bar, and grinning at me. He winks as I close the door and put my back to it.

This is sort of the last conversation I want to have right now.

"Already looking for a threesome?" the Mad Hatter asks, staring me down like he thinks he can intimidate me with a cocky attitude. *I made him beg,* I think, steeling my shoulders and crossing my arms over my chest.

"Imperial fiddlestick," the King snorts which is probably about the most hilarious curse I've ever heard in my life. He leans back against my mother's bookshelf and stares me down with eyes like obsidian. "Surely after one coupling with you, the Alice is quite done."

"I, uh," I start, exhaling, knowing there are more important things right now than erm, sexual worries. But I can't help myself. I'm just a little bit anxious, a little bit OCD. "I talked to Rab about sexually transmitted diseases—"

"Diseases?" the King asks, wrinkling his nose up and staring down at me with a baffled expression on his handsome face. "Don't be ridiculous. The King and Queen of Hearts are pillars of good health." He tilts his head to look at me and his crown slides across his bloodred hair. Oh. Crown. That's right. Mine's around here somewhere. I should probably take it with me. "Did you give me a disease?"

"No! Not me, I …" I start as the King looks at me like he wants to strangle me, and the Hatter looks on bemusedly. "I was worried about you, actually." I glance toward the sideboard against the dark red wall, and the sea of framed photos resting there. Rhoda isn't in a single one of them; Fred is in all of them. "Never mind. What I wanted to ask about was, uh …" *You're a big girl Allison. If you're old enough to fuck, then you're old enough to ask hard questions.* "About pregnancy."

"Pregnancy?" the King asks, as Raiden laughs. "It's a tad early to discuss heirs, isn't it?"

"Perhaps not, with nine to make. Best start early," Raiden Walker says, giving me a vampire grin as a tiny bat peeks out from under his hat, staring at me with dark, round eyes. When he sees the look on my face, he just loses it, doubling over and tapping his cane on the wood floors. "Oh, Alice, how delightful! What a question!"

Brennin Red still looks confused, fiddling with his gloves and staring at me with flared nostrils, like he isn't sure what to make of me.

"Fine, don't tell me," I growl, getting frustrated and embarrassed at the same time. "I believe I can make an educated guess." I start to leave, but the King puts a gloved hand on my shoulder and stops me dead in my tracks. Even with a glove between us, I like the feel of his fingers on me. There's power in his touch, power that draws me in like a bee to a flower. I just hope that *I* am the one with the power to sting.

"Do you mean that you think you can find out the answer?" the Mad Hatter asks, standing up straight and adjusting his hat. His marmalade colored eyes glow briefly, reminding me of that wild, snapping frenzy he was in just yesterday.

"I do," I hastily reply, pushing the King's hand off my shoulder. "At least—at least I mean what I say—that's the same thing, you know."

"Not the same thing a bit!" says the Hatter. "Why, you might just as well say that 'I see what I eat' is the same thing as 'I eat what I see'. And Alice, I do like to eat what I see." Raiden grins at me, his gaze flicking to the thundering pulse in my throat. All of a sudden, I don't feel like the aggressor here, but the prey.

All of a sudden, I don't feel safe in this room with these two very dangerous men.

My heart pounds, and I swallow past a tightness in my throat.

"Or," Raiden continues, moving toward me as the King watches on. The Mad Hatter pauses next to me and tucks a few loose strands of rainbow-streaked hair behind my ear. "You might just as well say that 'I like what I get' is the same thing as 'I get what I like'." He leans down and nibbles my upper earlobe. "And I *do* always get what I like, Alice."

"I made *you* beg," I whisper, but I can feel my body trembling, my blood heating, my loins burning with sudden need. Burning? Okay, so that makes it sound like *I* am the one with the STD. Which is, of course, nonsense because I've had *two* separate tests at the local clinic, just in case. I read a book called *Groupie* once where the main character was given an STD by her cheating ex; I was not about to let the same thing happen to me.

"Did you?" Raiden asks, biting me so gently on the ear that there's no pain, just pure pleasure. "You act as if *you* making me beg precludes *me* from making you beg. I think that's false logic, don't you, Alice?"

"I …" I can't breathe all of a sudden, and my lids feel heavy, and my knees are weak. Raiden grins, pulling back slightly.

"You *might* just as well say that 'I fuck when I'm horny' is the same thing as 'I'm horny when I fuck', eh Alice?" The Mad Hatter pushes me against the bookcase, and I let out a small sound. My hands come up and rest on his shoulders as he slides his jabberwock-horn cane up the inside of my thigh. He teases the already wet crotch on my pj pants, and makes me moan. "So, *are* you horny, Alice? Will you beg?"

"I'm not begging for shit," I whisper, and even though I know the King is in the room with us, that we have far more important things to do, I can't help myself. When Raiden puts his mouth to mine, I kiss him. All of that wild, primal fire from this morning rises up inside of me, and my body screams for them both.

His tongue teases my own, and his fangs make little nicks that he plays with mercilessly, bleeding and pleasuring me at the same time. I feel like both food and sex for him, satisfying his most primal needs in one go. The Mad Hatter drops his cane to the floor with a clack, and replaces it with his fingers. He slides his pale hand into my pants, teasing his middle finger along my slick front.

"Beg me," he demands, but I'm too proud.

"We need to have an adult talk," I whisper, but Raiden has moved his lips to my neck. He nibbles my skin gently as the King saunters over to stand beside us. He stares down at the pair of us with lust flaring in his dark eyes.

"You want to know if you might be pregnant?" the Mad Hatter asks, sniffing the blood welling from the two pinpricks on my throat. "I suppose there are ways to find out."

"Ways?" I choke out as the King touches his fingers to my bloody neck. His scar pulls at his beautiful face as a wicked slash of a smile takes over his lips.

"Well, certainly. But they take time. Ask the Caterpillar for a test, later on. In two weeks, perhaps, if we're all still alive then."

"Two weeks?!" My eyes widen as the Mad Hatter's fingers slide into my slick heat. "That's …" I can barely find the strength to speak. "That's the same as a Topside pregnancy test."

"Not all solutions are convenient, Your Majesty," the King drawls, pushing me forward and into the Hatter. He steps behind me and begins to kiss the other side of my neck. I have two, tall, cruel men on either side of me … and yet, despite the horror of our current situation, I can't help but like it. Love it, really. "Not all problems wrap up in little bows."

His gloved hands slide around to my front, cupping my breasts through my tank top and giving them both a hard, greedy squeeze.

"Do you want to see what I can do with my bare hands?" Red whispers against the back of my scalp. "When I'm not taking heads anyway."

"I …" There are no words for how I'm feeling right now. Guilty, scared, confused, horny, desperate—all at the same time. The room has a musty, unused sort of smell, like an old library. The scent mixes with the Hatter's blood-and-tea smell, and the King's flower-and-thyme aroma.

"Beg," Brennin repeats, sliding his hands down my body. Then, with agonizing slowness, he begins to remove his gloves. First, one falls to the floor in a flutter of white, and then the other. His palms are red as he pushes up the front of my shirt and presses them to my bare belly. "Beg, Your Majesty."

"Eat shit." My voice comes out in a weak tremble, like a lost soul drifting in an autumn breeze.

"Do you want to know why I was sucking the King's blood before?" Raiden asks, pushing a second finger inside of me. I can't keep my eyes open; my lids are too heavy. I sag back against the King, and he takes me in his arms. "Do you, Alice?"

There's a warmth coming from the King's palms, and despite the fact that I'm moderately terrified he's going to rip my head off with his magic, I relax into it. That warmth soon becomes a pleasantly scalding heat, like dipping cold feet in the bubbling waters of a hot tub. It's as if I can feel each one of Brennin's fingerprints inside of me, little strings of magic infiltrating my blood, calling my own power to the surface.

"I do," I whisper, feeling like I'm falling again, tumbling down the Rabbit-Hole into the arms of these two men.

"Because …" Raiden adds a third finger at the same time the King moves his warm, red hands to palm my breasts. When he flicks a thumb across either of the pert pink points, I lose my shit. Hot, wild magic takes over every inch of my body, drawing me toward Brennin Red's hands. It's like that day in the garden when I tried to use my power and was overwhelmed by it, except this time, there's someone more experienced to guide me in my exploration. "I like the taste of it, you see."

"He likes the taste of it," the King repeats, moving his left hand down and covering the Hatter's. Raiden switches out two of his three fingers, so that Brennin can take their place, thrusting two of his own inside of me. "Please, he likes the taste of *me*. I do dare say that truthfully."

"He does dare say," Raiden repeats, "a bit of blood, a kiss, a hug, what more could I well need?" The two men share a kiss over my shoulder that does nothing to quell the need between my thighs. Oh no, I *love* it.

"You two are lovers?" I ask, but Raiden shrugs his muscular shoulders in response.

"We like to share, Alice." He kisses my lips next, and I love that I can taste Red on his mouth.

"You like to share, what?" I repeat, swallowing hard, and then bucking my hips violently when the Hatter runs a thumb over my clit.

"We like to share *Alice*," Raiden repeats, and then he's kissing me hard enough to steal my breath away. "Now beg."

"Fine, *fuck me*," I snap, and it's more of an order than a beg, but it does the trick. The men withdraw their hands, and the Mad Hatter uses his *boot* to push my pants down my legs, crushing the crotch to the floor with his thick sole. "But you have to use protection." *Woo. Not sure how I even managed to get that out.*

"How dreary," Brennin drawls with a sigh. But he does remove two small paper packages from his robes.

"What are those?" I whisper, and Brennin quirks a red eyebrow at me.

"They are known as *condoms*," he says, with all the arrogance and authority of a King.

"You carry condoms around in your pocket?" I start thinking about Tee, and how he just *happened* to have lube on him when we needed it.

"Safe sex is important, don't you think? One should always be prepared." Red hands over one of the packages to the Mad Hatter; he opens it to reveal a white condom with little red hearts all over it. How quaint.

The men suit up, and then I find myself being lifted between them. My legs wrap around Raiden, his hands under my ass, while Red curls his beneath my thighs. I feel weightless with the two of them on either side of me.

The King of Hearts, and the Mad Hatter, the biggest, baddest mercenary in Underland.

And they're both … mine? Or they could be mine, if only I laid claim to them.

Raiden guides himself to my opening first, locking eyes with me as he pushes himself in with a grunt. My hands curl together behind his neck as Brennin kisses the side of my throat. Instead of heading for my ass the way Tee did, he lines himself up with my pussy.

"What—" I start, but then he's slowly pushing himself in, and my body is stretching to accommodate the pair of them. At first, I feel like it might hurt, but I quickly get accustomed to that feeling of fullness, magic swirling in my belly like a storm.

"My Queen of Hearts," Red whispers, and then power is surging through his palms and into me, drawing an orgasm from my throat in a pleasured scream. I come around the two men, muscles pulsing, and feel power igniting in my chest. It's like he's just turned a key and broken open all my barriers.

The two of them begin to move, alternately kissing my throat, Raiden kissing my lips, running their tongues along the shell of my ear.

It's all sweat, and magic, and groaning, just three bodies twisted up in primal wonder. And it feels *so* goddamn good with the King churning the magic in my body with the power in his hands. He pulls another orgasm from me with his magic, and I swear, I come undone in their arms.

I could very well be fucking two villains, I think, but it doesn't matter. Their cruelty is delicious, their cocks thick, my body full. Everything feels so good, like I'm drowning in a haze of pleasure. I'd die happy like this, surely.

Red moves one of his hands to my breasts, making my nipples tingle, like they've been dipped in glitter. It's hard to explain, that tickle of wild energy teasing my most sensitive parts. Their moans fill my ears like music, their shafts fill my body like steel, and a *third* orgasm sneaks up on me, one sent by my body and not by Brennin Red this time.

My mouth opens in a silent groan as my muscles flutter, squeezing two of the most powerful men in Underland between my thighs. Doesn't feel so much like I begged now; it feels like *I'm* the one with all the power, the magic, the control.

They both come within a minute of one another, their hips giving those last few, fatal thrusts, their breathing harsh and ragged and panting along with my own.

When they finally set me down, I can't quite find my feet.

"You make orgasms with your hands?" I ask Brennin, flopping down onto my mom's favorite wingback chair. He fixes his pants and then looks at me, red hair sticking to his sweaty forehead. His dark eyes don't look black anymore; instead they're navy swirls of stars, shining with power.

Red bends down and picks up his gloves, carefully sliding the white fabric over the long fingers of his right hand.

"I move free and wild magic around. Not as well as you; I don't hold onto it." He stands back up and smirks at me. "I just move it."

"That should just about do the trick?" Raiden asks, exchanging a look with the King. They have a strange relationship, the two of them. Even after what just happened, I'm not sure what to make of it. "Don't you think?"

"Get that damned breastplate, and then we'll see," Brennin says, moving over to open the door.

Rab is waiting outside, holding out the Breastplate of Courage that the White Knight gave me. Knowing now that she has her own agenda, I not only feel like an idiot, but I want to know what, exactly, that piece of armor does.

Blushing, I scramble to get my pants and put them on as Rab smirks at me.

"Don't get caught with your pants down, Sonny. Oldest rule in the book."

"Knock first, perhaps *that* is the oldest rule in the book?" I retort as I flush and sweep my fingers down my mussy braid. One of Rab's ears falls over his red eye, and he reaches up to straighten it with tattooed fingers.

"Pants down, it's the oldest: *trust me*," he drawls, handing over the breastplate to the King. "Rule number forty-two."

"That's not at all true; you invented it just now," I snap, watching Brennin Red run his bare left hand over the white material with its fancy shoulder clasps.

"It's the oldest rule in the *book*." Rab snaps that last word off the end of his tongue and props a fist on his hip, like he thinks he's the universe's gift to women.

"Then it ought to be number *one*." I give him a look of smug, female triumph, and move over to stand next to Brennin and the breastplate.

"Get me Lar," he says, and Rab nods, lighting up a cigarette as he saunters away and returns with the Caterpillar.

"There's a simple cantrip on this for courage," Brennin says, gesturing at it with his red palm. Lar looks at him, at the Hatter's smirking face, and then over at me. He winks and tugs at one of his earrings before turning back to Chevalier's gift. "Other than that, there's nothing. It's just a stupid, useless piece of armor with *clasps*." The way he says this last word shows he doesn't much care for the Knight's inventions.

Lar sweeps blue-blonde hair behind one ear and leans over, showing off all those glorious muscles in his back and shoulders. They have to be pretty strong, don't they, to hold up such an impressive wingspan. Those blue-gold-black windows to the world, they sway like petals in the wind as Lar folds his wings and opens them, like a butterfly resting on a daisy.

His pale fingers draw a gold sigil over the item, but it pops like a bit of confetti, showering glitter all over the study floor that soon dissipates.

"Hmm." He lifts it up and turns it over, rubbing his thumb along the matte interior. "I studied this before the ball, but I didn't find anything. I don't see how I will now." I step up next to them as Lar turns the armor over again. There's a crest on the upper left front, with the emblem for the Kingdom of Hearts—a broken heart intersected by a sword. I pick at it for a moment, and then frown.

"Did you pry this up?" I ask, but the Caterpillar, the King, and the Mad Hatter all look at me with this *why?* sort of expression.

"Magic can't hide beneath a simple metal design," Brennin huffs, but Rab is stepping up close and looking at me with bright, red eyes.

"*Fuuuuuck*, Sonny," he whispers, handing over the Vorpal Blade. I take it from its sheath, and then use the sharp tip to pry up the emblem. Underneath, there's a tiny gray circle with a little heart symbol on it. I purse my lips tight. "Useless in Underland, very useful Topside."

"What is it?" Lar asks as I pick up the little device. I only know what it is because I bought one for Dinah, to hang from her collar.

"It's a GPS tracker." I hand the item over to Rab to examine. "That's like … it's like having a spell that shows you where someone is at all times."

"Crush it," Brennin demands, but I'm already shaking my head.

"No, let's use it." I take the item back, stare it down, and start to form a plan.

"Why would the White Knight work with the Walrus anyway?" I ask as I finish tying up my combat boots. Dee helps me to my feet, and steals a little moment by yanking me into his arms. It feels good, to be pressed up so close against him.

His fingers brush my hair away from my face. The rest of it is still braided, thanks to the Cheshire Cat.

"I have no idea," he whispers, looking down at me like he really would give his life for mine. I can't imagine it's all because he … like, loves me or whatever, right? It's probably just because I'm the Alice, the supposed savior of the world he loves. Okay, so *mostly.* I mean, I could see this relationship going places. My parents are … were … are? … hashtag relationship goals. I could see me and Dee getting there someday. "But we'll figure it out. We'll make it alright again."

"I hope you're right." I pull away from him and head back into the upstairs foyer to find the Mad Hatter waiting outside of Edith's room.

Our eyes meet.

I can't believe I just fucked this guy again.

I try to be adult about it, clearing my throat and opening my mouth to ask about my sister, but he just chuckles at me, and I end up snapping my lips closed.

"What?" I put my hands on my hips and stare him down. "Do you have something to say?"

"Your sister is awake, and well, what do you want me to do about it?" Raiden tilts his head at me and removes one of his hats, revealing yet another one underneath in orange and purple stripes. He pulls this one off, and then removes a green one, continuing on with his game of nesting hats until he finds a … teapot and teacup. He sets his hats aside, pours himself a cup, and then replaces the pot and the stack of top hats.

And, what do you know, the tea in his cup is steaming.

"How do you do that anyway?" I ask, staring at Edith's bedroom door and the myriad bumper stickers all over it. She has political stickers that say things like *Any Functioning Adult, 2020* and *I Support #MeToo.* She also has rainbow sharks, pink cats, and dancing sea turtles. I smile.

"How do I do what?" the Mad Hatter asks, as I hear shuffling coming from Edith's room. "Charm people?"

"Exactly that." I try to figure out how to accomplish what needs to get done while keeping Edith in tow. It's not an easy feat. Sorry to say it, but my sister can be difficult at times, so difficult that she makes me look like a fucking peach. "You hypnotize them, but how?"

"If I take enough blood, enough *powerful* blood"—Raiden looks very purposefully at me—"then I can manage a few rounds. Better deal than making doors. Do you know how I pay for those?" I shake my head and he grins, taking another sip of his tea. "One tooth per door."

"One tooth?" I ask, thinking of the door he created that led straight into the King's garden. "What do you mean?"

The Mad Hatter sets his cup aside, on a decorative table next to a bowl of rotten fruit. It didn't always used to be rotten; Mom replaced it on a regular basis, and Fred … well, Fred always ate it. But now Fred is gone, and Mom is gone, and so it just sits there and spoils.

Raiden opens his mouth and points inside, to the spot where his molars should be.

"One tooth, one door," he says, shrugging. "I don't pretend to understand how the magic works; it simply … *does.* I make a door, and I lose a tooth." He picks up his teacup again as Edith cracks her door and stares out at me with wide, wide eyes.

"What the fuck, Allison?" she chokes, sparing a glance for my gun and knife holsters, the crown on my head that doesn't fall off no matter how I move, and the shredded ballgown I'm wearing over my jeans. I repurposed my outfit from the ball, tearing off the skirt and slipping the rest over denim. I kept the corset though because, like, *dope*. "Your new boyfriends are back?" She stares at the Mad Hatter, squinting and wrinkling up the skin on her forehead. "And who the hell is this?"

"Edy," I start, as her eyes move to Dee's wings again. She stares at them *hard*, like in her heart of hearts, she knows these are not cosplay cardboard and glue-on feathers. "We need to talk."

"Uh, oooooookay," she says, moving out of the bedroom and pausing to stare at the black and white cat that's now weaving between my legs. "What's going on? Where's Dad?"

I exhale sharply.

"I need you to trust me. Can you do that?" She just stares with eyes as blue as a winter sky, cold and cloudless. Edith's been hurt, and she's been hurt by everyone in our family, whether they meant it or not. Hell, she's been hurt by me. "I want you to know that I didn't leave by choice, and that I came back as soon as I could. If you just, well, not to be rude, but if you shut-up and follow along, you'll see."

Edith narrows her eyes and opens her mouth to snap back at me, but stops when she notices Chesh shifting right there in front of her face.

"Well," he purrs, swishing his tail around and winking at her. He makes a little paw with his hand and bats at the air near her face. "Before you sass your sister—and normally, I do enjoy a bit of sass—just look at me and think for a moment. Could you believe the unbelievable, just for a single moment? Could you believe in the impossible? Like, say, a cat who becomes a man, or a man who becomes a cat?"

Edy's mouth opens and closes, like those goldfish Dinah ate as a kitten. I never really mourned them, stupid things.

"I can't believe that!" says Edith, frustration, confusion, and disbelief written all over her face. I simply cross my arms over my chest and give her and her flustered cheeks and sweaty forehead a look. It's all I can do not to laugh. Even with the evidence right there in front of her face, she denies it. That's Edith for you, stubborn to the last drop.

"Can't you?" Chesh asks, disappearing until only his grin is left. "Try again: draw a long breath, and shut your eyes."

"There's no use trying!" she snaps back, clearly pissed off and reeling. It's a lot to take in, I must admit. "One can't believe impossible things!"

"I daresay you haven't had much practice," says the cat. His body reappears, but this time, he's back in puss form. "When I was your age, I always did it for half an hour a day. Why, sometimes I've believed as many as six impossible things before breakfast." He shifts yet again and lands on his bare, human feet, cocking his head to one side as if to say *I dare you*.

"Are you bloody ready yet, Doll?" March asks, coming up the stairs and fingering the vials of poison around his neck. In his other hand, he's got a spray of knives, one each held between his fingers, four in total. He folds them together, and then flashes them again, like a fan. "Thought you might like an extra weapon or two."

His ears swivel on his head, and Edith's eyes zone right in on them.

"Pick your poison, Alice-Doll," March continues, towering over me with his massive form. Not for the first time, I look up at him, and I wonder what it'd be like to be enfolded in such huge arms. I wonder if the Mad Hatter knows the answer to that question? "Paralysis—lasts about four minutes, flesh-eating—don't nick yourself with that one, or flames—like fire ants crawling through your veins." He tinks the glass vials together, but doesn't bother to explain the last one.

"What's in that, the white one?" I ask, peering close. The March Hare flashes me a huge grin, his brown eyes darkening with a naughty little look that gets my panties all twisted into a knot.

"That ain't poison, love, it's lube—for *her* pleasure." March chuckles as I rip the yellow poison—the paralysis one—off of his neck. Edith is still staring, gawping really, but I figure there's no better way to learn to swim than to be thrown into the deep end? Even if the deep end is swimming with sharks, right?

"Help me apply it?" I ask, and March smirks. His ears flatten back against his dark hair.

"Oh, I'll help you apply it, but we might want some privacy from your sister first, don't you think?" I shove him in the chest as he laughs, but of course, he's built like a goddamn mountain, so he doesn't exactly go anywhere. "Let's go with this knife then." He tosses one knife up into the air—I recognize it as one of Dad's fancy kitchen knives—and then throws the other three in quick succession. They stick into the wall next to the study in a perfect vertical row.

"Sonny," Edith chokes out, but as much as I'd like to sit down and explain things to her, we don't have the time.

Nah, we *definitely* don't have the time because we're planning a prison break, y'all.

"Just listen to me," I beg, stepping forward to put my hands on her shoulders. Our eyes, our nearly identical fucking eyes, meet, and I hope to Hearts she can see how desperate I am here. "For once in your life, please."

"Do I need to charm her?" Raiden asks, but I shake my head. No, I want Edith to see what's happening, and I want her to know exactly what's going on. Because I'm taking her back to Underland with me; it'll be her choice if she decides to stay.

My sister doesn't say anything as I step away and hand the poison vial back to March. He slides the knife into the cork on the top, turns the vial and knife over, and then slips the blade back out again. The single slice in the cork makes the perfect slit to coat the metal with the glowing yellow poison. When he's done, he hands the knife to me, checks under his hat, and finds a new cork to replace the old one with, tossing the poison coated cork into the trash can.

I tuck my new knife into the Vorpal Blade's sheath. Last time, that poison knife saved Tee's and my asses. I'm glad I have a new one to take its place.

The stairs creak, and I glance over my shoulder to find the Duke waiting at the bottom of the steps with Tee and the Black Rabbit.

"Are you ready, Miss Liddell?" he growls, eyeing me up and down with a lover's gaze. His gold eyes are glittering as he takes in my outfit with intense, lustful approval.

"I'm ready," I say, reaching out to take Edith's hand.

Today is probably going to be a shit-show, but at least … at least my sister doesn't pull away from me.

The GPS tracker goes in Mrs. Jones' minivan, and off *she* goes to the grocery store.

The Mad Hatter doesn't even need to charm her; I just know she never locks her car doors, and that she always goes to the overpriced local co-op to shop around this time on weekdays. She's so predictably predictable that she's going to help make *us* a little less predictable.

"My mother's in prison for killing the men who tried to rape me," I say, and my voice sounds horribly loud inside the quiet vehicle. With Rab and Chesh in their mouse and cat forms, and the March Hare and the Mad Hatter borrowing Fred's old car, there's just enough room for the rest of us in Dad's SUV.

I'm driving, and Edith is sitting petrified in the front seat with Dinah's carrier on her lap, but I know without even bothering to look that the men are listening. I told them earlier about my plan, to move our fight to the prison since it's on the edge of town, surrounded by empty fields and a state park. And I explained that I was taking my mother back to Underland, but I didn't really tell them *why.*

It feels easier, somehow, to do it while I'm driving, like if I keep my eyes on the road, I won't really have to think about what I'm saying. I can form words and string sentences together, and that's all they'll be: just letters hanging from my lips like smoke.

"Well, I guess she killed them because they were my brother's murderers, and I suppose even then she only did it because they walked from the ..." I almost say courtroom, but decide for ease of understanding that I'll go with a different word. The King of Hearts holds a weekly Trial, right? I'll go with that. "Trial with no punishment whatsoever."

"That's the Alice for you," Dee says, sounding proud. "And her illustrious family, slaying bad guys." He shifts his wings and draws my sister's attention back around to stare at him in shock and confusion. She hasn't said a damn word since I pulled her down the stairs and out the front door. "Always on the side of good, whether that's on top of it in Topside or under it in Underland ..." He trails off with a wistful sigh. "Once upon a time, there were rumors of *other* lands the Looking-Glass could connect to, places Beside or Between."

"But they've been lost," Tee finishes with a more mournful sounding exhale. "Or else they never were."

"And even if they *were,* they *aren't*, so I suppose there's no sense in talking about it, unless we're talking nonsense in which case *there* is some sense in the latter part of the word." Dee pauses as we take the exit toward the prison, and I park at the edge of the nearly empty lot outside the gates. We *could* go in jabberwock's a-blazing, vampires a-biting, and magical kings a-decapitating, but that's not really my style.

Instead, we'll ... *charm* our way through the doors.

Rab-mouse is in my pocket, and Cheshire Puss is on my shoulders. I glance around at the rest of the men, giving the Duke in particular a look. If it were up to him, he'd shift into his massive dragon form and guard me with fire-breath and scaly, black limbs.

"You're my *mate,*" he says, but he's snarling, and his big, thick arms are crossed over his bronze chest. He, too, has replaced his clothing with what he was wearing the night of the ball. Seems to be a signature of his to leave the top few buttons undone, probably with the sole intent of attracting beautiful young ladies. I know for a fact that he managed to attract this one. "But I'll guard your sister, if that's what you wish."

"It's what I wish," I say, turning my gaze to the twins, to Lar, to the King. Finally, I look over at Edith. She refuses to look back at me, staring instead at the torn black tights covering her knee. "I'm coming back with Mom."

"You're coming back in cuffs—or a straitjacket," she mumbles, but I don't have time for her games. I leave her there, trusting in the remaining five men to protect her. Just before I get out, I reach up and take off my crown, leaving it in Tee's care. We checked it for a GPS tracker, too, but there's nothing that's not supposed to be there.

March and Raiden are already waiting outside for me.

"It's still visiting hours, so we should be able to get in, and get out pretty quickly." I look toward the chain-link fencing, surrounded by empty fields, and the huge concrete building rising up out of it. Swear to god there are creepy gray clouds clinging to the horizon in just that particular spot.

"Your wish is our command," March drones, biting the end off of a banana and staring at the prison like he's seen worse. Hell, I know very little about his history, so maybe he has? "Just tell us what to do, and we'll fetch your mum."

"Try not to shoot anyone," Rab says from inside my pocket. "He's quite mad, Sonny. You do know that, right?"

"As if you're sane?" March retorts, giving the mouse a rather disdainful sort of look. He's got on his purple velvet trench coat, and his black hat, and he certainly doesn't give two fucks about the mission we're about to take on.

Me, I'm nervous as hell.

But this can't wait any longer. Who knows what's happening in Underland, what the Walrus and his crew are up to Topside, where my poor father is. We need to get back, and we need to get back *now*.

And if I'm going back, I'm taking Mom with me.

We move toward the front gates with Chesh purring in my ear, and head inside, waltzing right up to the front of the line like the Mad Hatter did last time.

"Hello there, dear," he whispers, turning the employee's dark brown eyes to a lustful, needy black. "We're here to see Hannah Reeve Liddell. We've already checked in with our IDs, so would you mind letting us on through?" His eyes flash a bright orange, like those pumpkin lights my mom used to string up on Halloween.

"And hand over that sandwich, too," March adds, stealing the poor woman's half of a salami sandwich. He chows down on it as we saunter over to security, the Cheshire Cat purring in my ear, and grooming my blonde hair with his sandpaper tongue. Now that Chesh and I have had our first kiss, at least I know for a fact that his human tongue is very much *not* like his cat form. It's slick and smooth and hot …

With a groan, I rub at my forehead and try to banish horny teenager thoughts from my brain. Seeing as I'm still eighteen and riddled with hormones, that's virtually impossible, but I give it the ol' college try, at least.

People are staring at the weird cat on my shoulder, but I guess it's *just* weird enough not to warrant people whipping out their smartphones to record the moment with. Well, either that or the *No Cellphones!* sign on the wall is doing the trick.

Raiden uses his, err, *charm* to get us through security, and then there's nothing to do but wait. Mom isn't expecting visitors today, so it might be a few before she's escorted up here by the prison guards.

My stomach is alive with butterflies, and my palms are soaked in sweat.

We're … going to walk my mom out of prison, like literally. Just walk her out. And sure, maybe something like this wouldn't work if we were to stay in this world. Security cameras would be checked, records wouldn't match up, and there are just too many people to charm for this to work out long-term.

The nice thing about this plan is, it doesn't *need* to last long-term. No, it only needs to last *right now.* Too bad I failed to remember that prisons and jails generally have a central control room full of cameras. You know, a room so well-protected that it's impenetrable even during a riot? Yep. Forgot about that one.

"I'm freaking the fuck out," I whisper as Chesh rubs his cheek against mine. I have no idea how I ended up screwing the Mad Hatter before him; I actually *like* the Cheshire Cat. *Note to self: make all of the sex rounds later.* Like, all of them. There's nothing like thinking you might die to get a person in the mood, eh?

"Over what?" March asks, staring at me. I feel naked without the Queenmaker and the Vorpal Blade, but I had to leave them in the car because, you know, charming a few guards in a prison is a bit different than letting dozens of other visitors see me waltz in wearing weapons. "Springing your mum from the joint?"

He doesn't even bother to keep his voice down, and I cringe.

"Yeah, exactly that," I say with a roll of my eyes. March just grins at me as I stroke both the cat and the mouse at the same time … and wonder what it might be like to stroke them in a very different sort of a way. See what I mean? I guess I get horny when I'm nervous. It's so inappropriate, I sort of just want to curl up in a ball and laugh myself into madness.

The door on the opposite side of the room opens, and my mother enters, looking horribly confused.

"Allison," she says when she recognizes me, taking in my strange outfit with stride. My mother has seen me wear weird for years. It's just my thing. "What are you doing here? Where's your dad?" She gives the Cheshire Cat a very peculiar look, her blue eyes darkening with concern. "What is … *that*?"

"Mom," I start carefully, giving her a very brief hug as the Mad Hatter saunters off with a whistle, making his rounds to all the guards in the room. Over my shoulder, I've got a satchel with clothes in it. Can't very well have Hannah walking around in an orange jumpsuit, now can I? "There's been a reversal of the court's decision," I blurt, hating myself for lying, but knowing my mother's far too intelligent to just waltz out of the jail without an explanation. Again, I could have the Hatter charm her, but I want her to be present for this.

I *need* her to be.

This is her new reality.

"A what?" she asks, giving the March Hare a very curious—and very suspicious—sort of a look. She flicks her eyes back to mine, searching my expression with that penetrating gaze of hers. "What are you talking about?"

"Time to go, little Alice," Raiden whistles, waltzing on by and heading straight for the door. He presses the buzzer, speaks to the man behind the bullet-proof glass, and then waits for us to join him.

"*Tick-tock, Allison, you're late,*" Rab murmurs from inside my pocket. Mom definitely hears that, but she looks around the room like she's searching for the source. I clear my throat to get her attention again.

"Mom, you're *free,*" I say, taking her hands and trying to pull her toward the door. She resists for a moment, confusion clear on her face. *Goddamn her for being practical!* She's not buying any of this shit. "But we need to go now. Dad is … having a crisis. He needs you."

Hannah Reeve looks at me with her forehead all wrinkled up, lifting her gaze to study the March Hare again. One of the guards on the edge of the room gets a buzz on their radio, and I feel a bead of sweat begin to drip down my spine. The woman says something that's too low for me to hear, but I see March glancing casually in that direction. Even without his brown rabbit ears, he seems to have excellent fucking hearing. Guess you'd need it, too, if you were going to be an assassin or a bodyguard or a master thief who steals peanuts.

"Oh dear, love," he says, turning back to me. Raiden Walker is still waiting at the exit with his brows raised, tapping the fingers of one hand against the back of the other. "We may want to, uh, speed our exit strategy up a bit."

I notice the female guard walking over to us, and a sick feeling roils in my stomach.

"Oh dear," Chesh murmurs, going completely invisible. Lucky him. Wish I had that ability right now.

Glancing up, I see the beady black eyes of several cameras embedded in the ceiling.

Someone who *isn't* hypnotized by Underland vampire bullshit is staring at us, I'll bet—and they know we're up to no good.

"Excuse me, Inmate Liddell," the guard calls out, but she doesn't get to finish her sentence because March is spinning and chucking a small knife in her direction. It hits her in the shoulder as I gape in shock and watch as she collapses to the floor. It can't have killed her though or even really hurt her as it's the size of a fucking sewing needle.

"Sleep tonic. Lasts a few hours. Killer headache, awful dreams, but not much can be done about it." March grabs my arm in one hand, and my mother's wrist in the other.

"What are you doing?" she shrieks as the room explodes into chaos. Even the guards that Raiden already charmed look upset. "Who are you? Allison?!"

Sorry Mom! I think as the March Hare finally gives up and throws her over his shoulder like a sack of potatoes. Raiden holds the door for us as we take off past the security checkpoint and into the lobby, just as the alarm begins to go off. Sirens blare and red lights flash from various points throughout the room. We *barely* make it out the doors before I hear the click of an auto-lock, and metal bars slide into place over the windows.

This is, like, some *Prison Break* shit or something.

There are already guards waiting outside for us, but really, they're not even a joke to the Mad Hatter and the March Hare. Raiden kicks the legs out from underneath a man with a gray beard, and then has the audacity to *yawn* as he throat-punches a man holding an automatic weapon. There are other guards, up in the towers positioned around the property. It's literally just a matter of time before they start shooting at us.

That, and my mother is screaming something fierce, yelling her lungs off and biting the March Hare's shoulder, punching him in the spine. I have to give it to her: Hannah knows how to fight back.

"Oh bloody hell," March groans as Raiden steps around behind him, grabs my mother's face between his palms, and looks her dead in the eye.

"You feel like you need to relax, or you're going to get your daughter shot and killed. You can wait for a proper explanation of the events taking place here today, now can't you?" He lets go of her and then shatters into pieces, black bats swarming up and into the sunny sky.

The March Hare doesn't stand there gawking the way I do. He reaches down, grabs my hand, and yanks me down the hill toward the front gates. Whatever the Mad Hatter does to the guards in the tower, we don't get shot. And when we come up to the closed and locked gate at the front of the property, March simply removes a vial from his hat and chucks it. The glass shatters and the metal gets eaten away by some sort of … hot pink goop. Yep. Hot fucking pink, like troll snot or something.

We jog down to the cars together, just as the sound of police sirens echoes in the distance. March sets Mom down and she sways briefly before finding her feet.

Hannah Reeve, out in the sunshine, a free woman for the first time in what feels like forever. And I can't even enjoy it because we have to book ass or risk getting shot or arrested.

Life's a bitch, right?

Chapter Three

Humpty Dumb-shit

Springing Mom from the joint feels a little like … kidnapping, especially when I open the back door on Dad's SUV, and she finds Edith surrounded by a bunch of strange men. Fortunately, she's too busy staring at them to notice the Mad Hatter reforming out of bats.

"Allison," she starts, and I can hear the fear in her voice. Mom is fucking terrified.

"I know what this looks like." *Okay, well, actually I have no idea what this looks like.* "You just have to trust me." I hand over the satchel, and Hannah takes it with a baffled expression on her face. She turns over her shoulder to stare at the Hatter and the Hare again. I admit, they *do* look intimidating.

"We don't have a lot of time for explanations," March says, exchanging a dark glance with his boss. "Should we, uh, take care of your mother for you, Doll?"

"Doll?!" Mom asks, rearing back, completely aghast. "Take care of?!"

"Please get in the SUV, Mom," I beg, pushing the satchel against her chest as the police sirens grow louder. She takes it, but she doesn't seem convinced. As the moments pass, the confusion on her face sharpens to stark clarity, and she squares her shoulders.

"When I committed that crime, Allison, I knew what I was getting myself into. I killed those boys, and I'll take responsibility for my actions." She trembles when she says this, but whatever she thinks is going on now, she knows it wasn't a simple court reversal on her sentence. I mean, the sirens and the poison knife and the troll snot sort of gave us away. "Whoever these men are, they can … well, they can go home now."

"Home?" the Savage Duke drawls, propping his chin on his knuckles. "That's the plan, isn't it, love?"

"Love?!" Mom shrieks, flicking her gaze from me to the circle of men. There's something in her expression that sort of … clicks. She sees the way Tee is staring at me, the way Dee is smiling. *Oh, hell.* "Allison Pleasance Liddell, who are these men?"

"Your salvation," the Mad Hatter says, putting his hand on my mother's shoulder, eyes flashing when she whips her gaze around to meet his. "You are comfortable with this situation, for now. Get in the vehicle, so that we might be on our way."

"What are you doing to Mom?" Edith shouts, knocking Dinah's carrier over, lunging out of the front seat, and scrambling to put herself between Raiden and Hannah. "Leave her alone."

"Sorry, little Alice's sister," the Mad Hatter says with a shrug, eyes brightening to that neon orange color. "Why don't you climb into the back and take a nap for a little while?" He stares at Edy for an awful long time, so long that I honestly wonder if his vampire hypno powers are even going to work. Just when I think Edy might leap out and make a run for it, her gaze gets glassy and she moves to crawl into the back. "Well," Raiden finally says on the end of an exhale, "I won't be doing that again without a little … refresher. What say you, Alice?"

"You've had enough of her blood," Brennin Red snaps, legs crossed at the knee, dark eyes stoic and locked into an expression of haughty disdain. There's jealousy in his voice, despite the fact that he, Raiden, and I just, well, had a goddamn threesome. "You can have some of mine." He snaps his fingers, and Lar climbs out with a roll of his blue eyes, trading places with the Mad Hatter. "Get in."

My mother and Edith both find spots to sit, as pliable and blank as zombies. I hate that. I seriously fucking *hate* it, but Raiden Walker is right: we don't have a lot of time. Actually, I'm surprised we haven't been accosted just yet. Must've been the supernatural vampire bat swarm that bought us some time.

"Okay," I say, exhaling as everyone gets settled, and I slide into the driver's seat. "Over the river and through the woods we go." I start the car and pull out of the parking lot, Fred's old red Acura trailing along behind us.

My heart is racing as Tee, who's still in the far back with his twin, passes the crown, the Queenmaker, and the Vorpal Blade up to the Duke. North's fingers tangle with mine when he hands the items over, and not by accident.

"We've got this, Allison," Tee tells me, his voice as soothing as fresh raindrops on the roof. I always loved that, lying in bed in the quiet dark, wrapped in blankets, listening to a storm roll in. That's what Tee is, a refreshing drink for a parched earth. His and Dee's wings take up every available inch in the back of the SUV, feathers pressing against the windows. It might be easier without them, but we can't risk being attacked without the twins at their full-strength … or without Raiden's frenzy as a backup plan.

The Black Rabbit looks a bit terrified being squashed between them, but she's smart enough to keep her mouth shut.

"I sure hope so," I whisper as Edith lies on the floor at the twins' feet, and my mother sits beside the Hatter and the King. Her glassy eyes disturb me, so I look away, biting my lower lip as I start the car. "I sure fucking hope so."

There's a park about thirty minutes from the prison, one that I'm pretty sure will be empty this early in the morning on a … wait, what day is it? Anyway, it's the best place I can think of for a confrontation—better than suburbia anyway. I'll take a stray hiker or two over a full street of gawking bourgeois neighbors.

I grab an empty space near one of the more difficult trailheads, and turn off the ignition.

When I look up at the rearview mirror, I can see the Mad Hatter licking the last drops of blood from the King's neck. Of course, Brennin Red could just as easily be filling out his taxes, or contemplating getting a root canal; he hardly looks pleased, although I can see his gloved hands are curled into fists.

"Tee, Dee, I want you to keep an eye on my family, okay?" I turn over my shoulder to stare at the twins, knowing that I couldn't put Edith and Mom in better hands. "No matter what, I need them to be safe, okay?"

"Anything for you, Allison-who-isn't Alice," Dee says, as I kick open the door and climb out.

"Wait!" the Black Rabbit calls, and I pause, glancing back at her. Green eyes shimmer as they take me in, like a proud papa. It's too fucking weird. "I can help, you know. Really, I could be an asset. All I want is to keep you safe, Allison. The thought consumes my chest, in that space just beneath my ribs." I cock a skeptical brow.

"*I'd rather not fight beside the traitor's pet*," Rab drawls from my pocket, and I'm inclined to agree with him. Leaving the Black Rabbit alive is one thing, but trusting her in a fight is a whole other animal.

"Sorry—you stay in the car, too." I flick the lock button on my door, and slam it closed behind me.

Dressed in thick, leather combat boots covered in buckles, a torn ballgown, and a crown, I feel a little bit like a badass. Above us, the old sequoias tower like giants, their soft red-brown bark a pleasant backdrop for what's most certainly *not* going to be a very pleasant day.

"This reminds me of the Tulgey Wood," Lar says, tilting his head to one side. The gold bangles on his wrist jangle as he plays with them for a moment. "And these, they look a bit like Tumtum trees, don't you agree, Rab?"

The mouse crawls from my pocket and then hops to the pine needle strewn pavement, shifting back into his tall, inked form, tattooed clocks tick-tick-tocking away.

"I highly doubt that these trees bleed." Rab pauses, and his ears flop in opposite directions, crossing in an X shape on his head. "As a matter of fact, I bet they don't scream either."

"They don't scream, curse, or call young women named Allison *trollops* either," I grind out, thinking of the stupid flowers back in Underland. Even with all of the bullshit and the nonsense, all I want is to go back.

To the tune of *I Left My Heart In San Francisco …*

Ahem.

"Is everyone ready?" I ask, putting my hand on the Vorpal Blade holster and taking a deep breath.

Tee and Dee are waiting in the SUV with Edith and Mom, but the rest of the men are standing around me in a half-circle. And they're all looking at me, too, like my opinion matters, like I really *am* the future Queen of Hearts.

"The question is," Lar begins, tilting his head slightly. "Are you, Sunshine?"

I exhale sharply, the wet scent of pine and moss and earth filling my nostrils when I inhale. The forest is quiet, the great trees shifting in a breeze off the sea. We're close to the bay here, Humboldt Bay to be exact. It's the only thing I ever liked about this little California town: the sea.

"I'm ready." I look over at the King, and he smiles, so devilishly handsome, so goddamn wicked. He steps toward me, removing his gloves, and then places one bare hand on my chest. The magic I've brought back from Underland, all of that terrible, storming wild magic, stirs inside of me, twisted up by Red's powers. When I feel it all hot and heady, surging into my limbs, and filling my skull with white-hot energy, I whip out the Vorpal Blade and let it sing.

So it summons the Anti-Alice, they say. It brings her running. Well, I challenge the bitch now.

"Come and get me," I whisper.

For several moments, there's nothing but an eerie silence, nothing but the creak of boughs in the wind.

"Do the trees here bark?" the Duke asks, lifting his head up to stare into the canopy above us.

"They have bark," I say, but he's already shaking his golden-haired head, his dark horns casting shadows on the pavement behind him.

"Certainly they *have* bark, but *do* they bark? I mean, you do know the limbs of trees are called boughs, don't you?"

"And?" I ask, Brennin's hand still splayed open on my chest. "What does that have to do with anything?"

"Why do you think they call them that? Because they bark: *bough-wough*." The Duke grins, but I don't think he's intending to make a bad pun; I think he's serious. Bough-wough. Bow-wow, like a dog bark, get it? Oh, ridiculously wonderful, nonsensically magical, ludicrously un-understandable Underland.

"Would you just shift and cease your nonsense?" the King asks as the Duke smirks, his body growing and shifting, stretching across the pavement in shimmering black scales. He towers above us, crouching low to keep his head from hitting the lowest hanging tree limbs. Bough-wough, indeed.

The Duke of Northumbria is impressive, this glorious mountain of muscle, all beast and teeth and claws. I can't seem to help myself, and murmur part of the Jabberwock poem.

"And as in uffish thought he stood,
The Jabberwock, with eyes of flame,
Came whiffling through the Tulgey wood,
And burbled as it came."

"Good luck with that, *Duchess*," Chesh chortles as he leaps from my shoulders and shifts from his kitty cat form to his … *jungle cat form.* "Keeping the beast in line." He snarls this last bit, his huge muscular form rippling with power. Of course, it seems like the Duke could have Chesh as an afternoon snack if he really wanted to, but that doesn't make the big cat any less impressive.

He's a bit like a tiger, with those black and white stripes, but he's still got the piercings in his ears, nose, and mouth, and his paws are at least thrice the size of the orange and black cat I saw at the Sequoia Park Zoo last summer.

"Are we sure this is going—" I start, when I hear a crack in the canopy above me.

"Absolutely sure," March murmurs, yanking me out of the way just in time to avoid the Anti-Alice as she smashes into the parking lot pavement, cracking the cement into jagged pieces. The King steps to the side, and I notice he's *very* careful not to touch her. I wonder what would happen if his magic hands touched a literal magic void? "Pardon, Doll," March continues, his body melting into a completely foreign shape.

It's the fucking tove.

The tove, the tove, I get to finally see the goddamn tove!

March shifts into a tall, muscular horse with a chest like the front of a fucking freight train. He's bigger than a Clydesdale, with huge, sharp hooves on the ends of his long legs, a rack of glowing antlers on the top of his dark head, and a pair of huge leathery wings folding against his back. March looks like some sort of demonic warhorse, with bony growths coming up the front of his legs, like living ivory armor.

His mane and tail are like dark fire, swirling in the wind in flickering fits and spurts of flame.

The Anti-Alice rises to her feet, her black and white dress fluttering as she cracks her head on her spindly, rotten neck. It's her eyes, those too-blue eyes, that really get me. There are only three people in this world with those eyes: me, Edith, Mom. I'd recognize them anywhere. Besides, the shape of her mouth, her nose, the way her forehead slopes down … this is Rhoda Caroline-Anne Liddell.

And the only person that can defeat her … is me.

Shit.

I didn't fare so well last time, and I haven't exactly had any time to add training to my schedule in between then and now.

"*You've already murdered one sibling,*" a voice says inside my head, the slimy sound of a tongue sliding across crooked lips accompanying it. "*How hard can it be to take down a second?*"

The Mocking Turtle isn't here with us, not yet, but he is in my head again, the bastard. The Anti-Alice moves through time and space in her own way, in a way that the other four creeps with her cannot. She came for the Blade, but she'll stay for the ass-kicking.

I back up a few feet, yank the Queenmaker out and into my hand, and pull out the match I have hidden behind my ear. Hey, I *have* learned a few things from training with the guys. I strike it on the grip of the pistol, and then light up, firing off one of the massive metal balls in the Anti-Alice's direction.

I aim up, sending it flying in an arc across the parking lot. The SUV with Mom and Edith and the twins should be far enough away that they're completely out of the ring of fire.

"Hop on," March growls, his voice deeper and darker in this form, like an echo of shadows in a dark, dark cavern. I grab onto the fur of his neck as he kneels down, and haul myself up. The ripple of fire, wind, and heat from the Queenmaker knocks pine needles lose, sending a shower of green down on our heads. But at the very least, it disorients the Anti-Alice for the briefest of moments.

March's wings lift up, and then snap down in a quick, sharp motion, pushing us up and off the ground. He's fast as fuck, too, and I figure this must be why his queen—the Queen of Spades, was it?—chose this as one of his forms.

The Anti-Alice doesn't seem to respond to gravity. Fuck, why should she? She's an undead monster, right?

She jumps, her skirt billowing out around her like a mushroom cap. She floats up to us with her Liddell family blonde hair, her glassy blue eyes shimmering. Her skirt and hair are singed, and there are flames dancing along the front of her skirt, but that doesn't seem to bother her. She's completely and wholly focused on the Vorpal Blade. Or me. Maybe both of us.

"Let me navigate," March growls through teeth far too sharp to belong to a horse. What did Tee say? That a tove was like a Pegasus? A tove is *nothing* at all like a goddamn Pegasus. It has the giant glowing antlers of some like, prehistoric fucking deer, the wings of a giant bat, and natural bone armor like a triceratops or some shit.

Pegasus, hah. And here I was, imagining some glimmering beast, white as snow, with an angelic smile, and feathered wings like the twins'.

This … well, I guess this would be the Underland version of a Pegasus, huh? Like some sort of nightmare horse-bat-elk creature on steroids.

I tuck the Queenmaker back in its holster as the Anti-Alice spins her bone-sickle scythe in the air, coming down so hard and fast that I'm convinced I'm going to end up with more than just a broken arm this time. But the March Hare has my back, dropping low and putting us *just* out of reach of her weapon. I'm still close enough to take a swing, so I do, whipping the Vorpal Blade out hard and fast; I catch the Anti-Alice in the ankle and feel the blade catch on bone.

Crimson blood spatters across my face as March dives down, forcefully tearing my knife from my dead sister's leg. The smell of dusty old tombs mixes with the reek of rot as I struggle to control an involuntary tremble in my body. On the best of days, I don't like killing things. And this is hardly the best of days. The Anti-Alice is my flesh and blood, my *rotted,* reanimated flesh and blood maybe but still … she's family nonetheless.

The feeling of my weapon catching on her bone is making me sick, but I can't let it get to me. One mistake here—*one*—and I'm fucking dead.

"*Look at you*," the Mocking Turtle chastises, his voice still ringing in my head, "*do you like tearing your own sister apart? Feeling her hot blood splatter across your lips? What does she taste like, this forgotten soul you haven't bothered to spare a single thought for your entire, selfish life*?"

Gritting my teeth, I squeeze my thighs against March's thick, muscular back, trying to predict his movements. He turns on a dime, throwing me this way and that. When I reach out with my left hand on reflex, grabbing at his seemingly non-existent mane, my fingers come in contact with warm, sultry smoke. It curls around my hand and gives me a grip, something solid to hold onto as March wheels and dives, flaps his massive wings and propels us even higher into the canopy.

None of the other men follow, not that some of them could if they wanted. But even North stays put down below. They can help defend me against her attacks, keep her from killing me, but the only one who can stop her is me.

And I have to. I fucking *have* to.

Our entire plan hinges on getting rid of the Anti-Alice and the Gryphon, the only two members of the Walrus' parade that can fly. That is, unless he's brought reinforcements through the Looking-Glass, something we probably won't know until it's too late.

The sound of breaking branches precedes a massive shriek, one that North mimics with a roar of his own. The Walrus' huge, blubbery form shuffles into view, tusks catching a stray shaft of sunlight and blinding me at the same time I feel blood dripping from my ears.

"Duck!" March shouts, and I feel us plummet down so fast that my stomach lodges in my throat, and I start to choke and cough. But I do duck as best I can on the tove's huge back, feeling a gust of air as the Anti-Alice swipes at the spot where my head was only seconds before. March drifts to the right with a flap of his wings, and then pushes us up in a draft of warm wind. It takes me a moment to figure out where all of that heat is coming from, glancing down to see North unleashing a red-orange blast that swallows the Walrus' massive form in flames.

The heat from those flames is what gets us airborne, sending us above the Anti-Alice.

March is doing an excellent job keeping me from getting injured, but I'm not doing a particularly great job at taking the openings I'm getting. I need to get the Vorpal Blade in the Anti-Alice, and *keep* it there. Even towering over my neighbors' houses with a blade as big as a car, even severing her in half, that didn't work.

I need a new plan.

Looking down again, I see the King holding out his decorative blade, right arm outstretched, the tip pointing at the Carpenter and his skull-topped axe. The man is tall, disturbingly skinny, and he moves like a fucking spider. I can just imagine articulated legs bursting from his back and carrying him across the pavement as he moves. Brennin doesn't look particularly worried, but when does he ever?

Rab—in bandersnatch form—faces off with the Mocking Turtle while the Mad Hatter takes on the Gryphon, and Lar provides backup support to them both. I remember they didn't much want him near M.T. during the Torrid Tea Party. Maybe we should've left him in the car, too?

The twins are still safely tucked away with my family, and the Cheshire Cat … is nowhere to be seen.

If he can find the Looking-Glass while the rest of us are engaged in combat, I'll consider that a *win.*

The Mocking Turtle smacks his toothless gums, and the sound is so goddamn loud that my already bleeding ears ring. I imagine if he gets that mouth of his on any part of the Mad Hatter, bones will break. I wonder how the vampire heals himself anyway? Does he drink his own blood?

March rears up as the Anti-Alice comes down fast and hard, the bloodstained skirt billowing around her torn black and white tights. This time, she doesn't swing at me—she goes for him. Her bone blade slashes March right across the muzzle, drawing a frenzied whinny from him, and a sea of red blood that splashes down and drenches the Caterpillar.

He looks up just in time to get the hot liquid in his eyes, as the Anti-Alice comes at us again, swinging her blade toward March's right wing in a sharp arc. Even snorting in pain, and bleeding everywhere, he dodges the second blow, sending us up even higher into the trees.

We're above the Anti-Alice now, but only for a second; it won't last. She's fucking relentless.

"Can you catch me if I fall?" I ask, and March lets out a strange snort.

"Bloody what now?" he asks, and he doesn't feel nearly as steady as before. That blow to the face is hurting him—*bad.* "Catch you, Doll? Why would I need to catch you?"

"Yes or no!" I snap, and he growls at me, clacking his sharp teeth.

"Yes!"

I shove up to my feet and jump, before I can think anything of it. I hate heights remember; I'm fucking terrified. And yet I do it anyway, leaping and landing on the Anti-Alice's back and shoulders. The Vorpal Blade slides across her throat, soaking my hand in thick, hot liquid. She lets out a strange shriek, like wind whistling between tombstones, and struggles to throw me off. I stab her again with the blade, hating the way the knife feels as it enters her belly.

Touching her like this, I can feel it, the lack of power and energy. No, not just a *lack*, but an active vacuum, sucking the life out of me. I keep the Vorpal Blade where it is as she drops us both toward the pavement.

The only thing that keeps me from getting splattered to bits on the concrete is March, throwing himself underneath me. It still hurts, probably hurts him, too, and I think I break a few ribs, but I'm still alive. Our tangled bodies roll off March's back and onto the hard ground.

Anti-Alice has her scythe in hand, but I'm underneath her, and my blade is buried in her rotten belly. She can't exactly swing at me from this angle, now can she?

Footsteps pound across the pavement toward me, and I look up to see the Mocking Turtle's big, pink mouth gaping between his crooked lips. I scream, but Lar gets between us, flicking his wings forward and showering the bald man with blue, black, and gold glitter. M.T. screams when he gets it in his eyes, clawing at his face with pointy, broken fingernails.

I shove the blade even further into the Anti-Alice, refusing to let go. I won't get another chance like this. Already, I can feel her weakening, sucking magic out of the endless flow of the Vorpal Blade, filling up like a water balloon getting ready to pop.

March struggles to his feet, swaying slightly. I can see bone on his muzzle as he shifts. When he's back in, err, let's call it human form, it's even worse. His nose is a mess of blood and flesh, but that doesn't stop him from snapping off one of his potions, swinging around behind Lar, and slamming the glass vial into the side of the Mocking Turtle's round head.

I've got the poison knife, but whether it'll work on the Anti-Alice or not is a gamble. To get to it, I'd have to let go with one hand, and if I do, I'm not sure that I can maintain my iron grip.

The Mocking Turtle unleashes his creepy ass tongue, wrapping it around Lar's neck and yanking him forward, even as the flesh on M.T.'s bald head begins to melt away from March's poison. It's like he doesn't give a shit that he's literally falling apart.

The Anti-Alice struggles, elbowing me so hard in the gut that I lose my breath. My right hand comes loose from the Vorpal Blade, and for a terrifying minute, I think I'm going to lose her. But then my left hand finds purchase, digging the blade in an extra half-inch. The undead monster I'm clinging to finds her feet, and even though my ribs are screaming in pain, I force my hand down to the holster on my thigh, yanking out March's tainted kitchen knife.

With every last bit of strength I can muster, I slam it down into her leg, making her cry out in that strange, haunted voice of hers, like bats in a graveyard. There's nothing human about the Anti-Alice. She's a monster, through and through. No soul left. At least … that's what I tell myself because I have no choice.

Otherwise, I'll fall apart.

I found Fred's body; I saw him with glassy eyes and a bloodied grimace, frozen forever onto his handsome face. That image will haunt me the rest of my life. And the Anti-Alice, as her body goes limp and she collapses to her knees with me still clinging to her … that will haunt me, too.

"I'm sorry," I whisper, over and over and over again. "I'm so fucking sorry."

"Hello, Allison," a voice whispers, drawing my attention up to find … Liam. It's Liam. His dark eyes slide over my face, making it feel like it's coated in a slimy film. He runs his tongue across his lower lip as I tear both my blades from the Anti-Alice and stumble back.

"Hey there," another voice says, and I spin around to find Fred behind me. Poor, beautiful Fred with the dark hair and dark eyes, the big brother of every girl's dreams. I stare at him, my hands quivering. I drop March's knife on the ground, but manage to hold onto the Vorpal Blade. "I've missed you."

"You're not fucking real," I grind out, closing my eyes and pressing the heels of both hands against them. "This is the Mocking Turtle playing with my mind." Hands close around my wrists, pulling my arms down, and I flick my eyes open to see Fred standing there, solid and warm and comforting. He has that look on his face, the one he'd get before he'd laugh, call me Sonny, and then sweep me into his arms.

Oh, Fred.

"I'm here, Alice," he whispers, moving his fingers over to the Vorpal Blade, like he's planning on taking it from me. I almost let him, too, until I realize what he's just said.

Alice.

Fred would never call me Alice. Hell, he rarely called me Allison. It was Sonny or Alli or Little Sis or Asshole or Bitch-face. But Alice?

"Allison!" Tee shouts, knocking a pistol from the Liam-lookalike's hand.

I have about two seconds before I realize that the Fred standing in front of me … is a goddamn Rabbit.

A Rabbit with a gun.

Fred lifts the weapon up, whips a match out from behind his ear, and lights up. But when he points the gun at me, he hesitates. *Rabbits take on the essences of their forms.* For a split-second there, it looks like he might have changed his mind. The Rabbit shifts back into what I'm assuming is his original form, like he's trying to clear his head. His ears are a golden caramel brown to match his eyes, twitching as he locks his hard stare on me.

I try to move out of the way, but my body is sore all over, my ribs are cracked, and no matter how fast I try to move, Rabbit-Fred keeps his gun trained on me. The fuse burns down and … then the Black Rabbit is stepping between us, shielding me with her body.

The weapon fires with the crack of sulfur and gunpowder, sending a small projectile straight into her chest. She staggers with the force of the impact, and slams into me, knocking us both to the ground.

"Allison-who—" Dee is panting so hard, he can't even finish his nickname for me, yanking me out from underneath the Black Rabbit's body. I stare down at her face as he drags me aside, and I can't help it: I touch my fingers to her bloody lips.

"Allison," she murmurs as I hold back on the tears. The way she's looking at me right now, I can see it, the little bit of my father that she's absorbed. She really *did* care about me and Edy. "My little girl." The Black Rabbit coughs up blood as Dee yanks me into a standing position. Fred-Rabbit points his weapon at us again, but Dee shoves me aside, sending me sprawling to the pavement.

With my wounded ribs, it's definitely not a pleasant sensation. I can *feel* the bones rubbing together, shards of my own body scraping across one another. The pain is fucking *exquisite*, breaking my vision up into jagged, white-hot lines, like lightning bolts in my brain. A groan escapes me, and the sheer, raw agony of the sound hurts my already bloodied ears.

"Allison!" Mom screams, and I hope to Hearts that she doesn't try to come over here.

I glance up just in time to see the Gryphon coming down at me, his legs curled up against his body like a hawk descending on its prey, toes stretched wide, talons extended. He just barely scratches the surface of my chest when Lar steps up beside me, drawing a gold sigil with his fingers. A protective shield comes up between me and the Gryphon, knocking him momentarily aside.

"Up, Sunshine, hurry," Lar breathes, pulling off one of his earrings. He tosses it at the Gryphon, igniting the creature's ragged brown feathers. The flames crawl across his entire wingspan as he screams and thrashes. I take the Caterpillar's offered hand, getting to my feet just in time to see Tee shield my mother and sister with his wings, knocking aside a brown striped bandersnatch with a simple flick of one, feathered appendage.

I let Lar pull me into his arms, his red jacket still clinging to his shoulders. I imagine that it's spelled, much like my crown, so that it doesn't fall off. His tobacco and blueberry scent enfolds me, but it's tainted with the reek of blood and the cloying sweetness of rotten flesh. The skin on Lar's neck is peeling off, leaving red-red muscle and tinged black edges. From the Mocking Turtle's tongue, no doubt.

Frantically, I search around for the Anti-Alice, but she's nowhere to be seen. *I didn't kill her?!* I think, wondering where she could've possibly gone. She could barely stand up, for fuck's sake. Someone must've moved her. My gaze searches the parking area, and the trees, but I can't seem to find the Carpenter *or* the King. And, as large as they are, the Walrus and the Duke are conspicuously absent.

Rab bounds over, his claws sliding across the pavement.

"March and the Hatter?" I ask, breathless and hurting. I could *really* use a healthy dose of vampire blood, if you know what I mean. Lar shakes his head, but before he gets a chance to answer me, the three of us are surrounded by the Gryphon, the Mocking Turtle, and the two new Rabbits.

My mother and sister stand near the van with Tee and Dee in front of them.

"You dragged your brother into hell with your actions," the Mocking Turtle whispers, circling around us, flesh peeling from his face in rotten strips. The March Hare's poison is doing its job, but the fucker doesn't seem to be hurting for it. "And so it seems you'll take the rest of your family with you."

"Eat a dick," I whisper, but I can barely talk. In fact, it's getting harder and harder to breathe. My lungs feel wet, and there's the metallic taste of blood on my lips. *Have I punctured a lung or something?!* My heart thunders in my chest as M.T. smiles at us, his curved beak of a mouth twisting into a grotesque replica of a grin.

"Should we talk about the sweet taste of the White Rabbit's pet mouse? How he gagged, how he wept, after the former King of Hearts took its head and then made him eat it? Do you remember that, *Rab*, how your nose clogged with snot, your throat with bile, your heart with pain?"

"Shut your mouth!" the bandersnatch roars, tail flicking wildly, nails digging into the pavement. "Or I'll shut it for you."

The Mocking Turtle laughs as the Gryphon smiles at him from across our little circle.

"Oh, Caterpillar," M.T. murmurs as Lar closes his eyes and hums under his breath. He draws more gold sigils around us, but I can tell he's suffering under the stare of these two men. I remember what I felt like the night of the Torrid Tea Party. The Mocking Turtle and the Gryphon … there's a reason they're the right-hand men of the Walrus and the Carpenter. "Does your head hurt? Can you feel us inside your skull?" M.T. licks his lips, but I'm just fucking *done* listening to him talk.

The two Rabbits are standing there watching, waiting, guns in hand. They could shift into bandersnatch form at any moment and take us on. With Tee and Dee, we outnumber them but just barely. And if the twins join in the fight, that leaves my mother and sister exposed. I can't have that.

I step forward, feeling the magic swirling around inside of me. Those Rabbits … they have Liam and Fred inside of them. One of whom is so evil, he doesn't deserve to exist in any capacity. The other … too good to have his essence stolen.

The Vorpal Blade goes back into its sheath before I curl my hands into fists and close my eyes. There's so much power, so much magic, it tears through me like a storm. A supernatural breeze stirs my blonde and rainbow hair around my face, and even though it hurts to breathe, I know I've got this.

"Sunshine, don't," Lar whispers, but I'm already unleashing that magic, letting it curl from me like chains. It hits the ground at various points, summoning more of the little glowing mushrooms. They sprout up everywhere, lighting the dark, stormy parking area. Somehow, for a minute there, I manage to keep the magic in check. But then the Gryphon and the Mocking Turtle start toward me, and I let go.

Power explodes from me, like a ripple in a lake. It echoes out around the park, blowing back the boughs, pushing the SUV over onto its side, and knocking *everyone* around me down flat. I don't mean to hit the twins or my family, Lar or Rab, but it just happens and I can't control it. When the next surge comes, I push it into the four men that are trying to kill us.

My power latches onto them like lightning on metal rods, crashing down and burning the Gryphon's swampy brown eyes, the Mocking Turtle's dark pits, and the gazes of the two Rabbits. Their screams tear at my ears, like the jabberwock's roar, and I feel more blood oozing down the sides of my neck.

The Mocking Turtle recovers first, scrambling to get to me, lashing out with his tongue and hitting me dead in the face with it. It's as powerful as a fist, knocking me back several steps. I can feel bones crack in my face, but the magic is too wild for a simple thing like a broken jaw to stop. I turn back to M.T., just in time to see him grab my arm, bring it to his lips, and clamp down with those toothless gums.

So much pain floods through me that I let out a scream of my own. In the distance, I swear I can hear some of the men calling to me, but I don't stop. I throw my broken arm even harder into the Mocking Turtle's mouth, sending a wave of wild magic through him. Like with the women of Underland during the Riving, this magic tears through the Mocking Turtle, ripping him apart from the inside out.

Blood leaks from his eyes and nose, his mouth and ears. He stumbles back, clawing at his face, writhing and spasming in agony. *The School of Reeling and Writhing, my ass.*

"Sonny, stop!" Rab screams, suddenly standing in front of me, his hands on my shoulders. He tries to look me in the eyes with his bright, red ones, but I can't see much of anything anymore. All I am is power, magic, energy. I fling out my right hand and send a bolt of it into the Gryphon's wing, blowing his left one completely off. The smell of singed feathers reaches my nose as Rab curses under his breath and then slowly begins to shift.

His face softens, his lips get fuller, eyes rounder and bigger. His dark hair becomes bloodred as his ears sink into it, and within just a few seconds, I'm looking at a beautiful young woman that very much reminds me of the King.

"Allison Liddell," she whispers, putting her hands on my bare arms. As soon as her palms make contact with my skin, I feel the magic reigning itself in, drawing back. It's like Rab is pulling it all into me and tying it with a pretty bow, much the same way the King did earlier. He's *rearranging* the magic. "Let it go, the Alice," the Rab-woman whispers, and I do.

With a groan, I collapse into her arms, and she hefts me up like I weigh nothing. I'm having another seizure, thrashing and writhing, blood and spittle flecking my lips.

"I leave you alone for one second," the Mad Hatter snaps, carrying the Looking-Glass with the March Hare, his face still a bloodied, awful mess. The Cheshire Cat is with them, too, but he's most definitely *not* grinning. "Get the Alice and her family through." Raiden tears open his wrist, and shoves the bloodied appendage against my lips, draining as much of the hot, crimson liquid into my throat as he can.

"I'm not leaving without you," March drawls, but the look Raiden gives him is pretty fucking clear. He's not making a suggestion: he's giving an order. "Boss, you've lost the damn plot!"

"Get the Alice back to Underland, and we'll deal with the Topside Looking-Glass." The Mad Hatter sets the mirror on the ground as Tee and Dee move over to stand beside us, dragging my sobbing sister and fear-stricken mother with them. "Now."

Raiden holds a hand out to indicate the silver glass, but Rab doesn't need anymore convincing. With a curse that sounds oh-so mellifluous in his new, feminine voice, we step through and into the viscous warmth of the Looking-Glass liquid.

I'm not exactly all there, thrashing about, my body seizing in violent fits and spasms. The passage through the Looking-Glass is so much worse like this, the silver liquid coating me, choking me. It feels like we're falling forever, much further than my tumble down the Rabbit-Hole.

When we do pass through to the other side, with a gasp and a cry … the first thing I see is the horrible half-smile on the face of the Knave.

♦ ♠ ♣ ♥ ♣ ♠ ♦

Ines Fripon peers at me from between metal bars, her dark hair disheveled and hanging in loose strands on either side of her face. My first thought is that we've woken her up, but that's probably just because I'm knee-deep in the middle of another magic-induced fit.

"Allison," Tee moans, helping Rab lower me to the ground. This time, it's Dee who puts his fingers in my mouth to keep me from biting off my tongue. *This* time, I have an audience of more than just nine men and some card servants.

The Knave is watching; her husbands are watching; my *mother and sister* are watching.

"My baby," Mom weeps, taking my hand in hers and looking around at the men that've passed through the Looking-Glass with me. Tee, Dee, Lar, Rab, Chesh, and March. That means the King, the Duke, and the Mad Hatter were left behind. Logically, I'm aware that *someone* has to stay on the other side until the Topside Looking-Glass is secured. Doesn't mean I have to like it though. "What can I do? What's happening to her?"

To her credit, Hannah Liddell sounds strong and sure of herself, like she could take on any crisis. Her demeanor reminds me of the day she was arrested, how she let the police put her in cuffs, how calm she was when she walked out to the squad car.

"There's nothing you can do," Lar whispers, kneeling next to me. Rab is back in his usual form, but he looks shaken, his red eyes dropping to mine. Our gazes meet, and even though my body won't cooperate, my mind is sharp as a tack. "Sunshine, do you want to fall asleep?" I shake my head and Lar nods, drawing magic in the air above me. It feels like he's cutting little slices into my soul, letting the power bleed out into the cool, damp air around us.

"I'm surprised to see you back in Underland," the Knave says, and I can't tell if she's addressing me or the men, or all of us. "But you've left the King of Hearts behind, that's unfortunate."

Rab takes a step toward her, crossing his tattooed arms over his chest as the Cheshire Cat sniffs at the metal bars. After a moment, he sticks a paw between two of them and yelps, stumbling back with missing fur and a blackened toe. He stares at it for a moment, the smell of rot tingeing the air, and then pads over to me to lick some of the Hatter's blood from my face. It's enough to heal the wound, but I doubt he'll be doing that again anytime soon.

"Focus on me, Allison-who-isn't-Alice." Dee takes my face in one hand, the fingers of his other still stuck between my lips. I'm not biting him this time though, not like I did Tee. Already, I feel like I'm starting to calm down. Whatever happens, I *won't* let myself pass out. "Just keep looking at me."

"I'm surprised to see *you* behind bars." Rab nods his chin in the Knave's direction. It takes every last kernel of strength I've got, but I tilt my head slightly to look at Ines again. She's not just behind *one* set of bars, but two. We're in a dungeon of some sort, very like the one in Castle Heart, but this one … doesn't seem quite as, um, *unused*. I can see the March Hare examining the stone walls with his palms, nose twitching at the awful smell.

If I listen carefully, I can hear screams and cries echoing down the stone corridor. The reek of sweat, feces, and urine is strong, so strong that if I weren't still seizing, I might puke. Tee pulls me close to him, curling one wing underneath me to cradle my bleeding body. My ribs are already starting to knit together from the Hatter's blood, but I'm still choking on the fluid in my lungs.

"Mom, I'm scared," Edy whispers, clinging to Hannah's back like she's five years old all over again. My mother ignores her, face stoic and determined, even with tears dripping down her cheeks. She's wearing the chunky, oversized white sweater I brought her, but I can see the orange jumpsuit underneath it still.

"She's calming down, I think," Dee whispers as Lar continues to draw sigils, and Chesh shifts back into his human form to let Dinah out of her carrier—thank fuck somebody remembered to bring her with us. Mom's eyes widen, but she doesn't say anything—not aloud anyway. *"Cats turning into people, well, that's certainly interesting, but my daughter is bleeding everywhere, and I have more important concerns to address."* That's what I imagine that she's thinking. Hannah Reeve Liddell, folks, always a trooper.

Tee nods his head, but doesn't say anything, sweeping hair off my sticky forehead. When I close my eyes, I can smell him and his brother both, their sweet scents cutting through the blood and the bullshit. But I dare not keep my eyes closed too long for fear of drifting off.

"Surprised to see me here?" the Knave answers at least, glancing over her shoulders at her husbands, the Lion with his golden hair and grizzled beard, and the Unicorn with his silver topknot and pale eyes. "And why is that? Because you and the King were too busy trying to frame *me* for treason when all along, it was his precious White Knight?"

"You're telling me," Rab says, pulling out a cigarette from his pocket and lighting up. He doesn't seem at all concerned that we're trapped in such a small cell with nothing but a dirty bucket and piles of wet, rotten straw to keep us company. March snatches the lit cig from Rab, forcing him to get out another with a scowl tainting his lips. "That you had no hand or foot in any treason, duplicity, traitorous intent, or deception?"

The Knave smiles and shakes her head, her crown still perched atop her mussy brunette hair.

"That's exactly what I'm telling you," she says, her green gaze snapping up at the same time March shouts and Rab turns, only to find the Looking-Glass being spun around, its gilded back against the stone wall of the dungeon. It's a trick fucking wall, and it turns around so quick, slamming back into place so fast that even though both Chesh, March and Rab all lunge for it, they come up against nothing but stone.

"What the fuck?!" Rab shouts, turning back around and heading straight for the dungeon bars. He attempts to curl his fingers around the metal, only to find himself seared with rotten burns, like Chesh. Cursing, he sucks at his skin and tilts his head to the side, one white ear flopping over completely. "This …"

"A gift from the Carpenter," a soft voice says, preceding an entourage of boots down the corridor. I'm calming down enough that Dee slides his fingers from my lips, and Tee helps me sit up. My body is still spasming, and I highly doubt I could string two words together if I tried. Chevalier pauses in between our cell and the Knave's, looking down at me with lavender eyes. She doesn't look gleeful or maniacal, just sad, like this is all a necessary evil. "That is, his very last gift to me. He won't be coming back through the Looking-Glass, him or the Walrus."

"I should've blown your head off when I had the chance," Rab says, in a very casual sort of way, his red eyes tracking across the rest of the gathered crowd. He pushes his shirtsleeve up and taps at a ticking clock. "This was a countdown to betrayal, and as you can see, we're way past due."

"If you suspected me before, why not take me down?" Chevalier asks, tilting her head to one side. Blonde hair cascades over her shoulder like a waterfall.

"*King's ... orders ...*" Rab drawls, pulling out his pistol and tapping at the side of his head with it. Nobody seems concerned that he's got a gun inside the cell with him. I imagine there's not a snowball's chance in fucking hell he could fire it out between the bars and hit the Knight. Whatever this strange magic is, keeping us in here, I bet it protects everyone *out* there as well.

"Well, the King is a fool," Chevalier curses under her breath, glancing over at a big, round man standing near her. His face is as pale as an egg, and oval like one, too. He looks like a stuffed figure, rather than a king, with his protruding belly, pale blonde beard, and scruff of hair tufted around his crown. Comparing him to Brennin Red would be like, well, comparing a child to a man, although I'm certain *this* king is far, far older.

"No, I do believe the King of Diamonds is the fool if he believes this *purr-lan* will work itself out," Chesh growls, the tip of his furry tail stroking my cheek as he stands beside the White Rabbit. His claws are extending and retracting from the tips of his fingers as he curls and uncurls his fists.

"It's *very* provoking," the King of Diamonds—because based on his red robes, covered in white diamond shapes, and the enormous white diamond at the front of his crown, he must be—says after a long silence, looking away from me for the first time since arriving in the corridor. "To be called a fool—*very*. I mean, considering Brennin Red is nowhere to be seen. For servants to pass through the Looking-Glass when the very ruler of the Kingdom of Hearts is missing? How queer."

The King of Diamonds twitches his nose, his bristle white mustache quivering with the movement. At his side, the queen—if that's who she even is—stands with her shawl crooked, her hair in a mess, and her hands quivering. She's as timid as a fucking sheep, and I can't help but wonder if she's some sort of puppet queen, a woman on the throne that the king is manipulating. She's so out of sorts that she's even got a silver-handled brush stuck in her matted, white hair. She doesn't say a word as the king harrumphs.

"Some people have no more sense than a baby," he says, beginning to turn away. "Make yourselves comfortable in there, my friends. Once we've ensured the Walrus and the Carpenter won't be crossing the Looking-Glass, we'll stomp their army and *then* you lot of idiots can return home. At least we've still got the Queen of Hearts, at any rate. I've no interest in killing idiots whose only crime is their abject failure at upholding the prophecy."

"They haven't been married," the Knave interjects, like she's simply furious at the thought of me taking the throne. "And the King will come back. Death could not keep him from his throne."

"*Humpty Dumpty sat on a wall,*" the Caterpillar begins, rising to his feet and tucking his hair back behind the ear that still has the red earring dangling from it. "*Humpty Dumpty had a great fall.*"

"Silence!" the king shouts, turning back around and getting so very close to the bars. The guards and servants accompanying him seem to be human. Well, as human as anything gets in Underland, but they are most certainly *not* card people. At any rate, it seems the magical bars work both ways because nobody moves to open the door. "Heresy!"

"*All the King's horses,*" Lar continues as the king throws his robes violently over his shoulder and takes off down the corridor, past Dor—who I hadn't even bothered to take note of until now—and toward the heavy wooden door he came in from. "*And all the King's men, couldn't put Humpty's mangled body together again.*" Lar grits his teeth and leans in as close to the bars as he can get. "This is prophecy! You will fall, I'm certain of it."

The door slams closed as the Caterpillar redirects his attention to the White Knight.

"You should be ashamed of yourself," he murmurs, looking her up and down with his pale, blue eyes, wings crackling with glitter and light. It looks for a moment like he might have a vision to share, but nothing comes of it. Perhaps the Mocking Turtle broke him again? "Doubting our ability to handle the prophecy. Don't you think if you had a role in it, your name would've been mentioned?" Lar swipes at some of the silver goo coating his arm, but it doesn't do any good; we're all covered in it.

"And you," March says, striding forward, swiping blood and ... whatever else away from his face. I think it's bits of flesh. His nose seems to be healed, but there's some, uh, leftover chunks from it nearly getting severed. He steps up beside Rab, shoulder-to-shoulder, Rabbit-to-Rabbit. His chocolate-colored eyes take Dor's huge, hulking form in with a scowl. "Shoulda pegged you for a double-double-crosser," he murmurs under his breath. Am I the only one who's taking note of the *double-double* in that sentence? "But serving the White Knight, really? Surely, *you'd* throw the towel in with someone who has better odds of winning their hand at cards, eh?"

"You and the Boss left through the Looking-Glass," Dor says with a hefty shrug, taking in our ragtag crew and smiling when he notices the Duke is conspicuously absent. "'Sides, they gave me a better deal. What was it you said? People gives us monies and prays they ain't outbid? Well, you been outbid, *pet*." Dor crosses his massive arms in front of his body, lifting his chin. His tiny, round ears wiggle in his dirty brown hair. After a moment, like he's only just thought of it, he reaches up and takes the tiny top hat off his head, chucking it aside.

March just smiles, his brown ears flattening against his skull. He definitely knows something he's not saying. He adjusts his own hat, shrugs his own broad shoulders, and shakes his head.

"The Mad Hatter … he doesn't exactly sew and sell hats, now does he, Dor? Do you know what he does to disobedient *pets*?" The Dormouse ignores his ex-comrade's words and stares straight at the wall, like a very well-behaved … or very well-paid employee.

"Enough conjecture," the White Knight says, squeezing a small flower on her shoulder. It sneezes and fills the air with a glittery pink cloud and the summery scent of sweet peas. "This," she continues before anyone can even ask, "this is my own invention. It's a spray that clears the head, keeps the mind focused, and lowers frantic heart rates." What I want to say is, *sounds like a load of bullshit, and a dash of aromatherapy, bitch.* "Look, I made a small bargain with the Walrus and the Carpenter, but I did it for the good of Underland." She pauses, narrowing her round, lavender eyes on the floor, like she's thinking rather hard about something. "No, I did it for *Wonder*land, because when I'm finished, this world will bloom like flowers in a spring storm."

"It'll wither and die like roses in the desert," Rab drawls as Tee and Dee help me adjust myself. I'm fully sitting up, but my body is still twitching and spasming, and I can't seem to find my voice. "But keep at it. You'll soon be dead. You don't think the Walrus and the Carpenter expected betrayal? They eat, live, and breathe it."

"I know what I'm doing," Chevalier snaps, sighing and then glancing back at the Knave. "I know what I'm doing, and I'm the only one qualified to get it done." She looks at me next, and then smiles. I don't think she hates me. No, she really does believe she's doing what's best for the world, misguided as her actions are.

"Where's my dad?" I gasp, fingers of fire clawing at the inside of my throat. It's like having strep, but a million times worse. My tongue may as well be held between fire-warmed iron pinchers, and there could very well be a scorpion living inside my throat. "I want to see him."

The White Knight pauses, sighs, and then waves her hand for the guards. I notice they're wearing red surcoats covered in white hearts. If there's anything to do with color in this world—black, red, white—I can't tell. The suits seem to be the only important part of the equation, other than preference. The King of Hearts likes red, the Knave prefers black, and the White Knight … well, her name is quite literally *white* in French.

"Throw her father in with the Knave. We can't risk opening the Alice's cell." Chevalier leaves the room as the guards do as she's asked, opening one of the other prison cells with the creak of iron.

"Your father?" Mom asks, looking confused as hell. She watches as the guardswomen drag Dad down the stone corridor. He's not wearing shackles or anything, just an old bandage on his left arm. I wonder if that's where the Black Rabbit … you know, got her meat from.

"Henry!" Hannah shouts as Edith lets out a tiny squeak, cowering behind my mother's strong form. They both watch as Dad is pushed into the Knave's cell, the iron bars are slammed shut, and the Carpenter's spell is reactivated with a special sigil.

Dad looks at us through dirty, cracked lenses, his brown eyes wide with surprise and fear.

"Edy, Allison … *Hannah*," he chokes, sitting up to wrap his fingers around the bars. "How did you get here?"

"How did *you* get here?" Mom repeats, blinking confusedly.

"I ... *I fell through a mirror,*" he chokes, glancing away unashamedly. For an atheist who teaches women's studies—one of barely a dozen men in the USA to carry a doctorate in that field, go Dad!—all of this mystical, metaphysical, supernatural bullshit must be making him crazy.

"So did we." Mom lifts her hands up, examining the viscous, silver liquid on her skin. "At least, I think we did. I feel like I'm losing my mind."

"Well," Rab purrs, tucking his brightly inked left hand into his pocket. He lifts his chin, salutes with his burning cigarette, and gives a smile sharp enough to cut. "That's the norm here, folks. Welcome ... to Underland."

♦ ♥ ♣ ♠ ♣ ♥ ♦

Try as I might, I end up falling asleep, soaked in that strange, silver liquid, wrapped up in the twins' arms. My mother is beside me when I finally give in, floating away on a river of dreams. The very last thing in the world I want to do right now is drift off, but I'm too weak from the magic to fight it.

The first thing I hear when I do wake up, is my mom arguing with the twins.

"She may—if she chooses," says Dee, "we've no objection. Contrariwise."

"Selfish things!" my mother huffs, and as I crack my lids, I see her nostrils flaring in anger. "You can talk all you want about this ... this *prophecy* or whatnot, but Allison is *my* daughter. I'm taking her home immediately."

"How so?" Tee asks, and I can tell by his tone of voice that this argument must've been going on for some time. "I already told you: the only way home is through the Looking-Glass. How do you propose to get out of this cell, find it inside Castle Diamond, and then get back through without being skewered by the Walrus and the Carpenter?"

"This isn't real," Edith whispers, sitting back against the stone wall with her palms over her ears. Her mascara has crawled down her face along with her tears, just two black streaks on her pale cheeks. "I dropped acid and—"

"You're dropping acid now?" Mom asks, her voice breathy and rife with frustration. "Since when?" She turns around to give Edy a look, but my little sister is completely out of it, her blue eyes as glassy as a still lake in spring.

"Aren't you rather relieved that *she* is not the Alice?" Chesh asks, peering into my sister's face with a pussy's sharp-toothed grin. "A ten percent chance at saving Underland ... no, no, that's not right. I imagine there's an extra zero added to the end of her chances." Chesh pokes Edith's shoulder with his tail, and she shrieks.

"I don't imagine I'd have been as pleased had the King gifted us to her instead," Dee agrees, as my mother resumes her stare-off with Tee.

"I may if I choose, what?" I choke out, and then break into a coughing fit, drawing the attention of everyone in both cells.

"You may stay in Underland," Tee says, turning to look at me. I can tell when I look into his amethyst eyes that he already knows my plan. His wings are gone, the only clue I have as to what time it is. He reaches out to cup the side of my face, showing off those intricate black and purple tattoos on the back of his arm. Honestly, once the curse is broken, I might ask him if he'd consider getting some new ink. It looks damn good on him.

Speaking of ink, I'd almost forgotten about mine. Of course, the jeans I'm wearing have ripped at just the right spot to show it off, that clock buried inside a lace cameo. Mom notices me looking at it straight away, and both her brows go up as she lifts her gaze to mine.

"Mom," I say, taking Tee's hand from my face and holding it in my lap. "I'm guessing you got a debrief while I was out?" I glance over at Dad, sitting as close to the bars of his own cell as he can get without being burned. He meets my eyes and smiles softly, tears brimming on the edges of his eyes. His expression makes me think of the Black Rabbit yet again, how even a tiny sliver of Henry's essence could brim with love.

I'm lucky to have the family I have left.

No wonder I was so conflicted about staying here at first.

But I'm not conflicted now.

"I … was informed," Hannah says, looking at Dad, then back to me again. "But Allison, it's rather hard to believe."

"Except that your clothes are soaked in Looking-Glass goo, you're sitting in a stone dungeon, and you saw that battle with your own eyes. Mom," I plead, leaning toward her. "Disbelief and denial are the tools of the ignorant and the uneducated. You've said that to me my entire life. Look around you."

I try to stand up, but all that happens is that I fall into Dee's arms.

"I'm looking, Allison. It's just … it's a lot." Mom stands up, looking between me and Dee with a curious expression on her face. *Curiouser and fucking curiouser, huh, Mom? Hey, I bet you're wondering if one of these guys is my boyfriend. Turns out, I have nine boyfriends! I've only fucked five of them so far, but don't worry: I'm sure I'll get to the rest soon.*

Yeah, no.

"And you've met …" I start, gesturing at the guys. I'm already in a near panic thinking about the three I've left behind. Hook, line, and sinker, these assholes have gotten my panties in a permanent wad.

"Your nine big cocks?" Edith asks, finally lifting her head up to stare at me like I'm an alien from another planet. "Yeah, we've met. And don't worry: they've *all* mentioned how they're your boyfriends."

"Boyfriend is such a weird word," Dee says, his voice taking on a bit of that special Underland singsong quality. "Because it denotes a boy who's a friend which, in reality, would be any person who's a friend who has a penis who's under a certain age. Then again, that age varies from person to person, but I'm fairly certain neither Rab nor Lar nor March would qualify as a boy." He pauses and taps his lips, but Edith just stares at him like she's losing her mind.

"Boyfriend," Chesh says with a huff, hooking his fingers together behind his dark head. "No, we never said boyfriend. We said a few of the men you were looking at belonged in the Alice's harem, and then several more that got left behind were in the Alice's harem, and then the rest of us are … just wannabes."

"Harem," my mom says, nodding briefly as she glances at Tee and Dee. I'm guessing she's made the leap of logic that sex is involved. I know I'm eighteen, and sex is perfectly normal and natural, but having your Mom stare at you with this look that says *I get ya banged a lot of these dudes* is just … uncomfortable.

Stride of pride, Allison, not walk of shame. Stride of fucking pride!

"Midnight Knicker Dancer here is the future Queen of Hearts," Chesh declares proudly, stroking Dinah's back. The cat glares at me with her bright yellow eyes, and I swear, if I didn't know better, I'd say she was smirking at me. "Which means you're the mother, father, and sister of the future Queen of Hearts. That's quite the honor."

"Quite the honor," Dee agrees as I hear the Knave sigh from across the corridor.

I turn to look at her, and even though she's still a judgmental buttwaffle who cursed my poor twins, I feel bad for suspecting her just for being a bitch. She's not working with the Knight, so she must really be on the King's side. I should've known, considering the depth of her crush on him.

"So how do we get out of here?" I ask, because being stuck in a dungeon while a war rages on does not sound like a particularly good time to me. "Red said his soldiers, plus the Hatter's, were poised to go to battle with the Walrus and Carpenter's army. Is that still happening?"

"War rages regardless of the whims of women and men," the Knave says, blinking her spring green eyes at me. She glances back at her husbands, both of whom I still find weird, but at least respect for standing up for their wife. Sure, the Lion may have punched Brennin in the face, but I *did* hold a very powerful blade to his wife's throat. A blade that, I might add, is still in my possession.

The White Knight and the King of Diamonds must really have a lot of faith in this fucking cell.

"The soldiers have moved out, yes. They're unaware of the White Knight's betrayal and she is still the general of Red's army." The Knave looks to March with one of her perfectly manicured brows raised.

"Raiden's army will follow along until they hear otherwise … or until their pay runs out." March sighs and digs around in his velvet trench for something to eat. When he doesn't find anything, he lifts up his hat and pulls out a cupcake.

It has a tiny, candy-coated grasshopper on the top, pink frosting, and white sprinkles. After a moment of gazing at it, he moves forward and kneels down beside me, his trench fluttering around him. When he offers up that cupcake like it's a diamond ring, I get a little flutter in my belly.

"Thank you," I whisper, and although I wouldn't normally accept food when I'm sure everyone else is hungry too, the magic I used on the Gryphon and the Mocking Turtle has drained me dry. I need this; I feel weak and dizzy enough as is. This time, I even eat the grasshopper.

"Once the King, the Duke, and the Hatter are back, they won't be able to hold us here," Lar says, exhaling and running his fingers through his long hair. "But who knows how long that will be." His wings beat gently, stirring bits of rotten straw up on the floor. The supernatural breeze that always surrounds him is here even now. "The Vorpal Blade, it can make doors, can't it?"

"Not without a hefty price," Tee scoffs, shaking his head. "And even then, it's a rumor. I thought we'd already established that?"

"It's a shard of the Looking-Glass," Lar says, staring the angel prince down. "Perhaps it could be our way out?" He moves forward and holds out his hand, asking for the weapon. I know how precious it is, so giving it over to him is a huge leap of faith and trust.

The Caterpillar takes it and runs his fingers down the shiny, silver surface, examining the blade itself, and the carved black jabberwock horn that makes up the hilt. After a moment, he glances up and over at the bars of the cell.

"We've tried everything else to get out of here," Rab says, lighting up another cigarette. "It's tight enough to keep a mouse locked in. The stones reflect our magic back at us. And, well, I'm not even going to try to shoot our way out. I have *some* sense, you know. So unless you can pull a rabbit out of a hat"—he flashes his knife-sharp grin—"then we're shit out of luck."

"It's the Carpenter's necromancy that makes up these cells," the Knave says, looking up at the moss-covered ceiling. The moss itself glows in all sorts of different colors: neon pink, spring green, pumpkin orange, but it collects water from leaks between the stones and drip-drip-drips moisture on our heads. "These are years in the making, probably decades, maybe close to a century."

I follow her gaze up and around, peering at the thick, dark stone, the moss, the tiny clusters of mushrooms sprouting up here and there. Even though we're in Underland, in a dungeon, in a terribly terrible predicament, I feel better. The air feels different here, charged, like there's possibility in every molecule. I didn't feel that way when I was Topside.

"If North were here, maybe he'd know what to do," Chesh yowls, sitting on the ground with the soles of his bare feet pressed together, elbows resting on his splayed knees.

"Why would North know any better than any of you?" I ask, frustrated to hear that my voice still sounds like a chorus of toads, all of them with strep-fucking-throat and smoker's lung.

"The Northumbrians used to make the Looking-Glasses," Lar says, sitting down next to me and handing back the blade. "They *loaned* their creations out to the four Kingdoms of Suits, as well as other nations: the angels, the neko, the … fae." Lar pauses and exhales. *Neko—that means cat in Japanese, right?* I glance over at Chesh and find him staring at us with dilated pupils. I can hardly see any of the gray in his irises. "They were supposed to get them back, should they ever ask. And when the Riving happened, the art was lost, and the warring started … the Northumbrians *did* ask for them back—all of them." He turns the blade around in his hands. "Of course, no Kingdom was about to honor that request."

"Except for the King of Hearts?" I ask, touching the blade. '*It was* owed *to me,'* North had said, tail thrashing. "And even then, only a shard." Lar nods and leans back, flicking one of his wings in frustration when the moss drips several icy cool droplets down his back. "So he might know what to do with this—if he's not already dead."

Dread lodges in my throat, but I refuse to think about losing North. I've only just gotten him. And I don't think I've even really allowed myself to accept *or* enjoy the fact that I have him in the first place.

"Maybe," Tee says, but he sounds skeptical as fuck. "But I doubt it."

"Well, it was worth an errant thought." Lar waves his hand dismissively as I study Tee's lips. Before I can let self-doubt creep in, I sit up and lean forward, thrusting my mouth against his. It's a quick kiss because, eww, Mom and Dad are staring at me, but it does the trick: his wings open up in glorious ebony and amethyst folds.

Dee is next, and he very cheekily pulls me into his arms and tongues me while Dad gawps, and adjusts his glasses with a middle finger. Doubt that move was incidental.

The chains are ridiculously loud as they hit the floor, and I lift my face up to glare over Dee's shoulder in the direction of the Knave.

"If we spring you out of here, you remove the twins' curse," I say, but she shakes her head, infuriating me even further.

"Once I see the twins earn it, I'll release them."

"Don't bother with her, Allison-who-isn't-Alice," Dee says, pushing back just enough, so that he can look down into my face. "She won't change her mind, but *you* can, eventually, remove the curse."

"That's all fine and dandy, isn't it, love?" March says with a sigh, his brown eyes heavy and tired looking. He's worried about the Mad Hatter, I'll bet. Funny thing is: so am I. The Duke and the King, too. "And yet, we need to get out of here and we need to take the Looking-Glass with us." He wedges the tip of his knife in between two of the stones and curses under his breath, something like *bloody, cocksucking, wankers.* It sounds very, I dunno, British. I find it sexy as hell.

I look up again and find a bug with wings like holly leaves, resting upside down on the moss clusters.

"What *is* that?" I ask as Rab steps up beside me, following my gaze with his beautiful red eyes.

"It's a snap-dragon-fly." He reaches up and grabs the poor thing by its wing, bringing it down to my eye level. "Its body is made of plum-pudding, and its head is a raisin burning in brandy."

Noticing the small flames on the creature's head, I cock a brow. Now *that* is some freaky Underland shit right there.

"It's perfectly edible," the March Hare says with another roll of his eyes.

"And what does *it* eat?" I'm having trouble even believing such a creature exists, let alone that it takes care of itself. I don't even see a mouth.

"Frumenty and mince pie." Rab doesn't even blink as he relays two items that I've never heard of in my whole life. Okay, so maybe I've heard of mince pie, but I don't really know what it is. And Frumenty? "Cracked wheat boiled with milk or broth, and a sweet pie filled with dried fruit and spices."

"Fucking gross," Edith murmurs from her corner of the room. I notice she's picked the corner opposite the one with the trick wall. Wouldn't surprise me if there was another though.

Rab pops the flaming head off the bug, cursing and shaking his fingers out. He offers up the pudding-body to me, but I wrinkle my nose. March takes it and eats it while Rab finishes off the head.

"Guess we know we could survive in here long-term, even if they don't feed us," I joke, but the words fall flat. My mom is staring at me like she doesn't know who I am, my sister is staring at the floor like she wishes she could melt into it, and my dad is gazing at me with shock and awe from across the corridor. "They will feed us though, won't they?"

"Presumably, if they have any sense," Rab says, pacing along the length of the cell.

For a while there, it's silent but for the dripping of the moss onto the stone. A new mushroom grows from between the pavers, yellow with orange spots. That reminds me … I undo the clasp on the Vorpal Blade's holster and pull out the last of my mushroom flesh. Of course, I could always suck Tee or Dee off if I need more. Just … not in front of Mommy and Daddy, no thank you.

"Even if you shrink, you can't get between the bars," Rab says, but I just lift my gaze to his and cock a brow.

"*You* can't, but you're not the Alice."

Rab smiles at me with murderously carnal intent. I shiver.

"I thought you weren't the Alice either, such protests you made." He strokes his hands over his ears and then pulls a stopwatch from inside his pocket. I recognize it as the one he used to activate his time magic earlier.

"No," I say, standing up and moving over to him. I curl my fingers around his and look him straight in the eye. "*Stop using this.*" He watches me for a moment and then clicks the button anyway. Everyone around us freezes, leaving just the two of us in that damp cell. "Rab, stop, please."

"Why?"

"We've been over this," I whisper, not at all sure why I'm whispering in the first place. I glance back at the room, noticing that my mom is staring at my sister now, and so is my dad. I'm glad that they're not frozen in judgment, gazes trained on me. That'd make me way too damn nervous. "I don't want you wasting your life. Every second we have is precious, and nobody knows what comes after. Please don't." Two heartbeats pass, then three. Rab is still just staring down at me, but I can see the pulse in the side of his neck thumping wildly. "I care about you."

"I can't imagine how that happened." He tries to sound nonchalant, but his voice is too rough. Rab reaches out one of his inked hands and caresses the side of my face. His fingers feel too good for words, the whorls of his fingertips teasing across my mouth. "Although … despite my psychopathic tendencies"—the corner of his lip curls up in a teasing smile—"when I saw you getting your ass kicked earlier, it hurt … right here in the dark cavern of my heart place."

"Your heart place, huh?" I can't take my eyes off of Rab's, even as I'm aiming to snatch that stopwatch from his hand. When I get the opportunity, I grab it, hitting the button hard with my thumb. Nothing happens. It's still just him and me, and frozen droplets of water clinging to the air.

"Only I can activate or deactivate this magic." I stuff the stopwatch into Rab's vest pocket, and sigh.

"So what do you want, hmm? What do you want me to do so you'll stop with this nonsense?"

The White Rabbit just stares at me like he can't get enough of me, like *I* have *FUCKING DRINK ME* written across my forehead, and he can't swallow fast enough.

"Sonny," he whispers, his voice like frost. But then his arms slide around me, and it's like I'm wrapped in a plaid wool blanket, sipping hot cocoa, with a new book on my Kindle waiting for its pages to be devoured. "Sonny," he repeats, leaning down and touching his lips to mine so gently, it's like a snowflake settling on my hot mouth.

And, like a snowflake, he ends up melting against me. His hot tongue slides between my lips, his palm across my lower back. Rab curls the fingers of his left hand around my messy braid, and gives it a little yank. His tongue travels across my lower lip to my jaw, and then he kisses his way to my ear.

Every second of this is costing an hour of his life, I think, but when I repeat that thought aloud, Rab just chuckles.

"You think it's not worth it?" he asks, reaching for my corset and carefully undoing the clasps. He tosses the white and black fabric aside, then cups my waist with his inked hands. Our eyes meet, and my breath catches in my throat. "Because it is, to me."

He spins us around and pushes me against the wall, reaching under what's left of my tattered ball gown, and undoing my jeans.

The White Rabbit puts his mouth to my ear.

"Of course, we may want to make this first round a quickie." He shoves the denim down my hips, following it to the floor as I watch, everyone else around us frozen, locked in the still, silent shackles of time.

"Just this first time," I joke, but the sound is so breathless and heady that Rab just laughs at me. I let him untangle my pants and underwear from one foot, freeing my legs. He stands up and puts his inked palm on the wall next to my head, gazing down at me with a bloodred gaze.

"Just this first time," he repeats, a slow, cruel smile spreading across his face. I reach up and touch his cheeks, threading my fingers into his dark hair, running my palms over his soft, white ears.

"Oh," I murmur as Rab's eyes shutter closed. His body quivers and his lips part in pleasure. Hell, I may as well be stroking his dick. "I've always wondered …" I start, sliding my hand down his back and into his pants. And there I find it: a puffy fucking tail. I give it a squeeze and Rab, well, he *growls* at me. It's not like an actual bunny's tail, more like a wolf's. He can probably shift it on and off, like the Savage Duke does.

Rab takes my hands and pins them together at the wrists, holding them above my head.

I can't help but think of his other form, the woman with the bloodred hair, and how once he'd shifted into it, he had powers like the King.

"Your other form," I start and Rab curses, his hand tightening around my wrists. He leans in to kiss me, but my curiosity is burning a hole in my throat. "Who was that?"

The White Rabbit looks down, closing his eyes for a moment. Whatever spell he's under not to reveal his third form, it still seems to be keeping him from telling me, even though I've seen it. He finally looks back up, his gaze dark with lust.

"You know," he manages to grind out between his teeth, "that the King had an older sister, right?"

My mouth drops open, but Rab is already kissing me again, driving any thoughts of Brennin Red's sister from my mind. His tongue conquers my mouth, and I let my head fall back against the stone, relaxing into his touch.

"I hear you made the King use a condom," he whispers, chuckling again. I give a faux struggle against his hands, frowning, but then he bites my ear and any pretense of being unhappy flees right along with my moan. "That's quite ballsy of you, I love it. But," he lifts up an inked finger, releasing some of the pressure on my wrists, "I'm a shifter."

"And that means what?" I manage to choke out. *Damn me and my adult conversations to hell!*

"Shifters *shift* their own fertility on and off. Mine is *off.*" He takes my hand and puts it in his shirt, over his heart. "You're the Alice; you can tell if I'm being honest with you." I swallow hard, thinking of my foray into Dee's mind. Considering that Rab was forced to eat his own pet, I don't want those memories. Instead, I focus on his warm, beating heart, and the pert point of his nipple.

Rab kisses the side of my neck again, and I groan. The Mad Hatter's blood can heal basically anything it seems, so I don't bother to ask about STDs this time. I let more practical thoughts escape my mind like butterflies, letting the White Rabbit clean the vampire's blood from my lips to heal the rot-burns on his fingers.

"I want to be in your harem, Sonny," he says, kissing his way back to my mouth. I'm naked down below, and I can feel the cold stone on my ass, the warm heat of Rab's body on my front. And there's this telling bulge in his slacks that I can't get enough of, no matter how I grind my hips against him. He's standing between my legs, giving me just enough of a taste to make my mouth water.

I *want* him. Badly. This is killing me.

"You'll have to ask Tee," I whisper, as Rab reaches down and unbuttons his pants.

He releases my wrists, and cups me under my ass with his right hand, inked fingers digging into my flesh. My leg wraps around him automatically, and I thank fuck that I'm both tall *and* wearing wicked high combat boots. Otherwise, this position might not work at all.

Rab positions himself at the slick, wet heat of my cunt, staring me straight in the eyes for a moment. It's then that I know my mistake: he's not a psychopath at all, not really. He's a dark, twisted beautiful soul, but a *good* soul nonetheless. He has emotions, heaps of them. He's just afraid of them, running from them. I'd like to help him catch them.

"We'd best hurry," he growls out, pushing just the tip inside of me and making me gasp, "we're *late.*"

Rab drives his hips into me, filling me up all the way to my core. My gasp is cut short by a deep, hard kiss from his lips, his pelvis thrusting against me so hard that my ass scrapes against the wall. Doesn't matter though, not in the moment. I'm so turned-on I can barely breathe, that mind-altering, body-quaking, all-consuming fire that races through the veins and makes the heart thunder.

All I can think, taste, smell, feel in that moment is Rab.

He grinds us together, but he never stops kissing, not even for a second.

My hands find his ears and pull the soft, white lengths down on either side of his head. They feel so good against my skin, and they're so … *unusual,* I can't seem to get enough of them. Eh, maybe I just can't get enough of *him.*

I let one of his ears spring back into place, and it flops right in half again. This time, I use my palm to rub and caress his arm, enjoy his thick, muscular bicep, tease his brightly inked skin with the pad of my thumb.

I could do this forever, but I also hate the fact that each second of carnal pleasure is stealing an hour of Rab's life away.

My other leg wraps Rab's body, and I make no shortage of movements of my own, meeting his thrusts with undulations of my hips, grinding and fucking him at the same time he's fucking me.

Rab uses his one free hand to grasp my breast through my dress, fingering my nipple through the fabric as his groans grow so much less civilized, and I love him like that: un-fucking-civilized.

He rams me into the stone wall, and comes with a mighty groan, burying his face against my neck, panting wildly. My own body is gripping his shaft like a slick glove, holding him tight as he reaches between us to find my clit.

"I finish what I start," he growls, rubbing and caressing me, making me moan and thrash. Either he's a god or shifters just have more stamina than a normal human man, because there's no refractory period—that annoying amount of time after a dude cums when he can't get hard again—for the White Rabbit.

He starts moving again, making me scream and claw at his back, like we've both got a little bandersnatch in us.

My climax tears through me like a shooting fucking star, this bright, hot light that chases away all the dark, and I'm left sobbing and clinging to Rab like he's a life raft.

It only lasts a few seconds, this weird tenderness between us, and then he's setting me down, and we're both fixing our pants. I wipe some of the sweat from my face, and then grab the mushroom meat from the holster again.

"I don't want to look at my mother with sex hair," I say, and he laughs, steepling his hands and putting them against his lips as he lets his head fall back. "I'm shrinking, and then you can start time again."

"Deal," he says, with a very wicked little grin.

Shoving the spongy yellow-white flesh in my mouth, I close my eyes, count my lucky stars, and ride out that awful, awful roller-coaster feeling. Since I've freshly orgasmed, I'm a bit more chill than usual, and it's not nearly as bad as I remember.

Of course, when I finally do open my eyes, I end up stumbling and falling on my ass. I'm still riding that horrible wave of magic I summoned when I was Topside; I could really use more than a cupcake, a nap, and a fuck.

Not that I'm complaining.

Time speeds back up in a rush, and the first thing I hear is Dee asking a horribly embarrassing question.

"Why is Allison-who-isn't-Alice's corset lying in a crumpled heap on the floor?"

"Excellent question, *White Rabbit*?" Tee growls, and I'm sort of glad I'm so shrunk he can't possibly get a read on my expression.

"I haven't the *faintest,*" Rab drawls, smoking a cigarette. "But I am going to give Sonny something to *mount*, if she'll have me." As he talks, his body begins to shrink, white fur sprouting through his clothes. He keeps the cigarette all the way down to the ground, until he's standing before me in mouse form with it clutched between his teeth. Rab takes one last inhale, and spits it to the ground. "Hop on."

"You want me to ride you?" I ask, popping a hip. Above me, my mother looms over us, this gargantuan beast of a woman.

"Allison?" she chokes out, and I'm sure a lesser woman would faint. "Oh my god, Allison!"

"I'm fine, Mom!" I shout, cupping my hands around my mouth. I'm not sure she can hear me, but Tee holds her back, and I can hear him attempting to explain.

"You see, if Allison eats the mushroom flesh—"

"Or my brother's semen," Dee interjects, rather unhelpfully.

"Do you mean," Rab-mouse says, walking up to me, "do you want to ride me *again*?" I ignore him, studying the tattoos on his naked pink rodent legs. Trippy. He's as big as a pony to me now. Not a full-size horse, but a good-size pony. I decide to take him up on his offer and climb on, grabbing a handful of white fur to keep myself on his back.

Rab turns us toward the bars, and the strange magic that seems to rot the flesh when it's touched. I don't want to mess around with this; it's fucking dangerous. So we're going to take it one step at a time.

"Be careful, move slow, and don't take any risks," I warn him, squeezing him with my thighs and finding myself rather pleased when he moves forward like a proper horse. Rab takes us up to the very edge of the bars. He sticks one of his tiny claws between them, and after several seconds, it begins to shrivel until it falls off entirely, leaving just a stump of nail behind.

"How … disturbing," he growls as I take the Vorpal Blade from my holster and stare at my reflection in the shiny silver surface.

I hardly recognize myself, with those big, open blue eyes, that golden hair, the vibrant rainbow streak. My face is determined, my expression hard, and I know for a fact that I am *not* the same girl that fell down that Rabbit-Hole.

No, this Allison … *is* the Alice.

Exhaling, I lean forward and extend my arm, fingers clutched tight around the Vorpal Blade. As soon as it slides beneath the Carpenter's necromancy magic, it reflects back a sickly, green light. How else can I describe it but to say it's the color of *rot* and fucking *ruin*?

My hand follows along after, so slowly that if my flesh does begin to peel off, I can save myself from a rather horrific injury. *So far, so good,* I think as Rab takes a few shuffling steps forward.

I lift the Vorpal Blade straight up over my head, creating a sort of protective shield, like an umbrella. Rab takes the plunge and scoots in between the bars. Nothing happens. It's the best fucking nothing I've experienced in years.

We scoot on through until we're standing in the corridor between cells.

"How clever," the Knave says, looking down at us, and I'm actually quite pleased to hear she sounds impressed. Surprised, but impressed. I glance over and find my dad watching with too wide eyes. He looks like he's holding back tears or something. I guess this must be a huge relief for him, right? I mean, he's been trapped down here for over a month.

"Should I follow after?" Tee asks, flushing slightly. I guess he's thinking about how to get some semen without, you know, jacking it in front of my mom. Speaking of semen … fuck, I think the crotch of my jeans are wet. Oh well. Nothing to be done about it. And if Rab does get some on his furry mouse back, well, it's his fault it's there anyway.

"Stay in the cell in case the White Knight or that blubbering idiot of a king comes back," Rab says with a sigh. "Throw March's jacket over the sister and let her blonde hair show, make a good sport of it. If we all disappear from the cell, they'll know."

"And I'm not particularly fond of the idea of my mom, sister, and father eating Tee's jizz," I grumble, rubbing my hand down my face. The mushroom meat is gone, so unless we stumble upon some lucky FUCKING DRINK ME bottles, that's our only option if more folks need to shrink.

"Where, exactly, do you intend on going?" Tee asks, putting his hands on his hips as he glares down at Rab and me. His purple eyes are rife with concern, and I can tell he's simply worried about us. Truth be told: so am I.

"To find the Looking-Glass, of course," Rab says, trotting off down the corridor with me riding his back. I can feel the eyes of everyone on us as we make our way toward the dungeon door and slip underneath, past a chip in the wood. If we're quick, maybe we can find the Looking-Glass, and in turn, the King, the Duke, and the Hatter. I imagine with them on our side, we'll have a much easier time springing the rest of the crew out of Castle Diamond—especially since they've made it pretty clear they don't want to hurt us.

The White Knight, she fancies herself a good guy.

"Do you have any idea where you're going?" I whisper, grabbing one of Rab's round ears as we meander down yet another stone hallway. It doesn't look much different from the one we were just in, although I must admit that it smells heaps better.

"Not the faintest," he says, "but if one doesn't know where one is, one must keep going until one finds their way."

"That doesn't make any sense," I grumble, "if one is already lost then one doesn't just suddenly find the ability to know where one is."

"One can't, perhaps, but *two* can." Rab reaches a set of steps, but he doesn't climb them. He just stands there, looking up with his red eyes. "You see, and we've already done it. I know where to go now."

"Do you?" I ask, putting my hands on my hips. "How so?"

"Well, I know where *not* to go, at the very least, and that's *up.* Surely the White Knight and ol' King Humphrey are smart enough to know that eventually, some*one* or some*thing* will come through that Looking-Glass. It's either going to be our Brennin Red and friends, or the Walrus and his ilk. Either way, they'll need to keep it quite secure. It'll be down here somewhere, in the dungeons with the rest of their dirty laundry."

Rab pauses, and turns, sniffing along the wall until we're back at the dungeon door again. Meanwhile, I'm perched up on his back, my mind turning like a teetotum—that's a spinner covered in numbers—while I try to figure out where we should go. If we couldn't get past the stone in the trick wall back in the cell itself, I don't see how we'll find our way through the stone down here.

We pace back and forth for a while, until Rab takes up residence in the corner, underneath a pile of old brooms and dirty mops, their heads so dry it's quite clear they haven't been used in some time. Above us, a spider makes a web, and I'm disturbed to see how disproportionately large it is. Also, its face looks like that of an old woman with pincers protruding from her wrinkled lips.

"Black widow spider," Rab explains when he notices me looking. He continues his vigil, eyes scanning the hall. I don't question him. After all, he *is* the assassin among us. What do I know about sneaking around secret passages? The closest I've ever gotten was that one time I had to creep down the school hall and flush some weed I'd brought to class with me. Oops.

A section of the wall near the stairs spins around, revealing a guardsmen dressed in a diamond-covered surcoat.

"Oh!" I whisper, covering my mouth with my hands to stifle my excitement. "Now that we know where the wall is, we can sneak—"

Rab dumps me off his back, lunges out from under the broom, and shifts into his regular form. His hands come up and he grabs the guard's neck, snapping it with inhuman force. The man crumples to the ground in a lump as Rab turns back to me and holds out an inked hand.

"Come, Sonny, quickly … or else." He taps at his vest pocket, and I scramble to get out the very last of the mushroom meat, swallowing it whole and then cursing when I knock over all the brooms and mops, *and* end up with the black widow in my hair.

Instead of biting me though, she curses me out for ruining her home, lamenting the death of her husband-spider as she scrambles up the stone wall next to my head.

"Fuck, Rab, a warning would've been nice," I grumble as I take his hand, and he taps around the wall with the other, looking for the switch. "I thought we were going to sneak up in tiny form, sit on the wall, and wait for it to spin."

"Nah," he purrs, and then he finds the stone he's looking for, pushing it in with his palm. We spin around and come out on the other side in … yet another identical looking corridor. I bet this whole bottom layer is a goddamn maze. "That would've taken too much time. Subterfuge is not one of my strong suits."

"You think?" I scoff, rolling my eyes. Yeah, pretty sure I knew subterfuge wasn't his thing from moment one: he shot my crush in the face not fifteen feet in front of me, remember? I follow along behind Rab as he strolls down the hall like he's on an afternoon stroll.

This, of course, leads us to a dead-end on *both* sides.

This doesn't faze the King's right-hand man. In fact, he grins like this is a challenge he's trained his whole life for. And I suppose, in a way, he has. This is his job: take care of Brennin Red's dirty work—not to mention Brennin Red himself, it seems.

I walk along the stone wall, running my palm across the pavers. Each one is twice the size of my head, and a dark blue-green-gray color. There's moss in nearly every crevice, its phosphorescent glow doing as much to light the hall as the flickering torches.

I do my very best not to look at the corpse.

That is, until I glance over my shoulder and find the corpse looking at *me*.

"Rab," I whisper, eyes going wide as I watch the man with the broken neck rise to his feet, like a marionette being lifted from the grave.

"Oh my ears and whiskers," Rab snarls. "Sonny, if you would please, *duck*." I do as he asks, crouching low as the White Rabbit whips his gun out of its holster, aims with one extended arm, and fires off a shot. The projectile hits the … whatever-the-guard's-become, blowing blood and brains across the wall.

I rise to my feet, realizing that I'm shaking all over. And it's not because I'm scared. Well, I mean, If I told you I was fear*less*, I'd be lying. Then again, I'm not exactly fear*ful* either. I'm … fear-average. Yes, that sounds about right. Anyway, I'm shaking because I'm tired and stressed and, well, seeing a *zombie* isn't exactly the highlight of my day.

Without waiting a blink, Rab reloads, turns, and shoots the dead-end wall opposite us. He slips his weapon back into his holster and moves over to grab my hand, pulling me toward the settling dust and debris. Doubtless we'll have an army on us in minutes, but I suppose Rab's got that time magic—

No.

No fucking way, Allison! I've known about that shit for a handful of days and already, even *I* am trying to manipulate it.

Rab yanks me forward and then pauses, putting his arm out to stop my forward momentum. The dust settles a bit, and then out of the darkness, a figure comes flying at us.

I stumble back, but even with Rab's protection, I find myself swept up into a pair of powerful arms.

"Miss Liddell," North snarls, his blonde hair matted with blood, his huge black horns protruding from the sides of his head. He looks down at me with golden eyes, his tail already beginning to curl around my ankle. He scared the ever-loving fuck out of me, but I'll be damned if I let *him* know that. "My mate." The Duke nuzzles my cheek as Rab exhales a sharp sigh of relief at the sight of the King *and* the Hatter emerging from the dust.

The King has the Looking-Glass tucked under one arm.

His normally stoic face, however, is locked in violent rage.

"They left through the goddamn Rabbit-Hole!" he roars, and even though I'm a tad slow on the uptake, Rab gets it.

"The Walrus and the Carpenter?" he clarifies as Raiden pauses beside me, and gives a very loose half-smile. If even the lord of Underland's mercenary army is nervous, then so am I.

"And their slimy, little rabbits," Brennin snaps, looking me over as the Duke cradles me against his bronzed chest.

"I can walk you know," I murmur, but North just smirks and follows after the King, keeping me in his arms. I suppose it's not the worst fate that could befall a girl. "What about the Gryphon and the Mocking Turtle?" I ask, terrified to hear that slimy voice echoing around in my head again, giving voice to all the deepest, darkest, most self-damning thoughts I've ever had.

All four of the men give me confused looks.

"Little Alice," the Mad Hatter purrs, drawing my attention back over to him. He reaches up to adjust his top hat as Rab activates the trick wall again. "Your magic left them as stains on Topside pavement, don't you remember?"

"Not … particularly," I choke out as North finally sets me down, curling his tail around my waist this time. I let him, patting the thick muscular length with my palm. "It's all a bit of a blur. I remember the Black Rabbit dying and then … nothing."

"No matter," Brennin snaps, waving his hand as I try to let it sink in that I just slaughtered two of the bad guys. Me. Allison Pleasance Liddell. I *killed* people. Bad people, yes, and I don't regret it, but holy fucking hearts on crackers. *I fucking killed those dudes.* "They left through the Rabbit-Hole as soon as we secured the Looking-Glass which, of course, means they're *here.*"

"That would explain the animated corpse then," Rab muses as North kicks open the dungeon door with his boot, snapping the chains in the process. Either he's exceedingly strong or else the King of Diamonds and the White Knight aren't particularly concerned with anyone getting in there.

After all, stick your fingers through the bars and you literally rot.

That'd be enough of an incentive for me—if I weren't the Alice, that is.

"What's going on here?" Brennin asks as we pause between the two full dungeon cells. There are other people down here, too. I saw them as we passed, but I didn't really *look*. It smells like rot and desperation in here, but I can't just go about freeing prisoners when I have no idea *why* they were imprisoned in the first place. Besides, I hate to say it, but we don't really have the time for it anyway. My stomach clenches with guilt, and I wonder if this is one of those hard decisions that leaders sometimes have to make.

I wish I wasn't making it now.

"Your Majesty," the Knave breathes at the same time my mother calls out to me. I think I've got a bit of fresh blood on my tattered dress, but it doesn't really matter. Since the moment I met the White Rabbit, I've been covered in blood. "The White Knight thinks she does good; she damns Underland instead."

Brennin Red looks at my father first, and then my mother and sister. The corner of his lip curls, but he doesn't say anything.

"And the King of Diamonds?" inquires the Mad Hatter.

"Another bloody idiot," March says, tilting his head to one side, brown ears flopping over. "Now, hurry your arse up and get us out of here before the little one pukes again." He gestures with his thumb in Edy's direction. "Thank *fuck* she's not the fucking Alice."

"The King of Diamonds is in on it, too. Oh, and Dor," I add, lifting up a finger and hoping someone other than me has a plan to get everyone out of their cell. It'd take too long to shrink them all down and walk them out with the Vorpal Blade. Well, that, and like I said: cannot ask my family to err, taste my new boyfriend's … Never mind. I won't even continue that thought.

"Dor, hmm?" Raiden asks, exchanging a look with March.

"She double-crossed the Walrus and the Carpenter, the White Knight did," Lar adds, sighing and running his hands down his face. I think, like me, he's magically drained as well. We could both use a nap.

"Well, the Dormouse *is still* working for the Walrus and the Carpenter," Raiden says, and both my brows shoot straight up. "We've known it since before we picked up the Alice; he had a contract worked out with that blubbery fuck. We were never actually planning on visiting the Clubs, too dangerous."

"You were never planning on visiting the Clubs, and yet you extorted Miss Liddell and myself?" North growls, but Raiden simply shrugs. He sighs and pulls his hat off, removing his cane, and then experimentally tapping at the bars with the end of it.

"We've fed him just the right amount of information, here and there. Looks like the White Knight has found herself a *rat*. And surely one that'll bite her in the ass along the way."

"Or, a mouse, really," Chesh purrs, disappearing and reappearing next to the bars. Okay, so his smile reappears anyway; the rest of him is still invisible.

"We best get out of here quick then," Tee says, arms crossed over his chest as he exchanges a long, lingering look with me. I'm not sure if he's picking up on the fact that Rab and I had sex—I'm almost certain he is—or if he's sincerely concerned about us getting out of here. We need to have a talk, me and him. I've been with the King and the Hatter *twice*, and now Rab, and yet Tee's supposed to be my primary. I feel like I'm failing at this whole harem thing. "What if …" He flushes a bit, and rubs at his nose, and I just know I'm not going to like this suggestion. I *do* however figure he'll be practical about it; Tee always is.

"What?" I ask, my voice thick with suspicion. Tee looks right at me with those gorgeous amethyst eyes, and then he steels his shoulders and lifts his chin, looking very much like the angel prince he was meant to be.

"So it seems to me that the Carpenter's spell is meant to contain us magically, while the bars are meant to contain us physically." I lift a brow, but gesture like *yes, please, go on*. "The bars are probably made of black oyster shells, like the chains on our wings, the ones that held the Mad Hatter." *Ah, so that's where those chains came from!*

"Black oysters?" I ask, and Dee salutes me, clapping his heels together.

"*In water, when the waves are high,*
Don't let the frothy crests deny—

That in their depths, these monsters lie,
Black oysters eat their victims' eyes."

Dee exhales as he finishes the poem, and then grins at me.

"Black oysters are about the same size as a bandersnatch, and they're mean, and nasty, and they feed on flesh. Fortunately, they only live in the ocean, but their shells are harder than diamonds, though not as precious. I hear they're the Walrus and the Carpenter's favorite food—nice and salty and *mean.*"

"Non-sequitur," Tee growls at his brother, raking his fingers through his dark hair.

"Twas not," Dee murmurs, and his twin shoots him a look.

"Twas so."

"Twas *not.*"

"Regardless," Tee snaps, turning back to me with this look of apologetic pleading. I don't like that, like he's already saying sorry. "These bars, even the Vorpal Blade can't cut them. So we need the gate to open, and for that, we need a key … or a lockpick."

March raises a dark brow.

"I can't pick the lock with that awful spell in place, not without losing my hands to rot." He pauses for a moment. "And besides, a lock as complicated as this would require I had a full kit with me. And by full kit, I mean a bomb that wouldn't blow us up along *with* the lock."

"Perhaps … Allison could shrink and … pick the lock from within? Surely, I'm making leaps of logic here as I'm not a master thief, but it sounds reasonable, does it not?" Tee adjusts his peaked cap, pushing it more firmly down on his head.

The March Hare thinks for a moment, rubbing his chin with his fingers.

"That could work. I know the inner workings of the Diamond lock like it were my own hand. Only problem is, it's a bloody bitch to undo. There are about a dozen pin tumblers that must be put just so. However, if Alice-Doll were to follow my instructions, I don't see that we couldn't pick it."

"Once the bars are gone," Tee continues, glancing over at the Looking-Glass under the King's arm. It's huge, but he carries it like it weighs nothing, such is the majesty of his strength I suppose. "We'll make a shield of the Looking-Glass, much like an umbrella, and walk through."

"Well, get on with it then," the King orders, waving a gloved hand in our direction. He sets the Looking-Glass down on the stone, but keeps an arm wrapped around it. I'm dying to know where they hid the other half, but now isn't the time for questions.

It hasn't escaped me that I'm out of mushroom flesh.

"Does anyone have any, err, FUCKING DRINK MEs on them perhaps?" I ask, glancing back at the Knave, the Lion, and the Unicorn. They're all staring at me like this is some sort of test.

"Afraid not, Allison-who-isn't-Alice," Dee says with a small grimace. His eyes flick down to his brother's crotch, and I groan. Great. How did I know this would eventually come up?

"Only as much," the Mad Hatter says, removing a quarter-bottle from underneath his top hat. He hands it over to me, and I breathe a sigh of relief. The entire plan hinges on me getting back through those bars. But, if I have this, then surely I won't need any of Tee's cum, right?

I take the bottle with its tiny tag, my fingers tangling with the Hatter's and sending a rush of violent heat through me. He's a beautiful man, with his dark hair curling around his ears, his marmalade colored eyes, and his vampire grin. *I made him beg first!* I remind myself, uncorking the DRINK ME bottle and downing it in one go.

This time, the flavors run the fruit gamut, morphing from overripe banana to sour orange, to the summer sweetness of watermelon, and the strange, bitter bite of a kumquat. A squeak escapes my throat as my body makes a rapid descent toward the pavement.

Only, I'm not quite so small as I'd wish to be, more like Barbie-sized than pick-a-lock sized.

"Fuck."

I push my blonde hair over my shoulders and adjust my crown, pulling out the Vorpal Blade, and slipping quickly between the bars with it held above my head like a lightning rod. Once I'm back inside, I hiccup and I'm back to full-size, just like that.

"Not a lot left indeed," I grumble, rubbing my hands over my face. Not that it matters, since I needed more anyway. But I'm also rather disturbed to learn that the effects are not indefinite. What if I were to return to full-size while in the lock itself? Would my body squish out the keyhole like I'd been put through a meat grinder?

No fucking sense in asking now. I glance over my shoulder to see my audience, looking at me with expectation. *God, this sucks worse than that time Dad volunteered to come down to the school and help with the sex talk.*

"I could activate—" Rab starts, touching his breast pocket, but I shake my head. Tee and I will have to deal with this like grown adults. I look back at him and Dee steps up behind me, pushing me forward a step, and then fanning his beautiful azure and ebony wings out to block us from the rest of the cell's inhabitants.

Tee and I are, of course, just standing there and staring at one another like awkward teenagers.

"What's going on?" Mom asks as Chesh very carefully steps in front of her and keeps her from trying to peer past Dee's wings.

"Nothing, Mom, just give us a minute for this … spell."

"Less a curse, more of a blessing, I always said," the Knave murmurs, and although she's sort of half-right, I still want to punch her in the tit.

"Do you want me to …" Tee gestures down at his crotch with his hand. "And then I could get some on my fingers and—"

Curling my palms around his shoulders, I put my mouth next to his ear.

"Somehow, that's even more disgusting. Let me just … do it the usual sort of way, and maybe it won't feel like such a chore?" My lips whisper against his flesh, and he shivers, curling one arm around my waist and giving me the warmest one-armed hug, one so warm it most definitely outshines most of the two-armed hugs I've had before. "Although this may scar me for life, I must admit."

"Are you certain you don't want me to just—" I kiss him hard on the mouth to shut him up, taking control of the moment with my tongue, lips, and teeth. In a different time and place, I'm going to spend hours simply making out with him, tasting every nuance of his mouth, feeling up every inch of his body.

Just … not in front of my parents and sister, okay?

"Don't you keep lube in your pocket?" I whisper after I've kissed my way along his jawline to his ear.

"Any smart Underlander knows to keep safe sex supplies in one's pocket," he chokes out as I reach around inside his pocket and find the tiny glass bottle of lube. "It's standard-issue, you know. They give condoms and lubricant out at school, along with sharpened pencils and schedules that describe how much shorter the lessons get every day."

"Why would the lessons get shorter?" I ask, and Tee cocks a brow at me, sweeping some of my hair back from my face.

"That's the reason they're called lessons," he explains, smiling softly. I swear on an entire pack of cards that I could look at this man all day, every day, and never get bored. His beauty is angelic, seraphic, all-consuming. "Because they lessen from day to day."

This is quite a new idea to me, and I think it over a little before I make my next remark.

"Even you, in all your logicality, embody the wonder of Underland." I put some of the lube on my palm, and replace the bottle in his pocket, glancing over my shoulder to make certain we're hidden behind Dee's wings. The Cheshire Cat and Dee are playing off of one another's nonsense, and filling the air with enough blabber to shield any quiet sounds we might make.

Note to self: thank them profusely later.

My right hand slides into Tee's pants, finding him hard and ready for me. He closes his eyes and lets his head fall back when my hand curls around his shaft, slicking wetness along his thick, hard length. There's a certain desperation in the moment that I can't deny, an urgency that begs tight, tight fingers and a frantic pace, my mouth nipping and licking at Tee's suddenly sweaty skin.

He leans back against the wall, his wings bundled behind him in a cluster of shiny feathers, his heartbeat so loud I can hear it across the inches that separate us. As I work him with my hand, I realize that I despise those inches, that I want nothing more than to be joined with him, our sweaty bodies pressed tight together.

I want Tee, and I don't think I'll ever be able to let him go.

My cheeks heat with the revelation, but I have no choice but to pick up the pace, working him hard and fast, licking and kissing and biting. It takes only minutes, I think, but it feels like hours, like we're trapped in a carnal world of our own making.

When Tee gets close to orgasm, he lifts his hands up and curls them around my upper arms, fingers digging into my flesh, making me gasp. Before he can finish in his slacks, I bend down, unzip him, and take his cock into my mouth. It's hot and sweet, and tastes like a warm breeze off the mountains. His climax hits and he very gently wraps his fingers in my hair, desperately trying and failing to control a slight thrust of his hips.

The angel prince's seed fills my mouth, that salty-sweet taste resting on my tongue, and I swallow it, sliding his shaft between my lips with a pop. There's only the briefest of moments for me to take in a big gulp of air before I'm shrinking again … and shrinking, and shrinking. *Fuck,* I think as my stomach churns with nerves, *I swallowed too much!*

But then the awful downward momentum stops, and I'm left standing next to the sole of Tee's boot. He fixes his pants, and then very carefully picks me up by the back of my dress, much like one would grab a kitten by the scruff. He then plops me down on his palm and looks closely at me with one of his gorgeous, amethyst eyes. I can see every striation of color, every nuance of lavender and eggplant, violet and pansy purple.

"A vessel for you, little Allison," he whispers, and his voice is like a storm, sweeping over me and ruffling my hair and clothes. Tee offers up one, sleek black feather, and I climb onto it. Lar then uses his magic to float me down from Tee's palm and over to the lock.

The Vorpal Blade slides into my hand as if I've been wielding it my whole life, and I raise it up to protect myself from the Carpenter's spell, leaping off the feather and into the metal mechanism of the lock itself. I can't be more than half an inch tall now, can I? What a wretched height.

"Can you hear me?" March asks, and I cringe slightly. I can tell he's trying to speak softly, but it's like standing next to the speakers at a rock concert; I wouldn't be surprised if my ears bled. I peek my head out, cup my hands around my mouth, and shout at the top of my lungs.

"Yes!"

March leans down and puts his ear right up to me. I could probably crawl inside it, but like, eww, gross. So I yell again, and he nods, turning and giving me a bright grin. I'm about as tall as his front teeth.

"Get deeper inside," he says, and there's a strange purr in his voice that gives me goose bumps. "Look for a series of pins that're about as big as you are." I do as he asks, my boots loud against the black floors of the lock's interior. They're rough and uneven, and I'm quite certain the locksmith who made this never designed for an actual human person to walk along his work.

I feel so disoriented, almost like I might faint, but I don't dare—not when I'm this small. Could you imagine? I could be eaten by a grasshopper, stepped on by a shoe, crushed by a fall of just a few inches. Swallowing back my fear, I look around at all the mechanisms, studying the intricate combination of pin tumblers, wheels, and cogs.

"Since I can't very well hear you, I'll just prattle on like an old man sipping sweet tea." March puts his chocolate-colored iris up to the keyhole and peers in. "Align the pin tumblers so that all their tops are evened out. You'll need a bit of magic to hold them in place."

"Oh, *now* you tell me!" I groan, pausing next to a series of big, rectangular pins. Each one is a different length, and they look heavy as hell now that I'm the size of a gnat. I put the Vorpal Blade between my teeth—need both hands for this shit, I do—and start to push the smallest of the lot into place. The top hits another bit of a metal with a screech, and I stand there like an idiot, searching for that power inside of me.

"You rule the magic, Miss Liddell," the Duke's voice booms, "it does not rule you."

That's all well and good for him to say that, but what does it *mean*, really?

"Magic is simply energy," the Mad Hatter says, his West Coast accent unmistakable. "Identify what it is you want it to do, and then ask for it."

"More Underland nonsense," I grumble, but I close my eyes anyway and feel that awe-inspiring power all around me. It wasn't that Topside didn't have any, but down here … free magic is fucking everywhere. It swirls around me, molecules collecting against my skin; I swear, if I closed my eyes, I could count them.

Holding the pin tumbler above my head is hard work, so I imagine that the magic does it for me, that it sweeps underneath the metal, props it in place. When my arms finally do give out, and I stumble back to avoid being crushed … I see that it's worked.

"Spells are like songs," the Caterpillar says, the calm in his voice soothing some of my rapid-fire heartbeat. "One note at a time until it's complete. Sing it, Sunshine."

Working my way down the pins, I push them into place and then lock them there with the same magic I used to obliterate the Mocking Turtle and the Gryphon. Funny thing is, it's a hell of a lot harder to keep these pins in place than it was to simply blast energy through the bodies of my enemies. Why is it sometimes that minutiae can seem so much less manageable?

"Assuming you've finished your task," March continues as I take the Vorpal Blade and hold it in my hands. If I concentrate, I can feel the Carpenter's spell all around me, like a waterfall of invisible, rotten flesh, pouring entrails down on my head. If I were to let go of the blade and my magic, it would make a corpse of me in no time. "Find a silver cog and spin it three clicks to the right. Once you've done that, a small door will slide back, revealing a sequence of numbers. Let me know what they are."

"Some lock this is." I grab onto the wheel and use every ounce of physical strength I have to turn it just one click. I quite literally have to sit down and rest between cycles. Being tiny sucks. "Only in Underland would they have something as stupidly complicated as this."

A great pounding comes then, like elephants stampeding on the floor above us; I don't imagine that's a good sign.

"Hurry, Knicker Dancer," Chesh purrs, the sound vibrating through the air and making my tiny body quiver. "They're *coming.*"

With my muscles burning, I push the wheel twice more, wait for the inner door to open, and then race back to the keyhole to scream out at the March Hare.

"Six-nine-six-nine," I shout, and he grins, the expression quite disturbing at this height.

"Sixty-nine, sixty-nine," he rephrases, and I swear to fuck, I do three consecutive eye rolls. "Turn the sixes over to one and leave the nines. Once you've done that, set the clock to midnight."

"Clock? What clock?" But the March Hare can't hear me, so I do as he's asked, activating yet another door with a … miniature grandfather clock behind it?! Well, it looks huge to me, but if I were my real size, it'd be smaller than that horrid pimple on Brandon Carmichael's face. How the White Knight and her guards lock and unlock this cell with a key is beyond me.

I move the hour and the minute hand into place … and then I hear a click. At my current size, it sounds a bit like a thunderstorm, but I recognize that satisfying sound as *success.*

Heading for the keyhole, I end up leaping out into Tee's palm as the King takes the Looking-Glass, slides it between the bars, and uses it as leverage to open the gate. He doesn't seem concerned about it breaking, but I know it gives me mad fucking anxiety.

Once the gate is open, Brennin holds the mirror above his head, and steps right into the Carpenter's spell.

"I'm no Alice," he grinds out, sweat breaking out on his forehead. "Get *out* before the mirror snaps, and I rot down to the bone."

The lot of us file into the corridor … and then it starts all over again.

Same size keyhole, same fucking lock, only this time with a different sequence of numbers. Doesn't faze the March Hare however; he still gets it right.

Once everyone is free, I realize … that I sort of need to get big again.

"Don't look so nervous, Allison-who-isn't-Alice," Dee says with a smile, leaning in to look at me as I rest in Tee's palm. The whorls on his skin look like hills and fucking valleys from here. And when the younger angel prince offers me a massive finger covered in, you know, jizz, I don't have much choice but to take it.

One lick gets me to the size of a mouse, two back to doll-size, and three makes it so that Tee has to put me down on the ground. This time, I simply grab Dee's whole finger and suck it into my mouth, shooting back up to my full five-ten in the span of an instant. It happens so quick that I feel a little dizzy. Also, I'm still sucking cum off a dude's finger in front of my family. I shove Dee away and swipe my arm over my mouth.

"Can we get the fuck out of here now?"

"Well," the Duke growls, his voice like thunder in a wild magic storm. "The easy part's over with. Now, we shall see if we can escape Castle Diamond alive." He looks up at the ceiling as dust and stone crumble down onto our heads. "Or … if anyone can, for that matter."

CHAPTER FOUR

The Lion and the ... holy shit, that's a fucking Unicorn!

There's only one way out of the dungeon which sort of fucking blows, because that means we head out the wood door, up the stairs, and straight into trouble.

Castle Diamond is overrun with Clubs, card soldiers and humans alike, and they're not alone. There are ... *things* with them, horrible, horrible things that look like bloodied, broken dolls. As soon as Edith sees them, she passes out and only narrowly avoids cracking her skull on the stone floor because Dee catches her and hoists her into his arms.

The King of Diamonds, the White Knight, Dor, and the rest of the people we saw in the corridor are nowhere to be seen. If they're smart, I'm sure they'll run. I know we're planning to. We can't fight the big-bads *and* their army by ourselves. No, we have to fight fire with fire. Besides, we have my family, and we have the Looking-Glass, and we can't risk a full-on brawl right now.

"How did they get an army here so fucking quickly?" Brennin snaps, curling one gloved hand over the railing and looking down at a room full of torture devices ... and soldiers. But holy hell, torture devices?! The King of Diamonds, that Humpty Dumpty idiot, has a dungeon with a rack in it? If I find out my father was subjected to torture, Hearts help the man and his court.

"Clearly, they've got an ace up their sleeve," the Duke says, tail thrashing.

"Or a rat," March mutters, as I study North's tall form. I imagine he could shift and throw down, but the goal here is to get out *before* the Walrus and the Carpenter find us. North moves away from the railing and over to a small window. It's just large enough for him to stick an arm through, probably a murder hole or something. Hell, maybe it's medieval ventilation for all the horrific smells emanating from this nightmare of a room?

The Duke looks at the window for a moment, and then he simply smashes his fist into the stone, shattering the wall into pieces. The opening is now just large enough for a person to squeeze through. The Cheshire Cat, who's holding a disturbingly calm Dinah in his arms, leans over to peer out.

"Out through here," North says, bowing and gesturing with one arm in the direction of the cool breeze. Outside, I can see darkness, trees, and giant mushrooms—

that's fucking it. It reminds me of my first night in Underland, when I came out of that door and found myself at The Pool, with nothing but woods all around us.

"Pardon me, ma'am," Lar says, sweeping my mother up into his arms. She lets out a little shriek, but doesn't fight him as he leaps from the window, spreads his wings, and carefully ends up on the lawn one story down.

Dee steps forward to follow suit, when one of the rotten-doll monsters stumbles up the stone steps and lets out a hiss. It's followed by another, and another, and another. And then a *swarm*, like a cloud of bleeding, rotten insects. They look like zombies or corpses, but there are plastic bits, and faux smiles, big bouncy hair, and metal turn-keys in their backs.

The King hands off the Looking-Glass to the Duke, and reaches for his sword. What he doesn't see is the Carpenter crawling on the ceiling above us.

But I do. And so does Tee.

The angel prince doesn't even say anything. But his eyes meet mine for the briefest of seconds, and there must be something in my fearful gaze that overrides his hatred for Brennin Red. Either that, or Tweedledum is just a good fucking person. He shoves the King out of the way as the Carpenter drops with his massive bone axe, cutting off half of a wing in the process. Feathers, blood, and bits of bone splatter across the stone floor as I scream. And an accompanying rot begins to crawl its way up what's left of Tee's wing, right into his shoulder. As I stand there and watch, the entire side of his face turns black.

"Raiden!" I scream, and I grab the Mad Hatter's arm with an iron grip. Luckily for him, he's a smart man, because if he let Tee die there, I never would've forgiven him. Never. Even if it wasn't his fault.

With a curse, he tears into his own wrist, wraps an arm around my waist, and snatches Tee by the back of the neck, all in less time than it takes me to blink. He kisses the elder angel prince on the mouth, forcing his blood down Tee's throat.

He doesn't pull back right away either, kissing Tee deeper and harder. There's just so much red smeared around their mouths that I figure he's probably bitten his own tongue. *He needs more blood; the wound's that fucking bad.* Whipping the Vorpal Blade from its holster, I ready myself to right the Carpenter's scowling, skeletal face. If I have to, I'll defend Tee with my life.

When did that happen?! I knew it! When you crush, you crush hard, bitch! Hard enough to make fucking diamonds.

"I'm sorry," North growls, yanking me back with a length of sinuous, black tail. "Not on my watch, Miss Liddell." I struggle against him as he pulls me toward the night sky, but the Knave steps up between me and the Hatter.

"Don't ever say I don't serve the crown," she snaps, gritting her teeth and looking me dead in the eye. "And don't ever call me traitor." With a wave of her arm, dozens of soldiers go flying. With a snap of her fingers, the Lion and the Unicorn jump into action. And with a single kiss, blown through the air in Tee's directions, I see chains made of shadow appear on his wings. They snap like broken bones and fall to the floor in pieces; she does the same for Dee.

Wait. Wait, wait, wait … did she just break their curse?!

Tee shoves Raiden back, gasping and choking on blood, but his wing is already knitting together, feathers sprouting from the wound as it grows and morphs back to its original state. But Raiden Walker himself … doesn't look so good.

"You're gonna need a load of blood, Boss," March says, swinging the vampire over his shoulder. He moves toward the opening in the wall as I check to make sure my family is safe; I won't leave unless they're all safe first. But when I look, I see that the rest of the men have made good on getting them out of trouble.

When I flick my attention back to the Knave, I see her looking at Brennin with a loyalty and respect that I can barely understand. How someone can be that devoted to an asshole like him is beyond me.

"Get going," she tells him, making a small bow. "And don't doubt that I've always only ever been concerned with the Kingdom of Hearts' prosperity." She steps aside as her husband—is the Unicorn Rook or Knight, I keep forgetting—shifts into a massive warhorse with silver fur, hooves as sharp as the tove's, and a horn that looks like a goddamn drill.

"Holy fucking fuckballs, he turned into a fucking uni-fucking-corn!"

Goal: use fuck as many times as possible in one sentence. Goal complete.

The Lion isn't any less impressive, shape-changing into this massive beast with a golden mane, claws as big as my vorpal blade, and a tail like a scorpion. I'd stare more, but then, there are rotten doll-zombies crawling up the walls, and a necromancer with an axe made of bone coming my way.

"Allison, if you would," the Duke growls, sweeping me into the air with his tail, and launching us out the window and into the night.

The next moment, soldiers come running through the wood, at first in twos and threes, then ten or twenty together, and at last in such crowds that they seem to fill the whole forest. And they're monstrous, too, like broken dolls that stagger and fall apart at the slightest provocation. These distorted bodies may once have been human or fae or angel, but whatever the Carpenter has turned them into now, they're simply puppets. Whatever parts of them that were missing due to injury or rot, have been replaced with plastic bits and googly eyes, big fake curls, or frozen rubber smiles.

Ten times as scary as the card servants. A hundred times. A *thousand.*

When King Humphrey's soldiers attack them, they fall to pieces, like rows of rotten dominoes, just one after the other, they crumple. The hard part is, there are always more. That, and they don't seem to feel pain either.

We gather together behind a Tumtum tree, for fear of being run over, and watch them go by. In all my life, I've never seen a scene so tragically disturbing: the doll-zombie-soldiers are always tripping over something or other, and whenever one goes down, several more always fall over them, so that the ground is soon covered with little heaps of broken dolls.

"Let's go, while we've got a bloodbath as a distraction." Rab takes off into the woods, leading the way for the rest of our party. Mom, Dad, and Edith all hold hands with each other, like they're afraid of being separated, or maybe like they're afraid one of them will simply drift away into the ether.

Can't really blame them, right? Underland is pretty fucked-up. But then, so is our world. They might have doll-zombies, and Walrus monsters, and bugs with burning raisins for heads, but back home we have sex traffickers, and pedophiles, and countries with leaders who openly admit to assaulting women—and are damn proud of it. Monsters take all sorts of different forms, don't they?

"Could we make a door?" I gasp, when I feel we're far enough away from the carnage that I can talk without attracting one of the soldiers. My legs are burning, and I'm having trouble breathing. Mom, Dad, and Edith actually all look worse off. For once, I am not the slowest person in Underland. That, and I just really need to touch Tee and make sure that he's okay. My fingers brush the side of his face, and I find that I can't stop replaying that awful moment in my mind over and over again.

Did that just happen?! My eyes slide over to the Mad Hatter's. He meets my gaze dead-on … and then has the audacity to smirk at me. And yet, I won't forget what he did, not anytime soon. I also won't forget what March said about him needing blood. So, the magic in his blood is fueled by feeding on others? Interesting …

Rab, who's leading our little group, slows down underneath the glowing gills of a giant mushroom. It's a much different shape than the ones I'd gotten used to in the Kingdom of Hearts, more like a bell than a toadstool, really. And it's this brown-gold color like treacle pudding.

I don't imagine *this* particular mushroom has the ability to make us as big as a house or as small as a mouse. Based on my conversations with the men, it seems as if that's a particular flora that's unique to the Kingdom of Hearts.

"We could make a door, certainly," Raiden finally says, sliding two fingers into his mouth in a very seductive sort of way as he stares at me. My dad notices and his nostrils flare wide. Seems that even in a magical kingdom under siege, Henry is his usual overprotective self. The Mad Hatter ignores him, counting his own teeth.

If a normal adult human has thirty-two teeth—and Raiden Walker *did* start out as human—then certainly he's got a few left, hasn't he?

"Twenty-six," he finally says with a sigh, sliding his fingers from his mouth, a single thin string of saliva linking them to his lips. He licks it away, and grins at me like, well, a vampire mercenary lord. "Could spare another, I do say."

And yet, the problem of shrinking down to walk through that door still exists, unless Raiden happened to overlook a couple of FUCKING DRINK MEs in his nesting doll top hats.

"And where would that door go, exactly?" Brennin asks, voice low and dark. His black eyes are narrowed, and he's staring into the woods like he suspects an ambush around every corner. Good thing, too, since I bet there really is. "Castle Heart could be compromised, and if the Walrus and the Carpenter have an undead army waiting for us, we'll be dead before we can say *callooh, callay.*" I have no idea what *callooh, callay* means, but I'll take it.

I sit down with my back to a Tumtum tree—they are rather like fucking redwoods, aren't they?—and my sister does the same. Only, she does it a lot less gracefully, collapsing in a heap and choking back a sob. Mom puts her hands on Edy's shoulders to comfort her, while Dad snuggles Dinah in his arms.

"Could we visit your Eternal Tea Party?" Lar queries after a moment, pulling a pipe from his pocket and lighting up with a bit of flame on the tip of his finger.

Eternal Tea Party?

Now that's a cool fucking name.

"We could, and it'd be the safest place to rendezvous with the army." Raiden exchanges a look with the March Hare. "However, it requires a certain level of …" His marmalade colored eyes slide over to my family, and the corner of his lip twitches. "Footwork, to arrive there. It's better guarded than Castle Heart."

"Than the Castle Heart *grounds,*" Brennin corrects, giving the Mad Hatter a look. "Good luck getting into the Suit of Hearts."

"Not a soul could penetrate the Suit of Hearts," Raiden drawls, tilting his head to one side and giving me such a naughty little look that my mother bristles. "Unless one penetrates the Ali—"

"Okay," I blurt, shoving up to my feet. "If we head for the Eternal Tea Party, we'll be safe?"

"Safe … ish," March says, shaking the branches of a nearby tree. A black apple falls to the ground near his feet, and he picks it up, shining it on the front of his purple trench and then putting it to his lips. The flesh inside is as red as blood, as red as the King's hair. "We'll be near the front lines. We can have the Alice take the reins of the armies, and crush the Walrus and the Carpenter one soldier at a time. Besides, we *should* travel on foot for a while. You never know who could be watching and waiting for us to travel by magic."

March's eyes focus on the branches above us, staring at an owl who looks to be made of wood. It's only when it opens its beak and lets out a *hoot-hoot* that I realize it's alive.

"Spotted wood owl," he explains as it blinks big black eyes at us. I remember though, the night of the Torrid Tea Party, how there were eyes other than the Mocking Turtle and the Gryphon staring back at me from their faces.

The bird opens big, wooden wings, and with a crack like splintering wood, takes off into the night. Dinah lets out a hiss.

"If we travel through one of Raiden's doors, and get squished coming out the other side, that just wouldn't do, now would it?" March takes another bite of his apple, and tucks his right hand into the pocket of his coat. "Let's walk a bit, and take a train."

"A train?" I ask, thinking of that electric guitar with all the gears, the cell phones that blow up when you press the bomb icon, and all the other wondrous eccentricities of Underland—like indoor plumbing and toilets that flush.

"Oh, yes, the train," Chesh purrs, but it's only his teeth that talk, just a big, white feral grin in the darkness. "It's been years since I took the train."

The screech of a jabberwock shatters the brief silence, and most everyone but the Duke, the King, and the Hatter put their palms over their ears. Edith begins to sob. I try not to hold it against her, all of that fear and weakness, but I'm awfully glad that she's not the Alice.

"We should get going, and quick," North whispers, voice laced with ice-cold fear. He looks up and into the darkness of the boughs, his tail twitching, claws extending and retracting from his fingers. "The last thing I want is for my mate to see me raped and murdered by a musking female jabberwock."

His gold eyes turn pointedly in my direction, and he smiles, a very lascivious sort of smile that—you guessed it—my parents both hone in on. Edith is too busy weeping, I'm afraid.

"Perhaps the Rabbits could pick up some of the … slack?" Dee asks, smiling and weaving his fingers together in front of him. He looks a bit chagrined for even asking, but I get it: my family is struggling to keep up.

"March," says Raiden, snapping his fingers.

"Rab," says the King.

Both Rabbits turn to look at each other, ears twitching, and they sigh in unison.

"If you insist," March says, and they both shift into their bandersnatch forms, like two massive wolves with brown and white coats. One is striped, the other spotted. Their jaws are big enough to *snatch*, their claws sharp enough to *catch*. And they've got those long, puffy wolf's tails. "Hop on up, loves." March turns his massive head around and gives my family a beast's smile, all teeth and tongue.

"There is no way in fuck I am getting on the back of that … that *thing*!" Edith screams, but Tee is already grabbing her around the waist and lifting her up. He tries to set her nicely on Rab's back, but she fights him and ends up sprawling over Rab's massive shoulder blades.

"Let's go," Tee says, looking behind us into the blackness. Outside the glow of the giant mushroom, I can't see a thing. I sort of feel like we should be celebrating that his curse could be broken, but we won't know for sure until midnight, right? Also … I guess we should get out of the woods first.

"I concur," Dee repeats, shifting his wings nervously and holding up a finger.

"I concur with his concurring," Tee adds, adjusting his hat.

"And I concur with his concurring of the concurring," Chesh replies, fading back into view. He, too, shifts into his big cat form—which is about three-quarters the size of the bandersnatch—and gestures with his head for me to climb on.

I'm too tired to argue.

I mount pussy, and we take off into the wood.

Sounds dirty, doesn't it?

There are things that live in these woods that defy imagination's greatest bounds. The green pigs I've seen before, rooting around for truffles and toadstools, and the giant mushrooms, but there are shabby-looking birds with their feathers sticking all round, like live mops.

"Borogoves," Chesh growls from underneath me, his legs moving like well-oiled pistons, his muscles thick beneath his sleek black and white coat. "I'd certainly enjoy a borogove, if I had the time to catch one." He snaps his jaws and lets out a rumbling purr that vibrates right up between my thighs and makes me shiver.

"They look like stringy, nasty little things to me," I whisper, giving his furred ears a rub. He gives me another one of those delicious growling purrs, and I realize I better stop or all that rumbling between my legs is going to do inappropriate things to me.

"*The Lion, Knave, and Unicorn were fighting for the crown,*" Lar mumbles as he walks alongside the King and the Hatter. "How we misinterpreted that bit of prophecy." He holds up a single finger and sighs. "Although I have warned you time and again, it's my job to recite, not to decipher."

"I'll make a memorandum of it," Brennin drawls, reaching up to adjust his crown on his bloodred hair, although he makes no move to actually do so. Facetious ass.

"So, the Lion and the Unicorn were fighting *for* the crown, as in *on behalf of*, not *in search of.* How unfortunate. Do you suppose they'll live?" Lar glances at the King, but he doesn't say a word. Maybe he doesn't know, or doesn't care to think of it? After all, the Knave and her husbands quite literally risked their lives to let us escape.

Even if she did curse the twins, they're free … I think? And anyway, her selfless act has completely redeemed her in my eyes. Well, mostly. She still can't be the fucking Queen of Hearts, and … I hate Brennin, but … well, I guess I'll keep him.

I groan and put my head down against Chesh's neck, rubbing my cheek against his silky fur.

"Are you okay, Allison?" Mom whispers, holding onto Edy's sleeping form as Rab trots along the forest floor with his massive paws. Dad is snuggling Dinah and doesn't look like he has any intention of letting go. Not that the cat would leave, not with Chesh around. He seems to have an affinity for pussy.

I lift my head up to look at my mother, forcing a smile. She's taking this all in stride. I mean, my whole family is, but what choice do they have?

"I'm fine, Mom," I say, and I make sure to put some heart into it, so she knows it's true. Now that I'm back in Underland, I can only wonder if I've spent my whole life holding my breath, spent my whole life with screaming lungs, just drowning, drowning, drowning. Because here, I feel like I can breathe for the first time in forever.

Sometimes, when I'm reading a book, I get so into it that when I look up, I have to blink several times to remember where I am, who I am, what my life is really like. There have been so many times that I've wished I never did wake up, that I died in a dream of words and sentences and characters and romances.

And now I am. I'm here; this is happening. At least now my family, even if they do choose to return home, will know where I am, that I'm safe, and that I never intended on abandoning them.

"This is where you went, when you disappeared?" she asks after a few more moments of silence. I know my dad, and all nine guys are listening, so it's not really the best time for a heart-to-heart, but I can't leave my mom hanging.

"This is it," I reply, exhaling slowly. "And Brandon, well, the guy you're riding, he's the one that killed him."

"King's orders," Rab repeats with a shrug of his huge, muscular shoulders. The movement jostles Edy awake, but she just keeps her blue eyes focused on the woods ahead.

"Apologies, but we were under the impression that Rabbit was going to murder your daughter," the King says, clearly not thrilled that I've brought my family with me. He'll just have to fucking get over it though. Sorry, but my mom literally has a get out of jail free card here, and there's no way I'm going to blow that opportunity.

"Rabbit?" Mom asks, exchanging a look with my father. He's so dirty and disheveled; I can't imagine the fear he must've felt being trapped in the Diamonds' dungeon for so long.

"Assassin, shapeshifter, right-hand to Kings and Queens," the Duke replies, his voice this booming baritone that hits all the right notes for me. He's glorious to look at, like the finest painting or the most detailed statue, a work of art meant for the eyes. Mine, they positively drink him in.

"An assassin?" Mom echoes, eyes going wide.

"Clubs thought they'd poach Allison-who-isn't-Alice before she came into her own," Dee says, stretching his wings above his head. "Planned it years in advance, too, before the rest of the Looking-Glasses were shattered. Doubtless, even if Brandon had switched over to the White Knight's side, there were other assassins waiting around to kill your entire family."

"How many of these … magic mirrors are there?" Mom asks, her gaze sliding over to the Duke. He's now the one carrying the Looking-Glass.

"One," Tee replies softly, and that's the last anyone speaks for quite some time. I think we're all exhausted, worried, terrified, or some combination thereof. I wonder if anyone else is horny though, or if I'm totally fucking inappropriate?

"Shall we break in Potsville then?" asks Raiden to March.

The brown bandersnatch grumbles in way of acquiescence.

"Seeing as you're the only two assholes who know how to get to the Eternal Tea Party, we'll have to follow your lead. Puts us at your mercy, doesn't it, Hatter?" the King drawls.

"My only concern is the Alice," Raiden says, giving me a look that's equal parts curiosity and want. He looks like he wants to throw me down and fuck me right here. Can't say I'm opposed to the idea—provided it were in private. The last thing I need is a repeat of Tee's blow job: sex with an audience. Not my thing, not when my family makes up the audience. Gross. "But if you're worried, by all means, go a different way."

Brennin Red scowls, but doesn't say anything more as we approach the edge of the woods, the sun cresting on the horizon. The double moons have set, and the golden glow of morning is illuminating the hills and valleys of a small town made up of … teapots, cups, saucers, and little fences designed from dessert forks and teaspoons.

"Holy fucking Hearts," I murmur, eyes wide. There's a huge, brown river running alongside the town, and it's *steaming*.

"Potsville," Raiden repeats, adjusting his top hat. "We'll rent some rooms, gather some supplies, and book a ferry for tomorrow morning." He licks his lower lip as he stares down at the town, like he's got some other agenda in mind.

"Why do you look so fucking excited?" I grumble, and Raiden glances over his shoulder to grin at me, both of his fangs peeking over the edge of his lip.

"Because," the Hatter begins, as my father slides off of March's back and lands on his feet. The March Hare shifts back into his regular form and grins at his boss. "We do so like to gamble."

The town of Potsville is most peculiar, although I must admit: I'm in fucking love with it. It smells like freshly brewed black tea, and every time a door opens or closes, it's like hearing the soft clink of China at a tea party.

I don't even have to ask if we're still in the Kingdom of Diamonds: the pots, cups, and saucers are emblazoned with red, white, and black diamond shapes. We weave behind houses and shops, keeping a somewhat inconspicuous profile—and in Underland, even a group of people with Rabbit ears, angel wings, and dragon tails don't attract much attention.

The Hatter leads us to a stack of teacups, as if some huge hand in the sky has piled up their dishes for weeks. Each one has a tiny window with frilly curtains, and the yard out front is large and well-kempt. A wooden sign flutters in the breeze with the words *The Scented Rush—Bed and Breakfast* hand-painted onto the front. He pushes the small door open with an open palm and struts inside like he owns the place.

"Good morning, Brebis," Raiden says, strolling up to the front desk and tapping his cane on the wooden countertop. A woman with a large sheep brooch on the front of her dress looks up at him with wide, brown eyes, and a gaping mouth. She's got a pair of knitting needles in her frail hands, and at first, I think she's caught her yarn in her curly, white hair. Only upon further inspection do I realize that she's actually knitting her own hair. "I'll need at least three rooms for the night. And if the others aren't empty, pour their guests out into the street."

"What the fuck?" I murmur as the old woman rises to her feet and nearly knocks her stool over. The room is small, but cozy, with rounded porcelain walls, and a staircase made of forks. Dried bundles of tea leaf sachets hang from the metal bannister, leaving a pleasant herbal scent lingering in the air. I'm so tired at that point that I could curl up on the bandersnatch skin rug that covers the porcelain floor and fall right asleep.

"Allison," Mom whispers, giving my shoulder a squeeze. I don't really know what to say to her though except to copy what Rab said: welcome to fucking Underland.

"Boss," the innkeeper murmurs, digging out several thick, iron keys. To keep the pixies from stealing them, remember? "We have a few guests tonight, but I'll make sure they're out within the hour." Raiden takes the keys and starts to turn away when

Brebis calls out to him. "Oh, and the latest shipment is in, just thought you'd like to know. You've been … incommunicable for some days now."

The Mad Hatter simply smirks, and turns away, heading for the staircase and then pausing at the bottom to hold out two of the keys. The third he keeps for himself.

"March and I will secure passage on the ferry for tomorrow. Rest up, eat up, and be ready to move. Your Majesty, do you think you can handle keeping the Alice safe for me while I make … arrangements?"

"I think if you ask me such an insulting question again, I'll deny you what you're after." Brennin steps forward, snatches a key from Raiden's hand, and bares his neck. The rest of us watch on in silence as Raiden opens his mouth wide, bares his teeth, and bites down. The bloodletting is quick and painless, but I can't help feeling like I'm watching something that'd be better off behind closed doors.

The Mad Hatter pulls back, swiping blood from his smiling lips.

"Let's go," Brennin says as he reaches out for my hand, grabs it in his gloved fist, and starts to drag me up the stairs. The Duke is right behind me, urging me on, and I just barely manage to make eye contact with Tee. He takes the last key, and sends my family up the metal stairs before him.

Fuck, I don't know what I would do without him.

Without any of them, really.

I think I've just screwed myself six ways to Sunday because I'm starting to get attached. I was attached to Fred; I loved him more than anything. And I know what happens to the heart when that love is ripped away, when that attachment is snapped like so much bone.

The soul, it bleeds to death.

There's a *cat*erpillar on my nose, scrunched up like an inchworm. It's got fur like a calico, and six pairs of simple black eyes. When I open my own eyes and see it hissing at me, I just about lose my shit and panic, scrambling up into a sitting position and knocking the tiny creature into my lap.

"Why, it's just a little caterpillar," Lar says, picking the bug up between two, long fingers. He sets it in the windowsill, taps it with his finger, and two brilliant blue and black wings burst from its back. It takes off into the cool, evening air as I blink myself into full wakefulness. It's just me and him awake right now; the Cheshire Cat sleeps in a kitty ball next to Dinah, on the white ottoman over by the door. Its fabric glitters in the dying rays of sunshine, almost like a … oh, no wait, it *is* a giant sugar cube.

On the floor, curled up in a colorful quilt, is the Duke, tail twitching gently. And on the twin bed beside my own, sleeps the King. I reach up and rub at my matted hair with the heel of my hand as Lar sets the satchel Tee packed up for me on the end of the bed. I'd pretty much forgotten its existence since Tee's been carrying it this whole time. He must've dropped it off after I fell asleep.

"May I open it?" Lar asks, and I nod, watching as he pulls out a silver hairbrush and moves to sit beside me. I scoot forward and he takes up a position in the pillows with me between his legs, still blinking past the sleep and trying to remember when and how I passed out in the first place.

Lar takes my hair in gentle hands and begins to brush it, humming a song under his breath that feels vaguely recognizable. When he sings a few of the words, I recognize it as the same tune I was to dance to at the Ball of Broken Hearts and Stolen Tarts.

"*'Will you march a little faster?' said an Alice to a King, 'There's a Walrus close behind us, and he's treading on my win.' See how eagerly the monsters and the soldiers all advance! They are waiting on the signal—will you take a fighting stance?*"

I close my eyes and enjoy the music for a moment.

"My parents and sister are with the twins?"

"And the White Rabbit," Lar replies, his voice this soothing calm in a sea of madness. I feel like I need this moment, or I'll fucking explode into a million pieces, Mad as the goddamn Hatter. *Off gambling, what a crock!* He better not be. And he and the March Hare … they most certainly better not be entertaining lady friends. Hey, at least I know there aren't any brothels, right?

Hearts on cards, I hate how fucking jealous I am.

"They're on the floor just above us; they're safe." I nod, and even though I feel guilty about it, I'm sort of happy to have a break from them? I don't know what to say, what to do, how to act. It's like … I'm not as much Allison now as I am Alice. "Would you like some tea after I fix your hair?"

"You don't have to fix my hair at all," I say, but my eyes are already drifting shut, and it feels damn good to have his fingers massaging my scalp and working out all the knots. "Never mind, scratch that. Keep doing what you're doing." Lar chuckles, fanning his wings softly and teasing me with a blueberry and tobacco scented breeze. "My body feels like one, giant knot."

"The price we pay for big magic," he says, humming a bit more of the song under his breath. "I'm surprised you got as far as you did, after all that. The Mocking Turtle and the Gryphon … they were very old, very powerful, very mad." Lar pauses and moves his hands to my shoulders, kneading my flesh with big, powerful movements of his fingers. He's a lot stronger than he looks. At first glance, he's got this mage-and-scholar sort of persona, but I imagine he could punch a man out with a very carefully aimed hit with his ringed knuckles. "If you'd like to steep, I could run you a bath."

"Steep?" I ask, and he chuckles again. "Like a fucking tea bag?"

"You like tea bags, do you?" Lar asks, and there's a note of mischief in his voice that makes the position we're sitting in shift from pleasant to … pleasantly uncomfortable. My body perks up at the thought of turning around and kissing him, seeing how that carnal scene in his wings might play out. I imagine, though, that I should take a bath and change my clothes. Tee, at least, in his infinite foresight, brought me some.

But the rest of my family is probably still crusted with Looking-Glass goo, and blood, and dirty dungeon cell straw. We all need baths, and clothes, and most importantly: I need some fucking food.

"Not sure if I've ever really experimented with *tea bagging*," I drawl, teasing Lar as I glance flirtatiously over my shoulder at him. If you're not familiar with the slang, tea bagging is when … well, you know how you dip a tea bag into a cup of hot water? Well, tea bag is a euphemism for testicles and *cup of hot water* is, like, your mouth. "Never been with a guy that I'd cared to try it with."

"What a shame," Lar whispers, letting go of my hair. I stand up and stretch with a groan, feeling every muscle in my body scream in protest. They ache so damn bad, I could probably start naming muscles I didn't even know I had, so acutely do I feel them. "Let me know if you change your mind on that."

I give him a look and then open the door to the bathroom, the entirety of which is contained in the thick handle of the teacup. I have to duck to get inside the small door, but when I stand up, I'm pleasantly surprised to find a clawfoot tub, a small porcelain sink, and a toilet. The water inside the toilet bowl is steaming and smells of Earl Grey, but I'll take it. I pee as quick as I can, flush, and duck back down to crawl into the bedroom.

The sun is going down, but I'm *starving.* I wonder if a town this size has somewhere to eat? A restaurant, a bakery, a café, I'm not picky: hell, I'll visit a butcher's if I have to. My stomach grumbles, and I put my palm over it to quiet it down. If I'm going to live in Underland the rest of my natural life, I may as well get used to it here. There are no drive-thru fast food burgers to pick up, so I'll have to make do with what's on offer.

"Is there somewhere we could grab a bite to eat?" I ask, peeking inside my satchel and pulling out a black tank top that says *Village Witch*, along with a fresh bra, panties, and a black and white plaid skirt.

"I don't know the town well," Lar says, moving over to the decorative table near the window and opening a map. "But this should help." Stepping up beside him with my clothes clutched in my arms, I look down at the folded brochure made of parchment. There are ink drawings of several locales in the immediate area, with tiny flashing signs above each one, advertising their wares. It's a bit weird, seeing the medieval looking sheet of paper with its neon colors and blinking lights. *Magic.* "There's a twenty-five hour bakery," the Caterpillar says, tapping the map with his finger. "They have meat pies, it says."

"How can a bakery be open twenty-five hours if there are only twenty-four hours in a day?" I ask, and Lar smiles at me, this bemused little half-smile that says he's thinking a hundred things that he isn't bothering to say. That intrigues me. That, and his key-shaped nipple piercings, his visions, his magic. I want to know *more*.

"They're only open for twenty-five hours at a time, and then they close for an undetermined amount of time before reopening again."

"That makes zero sense whatsoever," I say as Lar gently closes the map, folding his wings together behind his back at the same time.

"It doesn't have to," he tells me, glancing over, blue-blonde hair falling across his pale forehead. "Sunshine, some things are just … *fun*. Relax a little." Lar steps back and turns toward the strange, small door that leads into the bathroom. As the handle connects to the teacup on both the bottom and the top, there are actually *two* doors that lead inside, although I can't imagine any sane person using the upper one. No fucking way. "I'll run you a bath, and let you steep those muscles."

He squeezes into the lower door, dragging his wings against the walls and ceiling, and leaving a trail of glitter behind.

"Just for fun, huh?" I ask, but it's hard to think of fun as being anything but extravagant while there's a war going on. With a shrug and a sigh, I follow after Lar, and I try really hard not to think about what I'm going to say to my family when next I see them.

The bakery is known as The Bread-and-Butterfly—very clever, slow clap for them—and it's not far down the road, situated inside an old silver kettle with steam billowing out the spout. The evening walk is pleasant enough … or would be if it weren't for the fucking flowers.

"*When the Walrus and the Carpenter take over this neck of the woods,*" a not-so-shy daisy comments as we pass by, "*I imagine the landscaping will go all to 'ell in an 'andbasket.*"

"*Well, certainly someone's landscaping is already gone to 'ell,*" says a purple larkspur, fluttering its petals in my direction. I *am* wearing skivvies this time, so they can fuck off. "*I can see little 'airs on 'er inner thighs! Look, there's one right there!*" it shrieks, pointing with a delicate green leaf. "*You do know when you landscape your naughty bits, you're to wax there, too, right? I'd not put up with a male with a single 'air on his balls. Would you, Daisy?*"

"*I most certainly would not,*" the daisy replies, waving little white petals at me as I walk by with my sister and parents in tow. What a lovely conversation to be having with them, a discussion about the few hairs I have on my inner thighs. Thank you, ladies, for making me feel beautiful today.

"Well, I am not a male, and I did not ask your opinion," I growl, stooping down and tearing a bunch of them at the stems. Shrieks and yowling accompany the move, and several pixies scatter, leaving me with a bouquet of bleeding flowers that I hand to Lar.

"Is this for me?" he asks, smiling as he takes it from my fingers. Our hands brush together, and we end up staring at each other for much longer than necessary. When I realize what I'm doing, I pull away and hurry toward the bakery's front door, holding it open for my family and the twins to pass inside.

Preeeeetty sure that they're all in shock of some sort. Just hope it doesn't kill them. I mean, I guess if they pass out, and I think their life's in danger, I can just wrangle up some vampire blood from my twenty-eight year old lover. Not sure they'd survive the trauma of *that*, but, you know, it's an option.

Inside the Bread-and-Butterfly, it's absolutely adorable. There's a full-service tea station (of course) and counters made of gleaming tile in all sorts of colors. The walls are painted with fantastical scenes of *Wonderland*—definitely not Underland because there's text that says *Before the Riving*—and chandeliers made of crystallized flowers. Little bells tinkle when we let ourselves in, and my nose tickles with the powdery scents of sugar, yeast, and flour.

"Could you order for us?" I ask Lar, noticing that my sister is still cowering, my father is gaping, and my mother is staring at me, completely stone-faced. "I wouldn't know what to get anyway." Lar nods and starts to move away when I reach out and grab his upper arm. He stares down at my fingers, curling around his beautiful bare bicep, his red jacket still hanging off his shoulders like it's draped there, and he smiles at me. "No boosted tea," I warn him, but all he does is wink.

Asshole.

"I'll keep an eye on him," Tee says, exhaling sharply. I remember what he said about being a tea addict once, and I wonder about it. But he'll bring it up when and if he's ready. So I just reach out and give both him and Dee a little rub on their wings. Tweedledum looks down at my hand and then back up at my face. "It's not over 'til it's over," he whispers, and I know both he and Dee are waiting for midnight with butterfly bellies.

"The curse is broken; I can feel it," Dee says, but his optimism only seems to annoy his twin. "You know you can, too. He just likes to see his glass half-empty, 'tis true."

"'Tis not." Tee declares, moving over a bit to study the menu board. "I'm simply practical."

"Pessimistic," Dee corrects, raising a finger, sapphire eyes sparkling. "Nothing wrong with that—it's just how you are."

"I got my wing severed today," Tee growls, exhaling sharply and giving his brother a look. "Can you cut me some slack please?"

"Actually," his twin continues, tucking his hands in his pockets. "That was *last* night."

"It was after midnight which means it was *today*. It's not midnight yet."

"*Today* implies after the moons have set and the sun's risen. You're all twisted, topsy-turvy like." Dee leans in conspiratorially toward me, and kisses my cheek. "He knows not what he says."

"Contrariwise," Tee grinds out, and they get into another of their verbal twin battles.

I decide to let them at it, heading over to a table in the corner to sit down; my family follows suit.

What happens next is the most awkward moment of my entire life. Thought that was when my dad walked in on me and the twins, but … well, that wasn't my dad, was it? That was the Black Rabbit whose face will haunt my nightmares for years to come. And anyway, this is worse. This is infinitely worse.

"We're having a group delusion," Edith says, looking between both my parents. She's the only one of us who refused to bathe before leaving the Scented Rush, so she smells fucking awful, and her blonde hair is a tangled mat, but she doesn't seem to care. "That can happen you know, like … like if the water is poisoned, or some toxic chemicals get in the air."

"This is not a delusion, Edith," my mother says calmly, staring at her youngest daughter. How do I go about telling her and dad that their oldest daughter is an undead nightmare? Fuck, maybe that's something I should never share? Yeah, no. In that moment, looking into their frightened, confused faces, I know that I won't.

I'll take that secret to the grave.

"How do you know that?!" Edith shrieks, her shoulders shaking with fresh sobs. Staring at her now, I already know something I should've figured out before I even brought her here: Edy will never be happy in Underland. *Fuck.* Staring at her now, I feel like a selfish asshole. I told myself I was bringing her here to protect her, but maybe that wasn't it at all? Maybe I brought her here because this is where I want to be, and she's my sister, and I couldn't imagine life without her?

That Looking-Glass … it cannot break.

Now at the next table over, Tee and Dee shift uncomfortably and cast me a twin pair of sympathetic looks. Their wings are glorious and full, swathes of dark feathers dotted with color. The Knave's curse is gone (probably), and I can't even enjoy it because I'm sitting here stuck in a family nightmare of my own making.

"Edith, you live and breathe the reality you're in," Mom says calmly, reaching out to take my sister's hand, but Edy yanks it back and cradles it against her chest like she's been bitten, like my mother's words have slapped her hard across the face. "It's the one nightmare you cannot wake up from." Hannah exhales and glances over at me; I can barely meet her eyes. "When Fred died, I wished and prayed and dreamed and screamed until I passed out, but when I woke, I still existed in that same, horrible reality. That's life."

"You're so fucking mean," Edith growls out, and I can see so very clearly in that moment that she's only sixteen, that she's young at heart, that she's jaded and afraid of the world around her. No, Edith has to go back through the Looking-Glass as soon as it's safe for her to go.

Lar approaches the table with a steaming pot of … something, and a handful of teacups.

"Hot cocoa," he says, passing the cups around and leaving the pot in the center of the table. "And I've ordered you all jubjub meat pies with plum cake for desert."

"What the *fuck* is a jubjub?" Edith snaps, but Lar just looks at her like *she's* the mad person at this tea party.

"You know, your sister fought with everything she had to get back to you. Do you know that? She was willing to risk crown and kingdom to make sure you didn't feel abandoned." Lar leans down and puts his palms on the table, his one remaining earring swinging with the motion. "Don't be a goddamn brat."

He leaves again to get the pies, while Edith just sits there, completely dumbfounded.

"Thank you for coming to get me," Hannah says, looking at me with those familiar blue eyes of hers. "I was willing to pay for what I did, but … I'd rather be here with you."

"Even in Underland," I whisper, feeling my cheeks flush as my mother reaches out to brush some stray hair behind my ear. She pauses a moment to finger some of the rainbow-colored strands.

"Even in Underland … wherever Underland might be." She glances up at my dad, who looks substantially better now that he's showered and changed his clothes. The innkeeper brought all three of my family members fresh items to wear and left them in stacks outside their door. Dad looks a bit weird in tight breeches and a frilly white shirt—much like the Duke wears—but he's handsome anyway.

"I'm sorry you got dragged into this," I tell him, reaching out for the pot and pouring a round of hot cocoa for the whole table. There's an extra teacup filled with marshmallows in the shape of clouds. I drop one into my drink and it melts right away, white puffs of cumulus cloud drifting up from my cup and dissipating in the warm air of the bakery. "This is Liddell blood lineage crap coming up to haunt us all."

Dad smiles and wraps his hands around the teacup. After a moment, he reaches for a few marshmallows himself.

"When I took your mother's last name," he begins, and my heart swells with pride. Take *that* patriarchy! "I knew I was marrying into something interesting. I thought it was going to end up being scandalous family secrets from the fifties or something, but … this makes a certain amount of sense."

"I don't see how you all can just sit there and laugh," Edith grinds out, refusing to touch her cocoa.

"You'd rather us sit here and cry?" Mom retorts. Silence reigns queen over our table for a moment, but it's much less awkward this time. Lar returns to the table first with our meat pies, and then with big, juicy slices of plum cake that smell like dried fruit and spices. He brandishes the plates about like a circus performer, spinning them across the table until they land just so.

"Dessert always sits to the right of the main course, hot beverages above, and cool beverages to the left." Lar leaves one last time and returns with a jug of ice water, one that's filled with dozens of colorful flowers that tease the liquid with a sweet, floral scent. "Is there anything else I can get for you, Sunshine?"

"Nothing," I whisper, feeling my cheeks heat. "And thank you."

Lar leaves to sit with the twins as my mother reaches out and gives my hand a squeeze.

"Somebody's got a little crush. I've been able to recognize that face on you since you were eight years old."

"Mom!" I snap, picking up the meat pie and refusing to think of that giant monster bird spewing spider silk as I take my first bite. "Nice to know you can embarrass me on either side of the Looking-Glass."

"Speaking of," Hannah continues, as Dad picks off an experimental bit of plum cake. "If your father and sister want to go back …"

"Hannah," Dad starts, but she stops him from finishing his sentence by lifting her hand. Her blue eyes bore into mine.

"What do we need to do?"

"You, nothing," I say with a sardonic half-smile, lifting my gaze to look between her and Dad. "Me, I have a war to win."

"Stay in the room with us," Mom says, after a game of vintage style jacks. The White Rabbit smokes a cigar that smells like strawberries and watches us, white ears swiveling on the top of his head. Dee, he actually plays, too, and he's goddamn good at it. "Sleep in here tonight, Allison. You can share a bed with your sister."

As appealing as that sounds … I think, but I don't want to be rude aloud.

"I bet Allison-who-isn't-Alice has a lot of work to get done tonight," Dee supplies, folding his wings tightly against his back as he tosses up the little black and white harlequin-patterned ball, and snatches up all ten jacks in one go. He grins big as the ball bounces on the table's surface. "But don't worry: I'll stay here with you and tell you about the game of jacks. Did you know in some circles, it's called knucklebones? Originally played with sheep bones."

"That's morbid," Edith snorts, sitting on one of the beds, arms wrapped around her legs so that she's as small and round as the harlequin ball. This room has four beds, as opposed to two. Tee is resting on one, holding his right wing in his lap and stroking his fingers over the feathers. I will never forget what I saw last night; I will never forget that I almost lost him.

"I really should go," I say, feeling fatigue wash over me. Sleeping next to Edith sounds as appealing as snuggling up to one of those cranky *cat*erpillars. That, and I'd like to at least speak with the King on our plans for the next few days. Also, my curiosity is *killing* me: where did they hide the other half of that goddamn Looking-Glass? "Dee's right." I get up and give my dad a hug, my mom a kiss. Edith, I simply pause next to the bed until she finally looks up at me. "I'll get you home, Edy."

"Sure, Sonny," she says, looking away sharply. "Sure you will." But the more she denies my ability to carry through on my word, the more she rolls her eyes and acts like I'm an idiot, the more determined I am to do it. Don't let anybody ever tell you that hate can't motivate. I mean, I don't hate Edy, but her attitude fucking *sucks*.

Dee catches the bouncing ball, stands up, and scrapes the wooden legs of his stool across the porcelain floor. His blue and black hair catches the light from the gas lamps, and his eyes look like two sapphire jewels in that handsome face. He smiles at my parents, tips his hat, and then threads his arm through mine. As I pass Tee, I give him the sweetest smile I can muster.

"I'm glad you're okay," I tell him, and he opens his mouth to say something to me, pausing when he notices my parents are staring at us. They haven't really asked about my little harem, and I'm not quite ready to talk about it. Sounds exhausting, and I am *beyond* exhausted.

"I'm glad you're okay, too." He reaches out and touches my hand, and I give his fingers a little squeeze. Dee leads me out into the hallway, closes the door behind us, and locks it with the iron key.

"Are *you* okay?" I ask as Dee turns around and cocks a dark brow at me. He adjusts his cap again, a nervous habit that both twins seem to submit to. "I mean, you saw your brother's wing get lopped off. That must be pretty fucking awful." He stares at me for a long moment with those big, beautiful eyes, his clean air scent mixing with the herbal tea blends drifting up from the lobby.

"It's not the first time I've seen something like that," he whispers, tucking his fingers in the pockets of his red military jacket. His eyes darken with memories that he doesn't know I know about. They sit inside me like shadows, swirling around and blotting out the sun. I can only imagine what it must've been like to actually live through it.

"Remember when you told me to put my hand on your chest and …" Dee lifts his head up and grins, and I stop talking, cheeks coloring slightly. Of course he remembers. Hopefully, he'll never forget. I know I'll remember that night the rest of my life. "I saw … well, I saw something else."

"Something else?" he asks, taking a step toward me. I move back until my body is pressed against the metal railing. Dee curls his wings around me and pulls me forward a few inches, sliding his hands around my waist and tucking me in close. "What else, Allison-who-isn't-Alice?"

Closing my eyes, I take in a deep breath, and then I lean my cheek against his warm chest, listening to his heartbeat. He's the only one in this group besides Chesh that I might describe as cheeky or fun or playful; it feels *good* to be around him, light, almost carefree. Almost. There's a darkness inside of Tweedledee that'll take years to heal, but that's okay, because I have my own darkness, too.

"You can just call me … Alice, if you want to."

"Or Allison?" he asks, and I shrug. I don't really care anymore.

"No point in going back to yesterday, because I was a different person then, and it's no use now, to pretend to be two people. Why, there's hardly enough of me to make *one* respectable person."

"I think there's *more* than enough to make a dozen respectable people," he says as I lean back and lift my chin, looking up into those glorious jewel-toned eyes of his. "Or even a baker's dozen, really, which isn't a dozen at all since it's oft considered to mean thirteen."

My lips twitch into a smile of their own accord.

"Dee, right before we had sex for the first time …" I drop my gaze and pick at the epaulettes on his shoulders, toying with the fringe. "I saw into your memories." He stiffens up, and I flick my gaze to his to see if I've overstepped my bounds. Only, he just looks sad, and when he looks sad, he looks like Tee. Contrariwise, when Tee looks happy, he looks like Dee. Two brothers, each half of one coin. "The night your mother was killed, I saw the card soldiers climbing the walls of your tower …"

Dee exhales and lets his head fall back, but his peaked cap doesn't go anywhere, another item spelled to stay put. Reaching one hand up, I touch my crown, and I think about what it really means to become the Queen of Hearts, to inherit a kingdom and a legacy soaked in blood. Staying in Potsville however has given me an interesting perspective. I sat in a bakery tonight and ate a moist slice of plum cake that smelled like ginger, candied orange peel, and brandy. I watched a pair of children play dominoes, and on their way out, the shopkeeper gifted them both chocolate covered strawberries.

This is the Underland I haven't seen enough of, normal people doing normal things.

These are the people I'm fighting for, aren't they?

"I'm sorry you had to see that," Dee whispers, his sapphire eyes dark and filled with shadows. "That was the worst night of my life, but the best part of the worst night of your life is that every night after feels like a blessing." The young angel prince cups my face in both hands, leaning down and letting his breath feather across my lips for a moment. "Each kiss after the worst night of your life feels as good as the Knave breaking that goddamn curse."

I lift up on my tiptoes and close the gap between us, kissing him, letting all the feeling I have in my body flow through my lips. Dee hugs me close with his arms *and* his wings, squeezing me tight, and tasting me slowly. *He* tastes like hot cocoa, and I wonder if I do, too. I let my fingers explore his wings, his silky hair, pushing his cap playfully forward until it hides his eyes. Dee chuckles and the sound takes over my whole body, lightening my mood a good dozen shades. Maybe a baker's dozen, really.

"On the run from the Walrus and the Carpenter, and we still have time to kiss like teenagers," I whisper, and Dee grins.

"You're eigh*teen* and I'm nine*teen*, so certainly we're both considered teens." He pauses and lifts his eyes to the ceiling in thought. "But if you think we're on the run, you're wrong. We're not running; we're being cautious. Rendezvousing with the army, taking solace in a safe space, figuring out just who's loyal and whose heads need to roll, that's what we're doing." *Loyal.* Like the Lion, the Knave, and the Unicorn. I hope they're all okay; I need a chance to prove myself to Ines, too. If she dies with all that disdain for me, it'll bother me the rest of my life.

"Do you think we can win?" I ask, and Dee smiles at me, a different sort of smile this time though. It's not goofy or silly or playful—there's hope buried in there.

"I've known that since the day I met you, Alice. Just remember that: I believe in you." Dee kisses me again, slow and soft, and when the clock in the lobby strikes midnight, we both freeze. But this time, there are no chains, no folding of his wings, no harnessing of his magic. It's just me, and an angel boy, and a kiss I'll remember forever.

Chapter Five

Fabulous Monsters

The King of Hearts is in the bath when I get back to my room, reluctantly leaving Dee behind at the door with a kiss that lingers like morning dew. I could kiss him forever and never tire of it.

"Never thought to close either door?" I ask as I stand there and stare into the strange upper door of the teacup's handle bathroom. Brennin Red is laid out in a steaming tea bath, naked and glorious, beyond self-confident in his appearance. His best bits are hidden by the water, but I can see the flat expanse of his chest, his muscular shoulders, his beautiful arms … and his palms, red as blood.

"Why should I? Only my soothsayer has a key, my queen has my hearts, and I'm sharing the room with two infernal cats." He taps his fingers on the edge of the bathtub as I narrow my eyes.

"Don't you mean *has my heart*? We've each only got one, you know?"

"I'm the King of Heart*s*, with an 's', Your Majesty. I mean what I say." He smirks at me, referencing our little conversation in Mom's study. Good thing she'll never have to know I had my first double-penetration in her office. I look back and find the Duke watching me, lying on his side of the bed, tail swaying lazily. The Caterpillar sits in the open window, one leg hanging out, smoking his glass toadstool pipe.

"North."

"Duchess," the Duke replies, and I raise an eyebrow because the damn Cheshire Cat's given him the idea, and I doubt he'll call me much of anything else at this point.

"Can one really be a duchess *and* a queen?" I quip, moving away from the bathroom to sit on the bed next to Dinah and Chesh. The latter crawls into my lap … and then shifts into human form, nuzzling a place that's already quite sensitive from my make-out session with Dee. I pat his head and playfully stick my fingers into the silver loops of his earrings.

"One can be a duchess who then becomes a queen. You were *my* mate first, and then you took on the King, so that means you've upgraded in status." North swings his legs over the edge of the mattress and leans across the gap between the two beds. He moves to kiss me, but I stay stone-still, letting him take charge of my mouth. He's the near opposite of Dee, as demanding and possessive as the other man is carefree.

"The King still needs to get permission from my primary," I say, and I'm not at all joking. I hear a frustrated scoff from the direction of the bathroom, and a pair of chuckles from Chesh and Lar.

"What about me, Knicker Dancer?" Chesh yowls, rubbing his face against my belly. He turns on his side and kisses my bare skin between the tank top that's ridden up, and my low-slung skirt. I shiver as he nibbles the flesh near my belly button. "I'd make the *purr-fect* lover, and I do like you so very much." He rubs his cheek all over me, reminding me that this is supposedly how Dinah named me the Midnight Knicker Dancer in the first place. What sorts of messages is the Cheshire Cat writing with his kitty scent?

"We shall see," I respond coyly, but my fingers are already buried in his hair, and I *am* quite fond of him. *For the love of all that is holy, bang the goddamn Cheshire Cat, please!* I think to myself, suppressing a secret grin.

I push Chesh off after a moment, give Dinah a scratch, and head over to the tea table in the corner. Somebody's already lit the fire in the hearth, and there's a fair bit of steam coming from the kettle. Do you know there really *is* a difference between a teakettle and a teapot? The former is where you warm the water, and the latter is where you steep the tea leaves. It's all very proper and important.

There are several jars on a shelf, each one with a handwritten label and tiny, colorful designs painted onto it. *Lavender-bergamot, lemon citrus, peppermint, chocolate cherry, Scented Rush signature blend*. I choose the last one and turn the jar over, reading the side effects. *May cause dizziness, fatigue, overwhelming joy, heat, lust, flushed cheeks, hardened nipples, strange dreams involving flying or falling, or the sudden blurting of platitudes.*

Oh well. When in Underland and all that.

I'm not on holiday anymore: I'm a local now.

"Excellent choice," the Cheshire Cat says, sliding up behind me. He fades from view, and I feel invisible hands cover my own, guiding my movements. I can't say I don't like it, having Chesh tucked up so close behind me. I can feel his hardness pressing into my lower back, and I bite my lip. "You've not made much tea in your time, have you *Alice*?" He hisses this last word in my ear, and I shiver.

"Not really. Back home, sometimes, when it was raining and I wanted to read, I'd stuff a Lipton tea bag in a cup of water, and microwave it."

"Microwave?" Chesh says as I glance over my shoulder and see his mouth and ears reappear. "What's a microwave?"

"It's an electric box that either makes items lukewarm, or so scalding hot they burn you. It's kind of a shitty invention, but impossible for lazy people—myself included—to live without." Chesh guides me through the steps of making a proper pot, and then a proper cup of tea, adding just the right amount of sugar and far too much cream.

I drink it anyway, closing my eyes and sipping sweet hints of smoke and ripe plums tethered in an earthy aftertaste. It's fucking *delicious*. I sigh blissfully as Chesh steps back, and I move so that he can make his own cup.

"Would either of you like some tea?" I ask, looking to both the Duke and the Caterpillar. Red is still in the bath, and I can't very well ask Dinah, now can I? Though I do see Chesh sneak her a saucer of cream on the bed. When she glances up at me, licking her lips, she has the smuggest fucking look about her.

"Not for me, my dear," North says, and the only way I know to describe the way he's laying right now is to say that he's *lounging.* "I must be on the alert, to defend you and your illustrious King in case of attack."

"Since when did he become *my* illustrious king?" I ask, but really, I'm just being contrary. There's no point in fighting myself on what I want anymore. I *want* to be here, and I want to have a harem, and I fucked the King twice and I'm dreaming about doing it again, so what? It's *okay* to let myself be happy, and it's *okay* to let myself have it. I don't need to keep up an internal diatribe to make myself feel like a better person. *Indulge a little, Allison, and enjoy that indulgence or else, what's the point in having it?* "Anyway, do you think we're safe here?"

"Safe is relative," Brennin says, squeezing his muscular body through the strange door. He stands up and shoves wet, red hair off of his forehead. "The citizens won't report us: there's nary a soul in Underland who fancies a world in which the Walrus and the Carpenter rule. If they do catch up to us, we'll smell the rot."

"That doesn't account for spies and Rabbits," I say, sighing and sitting next to the Caterpillar. I copy his pose, dangling one leg out the window only to find a balcony there that I never noticed before. There's no proper door to get to it though, just the window. How fucking queer.

"The Duke and I, *we* account for spies and Rabbits," the King says, *slowly* pulling his gloves down over his fingers. Looking at him standing next to the Duke like that, I can only imagine what it'd be like to take both of *them* to bed at the same time.

"Where did you hide the Looking-Glass?" I ask, and we all know I don't mean the one that's here. *That* one is underneath the bed, wrapped in a sheet.

"Irrelevant," the King says, waving his gloved hand. He lets his towel drop and doesn't seem to give a fuck that he's completely and totally naked *and* erect. I gape at him, but the other men hardly blink. Dinah looks a bit offended though. "And anyway," he continues, smiling in just such a way that it pulls at the scar on his lip, drawing my attention to the healed gash in his throat. "If you're worried about spies and Rabbits, is it not best that I don't repeat it?"

He has a point.

I continue to sip my tea, feeling my head getting a little woozy as I make contact with the Caterpillar's perfect blue eyes, like chips of ice in his pale face. He smiles at me, and I smile back. If I kissed him now, would he taste like the sweet plum cake we ate at the Bread-and-Butterfly?

"I saw the White Rabbit's third form," I drawl casually, preferring to bring it up when said Rabbit is not around, just in case the King gets angry. His mouth hardens into a thin line, but he makes no move to dress himself. "Who's the girl anyway?"

"What girl?" the King asks, quite clearly playing word games with me. "His third form is a state secret; you cannot possibly have seen it."

"But I *did*," I blurt, my teacup rattling on its saucer. It's only then that I notice the balcony outside is also made up of a saucer, sitting underneath our teacup room. "She had bloodred hair and dark eyes, and her magic—"

"I had two sisters," Brennin says, nostrils flaring. Clearly, he doesn't want to tell me any of this. Maybe he figures it's the right thing to do? Or maybe he thinks by telling me that I'll shut my mouth and stop asking stupid questions. With the latter, he's completely correct. "A much younger sister, just a child. And an older sister who should've been queen; all queens have Rabbits, you know. When my father went mad, he slaughtered my mother first, and the girls next. He took a throne no male has any right to hold on his own. And then he tried to kill me."

After a moment, the King removes one of his gloves and shows me his hand.

"Take a life, bear the mark," he whispers, and I remember that Rab's female form also had reddened palms. "My sister had already learned her cruelty from my father, but she had a good soul deep down; she could have been saved." He continues to stare at his palm for a moment longer, and then replaces the glove.

"And the decapitation magic ...?" I start, wondering if I'm pushing my luck. The King glares at me with obsidian eyes.

"A curse, brought on by a wild magic storm. Just like North. I wasn't born with the ability to tear heads from shoulders, you know. What sane child is?"

"And you're a jabberwock ... because of a curse as well?" I finish my tea off and set it aside as North nods.

"Precisely, but I can't say I regret it. I wouldn't cure it if I could." His words make me think of the Knave, and the twins. I wonder if she broke their curse to help keep the King safe, or if Tee's sacrifice somehow warmed her ugly, black heart? No way to know without asking her. My chest constricts, and I feel awful for thinking badly about her and her husbands. They're sort of weird, and awkward, and mean, but they're good people underneath.

Turning, I let both legs dangle out the window and then hop down onto the saucer balcony, putting my hands on the metal railing, the one made of dessert forks. I stare out across the town, and into the woods beyond. I can see several giant mushrooms glowing from here. There's one not too far from our balcony, even, a decorative toadstool in the back garden of the inn. It's shiny and purple, with glowing white gills, and flecks of silver across the top.

I feel like I could float to it, if only I just climbed this railing ...

"Hold up there, Sunshine," Lar whispers, his hair and earring dancing in the breeze. He exhales some blue smoke, draws a beating heart in it, and then rises to his feet. He hands me the pipe, and I take a few inhales before tucking it back in his pocket for him. "Will you, won't you join the dance?" Lar murmurs as he comes up close behind me, turning me around with gentle hands.

Automatically, I put one on his shoulder, and he puts one on my hip. Our other hands clasp together as he hums, and we start to waltz, right there on the smooth white porcelain of the balcony.

"*You can really have no notion how delightful it will be*," Lar sings, as our feet begin to lift up off of the balcony. His voice is mellifluous, as smooth as air and twice as clear. I close my eyes and lean into him, letting the high of the boosted tea take over me. "*When she takes her throne and rises up, with nine husbands for all to see! But enemies reply 'No way, no way!' and then they take a chance— The Alice kills them kindly, for they will not end her dance.*"

"You're making this song up right now," I whisper, but Lar just keeps humming, fanning his wings as we rise up above the railing. He moves aside, so that we're standing next to one another, holds onto my hand, and walks us through the air and over to the toadstool.

From up here, I can see the rest of the city, including the river made of tea, the tiny boats bobbing with little colored lights glowing in their windows. The breeze smells of cream and sugar, and the distant scream of a jabberwock seems far away and unimportant; even my ears don't bleed.

"It's not a made-up song; it's been sung in the Court of Hearts for years." Lar lets go of my hand and watches as I spin in circles with my arms spread wide. Fucking boosted tea. The warning label was fairly accurate, I must say. But I feel good, too, relaxed. Maybe that's a mistake, maybe something is waiting out there in that darkness to destroy me, but one can never know such a thing with certainty, now can they? "I find it pretty, don't you like it?"

"If you were to sing it, I'd like anything—even Britney Spears, I'll bet."

"Britney *who*?" he asks, pulling out his pipe and smoking it again. His wings glimmer, and I brace myself for a vision. But he simply flutters them softly and then folds them together behind his back. I haven't forgotten about that image of us, wrapped in carnal bliss, hands and mouths and bodies touching in every which way.

"Never mind," I chuckle, sitting down on the edge of the toadstool and looking down at the cobblestone path below. First thing I did after dinner was check to see if the Mad Hatter and the March Hare were back, but either they weren't or they didn't bother to open their door when I knocked.

"See something down there?" Lar asks, but I shake my head.

"I see nobody."

"I only wish *I* had such eyes," he quips, sitting down next to me with a bemused smile on his lips. "To be able to see nobody! And at that distance, too. Why, it's as much as *I* can do to see *anybody*, by this light."

I elbow him in the side, but he just keeps smiling, tucking away his pipe yet again. His hand emerges from his pocket, and when he uncurls his fingers, there are two blue teardrop earrings resting in his palm. Those are the same earrings he wore from the day I met him, until the night of the ball.

"Are those magical, like your red earrings?" I ask, flicking his one remaining one with my finger. "Or just sentimental?"

The Caterpillar doesn't answer, instead reaching over to brush my hair back from my ear. He slides the metal of the earring into my hole—sounds dirty, huh?—and then does the same on the other side.

"These are for you," he tells me as I reach up to tug on them. "If you're ever in a pinch, throw one."

"What will it do?" I ask, as the cool night breeze washes over us, tousling my hair.

"I suppose you'll find out, if you're ever in a pinch," is his response. Dickhead. He looks down at my thigh, reaching over a single thumb and rubbing it across my new tattoo. The clock is ticking down to a time marked with a black line. Ten after nine in the evening, several days from now. I wonder what it's counting down to?

"Thank you." My voice comes out in a thready whisper, and even though it's pretty goddamn cold out here, I start to feel warm inside. Looking over at the Caterpillar, his blue eyes intent on the horizon, I find that I can't help myself. I lean up and kiss him on the cheek.

His smile is more genuine when he gives it, and he pats his lap. I don't hesitate before I climb into it, sitting a good four or five stories off the ground with nothing keeping me up here but the Caterpillar's strong arms around me.

"What does the other key do?" I ask, reaching a palm inside Lar's shirt and rubbing my thumb over his nipple. His eyes get half-lidded, and he swallows hard. "One is for the main Castle Heart gate, and the other …?"

"Was a placeholder," he says, as I push his shirt back a bit more and notice that the second key is different than the first. It has a heart on both ends, and I recognize it as the one to the Suit of Hearts. "I never intended to try for your harem," he continues as I give it a little tug, and he lets out this strained gasp, like he's trying not to push too hard or too fast. I grin and start to do it again, but Lar clasps his fingers around my wrist. "I never intended to try, but … once you gave me that key, I knew I wanted to hold it close."

My fingers curl through his, and I look up, into those eyes that are just a shade paler than my own. My lids get heavy, and I lean forward, hovering my mouth close to his. Our kiss is slow and languid, like the Caterpillar himself. He moves at his own pace, questions everything, and hides an immense well of power underneath a civil façade.

Unleashed, he would be tremendous; I've seen glimpses of it. Lar is a powerful fucking curseworker, or witch, or whatever you want to call him.

We kiss with the sound of the city beneath us, that gently clinking whisper of China paired with the murmur of distant voices. The boats on the river toot their horns, and let out puffs of steam that rise into the night air like clouds.

My fingers play with Lar's nipples, teasing and twisting the keys around. He lets me tease him for a while, the hard length of his cock growing in his slacks. I can feel it when I wiggle around on his lap. Adjusting myself, I wrap my legs around him, my back to the edge of the toadstool. I reach over his shoulders to find his wings, brushing my fingertips gently across them at first. Lar moans and cups my ass, squeezing hard. When I start to move my hands away, he reaches up and takes my wrist, encouraging me to keep going.

I grab the edge of his left wing, giving it a tug. Lar seems to love it, squeezing my ass tighter, sucking hard enough on the side of my neck that I just know I'm going to wake up with hickeys in the morning. *Won't Mom love that!* The boosted tea is making me feel brave, so I pull a bit of his wing forward and then run my tongue along the edge.

"Hearts and Diamonds, Sunshine," he groans … but then I *bite* it, and Lar is rolling us over onto the toadstool, so that he's on top and I'm left looking at his blue-blonde hair falling in his face, framed by stars. "That was quite naughty of you."

"I do like to be naughty," I whisper as he slides down and puts his warm palms on my thighs, sliding them up and under my skirt. His fingers find my panties, and there's a pause there, like he's asking for my permission. I'm big on consent, so I appreciate that sort of shit. Although Underland doesn't seem to have near as much trouble with that kind of thing. I doubt they have to have posters that say *No means no!* around here. "Go for it."

Lar gives me one of his trenchant smiles and then takes his sweet goddamn time pulling my panties down. He fingers the black cotton for a moment, and then lights them on fire with his magic. I give a playful shriek as he tosses them aside, but they don't even make it to the ground, instead floating away as ash in the wind.

"You're not the only one who's naughty." Gently, Lar takes hold of my calves and pushes my legs up, encouraging me to bend my knees. I do, and slowly spread my thighs, just like Lar parts his butterfly wings.

The look he gives me is pure wickedness.

Leaning my head back against the surface of the toadstool, I bite my lower lip and stare up at the stars. Not only does Underland have two moons, but the constellations are different. I see a teapot and cups on saucers, a mountain of sugar cubes, and a row of dominoes. Hell, maybe I'm just high? Or maybe I'm basking in the sweet and sinful kisses that Lar is placing on my calves, the backs of my knees, my inner thighs.

Thoughts of constellations flee my head the closer he gets to my core. He doesn't rush it though, moving back down to take off my boots. His thumbs knead my arch, fingers teasing across the top of my feet. It's pure, fucking bliss. I've most definitely never dated a guy who gives foot massages.

He brings my foot to his lips, gently sucking on one of my toes. That just makes me laugh, and I tear my foot from his grip.

"You don't like that?" Lar asks, leaning down and licking his way up my inner thigh. "Shall I suck something else?" He slides his hands under my thighs, gripping them in his strong arms. My breath comes in quick, frantic gasps, anticipating the feeling of his mouth on my core. In stark contrast with my rut with Rab in the dungeon, Lar moves slow as molasses. He's as languid in bed as he is in life.

He kisses my thighs and then works his way around my clit, licking and sucking on every available inch of flesh that *isn't* my magic button. Sort of makes me want to strangle him. But then, I wouldn't get an orgasm out of that, now would I?

My body is in a frenzy, so much so that I can't keep my own hands off my breasts, squeezing and kneading the flesh, playing with my own nipples through the fabric. I'm soaking wet down below, and my muscles are fluttering in anticipation of being filled. It's tempting to grab Lar and beg him to fuck me into the toadstool, but I want to take my time. I've had a lot of quickies lately, and I'm going to enjoy this brief moment of peace if it kills me.

His tongue finally makes a gentle swirl around my clit, rewarding my aching body for being so patient with a rush of wild pleasure. It's like magic as it swirls through me, lifting my back up off the ground, curling my toes. I dig my fingers into the mushroom's springy flesh and hold on for dear life.

"Lar," I moan, eyelids fluttering as I bite my lip and try not to scream. The feeling of his mouth on me is just so goddamn intense. I want more, more, more at the same time I want to drag out this feeling forever. The orgasm is the happily ever after, but it's the journey that I really love.

The King's soothsayer is an expert lover with a magic tongue, flicking it over my clit, sliding it between the warm folds of my cunt. He draws a circle around my opening, tasting me. *I wonder what I taste like anyway?* Whatever it is, Lar seems to enjoy it, making sounds of pleasure as he works a single finger inside of me, kissing and sucking on my clit until it's so swollen it hurts. By the time he works in a second finger, the constellations and the moons have moved across the sky, and I'm panting and sweating with need.

"You're teasing me," I manage to choke out as Lar comes up for air, hooking his fingers inside of me and hitting a spot that makes me gasp. "Stop teasing me."

"Teasing implies there won't be a climactic outcome. But trust me Sunshine, there'll be one." Lar moves back up my body, using his free hand to pull my shirt down, teasing my full breast out of the bra so that he can suck and lick my nipple. His other hand continues to fuck me with slow, delicious motions. When we kiss, I taste myself on his mouth, and I swear it's the taste of starlight. I don't know how, considering I've never eaten a star before, but that's how it feels.

Somewhere off in the distance, the crickets and frogs start up a nightly chorus, an accompanying song to our lovemaking. Well, they sound like crickets and frogs, but for all I know they could be pixies or demons or who the hell knows. But I like the noise, and I like the way Lar is sucking my breast into his mouth, and the pace of his fingers as they move in and out of me.

My arms wrap around his back, fingers digging into his glittering wings, and I climax at the same moment that I realize this is the scene I saw in his wings while we danced, this is the future he predicted. Still, I know I made the choice to be here. This is me, choosing my destiny.

Lar holds me for a while, until I stop shuddering and shaking.

"I told you there'd be a climax," he says, his mouth so close to my ear that I can feel his breath tickle my new earrings. "Would you like another?"

"Yes, please," I groan as we both sit up, and I watch him undo his pants with deft fingers. The Caterpillar—whose nickname is a mystery to me since he looks much more like a butterfly—frees the thick, alabaster length of his cock. "What's your story, regarding … you know, pregnancy?"

"Pregnancy?" Lar asks, brushing some of his hair behind an ear with one hand while he strokes himself with the other. "I see." He chuckles, and his wings glow blue and gold. "Understandable worry. Would you like to use a condom? I've some in my jacket pocket?"

"No stories about how you're infertile, or how fae … I don't know, use magic to make babies, or anything like that?" Lar just laughs at me and lies down on the toadstool on my right side, his hand still working his shaft. He's using my wetness for lube, too, and it's sexy as hell.

"Nothing like that. If I come inside of you, maybe you'll have a child. I don't know the answer to that." He pauses the movement of his hand, reaches up and pulls the jacket from his shoulders. After digging around in the pocket, he pulls out one of the square paper condom packages and hands it over to me. I take it as he removes his shirt, leaving his chest bare and beautiful.

I straddle Lar's legs, and open the condom—it's another heart-patterned one—and then I slip it over his shaft while he groans, teasing him with little tickles from the tips of my fingers. If I look up toward the balcony of our room, I swear I can see the Cheshire Cat watching me from gray eyes. Doesn't bother me. Instead, it turns me on, thinking of Chesh watching me ride Lar.

I lift myself up on my knees and scoot forward, positioning Lar's cock at my wetness, and then I lock gazes with him. He plants his ringed hands on my hips and helps push me down, my body enveloping his shaft with hot, throbbing muscles. I take him all the way in, pressing our pelvises together, and then I begin to move.

Lar's wings curl up toward me, sweeping over my body and teasing my skin with glitter. He leaves my flesh sparkling like the night sky as I lean down, blonde and rainbow hair hanging in a curtain next to my face.

"Kiss me," he says, and I smile as I do, pressing our mouths together, splaying my palm against his chest so I can feel his beating heart. He groans into my mouth, kneading my hips with his fingers, encouraging me to work his body with my own. My breasts are hanging over the wires of my bra, my nipples pert and tight and pink in the cool evening air. After a while, I move one of his hands up to cup one. That's all the encouragement he needs, taking both breasts in his hands and squeezing them, massaging the eager flesh, and playing with my nipples.

I sit up and lean my head back, keeping my hands on Lar's chest while he continues to tease my aching body. We're both getting sweaty, and there's a lot of wetness between my thighs, making my rocking motion so easy and smooth.

Lar's groaning gets rougher and less polished, less practiced, and it is satisfying as *fuck* when he comes, thrusting up against me as he drops his hands to my hips and squeezes. I move a little faster and harder, bending low to kiss his neck and making sure my clit rubs when I rock my pelvis. As the waves of his climax roll over him, I give myself another one, crying out and collapsing into his arms.

My head is on his chest, and I can hear his heartbeat, I can see the stars, and I can feel him envelop me in his wings. Truth be told, there's no place in Topside or Underland that I'd rather be.

And despite the cold, he must feel the same way because we don't leave that spot until the sun peeks its head above the hills.

The ferry is perched on the edge of the Camellia Sinensis river—if you're not aware, the *camellia sinensis* is the tea plant—bobbing gently in the steaming current. It looks much like the Long Tale, but with a metal bottom dotted with dozens of holes.

"That's the strainer," Dee explains, pointing it out to me as I blink past a boosted tea hangover. He recognized right away that that was what was wrong with me this morning. Mom and Dad both pulled me aside separately to ask if I was being pressured into drinking alcohol with these strange men, and Edith has mumbled the word *hypocrite* under her breath about a dozen times. I guess drinking some spiked tea, and sleeping with a guy that I actually like is as bad as shooting meth with a dirty needle—at least in her eyes.

"The strainer?" I ask, cocking my head to one side. It's an Underland habit that I've started to pick up.

"They stuff it with fresh, dry tea leaves. It keeps the river fragrant which is a boon to the local wildlife, and it also helps the boat stay afloat." Dee points across the river, at the distant hills coated in rows of bright green plants. "Those are the tea farms there. Seventy-percent of all tea is grown in the Kingdom of Hearts, but this is actually the second largest tea plantation in all of Underland."

"Huh." I put my hands on my hips, still dressed in my outfit from yesterday—except for, you know, those panties that got lit on fire. Luckily I had some rainbow ones in my bag that say *Make America Gay Again.* I read a book once called *The Nine* by Tate James and … well, I think it was co-written by another author, but I'll be damned if I can remember her name. Anyhow, the sassy gay best friend character was rocking a shirt with that slogan, and I fell in love with it. "What sort of animals can live in a boiling hot river like this?"

"Manatea," Dee says, and he doesn't even smile when he says it. It takes me a good ten seconds of staring at him to realize that's not a joke. "Big, blubbery creatures with flippers and long whiskers." Right. Sounds like the mana*tee* that we have back home. "Only they have glorious manes of hair, and are sometimes mistaken for mermaids."

"Are there mermaids here in Underland?" I ask, trying not to get too excited. Dee looks at me like I'm a crazy person.

"Not in this river, silly. They need cold water." He laughs and tags me playfully on the shoulder as we wait for the gangway to be set up. My eyes drift over to the March Hare and the Mad Hatter. They both look exhausted, but not hungover. As I watch, the March Hare opens his trench coat up and pulls out a long wooden skewer with several dehydrated fish on it. He bites off one's head and smiles at me.

"Did you miss us last night, Doll?" he asks, but I just stare at him.

"Find any beautiful women to tumble with in the city proper?" I ask, not that I'd call Potsville a city. It's more like a town. A village. A rest stop. There just isn't a lot here.

"Not a single *single* woman in the whole of town," March says with a shrug. "And I'm not about to have a cock-race with some small-town bloke over a woman that I don't want. You know the only woman I'm interested in is you, love."

"I agreed to marry the Mad Hatter, you know, not you," I blurt, and March feigns injury. Also, my parents' eyes get wide as saucers.

"Married?" Mom asks, giving me a look of terrified indignation. Dad takes her by the hand and squeezes it before pushing his spectacles up his nose. Poor guy. They're cracked in the center of one lens. I wonder if they have eye doctors here in Underland?

"I've always warned you that marriage is an outdated tool of the patriarchy meant to control women, their children, and their finances, haven't I?" Dad says softly, and I just roll my eyes.

"Au contraire," Dee says, leaping at the chance to educate my ignorant Topsider parents. "In Underland, when a woman marries a man, she essentially owns him. His money is her money, his land is her land, his accomplishments her accomplishments. Sometimes I think women take the legal maximum number of husbands just to collect on the coins." He adjusts his hat and taps a finger against his lips in thought while my family stares on, dumbfounded. "Of course, Alice—that is, your daughter Allison Pleasance Liddell—she isn't taking on nine husbands for the money."

"Nine husbands?" Mom repeats, as I slide my arms over Dee's shoulders and put my hand over his mouth.

"Thank you, Tweedledee, that's quite enough of your cultural history lesson."

"Next time," he tells me as I let go and run my palms down his back, right between his wings. "The lesson will be shorter. That's why they call them lessons, you know. Because they lessen every day."

"You're such a font of information," Lar says as the captain of the ship—a man with wooly, white hair very similar to the sheep lady at the inn—unhooks a chain and welcomes us onboard.

"Aren't I, though?" Dee purrs as he starts up the steps, and I follow after. Lar is right behind me, and I can't help but think how we spent our night. We made love on the toadstool until the sun came up; I got two hours of sleep, at most. He follows me onto the deck and then leans down, kissing my ear and flicking my new earring with his tongue.

"I'm going belowdecks to sleep, if you'd care to join me." My breath catches, and I curl my hands into fists. I almost say yes, but then … I really want to talk to Tee. Okay, so I want to talk to most of the guys. Fine! I want to talk to *all* of them, but one at a time. I don't think I can do this in a group setting.

"If it's as charming as the cabin I stayed in on the Long Tale, then I'll pass." Lar winks at me as he passes by, moving across the deck as the Duke carries the Looking-Glass onboard. It's wrapped in several sheets and tied with thick bundles of rope. It's hard to tell what it is anymore.

Hiking my satchel up my shoulder, I take a seat on a bench facing the tea plantation and pull out my diary. It feels like it's been an eternity since I last wrote it in. To be honest, I'm afraid to read what's in there; it feels like a different life.

Tee sits down beside me as Dinah peeks her head out of the bag and looks around. With a yawn, she retreats back inside and curls up to sleep.

"I wish I had my journal," Tee says longingly, putting one of his massive wings behind me like a cushion. I smile softly as I flip the pages open and find line after line of carefully scribbled text. The very last entry I wrote makes me smile.

Dear Fucking Diary, Edy wants me to go to a party tonight. I fucking hate parties, but you know what? I'll go because Brandon Carmichael is there, and spending senior year alone would blow. Who would I take to prom? Also, I'm bringing a book with me. Even if something goes wrong, I can curl up in the corner and read. You're never alone with a book, right?

"Who knew I would see Brandon's brains splattered on the lenses of his glasses?" I ask, and I hear Rab's cool laughter from the opposite end of the deck.

"That Rabbit-Hole you stumbled down," Tee begins, looking across the water as the crew prepares us to set sail. According to North, our next destination—the city of Wabe—is only a day's journey from here. "That was the best thing that ever happened to me."

Oh Hearts, there he goes, I think, feeling this hot heat suffuse my cheeks.

"I wasn't inclined to agree with you at first," I say, fidgeting on the bench for a moment. "But now …" I look up and meet his purple eyes, feeling my stomach flutter with nerves. Clearly, he knows something happened between Lar and me last night. I could read it in his face as soon as I saw him standing in the lobby this morning. "Now, I'd have to say you're right." I grab a mechanical pencil from my bag, flip to the last page of the diary, and find a note that Edy wrote.

Love reading your entries, bitch! I narrow my eyes, switch the pencil out for a pen, and cross out her note with violent scribbles.

"I wanted to talk to you," I say as the boat lets out a shriek, shoots off a puff of steam, and lurches forward, knocking my shoulder into Tee's. "You know, because you're the primary and all that."

"I already know," Tee says, and his voice sounds choked as he stares out at a boat dressed in colorful ribbons. There must be thousands of them, and they flutter in the breeze like butterflies. "Brennin Red is the rightful primary; it's okay."

I just stare at him for a moment and then snort.

"No. Hell no. Fuck no." I shake my head violently and tuck some rainbow-colored hair behind my ear. "You're the primary; that's what I've decided." I flick my gaze over and find him staring at me so intently that I feel my blush work its way up to my scalp. I bet Tee can see red on my hairline. "But I … need to tell you about a few things that happened with … me and some of the other guys."

"Like Lar last night, or the White Rabbit in the dungeon?" he asks, smiling sympathetically. "I already know."

"You do?" I blink at him, and he shrugs. I love it when the winged guys do that, because their gorgeous wings shrug right along with them.

"I'm perceptive, always have been." He stares down at the dock. "I know about all of it, and it's okay. I knew you'd take nine husbands."

"I should've checked with you beforehand," I say, but Tee shakes his head again.

"You gave keys to nine men, and the paintings in the Suit of Hearts reflected that." He glances over at me. "You know that was no coincidence, right? Those paintings were blank until you showed up in the castle. Those images were there because those were the nine men in the world you were most interested in. If your tastes had changed, so too would the paintings."

My mouth hangs open in shock, and I snap it closed quick to avoid swallowing a rocking horse fly.

"I … didn't know that."

"I still get jealous though," he whispers, looking up at me. "I can't help that. I like being with you, Allison, and I'm only angel." Instead of *I'm only human* … I like that. I lean forward and kiss him on the mouth, savoring his taste. He's more than I ever could've asked for, more than I ever could've expected in *nine* men, let alone one.

I'm glad Tee's my primary.

I lean back and exhale, knowing I have other awkward conversations ahead of me.

There are some guys on this boat, like North and Dee, that I know are ready to be a part of this prophecy. There are others—like Chesh and March—that I need to work on. Okay, and by work on … I mean fuck. Because sex sort of seals the deal in a relationship for me. Before that, it kinda just feels like we're … friends? Or maybe I'm using that as an excuse because I just *want* to get those guys in bed with me.

"Do you want to write an entry together?" I ask Tee, and he smiles, letting me situate the diary half on his leg, and half on mine.

What I can tell you … is that Tweedledum's handwriting is *infinitely* prettier than mine.

The city of Wabe is situated around a massive tower in the shape of a sundial. It's much larger than Potsville, with stone cottages covered in green roofs. There's not a single building that doesn't have moss, grass, flowers, or food sprouting from its rooftop. When we dock, I see that the dockmaster's residence has a large apple tree on the top of it.

We unload the Looking-Glass, and stand clustered on the dock, looking down a long length of cobblestone street to a giant, colorful tent filled with stalls.

Welcome to the Wabe Market the sign says, and then underneath, it's labeled *Directions*: *Goes a long way before it, and a long way behind it!* Huh. Right. That makes no sense whatsoever.

The buildings here seem to have a mix of both diamonds *and* hearts, making me wonder how close to the border of Red's kingdom we really are.

"They have the most magnificent food in Wabe," March laments, glancing back at the river and the setting sun. As it sinks beneath the hills, it paints the steaming water a brilliant burnished gold. "Too bad we're here on business and not on pleasure." He looks back at the Hatter, lifting a dark brow. "Although, people do need to eat, don't they?"

"I suppose they do need to … *eat*," Raiden purrs, but when he says that last word, his eyes are most definitely on the throbbing pulse in my neck. "This is our last civil stop before we reach the Eternal Tea Party. Fresh clothing, food, and train tickets are the business for tonight."

"And I suppose you have connections for a safe place to stay here as well?" Brennin asks, but Raiden Walker just smiles wickedly at him. Even though Red maintains his ironclad control, I can tell he's out of his element. I highly doubt he travels incognito on a regular basis. I bet he uses a *royal escort.*

"What exactly makes up a royal escort anyway?" I ask the Duke as the Mad Hatter lifts his top hat, pulls out his cane and gestures for us to follow him.

"A royal escort," North declares, his gold hair feathering around his dark horns, "is made up of precisely the following: ninety-nine foot soldiers, nineteen cavalry, nineteen archers, nine Rabbits, one carriage, and a tea set with precisely nine choices of tea, with Darjeeling generally being served first. The escort always travels at a brisk nineteen miles per hour, and they only stop at nine in the morning or nine at night."

"Do all of these nines have anything to do with the prophecy?" I ask, but the Duke just gives me one of his bestial little grins, curling his tail around my waist and pulling me close. I always feel safe next to him, like I could take on the world. I mean, he can shift into a fucking dragon—err, jabberwock—who wouldn't feel safe?

The streets here are much more crowded than they were in Potsville, and the air smells like saffron, turmeric, and wildflowers. I bet the former two scents are coming from the market, while the latter is from the living roofs. We take side streets and back alleys until we come to a teahouse called the *Haigha and Hatta*.

"Take a guess how that's pronounced?" Raiden says, flicking the wooden sign. It has a painting of a hare wearing a hat. How clever. And how painfully obvious, too.

"Nice way to announce to the world that you own the place," I say with a roll of my eyes, but the Mad Hatter stops with his hand on the door and gives me a very serious sort of look.

"Actually, my dear little Alice, this tavern is the spot from which *our* names originate. Isn't that right, March?"

"Quite right," he replies, peeling an orange that he snagged from god only knows where. The two of them are staring at me, but they don't seem interested in explaining any further. Instead, Raiden pushes his way into the raucous of the teahouse. There's a band in the corner with instruments much like the ones I saw at The Pool—an electric guitar with gears and cogs, a set of drums, and a woman singing a tune so lewd and bawdy that my parents both blush.

There are women at every table, surrounded by men, but it's very clear who's in charge in Underland. Teapots are passed around, and the clink of china fills every shadowy corner. The sign behind the counter advertises dozens of different teas, and the hallway next to it is marked *Overnight Guests (and Lazy Arse Staff Members) Only.*

The Mad Hatter arranges payment with the front counter, and the barkeep removes the velvet rope, ushering us through. The walls here are made of stone, and they drip constantly, those tufts of moss I saw in the dungeon growing between the stones, glowing faintly.

"One suite tonight, many rooms." Raiden unlocks a door with a heavy iron key and steps aside while we all file in. The room is cozy, with a fire roaring in the fireplace, and I see a whole host of doors arranged on three of the walls. "This is known as a wife's suite," he tells me as he steps inside and locks the door behind us. "Meant for the discerning woman with many husbands—but only if she likes to keep them separate. Some ladies prefer a single bed. I'm inclined toward that myself."

"What's the point of keeping multiple husbands if you have to split your time between them?" I ask, moving over to the fire and holding my palms up in front of it. I'm dying to go check out that market, and like March said: we *do* have to eat, don't we?

My mother's the first one to experiment by opening one of the doors. It has a little sign on the front that says *Kids (and Dwarves, Pixies, and Drink Me Drinkers) Only!* From what I can tell, there are several twin beds in there which is pretty much perfect for Mom, Dad, and Edy. My sister seeks out the nearest bathroom, exhales a sigh of relief, and disappears inside.

She has yet to shower, and I don't think I'm the only one praying she bathes before she comes out of that fucking room.

"I do believe poor Dinah is hungry," Chesh says, pulling the black cat out of my bag and setting her on the tufted green sofa. She yawns, flashing a bright pink tongue, and then proceeds to scratch her nails on the fabric. The Cheshire Cat gets down to her level, flicks a black and white ear, and lowers his lids to half-mast. This seems to convey a very clear message to Dinah, and she stops, sitting back to lick her shoulder. "We'll need to buy some fish in town. Oh, and maybe some freshwater crabs. You'd like some crab, wouldn't you, Dinah?"

"Don't spoil her," I chastise, turning around and putting my hands on my hips. "She's already spoiled enough and besides, I think she's got a crush on you."

"Are you jealous?" Chesh asks, moving over to stand in front of me. He's always crawling around and shifting and fading from view, so that sometimes I forget how damn tall he really is. Or that I almost murdered him with the Vorpal Blade. He wraps his black and white tail around my waist as I reach up and yank at his septum piercing.

"Not particularly," I lie, even though I know it's dumb as fuck to be jealous of a cat. But, as Chesh is just as often a cat as he is a human, I don't see why he *couldn't* have a crush on Dinah himself? "You don't … fuck cats, do you? Like normal cats, you don't get romantically involved with them?"

The Cheshire Cat looks at me for a long moment, and then throws his head back with a yowl of laughter. My cheeks are flushed, and I try to move away, but he grabs my wrists and pulls me close, leaning down to purr in my ear.

"You're quite mad, aren't you, Alice?" He licks the shell of my ear, and I stifle a groan. "Do I fuck cats? No, I most certainly do not."

"Not even in cat form? Why is that any less of a ridiculous question than asking if you fuck humans?"

"*Because* humans can tell riddles, and cats can't take a joke. You, of all people, should know that, Alice." I raise an eyebrow, because here we go with the Underland singsong nonsense again. But I'll tell you a little secret, since you've read this far and all: it doesn't bug me anymore. Actually, I kind of love it. "Come, we'll go to the market for fresh fish, cream, and catnip—just the essentials."

"If you're going to the market," the Savage Duke purrs, sliding the Looking-Glass beneath the couch, "you'll need an entourage. I'll accompany you."

"Maybe *you* should babysit the family, and Dee and I can go with Allison?" Tee says, sitting down in the chair closest to the fire and stretching his right wing toward the flames. He lays it gently on the rug in front of the hearth, and soaks up the heat. "Or maybe March and the Hatter can do it?"

"We must procure the tickets," March declares, picking through several decorative crystal candy dishes of varying sizes. Each one is filled with something different: dried fruit, nuts, peppermints, chocolate coated cherries. He stuffs his mouth with a variety of goodies before glancing up, the remaining poison vials around his neck tinkling. "Train tickets are not easy to come by, especially on such short notice."

"Why don't you just ask Twinkle to come and pick us up?" I ask, moving over to stand next to March. He smells pretty damn good, like strong tea and gardenias. The March Hare snorts and shakes his head.

"That lazy fuck? That bat couldn't carry more than four people if her life depended on it."

"But we have enough people with wings here that we could probably make it work, right?" I pick up the lid on one of the candy dishes and snatch a pretzel. It tastes … not at all like a pretzel, more like a croissant. It's a bit disconcerting.

"Too far to travel, too conspicuous. The Walrus and the Carpenter certainly have enough eyes in the world to notice a jabberwock carrying human passengers, don't you think?" Raiden grabs a handful of pretzels before I replace the lid, watching me as I chew. "We've been over this, haven't we? And don't you have a thing about heights?"

"I used to," I say with a shrug. "I'm not sure if that's even worth being afraid of anymore." I sit down at the little table as Mom and Dad hover in the doorway to the bedroom, trying to look useful. I can tell they feel like they should be doing *something*, but really, they may as well just relax. This is all out of their hands. "Do you need more blood?"

"Are you offering?" Raiden asks, perking up substantially.

"I don't like you thinking of the Alice as a snack; have some of Rab's blood instead," Brennin Red says, having selected a room for himself and Rab. He hands the key over to his right-hand man and then takes a seat on the couch, snapping his gloved fingers in silent demand. I notice he gives Dinah a very narrow-eyed *stay the fuck away from me* sort of a look.

Rab rolls his eyes, pushing his shirtsleeves up as he checks through the candy dishes, taking the peppermints over to Brennin before filling up a glass of water from the tap at the wet bar. Yep. Our old-fashioned cottage teahouse room with the living roof has a wet bar. But, like, a wet bar for tea and not booze. They *have* booze here, just not much of it. Everyone prefers boosted tea, and I can't say I blame them. It's kind of fucking awesome.

"Yes, well, she's a snack and a fuck and a love and a savior all wrapped up into one."

"Don't you call my daughter a fuck," Mom snaps, embarrassing the shit out of me. I can defend myself, you know.

"*Mom*," I grind out as Raiden tosses a pretzel up in the air and catches it with his mouth. He smiles at her, and then sweeps his hat off, offering up a bow. Even though I know he has guns, and a cane, and food, and a million other hats underneath it, all I see is his slightly curly dark hair.

"My apologies, Ms. Liddell. You are quite right. Where *are* my manners?" Raiden replaces his hat and then lifts it up again, pulling out his cane. He taps the end on the floor and stares at me with marmalade colored eyes. "All I mean to say is, my fantastical healing abilities are predicated on my ability to find high quality crimson nutrients. That is to say, I need *blood* and lots of fucking blood, too."

I think about how quick he reacted to save Tee, and I know that I'm going to give him some. Shit, I'm going to give him as much as he wants.

"Take a bit of my blood to start," Rab drawls, serving the King his water, and then planting his hands on his hips. "It might be a bit cold to the taste, but I promise you there's some value there."

"Shifter blood tastes like dog shit," Raiden says, as the White Rabbit lifts his gaze up to look at him. "I only drink March's when I have to."

"Only when he has to," March repeats as Dee appears in a pair of black linen pajama pants and nothing else.

"They have loaners, in the drawers," he explains as I raise an eyebrow. "And thank fuck for that. Shifter blood might taste like dog shit, but I certainly smelled like it." I smile, because I don't think I've ever not thought the twins smelled good. Great, actually. Perfect. Maybe it's a crush thing? Because I'm so into them that I'm not perceiving reality anymore? That's love for you.

Not that I love them.

I mean … I mean, shit. Maybe I do?

Oh crap.

"So, if the Alice is okay with it—because it is *her* blood—then I'd like to drink before I go. March and I will escort her and whoever else into town. Like I said, buy some clothes. You *all* smell like dog shit to my poor, sensitive, little vampire nose."

Dee pads over to stand next to me, picking out the brightly colored marshmallows from one of the dishes. He pops them into his mouth, and goes for the candied ants next. Gross. But he still looks sexy with his blue and black wings, his shirtless chest, and that magnanimous smile of his.

"Let's get on with it then, shall we?" North asks in a low growl. He's clearly not pleased with my sharing blood with a vampire either, but it can't be denied: Raiden Walker has seriously come in handy. I literally cannot imagine having gotten this far without him: there's a reason he's the most powerful mercenary in Underland. "I don't care who else goes to the market with us, but *I* need some time with my mate."

"And there's that word again," Dad mumbles, but Mom shushes him.

"Shall we do it right here?" Raiden purrs as I sit down on a red chair with a black and white checkered cushion. "In front of everyone?" He sweeps some hair over my shoulder, and I shiver.

"You're the one who said you preferred everyone share the same bed. What makes this any different?" I close my eyes and tilt my head to one side, waiting for the delicious pleasure of the Mad Hatter's teeth to sink into my skin.

He hesitates, but only for a moment, kneeling down in front of me, right between my spread legs. I'm only wearing a skirt, too, and this is *way* too fucking sexual for me right now.

"I'd be happy to take you to the teahouse for a bite to eat?" says Lar to my poor, confused parents. "They serve cakes and scones, jam and fresh cream. Your daughters are well-protected here with the angels."

Tee sighs, but I can tell he's resigned to staying with his brother and watching over Edy. I meet first Dee's, and then Tee's, eyes over Raiden's shoulder, just before my parents leave with Lar, and the vampire bites down *hard*.

Pleasure rushes down from my neck to pool in my belly, making my lower tummy muscles ache as Raiden drinks deep and long, tongue playing with the sensitive skin on my throat. His right hand slides up my thigh and under my skirt, teasing my panties in the most delicious possible way. My fingers curl in his hair, and I hold him tightly against me as he drinks. Once again, I get the idea that this is about more than just food: there's a sexuality that's intrinsically woven into the act.

And a small amount of … affection?! Am I feeling affectionate toward him as I cradle his head and he drinks? Gross.

"Okay, enough," I gasp after a moment, pushing Raiden away and putting my palm over the bite. The Mad Hatter licks red from his lips and withdraws his hand.

"Thank you, *Alice*," he growls out, and he barely sounds half-human—*if* that. "Never know when you might need me." Raiden stands up and then leans down near my ear, his right hand taking hold of mine and pressing it against his crotch. "Strong, good blood … does come in handy for certain things." He gives me a moment to squeeze his erection, and then steps back, smirking down at me like he knows he's made an impression.

Prick.

Only question here is: which guy in this room is the biggest asshole of them all? Hint: it's not Tee, Dee, Chesh, or Lar. The other five are fair game. My guess though? It's probably the goddamn King or the a-hole Hatter.

Smearing blood off my neck, I accept a cloth napkin soaked in warm water from Dee's hand and blot at the wound.

"Now, can we go to the market please?" the Duke drawls, undoing an extra button on his frilly shirt for maximum chest exposure. I could just grab him by the horns and kiss his full mouth right now, I swear on the Ace of Hearts. "The Fabulous Monsters are in town tonight … and I intend to take advantage."

The way he looks at my mouth when he says that … gives the idea that maybe it's *me* that he's planning on taking advantage of.

The market is big, loud, colorful, and rife with myriad scents. My nose hardly *knows* what to sniff, if you know what I mean. There are spices and perfumes, soaps and fresh linens, animals of both the wild and domestic sort, all alongside weapons vendors, jewelry vend0rs, and open boutiques that've taken up residence in some of the cottages surrounding the market square.

"What are the Fabulous Monsters?" I ask, and North grins with his beautiful white teeth. Chesh has already purchased a pair of red ribbons with tiny white hearts on them, and tied big fluffy bows around each of the Duke's dark horns. It's hilarious and sexy both at the same time.

"Performing troupe, travels Underland and puts on quite the show." March glances over his shoulder, sucking on a candied apple as he stares at me with espresso brown eyes. "It's lewd and bawdy, and to be quite frank, it's the very essence of Underland." March snaps a bite off the apple, swallows, and then smiles. "Card tricks, nudity, and foul, foul language. You'll love it, I'm sure."

"Tickets cost either a smile or a frown, a laugh or a cry, an arm or a leg—most folks pay with a smile." An arm or a leg, huh? Right. Chesh stretches his arms above his head and yawns.

"Too bad they don't let you pay with one of those," I joke as we pass by a stall filled with birdcages of varying shapes and sizes. Each one of them is a work of art, sparkling with jewels, or made of metal so fine it looks like petals and vines. There's a bird inside each one, and they're as fantastical as anything else found in Underland. There's one with two sets of eyes—one pair on either side of its head. And another that looks like a little jubjub bird; it even has a thick web spanning across the bottom of its cage.

I shiver and move away from it.

"Hey, are there any Rabbits who take jubjub form?" I ask as North fingers some red silk with a wistful sort of look on his face.

"This would make a fine wedding fabric," he murmurs, and I pretend not to hear him. I *know* that soon after all this is over, I'll be marrying the King, the Hatter, and whoever else needs to be married to make these politics work. When that's all it was, just a political move, I didn't care. Now that my feelings are involved, I'll admit it: I'm a tad nervous.

"Rabbits take on the essence of their three forms, remember?" March says, pausing near a stall that advertises *Freshly Made Toad-in-the-Hole!* What the *fuck* is that? I mean, I vaguely—and I mean *vaguely*—remember that toad in the hole is a traditional British dish made with sausage and Yorkshire pudding. Not bad for an American, eh? But when I look at … whatever this is, it looks like literal frogs baked into weird green muffin cakes. "A jubjub is far too primitive, mean, and stupid to take on. If there were a Rabbit running around that was part jubjub, you would know."

"Is that why you're such an asshole then?" I ask as the March Hare flips a coin to the shopkeep, and picks up three small muffin wrappers filled with the mysterious treat. He hands one over to me, and I take it with a wrinkled nose, realizing as I do that it's not actually a toad or frog on the top at all, just more of the Yorkshire pudding baked from a mold.

I decide I almost like the asshole when he hands Chesh a goodie, too, and the cat purrs with delight.

"What are you trying to imply there, Little Alice?" Raiden asks, poking through the next stall—which sells hats, of course, what else?—with his cane.

"I'm implying," I start as I pick at the breading on the toad's head and try not to think of the Mocking Turtle's bleeding eyes as I obliterated him with my magic, "that the March Hare has taken on your essence, and that you are an asshole. What was unclear about that?"

"I never said my third form was the Mad Hatter, you cheeky little twat," March drawls affectionately, eating his toad-in-the-hole in two bites. He chews so nicely, too, and there's never food stuck between his teeth. Must be magic. "You done made that up, all tricky like."

"Lar told me; he has visions. And denial doesn't look good on either of you." I exhale, close my eyes, and take a bite of my food. It's actually pretty goddamn good. It tastes like a meat pie, sort of. Probably organic and non-GMO, too. Hah. "Besides, the King pretty much told me point-blank that all rulers have Rabbits that can wear their likeness."

"Not Brennin Red," the Savage Duke drawls, using his tail to play with my hair. "He's far too arrogant to let another take his skin."

"Well, that, and the White Rabbit was already promised to his sister." Raiden grins as I raise my eyebrows in shock. "Might be a state secret to some, but it's not *my* secret. Rab wears Scarlet's skin, not Brennin's."

"Scarlet?" I whisper, excited to finally get another piece to the puzzle. "But come on: Scarlet Red? Really?"

"Don't see how that's any weirder than the name March Hare," March says with a roll of his eyes.

"But that's *your* name, and *you* said you chose it!" I retort with an eye roll, taking another bite of my food.

"Yes, well, why should that preclude it from being absolutely ludicrous? I'm a Rabbit with the name Hare. Do you know the difference between a rabbit and a hare?"

Um. Actually, now that I think about it … "Nope."

"Neither do I," March says with a shrug, and apparently that's that. We keep walking, past a dozen different stalls that I could spend all day looking at, if I had the time. I glance down at the tattoo on my thigh; my parents most definitely saw it, but I guess that's the least of their concerns, considering they're trapped in an alternate universe full of mad people. It's still tick-tocking away, and that scares me, just a little bit.

Because sometimes, when the clock strikes midnight, the fairytale is over.

I never want my fairytale to end.

"There's an entire stall of clocks," I whisper as we pass by a booth so full of items for sale that the shop owner has to sit on the roof. Not sure how much business he gets all the way up there, but it's fascinating for sure.

"And an entire stall for kitty cats," Chesh says, pausing one row over and leaning down to peer at an array of colorful, felt cat toys. He licks his lips and his pupils get wide as he reaches out with curled fingers and paws playfully at the items. "Oh, and the catnip … I would trade boosted tea for catnip any day."

"Now that you mention it," the shopkeep says, and … I see that she, too, has a tail and ears?! It's another cat person, a neko, just like Chesh! She sways her fluffy white tail, and grabs a tin off the shelf in the back, presenting it to him with a little purr and a flash of fang. "Herbal tea with catnip. Gives you a playful high and then puts you right to sleep."

Chesh takes it from her hands and then yowls for the Duke.

"I haven't a coin to my name, pussy that I am," he says as North pats him on the head, and pays the shopkeep with several gold coins from inside his pocket. "You do treat me so nicely, Savage Duke."

"And you do keep my feet warm on cold nights, though I am not fond of you peeing on my freshly starched shirts." North watches as Chesh gathers up some jars with dead fish floating in them, several cat toys, bundles of herb that must be catnip, and a new collar—not for Dinah though, clearly for him seeing as it's rather large.

"I did it once, and only because you refused to scratch my rump." Chesh accepts a paper bag from the cat-girl behind the counter. She purrs flirtatiously at him, but he just taps a nail on his ID tag and she peers close to read it, hair bristling along her neck with a sigh.

"I've got four husbands already anyway," she says with a toss of her shoulder and a flick of her ear. I clamp down on the jealousy and keep walking. Interesting how I've been pushing Chesh away for weeks, and now I sort of want to drag him close. Must be all that wild magic in the air, poisoning my brain. I mean, how else could one possibly explain my attraction to the Duke, the King, and the Hatter? Assholes, all three.

"And remember: even if I pee on your things, or scratch your furniture, or cough up hairballs in your bed, I also protect you when you sleepwalk. I make sure you get home safe, and I never let the jabberwock take over the Duke of Northumbria." Chesh grins, fading from view until it's just his bag of goodies and his smile that are visible.

"Point taken," North growls, thrashing his thick muscular tail against the pavement. We head toward a busy intersection, and both the Hatter and the Hare pause to tip their hats at me.

"We'll be on our way to fetch the train tickets," Raiden says, staring down at me with his beautiful orange eyes, like falling leaves on a brisk autumn day. I wonder if they have seasons here in Underland the same way they do back home? "Rendezvous back at the *Haigha and Hatta* no later than midnight. Enjoy your Fabulous Monsters." He winks at me, and I get the idea that maybe when he says *Fabulous Monsters,* it's a euphemism for something else. Like, maybe North's and Chesh's cocks?

Or maybe I just want it to be a euphemism? Remember: still horny young person over here. I have not leveled-up in that arena since you began reading. I'm sorry, but I'm simply obstinate about remaining my own age through all three-hundred and sixty-four days of my un-birthdays.

"Come, come," North says, sweeping through the crowd in the direction of a striped tent. Really, it's a tent inside a tent, because the whole market is covered by one, big swatch of red fabric decorated with the symbols from all four kingdoms.

There's a ticket booth outside, but North simply smiles and he's handed a stub. Chesh frowns as hard as he can to get his, and I stand there like an idiot until the cat tickles me with his tail and a laugh bubbles up past my throat.

"Almost thought you couldn't pay your way for a minute there," the woman inside the booth purrs, half of her face hidden with a veil. She makes a little hissing sound, and I see a forked tongue flicker out from beneath the fabric. "Sad is the bastard who can't pay the toll."

"What happens if he can't pay?" I ask, even though I know I shouldn't, and Chesh is tugging on my arm in the direction of the stage.

"He joins the troupe," another voice says, and I glance over to the left of the ticket booth to find a man in skintight leather pants, tattoos, and nothing else, tossing a series of flaming knives into the air. He catches them all on his fingertips, blade side down, and then grins as red wells up from his skin and drips to the dirt. "Until he learns to show emotion, or else he's labelled a sociopath or psychopath, and he stays with the Fabulous Monsters forever. That's the rule."

"And who made up *that* rule?" I challenge. Sorry, I can't seem to help myself.

The man with the knives stares at me with eyes that swirl in rainbow colors.

"The most fabulous monster of all: the troupe master. Everyone knows that. What are you, a fucking Topsider?" he laughs and shakes his long, dark hair, moving away from the ticket booth as the snake lady checks out his ass. I peer a little closer at her … until I see that the lower half of her body is all snake, and not so much woman.

Fucking hearts on a card …

Chesh drags me away, following the Duke to the last row of benches in the center of the striped tent. He's already managed to get hold of some popcorn—No. No, wait, that's not popcorn. Sorry, my bad: it's just *kettle buds.*

"What the fuck is a kettle bud?" I ask as Chesh scoops up a mouthful, plops down on North's lap, and begins to purr. He gives his friend a nice rub, and receives a pat and a scratch in response, before bothering to move over to my other side to sit.

"It's a very tender young flower bud that's cooked in a cast-iron kettle with salt, sugar, and oil. Try some." He holds up a piece and I open my mouth, sucking on his fingers in a way that's a little overt—even for me. But then our eyes meet, and I can't help myself. I like the Cheshire Cat, have from day one. Well, maybe not day *one* because he's an ass who keeps bringing me dead rodents, but like day four or five at least.

Anyway, I should just put the poor cat out of his misery and ask him to join my harem.

"What is it you like so much about the Fabulous Monsters? Have you been to see them before?" North takes a few of the kettle buds between his fingertips, his black talons protruding just slightly from the tips of his fingers as he studies me with golden eyes. I can't believe I'm sitting here next to him, waiting for some bizarre show to start. The thing is, I'm *happy* here though. This is where I want to be.

"We're all Fabulous Monsters here in Underland," North says, staring right at me, his gaze so intense that I start to squirm. "I suppose … I like them because they remind me that being a monster isn't quite so bad as it seems. Everyone who performs here is cursed by the wild magic."

I look at him, and I wonder how old he was when he became a jabberwock. He seems to like it now, but that can't have been easy, taking on the persona of a … monster.

"I think monsters are beautiful, provided their monstrosity is on the *outside*. It's the ones who keep their monsters hidden that you have to watch out for." The Duke grins at me, like I've said something, well, *fabulous*, and then leans over to kiss me.

And oh, shit, if I had my diary right this second, I'd probably scrawl something like this:

Dear Fucking Diary, the way the Savage Duke of Northumbria kisses is … criminal. His tongue is a hot slice of carnal temptation, and his mouth is this possessive darkness that I want nothing more than to succumb to, submit to, surrender to. When I'm around him, I feel like a hapless heroine in a romance novel—one of the ones with a shirtless man on the cover—and I don't even mind it. He also makes me feel valued, and treasured, and interesting.

Dear Fucking Diary, if I believed in marriage, I'd probably marry this guy. As things stand, I'd like to share a Costco card, cohabitate, and also fuck his brains out. Thanks for listening!

The Duke and I pull apart as the gas lamps flicker, and several people in black bodysuits enter the stage with birdcages held in their hands. As the crowd goes wild and then quickly hushes themselves to the level of whispers and secrets, the performers hook their cages on chains hanging from the ceiling.

Music starts up, eerie and haunting as colored lights shimmer onstage and smoke filters across the wooden floor. One of the people in the bodysuits pauses to tap a silver wind chime with a small mallet just before several trumpets and a washboard sound up.

The birdcages rise and lift in opposition to one another, starting in a random pattern and becoming more and more nonsensical as the music progresses. The lights brighten up and a woman in a short, puffy skirt, corset that just barely contains her breasts, and high-high heels struts out with a whip in her hand, smacking the bars of each cage as she waltzes by.

Inside, the birds shape-change into humans in varying degrees of dress.

They open their cage doors and join the woman in the skirt, doing a dance that's nothing short of a come-on for the audience. When they get to the can-can, I can see that they really mean this show to be bawdy. Not a pair of panties in the whole bunch —men and women included. All of them are wearing skirts, and all of them are performing the same dance. I like that part, at least.

When they finish up and take a bow, people start to chuck flowers onto the stage.

I hear a Venus flytrap murmuring as it's chucked, pot and all, toward the dancers.

"*Not a pair of skivvies in sight!*" it admonishes, just before its pot breaks into pieces and the pixie escapes to sit in the rafters.

A new song starts up with one of the troupe members playing an accordion, and a belly-dancer dressed in nothing *but* snakes, comes out, swaying her hips to the slow, sensuality of the tune. She begins to remove the snakes, handing them off to more of the performers in black bodysuits. She's quite pretty, with the spotlight making her ebony skin glow, the black and white striped curtain a frame for her sexuality.

I risk a peek at both North and Chesh, their eyes focused on the stage. And then I take another peek at their respective crotches. Not a boner in sight. That makes me feel better, in a petty, annoying sort of a way. I shouldn't be getting jealous, but … I am. Crap. New relationship energy, that's what we'll call it. It's making me act like a crazy person.

Once she's entirely nude, but for a single glittering heart pasty on her *belly button*, she takes a bow and then whistles. A black and white striped tiger trots out onstage to meet her, balancing a ball on his nose. The belly-dancer takes it, rolls it down one arm and over her shoulders to the other side. She then tosses it up and the tiger knocks it back. She catches it again and then places it back on his nose, accepting a silver tray, set for tea, from the bodysuit folks.

She parades this across the stage, and then carries it over to the big cat, balancing it on the ball that's still resting on the tiger's nose. With a whistle and a click of her tongue, she convinces the beast to stand up on his hind legs. When he shifts into a naked man, she whips one of the teacups off of the tray and carefully sets it on the tip of his erect dick.

The crowd goes goddamn bananas—including my two boys—and people start to toss strange things in place of flowers: cards and dice, keys and jacks, even dominoes. Chesh chucks some kettle buds in that direction, but they fall over the empty benches in front of us.

"Oh, I do enjoy a good show," he purrs, teasing the side of my boob with his tail. I grab hold of it and he makes a sound that's more growl than groan. "But I love that even more. Stroke it, Alli Cat? Please." I look over and find his gray eyes watching mine. My tongue runs across my lower lip and Chesh follows the motion with his gaze.

I use my hands to play with his tail while the man from earlier, the one with the rainbow eyes, takes the stage next. He's still wearing tight leather pants and nothing else, juggling a set of nine flaming knives, and performing fantastical spins as he manages to get them all up in the air at the same time.

As he continues his act, the knives are replaced with brightly colored hedgehogs. Poor things. I almost feel sorry for them until, in the middle of the juggling, they shift into people and tumble off the sides of the stage.

The music quiets briefly as the man approaches the audience and bows low, his long hair hanging down like a curtain. He sweeps it back and then holds his arm out for a topless woman in a short, lacy skirt and a tie. She has a glittering heart pasty on her clit, but that's about it. She's also wearing six inch heels and fishnets, and doesn't look at all like she might trip and break her face. If that were me, I'd already be dead.

"The lewdest fucking performer in all the land," the man shouts out, encouraging the crowd to cheer by juggling pieces of the tea set as he walks. "She once married twenty men in one night, and divorced them all the next day. Her breasts each have their own fan clubs, and her cunt is running for mayor."

The man bows as the woman takes centerstage, looking out at us with glimmering pink eyes.

"I attract so many cock-races," she says in a husky voice, "I've had to start taking applications!" She raises her eyebrows, accepts a deck of cards from the man with the long hair, and then shuffles them with magic. They make an arc from palm to palm without her having to move a muscle. "And look, look, here are two of the cocksuckers now!"

The cards swirl around her like a storm, and she pauses as two men wearing Knight's helmets—like chess pieces—on their heads take the stage. They're both naked and erect as hell, carrying clubs in the shape of giant foam dicks, and they proceed to start beating the shit out of each other with them.

It's clearly meant to be humorous, as they fall over and tumble at every possible provocation. Sometimes the foam clubs don't even make contact, and they give a little cartwheel or a roundoff. Our leading lady watches in amusement until both men have knocked each other to the ground. She then grabs a few of the cards from the air, tosses them until they create a set of stairs, and walks right up it.

The audience is eating it up as the woman seems to choose between the two men, then shrugs her shoulders and wrinkles her nose, pointing at the long-haired man instead. He joins her on the card stairs, and then undoes his pants, revealing a cock tattooed in fantastical colors.

"What are they doing?" I ask as Chesh's groan turns into a chuckle, and the Duke smirks lasciviously.

The rainbow-eyed guy lifts the woman up by the hips and then helps her lean forward, so that she's in a plank position with her legs spread. It's acrobatic and quite beautiful … until he slides inside of her and starts to thrust. She's not at all shy with her moans either.

"Oh. It's *that* sort of a show," I whisper as Chesh takes his tail from my hands and wraps it around my waist instead. Seeing as the Duke's tail is already wrapped around it, they sort of twine themselves together. It's rather cute, actually. Or it would be cute if it weren't so hot and steamy in that tent.

The leading lady bends her legs at the knee and lifts her rib cage up, so that she's leaning back against the man's chest while he continues to thrust. Another troupe member, one of the ones dressed all in black, ascends the card steps, stabs metal needles through her upper back, and then gestures for another member to tug on a chain.

Suspension. Holy fuck. But not like anything I've ever seen. Instead of simply holding the woman up by the hooks in her back, the chain hauls her *and* her lover up, with just his dick inside of her, and his hands on her hips to keep them connected.

My mouth drops open.

"That's what I call a strong pussy," Chesh says, clapping along with the audience. The couple doesn't stay suspended for long, but once they're lowered down—all the way to the floor this time—the cards reassemble into a bed and they relax on it. As fire dancers fill the stage, and men and women drop from the ceiling wrapped in aerial silks, I watch them writhe and touch and sweat and kiss in the dim lights at the edge of the stage.

I find it hard to look at either the Duke *or* the Cat, because my nipples are pebbled and I'm wet between the thighs. I can't decide if it's the show that's turning me on or if a constant diatribe about sex has simply reminded my body what I'm missing. Maybe it was Chesh's groans while I stroked his tail? More than likely a combination of all of the above.

Swallowing hard, I reach down and put a hand on either one of the guy's laps.

"Oh, my mate is enjoying the show?" the Duke whispers as I lick my lower lip. The lights are dim enough, and there's no one sitting nearby. *I must be seriously losing my shit.* Either that or the heavily perfumed incense floating in the air is spiked.

"I don't know how I feel about the show," I admit, undoing both men's pants. My palms are sweaty, so I don't need any lube when I take them both in my hands. It's a unique experience, having one on either side of me. I've never done anything quite like this before.

"Oh, Alli Cat," Chesh growls, like he's as surprised as I am. "I do believe this is the first time you've touched my cock." He leans over and rubs his cheek against my shoulder, curling one of his hands around mine and encouraging me to keep going.

I keep my eyes on the stage, flicking them over only briefly to catch the expression on either man's face. The Duke's gold eyes are half-lidded and there's a snarling emanating from deep inside his chest that vibrates through the bench and into me. Chesh on the other hand is purring, but the vibration is just as pleasant.

The show moves to other strange, surreal events, but that couple in the back never leaves the stage. In fact, the two men she kicked to the curb end up joining them until they're embroiled in quite the fascinating foursome. Can't say that I don't steal any ideas for positions from the Fabulous Monsters.

My first time touching Chesh, and I make sure it's a voyeuristic exploit. Great, Allison, drinking the Underland Kool-Aid, are we?

My hands tease the men for the better part of the show, bringing Chesh to climax first. He curls his nails into the wooden bench and leaves grooves, turning his head and biting my shoulder hard as he comes. I let out a little yelp, but it actually feels kind of good, too, so I don't stop him. I finish him up, and then leave him to deal with his own mess.

Chesh tucks himself back into his pants and cleans himself by *licking* his hand clean, turning to watch me with the Duke. That dragon bastard is stubborn as hell though, and it takes me damn near into the ending bows to get him to thrust up and into my hand, coming hot and sticky against my palm.

I grab a handful of napkins, clean up, and shove them in his lap, blushing furiously and clapping as the show wraps up. Apparently, there aren't acts in this particular performance, probably because everyone's rushing out to go and fuck against a wall somewhere. I'm feeling pretty good about it, like maybe I got away with my double handjob, when a surprisingly familiar face appears out of the crowd.

"First time at a Fabulous Monsters show?" Lory asks, with Dodo, Eaglet, Duck, and Mouse behind her. She gives me a very knowing sort of look as I turn six shades of red in the face. Chesh is still licking his hand, cleaning out between his fingers with a long tongue. He barely acknowledges the pirates, fading from view, and then reappearing as a triumphant male smile on my shoulders. Even in kitty form, he's still being a dick.

"However did you guess?" I ask as the Duke helps me to my feet. "What are you doing here?" I try to act casual, like I didn't just jerk two guys off in a circus tent, but eh, it is what it is I suppose.

"Delivering a shipment of tea and trying to stay out of Castle Heart for the time being." She sighs and blinks brown eyes at me. "That ball went all to shit as soon as you left. I mean, the White Knight took control pretty quick, but I don't trust her as far as I can fucking throw her—and believe me, I'm strong: I could throw her from the Long Tale's stern all the way to the bow."

I stand up, spilling loose bits of kettle buds all over the ground near my feet. I swear to god the woman onstage catches my eye as she picks up her cards, and gives me a very dramatic wink that I pretend to ignore.

"Yeah, well, that's sort of an ongoing problem …" I rub at my forehead with the heel of my hand.

"Nobody crosses onto the castle grounds without the King's permission," Dodo growls, crossing his beefy arms over his chest and glaring at nobody in particular while the Duke scans the crowd with a very discerning golden gaze. He's alert, but not alarmed which makes me feel a bit better for missing the pirates' presence in the room. I'm sure he noticed them right away. "I want to know how those fuckers got themselves inside the walls to begin with."

"The Anti-Alice," the Mad Hatter says, appearing behind the crew of the Long Tale like he's just materialized there. More vampire voodoo, y'all. "She uses the Vorpal Blade as a point of reference to travel outside the realm of the regular. She just brought a few guests along with her."

"So if I hadn't gotten angry and pulled the blade …" I start, feeling that revelation hit me like a bucket of ice-water. March steps out from behind the Mad Hatter, snacking on our leftover kettle buds. I'm not even sure how he got ahold of them because I'm pretty sure I was just holding the box. Sigh. Master Thief, strikes again.

"She'd have had another plan to get you to take it out; don't fret. It was that hole in the wall that fucked it all up. If it wasn't one thing, it'd have been another, Doll." March studies the pirates with a cool, brown gaze. "Who are your friends, love?"

"We're bloody pirates, obviously," Lory says, straightening her tricorne hat.

"Obviously," March drawls, raising an eyebrow.

"We were thinking of having dinner, come and sit, stay a while." Lory nods her head in the direction of the market, and I glance at the four men with me. They all seem to be staring at *me* for confirmation.

"Okay, yeah," I say, reaching down to take North's hand—as opposed to his dick. I curl our fingers together. "Dinner sounds good."

"And then if your jabberwock's okay with it, I can kick your ass a little, make sure you stay on your toes." Lory moves off down the row of benches without waiting for me to answer, and I roll my eyes to the ceiling. There's a monkey up there, also eating kettle buds, with rainbow fur and eyes like glass. He just hangs there by his tail and eats his snack, ignoring me completely. I glance back down at the pirates' retreating backs.

"Right. More training. Because I do so love being put on *my* back on the mat."

"You seem to love it when I do it," North purrs, bringing my knuckles to his lips for a kiss. I pull my hand from his and punch him in the chest, but he just laughs and steals a kiss from my lips instead.

"Just … try not to stab anyone this time," Chesh drawls, his disembodied mouth floating near my ear. I roll my eyes at him, too, and let the Duke escort me out of the tent, the Mad Hatter and the March Hare trailing along behind us.

Several hours later, after I'm bruised and beaten to shit near the fountain in the courtyard outside our hotel, I have a much better understanding of how to hold my knife, how to feint and dodge and throw, but also … my muscles are sore as shit. I stay in the old-fashioned copper tub until the water is ice-cold.

Stepping out onto the plush rug in front of it, I dry off with a fluffy white towel, slip into my tank top and cotton boyshorts, and blow out the candles. When I pad barefoot out into the living room area, I find the Cheshire Cat dancing in front of a mirror.

He's wearing a pair of black linen boxers and singing into a candy cane with a skull shape on the end of it. That's Underland for you, can't even leave the sanctity of candy canes alone.

I cross my arms over my chest and smile, watching as he rocks out to a scratchy gramophone recording of a pretty goddamn decent rock song. Actually, I think it might be the same song that Dee and I danced to at The Pool my first night in Underland.

Dinah is rubbing all over his legs; she's fucking merciless.

"What are you doing?" I ask, and the cat pauses, glancing over his shoulder and flashing two tiny fangs. He flicks his silver lip piercings with his tongue and folds one black and white striped ear against his head.

"I'm practicing my midnight knicker dancing." Chesh turns around to look at me, tail swishing behind him, and points at his boxers with a black claw. "Knickers." He points at himself next. "Dancer." And then swings his hand over to point at the clock on the wall. "Midnight."

"Very clever," I say with a small roll of my eyes, moving over to stand next to him and the roaring fire. He's moved the mirror from the fireplace mantle onto the floor and stood it up vertically. It's no Looking-Glass, but it's pretty, with a frame embedded with what seem to be real diamonds. "How's that working out for you?"

"I feel …" Chesh starts, tilting his head to one side, flattening both of his ears, the silver hoops in them jingling. "That if I had a teacher, it would go much better." I reach over and poke at the tag hanging off his collar, the one that says *Alice* on it.

Well, I finally took the plunge: I jacked the goddamn cat off in public.

"I wanted to talk to you anyway," I say as the gramophone goes silent and Chesh moves over to play with the needle, starting the song up again.

"About?" he asks, taking a sip from a glass milk bottle on the table and then turning so I get full-view of him sensually licking white from his lips.

I grab another skull-topped candy cane from the jar on the coffee table—or is it a tea table since they don't have coffee here? I don't know the words to the song, but I can at least dance to it.

"I don't know," I say as he rejoins me in front of the mirror and we stare at our reflections, both wearing underwear and not much else, both rocking bare feet and candy canes. Dinah is rubbing all over me now. "Harem stuff."

Chesh makes a huffing sound and pushes the cat away with his foot.

"She's marking you with a new nickname," he says, licking his tattooed right hand and sweeping it over his head to clean himself. He's covered in black and gray tattoos that beg my attention, a story played out in ink across his skin. There are sad memories there; I can tell based on the expressions of the cats and people in them. They seem to get happier the further up his body they climb.

"And what's that?" I ask as I reach over and tug at the piercing in his nose.

"She's started calling you *In Heat Alice*." Chesh grins at me, and I punch him hard in his tattooed shoulder.

"She is not," I mumble, but he just raises his eyebrows and shrugs.

"Is so. Why would I lie about that? If I were going to make up a lewd nickname with the intention of embarrassing you, well, it would be much worse than that." Chesh lifts the candy cane to his lips and growls into it, on time with the singer of the rock song.

"I'm not even going to ask for an example," I say as Chesh bites off the skull on his candy cane, and then tosses it aside. He holds out a hand for me to take.

"Dance with me?" he asks, and even though we both sucked ass at the quintrille, I like dancing with him. He's easy to be with, and he makes me smile. He's a bit of a perv, sure, but he's fun and playful, the only one in the group besides Dee I could see sitting down to play videogames with.

"Why not?" I toss my own candy cane aside and take his hand, letting him swirl me around and then pull me close by curling his fingers under the waistband of my panties. His warm fingers tease the sensitive skin on my hip as we grind to the electric —or steam-powered?—guitars. With so much bare skin between us, every touch is torture. Every touch gets my heart beating faster, my pulse thumping a million miles an hour.

Chesh leans in and rubs his cheek against mine before turning me around so that he's pressed up against my back, meeting my gaze in the mirror. His tattooed right hand sneaks down over my lower belly, fingers dipping under the waistband of my panties.

I bite my lip, watching my own eyes flare with lust as Chesh finds my already wet core, steals a bit of lube, and then drags his fingers back to play with my clit. He's still swaying with me, holding me close with one arm around my waist.

Also, he's fucking purring. The sound rumbles into my body and gives me goose bumps all over.

"Cheshire Puss," I groan, leaning back into him and feeling his hard cock through his boxers. He just grins at me, flashing fang, and then uses his left hand to push my tank up and over my breast, exposing my nipple to the warm air. His fingers tease it mercilessly, rolling the pink point between them like it's a marble.

His tail tickles my inner thigh and then teases its way up my ass crack to slide over my belly. It's like being teased with a feather duster or something, this gentle whisper of pleasure to contrast against the hard yanking of my nipple.

"Tell me what you were going to say earlier, about the harem." Chesh licks up the side of my neck, and I shiver, pushing my ass into his crotch and making him grunt. "Tell me please, Alli Cat; I need to know."

"I was going to ask if … you wanted to be one of my nine," I whisper, and he groans like he's coming in his pants. Chesh pulls his hands from my underwear and turns me around, curling the fingers of both hands around my shoulders.

He kisses me with a startling amount of affection, sliding one hand up to cup the side of my face. When he pulls away, his eyes are sparkling.

"I've been crushing so hard," he groans, raking his wet fingers through his hair. Oops. It sort of … sticks up a little. Chesh lets go of me and pads over to the door, grabbing a basket that used to have loaner umbrellas in it. I remember seeing it when we got back earlier because it had a small sign that said *Please Do Not Get Semen on the Umbrellas! Thanks, Management.*

But now the umbrellas are all over the floor, and there's a smell like wet dog when Chesh brings it over and presents it to me.

It's filled with dead birds, rats, mice, and … a few animals that I can't identify.

"When you were training and bathing, I got these for you." He seems so happy about it that I'm afraid to tell him that I don't want them.

"That's … amazing. Thank you, Chesh." He grins and kisses me, handing over the basket. I make sure to put it as far away from the couch as possible and then move back over to stand next to him.

Chesh's eyes soften as he steps toward me, and I find it suddenly hard to swallow.

He takes the hem of my shirt as I raise my arms above my head, and then pulls it up and over, tossing it over Dinah's back as she yowls in protest.

"Let's mate—I promise I'm not as rough as the Duke." My heart pitter-patters at that, and I let Chesh back me up to the couch, lying on my back as he climbs over me, and we start to kiss to the crackle of flames.

My right hand massages him through the fabric of his boxers as he grinds his body against mine. We play with each other for more than an hour—I know because the clock strikes twice-over while we're in that living room—switching out who's on top, who's controlling the kiss, who's got a hand in the other's pants.

When I feel like I might break if we don't find some sort of conclusion to our encounter, I pull Chesh's hard cock out of his boxers, pushing them down just enough that his shaft and balls are free. And then I pull my panties aside.

I don't want to take them off.

Knickers seem … sort of like an important thing between us.

Chesh kisses me again as we figure out how to fit together like a puzzle. It's him who pauses at just the tip, and I feel I might scream. He blinks down at me with eyes like storms.

"I've been taking curseworker birth control for years," he blurts, and I give him an *eh?!* sort of a look. "It helps keep my fur shiny. I just thought you should know about that, as you're a very responsible individual." He taps his chin and I groan, wiggling my hips a little. I appreciate his candidness, and his honesty, but I just want to *fuck* right now.

The Cheshire Cat leans down and bites the side of my neck, thrusting into me at the same time. He moves with undulating motions that have me moaning and clawing up his back as he moves his lips back to my mouth for more kissing.

We manage to keep a good thing going for a long, long while, and when Chesh does come first with a growl and a snarl, he makes sure to return the favor with his mouth. Only … my dad walks out, screams like a murder victim, and passes out on the floor.

Yep, that's how I start my morning.

Chapter Six

"It's my own hearts-damned invention!"

"You keep *staring* at me," March says as we stand at the train station and I do my best not to gape at all the weird individuals huddled on the platform, hiding from the wild magic storm. It rolled in overnight and pelted the countryside in hail and lightning. I've already seen a man collapse into a puddle and shapeshift into a small, black kitten.

I'm definitely not going out in that mess. I can feel the magic from here, tainting the air, trying its best to find a way under my skin. I could probably topple mountains during a storm like this, only I'd probably topple the wrong mountains because I'm not fully trained yet.

After we revived my father with some *sal-volatile*—that's fancy-talk for smelling salts—I blushed my way through breakfast in the mess hall with the bawdy pirates, the nine men (eight of whom I've fucked), and a yowling Dinah. Lory made sure to kick my ass a little in training before boarding the Long Tale with Dodo and his crew. And the Mad Hatter … well, he did *try* to give me some magic lessons.

All I can say is that a lot of mushrooms grew in a circle around me, my hair briefly turned a bloodred color, and I managed to break the fountain in the courtyard. Well, maybe it's not broken, but it's filled with sticky treacle instead of water now.

"I'm not staring at you," I finally murmur, huddled in a furred cloak made of red velvet and lined with white rabbit—pun intended—fur. It's cozy as hell, and I snuggle into it as the rain pelts the glass roof overhead. "Okay, so I am, but who cares?"

"I care—very much so." March cracks a melon in his hands and offers half to me. The flesh inside is pink, and the seeds are white as ghosts. It smells like a mix between watermelon and grapefruit, so I take it. He even offers me up a spoon that he pulls out from under his hat.

"I was just … wondering what your motivations are, that's all." I sit down on the bench where Chesh is dozing in cat form, and I flush bright red when my dad looks our direction with wide eyes and flared nostrils. I dig into the melon and take a bite. It might *smell* like watermelon and grapefruit, but it tastes like a lemon tart.

"Motivations?" March asks, letting one brown ear swivel in my direction. The wind blows his purple trench coat all over the place, whipping it against his new black slacks. Most everyone's got a new outfit today, courtesy of the market. While I was training, Tee and Dee went out and picked up supplies. "What motivations? I serve the Mad Hatter; I'm his *Rabbit*."

"And his lover?" I keep picking at my melon as the sound of a train whistle echoes around the station. The black steam train with all the golden gears and cogs starts to move, wheels turning as it pulls out of *The Great Wabe Station* and takes off for a destination listed on a chalkboard as a very helpful *Somewhere.* So the two o'clock train is from Wabe to Somewhere. Very descriptive. Guess we missed the two from this morning which were scheduled for *Here* and *There*.

I kid you not. Could I really make this crap up? I mean, maybe someone could, but she'd probably be a crazy bitch.

"Since you so badly want to know if the Mad Hatter and I have fucked, I'll tell you something. Are you staring at me because I'm the only man in this group you haven't asked into your harem? Because I don't want you to feel obligated. I'm looking for love, Doll, not sympathy."

He finishes his melon and tosses it into a nearby trash bin.

The bin burps, too, which is weird as fuck. Also, it has little clusters of mushrooms growing all over its rim. Even sprouting from trash, they sparkle and glitter in a very pretty sort of a way.

"Well, you said you'd tell me something, so do it." I take another bite of melon and pretend I didn't hear the rest of what he said. But he's right, though. That's exactly what I was thinking. I haven't asked him yet. Am I going to? Should I? I like him, and I think it'd be awful nice to see what being held in those, big muscular arms would be like …

"I did tell you something. I told you I was looking for love, that's something." He grins at me, teeth white in his dark face. I flick some melon at him and he quite easily catches the round, pink ball in midair and pops it into his mouth. "But also, sure, Raiden and I have fucked." He shrugs his shoulders like it's no big deal, but I'm gaping at him. "We're both bisexual, heavily leaning toward a preference for women, but there aren't a lot of women around. And there certainly hasn't been anyone we wanted to date."

"I knew it." I keep scooping up bites of my melon, trying not to imagine the two of them going at it. Because if I imagine it, I'll want to see it, and then I'll start to get uncomfortably wet downstairs which will most assuredly ruin my new knickers.

Another whistle sounds in the distance, and I look up to see another large black steam train pulling into the station. It settles with a sigh in front of us, pulling a good two dozen brightly colored passenger cars.

"I've got our tickets," Raiden purrs, lifting up a handful of *huge* motherfucking stubs. They're half the size of the damn Looking-Glass we're still carting around. Makes me nervous, even if Tee and Dee are holding and guarding it like it's their firstborn child. *I* personally wouldn't be overly upset if it broke—I like it here—but I think Edith might shrivel up and die. "Let's do this an orderly fashion, shall we?"

He leads the way with his cane held high, and offers up the wad of massive ticket stubs to a man with a *goat head*. You heard me. This dude has the head of a motherfucking goat. And when he gets the tickets, he counts them, points to each person in the group, and then starts to eat them.

Nobody but my family seems concerned, so I just gawk my way past him and head up the stairs into the train car. Raiden leads us past rooms filled with tables and gas lamps, velvet curtains, and marble-topped bars serving boosted tea. The music that's playing is in a language I don't understand, with wailing vocals and steadily beating drums. I'm no expert, but it sounds very much like it could be Indian in origin.

We move to the back, to a private car with five separate compartments. One is a bathroom, one has tables and chairs, the third is a living room, and the other two are sleeping chambers with two sets of bunk beds. There aren't enough beds for everyone, but if we were to share … I mean, sleep in shifts, then we should be fine.

I have no idea how long we'll be riding the train as Raiden Walker refuses to say. Makes sense, I suppose. He doesn't want anyone knowing how to get to his hideout. Apparently, he has a separate, more public residence for folks to pay their respects or transact business.

Where we're heading now, its location is not public knowledge.

The Mad Hatter's private residence.

I get chills.

We settle in, and Dee rings a small bell that calls a snack cart. It's laden with pots of boosted tea, cakes and frosted cookies, candied insects, and warm rolls filled with jelly. There are berry scones, fresh cream, and pots of fruity jam. There's also a whole shelf of spicy foods whose flavor matches the music, curries that smell like turmeric and lamb, with little round spots of bread and yellow rice to go with it.

By the time we've cleaned our dishes, and Edith is asleep in a chair, the train is long gone from the station and we're traveling through wild countryside, the woods beyond the tracks so dark from the heavy cloud cover that it feels like night again.

There's a fire burning in the fireplace and Dee's positioned himself in front of it, warming his wings, feathers ruffled in pleasure.

"There's a library car, too, you know," he says, smiling brightly. "With all manner of books—plenty of erotica, too."

"Is that a hint?" I ask, as Dee leans forward, crawls over to me and presses a very hot kiss to my knee.

Dad coughs dramatically, and Mom pretends to look anywhere but at my face. Sigh.

"Do you suppose there's any poker on this train?" March asks the Mad Hatter, and they exchange a look. I'm actually starting to wonder if they might be addicted to gambling. "Gin rummy? Cock-races we might bet on?"

"There are certainly cock-races, at the very least," the Mad Hatter says, whipping off his hat and pulling out a stack of playing cards. "But I do have cards, and we do have players, if anyone is interested in a game."

He looks right at me when he suggests it, and I don't get the idea that we'd be playing for money.

No, the Mad Hatter isn't interested in any coin from me, seeing as he plans to marry me. According to Dee, that would make all of *his* money, my money then, wouldn't it? I smile to myself and stretch my arms over my head. After last night with the show and the training, the sex with Chesh, more training … I'm beat.

"Maybe later," I tell them as Dee crawls up onto the sofa and pulls me against his chest. The March Hare makes a sound of disappointment as Raiden shrugs, and puts the cards away.

"*Suit* yourself," he purrs, and the two men disappear into the train.

Me, I sip my tea and watch the scenery go by, the storm pelting the earth, and I fall asleep in Dee's arms.

It's the last good night of sleep I'll get for a while.

But I don't know that yet.

When I wake up, the train car smells like curry and Tee is sitting across from me, next to the Duke and the Cat. He's eating curry from a brightly colored ceramic bowl while North reads a book titled *The Alice: a Collection of Ancient Prophecies,* and Chesh naps with his human arms wrapped around Dinah's purring form.

Dee is still snuggling me, but I carefully move his arms, lifting my own above my head to stretch. I'm sore all over, and not just from getting my ass kicked by Lory and the Duke. I'm just chronically tired. As soon as this is over, I'm taking a hit on Lar's pipe and sleeping for a week.

"Can I get you anything, Allison?" Tee asks, but I shake my head, standing up and moving over to the window to peer out the velvet curtains. The train speeds through a forest of giant mushrooms, no trees in sight. They glow with their own inner light, brightening up the storm. I think I see strange white deer wandering around beneath them, but it's really hard to say, dark as it is outside.

"Where's everybody else?" I ask, letting the curtains fall back into place.

"The King of Hearts, the Caterpillar, and the White Rabbit are watching over your family," the Duke says, looking up at me with gold eyes. He reaches up and teases along the length of his horn, poking his finger with the tip as he smirks at me. "I haven't the faintest what the Hare and the Hatter have got up to. Bloody idiots, if you want *my* humble opinion."

"What about you is humble?" I snort, making for the door. I'm going to pee, and then probably grab something to eat before I collapse in bed again. North grabs me as I walk by, yanking me into his lap and kissing the shit out of me with his hot, hot tongue.

"Nothing at all," he snarls, rubbing his face on mine. "It's why they call me the *Savage* Duke."

I give his horns a rub, and stand up before I end up getting embroiled in a lewd sex act right here in the main compartment. The last thing I need is for my parents to walk in on me again. We're already working through a lot of issues here, don't need to add anymore.

"As long as you're not leaving this car, you can just crack the door open and we'll be able to watch over you," Tee says, his voice thick with anxiety. I smile at him and do as he's asked, leaving the sliding wooden door with a silver of light shining through.

The gas lamps in the train car flicker as we rumble over a rough patch, music piping through the speakers in a catchy, scratchy wail. I sway back and forth for a moment, dipping my hips to the sound. Quickly, I peek in the first sleeping chamber and find Rab alone on a bed, reading a book called *Dark Glitter*, and see that Edith's passed out on the top bunk.

"Sonny," he purrs in that icy voice of his. He has a pistol at his side, and absolutely no shirt on. His ears are lying flat against his skull as he smiles maniacally at me. "If you need a place to lie down, I've got you covered."

"Maybe later, I want to grab something to eat first." He nods and winks at me, his clock tattoos ticking away. Speaking of clock tattoos, I touch a hand to my new black leather breeches and rub my palm over the fabric. I still can't believe that my new ink used to be Rab's fucking skin. There must've been some significance to that ritual, but I don't know what that is yet.

I leave the White Rabbit to his reading and move over to the other sleeping chamber, finding the Caterpillar on his own bed, my parents on another. The King of Hearts is sitting upright with his dark eyes closed, but when I slide open the door and flood the room with light, he cracks one eye to stare at me.

"Thanks for watching over them," I say, and his eyes narrow. I'm about to back out and close the door behind me when I hear a faint whisper, so low that I almost think I've imagined it.

"You're welcome."

I smile and close the door, stopping in the bathroom to piss, and then heading over to the compartment with all the tables in search of food. What I find … satisfies a much different appetite.

The room is mostly dark, save a few flickering candles. Most of the tables have been pushed aside, save for the one the March Hare and the Mad Hatter are sitting at. They're both shirtless, with cards in their hands. And the way they both turn to look at me, it gives me serious chills.

Without giving myself a moment to second-guess it, I step inside and close the door behind me.

"So lovely of you to join us, Doll," the March Hare says, his smile bright in the darkness. He plays with the glass vials around his neck, giving special attention to the one with the lube in it. I raise an eyebrow and move over to stand next to the table.

"Couldn't find any cock-races to bet on?" I ask, my voice breathy in the smoky darkness. They've lit incense in here, something that smells like amber and musk. It only adds to the sensual shadows in the room. The dark wood paneling and crimson wallpaper with the black lilies doesn't hurt either.

"Oh we found some alright," the Mad Hatter says, grinning with his vampire teeth. "And we made good money, didn't we, March?"

"Excellent money, boss. Should help pay for your wedding to the Alice." They both chuckle, but I just stand there, looking down at their game, and their mismatched clothing. March has no shoes or socks on, while the Mad Hatter has but a single sock. They're both wearing pants, but no shirts, and there aren't any chips on the table, just cups of tea.

"Is this … what kind of poker is this?" I ask as a chair scoots up behind me and scoops me up. Based on Raiden's chuckle, I figure it's his magic that's done it.

"The best sort there is—lose a hand, take a drink and shuck a bit of clothing. Gets you naked and drunk, *fast*." March shuffles the cards, and then deals a hand. It seems like they might be playing Texas Hold'em, but since there's no Texas here, it must be something else.

I pick up my cards and tuck some hair behind my ear, making Lar's gifted earrings sway.

Fred taught me to play poker, so I'm not completely clueless on what to do.

"Crown doesn't count, nor does jewelry," March says, glancing over at me with dark eyes. The color reminds me of the earth after a fresh storm, soaked but resilient, ready to start anew. There's something resilient in his expression, like he's fought a long time to get where he is and he won't let it go without a fight. "You have pants, underwear, shirt, bra, two socks, and two shoes—that's it."

"You're starting me with a handicap?" I ask, and both men shrug.

"Oh hell no." I rise to my feet, slip out of my jacket, and kick off my shoes and socks, turning away from them and wiggling out of my bra without taking off my shirt. You know how it is, ladies, that careful strap-strap-twist-unsnap move you have to do before you can pull your bra out of your top. I toss it aside, unstrap the Vorpal Blade and Queenmaker, then turn back around, now with the same number of items as the Mad Hatter.

Three.

Three lost rounds, and I'd be naked—only, I don't intend to lose.

I sit back down and the round starts with the Hatter on March's left.

There's a cigar burning in an ash tray on the table that smells like fresh rain and lightning—I don't know how I know what lightning smells like, I just do—and I pick it up, taking a puff before I put it back. It makes me feel light-headed and courageous both at the same time. Uh-oh.

"Are either of you ever going to open up and tell me a damn thing about your past?" I ask, and Raiden chuckles, fanning his cards against his lips.

"You know I came from Topside; what else is there?"

I stare at my cards and shake my head.

"If I fold …" I start, wondering how it works since there's no betting in this game.

"If you don't have the winning hand, you strip and drink. If you plan on folding, decide what you're gonna take off, Alice-Doll." March glances between the Hatter and myself, but nobody's about to fold just yet. He deals the three community cards.

"What *kind* of Topside family?" I press, wondering what sort of house Raiden grew up in, what his parents were like, if he had any siblings. He ignores me and leans back in his seat.

"Check," he purrs, which simply means play moves over to me.

"Check," I repeat, and March deals another card called the Turn.

"That life is over for me," he says as he looks up and meets my eyes with his marmalade-colored ones. "What does it matter? This is where I am now; this is where I *want* to be. You feel it, too, don't you—the pull of Underland. It calls to the adventurer in us all."

Nobody speaks until we get to the last round in the hand, called the Showdown.

"It doesn't call to Edith," I whisper as Raiden grins and drops his cards on the table.

"Royal flush," he says, and the way he smirks … ugh, it's so fucking infuriating!

March and I simply exchange a look, toss our cards onto the table, and start to take off our pants. I'm so sweaty and hot all of a sudden, trying my best not to stare at him as he strips down to his black linen boxers. I love that they have boxers here in Underland, by the way. So much doper than like, I don't know, whatever underwear they wore in medieval times. Bet it was gross though.

"It doesn't call to Edith because she's weak and scared; she's a peasant, not a queen." I flick my eyes up to Raiden's as March downs a teacup of boosted tea, and then Raiden deals a new hand. I want to be annoyed at the Hatter for talking about my sister like that, but … he's right. He's so fucking right.

I drink my tea, too, and shiver at the smoky taste of it, like the tea leaves sat in a smokehouse for weeks before finding their way to my cup. It tastes like the forest after a summer fire, when the air is hazy and gray, but it feels right to see the earth cleansed. With my cards in hand, I glance over to the March Hare.

"And your backstory? How do I know so little about you? Master Peanut Thief, I get that." He grins at me as he checks his cards, then puts them down on the table so he can pour some fresh tea. "But where did you come from? You grew up in the Court of Spades, right?"

"Worst years of my life, serving an unworthy queen," he drawls, leaning an elbow on the table as Raiden deals the three community cards, and March curses under his breath. Either he has a really shitty hand … or he's bluffing. Hmm. "Even worse now that her horrid son's taken over. You heard the prophecy, Doll: *The kings had got no business there, because their time was done.*" He waves his hand to encourage Raiden to move the round along. "The current King of Spades is a weak, spineless nightmare of a man. Once the Walrus and the Carpenter are dealt with, and you're established as the Queen of Hearts, we'll kill him. Won't we, Hatter?"

"Absolutely," Raiden purrs, and we continue on until we reach the showdown.

Once again, Raiden kicks our asses.

"Off with their … *clothes*," he says, eyes sparkling as I sip my tea first … and take off my shirt next, bearing my heavy breasts to the smoky room. A bead of sweat drips between them, and both men watch it with hunger apparent in their lustful gazes.

"You're an ass," I grumble, as I take my seat and curl one arm over my breasts to hold them in place. When the next round starts, I see that my hand is shaking from the tension in the room.

"Anything else you want to tell me about your past?" I ask March. It's my turn to deal the cards, and it sucks doing it one-handed, but I refuse to let go of my boobs.

"Only that I've been hurt, had my heart broken and stomped to pieces. I don't ever want to go through that again. I told you: I'm looking for love, Doll." I pause and glance over at him, meeting his chocolate-colored eyes with my blue ones. March flattens his ears against his skull, and we just look at each other for a long-ass time, only stopping when Raiden clears his throat.

"Could we get back to the game, please?" he says, resting his head on his knuckles and raising two dark brows at me. His top hat falls forward and shields his eyes from view before he reaches up to fix it. "I'm so ready to see you both drunk, naked, and licking the wounds from your losses."

I smirk, and we continue on with the hand, but when it comes time for yet another showdown, Raiden is once again the winner.

I let my head fall back and groan.

"You've cheated, haven't you?" March asks, narrowing his eyes as I sit back up, and Raiden smirks at the both of us. It's a non-answer that says everything. "I was cheating, too, so how on earth did I miss that?"

"You were both cheating?" I choke as the March Hare stands up … and pushes his boxers over his magnificent hips. His Adonis belt—those gorgeous V-muscles on a guy—catch the light from the candles, making deep shadows underneath that emphasize how beautiful they really are. My mouth waters, and it takes everything I have in me to look away.

"We always cheat," the Mad Hatter says as he watches us carefully. "What's the point in playing if you don't?"

I don't even know how to respond to that, so I simply stand up, suck in a deep breath, and push my panties to the floor at my feet. Swear to hearts, I feel a rush of heat swirl around me. *Fucking wild magic.* It's storming like crazy outside, probably leaking some of those magic-mad molecules into the train.

March sits down hard on his chair, like the sight of me is too much for his deliciously muscular legs. I run my tongue across my upper lip to clean off the sweat, reaching up and fluffing my blonde hair.

"You don't want your heart broken?" I ask, and March makes a sound in his throat. "Do you think I'd break it?"

"I haven't the faintest," he whispers in a hoarse voice, watching as I walk over to stand next to him. When he raises his huge hands and puts them on my hips, I moan, letting my head fall back, my hair teasing my upper back. I feel so achy all over, like I might break apart from the storm. I wonder if this is how the women in the Riving felt, this fucking magnificence, before they were torn apart. "But I'm willing to give it a try."

He pulls me onto his lap and envelops me in his thick, muscular arms, just like I've been dreaming about for days. And oh, oh, it feels *good*, too. We're both slick and sweaty and hot, and I groan when he tucks my head under his chin, his breath stirring the hair on top of my head.

Raiden's chair scrapes across the floor as he stands up and moves around the table, sliding his hands over my shoulders and kneading the tender flesh. He leans down and bites my earring, yanking on it with his teeth and making me shiver.

March moves his head back as I adjust my face, tilting my chin to look at him. Our eyes meet and there's a seriousness to his expression that I don't think I've seen before, not even in the heat of battle. *Willing to give it a try, huh?* I'm so desperately curious to know who broke his heart in the past, but I'm also not willing to break the tension of the moment by asking.

Instead, I lean up toward him as Raiden kisses his way down my bare shoulder, just barely nicking my skin with his teeth. My mouth comes within millimeters of March's, and I hear him let out a small curse as he exhales, his breath against my lips.

And then suddenly we're kissing, and he's holding me so tight that I can't breathe, but in a good way, like he can't get enough of me and never will. His lips are so goddamn hot to the touch, and the tip of his tongue teases my mouth in ways that make my stomach flip-flop.

I'm so busy tasting him and savoring the moment that I hardly notice when Raiden Walker steps back, adjusts his hat, and slips out of the train car, closing the door behind him.

The music still trickles through the speakers, a light background noise that barely penetrates the fog of lust around my brain. Sure, the boosted tea is part of it, but I'm not drunk—not even close.

"Bloody cheater," March murmurs, kissing me harder, deeper. There's a romance to his kiss that I didn't expect, a longing that tears at my heart, and a commanding gentleness that makes me want to surrender to his kiss.

One of those big hands finally finds my breast, kneading and massaging the aching flesh until I cry out, covering his pecs with my hands and feeling him in a way I've wanted to do since I first saw him peeling that apple with his knife.

He smells like a tea party in a garden, his natural scent mixing with the amber incense into this fevered dream. I can hardly help myself, adjusting my body so that I'm straddling his lap instead of just sitting on it. The huge, hard length of his cock teases my clit as I scoot forward, trapping his erection between our bellies.

Cards fall off the table and flutter to the floor as he adjusts his hands and bumps the wooden surface, sliding his palms down to cup the roundness of my ass and giving that a squeeze, too. But then he moves his right hand up to cradle the back of my head, and looks into my eyes with this soulful depth that I never expected from the man.

"Is this an invitation?" he murmurs, sucking on my lower lip. "Because if it is, I'll take it."

"Maybe," I whisper back, reaching down between us with my hand and giving his cock a tease with my fingers. He's got that vial of lube around his neck, but I most certainly don't need it. He's sweaty, the tip of his shaft shimmery with a drop of pre-cum, and I'm beyond wet. It's almost embarrassing, considering I'm just sitting butt-ass naked on his lap.

"Maybe is the answer for backroom dealings that you haven't quite figured out how to manipulate yet, the thing you say when you're searching out the other party and secretly freeing your pistol under the table. I want a real answer, Doll. You don't have to say yes, but if it's no then I want to hear it."

I lean back and look at him, his face so far above mine. He's seriously fucking tall this guy, his espresso brown hair hanging across his sweaty forehead, sticking to his skin. His top hat sits between his brown rabbit ears, one of them flattened back against his head, and the other pointed right at me like he's desperately awaiting my final answer.

"Yes," I say with a small nod, and he grins at me. "And it's not just because you're sort of a package deal with the Hatter. If I didn't like you, I'd tell you to fuck off."

"I figured as much," he murmurs, his accent turning my knees to jelly. Good thing I'm not standing up or I might've swooned. And this Alice, she doesn't really do the whole swooning thing. Nah, not really my style.

"Is your fertility shifted to the *off* position?" I ask, and he chuckles, the sound fading to a groan when I reach up and rub at his furry ears. "It's a valid question."

"Valid, true. I doubt the White Rabbit took the time to school you in shifter biology, but maybe I'm wrong?"

"That's about all he explained," I say with a shrug, and March snorts.

"That fucker. Well, that's about all you need to know for now. I could explain more later, but it's a bit dull and frankly not anything anyone wants to hear about before a shag." We kiss again, and March swings his arm across the tabletop, knocking cards and teacups to the floor, shattering porcelain bits across the train.

I think he intends on moving us up to the table, or maybe fucking me on top of it, but I stand up and scoot forward before he gets a chance, reaching down between us to guide his shaft to my opening. When I position him at my wetness and start to slide down his cock, our eyes meet, and March bites his lower lip with a curse and a groan.

We come together as he takes my ass in his hands again, encouraging me to move. It's slow, but not languid like it was with the Caterpillar. We take our time, but our movements themselves are frenzied and rapid. March tucks my head under his chin, hips rising up off the chair to meet the undulating thrusts of my pelvis.

He lets me work him until we're both slick and frenzied, and then he encourages me to stand up and move over to one of the bar stools near the back window. It sits at a high counter and, when March flings the curtains back, shows our reflections in the dark glass that leads out to the balcony.

I put one knee up on the stool, the other foot on one of the metal rungs. At this height, I'm at the perfect level for March to take me from behind. He thrusts into me, bumping against my ass with a grunt, and then taking my palms and very purposely putting them against the glass.

I stare into the eyes of our reflections as he moves against me, slow at first and then harder, faster, far more desperate. Outside, glowing mushrooms pass by, buried in stands of dark woods. The clock strikes nine, and still, we keep going. I can see March studying me in the window, eyes dark with lust.

It's even better when he comes, and I see the pleasure on his face, the tightening of his muscles, the way his hands dig into my hips. His last few thrusts put me over the edge, but I don't come yet. No, I want to savor this moment.

March finishes and then slides out of me, helping me turn around, so he can lean in close and put his lips to mine, finding my slick core with his fingers. He puts three in, using his thumb to tease and torture my poor clit. He's gentle, but it's so damn sensitive, and I'm so ready to find my own climax. We kiss our way through that as my body is wracked with shudders, and I let out a sound of pleasure that's far too embarrassing for me *not* to blush.

"Well, at least I know I'm appreciated," he whispers with a chuckle, and I slap him, right in his broad chest. Like the White Rabbit, he doesn't seem to have a refractory period, and is hard before the clock on the wall says ten after.

Ten after …

I feel a strange sensation in my thigh, and glance down to see that the clock tattoo on my leg has hit the marked time.

"Oh," I whisper as March follows my gaze, and then suddenly, the White Rabbit is just standing there next to him.

I let out a shriek as March grabs a gun from under his top hat and has it pointed at the other Rabbit in less time than it takes me to blink.

"How did you …" I start, but I don't bother to finish the sentence. Clearly, there's time magic at work here. Rab waves my question away, his stopwatch held in his inked fingers.

"They're on the train, in some capacity. Might just be the Rabbits, but it's hard to say. And like I told you before: rule number forty-two is don't get caught with your pants down." He raises a dark brow at me, his red eyes taking in March's and my compromising position with amusement.

"They're not down—they're bloody *off*," March says with a roll of his brown eyes, but then he's kissing me and pulling me up, and we're both flinging our clothes back on. The Vorpal Blade and the Queenmaker get strapped into place as I glance at the clock.

Twenty-one seconds. Too long already. I don't want Rab wasting his fucking life away.

"Start the clock," I growl, and he nods, hitting the button on his watch with a dramatic press of his thumb. The world speeds back into motion again, the frozen scenery flying by outside as a pair of feet scramble up the ladder on the back balcony.

Holy shit.

Someone was out there staring at us?!

There's a thump and a crash, the sound of a struggle. When Rab moves to open the door to our compartment, it's either locked or jammed. Either way, he can't seem to get it open. My heart shudders, and I start thinking about my family, about the Looking-Glass, the other men.

Fire crackles, and smoke and heat seep underneath the door, making me choke. Someone's either lit a fire on purpose, or knocked over one of the candles or gas lamps. Either way, a fire in a closed train car is not a good thing by any means.

"On the roof," March snaps, and he doesn't bother to pull me along like I expect. Instead, he trusts me to find my own way which I very much appreciate. He flings the glass doors open to the balcony, shoving one of the spare stools aside, and lets in a burst of freezing wind and rain.

He grabs onto the ladder and starts to climb, swinging around the metal to the other side so he can get access to the roof.

This is where I start to get nervous, following after him, my boots clinging to the slick bars of the ladder. I move to the other side, too, much slower and much less gracefully, and find March reaching down to yank me up by the back of my new black jacket. He sets me down on the roof as the White Rabbit climbs up to join us.

I'm on the roof of a fucking *train*, with hail pelting me in the face, and lightning crashing down in the distance. The roar of thunder is audible even over the rush of wind. I'm not a trained court assassin like the two men with me, but I'll do my fucking best.

"Shouldn't we …" I start, cringing as yet another burst of lightning turns the sky white for a brief moment.

"Not be out in the storm?" March asks, and he shrugs his big shoulders. "No, we really shouldn't be." He takes off down the train, pausing as a hatch opens several cars down, and the Mad Hatter crawls out, his top hat soaking up the rain and lilting to one side as it gets soggy.

"Did you see—" he starts, but he doesn't get to finish because a shot goes off and just narrowly misses hitting him in the shoulder. March doesn't hesitate to defend his boss, chucking a small knife from inside his trench coat and making the air in front of us bleed.

A Rabbit appears right there next to him, fading into view like the Cheshire Cat. Actually, before he shifts into the Fred-Rabbit's form, I do see ears and a tail. So not only did this guy eat a little piece of my brother—before or after death, I'm not at all certain—but he's got some neko in him, too.

The Mad Hatter whips out a pair of guns from under his hat, spins around and fires, just as the other Rabbit comes into view, the Liam one. He's not in Liam's form at the moment, thank fuck, but I recognize him nonetheless.

But it's not just those two Rabbits.

The hatch on one of the frontmost cars opens up, and several women and men climb out of it. They all have rabbit ears, and they all look … not quite themselves. They've got turn-keys on their backs, and their eyes are dull as dark glass. Upon closer inspection, it seems that quite a few of them are … dead? Undead?

Shit.

"Sonny!" Rab shouts, shoving me forward and knocking me out of the way as the Anti-Alice comes crashing into the roof of the train. Shots are fired as the Hatter and the Hare try to deal with the influx of Rabbits and I, I whip out the Vorpal Blade and try to figure out how to deal with the Anti-Alice.

On the roof of a train. In the pouring rain.

It rhymes. Fantastic.

Wind rushes past me as I widen my feet and hope to hell that I don't fall off. Smoke is seeping from the windows of the car below, and I'm seriously *this* fucking close to having a panic attack. What if my family is trapped down there?!

Before the Anti-Alice can even lift her scythe, the train screeches to a sudden halt, throwing us all across the roof. I'm nearly knocked off, the White Rabbit's hand around my wrist the only thing keeping me from slipping and sliding to my death.

Our stop is so sudden that the tracks screech, and the car we're on is tossed up and over them, curling around like a snake and skidding across the wet earth, destroying bushes, small trees, and mushrooms that burst into glittering clouds of dust.

It's still hitched to the rest of the train though, dragging several other cars with it. We almost topple over completely, but the car rights itself at the last second, smashing into the dirt with a groan of metal.

When I look back over my shoulder, I can see that there's something blocking the tracks, a pile of … I'm not sure *what*, soaked in rainwater and writhing. When I squint, I see that it's a pile of those undead doll soldiers.

"Fucking hearts," I murmur, but then the Anti-Alice is coming for me, just as North tears from the window of the train, shifting into jabberwock form as he goes and tearing a massive hole in the metal wall. The Caterpillar is right behind him, helping my family out of the burning car and into the rain.

There's not much I can do but trust that they've got it covered.

No way the Anti-Alice is going to let me deal with my family *and* fight her at the same time.

She swings her bone scythe at me and I jump, just narrowly missing the pleasure of having my feet severed at the ankles. I land on the roof of the train car and then lunge at her. Dodging isn't going to work for any length of time. The Anti-Alice is better than me, faster, stronger.

I've got to be cleverer.

That's my only out.

Rab steps between me and the oncoming onslaught of undead Rabbits, shifting into … his Scarlet form? He tears the white glove from one hand, and grabs a male Rabbit with gray ears first. The skin on his enemy splits right down the front, like he's being unzipped, and blood sprays out, mixing with the rain. The Gray Rabbit's head snaps back so violently that I know his neck is broken, and then his corpse slides and stumbles off the train … only to get back up again when it hits the ground.

Fucking hell.

The Anti-Alice throws herself at me, and I move to dodge her again while I think of a plan. Honestly, the only reason I make it out of the way at all is because I slip and fall, tumbling to the muddy grass beside the burning train.

She follows me down, relentless in her pursuit, and I just barely manage to find my feet before she swings again, cutting across the front of my jacket and giving the fabric a neat little slice. I can't get away fast enough, slipping and sliding in the mud. My hair is whipped around my face by the relentless wind and rain, but standing this close to the Anti-Alice, I don't feel *any* of the magic. She sucks it right out of the air like a vacuum cleaner.

I'm losing ground fast and starting to panic, when I feel Lar's earring slapping against my neck. Without letting myself worry about what it might do, I just tear it from my ear and throw it. A sheet of ice comes up between the Anti-Alice and me, trapping her scythe not only mid-swing but literal inches from my face.

That's what buys me enough time to pull back, rushing through the water and the ice and the magic. The twins are there in just a few seconds, taking up either side of me like bodyguards.

"Thank fuck you're okay," Dee whispers, looking over his shoulder and toward the edge of a steep hill. "We thought maybe you were down there." I move over a few feet, so I can see past the row of shrubs blocking the view and … I feel my breath get caught painfully in my chest as I gasp.

There's an army down there, the scope of which I can hardly comprehend. I can't even begin to grasp at numbers as I squeeze the hilt of the Vorpal Blade and watch with wide, wide eyes. Those doll soldiers are *everywhere*, and even though they're clumsy and brainless, they're relentless. The tide of red-clad soldiers is being pushed back.

"How did we not know the battle had spread all the way over here?" I whisper as a roar shatters the sky at the same time a bolt of lightning crashes to the earth. "We didn't hear rumors or intel or … anything."

"The network is still compromised," Tee whispers, his voice nearly impossible to hear over the storm. Hell, I can barely hear the battle raging below and it's right fucking there in front of me. "Nobody could call us, nobody knew where to reach us with letters …" He trails off and looks back at the Anti-Alice as she struggles to free her scythe from the ice block. "And she, she sucks the magic out of everything. I still can't feel the battle, can you?"

I look back down at the melee, but Tee is right: I don't feel anything. And with the storm coming down this hard, I don't smell anything either.

"They just got on the train, too," Dee says, shoving wet, blue-black hair from his face. "Can't have been long ago either or we would've noticed."

I look down at my leg, wrapped in the leather breeches, and I think about that clock.

"Ten after nine," I whisper, just before we hear a shattering sound, glancing back to see the Anti-Alice tearing her weapon free. *Shit.* "I'm fucking scared," I admit as Dee leans toward me and presses his forehead against mine.

"True fear is fine," he says, giving me a small kiss on the mouth before he pulls away, drawing his knife. A screech echoes from behind us, like the sound of clattering nails, breaking up the monotonous drone of the rainstorm. Down the hill, a sea of dolls with rubber smiles and bleeding eyes crawls through the bramble toward us.

Dee steps forward, spreads his wings wide, and throws his head back.

Power explodes from him, throwing the entire horde back down the slope in pieces. It's one of the most beautiful, awe-inspiring things I've ever seen, watching Dee use his full powers for the first time in years.

That fucking curse … I'm so glad it's gone.

Tee gets ready to help defend me from the Anti-Alice while his brother watches our backs. Thing is, he can only protect me for so long. If I want this war to end, I *have* to kill her.

So when she comes at me again, I close my eyes for a brief, brief moment, and I pull as much magic from the air as I can. When my gaze flicks open on her striped skirts, black mouth, and the summer sky blue of her eyes, I unleash it, throwing up a wall of giant glowing mushrooms between us.

A horn sounds from somewhere nearby, and Tee grabs me, lifting me up in his arms.

"No, I have to do this!" I shout, but he just flaps his wings and takes off with Dee following behind us. The Anti-Alice will give chase, that much I'm sure of, but the twins seem to know where they're going and what they're doing, flying us over the horde of soldiers that stretches from the train car to the edge of the woods, covering *miles* of wet ground.

There's a white and red tent with diamonds and hearts on it, set just off the edge of the battlefield.

This is where Tee sets me down.

He strides forward, opens the curtain, and lets me inside

I must have a one-track mind because, despite all the craziness going on inside that tent, the first things I see are North, Chesh, and Lar. They've got my parents, sister, and Dinah with them, huddled in the corner with their hair dripping onto the plush rugs beneath our feet. There must be dozens of them, creating a cushioned floor for the massive white and red tent. It's about the size of my parents' living room, kitchen, and guest bathroom combined.

There's a table in the center, torches stuck in the ground around the edges, and chests overflowing with weapons and maps. I even spot a station set up for tea, with pots and cups and saucers, silver towers of cakes looming over the sugar-strewn surface.

The King stands at the head of a large rectangular table, staring at me with obsidian eyes.

Since the twins are with me, that means it's just the White Rabbit, the March Hare, and the Mad Hatter who are missing. But at least I know they made it out of the burning car. Hell, they might be dead already anyway, but … I feel like I'd know if they were.

"It's my own hearts-damned invention!" the White Knight screams, looking totally and completely disheveled. Her face is streaked with blood and tears, and her long hair is matted and messy. She looks like a completely different person, standing there and staring down at a massive chessboard with several broken or missing pieces—mostly on the red side. The black seems fairly-well intact. "It's my own invention," she repeats, swiping her hand down her face. "A nightmare of my own making."

"Yes, we all know you did this to yourself," the Knave snaps, and I startle because I was so busy looking at everyone and everything else that I'm just now noticing her. She has her husbands with her, too, which makes me feel a hell of a lot better. If she'd lost one of them, I think my heart would break a little for her. "Now, the question is: how do we fix it?"

The White Knight just stares at the board like she has no idea how to make the next move.

"I'll have your head," Brennin says, his voice as harsh and unforgiving as a tundra. "Just not right now. You'll fix the mess you've made before I kill you."

Chevalier hangs her head in shame, scrubbing at her bleary eyes with the heel of her hand.

"Where are the Walrus and the Carpenter?" the Duke asks, approaching the table. He swishes his tail angrily as he studies the board. As I watch, the black queen moves into position, putting herself several squares closer to the red.

Uh-oh.

"The Carpenter," the Knave says, pointing at the black king. "This pawn, that's the Walrus."

The piece she's pointing to just sits there, completely immobile. Not sure if that's a good thing … or a really scary one.

Dor is still in the tent, standing near the back with the rest of the guards. As soon as I see him, I know something's really wrong. He's a double-double crosser, right?

"And I really don't like the position of the red king," the Knave continues, giving her ruler a very stern look. "He's likely to be checked if he continues to stand there." Brennin Red ignores her, moving around the table and studying the board.

Dor's eyes stay on the far wall of the tent, and I wonder if everyone but me has forgotten that he's still working for the Walrus and the Carpenter. Or maybe since we've all just stumbled into this chaos, nobody's had a chance to address him yet.

"Exactually!" the King of Diamonds snorts, his mussy bride standing beside him. She's shaking, too, as she lifts a tissue to her nose, sniffles, and dabs at it. "We have this under control; we don't need your help here, Sir."

"To beg your pardon, *Sir*," Brennin snaps back, narrowing his eyes on the fat, round little man. "You're losing this battle and, in turn, the war. You've taken a shit all over the prophecy, and you've made a fool out of yourself as king."

"At least I'm here!" Humphrey roars, straightening his cravat. "I don't see that slimy, cocksucking King of Spades anywhere near this battlefield with his soldiers. I've donated mine, you see." I just stare at him, thinking how leaders are always so proud of themselves for sending their citizens in to die. It's easy, isn't it, to order others to die for you, but it's much harder to take that risk yourself.

"Humphrey dear," the Queen of Diamonds whispers, tugging on his sleeve. He ignores her for a moment, preferring instead to argue with Brennin. But when her eyes fly wide, and a strangled scream escapes her throat, Humphrey grabs her by the shoulders and looks into her eyes.

Like the Caterpillar's visions appear in his wings, it seems the Diamond Queen gets them in her irises. I can see a scene playing out from all the way over here.

"What is this …?" Humphrey starts as Lar sighs.

"*All the King's horses, and all the King's men …*" He trails off and then looks Humpty Dumb-shit dead in the eye. "I tried to warn you."

The tent explodes into chaos as blood spatters across the chessboard.

At first, I think it's Humpty Dumpty and his soothsayer wife, but then I realize that it's not them at all: it's fucking Dor.

An axe is protruding from *behind* his own rib cage, his own brown eyes wide with fear as he looks down to see the Carpenter … crawling out from *inside* his chest. The dude is literally in-fucking-side of him, like some macabre birthing nightmare.

Well, I guess we see how he's moving around so quickly, don't we?

The black pawn piece slides forward a square, getting closer to the red king.

But if the Carpenter, who's currently wearing the crown for the Kingdom of Clubs, is the pawn … then who's the black king?

The Anti-Alice steps out of the storm and into the tent, her black and white dress plastered to her body, white hair stuck to the gray skin of her face. I spot her right away and step back, readying myself for another fight, when the Carpenter launches himself at the King of Diamonds and his queen.

And Lar's right: his mangled body … will never be put back together again.

Chapter Seven

Shaking, Waking, and Decision Making

I am scared shitless.

If you're reading this, you should be, too. There's a necromancer spattered in the blood of a king, a chessboard set up for failure, and an army of undead dolls outside the walls of this tent. A wild magic storm is raging outside, and my dead sister is staring at me with eyes that are so familiar, I could cry. I see those eyes every time I look in the mirror.

Unfortunately, it's kill or be killed, and I am ready to *live.*

I'm so nervous that I start to shake, but I force myself to repeat Chesh's poem aloud. With the storm, and the chaos inside the tent, I can barely hear my own voice, but it soothes me enough that I get my head together anyway.

"She took her Vorpal Blade in hand: Long time the manxome foe she sought—" My voice cuts off as the Anti-Alice comes at me again … hopefully for the last time. Tee and Dee stay with me, but only as defense. They know better than to touch or attack the girl in black and white.

There's chaos all around me, but I only have eyes for Rhoda.

Nothing else matters right now.

We circle each other, moving around the table and past the King as he grapples with the Carpenter, past the Caterpillar and the Cheshire Cat protecting my family from the doll soldiers that're slipping underneath the fabric walls. The tent's perimeter is spelled, but even though their flesh burns and they scream like broken wind-up toys, the doll-zombies keep coming.

On the chessboard, our corresponding pieces move with us.

Back home, the game of chess is all about the King. Here, it's all about the *Queen.*

I run at the Anti-Alice, swinging the Vorpal Blade and catching her across the front of her dress. It's not a good enough move to make her bleed, but now that I'm close to her, that scythe isn't quite so useful. She uses it as a shield instead of a weapon, catching the Vorpal Blade on the handle and pushing me back.

This close to her, I can feel the magic in the air disappearing into her void, making my stomach feel like a block of ice, like I'm being cut off from every important thing in the world. Do I make her feel that way, too? Does my presence make her feel like she's breaking apart from the inside? Or does she even feel at all?

I guess I'll never know.

The Anti-Alice and I battle, weapons clashing, feet smearing mud and blood across the carpets on the ground. The Duke shifts into his jabberwock form as we fight, his huge body knocking aside the tent, sending cold rain pouring over our heads. The White Knight simply stands there in the downpour for a long, long moment, staring at the corpses of Humphrey and his wife. When she pulls out her sword to fight, she's almost instantly swarmed by dead dolls. They bury her, so quickly that she soon disappears from sight.

I wonder briefly if I might've just seen her death with my own eyes.

Rainbow streaked hair is stuck to my face, but I don't have time to push it aside, so I stare at the Anti-Alice through a curtain of color as a swarm of bats descends on the pile of rugs, reforming into the Mad Hatter. He's just in time to grab the Anti-Alice's weapon by the handle, giving it a yank and flinging it aside. It smashes into the chessboard, knocking pieces everywhere.

But just that one, small touch is enough to turn his hand an awful gray color, the rot spreading up toward his shoulder. Raiden wrinkles his nose, stepping forward and grabbing Dee by the back of the neck. The angel prince bares his throat, letting the vampire sink his teeth in deep.

Even if I have to fuck the Frenzy out of him later, I know we need Raiden Walker to go batshit—pun intended—on these assholes.

While the Anti-Alice is preoccupied with her missing scythe, I take another swing at her, grabbing onto her dress as I plunge the knife into her back. She stumbles, but keeps moving, like I'm a gnat she just hasn't had the chance to swat at. Her feet take her in the direction of the Knave, whose arms are wide as she casts a spell to push the encroaching army back, her brunette hair swirling around her petite face in the storm. The Lion and the Unicorn—their names Rook and Knight suddenly make so much more sense now that I've seen the chessboard—keep her safe while she draws sigils and whispers ancient words.

Tears pour from my eyes as I dig the blade in deep. Unlike last time, I won't let go. Not even if I see a Rabbit who looks like Fred, or a monster with Liam's face. My past … I'm not going to allow it to come back and haunt me ever again. Never a-fucking-gain.

The March Hare, in tove form, and the White Rabbit as Scarlet—riding March's back—show up next. But they're not alone. They're following the pair of Rabbits that I met Topside. They're both in bandersnatch form, but as soon as they near the tent, they begin to shift.

One of them … becomes the Carpenter. The other, the Walrus.

Holy fuck.

"Good thing only one Rabbit can ever share another's skin, don't you agree?" Rab drawls in this husky, feminine voice that sounds rather like a female version of the asshole King's. "Because this … this is not a good scenario." She—or he, but seriously fuck gender pronouns—climbs off of March's back with one of her red hands bared. The other is still dressed in a white glove and holding a pistol

Without hesitation, Scarlet-Rab lifts the weapon up and fires a shot through the Rabbit-Carpenter's skull. I don't have time to see if that drops the fucker because the Anti-Alice has found her scythe, using the handle of it to stab back over her shoulder and hit me in the face.

I stumble as the Duke's roar breaks apart the monotonous drone of the wind. As I slip and fall on my back, I look up to see the Walrus fighting with North just outside the rectangle of rugs that mark the spot where the tent used to be. I don't know if he's fighting the real Walrus, or the Rabbit, but does it really matter?

They tear at each other, spattering blood everywhere, blood that's quickly consumed by the rain.

It's at that moment that I spy the Looking-Glass, wrapped in its sheet and sitting all alone on the ground near the huddled cluster of my family. Lar is nearby, but he's busy with a horde of the Carpenter's soldiers, casting a shield first to keep them back, and then a series of golden sigils that blow through the monsters like a tornado.

I shove up to my feet, but I force myself to stop staring at the Looking-Glass. Bringing attention to it will only make things worse. I start to wonder if we shouldn't have left it behind in someplace like Potsville. But then, it would've been unprotected and alone. And how could we have known how the events of today were going to play out?

March is rearing up with a roar, coming down with those sharp hooves on the Carpenter's double. At least … I think it's his double? The other bone-axe wielding asshole is fighting the King not a dozen feet away, their movements as impressive as a choreographed dance as they move around one another. I wish I could move that way with the Anti-Alice, but as things stand, it's hard enough for me to simply keep my feet.

Dee and Tee are watching my back, and working on the rush of soldiers at the same time, beating their way forward, toward the bulk of the army. If we only had a moment, I bet the ten of us could turn the tide pretty quick. A Frenzied vampire lord, a King who tears off heads with his hand, a jabberwock with fire breath …

We just need to deal with this mess first.

The Hatter breaks apart into a sea of bats again, and then reforms about a hundred yards away, meeting the stumbling, undead Rabbits that're left over from the fight at the train. He tears into them like a hot knife through butter, spilling blood into the cold mud at his feet.

It feels like everyone is making at least *some* progress, while I'm left in this limbo with the Anti-Alice, making zero progress whatsoever. If I don't kill her, then everything else is for naught. She's the lynchpin of this entire operation, an Underland queen to push back a Wonderland hope.

"*Twinkle, twinkle, little bat,*" Raiden's voice booms out, and within seconds, I see the huge shadow overhead, sweeping down and heading right for the Looking-Glass. *Thank fuck.*

But the Anti-Alice sees it, too, and before I can think up a way to stop her, she's running, heading straight for the Cheshire Cat as he slides in front of the mirror to protect it. I see it before it even happens, that swing of her scythe that could easily take Chesh's head from his shoulders.

What I don't expect, is for the King—a man who hates the Cheshire Cat more than anything—to step in between them and defend Chesh with his sword. But saving the cat comes with dire consequences, and the Carpenter takes advantage of that.

He lifts the Looking-Glass up, tears the sheet off, and then whistles for the Walrus. The blubbery beast tosses North aside by the neck, sending the dragon crashing into the trees, and then he shifts back down to his ogre-like visage. Both men flee the glass, and the Anti-Alice follows, throwing Red into Chesh and knocking them both over.

I have no idea what their plan is, but just when I'm considering breaking the Looking-Glass myself to keep them trapped, a screech sounds from behind me and I spin to find the Carpenter crawling out of the burst stomach of one of his doll soldiers, like he's from fucking *Alien* or something.

He grabs me and throws us both through the Looking-Glass and into Topside.

We emerge in a garbage dump, a literal fucking trash heap.

Good hiding place, though. It's really the last place I'd ever look.

I crawl away from the Carpenter, covered in silver goo and praying I get some back-up before the necromantic monster turns me into one of his doll zombies. Spinning around, I kick him in the face as hard as I can before the Walrus is grabbing me under the armpits and hauling me to my feet.

"The time has come," the Walrus says, "to talk of many things. Of pain—and bones—and murdering, the Alice and her kings." He licks my ear as I fight and scream, swinging the Vorpal Blade around and managing to catch him on the arm with it.

He hisses, but he doesn't let go, not even as the Carpenter raises his axe above his head.

I watch in abject horror as he brings the weapon down … and shatters the Looking-Glass.

A scream tears from my throat along with their laughter as the Anti-Alice moves up to stand in front of me, staring at me with blank, blue eyes. They're still pretty, but there's no soul in there, none at all. *The Looking-Glass!* my heart screams in pain, already wondering how I'm going to get back. If I were trapped here … but no. I refuse to think about that. My logical mind screams for a different reason, now fully aware that there is no back-up coming. Unless one of those men back there knows how to travel worlds by crawling out through other people's insides … I'm fucked.

The Anti-Alice spins her scythe around, and then carefully, meticulously … slices my throat with it. At the same time, the Carpenter lights the Looking-Glass on fire, and I find myself with the privilege of watching it burn as I bleed to death at the same time.

I can feel hot blood ooze down my throat as my lungs begin to scream for air, already acutely aware that there's something wrong with my body, that the oxygen isn't going where it's supposed to. There's a burning in my chest as I gape like a fish out of water, mouth opening and closing as the Anti-Alice leaves her blade embedded in my skin.

It's like she's plugged into me, tapped into the very essence of my soul. My life and magic drain from me, sucked into a void as cold as space, as empty as an eternity devoid of stars. *Nobody is coming for me; nobody can save me.*

But do you really need them to? a voice whispers from inside my head, the sound echoing around my skull. *They're just the nine, the Alice's helpers, guides for her journey. Those men, as fabulous as they are, they are not the Alice.*

I cough on the fluid filling my lungs as I think about Dee, telling me how much he believed I could change the world. But how can I, if I die here in a retired garbage dump? My body will be tossed aside like so much trash, buried underneath plastic straws and grocery bags, rotten food and old refrigerators.

I'll sink into the muck, just rot and ruin, a feast for the worms.

As the Anti-Alice drains my magic, her skin begins to change color, from an awful charcoal gray to a fresh pink-peach that's much the same as my own. She's quite literally filling her own void with my essence.

I'm the fucking Alice, I think, fingers twitching, the Vorpal Blade still in my hand. The Carpenter reaches forward to remove it, fingers curling around the hilt. *And there's magic everywhere, even in Topside.*

With a gurgling gasp, I suck in as much magic from the air as I can, pumping it into the Anti-Alice, overwhelming her connection to me. She shrieks and stumbles back, pulling her weapon out just far enough that I get a brief moment of reprieve from that ice-cold nightmare.

The next surge of power I collect goes right into the Vorpal Blade and up the Carpenter's fingers. It's not enough to truly hurt him, but he does stumble back, giving me the opening I need to hit the Walrus in his solar plexus. I'll have to thank Lory for that one later.

The blubbery bastard stumbles back as I scramble to escape, gasping and choking. I'm starting to get dizzy from the lack of oxygen, and there's certainly no vampire blood around for me to drink, so I need a different plan.

I call out to the universe for help. After all, the special power of the Alice is that she can draw on *all* magic, not just the magic she was born with. And surely there must be enough power in the world to heal my wound, no matter how severe it might be.

Drawing energy into my body, I channel it toward the slice in my throat, sealing it up, skin and flesh knitting together as tears escape unbidden from my eyes. Oxygen never tasted so damn good, and I suck in several greedy mouthfuls of it before the Anti-Alice tackles me again, sending us both rolling down the side of the slag heap.

It smells so fucking awful here, like blood and rot, but I don't care—as long as I can breathe, I'll take whatever ugly scents the world throws at me. I put as much distance between the Anti-Alice and myself as I can, using the magic to push the ground up beneath my feet. It lifts me into the air, giving me a perfect view of all three enemies down below.

The Carpenter seems like the biggest threat, has all along actually. But I remember the way the pawn moved on the board with him, and how the black king sat still. That, and in the original Lewis Carroll books, the Walrus betrays him.

"Filthy whore," the Walrus snarls, spittle and blood flying past his tusks. "You would've been a lovely, little oyster to add to my collection." He grins at me and then reaches out to grab the Carpenter around the throat. "But I suppose if I leave you here to rot, you'll die eventually. That's all I really need—you, *gone*. And to get out of here, I need only a single sacrifice. Au revoir, the Alice." He snaps his brother's neck, and I realize how ridiculous we've been: the Carpenter isn't the only necromancer in the family.

With hot blood pouring down his hands, the Walrus opens his jaws wide, and *eats* the other man in a few, hideous, gurgling bites. Once his brother's disappeared down his throat, the Walrus' body folds in on itself, like it's turning inside out. I see blood and bone and throbbing organs before he begins to fade from view.

No! You're not fucking leaving! I think, letting my head fall back, throwing my arms wide like I just saw the Knave do. Like I did with the Gryphon and the Mocking Turtle, I tap into the energy of the woods behind me, just outside the dump's rusty chain-link fence. Pulling that power into me, I redirect it into the Walrus. All I'm trying to do is stop him from manipulating his brother's life energy to make an escape. I don't even try to hurt him, just … keep him here.

But the process of hopping worlds with a blood sacrifice instead of a mirror must be a real bitch because as soon as I interrupt him, he starts to scream. The sound is this horrific blood-curdling screech, made all the more macabre by the Walrus' inside-out face. I can see all of his teeth as his mouth opens wide and inhuman sounds begin to pour out.

With another wave of magic, I fling my hand and send him flying across the yard. He smashes into the fence … and through it, like meat in a sausage grinder, falling to pieces on the other side. My stomach churns with bile, but I don't have a spare moment to dwell on what I've just seen.

The Anti-Alice leaps into the air, her skin much less gray, her eyes more blue. She launches herself at me, knocking us both out of the air. On our way down, I call up the wet earth to catch us as rain pours down from a gray sky.

Heh.

It's storming in both Topside *and* Underland.

My magic creates a little nest that the Anti-Alice and I fall into, knocking our weapons aside. We struggle together, just hands and fingers and legs, kicking and clawing and screaming. It's a primal struggle between two sides of the same coin: life and death.

That's what this fight is, a fight for *life*.

I think about the little kids at the Bread-and-Butterfly, taking their chocolate strawberries in hand. I think about my parents and Edith, huddled in the pouring rain. Mostly, I think about the nine men that I'm falling in love with, and how desperate I am to see the seeds of our affection grow into mighty trees.

With the Anti-Alice touching me like this, I shouldn't be able to pull magic. I can still feel her void-like emptiness, but … whatever she did when she started sucking my life out seems to have weakened that aspect of her powers. Using the tiny bit of energy I manage to summon, I use the wind to grab the Vorpal Blade and drop it in my hand.

A scream escapes me that's fabulously monstrous, and I thrust the Vorpal Blade up and under the Anti-Alice's chin, sending it straight through her skull. It's no normal blade, channeling the magic I pull from the world, and cutting through bone like butter.

The Anti-Alice scrabbles at me with her nails, blood leaking from her eyes, desperately searching for purchase. If I were to remove the blade now, she'd come at me again. But I don't. Instead, I sit there in the rain and cry, my wet hair plastered to my face, my heart in pieces.

It takes the better part of an *hour*—I know because I can hear the clock tattoo on my thigh ticking again—before she collapses to her side, her body withering away to ash in the wind. I smell rot and dust and tombstones … but also, the salty taste of tears. A flicker of light leaves the ashes and floats away like a faery in the wind.

"Goodbye Rhoda," I whisper, watching her flitter away, my hands soaked in hot blood, my heart hoping she finds some peace in whatever comes after.

My head drops back into the mud … and my body begins to convulse.

All alone in Topside, I have a magic-induced seizure with no one to hold me, hug me, help me.

No … this time, I'm all alone.

When I wake up, shaking and ice-cold, it's still dark.

Or rather, when I use the Vorpal Blade to cut my pants open and check the time, I see that an *entire day* has passed. I've just been lying here comatose and alone for twenty-four fucking hours. Shaking, soaking wet, and starving, I crawl out of the mud and wash my hands in a puddle. Once they're clean, I bring them to my lips and drink deeply.

It takes a while, but as soon as I have the strength to stand, I get up and I start to walk.

Once I get a ways from the garbage dump, I start to see street signs, following one after the other until things begin to get vaguely recognizable. People stare at me as I pass, covered in mud and soaked to the bone, but nobody stops me. Honestly, in Topside, that's a blessing. I'd rather not get raped and murdered on my way home, thanks.

I head back to my parents' house. It takes *hours*, but I make it there around sunrise, teeth chattering as I head into the backyard, and dig up the spare key, the one Mom buried in the center of her heart-shaped tulip bed.

I let myself inside, and don't make it five feet before I collapse again. But this time, I'm determined to keep going. I make myself get up and eat some lunch meat from the fridge, nab a banana from the counter, and drink a huge glass of orange juice. After that, I feel okay enough to strip down and crawl into a hot shower in the downstairs bathroom.

That's where I have the second seizure, my body slamming against the glass walls of the shower as the power punishes me for overusing it, for channeling it through my undisciplined and weakened body. But I live through it. I fucking *live*.

After I'm dry and dressed, I head into Edith's room and get on her computer—she might know where my diary is, but I know *all* her fucking passwords. I log into her social media and start checking messages until I find one talking about the party where Brandon died. I scribble the address down, steal some money from Dad's sock drawer, and call a cab with the house phone—who knows where the fuck any of our cell phones are.

Once I get there, I pay the driver, and rush up to the back gate, letting myself in and not giving a shit if there are people home. I have no idea if there are; I don't *care*. Instead, I race through the rain, across the lawn, and into the bushes where I tumbled down the Rabbit-Hole.

Falling to my knees, I search across the ground like I'm hunting a diamond ring in the dirt.

After my first round in the bushes, I feel like maybe I'm losing my mind. It *should* be here, right? But in my heart, I know the truth …

"The Rabbit-Hole is like a stream off a river," the Mad Hatter says, adjusting his top hat and glancing down at my sister like he's just seen her. She's shaking now, her eyes so wide they look liable to roll right out of her face. "This is the river," Raiden says, caressing the edge of the mirror suggestively.

And the river's been … smashed.

But still, I keep searching that yard, going over every fucking inch as the storm rages around, me, rainwater soaking me to my bones. When a new sunrise begins to take over the sky, I sit on my knees, lean back on my ankles … and I cry.

Chapter Eight

I Dreamed It?!

I wake up in a great panic, my mind cluttered with dreams of brightly colored toadstools and men with wings. There are moments of great passion mixed with flashes of violence and blood-soaked fields. I hear music and the sound of waltzing feet in ballrooms made of glass and hearts.

Rubbing at my eyes, I try to remember where exactly it is that I am. The room is vaguely familiar, but it's not right; something *isn't right*. And that's when I remember: I'm at home, in suburbia.

I am fucking Topside all alone.

I scramble out of bed and find the calendar on the wall, the one with all the red Xs. It's been nine days since I found myself trapped on the wrong side of a broken Looking-Glass. Nine days of pure hell. The red Sharpie squeaks as I draw another X on yesterday's date, turning around and leaning my back against the wall. I slide to the floor and sit there in a heap. There's a possibility that I'll sit here for hours. Maybe all day. That's what I did yesterday.

I just can't find it in myself to care.

My mother, father, and sister are in Underland; the men I've grown to love are in Underland.

My fate, my magic, my kingdom, my happiness … it's all in Underland.

And I'm here.

Life. Fucking. Sucks.

Putting my face in my hands, I suck in several deep breaths, fighting off the cold fingers of a panic attack. I haven't had one yet—I've stayed strong—but the reality of my situation is starting to set in.

There is no way back to Underland. No matter how many days I sit here on the floor of my childhood bedroom and stare at the window and the huge oak tree outside of it, nothing changes. No matter how long I wait, nobody is coming.

Well, nobody from Underland anyway.

Yesterday, the police came, and I hid on the roof while they yelled about a search warrant and barged in, searching the house high and low. That was the most company

I've had in nine days. The food in the cabinets and the refrigerator are gone, and I've started having pizza delivered. Eventually, my parents will run out of money. Eventually, the house will be foreclosed on. Eventually, I won't have a safe place to call my own.

So, really, I only have one option, and that's to make a life here … all by myself.

No Fred … no Edy … no Mom … no Dad.

Just me.

Putting my head in my hands, I curl forward and rest them on my knees, dreaming of rivers made of tea, towering castles with closets full of fantastical clothes, and men who call me by a dozen different nicknames. That's all gone now, and I have no choice but to accept it. Get a job, earn some money, try my best to explain to the cops that I didn't kill Brandon … try to explain how I sprung my mother out of jail.

I'm eighteen; I might get time for what I did.

Tears come then, and even though I said I don't cry, I do. I sob and sob and sob, because it's not just Fred that's gone this time, it's everyone. Everyone I love is gone, and I'm alone in a world that doesn't care whether I live or die. All readers dream of finding the fantastical, of escaping into another realm, a realm that's better than this one, that's full of hope and magic and love. But they never find it, so they don't know what they're missing.

I do.

I had a taste of forever, and I lost it all.

Falling onto my side, I cry into the pile of dirty clothes on my bedroom floor, and then I fall asleep again. At least in my dreams, I can see them all again. In my dreams, I am Queen.

♦ ♠ ♣ ♥ ♣ ♠ ♦

When I next wake, it's dark outside, and no less depressing. I sit up and rub at my crusted eyes. Maybe I'll go back to Rabbit-Hole again? It wasn't there last time, but … maybe I wasn't looking in the right spot? It's worth another try, at least. What else am I going to do? The thought of moving forward with a normal life now, a life that's devoid of the only family I had left … it's devastating.

Those men, those nine, beautiful men, they had me believing in the prophecy. They had me believing I could live a life, fall in love, live in bliss. They had me believing I was queen and that I could change the world. And now those dreams I never wanted in the first place, the ones I grew to embrace, they're dead, like bloated corpses floating down a river of disappointment and despair.

I stand up and pull the Vorpal Blade from its holster, staring in the shiny surface at my reflection. Now that I'm back in Topside, my hair isn't quite so golden, and the rainbow streaks are starting to fade. Maybe it's because my spirit is fading, too?

"Fuck you," I tell the blade, because no matter what I do with it, no matter how hard I try, I can't get it to be anything but a blade. My magic is still inside of me, sure. I can still feel that, but it's so much harder to collect here in Topside, and it tastes different, smells different, feels different. I've tried casting spells, and I've managed to accomplish things, too. I've stuck a table to the ceiling and left it there for days. I've blown up the old swing set in the backyard. I've lit a few candles and watched them melt into puddles of wax.

But I can't get back to Underland.

"You can sacrifice a shard to make a Rabbit-Hole, can't you?"

Chesh said that, and Lar confirmed the rumor. Yet, here I am, standing here with a Vorpal Blade and no Rabbit-Hole. I haven't been in Underland long enough, haven't trained with Lar or the Duke or the Mad Hatter enough to know what to do. If only I'd had more time, maybe I could fix this? After all, once upon a time, there were no Rabbit-Holes and no Looking-Glasses, right? Somebody had to make them.

I sigh and tuck the blade away, heading down the stairs and into the kitchen. There's leftover pizza and a few drips of my dad's favorite brandy—that's about it. I take a slice of cold pepperoni in one hand, the bottle in the other, and I go sit on the couch in the living room, remembering my horror and fear when I first tumbled through the Looking-Glass and thought I might be trapped.

Fucking hearts, the relief I felt when the twins came tumbling after … I'm not sure if I've ever been that relieved. The closest maybe was when Fred saved me from being raped. But then, we all know how that turned out. Maybe it's the universe's way of seeking balance, offering up something beautiful and then evening out the scales with a dose of horror?

I finish off the pizza, down some of the brandy, and then turn on the worst horror movie I can find, something where everyone suffers and nobody lives happily ever after. Because it's all just a bunch of bullshit, isn't it?

I'm a bit buzzed, so my mind wanders, and I start noticing random things, like how much smaller this new rug on the floor is. The one that was ruined by the Looking-Glass goo was at least twenty-five percent bigger than this. Lifting the bottle to my lips, I notice the mirror above the fireplace next. It's certainly *not* the original Looking-Glass—that one was smashed into pieces and *burned.* This new mirror isn't nearly as ornate, not nearly as impressive. But it is about the same size.

Since I'm on the path to being drunk anyway, I decide it can't hurt to grab what's left of the original Looking-Glass ashes. I've tried everything with them: rubbing them on the Vorpal Blade, smearing them on my skin, *eating* some. Nothing happened.

This time, I take the little baggy and rub the ashes over the new mirror, making sure to cover every inch of the glass. When I'm done, I set my brandy bottle aside, and take hold of both it *and* the Vorpal Blade—one in each hand. Closing my eyes, I pull as much magic from the air as I can, channeling it into the two objects, imagining the power of the ashes and the blade fusing into the mirror.

I'm not sure how long I stand there, but when I finally let go and stumble back … nothing has changed.

Of course it fucking hasn't.

Tears stream down my cheeks as I grit my teeth in frustration.

When Fred died, I wished for anything to bring him back. Eventually, I had to accept that I never could, that he was gone forever. That's what I have to do now: I have to accept that this is my new normal. This is my new reality.

"Imagination is the only weapon in the war against reality."

"Fuck reality," I growl, imagining falling into that mirror, tumbling back into Underland, landing in Rab's arms the way I did the first time I fell into the Rabbit-Hole. "Fuck reality!" I swing the Vorpal Blade at the mirror with every last ounce of strength I have, and it shatters. They *both* shatter—the mirror *and* the blade.

Hot, wet heat spatters my hand as I stumble back, and I realize that I've just shredded my hand and wrist into ribbons with the glass. The crimson spray coats the ash-covered shards of the mirror and the Vorpal Blade, drip-drip-drips down the front of the mantle, and spatters on the bricks below.

"Even if you shrink, you can't get between the bars," Rab says.

"You can't, but you're not the Alice," the King replies.

The Alice. I'm the fucking Alice. I step forward and touch my shaking, bloody fingers to the frame of the mirror. Magic pours through me and into it, lifting up shards of the Vorpal Blade from the ground. Like I did with the pin tumblers in the lock, I put the pieces where I want them, and I hold them in place.

No sooner has the last piece clicked into place, then the shattered mirror begins to swirl. I can barely breathe; my throat feels tight; my heart thunders. Reaching my fingers forward … I find the hot, viscous liquid of a Looking-Glass.

"Oh fuck," I sob, pulling it down from the mantle and setting it gently on the floor in front of me. There is no way in hell I'm waiting around to see if my good luck runs out. No, I put one foot forward—carefully, so as not to break the mirror any further—and I set it down, watching as my bare toes disappear into the swirling, silver goo.

And then … then I jump.

Chapter Nine

Queen Alice

My body hits the floor so hard that bones break; I can hear them.

The scream that so desperately wants to come out of me is cut off by my lack of breath. Not only am I choking on that horrid goo, I've hurt myself pretty goddamn badly. I shouldn't have jumped so … enthusiastically.

For a brief moment there, I'm completely disoriented, wondering where the second half to my new mirror might lead. For all I know, I could be in the Kingdom of Clubs. The Walrus and the Carpenter might be dead, but that doesn't mean the corruption fades overnight. There's still a lot of work to be done in Underland.

"Allison!" I hear Tee's voice, his perfect, seraphic, heroic voice, calling my name. And there are his hands, all over me, gently turning me over so that I'm staring at the ceiling in the Suit of Hearts. I'd recognize it anywhere, this room. It feels a thousand times more *mine* than my childhood bedroom. Even with blood burbling from my lips, I laugh. "Get the Hatter!"

Within minutes, I'm surrounded by a sea of concerned faces that fade in and out, that quiver and shake and make me wonder if I'm still dreaming. But I'm not. I can't be. I never *was*. Underland, it was always real.

"Drink, Little Alice," Raiden Walker breathes, tearing open his wrist, sucking in a mouthful of blood, and putting his lips to mine. Like a prince waking a princess at the end of a fairytale, the Mad Hatter kisses me with tongue and teeth and the passion of lost love returned. *He's missed me,* I think, knowing that later, I'll gloat like crazy about it.

For now, I enjoy my fairy-tale kiss, and even though it's a hell of a lot bloodier, a fuck of a lot more morbid, than the usual … I'll take it. Because this isn't Wonderland, it's fucking Underland.

This … this is home.

Waking up in that massive bed, with the Cheshire Cat curled around my shoulders, Dee sprawled and drooling across the red comforter, and the Duke sitting side by side with my mother in a pair of chairs, it's like winning the lottery times a thousand.

Fuck, it's *everything.*

Tears spring to my eyes, but I push them back. Crying was appropriate when I was at home alone with nothing but old pizza and alcohol to keep me company. I don't need them now.

"Allison," Mom whispers, standing up and giving me a huge hug. *She* is crying, but I'm not going to. "I thought I'd …" She stops talking for a moment, holding me close, strangling the life out of me with her love. But holy fuck, after the week and a half I've had alone, I will take it. I'll take a million hugs because you know what? You never know how important the people you love are until you lose them. Call me clichéd, but it's true: it's hard to understand loss if you've never experienced it. "I thought I'd lost you like I lost Rhoda and Fred."

My own throat stops up, but I refuse to cry, and I'm a stubborn bitch, so I'm not going to.

"I didn't think I'd ever get back," I whisper, exhaling and glancing over to find North's golden eyes watching me. There's a tenderness there, buried beneath all of the beast. Just by looking at him, I can see that he means it: he really does think of me as his mate.

Would it be too soon to say I'm proud to be his Duchess? Maybe. But I am anyway. The heart wants what it wants.

"I tore apart my palace looking for clues on the art of the Looking-Glass," he whispers, voice gruff and low, like gravel scraping across my heart. I want to hug him, hold him, kiss him … and other things. Mom sits there staring at us for a moment, and then stands up abruptly.

"I'll get your father and sister," she says, and then pauses. "Just … please don't have sex while I'm gone; I won't be long."

"*Mom*," I choke out, but the Duke of Northumbria just laughs, his chuckle like bells in the wind. As soon as my mother leaves the room, I gently push the sleeping Cheshire Cat aside, onto a pillow next to Dee, and I climb into the dragon's lap.

My fingers trace his horns as his tail wraps around my waist. He's so fucking excited that his huge, leathery wings explode from his back.

"Miss Liddell, I started every man in my dukedom on the task of creating a new Looking-Glass. I would not have rested until the art was reclaimed, and Topside was reunited with Underland." He rubs his cheek against mine, and then he kisses me with so much passion that I feel dizzy.

"Allison-who-isn't-Alice?" Dee murmurs, shaking the black and white striped cat. It cracks one gray eye, and then the other. I see the hair on Chesh's back stand on end.

"Midnight Knicker Dancer, you're awake!" he throws himself at me, shifting as he does, and then ends up in the Duke's lap with me. The jabberwock growls, but Chesh hardly gives a shit, rubbing himself all over me until I end up in fits of giggles. "I was *meow*-serable without you!"

I grab his face between my hands and kiss him, too. I could kiss them all for hours, just lie here in bed with all nine men and luxuriate in their nearness. Hell, maybe I'll do just that? The Walrus and the Carpenter are dead; that doesn't mean the fight is over in Underland, but I do deserve a week off, right?

"Oh, Allison-who-isn't-Alice," Dee moans, and I turn back around to find him waiting for me on the edge of the bed with open arms and open wings. *He* doesn't seem to have any trouble with crying, not like I do. He just bawls these big, happy tears, holding me close and squeezing me like his crush on me is as hard as diamonds—and twice as precious. Our kiss is sad and happy, both at the same time.

The doors fly open and smash into the wall, but when Dee moves his wing out of my way, so I can see who it is, it isn't my mom. No, the King is here, and he's brought his entourage: the Caterpillar, the White Rabbit, and the fallen angel prince.

"The Alice is awake," Brennin breathes, pausing at the end of my bed. Tee doesn't bother with formalities, coming around and stealing me from his brother's arms, looking into my eyes like I'm the only girl he's ever dreamed of. I might have nine lovers, but for him, I'm the only one there is.

"You scared the shit out of me," he says, just before my family files into the room and stands awkwardly off to one side. I can practically hear Edith drooling over the sight of the Looking-Glass, but I'm not upset. No matter how many bad things have happened in her life, that's home to her, and she wants to go back.

I respect that.

"*I* scared the shit out of me," I whisper, unable to raise my voice above the level of *hushed* for fear that I very well might give up and cry. And that just wouldn't do, would it? This is a happy ending, not a sad one.

"You're very, very late, you know," Rab says, his voice like bones and ice. He crawls onto the bed and looks at me with those beautiful red eyes of his, like rubies in a handsome face. With only a vest covering his gorgeous body, I can see the sweeping lines of his brightly colored tattoos. There's a new one that I swear wasn't there when I left, a very familiar face with blue eyes and blonde hair, and she's staring back at me from his inner elbow.

The White Rabbit reaches over and grabs hold of the dressing gown I'm wearing, one that I distinctly do not remember putting on after I drank the Hatter's blood. Thank fuck though, because the clothes I was wearing when I got here were B.O. central. He unbuttons his vest and shows me the clock in the center of his chest. It's past its marked time by several days.

"This, this was supposed to be your *wedding*," he whispers, and then he reaches up and cups the back of my neck with brightly colored fingers, pulling me in for a kiss that tastes like the first brush of frost in winter. "And you're late for it. The Knave has given her approval, and the festivities are already under way."

"But I wasn't even here," I whisper, heartbeat quickening, pulse thumping. "How can you plan a wedding without a bride?"

"Dreaming, Sunshine," Lar says, sitting on the bed beside the White Rabbit. "We were planning, and hoping, and dreaming. The universe is all about intent: don't just sit and wish for something you want. You must make it happen. And we've planned a wedding."

"I never actually said yes to that horrid King," I mumble, crawling over and curling up in Lar's lap, letting him hold me and play with my hair. His tobacco and blueberry scent surrounds me, soothing away some of my anxiety. When I look up, I can see that he was afraid; he didn't know if I was coming back. I guess his prophecies don't tell him everything, do they?

Lar and I kiss, but it doesn't last long. Hard to get into it with my parents staring. That, and I've got other men to greet.

I stand up and face the King, feeling pretty damn brave, even in bare feet and a nightgown.

"You made it back, Your Majesty," he says, and the scarred corner of his lip twitches, like he's trying to smile. I'm just about to ask him where the March Hare and the Mad Hatter are when they waltz into the room, side by side, dressed in trench coats and top hats.

March has half a cupcake clutched in his hand, like he started eating it and then just plumb forgot it was there. Raiden smirks at me, but there's no arrogance to that expression. Even he's glad that I came back. Still not sure how I managed it, but I did.

"You haven't agreed to marry me?" Brennin Red asks, pushing his gloved fingers through his hair. "That's quite a silly statement, as it should be *you* who does the asking. Men don't ask; women are in charge of marital arrangements."

"Oh, is that how it is?" I ask, putting my hand on my hip.

I'm feeling pretty spunky and on top of my game until the Knave and her husbands move into the room, coiffed and beautiful and blessedly alive. That's when I realize my hair is matted as fuck, my armpits still stink, and I'm not wearing any panties under these damn pj's.

"I've approved the wedding," she repeats, exhaling a low, disappointed sort of sound. She's still in love with the King of Hearts, but I suppose she'll just have to get over it. He's mine now, whether I like it or not. Well, okay, I love it, but don't tell anyone! Just because you've read all my secrets, doesn't give you the right to blab. "All you have to do is make an official proposal, and it shall be done."

"Go on then, Doll," March says, grinning as he breaks off from the Mad Hatter, moving over to stand beside me. He's so fucking tall, and his espresso skin ripples with muscles. I could fall into his brown eyes and stay a while. When he leans down to kiss me, he tastes like herbal tea and sugar, and his big hand slides around to my lower back, holding me close.

It's interesting, to kiss all of these different men, one after the other. They all taste different; they smell different; even their auras are different. Like a rainbow, each one flickers a different color behind my closed eyes.

"Okay then," I say, feeling my cheeks flush as I catch my dad's brown-eyed stare. Edith is still gazing at the Looking-Glass, but even she glances back when I take a deep breath. I thought I'd lost this place forever; I'm not waiting another moment, hoping for some 'right time' or magical alignment of stars. If I'm going to do this, I'm going to do it now. "Will you marry me then?"

The Mad Hatter is the first to step forward, raising his cane in the air, before he grins down at me with his vampire fangs flashing.

"I accept!" he shouts, and then he's pulling me into his arms and kissing my neck, taking just a drop of blood before he moves his lips to mine. I make out with Raiden, but only for a minute, pulling back and giving him a look. I *did* agree to marry him, but … I was only asking the King just then … right?

"I accept," Tee says, chest puffing up with pride as he lifts his chin. Our eyes meet, and I can see that his are sparkling.

"In Underland, if you have more than one male in your harem, you generally propose at the same time—unless you don't want one of them. Then it would be customary to dump them *beforehand.*" Raiden pauses and narrows his orange eyes, grimacing slightly. "And I'm most certainly not one to coerce the girl I fancy into marriage. When I disliked you, it was different. Now that I'm fond, I couldn't possibly. Did you want to dump me then?"

"I don't want to dump you, you dolt," I chuckle as I pull away from him, and Dee offers up a salute.

"I accept," he declares with a massive grin.

"Ditto," Chesh purrs, bumping the Savage Duke with his elbow.

"Yes, of course, my sweet mate, my *Duchess*." North rises to his feet. Hell, they all do—and it is embarrassing as *fuck*.

"Humbly, I accept," March and Rab say in unison, and then their ears twitch and they're glaring at one another like a fight's about to break out.

"Formal words used at the Inaugural Feast," the Caterpillar whispers, pulling my hair behind my ear. "And if you'll have me, I, too, will accept."

The room goes silent as every asshole in there turns to look at the stupid king.

But holy *shit*, Brennin Red is gorgeous with his ruby-colored hair, that scar on the edge of his lip that makes his perfection bearable, and those eyes like shards of obsidian. If he says no, then … I'll still be the Alice, and I'll still have my other men, but I'll never get to hear him whisper *'My Alice, my Queen of Hearts'* in the throes of passion again.

And I want that. I fucking *need* it.

Before I even realize what's happening, there's a bit of wetness on my cheek and Brennin Red is stepping forward to swipe a tear away with his gloved thumb. His eyes meet mine just before he leans down and steals the last kiss.

"I look forward to our wedding, *Your Majesty*."

Our lips meet and outside, I hear the raucous cheering of a thousand flowers, card servants, and citizens of the Kingdom of Hearts.

I hear the cheers of a future Wonderland.

A wedding in Underland is both disturbingly similar to one in Topside … and also completely different. Nobody is giving me away—no one has a right to—and there are nine grooms, not one. But it does, unfortunately, come with a massively poof-y dress and a train that's longer than my entire bedroom in the Suit of Hearts.

The dress itself is, of course, red, and I've modified the top hat that the Mad Hatter gifted me so that my crown sits on the brim, and my veil is tucked underneath that. It's just a scrap of veil, too, just enough to fan over my forehead. Guess they used the rest of the fabric on that fucking train and ran out.

I play with the single blue earring that I have left, and contemplate myself in the mirror. Never thought I'd be getting married, to be honest with you. If I were Topside, I probably never would. But things are different here. In Underland, the fairytales you dreamed of come true—only sometimes they're nightmares. But that's the risk a person takes, isn't it? There are always obstacles, stumbling blocks to the future. It's how we overcome them that determines our character. And every once in a while, we collapse, we break down, we scream and cry … *that* is what makes us human.

My corset is made of silver, and I've got the Queenmaker and the King's sword in holsters under my dress. I feel … different without the Vorpal Blade, like I've lost a familiar friend. The sacrifice though, was worth it. So fucking worth it.

"Are you sure you want to go home?" Mom is asking Edith for the hundredth time, straightening the sleeves on *her* puffy dress. Yeah, my mom's wearing one, too, and she looks about a hundred times more graceful than I do. "Because … I'll miss you. You could at least stay until after the White Knight's beheading?" I grimace because even though her public execution for treason is on the Court of Hearts' schedule … I want to cancel it. She's a traitor, but she was trying to do good in a misguided way; I don't want her to die.

"You've been asking me for the last week," Edith groans, rolling her eyes. "I don't want to stay here; I want to go home." Dad sighs and exchanges a look with mom, one that's so full of passion that … it's kind of gross. But also, like, I'd love it if my men looked at me that way for the rest of my life.

The current plan is for Henry to head Topside with Edith, and for Mom to stay. They'll visit on Sundays, and as soon as Edith is on her own in the world, Dad'll come back to live here full-time. It's not ideal, but at least I know that they'll have a contingent of Rabbits up there to keep the Looking-Glass safe, as well as watch over them.

That's what's important.

Mom touches the side of Edith's cheek and then moves back over to stare at me in the mirror.

"I still don't think you should be getting married at age eighteen."

"Same," I tell her with a smile, and a shrug, "but it's a political move, really."

"If it were just a political move, I wouldn't let you do it." Mom plays with some loose strands of hair that're hanging near my face and then steps aside as the doors open, revealing all of my men save the King … and Tee. Because while the former might be the blooded ruler of this kingdom, the latter is still my primary.

"Hey," Edith calls out as the guys move forward to pick up my train. "Since it's your wedding night and all, don't forget: the pullout method doesn't really work." She chuckles at her own joke as my dad tries to shush her.

"You're right: it doesn't work … *for most people*. Because they don't do it right." I turn over my shoulder and give her a little smirk. "Maybe you'd know that if you weren't a virgin?"

"I am not a virgin!" Edith shouts which, of course, draws my parents' attention back over to her, making her flush from head to fucking toe. *Nailed it.*

"Nobody's embarrassing you on your wedding day, are they?" Dee chuckles as he lifts up the mountain of fabric and adjusts his wings, his curse-free fucking wings.

"Definitely not," I whisper as we turn in a slow circle and head out and down the stairs, toward the ballroom. *Especially not after I finally got that negative pregnancy test back, bitches.* Talking to me about the pullout, please … but even sex-perts make mistakes sometime. I should sit Edith down and talk to her … but I'll do it next Sunday.

This Sunday, this bitch is booked.

Also, never knew there were pregnancy tests involving butterflies, blood, and magic, but that's a story for a different day. Plus, I got all negative results from the tests I had one of the Court's Rabbits buy me Topside. 'Cause, you know, one can never be too careful and all that.

"Did you know?" Rab says casually from my other side. "That I have a tattoo that counted down the moments until I met my true love." My cheeks flush, but I pretend not to be listening. He's probably full of shit anyway. "It stopped counting down the moment I met you at that party. Did you know that, Miss Alice?"

"That's such a crock," I choke out, but really I like it, and I'm just trying to be tough because … this day is surreal. It's surreal and nonsensical, and there's a buffet table with a roast that's walking around and greeting guests with little paper frills on the ends of its legs. There are bread-and-butterflies flitting about, pots with flowers that are telling me how fat I look in my dress, and a red carpet that leads to a dais where the King and Tee await.

"Are you ready, Allison?" Chesh whispers, and I nod.

I'm more than ready.

"Let's do this," I whisper back, and then I start down the steps toward the ballroom, and toward a future that's as uncertain as it is exciting.

Nothing is predictable in Underland—and I wouldn't want it to be.

When the audience, some of whom had eyes wet with tears, have gotten positively dry from such a long and boring speech (a rather *dry* speech, to be specific)—and I've caught the eye of Lory the pirate, Captain Dodo, and the rest of the Long Tale crew making lewd and inappropriate gestures a good baker's dozen worth of times—the Knave hands the crown she made over to the King.

Once he looks me in the eye and places it on my head with his un-gloved hands, the crowd lets out a collective gasp as my blonde hair turns red as blood.

"The Queen of Hearts," they whisper as my own heart thump-thump-thumps in my chest, and my lips find Dee's then Chesh's, March's then Raiden's, North's and Lar's, Rab's … and finally Tee's and Brennin's.

Nine kisses, nine big cocks, and a clock that strikes midnight without any one of them turning into a frog, pauper, or any other sort of small, annoying, creature.

Now, I call that a fucking win.

"This is not the easiest dress to get off," Brennin Red whispers, standing behind me and helping the Caterpillar take my metal corset off. Lar puts it aside as the King's gloved hands undo about a dozen satin buttons on the back of my dress.

"Are you certain you don't want to have a holiday in Brillig?" Dee asks, slipping out of his red and black jacket and tossing it onto the chaise. We're back in the Suit of Hearts because, well, a ten hour carriage ride in a giant teapot to a vacation destination just isn't on the top of my to-do list. I want to be here, in this castle, in this room.

"And postpone the sex?" Chesh purrs, and I blink in shock to find that he's already naked. How he did it that fast, I haven't the slightest clue—must be a cat thing. His gray eyes mimic the wild magic storm that's rolling in outside, pelting the glass with tiny, round balls of ice. Edith hates hail, but she's not here to see it: her and Dad have already left through the Looking-Glass.

And they left *before* the soup ladle hopped out of the tureen, walked up toward my chair, and beckoned impatiently for me to get out of the way. It was quite the sight, like fairy princess bullshit on crack. Well, it wasn't the talking spoon that made it creepy: it was when the leg of mutton murdered the spoon, right there in front of us all.

There's a lot of wild magic around here, and it seems to seep into everything. Some people, like the Duke of Northumbria—my new *husband*, God that gives me chills—get cursed and turned into jabberwocky. Some items, they come alive. It's definitely a learning curve, figuring out how to deal with it all on a daily basis. Why, just yesterday at dinner, I had to stand up to the card servant staff and say: *"I won't be introduced to the pudding, please, or we shall get no dinner at all"* only to hear *"Pudding—Alice; Alice—Pudding. Remove the pudding!"*. It was whisked away so quickly I hadn't time to return its bow.

"Did you enjoy the feast?" North growls, loosening his cravat. He had quite the laugh earlier when I called it a belt on accident. What can I say? Not a lot of dudes wear *cravats* back home. My stomach rumbles and I raise an eyebrow as Tee helps me with my hat and veil. The crown though, we leave the crown on my bloodred hair.

I've probably looked at it a dozen times already, admired the color in a curve of a silver dessert spoon that very soon after ran off to fuck some forks. My stomach rumbles, and I cock a brow.

"I didn't get to eat much of it; the damn dishes kept sprinting off to join the dance." Lar chuckles at me, wearing his jacket the way he likes it, draped over those handsome shoulders. The men are all decked out in varying patterns of red, white, and black, and the Caterpillar's jacket is a rather handsome ebony color with red leather epaulettes.

"You didn't step on my feet today though; you're improving." He watches as Rab removes my cloak, and March … stands off to the side and finishes a plate of wedding cake. It had ten tiers, you know, and a very unflattering figurine of myself on the top, made entirely of white chocolate. Whoever sculpted it gave me three breasts though which is entirely inaccurate, if I do say so myself.

"Gee, thanks," I murmur with a dramatic eye roll. It doesn't last long though, because my dress is being slid over my shoulders by the King, falling into a red puddle around my booted feet. Yes, I wore combat boots today—heels look pretty but they hurt like hell and they're sexist as fuck. Sorry, I know, I *said* they were cute, but they're also a tool of the patriarchy. And here in Underland? There *is* no patriarchy. Win.

"You look scrumptious," Raiden murmurs, holding out a hand and helping me step out of the dress. His orange eyes take in my lingerie with a sparkle of appreciation. "The gods themselves couldn't have picked better undergarments. That is, if there were such a thing as gods."

He gives me a little spin and lets go, so that Tee can catch me, enfolding me in his wings for just a brief moment, so we can have some privacy. He looks at my red corset, thigh-highs, and garter belt like he's never seen debauchery so decadent in the whole of his life.

"You look stunning," he whispers, kissing me softly on the mouth and then stepping back.

"As do you," I say with a lift of my chin, trying my best not to feel like a wannabe playing dress-up. I can't feel like that, if I want to make any significant changes in Underland. The prophecy only got me so far: the rest I have to do on my own. "You'd look better if you were naked though."

Tee grins as I move toward the bed, crawling onto the sprawling mattress and rolling onto my back with a groan. It feels so goddamn good to lie down, I could fall asleep here right now. My eyes close, but Chesh is already crawling over to me, running his tongue along the top of my corset.

"I'm all for a cat nap," he murmurs, kissing the white swells of my breasts, "but all good beasts know that mating comes before sleep. Don't you agree, Savage Duke?"

"Oh, I very much agree," he growls, his horns and tail the only part of his outfit left from earlier. "I'm all for taking advantage of this *honeymoon* concept."

"Who knew that the prudish Topsiders would have an entire holiday dedicated to fucking." Dee crawls onto the bed, sharing my right side with Chesh. He takes one of my stockinged legs in his hands and carefully pulls off my boot, chucking it onto the floor. "Explain how it works again?"

"After a wedding, you're supposed to take a vacation and fuck a lot." I start to chuckle because it sounds pretty ludicrous when you put it that way. That chuckle very soon devolves into a moan when Chesh's tongue gets a little more adventurous. His fingers tease down the boning of the corset, making me wiggle.

"Why?" Rab drawls, lounging above my head with a cup full of boosted tea. There's a silver tray covered in steaming pots that was left on our dresser by the card servants. I still find them creepy as fuck, but that's a problem for another day. "Don't lovers in your world fuck a lot *before* the wedding as well?"

"I'm sure they do," March says as Dee kisses his way up my leg, pausing only to accept an offered sip of tea from the White Rabbit's mug. "But who would ever complain about a night off dedicated to sex?"

"Only a very mad person would complain about that," Raiden agrees, stripping down all of his clothes … except for his hat. I don't mind it though. If I had to admit it aloud, I'd deny it, but I find the top hat sexy as hell.

The Mad Hatter watches Dee worshipping my right leg, and decides the left looks rather lonely.

March gently pushes my thighs apart and takes up residence between them. He's always eating something, so he may as well eat me, too, right? That's what's printed on the front of my panties, by the way: eat me. Anyway, March's warm breath fans over my inner thighs as he teases my silky panties with a finger, and then replaces it with his mouth.

The Duke takes over my lips, kissing me and teasing my tongue with his own, possessive little growls escaping him as Chesh starts to undo the clasps on the corset. As soon as my breasts are free, North sneaks his hand down and takes one in his bronze palm, massaging and kneading it as I moan and luxuriate in my worship.

Because that's what's happening here: I'm being *worshipped*.

By nine dudes.

It's surreal as *fuck*.

My hand reaches out for someone to touch, to pull into the bacchanalia, and I soon find myself with my fingers curling around the waist of Lar's slacks. He helps me work them open and take his cock into my hand; I tease his shaft with my fingers for a moment before he lifts them to his mouth and sucks on them.

I swallow hard as March pleasures me with his tongue and then trades places with the Mad Hatter, licking the bottom of my stocking-covered foot instead. Raiden wastes no time in adding blood to the equation, because really, what would an orgy be without a little crimson spilled?

Tee finally joins us, finding a spare spot on my other side, and I reach for his pants next. He drops a wingtip down and teases my belly with his feathers as the Cheshire Cat peels the corset open and leaves my upper body naked and sweaty and wanting.

Chesh drops his mouth to my right nipple, licking the pert point and taking it into his mouth while North rolls the other between his thumb and forefinger.

My head gets dizzy as the Mad Hatter takes just enough blood to make the room sway above me. It's like I've had a cup of boosted tea without taking a single sip. And then he moves his mouth to my aching pussy, kissing and teasing with his tongue through the thin, red fabric. Dee and March undo the clasps on my garter belt and each take their sweet, sweet time in pulling off my stockings, turning the act into a carnal affair.

My hands work Lar and Tee as Raiden bites my panties and starts to pull them down with his teeth. He makes it all of a few inches before he gets frustrated and sits up, tearing them off with the sensual sound of snapping fabric.

"Tired of waiting?" I whisper as North pulls back from my mouth slightly, and the Mad Hatter slides up to kiss my neck. "What happened to that infuriating patience of yours?"

"When it comes to you, Little Alice … I'm an imperfectly impatient imbecile. I can't think straight." He kisses his way from my throat to my lips, kissing me with the faint copper taste of blood on his lips. I'm so slick and ready that when he lines his pelvis up with mine, he slides right in.

Did you know Underland has its own all-natural, hormone-free birth control? Curseworkers mix it up from the whiting plant, a special breed of glowing pink mushroom, a mix of three different types of truffles, and a bit of magic. Oh, and it's for *men* to drink. So I don't have to worry about a thing.

Raiden's pelvis meets my own, and my back rises up off the bed in a gasp as he fills me with his cock. His teeth graze my neck, but he doesn't bite down. He knows exactly how much blood to take to make me dizzy, but he doesn't cross that line.

He wants me to trust him.

My hands stop working so well on Lar and Tee, so I wrap them around the Mad Hatter's neck instead, noticing that Brennin Red has finally gotten his pompous ass on the bed with the rest of us. I lock eyes with him while the Mad Hatter fucks me into my heart-shaped wedding bed, soiling those perfect sheets with the evidence of our arousal.

I find his stamina impressive, but I'm not sure the other guys do. Still, they're patient about it. They're not about to rush our wedding night. Raiden rolls us over after a while, encouraging me to ride him. I reach up to adjust my crown, bloodred hair falling around my shoulders.

My gaze lifts up, and I glance over to find the March Hare watching us with dark, lust-filled eyes. I invite him over, and he comes up behind me, his huge muscular arms enfolding me as I rock his boss' cock off. See, even I can make Underland rhymes.

March licks the shell of my ear, sliding his brown hands up to my white breasts, making the most beautiful contrast of our skin as he slides his shaft between my cheeks.

Moans escape my lips, sensual sounds that I hardly recognize. I'm riding a wave of bliss here today, because, as I'm sure you've figured out already, my happily ever after doesn't come without a few naughty bits woven in. Otherwise, what fun would it be?

I hear the tinkling of glass as the March Hare lifts up a few of the vials around his neck, shaking the white one over my shoulder so I can see it.

"For her pleasure, remember?" he whispers against my ear, and I shiver. I *do* in fact remember. "You asked me to apply it for you, so here goes." I laugh as he moves back a bit, uncorking the vial. I can hear the slick sound of his hand moving up and down his shaft before he puts it to my opening again. He teases both my ass and cunt, rubbing his dick against the Mad Hatter's a bit before he starts to push inside.

My lips part with a pop as March works himself inside of me, sharing the slick heat between my legs with his boss. It takes a lot of breathing, and a lot of lube, and those big hands rubbing my clit, but once both guys are settled and March takes over the thrusting, I lose my shit.

An orgasm takes over my body much faster than I expected; there's just something about that feeling of fullness that gets me. My muscles wrap the two men I'm currently fucking, making Raiden buck and groan as he spills himself inside of me. March, he's not done yet.

"Have a cup of tea," Rab whispers, leaning over the panting face of the Mad Hatter and offering me a sip of the steaming liquid. I drink, drops of moisture escaping my lips and running down my throat. The warmth of the tea feels so damn good that when Rab gets this little twinkle in his eye, and then starts to pour it over my breasts, all I do is moan.

"I'll get out of your way," Raiden whispers, and we shuffle around, so that he can slide out of me, making me groan as my muscles flutter in pleasure. That's something you learn quick about orgies: there's a lot of awkward shuffling to get to the sexy bits. I learned a lot about that when I read that book, *Groupie*. Only, the main character in that book had five lovers.

Yours truly, she has *nine*.

My body is going to be hurting after this, but I refuse to stop until I've fucked all nine of my new husbands. That's just how I roll. Besides, I've always sort of had fantasies like this, where I conquered an entire group of guys. It was almost ruined for me when Liam and his friends assaulted me, tainting my sex fantasies. But I've learned since that trauma doesn't define me; it's okay to move on and like what I like, no shame.

The White Rabbit takes my mouth with his own, tasting of tea and sugar. His tongue swirls against mine before he gently takes my lower lip between his teeth, giving it a little yank. He sits back against the pillows, and I readjust myself so that I can have him and March at the same time—both Rabbits at once.

There's a rivalry brewing between them that turns me on, this competitive energy that sparks and ignites. It's not malicious, just sharp enough to cut. Feeling them both inside of me at once takes my breath away as we move together in slow, undulating motions, rocking the bed and the rest of the men on it.

My hands tease the tattoos on Rab's chest, fingertips playing with his nipples, sliding down the valleys between his muscles. He takes one of my breasts in his mouth and sucks at it, while the other men watch, hungry for their own moment in the spotlight. Little do they know, they aren't getting one: the only person in the spotlight tonight is me.

Chesh manages to sneak his way into the fray, taking over my mouth with sensual kisses that curl my toes, and make my heart flutter inside my chest. Must make my lower stomach muscles flutter, too, because both March and Rab make pained sounds, like the pleasure is just too much. March finishes soon after, and I take advantage of being alone with just the White Rabbit inside of me.

My hips rock furiously as I make out with Chesh, my right hand being pulled away and wrapped around the base of a thick cock. I'm stroking someone I can't see because my eyes are closed and I'm engulfed in a wave of hazy pleasure.

The next person to orgasm is me, my entire body going ice-cold and then white-hot. It feels so damn good that I let out a small scream, taking Rab over the edge with me, massaging his body with my wet heat.

When I roll off, panting, a burst of wild laughter escapes my throat.

"This is like a marathon," I whisper, covering my eyes with my hands. That foursome I watched during the Fabulous Monsters show springs to mind …

"You don't have to please us all at once, you know," the Savage Duke growls, but I pull my hands away from my face and give him a look.

"It's my wedding night. I want to claim all of my men."

I sit up and push my hair away from my sweaty forehead, looking over the sea of naked bodies in my bed. At least the bed truly is large enough to hold us all. Pretty goddamn impressive. I don't know that we'll all sleep in here every night, but this night, that's what I want—more than anything. I want to be surrounded by love and romance and fresh starts.

"North, lay down," I command, pushing his big, bronzed body onto the bed. He growls and yanks me over to him with the muscular length of his tail. "Lar, here." I point behind myself and then crook a finger at the Cat who purrs excitedly. "I saw this at the show …" I start, and Dee chortles with laughter.

"You're not the first person to steal a sex position from the Fabulous Monsters," he says with a grin, wrapping his wings around himself and making a cocoon of feathers. He peeks out at us with one, sapphire eye.

I look back down at North, with his glorious black horns coming from his golden hair. I sweep a few strands off his forehead, lean down, and kiss the shit out of him. Pretty sure I'm making a mess all over this bed, but it doesn't matter. Not right now. This is our fucking honeymoon—even if I'm the only one that thinks of it that way.

I straddle North, sliding his shaft between my wet folds before I take him into me, groaning and arching my back until he's fully sheathed inside. Lar moves up behind me, taking my breasts in his hands, squeezing and kneading the flesh while he kisses my neck, fanning our sweaty bodies with his wings. And Chesh, I encourage him to straddle the Duke's head, so I can lean forward and take him into my mouth.

Good thing North actually likes Chesh, or else this would never work. Pick your battles, right?

My tongue slides around the head of Chesh's cock while my fingers grip the base of his shaft, taking him in as deep as I can, humming low in my throat so that the vibration travels through my tongue and into him.

I don't manage to pull it off like a show, not the way the Fabulous Monsters did, but it feels damn good, and I'm pleasuring three of my men at the same time. There's so much moaning, so much sweat, and everything is slick. It's one of the most primal things I've ever experienced.

Outside, the storm rages on, filling the castle with magic, making my blood sing.

When Lar finishes, Chesh takes his place, kissing me and teasing my ass with his fingers until I'm ready to take him.

I'm sore as hell when I fall onto my back next to the panting Duke, more than ready for a shower. But not until I'm done, not until I've completed my wedding night mission. Tee and the King are next, one of them on either side of me, the two men who stood at the dais today.

They worship me from either side, their hands tangling as they touch my body—Tee's bare fingers mixing with Brennin's gloved ones. There are too many people in here for him to risk his naked palms.

When I take them, I take them one at a time, riding the King's cock first while Tee provides the foreplay and the backup, kissing my neck, palming my breasts, massaging my clit. Brennin might think he's a badass, but he comes fairly quickly, looking into my blue eyes and whispering under his breath.

"My Queen of Hearts," he croons, and this time … he's right. I've finally accepted it, and it feels so goddamn good, like the last puzzle piece of my life is sliding into place.

Tee and the King switch places, and when I look into the angel prince's eyes, I see that he's as much a king as Brennin Red is—possibly more. Now that he's mine for good, that we've got this seat of power to work from, I'm going to make sure the world stops treating him like a slave.

We finish up together, after what's probably a very long, very boring lovemaking session to the other men. And I smile as Tee collapses right next to Brennin Red and doesn't bother to move—he's too fucking tired to do it. I'm tired, too, and sore, and achy, but it feels good and I'm not ready to stop. The magic is riding me, using me as a vessel. My next goal in my new life is to figure out how to ride *it.*

Dee is the last man in the bed that I haven't taken, the only one sitting there with a hard-on and a smile, waiting for me. I saved him for last on purpose, because I want to take that cheer and that playfulness into my heart and hold it close. He believed in me. From moment one, he fucking believed in me.

"Hello, my Queen," he whispers as I climb onto his lap and take him into me, his wings sweeping around and holding me close, cocooning us in this little bubble of warmth. I ride him for so long, my hands on his shoulders, our eyes locked on one another, that when we're both finished and panting together, we look over and find that the rest of the men are asleep.

"That was *intense*," I whisper, and Dee chuckles, hugging me with his arms *and* his wings.

"Don't see yourself doing that on a nightly basis, huh?" he asks, and I groan, nuzzling the sweet-smelling spot between his neck and shoulder.

"Maybe annually. Bi-annually, if you guys are lucky." Dee gives me another squeeze and leans forward to whisper in my ear.

"Allison-who-isn't-Alice, no matter what happens in the bedroom … we already are."

The moons are out when I finally climb from bed, sore in all the best places, and slip on a satin robe. Before I open the French doors that lead outside, I grab my diary and that copy of Lewis Carroll's book that Tee gave me. I have to read it, all over again, just to see if I've missed anything.

Even on my wedding night, I'm incapable of taking a break.

With a sigh, I lean my elbows on the balcony railing and look out over the castle grounds towards the wood. There are owls out there, hooting softly, and bats with multi-colored eyes that shimmer like jewels. Somewhere way, way out there, I can hear the scream of a jabberwock, but it's not close enough to make my ears bleed.

Home.

I finally feel like I'm home.

I reach up and touch the crown sitting atop my bloodred hair. I still can't believe it's not blonde anymore, although that stubborn rainbow streak refuses to fade. I also can't believe I got fucked by nine different dudes while wearing it. Lucky me for stay-put spells, huh? Otherwise this baby would've been lost in the sheets before the foreplay was over.

"Allison?" Tee asks, padding out to stand beside me. Dee is with him, and they flank me like guards, their beautiful wings shimmering silver in the moonlight. "Are you okay?"

"Are you alright?" Dee repeats, and I smile. They remind me of the moons, these twins, destined to rule the skies together, shining brighter because they do it together.

"I'm just … marveling," I whisper. It feels sacrilegious to speak too loudly, not on this night, my wedding night, the first night I sat the throne as the Queen of Hearts. One day, I may very well be the Queen of Underland … or Wonderland, even. Not yet though. I still have some growing to do.

"Marveling is good," Dee whispers, kissing me on the cheek. "When we forget to be surprised by the world, the world no longer surprises us." I grin at his nonsense as he takes a seat on the stone bench next to me and leans his head back, looking up at the stars.

I pull my diary from my pocket, so Tee can see it, and he smiles.

"Care to make an entry together?" I ask. He reaches out and cups the side of my face, running his thumb over my lower lip.

"I'd like nothing more."

I sit down on the bench next to Dee, and Tee sits down on my other side, curling his left wing around my shoulders and tucking me close to his warm side. I pull out my omnibus copy of *Alice's Adventures in Wonderland* and *Through the Looking-Glass, and what Alice Found There,* and open it up, just for a moment. Already, I see things that I don't recognize, moments that haven't happened yet.

The prophecy of the Walrus and the Carpenter might be over, but it looks like there are still several more stories to come.

Bring it on, I think, shutting the cover on those famous stories of little Alice, pushing it aside, and taking out my diary. Together, Tee and I make an entry.

Dear Fucking Diary, there was a wedding today, and a feast, and then, in usual Underland fashion, there was an orgy. I said goodbye to Dad and Edy—after the feast, before the orgy—and watched Mom cry. She knows she can see them whenever she wants, but our lives are changing, and even if that change is good, it's still scary.

After the ceremony, the food, and the sex, I put my crown on my head, and I walked out onto the balcony to watch the sun come up. It's a new day in the Kingdom of Hearts, a new day in Underland. It can't be Wonderland overnight; I have a lot of work to do here. But I have a lot of help, too.

She has a ton of help—mostly from me because the other eight are useless.

Dear Fucking Diary, that was Tee. You can probably tell, because his handwriting is a million times better than mine. He's in this with me, one of my nine big cocks. Hah. If there was one thing that stupid prophecy got right, it was penis size.

Well, okay, so it got two things right: I was always destined to fall in love with Underland. These men, I fell in love with them by accident. And all of those things that I did and said, the way I felt compelled to follow the White Rabbit down the Rabbit-Hole ... I figured it out.

That was just me.

That was me, choosing my own destiny.

Because I'm Allison Pleasance Liddell, the Queen of Hearts, partner to nine handsome men, daughter of Hannah and Henry, sister to Edith, Frederick, and ... Rhoda.

I'm Allison, but I'm also the Alice.

And the Alice, she lives happily ever ... for now.

Because we're all mad here, and there are no happy endings. This is just the beginning.

And if you're reading this ... you must be mad, too.

So welcome, welcome to Underland.

Sit down and stay a while.

JOIN THE C.M. STUNICH

DISCUSSION GROUP

Want to discuss what you've just read?
Get exclusive teasers or meet special guest authors?
Join CM.'s online book clubs on Facebook!

@

www.facebook.com/groups/thebookishbatcave

STALKING LINKS

BUY C.M. STUNICH BOOK MERCH– Want to represent your favorite book with a blanket, sweatshirt, mug or sticker.

LISTEN TO MY BOOK PLAYLISTS – Share your fave music with me and I'll give you my playlists

TikTok – Okay, I'm really bad at social media but if you want to hear me talk about writing my books or just order a signed copy in the tiktok shop this is the place

AMAZON, BABY – If you click the follow button here, you'll get an email each time I put out a new book. Pretty sweet, huh?

LIKE ME ON FACEBOOK – Pretty please? I'll love you forever if you do! ;)

FRIEND ME ON FACEBOOK – Okay, I'm actually at the 5,000 friend limit, but if you click the "follow" button on my profile page, you'll see way more of my killer posts

INSTAGRAM – Want to know whats up with my life. Nothing fancy just pictures from my everyday life.

www.ingramcontent.com/pod-product-compliance
Ingram Content Group UK Ltd.
Pitfield, Milton Keynes, MK11 3LW, UK
UKHW041312100125
4051UKWH00020B/56/J

9 798330 386604